# THE COMET CHRONICLES

# THE COMET CHRONICLES

**By Brian Herbert**

**WordFire Press**
Colorado Springs, Colorado

**THE COMET CHRONICLES**
*Sidney's Comet*

First publication Berkley Books 1983

*The Garbage Chronicle*

First published by Berkley 1985



ISBN: 978-1-61475-404-6

Cover design by Duong Covers

Art Director Kevin J. Anderson

Cover artwork images by Dollar Photo Club

Book Design by RuneWright, LLC
www.RuneWright.com

Published by
WordFire Press, an imprint of
WordFire, Inc.
PO Box 1840
Monument CO 80132

Kevin J. Anderson & Rebecca Moesta, Publishers

WordFire Press Trade Paperback Edition May 2016
Printed in the USA
wordfirepress.com

# Sidney's Comet

# Prologue

Humming the Hymn of Freeness, Sayer Superior Lin-Ti motoshoed over the top of the hill as he had done each morning for centuries on the domed asteroid of Pleasant Reef. This was in a distant, private corner of the galaxy, the breeding and training ground for the young men of Uncle Rosy's Sayerhood.

Now, in the verdant valley below, Lin-Ti could see the silver-tipped spires of the Great Temple punching through a low fog that lay across the valley floor. From their cave habitats in the hills, white-robed youngsayermen hummed softly as they rolled down along winding motopaths toward the temple. The horizon was close on this little asteroid, and a hazy red outline along the limit of Lin-Ti's vision marked the approach of the new day's sun.

With a new vinyl-bound history primer under his arm, Lin-Ti felt excitement at the prospect of the lesson he would begin teaching today. *This garbage comet matter has been a mystery for too many years,* he thought, *and now, thanks to the Sayerhood history writing team …*

As he reached a fork in the motopath, a ground squirrel darted across the path and disappeared into a clump of Scotch broom. Lin-Ti slowed to roll over an arched bridge to the left, then mentocommanded his shoes to resume speed.

Twenty minutes later, the Sayer Superior stood somberly at a podium with the history primer in front of him. An odor of newness from the book touched his nostrils, and he smiled. *My Rosenbloom, but I love the smell of new things!* he thought.

Lin-Ti glanced around the sunny ordinance room at a seated assemblage of youngsayermen in their hoodless white smocks of purity.

Each held an open edition of the primer, and waited to read along with the instructor. One youngsayerman in the first row reminded Lin-Ti momentarily of Onesayer Edward, with the same long body and fat features. Lin-Ti recalled nearly four centuries earlier, when a then Youngsayer Edward had stood with him at the tutelage console … such a bright youngsayerman, with so much promise. …

A wave of sadness passed over Lin-Ti as he thought of Onesayer Edward's tragic fate. But as he gazed around the cheerful room and saw attentive young faces looking back, Lin-Ti began to feel better. It was still in the room, and Lin-Ti heard his own muslaba robe rustle as he shifted on his moto-shoes. He leaned one arm on the podium for a moment, then pulled it back and stood erect.

The Sayer Superior was a large man with the shaven head of the Sayerhood, made to look larger by the platform on which he stood. His face had the lineless clarity and serene countenance of one who had never deviated from the Master's path. In fact, you had to look upon the man for only a short time to know why Uncle Rosy had selected him. Lin-Ti cleared his throat, then read from a looseleaf introduction sheet. Words flowed quickly and smoothly across his lips, like a brook racing over stones to the sea:

"There are special places in the universe, places which even Uncle Rosy never imagined. Of this there is little argument today. Some say God dispersed varying life forms for the purpose of determining the most perfect state of life other than His own. Others are not so certain about the reason for the creation of such special places.

"Imagine one of these places … a magical realm having no land or water mass occupied by beings without bodies or flesh, but possessing the most highly developed senses imaginable. Senses without flesh? A realm without land or water? We did say the realm was magical, did we not?

"We can only speculate concerning the party these beings were having when the first load of catapulted Earth garbage came through their realm. We know they were partying, for that was all they had ever done. They were known to revel in the pleasures of non-flesh, and this particular party must have been no exception. Gentle, lilting music and delicate fragrances carried by the sweet solar breezes that moved between the stars and flower planets near their realm probably wafted across their non-human tympanic and olfactory sensors.

"At their party, they undoubtedly had non-physical things which tasted or sounded good, looked attractive or smelled divine. They even had things which felt good to them. It was like any human party in these respects, except all sensual pleasure experiences were accomplished without flesh. For as these beings knew, 'Flesh clings to senses. Senses do not cling to flesh.' In their experience, senses were pure and magical. On the other hand, flesh was believed to inhibit sensual enjoyment, and was associated with dirty and distasteful things. As they often said, 'Flesh stinks when it gets old or when it perspires. Dirt clings to flesh.'"

Lin-Ti looked up, catching the gaze of the youngsayerman who reminded him of Onesayer Edward. Lin-Ti looked back at the looseleaf sheet, flipped it to the other side. The swift-flowing words began anew:

"Students of such phenomena understand that there is a point at which flesh, aided by technology, approaches a more perfect state. But flesh never quite measures up. This is the problem of infinity and of geometrical lines that cannot intersect, of time warps that do not overlap and of lives that never meet. An entity can be there but not there at the same moment, making it impossible to capture from outside its dimension.

"We have reliable reports indicating that the beings of which we speak spent thousands of years enjoying one party. It took them that long to reach a crescendo of pleasure, the point at which all sensual receivers were fully open. It was somewhat akin to a citizen of the American Federation of Freeness on 'full automatic' with respect to consumption, and was a very high state of existence for that particular realm.

"With their olfactory sensors fully open to pick up delicate solar fragrances, it is not difficult to imagine the outrage felt by these bodiless beings when they smelted the reek of Earth garbage! The 'fleshcarriers' could not have selected a worse place to hurl their poorly constructed, dripping containers!

"After accumulating Earth's waste for nine years, these beings implemented an appropriate method of returning all of it to the senders. For life forms having their durations measured in thousands of human years, this was quite an immediate response."

Lin-Ti slipped the looseleaf sheet to a shelf in the podium, and looked up. "In examining the new primer," he said, "you will note marvelous detail, down to precise conversations … even emotions and thoughts. You all understand how this information was developed?"

"Yes, Sayer Superior," a youngsayerman in the center of the room said, "from the lifelog tapes we have on each government employee—from cell memory readings taken when they touch security monitor identity plates. We have the minutest details on their lives!"

The youngsayerman who resembled Onesayer Edward was not paying attention. He flipped ahead in the text, read a conversation in the middle of the first chapter.

"'"... It's a garbage comet, Mister President,' Muñoz said. 'Our own damned trash is coming back! ..."'"

The youngsayerman looked up, catching the full impact of Sayer Superior Lin-Ti's disapproving stare. The offender blushed, then turned back to the title page....

# Sayers' History Primer

**August 24, 2605–September 1, 2605**

*Dedicated to the memory*
*of our Beloved Master,*
*Willard R. Rosenbloom*

PLEASANT REEF PUBLISHERS

NEW SERIES 2698

# Chapter One

## BACKGROUND MATERIAL, FOR FURTHER READING AND DISCUSSION

[1] *mento/ 'mento / vb: activation of a mechanical device through thought transmission.*

[2] *mento/ 'mento / adj: used as modifier, as in "mento thought transmitter" or "mento brain implant."*

From the *New AmFed Dictionary*
(Seventy-First Edition)

***Thursday, August 24, 2605***

At shortly past noon on Garbage Day minus eight, General Arturo Muñoz slapped on his gold-brimmed military cap angrily as he and a larger man moto-shoed toward the door of Muñoz's private lunchroom. The windowless little room was chrome and white plastic, illuminated by rows of overhead fluorescent cubes. Some said the room was too austere, particularly for a council minister. "Council ministers should be models of consumption," they said. But the general did not listen to such talk. A plate of aromatic syntho-steaklets lay untouched on the table behind him. Despite hunger pangs, he felt too upset to eat. The president had called an emergency council meeting, and General Muñoz did not know why.

"I don't have time to discuss the Black Box of Democracy with you now!" Muñoz snapped as he mentoed the hall door. He felt a *click-thud* in the back of his brain, waited impatiently for the door to open. "The Black Box is bluffery, I tell you! The most monstrous bluffery imaginable!"

Muñoz slammed, a clenched fist against the stubbornly immobile door, heard the other man mumble something. Then Muñoz snarled, "Dammit, Dick. This brain implant you gave me is acting up again!"

The much taller and consumptively heavy Dr. Richard Hudson was in his usual place at the heels of his superior. Hudson held two typed sheets. His gaze flitted away nervously under Muñoz's ferocious glare. "The implant is not standard consumer issue, as you know, Arturo," Hudson said. "That's why you and I can read one another's thoughts ... and those of anyone else."

"I know, I know...."

Hudson wore a hoodless white, gold-sashed ministerial robe with a gold cross and chain about the neck. General Muñoz's robe was identical, except his garment had multi-colored battle ribbons across one side of the chest. Both men were in their early forties.

"There were bound to be bugs," Hudson said.

"Yes, but why me? You installed twelve of these 'special' devices ... in our brains and in the brains of my most trusted people. But my implant is the only one to act up! I'M THE LEADER, DAMMIT, AND I CAN'T EVEN MENTO DOORS LIKE THE LOWLIEST CONSUMER!"

"I'll laser-set the frequency for you again, Arturo." Hudson fumbled in a robe pocket with his free hand. "Now where did I put that laser pen...? Must be in the other pocket.... "

Muñoz glared at the still-closed door.

"Just listen to this Bu-Med report for a minute," Hudson said. "It is most unusual." He smelled heavily spiced steaklets.

General Muñoz shook his head slowly in exasperation. To Hudson, the cap worn by the orange-mustachioed general appeared laughably large on such a small man, but he suppressed the thought.

"Make it fast," Muñoz said, glaring sidelong at Hudson. "We're due at an emergency meeting."

Hudson was a nervous, bespectacled man with a bald pate and a fringe of black hair. His influential position as Minister of Bu-Tech had been arranged by Bu-Mil's powerful minister, General Muñoz. Hudson shifted uneasily on his mento-locked moto-shoes as he glanced down at the report.

"There is great power in the Black Box of Democracy," Hudson read. "Uncle Rosy may still be alive and living inside the structure."

"We've heard this nonsense before," Muñoz scoffed. "The Black Box is our 'guardian of democracy.' It will respond to any threat, 'internal or external.' It's all conjecture, Dick. Wild conjecture."

"Maybe not. Bu-Med says they brought in an unusual client two weeks ago … a fellow who said he had once been a Sayerman inside the Black Box. He wrote an article on the subject, was trying to get it published."

"A Sayerman?"

"According to the report, Sayermen are those brown-robed fellows who never speak … the ones who come out of the Black Box to perform mysterious rites at the electronic security monitors. As you know, Uncle Rosy mandated the placement of these monitors at the entrances to all government buildings."

"More fakery," Muñoz said with a sneer. "Those 'legendary and impenetrable' security units they assemble inside the Black Box … I say it's all for show."

"Listen to this," Hudson said, looking down at the report as he flipped to the second sheet. "Their client's exact words: 'Uncle Rosy has a great chair in the central chamber of the Black Box of Democracy. Adjacent to this chair are three chrome handles. If actuated, the first handle is capable of blowing Earth apart….'"

"Oh, come now!"

"'… The second can alter the planet's orbital trajectory and speed. The third would release an army of ten thousand armadillo killer meckies to do Uncle Rosy's sacred bidding.'"

General Muñoz tilted his head back and laughed squeakily. Holding his oversized cap to keep it from falling off, he said, "Sounds like they've got a real live one over there, Dick. We'll visit the Bu-Med psycho ward to consult with him, of course."

"According to the report, this man does not appear to be deranged. They've done brain-chem tests for schizophrenia and other disorders. Additionally, a complete memory scan was performed. He has full and coherent recollections of all the events described."

"There must be a logical explanation for this." General Muñoz caressed his mustache as he thought.

Hudson met Muñoz's gaze, said: "The fellow claimed a 'selective memory erasure' procedure was performed on him when Uncle Rosy released him from the Sayerhood for relocation in mainstream society. But unknown to Uncle Rosy, something apparently went wrong with the erasing equipment and the memories remained intact."

Muñoz's dark eyes brightened. "Couldn't this have been a dream that was very real to the man? So real that he thought it actually occurred?"

Hudson's brow furrowed. "I don't think so."

"My intuition tells me you aren't so certain." Muñoz smiled as he read Hudson's thoughts.

Flustered, Hudson said, "In large part, the human brain remains a mystery to us. We're always learning new—"

"I thought as much!" General Muñoz snatched the report. He rolled it up and hurled it across the lunchroom. "NOW RESET MY TRANSMITTER!" Muñoz removed his cap.

Hurriedly, Hudson folded the report and slipped it into a robe pocket. Then he brought forth a white, pen-shaped device, placing the tiny silver tip of it against the back of Muñoz's head.

"Wonder what that fool President wants now," Muñoz said.

"Don't talk for a minute." Hudson mentoed the device, saw a tiny lance of red light flash against Muñoz's head.

Muñoz jerked.

"All right," Hudson said, replacing the unit in his robe pocket. "You can open the door now."

O O O

Sidney Malloy's galaxy blue autosedan accelerated up the onramp to the Campobello Expressway, pressing him against the back of his bucket seat as the car picked up speed. Following the magnetic lure of buried wire, the car fell silently and smoothly into place in midday traffic. Sidney glanced over his shoulder, watched the grey-glass tower of his condominium building disappear behind other similar structures.

The sameness of his lifestyle with that of most other people depressed him momentarily. Sidney knew this was a bad thought, a selfish thought. He turned forward, trying to think of something else.

As Sidney turned his head, a yellow autosport darted past on the left and cut in front of him. This activated the collision sensor on Sidney's vehicle, and his car braked suddenly, slamming him against his shoulder harness.

"Damned hot dog," Sidney cursed softly. "His manual override ought to be jammed down his throat!" Sidney mentoed his rooftop signboard, flashing an angry message to the offending driver:

"SLOW DOWN, YOU FOOL!"

The reply came quickly, in bright green letters half a meter high:

"EAT MY DUST!"

The yellow autosport darted to the right, taking an exit into New City's central shopping district.

Sidney's pre-programmed car took the next exit, negotiating a spiral offramp onto American Boulevard, a broad avenue dotted with pink, lavender, and yellow synthetic flowers and plastic maple trees. On each side of the boulevard, miniature expressways for moto-shoeing people carried four lanes in each direction. Sidney saw moto-shoers entering and leaving the skating thoroughfares via ramps. They traveled in lanes of varying speeds, from a slow right-hand lane to faster lanes at the left. Many wore multiphonic headphones over their ears, and Sidney saw their pudgy bodies undulate to the music he could not hear.

*They shouldn't move like that,* Sidney thought. *The Conservation of Motion Doctrine.... I'm not the only one with shortcomings!*

At a stoplight, Sidney watched a maple tree shed plastic leaves and sprout new ones. Workcrews in bright orange windbreakers carried plastic bags emblazoned with the Bu-Maintenance crest, which they filled with leaves and litter. The air was still.

The car accelerated, gliding on its air cushion past the Black Box of Democracy, an opaque doorless and windowless megalith surrounded by rolling green plastic lawn. There were people reading an inscription plaque on the structure, and others taking pictures. Children played on the lawn.

In the next block, the Uncle Rosy Tower fronted a curving section of the boulevard. Sidney looked up through the glassplex top of his autocar as it rolled by the tower, he could barely make out the ring of the revolving Sky Ballroom on top of the structure.

*It's Thursday,* he thought. *Only two more days until my reunion. Just think ... twenty years....*

Now Technology Square was directly ahead, and Sidney saw the sun peeking through a swirling cloud over New City's skyline, reflecting off tinted glass windows on the government office towers that ringed the square. A Bu-Cops car sped by, its purple lights flashing and siren wailing. Other sirens screamed in the distance. Throngs of people stood in the square, and more streamed in from all directions.

*Something big's going on,* Sidney thought.

His car stopped as programmed several hundred meters from the square, and he short-stepped out onto a platform. As his car disappeared into an underground parking tube, Sidney mentoed his moto-shoes. They flipped out of their plastic ankle cases and lifted him gently onto their wheels, and he began to roll down a ramp to the skatewalk. A warm breeze blew across his face as he picked up speed. Changing lanes expertly on the crowded skatewalk, he moved to the slow lane and took an exit designated TECHNOLOGY SQUARE."

The square was dotted with planter boxes, white plastic benches and modernistic government-commissioned sculptures. A large fountain at the center adjacent to Uncle Rosy's towering mechanical likeness sprayed the air with a thin, metallic moisture. The air was alive with people noises. *Angry noises,* Sidney realized.

Recognizing his regular datemate in the crowd of jeering onlookers watching a demonstration, Sidney rolled up beside her. As he came to a stop, Sidney focused upon Carla Weaver's high cheekbones with a red painted beauty mark on one side. Her nose was distinctly Roman and classically perfect. Curly, golden brown hair swirled about the shoulders of her carmine red pantsuit.

"What's going on, Carla?" he asked.

"Doomies," Carla said with a glance in Sidney's direction. "Real freakos. They say a comet is coming!" She laughed, looked full at Sidney with heavy-lidded lavender eyes. "It's supposed to destroy us all!"

Carla studied Sidney, noted fat pouches and chubby cheeks beneath large round hazel eyes which stared back innocently. Dark, curly lashes framed the eyes, overhung by thick, dark eyebrows, a high forehead and curly black hair that was thinning at the temples. *He's not very good-looking,* she thought, concentrating upon Sidney's pug nose and ears which protruded like wings. *And he couldn't be as good in bed as my new pleasie-meckie.*

"We've all heard rumors the past few days," Sidney said, wondering why Carla continued to stare at him.

"Lies," she shot back without a shade of doubt in her tone. "You saw the President speak last night, of course."

"Yeah. I saw." Sidney shook his head negatively as a young girl with straw-blond hair attempted to hand him a pamphlet. On the cover he saw a picture of a terrifying fireball streaking toward New City while people panicked in the streets below. Large red and yellow letters on the pamphlet proclaimed: "ARRIVAL OF THE GREAT COMET!"

"Go on, get out of here," Carla said to the girl. Then Carla touched a button on her belt to activate a synchronized autoclapper recording and joined in as a group of onlookers jeered, "Chicken Little! Chicken Little! The sky is falling!"

Uncomfortable in the crowd of jeerers, Sidney considered an excuse that would permit him to leave. But a sudden numbness hit his brain. With it he heard the echoes of distant, murmuring voices. It was an angry cacophony of sound, and Sidney thought he heard the words "filth" and "unfit." As he rubbed his forehead, the murmuring receded, and he peered through the crowd at the focus of their attention.

A tall man with pale skin and high cheekbones stood at the base of Uncle Rosy's mechanical likeness, speaking through a bullhorn. Thick clusters of standing supporters protected him on all sides, their arms locked in defense against a contingent of electro-stick-wielding Bu-Cops. As each supporter fell to the onslaught, others rushed to close the hole. Sidney saw them bear their pain heroically, silently. Other doomies attempted unsuccessfully to distribute literature through the crowd.

In an emotion-laden voice, with his Adam's apple bobbing, the tall man implored, "FLEE WHILE YOU CAN! A TERRIBLE BLOOD-COLORED FIREBALL WILL DESCEND UPON US! AS THE GREAT COMET NEARS, THERE WILL BE PANIC, LOOTING, AND MURDER! THE SEAS WILL RUSH ACROSS THE LAND! SEEK HIGH GROUND! FLEE WHILE YOU CAN!"

Although the man was fervent, Sidney detected an inner serenity about him … a deep strength that showed when he stopped speaking, lowered his bullhorn and looked from face to face across the crowd. Sidney felt a sudden urging to catch the man's gaze, to be recognized as someone different in a sea of sameness.

But as the speaker's gaze moved toward Sidney, a woman with dark, ringletted hair interrupted his concentration to call out, "HOW ABOUT A BOAT, NOAH? SHALL WE BUILD A BIG BOAT?"

The crowd roared with laughter.

"I KNOW WHAT!" the woman exclaimed, moto-shoeing forward and turning to face the crowd. She removed a vial from her purse, held her hands high and poured white pills into one hand. "COMET PILLS!" she screeched. "THE VERY LATEST ITEM, LADIES AND GENTS, GUARANTEED TO WARD OFF ANY EVIL INFLUENCES THE

DREADED STAR MAY IMPORT! ONLY THREE FOR A DOLLAR! STEP RIGHT UP!"

Catcalls and the staccato thunder of auto-clappers drowned out the man with the bullhorn.

Sidney looked past him and up to the giant mechanical likeness of Uncle Rosy. A rotund, friendly-looking fellow, Uncle Rosy sat in a great armchair with his hands outstretched, palms turned to the heavens. In his left hand he held a cross, and in the right a machine gear, symbolizing the unity between religion and technology. Sidney looked beyond this to the new Bu-Industry Tower under construction on the southwest side of the square, and then over the building tops to scan a cerulean blue, nearly cloudless sky. *Could it be?* he thought.

"Do you notice anything strange about his appearance?" Carla asked.

"Eh?" Sidney dropped his gaze, met the eyes of his questioner. "Sorry, Carla. What did you say?"

Carla glared disapprovingly, as if to say that only non-patriots dared look for fireballs in the sky. "I SAID," she repeated angrily, "do you notice anything strange about his appearance?" And she cast her gaze toward the man with the bullhorn.

Sidney studied the demonstration leader again, noted wrinkled, worn clothing, milky white skin and a mane of disheveled black hair. "Yes." Sidney spoke carefully: "His skin is unusually pale. He doesn't glow like the test of us."

"Right! Obviously, he's had his mento thought transmitter disconnected. Some of those other freaks are the same way. It's positively un-AmFed and unconsumptive!"

"Yes," Sidney said. Then he intoned: "Truly we are blessed."

The police reached their prey now, pouncing upon the man with the bullhorn in a great phalanx of blue uniforms, gold buttons and flashing electro-sticks. The bullhorn was ripped away, and Sidney grimaced as he saw a club smash against the man's face. With the blow, Sidney felt a surge of intense pain on his own cheek and nose.

The reality of this sensation was more shocking to Sidney than the pain. *How can I feel what is happening to him?* he wondered, lifting a hand to his face.

"Oh my … oh!" Sidney exclaimed.

"What's the matter with you?" Carla asked.

"I'm okay," Sidney lied, closing his eyes while trying to overcome the pain. He dropped his hand, opened his eyes and saw Carla staring at him with a perplexed expression. "I shouldn't feel this way," he said, "but the violence is so sickening…." Sidney watched in horror as the demonstration leader clutched at his face. Blood oozed through the man's fingers, trickling down his arm.

"That doomie deserves it," Carla said.

Now the murmuring, angry voices returned to Sidney's awareness, and they grew louder quickly until he was able to make out complete sentences:

*"You suffer, eh, fleshcarrier?"* a tenor voice said. *"Think of our plight then, mired in the decaying rot of Earth garbage!"*

*"What a stinking, terrible thing to do!"* shouted another, deeper voice.

The voices faded as quickly as they had come, leaving Sidney stunned. He glanced around nervously, caught Carla's inquisitive gaze.

"Are you all right?" she asked.

"Yes, yes," Sidney snapped.

"You're behaving so strangely…."

"Don't worry. I'm fine." Sidney cleared his throat, looked away.

They watched three policemen kick the demonstration leader along the ground with steel-toed boots. The man curled into a ball in a pitiful attempt to protect himself. Strangely, Sidney felt sharp pains on his head, arms, and torso, as if he too were being kicked and beaten, and he heard cruel, cackling laughter in a distant cavern of his brain. Sidney chewed at his lower lip, struggling not to show discomfort. The crowd clapped and called out derisively as the man's unconscious and bleeding form was dragged to a waiting van.

When the van doors slammed shut and it began to roll away, Sidney's pain subsided. *That was the damnedest thing,* he thought, turning to leave. "See you at coffee," he said, feeling his moto-shoes click into gear.

Carla nodded, but she continued to stare at him curiously.

Now the comet pill woman called out again: "THESE DOOMIES ARE DOING US A GREAT SERVICE! MORE NUTS FOR OUR THERAPY ORBITERS MEANS MORE EMPLOYMENT IN BU-MED!"

Saddened at the spectacle, Sidney moto-shoed across smooth concrete toward a massive white-glass office tower which bordered the square. Pausing at an electronic security monitor just outside the main entrance, he pressed his palm against an identity plate and mentoed: *GW seven-five-oh, Malloy, Sidney … Central Forms.*

A vacuum surge pulled against his hand, then released him as a red light on the monitor turned to green. Glass doors slid open, and he rolled into the lobby.

Sidney paused at the elevator bank marked "SUB 501—SUB 700," gazing above the hypnotic dance of blue floor indicator lights to one of many pictures of Uncle Rosy that ringed the lobby. The soft background notes of Harmak played a "Melody For Progress," causing visions of home furnishings, autocars and bright clothing to float across his brain. Uncle Rosy seemed to look directly at him with concerned, benign eyes, and Sidney felt a force compelling him to reach for his back pocket. Dutifully, he brought forth a tiny red, yellow, and blue volume. Gold leaf lettering on the cover announced its title: *Quotations From Uncle Rosy.*

Touching a button on the book cover, Sidney auto-leafed through the pages, only half-conscious of people around him doing the same thing.

"I can't believe our Uncle Rosy wrote this more than three centuries ago," a woman said. Then, in the precise and emotionless tone of a Freeness Studies Instructor, she commanded, "Turn to page one-three-four."

She paused momentarily as pages auto-flipped.

"There will always be non-believers," the woman read reverently, "dangerously insane people who will stop at nothing in their attempts to disrupt our holy order. They will predict all manner of plague and catastrophe, insisting that God disapproves of the manner in which we live." She closed the volume, and Sidney looked up to see her smile softly. She had flaxen hair, and with a glance toward the square she said, "They are wrong, citizens. This is God's land."

The group closed their volumes, murmured, "Truly we are blessed."

Sidney waited as people destined for lower floors took places in the back of a large elevator, then he roiled on and stood at the front. Mentoing *sub-five-oh-three,* Sidney felt a click in the back of his brain as the car's computer accepted his command. The doors closed.

* *

Sayer Superior Lin-Ti looked up, and his words slowed as he stopped reading from the text. "Those voices," he said, "you understand who they were?"

A short youngsayerman rose and responded: "Yes, Sayer Superior. They were the beings whose realm was invaded by Earth's garbage. The ones who turned the garbage into a fiery boomerang comet."

"And why did they speak to Malloy?"

"We have heard stories, Sayer Superior. I believe Malloy was a … well … a dolt of some sort. And they wanted him to botch up Earth's plan to stop the comet."

"That is correct. To put it bluntly, Sidney Malloy was a no-talent jerk … working in the lowest level of the most useless department in the government.…"

* *

It was shortly after noonhour, the beginning of Carla's daily shift. Her rotatyper platform stood to one side of the sprawling Presidential Secretaries Pool, and beyond the tap-tap-whir of memo-activated machinery she heard the faint, gelatinous purr of Harmak.

She thought of Sidney as she adjusted her earphones, of the strange way he had behaved at the demonstration and of his attempts to be more than a datemate with her. Lately, Sidney had been most persistent.

Carla watched the letter "e" appear on her rotatyper screen, then called out, "Lower case 'r,' period, return, tab, upper case 'j.'"

She paused to make an entry on a Time and Motion form, then watched the typists encircling her platform as they mento-activated the keyboards in front of their chairs. One did upper case, another lower case, yet another was responsible for numbers, and so on. Six typists sat around each rotatyper caller, although Carla had heard of a new machine developed by the Sharing For Prosperity people that would accommodate ninety-five typists, each having only one key to operate.

All across the floor Carla could see great mounds of paper. There were stacks of paper on desks, on sidechairs, on windowsills, on the floor, spewing out of computers and in autocarts which rolled back and forth down each aisle delivering and removing. Brown and gold pamphlet meckies rolled along the aisles as well, full to bursting on all four sides with red, green, yellow, and blue government pamphlets. A round, four-faced head on a stick neck rose from the center of each meckie's rack, above which was a square top hat that proclaimed "TAKE SEVERAL" in flashing purple lights on all sides. Department of Quality Control personnel wearing black uniforms and shiny yellow half-lemon helmets rolled from machine to machine, checking to be certain that all equipment malfunctioned according to standard.

Carla focused upon a sign on the back of one Quality Control Technician which read, "EACH BREAK IS A NEW TASK." Then she noticed a typist glaring at her and removed her earphones to ask, "What is it now, Margaret? Don't you like the way I'm calling out punctuation again?"

Margaret shook her puff-curled silver hair before replying haughtily, "I don't like the way you call out anything. You think you're better than we are." She glared at Carla, then added in a sing-song tone: "We've all seen you making goo-goo eyes at Chief of Staff Birthright!"

"I don't think I'm better than any of you," Carla huffed, looking back with hostility in her lavender eyes.

"You don't even go to coffee with us now that you're a GW two-five-four. Well lah-dee-dah!" Margaret rolled her eyes upward. "That's still only one two-hundred-fifty-fourth of a job! My brother is a GW fifteen!"

"You're just bitter because you didn't receive a higher calling, Margaret. I got the assignment you wanted."

Margaret whirled around angrily on her swivel chair, rose and then sat back down abruptly. A hush fell across the floor as ten white-robed men carrying grey urns emblazoned with the Presidential Seal rolled single file into the department. Margaret recognized General Muñoz at the head of the procession.

"The Council of Ten!" Carla whispered excitedly. "But they were just here yesterday for their regular—"

"Shuttup!" Margaret commanded, her voice a hostile whisper. "We can see who it is!"

Everyone rose silently, bowing their heads.

"Bless this mess," the council ministers called out, reaching into their urns and scattering confetti as they rolled through the department. "Bless this mess...."

O O O

From his oval office on the two hundred eighty-fifth floor of the White House Office Tower, President Euripides Ogg heard the distant whine of police sirens. The President was a massive black man in a satin gold leisure suit—in his early fifties but with a lineless face. The eyebrows were dark and bushy, contrasting with a wave of golden hair that was combed straight back from a widow's peak.

Ogg stared intently at a desk-mounted video screen as the Technology Square demonstration broke up, squinting his blue-green eyes as sunlight from a solar relay panel outside the window glinted off the screen. He took a deep puff on a tintette, and exhaled blue smoke thoughtfully. Ogg snapped a glance at a sign above the doorway, mouthed the familiar words: "Faith, Consumption, Freeness." A half-read Sharing For Prosperity report lay on the desk in front of him, and he tried to get back into it. Forty-two additional tasks that could be shared.... Uncle Rosy's Thousand Year Plan....

He sighed.

The President looked up, and through drifting blue smoke saw Chief of Staff Billie Birdbright standing in the doorway. A handsome, tanned man of middle years with bright yellow hair and a small dimple in the center of his chin, Birdbright was in constant demand as a bedmate with the ladies of the office.

"The Council is here, sir," Birdbright said. "Shall I send them in?"

Ogg nodded.

As the council ministers moto-filed in, Ogg tapped impatiently on his desk with one finger. General Muñoz led, followed by Dr. Hudson, who moved along behind the tiny Mexican-American general like an oversized shadow.

*Can't trust those two,* Ogg thought *Something disturbing about their alliance ... and Hudson made moves on my sister ... until I appointed her mayor of that therapy orbiter.*

Muñoz and Hudson were followed by all the ministers of the various governmental super-bureaus. Each wore a hoodless white ministerial robe with a gold braid sash and a gold cross and chain which dangled from the neck. Muñoz carried his military cap in one hand.

Cassius Murphy, the jovial Minister of Bu-Bu, followed, then Bu-Free's tall and angular Jack Ramsey. *Both are neutral,* Ogg thought. He glanced at Bu-Health's Salim Bumbry and at the reddish-skinned American Indian Jim McConnel of Bu-Med, who entered eighth and tenth. *So are they.*

As the ministers took seats silently in comfortable red nauga suspensor chairs which formed a half circle in front of Ogg's desk, Ogg singled out Kevin Osaka, the small oriental minister of Bu-Construct. *Still not sure of him,* Ogg thought Osaka noticed the President staring at him and looked away nervously.

"Good afternoon, gentlemen," President Ogg said, scanning the faces in what he hoped was a somber manner. He nodded to Ezrah Sims of Bu-Cops and to Bu-Industry's Marc Trudeau, men he considered loyal, then looked at his lifelong friend, Pete Dimmitt of Bu-Labor and said, "Nice to see you, Pete. Feeling better?"

"Yes, Mr. President The leg's doing fine." Dimmitt touched a star-shaped Purple Badge on his left lapel proudly. This was the nation's highest mark of valor, evidence for all to see of Dimmitt's "conspicuous bravery" in the face of a disintegrating product: his moto-shoes.

General Muñoz placed his cap on the lap of his robe as he sat down crisply. *Why in the hell has he called us in?* Muñoz wondered. *Probably another foolish Job-Support idea to waste my time....*

Muñoz studied President Ogg closely, noted anger as the big black man crushed out his tintette in an ashtray. Ogg's penetrating, blue-green eyes flashed at Muñoz for a second. Then Ogg looked away and mentoed a "coffee" button on his desk panel. "Gentlemen," he said, "in a few minutes you will see something extremely important."

*That procession of coffee secretaries again,* Muñoz thought, reading the President's thoughts with the brain-implanted transceiver given him secretly by Dr. Hudson. Muñoz flicked a piece of confetti off his robe angrily. *How many times is he going to show that to us?*

As Ogg watched, Dr. Hudson cleared his throat and squirmed into a chair next to the thin and mysterious General Muñoz. The pupils of Muñoz's eyes were almost pure black, and he stared back at the President in cool disdain.

*Something about his eyes,* Ogg thought. *He almost seems to be laughing at me.*

*I am laughing at you,* Muñoz thought, reading the President's mind again.

Ogg saw Muñoz sneak a glance and a smile in Hudson's direction.

Only Muñoz, Hudson, and ten trusted conspirators had received the mind-reading units. Muñoz recalled his doubts when Hudson installed the transceiver....

"... Will I really be able to read minds with this?"

"You'll see for yourself in a few minutes," Hudson had said.

Muñoz remembered his response: "Now I will see who is loyal to me and who is not!"

"This transceiver will operate electronic gadgets like any consumer-issued unit," Hudson had explained as he worked, "but it has a nice additional feature...."

Muñoz returned to the present, watched President Ogg clasp his hands on the cluttered desktop and glare around the room. Unaware of Muñoz's prying, Ogg said, "I have called this emergency session because the Alafin of Afrikari is due to arrive in my office at seven-thirty tomorrow morning."

Muñoz read the President's thoughts and cursed under his breath.

Ogg rubbed a finger on the edge of his desk as the ministers whispered in surprise. "I should say a projecto-image of him will be here," Ogg explained. "The old fool is still afraid to fly."

"He has demanded an audience?" Bu-Cops' craggy-faced Minister Sims asked.

"Yes. By telephone just an hour ago." Ogg chewed his lower lip. "The Alafin says his astronomers have seen a comet which appears to be on a collision course with Earth."

"I thought that was just a rumor," Sims said.

The council ministers whispered to one another again.

President Ogg fixed an icy gaze on Hudson. "What I want to know is this, Dr. Hudson. You *have* told me everything about this alleged comet? It is a bunch of garbage, isn't it?"

Hudson wiped his brow with a white kerchief, glanced at Muñoz.

*Tell him,* Muñoz mentoed. *Better to hear it from us.*

"Uh, no sir," Hudson replied nervously. "I mean, yes sir. It *is* garbage."

"Dammit to Hooverville, Hudson!" President Ogg thundered. "IS IT GARBAGE OR ISN'T IT?" A bulky mechanical arm popped out of the desktop, smashed a clenched fist down with tremendous force on the desk. WHAM! Papers scattered in all directions. CRASH! A brass lamp rocked and fell to the floor. The arm flexed back into its compartment.

Hudson shivered with fear, smoothed the fine muslaba robe he wore across his lap with one hand. He glanced at Muñoz for support, then stammered, "S-sir, it's d-difficult to ex—"

"It's a garbage comet, Mr. President," Muñoz said. "Our own damned trash is coming back!"

President Ogg sat back in stunned disbelief, slack-jawed and mute.

"The th-thing is huge, sir," Hudson said, "and Earth is directly in its path!"

Hardly able to speak, Ogg said, "I can't believe ..." His voice trailed off, and a pained silence fell over the room.

Bu-Bu's Cassius Murphy broke the silence. Looking at Hudson, he said, "You mean it stinks?"

"Why yes," Hudson replied. "I suppose it does."

"That's interesting," Murphy said with a wry smile. "If it kills every last one of us, will it still stink?"

Hudson shook his head, rolled his eyes upward.

"Those deep space shots we've been making for the past nine years," Muñoz explained, looking at Ogg. "A Bu-Tech computer miscalculated their trajectory."

"Now w-wait just a minute," Dr. Hudson protested, staring through sweat-fogged glasses at the battle ribbons on General Muñoz's chest. "The electro-magnetic catapults are operated by Bu-Mil people. Your staff should have checked the figures before making the shots!" Hudson took a deep breath, realizing he was treading on dangerous ground in speaking to the general this way.

"I don't know about that, Dick," Muñoz said calmly. "There's nothing in the procedures manual to that effect."

"It was only a tiny miscalculation," Hudson said plaintively, looking at President Ogg. "Just one-nineteenth of a percentile!"

"A tiny miscalculation!" Ogg half rose out of his chair. "It doesn't seem so tiny to me!" He sat back, lit a tintette and blew an angry cloud of yellow smoke in Hudson's direction.

"Tiny in galactic terms," Hudson insisted. He removed his horn-rimmed glasses with shaking hands, wiped the glasses on his robe and put them back. "And besides, *my* bureau didn't manufacture the Comp six-oh-one computer. Bu-Industry did that, and they didn't follow Bu-Tech's specifications. The circuit board that failed and caused a one-nineteenth of one percent trajectory error was constructed to consumer quality instead of industrial quality."

"Hold it right there!" All eyes turned to Marc Trudeau, the Minister of Bu-Industry. Seated at the end of the semi-circle on the President's right, Trudeau's heavy brown face sported a bright pink mustache that had been dyed to match a new line of kitchen appliances. With his features contorted in indignation, he gripped the chair arms and said, "All circuit boards are manufactured in space … on therapy orbiters. How can we be expected to monitor quality with crips and retardos doing all the work?"

The President's gaze was bone-chilling as he asked: "Why did you entrust such a critical part to the therapy orbiters?"

"It wasn't our fault," Trudeau said. "Some therapists from Bu-Med came into my office one day and asked to be given tours of our manufacturing and assembly lines. I didn't see anything wrong with that, and a couple of days later they came back with a list of tasks they felt could be better performed by handicapped personnel. One of those tasks was the assembly of circuit boards."

Jim McConnel, the portly Indian minister of Bu-Med, rose angrily and snapped: "I'm not going to let this mess land in my lap! No one told us we were manufacturing critical components! And don't forget that Bu-Construct pressured us to build more orbiters!"

Immediately, all the other ministers leaped to their feet, clamoring for attention. They argued heatedly for several minutes, with the ones who had not yet been blamed choosing sides. Ogg let the mêlée continue awhile to see if he could make sense out of the alignments among those ministers of doubtful loyalty. But no clear patterns emerged, and as the alliances shifted back and forth, Ogg finally demanded: "STOP THIS FOOLISHNESS! TAKE YOUR SEATS IMMEDIATELY!"

The ministers fell silent and resumed their seats.

"Now I will show you what the President's office can do," Ogg said.

Muñoz knew what was coming.

The office door swung open, admitting a procession of coffee secretaries. They rolled in single file, dressed in dark brown mini-dresses bearing the gold encircled lapel crest of a steaming cup of coffee. The first in line was a consumptively rotund redhead carrying a trivet. With a curt smile, she placed the trivet on the President's desk, did a one hundred eighty-degree spin on her moto-shoes and rolled out the door. The second girl carried a large coffee pot, which she placed on the trivet with equal fanfare. Next came eleven pudgy saucer bearers, and a saucer was placed in front of the President and on the little tables next to the ministers' chairs. They were followed by eleven cup bearers and then by a pneumatic brunette who poured the coffee and returned the pot to the trivet.

"Very impressive, Mr. President," several ministers said as they watched buxom blond twins remove the coffee pot and trivet. "Very impressive, indeed."

*I call that showing off,* Muñoz thought as he watched the women leave. *Twenty-seven girls to serve coffee to eleven of us!*

"Thank you," the President said as he mentoed the door closure. "Now let's get back to the matter at hand." Addressing Dr. Hudson, he said, "Just forty-eight hours ago you assured me that no comet was heading toward Earth."

"That's true, sir. I replied so at the time because I did not believe it to be a comet."

"Why not?"

"Many bodies of matter move through the heavens, sir, not all of which are comets. This particular object is of unique origin … and unlike any comet I have observed, it has an extremely dense mass. Most comets are a 'bag of nothing,' in that they consist of gas particles surrounding an ice nucleus. While their tails may stretch for millions of kilometers across space, they typically don't have much mass."

"Tell him about the spectral analysis, Dick," Muñoz said.

"It's burning common garbage, meteorite chunks, nuclear matter, and the like," Hudson said. "I suppose it's a comet, Mr. President. It's closer to that than to any other phenomenon. But this baby's unlike any other comet in the universe!" *It's also burning human bodies from our burial shots,* Hudson thought. *Such a nasty detail.*

Ogg took a sip of coffee, asked angrily, "Why didn't you level with me in the first place? You knew something was heading toward us."

"You don't like to be bothered with technical details, Mr. President. Besides, until now, we didn't have enough photographs to plot the course."

"It'll hit us? For sure?"

"It is on a definite collision course with Earth. We were trying to save you a lot of trouble. …" Hudson's voice trailed off.

President Ogg spun his chair around to stare out the window. He focused on an imposing grey General Oxygen factory in the distance, with seven tall stacks rising out of a domed base. *Maybe we should turn this over to a committee,* he thought. *A lot of people could be kept busy. …*

After several minutes of pained silence, Salim Bumbry, Minister of Bu-Health, said, "Shouldn't we make an evacuation plan, sir … to help people reach higher ground?"

President Ogg did not turn around. He could imagine Bumbry sitting there—the youngest minister, precisely-trimmed brown hair, a neat beard and pale green eyes. Definite presidential stock. "No, Bumbry. We can't do that now, don't you see? I've told the world it isn't coming."

"Announce new evidence."

"No. Too embarrassing … and I'm up for re-election Tuesday."

Muñoz, monitoring the thoughts of the speakers, noted that the President was worried about losing votes. Bumbry was genuinely concerned about human life. *Always knew Bumbry was poor political stock,* Muñoz thought.

"How much damage will it do?" Ogg asked, turning around to face Hudson. "And where will it hit?"

"It isn't a question of damage, sir. Nor does it particularly matter *where* on Earth it hits." Hudson squirmed in his chair. His eyes flitted around nervously behind the glasses. "This comet is very large, and grows as it accumulates space debris. If that baby hits us, the entire planet is going to be garbage!"

Ogg felt numb. He could not think of anything to say.

Hudson tried to take a sip of coffee, but his hands shook so badly that he sloshed liquid on his white robe. He placed the cup on the sidetable, coughed. "Laser penetration readings and gamma ray cameras show this to be the heaviest mass ever to approach our system. We think our garbage shots ended up in the Fourth Columbarian Quadrant … near a black hole."

Hudson paused as he noticed President Ogg shaking his head from side to side in disbelief. Angry words seemed on the tip of Ogg's tongue, but were not uttered.

"Our garbage shots probably reactivated a dead sun," Hudson said. His gaze darted away under the President's intense scrutiny.

"My Rosenbloom!" one of the ministers exclaimed.

*We can't admit the truth,* Hudson thought, feeling uncomfortable. *No one has any idea why that stuff is coming back!* "If put on the periodic scale," Hudson said, "where the highest present density is one hundred eighty-six, this fused mass would have a reading of five thousand, three hundred eighteen. It would crack our planet like a wrecking ball hitting glass."

"We plugged the problem into Comp six-oh-two," Muñoz said. "That's the computer which replaced the six-oh-one."

*I'd like to get rid of all computers,* Ogg thought. *The tasks they steal from people....*

Muñoz read this thought, then said, "We can deflect the damned comet, Mr. President."

Ogg brightened. "Ah!" He turned to Hudson. "For sure?"

Hudson nodded. "The best plan has us changing the comet's course by using an E-Cell powered mass driver. We'd push the comet as it passes the Leviathan planet of Kinshoto in the Bardo-Heather Group. Lots of nitrogen in that planet's atmosphere."

"We're reviewing military dossier files now," Muñoz said, "searching for the best man to head up the mission." Muñoz felt a numbness in his brain, heard echoing, far-off voices. *"Forget the dossier files"* a voice said. *"Choose Sidney Malloy. He's the only one...."* Muñoz shook his head, tapped at the rear of his skull above his implanted mento transceiver. *Dammit,* he thought. *It's acting up again.*

When Muñoz's head cleared, he heard Hudson speaking: "Kinshoto's atmosphere is nearly seventy thousand kilometer's deep and supports no known life forms. If we can lock onto the comet with fire probes and guide it through that nitrogenous region, it may burn up."

"That planet is BI-I-IG!" Muñoz said.

"What's the likelihood of this comet hitting Earth?" Bu-Med's Minister McConnel asked.

General Muñoz reviewed the speaker's thoughts, noted something new. An escape plan ... bribe money paid to a shuttle commander ... intended refuge on one of the orbiting solar power stations. *How did he find out?* Muñoz wondered.

Hudson, responding to McConnel, said: "Ninety-eight point nine-one percentile. We've been monitoring it from deep space tracking stations. It's coming back along the identical course of our garbage ... and burial ... shots. We've since corrected the error, of course."

"Wonderful," President Ogg said, his voice dripping sarcasm. Mumbling something about bodies coming back, he spun his chair again and watched a distant transport shuttle land at Robespierre Magne-Launch Base. "How much time do we have?" he asked.

"Fourteen days," Hudson said, trying not to betray uncertainty in his tone.

O O O

As the ministers left the oval office single file, President Ogg singled out Hudson: "Dr. Hudson, I would have a word with you in private."

Surprised, Hudson turned back and resumed his seat. "What is it, Mr. President?" he asked, timidly.

Ogg scanned the papers which had fallen to the floor, leaned down and retrieved a long, narrow piece of electronic billing paper. Looking at Hudson, he said stiffly, "This is the monthly microwave radio call log for the therapy orbiter of Saint Elba."

Hudson gulped.

"It states that you called my sister six times this month, all on scramble code." Ogg glared ferociously. "What did you discuss with her?"

"N-nothing important, Mr. President."

"Then why was it necessary to use a scramble code?"

"P-personal matters, sir."

"Personal matters?" Ogg sat back, a sneer on his face. "How can you have personal matters with someone tens of thousands of kilometers away?"

"L-look, Mr. President. I know you don't like me. That's why you made Nancy mayor of Saint Elba three months ago … to get her away from me." Hudson read Ogg's thoughts to confirm this statement.

A faint smile touched the edges of Ogg's mouth.

"I love her, Mr. President. And … she loves me!" Hudson took a deep breath. He stared at the broken lamp on the floor.

"Love? You're right about one thing, Hudson. I *don't* like you. You're a weak, sniveling—"

"I'm not good enough for your sister, right, Mr. President?" Hudson said, feeling his face flush hot with anger. He adjusted his glasses, focused upon the massive black man seated on the other side of the desk.

"That's exactly right, Hudson. If not for Muñoz's influence, you'd still be a lab technician." Hudson had read this thought previously and was not surprised to hear it spoken.

*I'll ruin you,* Hudson thought. *I'm going to show General Muñoz an invention this afternoon that will knock you out of the oval office!* "I do have certain … talents, shall we say?" Hudson said, beginning to taste the pleasure of prospective revenge.

Noticing a twinkle in Hudson's eyes, Ogg was thrown off balance momentarily. Ogg fumbled with the call log sheet, glanced down at it and said, "I notice you called her almost daily in the early part of the month … but in the past week and a half there have been no calls. Why is that?"

"A minor disagreement, Mr. President."

"Over what?"

Hudson felt the advantage swinging to Ogg again. "She wants me to s-stand up to you, sir."

Ogg laughed cruelty. "And tell me what you think of me, eh, Hudson? You don't have the guts!"

"M-maybe I do, sir."

"Eh? What's that?"

"May I speak candidly, sir?"

"Yes." Ogg set the call sheet down, clasped his hands on the desktop and glared ferociously at Hudson.

"YOU'RE A BIGOT, MR. PRESIDENT!" Hudson said, blurting it out. Hudson's eyeglasses slipped to the end of his nose. He pushed them back.

"A bigot!" Ogg rose out of his chair, hulked forward over the desk. "A bigot, you say?"

"That's the real reason you don't want me to be permies with Nancy, isn't it? I'M WHITE AND SHE'S BLACK!" Hudson felt relief at getting the long-suppressed statement out, but was fearful of the consequences.

"Look at my council of ministers, Hudson! An American Indian, an oriental, six whites, a Mexican, a black. Does that sound like the council of a bigot?"

"You didn't select them, sir. They were chosen by council votes when vacancies arose."

"I could have vetoed any one of them, including you." Ogg sat back down, glared at a wall.

"True enough, Mr. President. But even so, this represents your public self. I'm speaking of your real self."

A shocked President Ogg felt Hudson's words slash into an area of consciousness he had not considered. *Can this be so?* Ogg thought. His gaze snapped toward Hudson as he asked, "Who put those words into your mouth?"

"They are my own, sir. I have discussed the matter with Nancy, but the words are my own."

"She agrees?"

"I believe she does."

"You surprise me, Hudson." Ogg lit a tintette nervously, blew a wisp of lavender smoke across the desktop.

Hudson saw near admiration in the President's dark brown eyes, that and confusion. Deciding not to press his advantage, Hudson said, "I have to call Nancy right away, sir. An official call."

"Concerning what?"

"Saint Elba is on the route of the comet intercept crew. It is the first recharging station ... and the place where the two mass drivers will be constructed."

"Mass drivers?" Ogg tapped his tintette on an ashtray.

"Remember we discussed that during the meeting, sir? They will connect fire probes to the comet's nucleus, and guide it...."

"Yes, of course. Do what you must, Hudson. Do what you must."

Hudson rose. "Unless you have something further, sir, I should leave now."

Ogg nodded, stared at his tintette despondently. *I should control everything,* he thought. *I AM PRESIDENT! But even the tiniest matters elude me.... My own sister opposes me?*

As Hudson left the oval office, he realized he had seen a heretofore unexposed side of the President ... unrevealed even to one able to read the thoughts of others. Maybe Ogg was not so bad after all. Still, forces had already been set in motion, and within days Hudson was confident that a new government would take power.

O O O

Mayor Nancy Ogg held a red towel in one hand as she turned sideways to admire herself in a poolside mirror. Her skin was sleek, wet, and light brown, the swimsuited figure trim and regal. Three red clasps secured the wet, black hair in a Mohanna Dancer's tail. A triangular Bu-Med crest graced the waist of her suit, and superimposed over that was the tiny silver cross denoting her mayoral rank.

In an adjoining area of her suite on the $L_5$ therapy orbiter of Saint Elba, the pool constituted a private place for her, and was, as she often liked to mention sarcastically, "one of the perks of power." Overhead, a reflected midday sun flooded the room with light, and as she looked up she saw one edge of the orbiter's night shield.

*Five more hours,* she thought dejectedly, *and that shield will block the sun again, My Rosenbloom, but I hate this place!*

She dropped the towel and stepped quickly onto the diving board. Springing twice at the tip of the board, she leaped into the air, bent gracefully and touched her toes before cutting neatly through the water. The pool was pleasantly warm.

When Mayor Nancy Ogg came to the surface, Security Sergeant Rountree stood at the pool edge, looking down at her. Trim, tall and muscular, he cut a dashing figure in his gleaming black and gold Security Brigade uniform. She was attracted to him, but had done nothing to fulfill her desires. A person of her status could not mingle with inferiors. A telephone cord at Rountree's side had a cordless tele-cube which danced in the air above the phone cradle.

"Telephone call, Honorable Mayor," the sergeant said, delivering the crisp rotating wrist salute of the Brigade.

"I am not to be disturbed in here!" Mayor Nancy Ogg snapped, treading water at the center of the pool. Her eyes stung, and she blinked, thinking, *Too much chlorine in the pool again.... Doesn't anyone ever listen to me?*

"But it's a radio call ... by microwave from Earth."

The Mayor scowled, then muttered something and swam smoothly to where the sergeant stood. As she grasped the plasticized pool edge, the tele-cube dropped to meet her, hovering in midair before her mouth.

"This is Mayor Nancy Ogg."

"Nancy?" Hudson's voice crackled over the distance and immediately there came a scramble-code beep.

She motioned the sergeant away. Her eyes followed Rountree's buttocks, then moved up his muscular back to the broad shoulders and wide neck.

Rountree flicked a glance at her as he pushed through a double exit door. She saw him smile.

"Yes, darling," Mayor Nancy Ogg said to Hudson.

"I've just come from a meeting with the President," Hudson said, breathlessly. He sat on the edge of his desk, spoke into an intercom.

"And how is my dear brother?"

"He is well."

"Do you love me, Richard sweets?"

"You know I do."

Mayor Nancy Ogg detected irritation in the tone, then asked: "And that is why you called? To tell me you love me?"

Hudson scowled. "No. There are problems here on Earth."

"You haven't called me for almost two weeks. Why not?"

"I've been busy, Nancy. You know of the comet?"

"Rumors," she said, kicking the water playfully. "Tell me you love me."

"Nancy, I don't have—"

"Say it."

The line beeped.

"All right. I love you. Now will you listen to me?" In his New City office, he could hear water splashing at Nancy's end and realized she was in her pool. Hudson shook his head slowly in exasperation while staring out the window at an autocopter as it landed in a cloud of dust on a nearby rooftop. Sunlight flashed off the windows of the autocopter.

Mayor Nancy Ogg swam on her back to the center of the pool. The tele-cube followed her, remaining in midair several centimeters above her mouth. "I'm listening," she said.

"The comet is not a rumor, Nancy."

"Oh come now, Dick. Our therapy cells are overflowing with doomies. But you're not going to tell me that—"

"I don't have time to explain, but the danger is very real."

Mayor Nancy Ogg swam to the opposite side of the pool. The tele-cube followed her, and she spoke as she climbed out of the water. "Can it be stopped?'

"Saint Elba is the closest orbiter to the flightpath of a ship we're sending … and you have the manufacturing facility we need…."

"I get the feeling I'm not going to like what you have to say next," she said, throwing a towel over her shoulders.

"Pay close attention to this. You must construct two E-Cell powered mass drivers, type J-sixteen with twin R-eleven fire probes on each. Scale everything up twenty-eight times."

"Twenty-eight times? Are you kidding?"

"Our calculations show it will scale up with no problem."

"No problem? We'll have to hand-make a lot of this, with no molds, no standard parts that big. That will take time!"

"Put everyone to work on it. This is a Priority One."

"We don't have an assembly area that large."

Hudson hesitated as he heard a scramble code beep, said, "Knock out the partition walls in Hub Sections A and B."

"But we have work in progress in those areas, government contracts to fill ... deadlines to meet."

"Stop everything else, and I do mean EVERYTHING. Move it all out. Catapult it. Whatever, but get it to hell out of there."

Mayor Nancy Ogg dried her legs angrily with the towel, said, "And even if we get the damned things built, how are we going to get them out? The space doors are too small! I know, I know ... put a crew to work on that too—"

"Finish the mass-drivers by Friday of next week. At noon."

"A week from tomorrow? All I can say is we'll try—"

"Not good enough. No excuses on this one, Nancy."

"I'm an administrator, not a technician!"

"Delegate it!"

"Will that be all, Dr. Hudson?" she asked, coolly.

"Nancy, please believe me when I say that I WILL get you off that orbiter." *I can't tell her how we're going to beat her brother in Tuesday's election,* he thought. *The ties of blood....*

"Why did my brother have to send me here?" she wailed. "I've been on this Godforsaken orbiter for three months!"

"Be patient. We can't let personal problems interfere with a world crisis."

"Such a convenient excuse. If not for that one, you'd have another."

"One more thing, Nancy."

"Personal or official? I'm ready to hang up on you!"

"Official. Have a charging bay available for the ship when it gets there. Use Number One Argonium Gas. Check the charger now for malfunctions. There won't be time for that later...."

Hudson heard a click.

"Nancy?" he said. "Are you there?"

The line beeped, went dead.

* *

At a study carrel in the Pleasant Reef Library, a youngsayerman read the first question of his homework assignment:

1. State two reasons why Uncle Rosy led the AmFed people to believe he had died and then went secretly to the Black Box of Democracy.

In ornate script, the youngsayerman penned the answer on a separate sheet of ruled paper, "a.) Our Master felt strongly that the AmFed system eventually had to survive on its own. He chose to monitor electronically all aspects of AmFed life in secrecy, adopting a policy whereby his control would be withdrawn gradually. In essence, it was a weening, b.) ..."

The youngsayerman scratched his shaven head, trying to come up with the second part of his answer. Glancing at the adjacent carrel, he read another student's answer and then copied it onto his own paper: "b.) Uncle Rosy discovered the secret of long life, which he dispensed only to himself and to his sayermen. He did not feel an economic system could survive if such knowledge was released to the entire populace...."

# Chapter Two

**BACKGROUND MATERIAL, FOR FURTHER READING AND DISCUSSION**

Javik, Thomas Patrick—D.O.B. 10/20/68—Atlantic City, NJ—
Skill Quotient: 1000 (perfect)
Attitude Quotient: 135 (poor)

2585: Graduate of PS 502, New City, MD.... aptitude in math and physics ... disciplinary problems.

2588: Graduate of Space Academy ... Mass Driver Mechanics ... 3.93 GPA ... 5-day suspension for fighting.

2588-2593: 2nd Lt., Space Patrol, light cruiser duty in the Ross Asteroids ... Promoted to 1st Lt. ...

2593-2602: Resource Protection Patrol, Dune Region, Moon .. one AWOL reprimand ... promoted to Captain and given command of a Baltimore class cruiser at the outbreak of the Atheist hostilities.

2603: Distinguished service in the LaGrange Four region ... saved 2 AmFed base ships and destroyed an entire enemy fighter squadron ... dishonorably discharged for striking a superior officer ... no court-martial due to exemplary war record....

2603-present: Garbage shuttle pilot, New City, MD

Excerpts from one of 300 military dossier files known to have been in the possession of General Muñoz

## *Thursday, August 24, 2605*

On the afternoon of Garbage day minus eight, Tom Javik found himself looking forward to the class reunion. He thought of Sidney as he switched off the autopilot and pushed the control stick forward with an effort that made the muscles on his arm standout.

*Good old Sid,* he thought. *Hard to believe it's been twenty years….*

The heavy lift garbage shuttle *Icarus* rumbled and shook like a great awakening beast, then banked right slowly and made its way around New City's field of solar power microwave dishes. Now Javik could see Robespierre Magne-Launch Base beneath the sun to the west, with its grey E-Cell silos, compactor buildings and mass driver tracks.

"Robie clears us for landing," a gravelly voice to his left said. "Pad four."

Javik glanced at his wiry-thin co-pilot, Brent Stafford, nodded. Stafford's face was creased beyond its years and made him look more like forty-eight than thirty-eight. The hair was blue-black, tousled. He sat hunched over a computer screen, perspiring in the mid-afternoon heat. This summer had been a scorcher.

Javik verified the clearance on his own screen, cracked: "Tell 'em to evacuate the area. This heap handles like a flying sack of potatoes. No power, controls shot to hell…." He wiped his brow, scowled. "And no air conditioning. Jeez that load stinks today!"

"Cattle carcasses," Stafford said, nodding in the direction of the underdeck cargo hold. "They didn't seal up those drums worth a damn. Saw 'em load on a bunch of cobalt and zirconium waste, too. The packages were dripping radioactive…."

"Don't worry about it," Javik said. "You knew what you were getting into when you signed on for garbage duty."

"Aw, what the hell. Guess it beats pushing paper at some desk." Stafford smashed a fly against the side of his keyboard with one fist, wiped the insect off on his pantleg.

"Not like the old days, is it?" Javik said, glancing down at his stained grey and blue garbage workers uniform. "Remember those Space Patrol outfits? White and gold with ribbons across our chests?"

"Yeah. The ladies sure went for 'em."

Javik grinned, wiped a hand through his shock of amber hair. "Uh huh! Hey, remember that Polynesian girl I met in the astro port?"

Stafford smiled, glanced out his starboard window as he heard the sonic thump of a catapulted load. "Port Saint Clemente," Stafford said. "Greatest little spot in the asteroid belt. You met her at the hot springs … love at first sight."

"Thought I was gonna go AWOL. and become permies with that lady," Javik said. "But the war …" His voice trailed off. "Well, you know.… "

The *Icarus* hovered over its landing pad now, and Javik watched grey-uniformed men below scurry to get clear.

"Never saw you any closer, pal," Stafford said. He studied his friend, noted that Javik's long legs had to be turned to one side to fit under the instrument panel. Lines were beginning to appear around deeply set blue eyes. The aquiline nose had a scar at the bridge from one of many barroom scuffles. A little pouch of fat had begun to adhere beneath Javik's chin, evidence that he no longer sustained a rigid conditioning program. In the old days, Stafford could hardly keep up with this man. Of late, it had been the other way around.

Javik hit the retro rockets button, flipped a switch to activate the para-flaps. "C'mon, c'mon," he husked impatiently. He was cursing when the rockets finally ignited, but Stafford could not hear the words in the roar. The *Icarus* settled onto a concrete landing pad. "Okay!" Javik yelled, hitting switches and pushing buttons. "Shut her down!"

Javik was first to the door. He waited as one of the base crewmen drove an escalator unit into position. Javik mento-locked his moto-boots and was bounding down the steps before the mechanism had clicked into place against the *Icarus*. Stafford followed.

"Hey you guys!" a pig-faced base sergeant called out. "Remember the Conservation of Motion Doctrine! No exercise outside a Bu-Health gym!"

"Stuff that full-employment hype, Peterson!" Javik barked. "We're doin' our bit hauling garbage to the catapults!" Javik reached the ground short-stepped to the sergeant and pushed him in the chest. "You wanna ride in that ship full of stink, buddy?"

The sergeant rolled back against the escalator, nearly falling over. "You're not in the Space Patrol anymore, hot-shot!" he screamed. I'm gonna teach you a lesson!" The sergeant locked his moto-boots and grabbed a wrench from the escalator cab.

Javik hit him before he could swing the wrench. Two clean belly punches and a forearm across the face put the big man down, writhing in pain.

"One of these days, hot-shot!" the sergeant moaned. I'll get you!"

"Yeah, yeah," Javik sneered. "Can't you see I'm scared to death?" Javik activated his moto-boots, rolled toward a waiting autocar at the edge of the landing pad. "C'mon, Staf," he said. "Let's hit the baths."

O O O

General Muñoz closed a manila file folder, added it to a large stack on the left side of his desk. He squirmed in his chair from sitting too long, rubbed the corner of one eye. *Which one?* he thought. *Which one do I choose?*

He felt stiff, and stretched his arms straight out in front. There was a buzz in his left ear, and he picked at it, squinting one eye as he did so.

*"Over here, fleshcarrier!"* a voice said. It seemed to come from the corner to Muñoz's left.

"Huh?" Muñoz said. He lowered both hands to the desktop, and slowly ... ever so slowly ... his jaw dropped, leaving his mouth agape. For as General Muñoz looked at a small round trash can in the corner near a disconnected disposa-tube, he saw a banana peel fly out and hover in the air. A candy bar wrapper followed, then a paper cup and half a cheese sandwich—all remains of the General's lunch. The items hovered for a moment, then began to spin rapidly in a ball.

"What the hell?" Muñoz cursed.

Suddenly, the ball of garbage became a ball of fire. *"Die, fleshcarrier, die!"* a voice screeched. The fireball flew toward Muñoz's face at blinding speed, and it was all the frightened little general could do to duck out of the way. As he ducked under his desk, the fireball whizzed overhead, striking the wall behind his credenza.

When Muñoz looked back, terrified, he saw the ball of burning garbage drop to the credenza top and spark. The fire smoldered, and Muñoz wrinkled his nose at the odor.

*"Not very pleasant, is it, fleshcarrier?"* the voice said. This time, the voice came from the smoldering fireball. *"I'm a sample of my big brother! You won't be able to dodge him when he comes!"*

"Who are you?" Muñoz asked, still cowering under his desk. "And why are you doing this?"

*"Listen, fleshcarrier, and listen carefully. For you don't have much time. Sidney Malloy is the pilot you need."* The voice gave Sidney's consumer identification number, then faded away.

Muñoz inched out from under the desk. He fell into the chair, fumbled for a pen and a sheet of paper. With shaky handwriting, Muñoz scribbled Sidney's name and I.D. number.

*Who is this guy?* Muñoz wondered, staring at the note. He reached for an unread stack of dossier files. *Maybe we have something on him here....*

O O O

About ten minutes before the afternoon envelope stuffing session, Sidney sat at his desk on the Job Station Beasley Floor, thinking about the violence he had seen on his way to work. It troubled him deeply, although he was sure he should not feel this way.

Sidney stared at the five meter high metronome mounted on a high octagonal platform at the center of the department. Light from an overhead fluorescent fixture glinted off the metronome's shiny brass surfaces. A simple plaque on each face of the platform bore this inscription:

**SHARING FOR PROSPERITY.**
**Another way to share as we build a better future.**

Sidney had seen the plaque in other places, the axiom having been taken out of *Quotations From Uncle Rosy.* Both his motorboat and vacation condominium were owned on a time-share basis, with Sidney holding a one-fifty-second ownership in each. This gave him the use of each for one week out of the year.

He mentoed a desk-mounted automatic thumb. It flipped through a thick stack of mail in front of him. A letter bearing the seal of the Presidential Bureau caught his eye. Stopping the thumb, he read the letter to himself in a low tone: "Mister Malloy:... We are making the following recommendations after reviewing the activity at your work station. As you know, energy management is a top priority of this administration, since energy expended outside a Bu-Health facility is not Job-Supportive. Our recommendations cover hazards which, if not remedied ..."

Two packing meckies appeared at a recently vacated desk in the next aisle, carrying cardboard cartons. Short and squat, they had blinking red and yellow lights and tin can heads. One eye was centrally positioned. No mouth, ears, or nose. The meckies emptied the contents of the drawers on top of the desk, then lifted one end of the desk, causing the items to slide neatly into waiting boxes. They worked quickly and efficiently, and soon rolled away with their loads in the direction of the elevator bank.

Sidney heard a familiar voice, turned his head to the left and glanced at Malcolm Penny, the owlish Second Assistant to the Assistant Administrator. Penny was conducting a departmental tour, and a group of GW eight hundred trainees rolled along behind him, hanging on every word.

"The Presidential Bureau has seventy-nine departments," Penny explained in his high-pitched voice, "one of which is Central Forms. Job Station Beasley is one of the authorized jobs in Central Forms." He waved an expansive arm, added, "This station takes up an entire floor." The group rolled slowly by Sidney's desk, made a right turn onto the main aisle.

Someone sneezed at a nearby desk.

"May Rosenbloom bless you," a woman said.

"Beasley Station has twenty-six sections," Penny continued. "Each section has five item counters, two projection-graph operators, three trash can auditors, one manual sergeant, and one attendance monitor. All draw up reports, in exquisite detail, of course. Comprehensive reports are the life blood of the government."

The trainees nodded in agreement.

Sidney looked back at his letter from the President, read its first recommendation: "On numerous occasions, you were observed balling up pieces of paper and hurling them into the waste receptacle. Papers should not be balled up, and should be slipped into the waste receptacle with a minimum expenditure of energy...." Sidney yawned and looked around the room.

From his desk near the metronome, he could barely make out a row of red, yellow, and blue alpha-numeric charts along a distant wall directly ahead of him. That was the file department. A double swinging door in the wall led to the departmental archives. Along an equally distant side wall were the committee rooms, and along the other side were the managerial offices and supervisorial cubicles. The tiny figure of Administrator Nelson could be seen approaching from his office. The KWAK! KWAK! of automatic name-date stampers rang from all around, accompanied by the sounds of auto-staplers and collators and the punctuating squeaks of autocarts as they stopped at each worktable to pick up paper. It was warm in the room, and the ever-present, gelatinous purr of Harmak forced Sidney to fight drowsiness.

Sidney shook his head to clear it, turned around to face Melinda Brown, a yellow-haired GW seven-five-oh at the desk behind his. As she slipped a green plastic paper clip onto a file, the paper clip broke. Smiling winsomely, she reached into a dispenser for a replacement.

"Plastic is fantastic!" Sidney intoned.

"Yes," she agreed. Still smiling, she placed a new, orange paper clip on the file. "Every break is a new task."

The noise of machinery and buzz of conversation gradually slowed and stopped. Sidney turned to watch Administrator Nelson ride a lift to the top of the metronome base. It was nearly time for the afternoon envelope stuffing session, and every employee had a stack of form-change announcement cards and a stack of white envelopes in an automatic stuffing tray. Sidney glanced at the large red button on his desktop near the base of the stuffing tray. He placed the forefinger of his right hand over the button.

Administrator Nelson was a small man with a friendly, elf-like face. Tiny eyes peered from under a translucent green visor that nearly covered the upper part of his face. He cleared his throat, amplified his melodic voice with a tiny silver microphone clipped to his tie: "Good afternoon, employees of Job Station Beasley! Before getting on with the important task at hand, I would like to take this opportunity to give thanks to our gracious benefactor, Willard R. Rosenbloom."

Murmuring their lines on cue, the employees intoned: "Thank Uncle Rosy. We are all employed."

Administrator Nelson continued: "Uncle Rosy is proud of each of you. Every person in this room holds a share of the Sacred Job that was created for our benefit."

And the employees murmured: "Praise be to Uncle Rosy. He loves us all."

Nelson touched a heat switch on the metronome, setting the device into operation. Click … click … click … click. The pendulum swung back and forth, a passage every fifteen seconds. Sidney pressed his red button with each metronome click, activating his envelope stuffer at the rate of four per minute.

After several minutes, the metronome automatically slowed, making a click every twenty seconds. Then it slowed again, to a thirty-second click. Sidney's eyelids grew increasingly heavy. He dozed off. Then, half awake, he tried to catch up by pushing the button several times in rapid succession.

"No, no Malloy!" a voice said. "You're going too fast!"

Startled, Sidney looked tip to see the scowling face of Malcolm Penny staring down at him through round spectacles perched on the end of a disapproving nose.

"Oh!" Sidney said, sitting up straight. "I'm terribly sorry!"

Penny shook his head disapprovingly, set his jaw. "And your desk, Malloy … it's not organized according to standard!"

"But I thought it—"

"Your day calendar and auto-staple remover, man! Don't you ever look at the manual?"

Sidney heard a metronome click, pushed the stuffing tray button. "I'm sorry, Mr. Penny," he said. "I'll correct it right away."

The Second Assistant to the Assistant Manager straightened, still shaking his head. "See that you do," he snipped. Then he rolled down the aisle to look for other violators.

* *

Still angry over his encounter with the base sergeant an hour before, Javik stepped out of a Bu-Health surge-pool. Smelling the back of his hand, he shook his head and thought: *Still a trace odor of that god-damned garbage. The skit permeates every pore in my body….*

Javik shivered as he walked dripping wet across the blue Italian tile of the main bathhouse toward a line of naked men and women waiting to get into Tanning Room Five. His leg and arm muscles ached from the weight exercises he had completed fifteen minutes earlier.

"This old body can't take it anymore," he muttered.

Finding a place in line, Javik looked around and motioned to a towel monitor standing nearby. A dark-haired young man wearing the silver and gold leotard of Bu-Health moto-shoed over, draped a long white towel over Javik's shoulders.

"Sign here," the young man instructed, thrusting a Tele-Charge board under Javik's nose. Javik unsnapped a transmitting pen from the board, squiggled his name across the tiny screen. A green imprint of Javik's signature appeared on the screen as he wrote, and as he finished, his consumer identification number and the amount of purchase appeared. All this faded quickly, being replaced by a flashing orange

"Thank You." The young man retrieved his Tele-Charge board and rolled back to his post.

Javik pulled the towel around his shivering body and felt its warmth take hold. The line moved quickly. Soon he had signed another Tele-Charge board and was in the warm, brightly lit tanning room. It was a high-ceilinged room, with eighty-eight levels of tanning slabs stretching upward, connected by steel ramps and clanking conveyor lifts. Harmak played "Dreamer's Lullaby," one of the new restful background tunes. The smell of perspiring bodies wafted across his nostrils.

"Hey Tom!" the voice came from above. Javik looked up, saw the goggled, ruddy face of Brent Stafford smiling down over the edge of a thud-level tanning slab. "I saved you a place!" Stafford motioned for Javik to come up.

Javik stepped onto the clanking conveyor lift, rode it to a third level ramp. From there it was only a few short steps to the tanning slab beside Stafford. Javik removed his towel, donned a pair of goggles and dropped face down onto the warm, clear glass of the slab. Heat lamps all around warmed his body, soaking into every aching muscle. "Ah!" Javik sighed. "That feels good!"

Stafford turned to face Javik, peering through his goggles as he asked, "When's the big reunion?"

"Saturday night." Javik focused upon body smells carried by a downdraft.

"Twentieth, isn't it?"

"Uh huh. Old PS five-oh-two. Be nice to see the bunch again … Charlie, Bob, Sidney … Hey, I wonder if Sidney ever permied up with Carla…."

Stafford sat up, sprayed water over his body with a passing porta-shower. "You know, Tom," he said, measuring his words carefully, "You'd do well to watch that temper. With good behavior, I've heard it said you can get another commission."

"Yeah, yeah. I know." Javik shifted on his belly, turned his face away from Stafford.

"Could have been worse, buddy. You might have been court-martialed and shot for that … but they took your war record into account."

"Am I supposed to thank them for that? Hell, they should thank *me* … and you too … for what we did."

"You've got to see their point of view."

"*Their* point of view?" Javik felt rage rising inside. "I belted that wet-behind-the-ears gay major after you and I were almost shot down by an Atheist fighter squadron!"

"They don't see any justification for hitting an officer, Tom. You know that."

"We saved two base ships with a little initiative, and that armchair fairy read us out for not getting the proper authorizations!"

"I know, I know." Stafford sounded sleepy.

"Now it's happening again, Staf. That damned garbage shuttle's driving me crazy."

Stafford turned to his back. "You're right. I can't argue with a word. But we've got to use our brains … you know, play their silly games a little."

"We bust our asses and what do we get? Some creep spouting off about rules and procedures! Well for Christ's sake! I'm a Star Class Captain, not a stinking garbage shuttle pilot!" Javik paused, breathing hard, turned to face Stafford. "Get the hell off my case, will ya, Staf ?"

"Damn you!" Stafford said. His creased face stiffened. "I'm trying to help you, you hothead! Can't you see that?"

"I don't need your help!"

"Yeah? Then get the hell away from me!"

Javik rose with his towel. "You're a little old lady, Staf. Always telling me the safest things to do, aren't you? Well, I've had enough! DO YOU HEAR ME? ENOUGH!"

"Everybody in the place hears you," Stafford sneered.

Javik turned without another word and stalked off. *Pleasure domes,* he thought. *Maybe a forest maiden will calm me….*

O O O

Sidney did not have to look at his watch to know it was time for the second afternoon coffee break. He was already nearing the elevator bank when the bell rang. Carla waited in the elevator as usual, holding the door open. Sidney rolled on without a word.

"Perfect timing again," Carla said as the doors whooshed shut. She placed both hands in the pockets of her carmine red pantsuit and mentoed: *Sub-nine-sixty-six, Presidential override. Code twenty-four.*

"That Presidential override is nice," Sidney said, knowing what she had done. "Our car used to stop at every floor before you got it."

"Just don't tell anyone about it," she said focusing on Sidney's receding hairline and high forehead. "I had to pull strings to get it."

"How did you manage it?"

Carla smiled. "Leave a girl some secrets, Sidney." She thought of Chief of Staff Billie Birdbright. *Billie likes me enough to give me an override. But when will he get around to asking me out?*

The car dropped quickly and silently, depositing them at the entrance to the Cave Coffee Shop. It was an immense, dimly lit restaurant, dotted with hundreds of tiny tables. Each of the four perimeter glassite walls looked out upon one of the iridescent bat caves that honeycombed the ground beneath New City.

"You're quiet today," Carla said as they took a seat at their usual window booth overlooking an underground waterfall. She looked at his soft-featured face, with its familiar pug nose and wing-like ears at the sides. "You aren't worried about a comet coming, are you?" She laughed.

"No. The doomies are crazy. I was just thinking about my job again … and wishing to Uncle Rosy I'd taken a physical for the Space Patrol twenty years ago."

"But your …"—Carla looked around, whispered—"… disability. It would have shown up." She touched a tiny dice cage mounted on the table, looked at him intently with understanding in her eyes.

"Maybe not." Sidney watched people beginning to stream into the coffee shop. "The incorto dispenser my father implanted … in place of my appendix … has an x-ray scrambler. It takes special equipment to detect it."

"Your father was a great surgeon," she said, looking at him tenderly. "You seem so unhappy in Central Forms. Could it be that you would prefer life on a therapy orbiter?"

"With the exception of missing you, it might be more interesting." He laughed nervously. "Look at me, Carla. I want so desperately to be a gallant captain at the controls of a space cruiser, on a great mission to the outer reaches of the galaxy. And here I am … hundreds of floors underground!" He fell silent, gazed out into the cave as a flurry of large butterfly bats passed in front of the waterfall, then disappeared behind a blue and white stalagmite formation.

"I'm sorry," she said. "Really I am." She reached across the table, took his pudgy hand in hers. "You always had that romantic dream of running away to the sky … even when we were kids."

Sidney fought back a tear, turned to study her classically featured face, with its straight Roman nose and high cheekbones. A red painted beauty mark dotted the left cheek, and long curls of golden brown hair cascaded onto her shoulders. People thought Carla of average build, and the muscle tone of her body provided evidence of time spent in Bu-Health gyms. Sidney tried to smile, said, "I remember we used to play condominium together. And we promised to become permies someday...." He cleared his throat.

"The grown-up world isn't simple," Carla said.

"Can't we find some way to work it out?"

"No!" She spoke firmly. "We've been through that before ... the probability of cappy offspring and all. It wouldn't be fair to them."

"But that's only a fifty-fifty chance. And even if there was a handicap, maybe we could find a doctor who would—"

Her voice grew cool. "No," she said. "Absolutely not." She pulled her hand away, noticed Chief of Staff Birdbright slide into a booth two tables behind Sidney. Birdbright smiled at Carla. She looked away, said to Sidney: "Let's order now. Everyone's arriving."

They mentoed orders into a tabletop receiver. Then they fell silent while waiting for the order to arrive, glancing at one another for several agonizing moments without speaking.

The coffee shop was full now, and Sidney listened to a talkative silver-haired girl at the next table. "I don't know what happened to Abercrombie," the girl said. "One day I came to work and he wasn't there. Then packing meckies cleared his desk. Judy asked her supervisor, but he just said, 'Abercrombie is no longer with us.' It's all kinda weird, if you ask me."

A tray holding two Styrofoam cups of coffee and a plate of mini-donuts popped out of the table between Sidney and Carla. Carla signed a Tele-Charge board mounted next to the dice cage, then mento-spun the dice. Her results appeared on the Tele-Charge screen.

"Five sixes!" she exclaimed. "That puts me in the Trip to Glitterland Sweepstakes! Now you try it!"

Sidney signed the board, mento-spun the dice cage.

"Aw," she said, her voice reflecting disappointment. "Only a pair of fives."

"Oh well," Sidney said, reaching for his coffee cup. "Guess I wasn't meant to do anything exciting."

"I can't believe it!" she said. "Just think! I could be a winner!"

"Uh huh."

"Isn't Freeness wonderful?"

"Yeah." Then his voice grew more cheerful as he said, "I'm happy for you."

Carla knocked over her coffee cup in her excitement, spilling liquid on her dress. "Darn!" she said, quivering as she reached for a napkin. "I'm so excited I can't stop shaking."

Sidney used his napkin to wipe the table.

"Thank you," she said, dabbing at the dress with her napkin. "I'll change as we leave. There's a venda-dress machine in the lobby."

"That reminds me," Sidney said. "What are you wearing to the reunion?"

"I don't know." She lifted her gaze to the attentive eyes of Billie Birdbright. "I'll shop for it tomorrow."

* *

General Muñoz did not like to be kept waiting. Slapping his gold-braided military cap rhythmically against his thigh, he moto-paced the length of Dr. Hudson's office. Passing from sunlight to shadow, he mentoed the digital cuckoo clock on the wall, noting the readout beneath the closed cuckoo bird doors: PM 3:39:26. He spun angrily as he reached an end wall, then saw Hudson standing in the doorway, holding a red velvet box.

"Sorry I'm late," Hudson said nervously. He entered and set the box on his desk. Adjusting his horn-rimmed glasses, he said, "You're going to like this."

Muñoz's dark eyes flashed. "Hrrumph! Nearly ten minutes wasted! My time is valuable, you know!"

Hudson kept his gaze on the box, smiled proudly at the corners of his mouth. "Open it."

Muñoz rolled to the box with his orange mustache curled into a scowl, but there was a glint in his eyes. Setting his cap on the desk, he opened the box, then stared at a burnished gold cross and chain which lay on red velvet. "A cross? But I alrea—" He stopped, noting Hudson's bemused expression. Muñoz lifted the cross out, studied it intently.

"It looks like the cross you've always worn, General. But it's more. Much more. The wearer of this baby commands all AmFed weather control machinery. Simply touch the cross with either hand and mento-transmit."

Muñoz looked at the cross with disinterest.

"This is a nicer, more compact system, General. We can dismantle the weather console now.... All that bulky equipment has been replaced by one little device. You can play God with this little unit, changing the weather as you please, wherever you are."

Still no response from General Muñoz.

"To monitor the results, you simply close your eyes and there it will be, dancing on the insides of your eyelids."

"Uh huh."

"Try it."

Muñoz took a deep breath, touched the cross with one hand and thought of a tidal wave hitting an unpopulated stretch of Kamchatka coastline. He dropped his eyelids and saw a great wall of blue green ocean thundering toward shore. There was no sound in his vision, and the tidal wave hit land with unharnessed fury, destroying trees and land shapes in its path.

"Interesting," Muñoz said. He opened his eyes, looked at Hudson with the expression of a spoiled child who wanted a better present. "Nice gadget, Dick," he said.

Hudson gathered his robe and sank into his big chair. Slipping into their unspoken conversation mode, he mentoed: *It's a subliminal transmitter, too, Arturo.*

Muñoz brightened. *Yeah? It'll change votes in Tuesday's election?*

*You bet. As you know, every consumer-issued brain implant has a subliminal receiver, originally for the purpose of picking up advertising suggestions from Harmak and from National Home Video.* Hudson noticed Muñoz looking out the window, added: *Now we don't have to worry about retaliation from the Black Box to a military attack. You can take power peacefully.*

*Uncle Rosy was a crafty bastard,* Muñoz mentoed. *I still think he spread that retaliation story as a bluff.*

"What time shall I arrive for dinner Sunday?" Hudson asked, making harmless conversation for the benefit of anyone who might be eavesdropping.

"Six or six-thirty. We'll play a little Knave Table afterward."

Hudson took the old cross and chain to a wall-mounted disposa-tube, dropped it on a shelf door which opened as he approached. *I thought you would be pleased with the new cross,* he mentoed. *But you don't seem to appreciate it.*

The shelf door snapped back into place. Machinery inside the wall whirred.

*It pleases me,* Muñoz mentoed. *But wait until you hear what popped out of the trash can in my office this afternoon. You know how you're always telling me I should reconnect my disposa-tube? Well, listen to this....*

O O O

That night, Sidney mentoed his bedside dream machine, instructing it to take him on an ego pleasure space fantasy. He fell asleep within minutes, imagining a wonderful, magical adventure....

"Fsssing! Fsssing! Fsssing!" Death rays from his one-man gunship, the *Galilee*, cut though space, making sounds that were only possible in fantasies. Three exploding balls of orange and purple ahead marked the dream-precise hits: three Slavian warships!

"Half-human monsters!" Captain Malloy cursed under his breath. He mento-banked the gunship, headed back to astro-port.

"Captain Malloy!" the speakercom blared. "The President wishes to speak with you!"

In his dream, Sidney listened as President Ogg explained: "The Slavians have diverted a great comet, Captain! It's on a collision course with Earth!"

"How diabolical, Mr. President!"

"The reason they are masters of the Humboldt Star System, Captain. There is strength in being evil!"

"What are my orders, sir?"

"The comet will pass near you in sixteen minutes," Ogg's dream voice said. "Stop it, Malloy. You're the only force between us and destruction!"

"I'll do my best, sir."

"If you succeed, there's nothing you can't have ... riches, beautiful women ... even the AmFed Presidency!"

"I don't want any of those things," Sidney's imagined self told the President. "I'll do it because ... because ... duty calls!"

Sidney saw his dream ship now from a detached vantage point, watched it bank gracefully and slide through frigid black space toward a huge rainbow-colored fireball that was bearing down on Earth. Then he saw himself lying in bed with a determined but contented expression as he experienced the dream.

*"Awaken, fool!"* a voice from afar said. Then another voice, equally distant and echoing, said, *"We refuse to tolerate the stench and degradation of AmFed garbage! Take it back and die, fleshcarriers!"*

Sidney turned in his sleep, flailing and kicking as he struggled desperately to awaken. After what seemed an interminable period, he opened his eyes. Sticky and hot with perspiration, he stared into the blackness of his room.

*Those voices again,* he thought. *Am I losing my mind?*

Unable to return to sleep, Sidney mentoed for his pleasie-meckie. He heard the closet doors open, and the smooth whir of machinery as the meckie approached. *It's not Carla,* he thought, feeling the bed shake as the meckie got in and climbed under the covers. *But at least I'm not alone....*

* *

In the privacy of his rock-walled cave room, Sayer Superior Lin-Ti popped a minicam cartridge into the video machine. The machine was bright red plastic, with a wide oval screen. As the film began, black gothic letters announced its title:

**Pleasant Reef**
**August 14, 2605**

*Two days before anyone knew of the comet,* he thought. He watched his own image appear on the screen, standing at a tutelage console with a hooded youngsayerman....

Sayer Superior Lin-Ti: "Following the questioning period today, I will make an announcement concerning your future."

Youngsayer Steven: "My primer tells me that Uncle Rosy granted non-revocable trade status to the Afrikari nation. It does not say why this was done."

Sayer Superior Lin-Ti: "Uncle Rosy developed a special friendship with the first Alafin of the present line, Alafin Inaya, more than three centuries ago. The Master does not reveal such details to the history writers, of course, but he and the Alafin struck up their friendship during a game of Swahili Croquet in the Alafin's capital city. After that, they often vacationed together during Uncle Rosy's last years in public life."

Youngsayer Steven: "I have no other questions today. What is the announcement?"

Sayer Superior Lin-Ti: "An opening is available in the Black Box of Democracy. It is the Sixty-Six Sayer position. If you accept, you will be known as 'Lastsayer.' Do you accept the calling?"

Youngsayer Steven (without hesitation): "I do."

Sayer Superior Lin-Ti: "You are to replace Twelvesayer Robert, with everyone below that level moving up a notch. Twelvesayer suffered from Box Fever and had to be removed."

Youngsayer Steven: "I am not familiar with that malady."

Sayer Superior Lin-Ti: "Alas, he went mad from the regimentation and confinement to the Black Box. The poor man wanted to be like any consumer, even spoke with apostrophes."

Youngsayer Steven: "How unfortunate! What became of him?"

Sayer Superior Lin-Ti: "Uncle Rosy personally administered selective memory erasure and gave him AmFed identity papers. I understand he is going to work in the travel division of Bu-Free."

Youngsayer Steven: "That should make him happy."

Sayer Superior Lin-Ti: "Uncle Rosy is most compassionate!"

Youngsayer Steven: "Peace be upon you, Sayer Superior. . . ."

Lin-Ti flipped off the video machine and rolled to a brown nauga chair next to his bed. There he re-read the following day's history lesson. . . .

# Chapter Three

## UP CLOSE WITH THE MASTER, FOR FURTHER READING AND DISCUSSION

*"I feel complete. This is my legacy to the nation."*

Remarks made by Uncle Rosy to his personal secretary, Emmanuel Dade, concerning the recently completed Black Box of Democracy. Uncle Rosy disappeared three days later (on May 16, 2318) after personally supervising selective memory erasures on everyone involved with the project.
(From E. Dade's unpublished notes.)

***Friday, August 25, 2605***

"What the hell happened?" General Muñoz demanded. His orange mustache bristled as he glared at Dr. Hudson. "Another miscalculation?" Muñoz stood in the center of his living room module with his hands thrust deeply into the pockets of a dark brown robe. His new gold cross hung about his neck, outside the robe. It was well past midnight, the first hours of Garbage Day minus seven, and his hair was sleep-tousled. A brass table lamp near the window cast yellow light against the general's side, leaving half his face in shadow.

A fair-haired, taller man of perhaps thirty-five stood in a gold robe at the general's side. Hudson recognized Colonel Allen Peebles, the general's adjutant and lover. The younger man had pale blue eyes which to Hudson seemed to look at some indeterminate point in an unfocused distance, as if Hudson was not there. Hudson had long since learned to control his thoughts of revulsion in the presence of these two, since they, like Hudson, were fitted with mento transceivers.

"We have problems," Dr. Hudson said, a bit out of breath. He removed his overcoat, slung it over the back of a white nauga chair and slumped into the chair. "As I told you on the phone, our biggest concern is that the comet's speed has increased dramatically. We now estimate its arrival in seven days rather than thirteen."

"Oh damn!" Colonel Peebles said, speaking in an exaggerated lilt. He took a seat in an adjacent chair, crossing his legs gracefully.

"I hate surprises," Muñoz said. Continuing to glare at Hudson, he popped a sleep-sub pill and washed it down with a water capsule.

"And I've just discovered a second computer error," Hudson said.

"The new Comp six-oh-two?" Muñoz asked.

"No. This time it was the Willys twelve-forty that calculated the comet's ETA … off by six hours."

"In the wrong direction, I presume?" Muñoz said.

"Naturally."

Muñoz shook his head, stared glumly at the floor.

"The comet is not behaving according to known laws of physics," Hudson said, rubbing the fringe of black hair on one side of his head. "Just one hour ago, it made a ninety-four degree turn, veering off into space for a time. Then it made another sharp turn, back to a collision course with Earth."

"How odd!" Peebles said. "What are we to do?" He sat sideways in the chair to look at Hudson, an arm draped across the chair back.

"Silence!" Muñoz commanded, shooting a fiery glance at his adjutant. "I have to think!" Muñoz moto-slippered to the couch, sat down with his hands grasping his thighs. "How could the comet change like that?" he asked, staring at the floor.

Hudson shrugged. "I don't know. This thing's a complete mystery to all of …" He stopped as Muñoz looked up and glared at him. Such words had been spoken before.

"Get out new orders, Allen," Muñoz said. "Have the crew ship ready three days earlier … by Tuesday afternoon at fourteen hundred hours." He turned to Hudson.

Hudson spoke as Muñoz was formulating a new thought. "I'll call Saint Elba and have the mass drivers moved up too."

"Right," Muñoz said. "And tell 'em to double-check the E-Cell charging bays. We don't want any last minute problems."

"I'll reiterate that."

"Anything else?" Muñoz asked.

"We'll have to set up new recharging stations along the route in deep space," Hudson said. "The others are placed incorrectly for the new course and time. I'll refigure it right away."

"Good," Muñoz said. "We still have the matter of the pilot. There's no time left...."

"Have any more garbage balls spoken to you?"

"What do you mean by that?" Muñoz snapped.

"Maybe you were tired. The mind and eyes can play tricks...."

"It was in flames, and came right at my face! I was there! And listen to the clincher: there is a Sidney Malloy!"

"Yeah?"

"He's a nobody in the Presidential Bureau—Central Forms."

"You're not actually thinking of using him?" Hudson asked.

"I have a strong feeling—call it intuition, I don't know. Something tells me...."

"We need to go on more than intuition," Hudson said. "Everything rides on this mission, Arturo. This calls for the best, only the very best."

"I know."

"Did it occur to you that your trash can magic trick might have been performed by the Black Box?"

"No," Muñoz said. "I'm sure they had nothing to do with it."

"On what evidence? You puzzle me, Arturo—relying so heavily on intuition for critical decisions."

The General's black pupils became steely hard. "And you are a man of facts, Dr. Hudson. Precise scientific facts." Muñoz fingered the burnished gold cross which hung from his neck.

"I am—and there is a concise scientific answer for every question."

"Don't be so sure of that. I'll tell you one thing. Anyone that can make a ball of burning trash speak to me has my undivided attention. The voice told me to use Malloy, and I'm damn sure not going against its wishes. Hell, Dick—maybe that was God himself. Speaking to ME!"

"Okay, okay. This Malloy—can he be trained?"

"Anyone can be trained," Muñoz said. "You know that. And Malloy knows a pilot—one of the three-hundred on whom we have files."

"Oh?"

"Javik," Colonel Peebles said. "He's a ruffian."

"Funny thing though," Muñoz said. "This Javik is sharp, maybe the best we can find. He knows the Akron-class space cruiser and has exceptional reaction times." Muñoz lifted a manila folder from the coffee table, handed it to Hudson.

Hudson thumbed through Javik's dossier file. "He's had mass-driver mechanics training, too.... Odd that he'd know Malloy.... They went to high school together...."

"Javik is bull-headed and quick-tempered!" Peebles said.

Hudson nodded. "Poor attitude quotient," he said, reading from the report. "Gets in fights all the time."

Muñoz shook his head in exasperation, spoke tersely to Peebles: "His bull-headedness ... as you call it ... was actually independent decision-making. He took out an entire enemy fighter squadron with one star-class cruiser—"

"And a major's jaw with one punch," Peebles said. "I saw him knock Neil Smalley down. In fact, it was my testimony that got Javik tossed out of the service."

"The decisions he made were absolutely correct," Muñoz insisted. "His only error was in striking an officer. Major Smalley shouldn't have pressed him about procedures."

"It won't matter anyway," Peebles said, raising his blond eyebrows. "He's on a six-day pass and is nowhere to be found ... I'll bet he's shacked up."

"You're going to send Javik and Malloy on this mission together?" Hudson asked, looking at Muñoz.

Muñoz nodded, then glanced at Peebles. "You'll find Javik, Allen," Muñoz said, smiling knowingly, "... when you hear what I have in store for him."

Peebles did not reply, stared at the general impertinently.

"The ejection pods on his ship will be disconnected, and the rocket engines will have a certain ..." Muñoz paused, glanced at Hudson with a mischievous smile.

Hudson returned the smile. "I believe planned obsolescence is the term for which you were searching, General," he said. "The radio has been prepared similarly."

Peebles brightened. "That sounds pretty good...."

"And no rescue craft anywhere in the vicinity," Muñoz said. 'The world will never know that a comet really threatened us, or that he stopped it."

"What about an enforcer?" Peebles asked.

The general raised an eyebrow. "An enforcer?"

"Yessss," Peebles said, his voice a cruel purr. "Conceivably, Javik could repair anything you disconnect. And we don't want any chance of him getting off a distress call."

"True."

"Let's send along Madame Bernet." An evil, purse-lipped smile danced along Peebles's mouth.

"Ahh!" Muñoz caressed his mustache. "The Montreal Slasher!" He turned to Hudson. "The meckie is available?'

"Yes," Hudson said. "Just back from a mission. Madame Bernet silenced eight guys on that one … permanently."

"This will be delicious," Peebles said, smiling like a death's head. "But alas," he added sadly, "it will be the last mission for our finest killer meckie."

Muñoz rubbed his temple. "Bring Malloy and Javik to me," he said.

O O O

Four hours later, inside the Black Box of Democracy …

With his ankles crossed beneath his body, the tall fat man known as Onesayer Edward sat naked on a blue and gold prayer rug with one hand resting on each knee. Soft morning rays of sunlight from an overhead skylight warmed his bare shoulders and the back of his shaved head. Flicking a downward glance at his pendulous stomach and at the great folds of flesh which cascaded to the rug from every part of his body, he imagined that he must resemble a wallowing hippopotamus. Onesayer grimaced at a surge of pain from one ankle, tried to think the things he was supposed to think.

The prayer rug was on a loft of Onesayer's private Black Box of Democracy penthouse, and in the background he heard the soft, lilting notes of the Hymn of Freeness. Uncle Rosy had written that tune. It was the theme song of the Sayerhood.

Gazing at a burnished bust of Uncle Rosy which rested on the leading edge of the rug in a pool of sunlight, he noted the floating red arrow at the sculpture's base pointed straight ahead and sharply down. This indicated the precise location of Uncle Rosy's immense chair on the main level of the building. An inscription on all four sides of the bust's pedestal carried the admonition: "Keep The Faith."

*I cannot get into this,* Onesayer thought. *And it used to be so easy!* He sighed twice, causing his flabby chest to rise and fall like an undulating wave, then stared at the sculptured, cherubic face of Uncle Rosy.

He thought back to his boyhood on the asteroidal sayer's retreat of Pleasant Reef, and upon the two hundred eighty-seven years he had spent in the Black Box. Remembering the first day he had seen Uncle Rosy sitting upon the great chair, he recalled being in awe of the Master's presence. To Onesayer, Uncle Rosy seemed godlike, always sitting in the shadows and never revealing his face.

Flicking a fly off his leg, he thought, *I was one of the original sixty-six ... the Master brought me from Three-Sevensayer to Onesayer in ninety-three years, skipping me ahead of others, putting me in slots that became available....*

Onesayer glanced at his onyx class ring angrily, recalling Uncle Rosy's exact words to him, spoken nearly two centuries before: "I will step down within fifty years, Onesayer Edward. You will become Master. Be patient, and all will come to you."

*Be patient!* Onesayer thought bitterly, looking up at the ceiling in dismay. *How long do I have to wait? I know all about Freeness and Sharing For Prosperity.... I have served on twenty-seven bureau monitoring teams....*

Uncle Rosy's words came back once again: "You will be the Protector ... the Chosen One...." Onesayer lowered his gaze. *Ha!* he thought, glaring at the bust of Uncle Rosy. *He is always coming up with new excuses for not stepping dawn, saying I have much to learn....*

His thoughts were interrupted by an intercom buzzer whose rapid-fire tones told him the Master was calling. Onesayer mentoed the circuit to open it, replied aloud, "Yes, Master?"

"The new Bu-Industry Tower, Onesayer. You are prepared for our ten AM dedication?"

"Yes, Master. There is plenty of time."

"See that you are prompt."

"I have never been otherwise, Master."

There was a long silence at the other end of the line, followed by, "Our new Lastsayer will meet you at the helipad."

"I am aware of this, Master. He will be trained properly."

"Very well, Onesayer. And do not forget to show him the Bureau Monitoring Room afterward."

Onesayer Edward rose wearily after the conversation ended and short-stepped across a hardwood floor. He rode the escalator downstairs, then made his way across the cool blue slate of his dining room module to the bedroom module. There he looked at a row of identical friar brown robes in the closet and said to himself mockingly, "Let me see now.... Whatever shall I wear today?"

O O O

Mayor Nancy Ogg stood at the Hub Control Room viewing window, watching as two space tugs pulled containers of raw materials to a loading dock near the newly enlarged double doors leading to Hub Sections A and B. It was midmorning Friday, and she had supervised all night as meckie and human workcrews enlarged the doors, tore out partition walls and removed work in progress to make room for assembly of the mass drivers.

*It's going well so far,* she thought, yawning as she stared at a box of sleep-sub pills on the console. A hunger pang shot across her midsection.

Mayor Nancy Ogg glanced to her left at a tap-tap-whirring sound, watched a floor-mounted electronic mail terminal spew out a letter. One of three electronic mail terminals, this unit was reserved for classified correspondence. A flashing blue light on the machine indicated it was a Priority One transmittal.

Gliding gracefully to the terminal, she tore the letter off and examined it.

*From Dick,* she thought angrily, reading the heading. *Well I don't care to hear from him!* She rolled the letter into a ball and hurled it across the room.

Mayor Nancy Ogg returned to the viewing window, watched through tear-glazed eyes as the space tugs released their containers on the loading platform and then left via the docking tunnel to retrieve additional containers.

She turned to stare at the ball of paper as it lay on the floor near the Control Room's bank of CRT screens. *I'd better look at it. Duty before personal matters.*

She knew this was a rationalization. Actually, the personal aspect interested her more than any professional message the letter might contain.

Mayor Nancy Ogg unrolled the ball of paper and pulled at the sides to flatten crinkles. This is what she saw:

CONFIDENTIAL—FOR EYES ONLY

TO: HON. N. OGG, ST. ELBA MAYOR, L5. EARTH QUADRANT

FROM: DR. R. HUDSON, BU TECH MINISTER, NEW CITY, EARTH

HAVE M.D. SHELLS READY TUES NOON STED FOLL FRI—ASSIGN DISPENSABLE CAPPY CREWS TO FIN INT WORK IN FLIGHT.
PERSONAL—DO NOT REPEAT—EXTREME DANGER— KILLER MECKIE ON SH V. WILL SILENCE CREW AFTER MISSION.
KEEP PATIENCE. CHANGES SOON. TOLD YOUR BRO HE IS BIGOT. LOVE YOU.—DICK

Mayor Nancy Ogg wiped tears from her cheeks, mentoed this response via the same terminal:

CONFIDENTIAL—EYES ONLY
TO: DR. R. HUDSON, BU-TECH MINISTER, NEW CITY, EARTH
FROM: HON. N. OGG, ST. ELBA MAYOR, $L_5$, EARTH QUADRANT

WILL DO BEST. AVOID CHANCES—WELCOME HERE IF MISSION ABORT. BRING BIGOT WITH YOU. I FEEL SAME!—NANCY

* *

Ninety-three years later, these electronic letters would be reprinted in a Sayers' history primer....

Sayer Superior Lin-Ti held the volume after reading from it and gazed around the Great Temple ordinance room at youngsayermen who eagerly awaited the continuance of his reading.

It was late fall on the domed asteroid of Pleasant Reef, and through a tiny northeast window Lin-Ti could see golden brown leaves dropping one at a time from a gnarled old oak. Already, he had read the new history primer twice—so he knew what came next.

"I will skip the following section," Lin-Ti said, touching a button on the book to flip several pages. "Nothing of note occurred at the meeting demanded by the Alafin of Afrikari. He sent a projecto-image of himself to the oval office on the morning of Garbage Day minus seven. You can read details of the meeting if you wish on your own time. Suffice to say that President Ogg and the council ministers denied the projected Alafin's charge of a comet heading toward Earth along the same path as the AmFed deep space garbage shots. A malfunction of the Alafin's telescope was suggested."

Lin-Ti glanced up at the ceiling as he recalled the story: "A confrontation occurred during the meeting when a projecto-image of the Atheist Premier demanded inclusion in the meeting, fearful that the other two nations of Earth were plotting against him. His projection was permitted to enter. After learning of the alleged comet, the Premier made his customary complaints, alleging that the AmFeds had overcharged the Union of Atheist States for E-Ceils. As usual, the Premier felt the AmFeds were sabotaging his nation's energy development programs for the purpose of keeping them economically captive. We will discuss the 'Economics of Freeness' next week. For the present, we will pick up our studies immediately after the meeting...."

* *

Hudson and Muñoz moto-shoed across Technology Square after the meeting with the Alafin of Afrikari. Deep in thought, Hudson scarcely noticed bits of paper from the prior day's doomie demonstration which swirled in a gentle breeze at his feet. "Have you spoken with that officeworker yet?" Hudson asked. "What's his name?"

"Malloy. No. We're waiting for them to find Javik. The guy's a real carouser—we lost his trail at the pleasure domes."

Hudson focused upon the giant Uncle Rosy meckie perhaps twenty-five meters to his left, saw it rise and stand with its hands clasped in front. "It's time for the hourly address," Hudson said, slowing his shoes. He glanced right at the much smaller Muñoz.

"Keep rolling," Muñoz said irritably. "Another minute of horse—"

"Arturo!" Hudson rasped in a low tone, catching Muñoz by the arm. "Remember appearances!"

General Muñoz scowled, stopped reluctantly with Hudson to watch the meckie. The meckie spoke loudly in the kindly voice of Uncle Rosy, recorded three centuries earlier.

"Right living means consumption, citizens. It means buying and using the fruits of another person's labor. As you use what another man has wrought, keep in mind that he also uses what you have wrought. This is a wonderfully balanced system, but it depends upon YOU."

With these words, the meckie pointed a bulky forefinger down at the people who stood in the square. It closed with an appeal for all to report shirkers to the Anti-Cheapness League, then resumed its seat.

"I'm skeptical about the comet intercept plan," Hudson said, glancing down at Muñoz. "Two mass drivers with fire probes on each side of the nucleus, attempting to shift a comet's direction...."

"We've done it before," Muñoz replied, staring at the Uncle Rosy meckie. He resumed moto-shoeing. Hudson fell in at his side.

"Sure," Hudson said, "In the lab and on seventeen small comets that followed predictable courses. But this thing's huge and jumps all over the place. I wouldn't bet on it being cooperative."

Muñoz shook his head. "You're a chronic worrier, Dick. Comp six-oh-two worked it all out."

"A computer. We know why the six-oh-one was scrapped."

"Uh huh," Muñoz said, rolling around a pebble. "The trajectory error on our garbage shots. But we don't know for sure that this error caused a pile of junk to come back at us. We used it as an excuse."

"And don't forget the ETA miscalculation by the Willys computer," Hudson said ominously.

"Freaky errors that will never happen again. The odds have to be in our favor now."

"You're an expert on odds, Arturo ... at the Knave Table. But this is no card game."

"I have a feeling," Muñoz said. "Call it the intuition of a winner."

Hudson rubbed an itchy eyelid and fixed his gaze with the other eye on a woman in a red taffeta dress who stood in the motopath ahead feeding pigeons from a package of vendo-crumbs. "I wish to hell we had more time to figure this out," Hudson said. "Everything's too damned rushed."

"I agree with you there."

"Consider this, Arturo. We know a great deal ... can control voting patterns, even the world's weather and economy. But stop to think. What *don't* we know?"

"I don't see what you're driving at."

"Start with the comet—and those strange voices that give you commands."

"Commands?" Muñoz said, haughtily.

"Suggestions, then."

"It's true we don't know the comet's origin," Muñoz said, slowing to roll around the woman in the red dress.

Hudson followed, again falling in at the General's side. "Or why it follows an erratic path," Hudson said.

They looked up at the sound of thumping rotors, watched an auto-heliwagon as it landed in front of the new Bu-Industry Tower several hundred meters ahead of them. "More security monitors from the Black Box of Democracy," Muñoz said.

"How do they work?" Hudson asked. All we know is that they come from the Black Box and are required at the entrances to all buildings."

"You're the scientific whiz," Muñoz said, scornfully. Penetrate the Black Box … or get one of those monitors into your lab."

"One doesn't go about tearing into Uncle Rosy's creations indiscriminately. They're sacred, you know."

Muñoz spit on a plastic petunia garden beside the motopath. That's what I think of Uncle Rosy," he said.

Dr. Hudson glanced around nervously. "You shouldn't do that," he said in a low tone.

"You told me they use indoor surveillance units the size of a pin tip," Muñoz said. "If that's true, I can say anything I please outside!"

"I said I *thought* they were doing it that way. I have no proof! A beam might be trained on us right now, picking up every word. We don't know how it's being done."

"Or IF it's being done. This whole Black Box thing smacks of bluffery to me."

"The card game expert again …"

"Well, find out, dammit! You can check anyplace for bugging equipment … on the premise that an enemy of the state might have put it there."

"We shouldn't talk this way," Dr. Hudson said. He rolled along silently, and as he watched, four security monitor units slid off the rear of the heliwagon and rolled to positions at the building entrances. Dr. Hudson glanced at Muñoz and mentoed: *We've taken hundreds of specks to the lab. All have turned out to be paint or dirt. They could color the micro-units to match any paint color … and with today's signal camouflage technology….*

"Jesus!" Muñoz said.

Hudson glared down at him, mentoed: *And add Uncle Rosy's disappearance to the list.*

"Suicide," Muñoz said. He picked up Hudson's glare, mentoed reluctantly to finish his statement: *He didn't want to grow old; he arranged for someone to hide the body.*

*Maybe,* Hudson mentoed. *And maybe not.*

They took a narrow side motopath toward the Bu-Mil and Bu-Tech towers, watched through widely spaced plastic poplar trees as two men in brown friar robes touched a security monitor unit and then raised their hands heavenward.

Hudson shook his head, looked away. He had seen the ceremony many times and had no idea what it meant.

"They don't speak," Muñoz said, feeling his words were safe. "Rumor has it they're mute."

"Impossible," Hudson said. "Uncle Rosy would never permit cappies to remain on Earth."

Muñoz picked at a front tooth with his forefinger. He nodded without saying anything.

They watched as the robed men rolled up a ramp to enter the heliwagon. When the men were inside, the heliwagon rose swiftly into the air, banked and flew off in the direction of the Black Box of Democracy.

Moments later, Dr. Hudson rolled alone up an entrance ramp to the Bu-Tech Tower. He pressed his palm against the electronic security monitor's black glass identity plate, mentoed: *GW one, Dr. Richard Hudson, Bu-Tech Minister.*

He felt a strong vacuum against his hand. Then it released, and a red light on the monitor turned to green.

O O O

As Dr. Hudson stood at the security monitor, two sayermen wearing brown-hooded robes rose above Technology Square in a pilotless heliwagon. Onesayer Edward squinted in sunlight from the east, extended his left hand to Lastsayer Steven, who sat to his right. "Peace be upon you," Onesayer said, raising his voice over the thump of rotors.

Lastsayer touched his brown-and-gold onyx ring to a like ring worn by the other man, coughed and replied, "Peace be upon you, Onesayer. Thank you for instructing me in the Holy Order," Again, he coughed.

"Nasty cough," Onesayer observed.

"Felt it coming on yesterday," Lastsayer sniffed, looking at Onesayer's wide, puffy-fat face. "I have been tired since arrival."

"Rocket lag. I see it all the time." Onesayer reached into his robe pocket, removed a chrome pillbox. He selected two yellow pills and handed them to Lastsayer. "Take a Happy Pill and a water capsule," Onesayer instructed. "You'll … uh … you will feel better." *My speech,* Onesayer thought. *It slips into apostrophes … another sign of my break with the Master….*

Onesayer watched the younger man hesitate and then accept the pills. Lastsayer had clear, wrinkle-free skin, like that of all sayermen. Moderately plump, he had an upturned nose and light green eyes that darted nervous glances around the edge of his hood. *He looks so innocent,* Onesayer thought, recalling a time nearly three centuries earlier when he had been the same way.

Lastsayer held the pills in an open palm, looked at them inquisitively. "These are allowed?" he asked. "I have heard—"

"They are not *allowed*," Onesayer said, "but take them anyway." He smiled, adding, "We do not take many of them, you understand … maybe seven or eight a day. You never had one?"

Lastsayer smiled nervously, coughed again. "No, but I see no harm … if you approve." He popped the pills in his mouth and swallowed them.

"How are things on Pleasant Reef?" Onesayer asked.

"In turmoil. Our women have demonstrated the past two weeks. Can you imagine? They demand positions in the Sayerhood!"

"They share the Sayerhood now!" Onesayer said angrily. "Is it not enough for them to raise the youngsayermen of our order?"

"Apparently not." Lastsayer gazed out the window, saw a white Product Failure van speeding along the expressway below, red lights flashing. He was unable to hear the sirens over the thump of rotors.

"And Sayer Superior Lin-Ti … He is well?"

"Yes. He spent countless hours tutoring me."

"Your tutelage is far from complete. Uncle Rosy even reminds *me* that I have much to learn."

Lastsayer nodded. Presently he said, "I saw the Uncle Rosy meckie on its feet as we landed."

"A message on right living."

"The history primer told me of this, Onesayer. The meckie holds a cross and a machine gear, and I was taught the significance of these symbols."

Onesayer looked out the window, saw the Black Box of Democracy two blocks to the right. Feeling a need to say the correct things, he said, "You studied the near civil war between the Christian Church and the technologists, I presume?"

"Yes," Lastsayer said. "Two armed camps ... bitter feelings...."

"Over petty matters, as the Master pointed out at the time. He brought the adversaries together."

"By protecting the economic base of each side," Lastsayer said, demonstrating his knowledge. "In the end, it all boiled down to economics, with each side wanting more followers and more property."

"It is good that you paid attention to your lessons. That is why you were selected for Earth duty." Onesayer watched another heliwagon prepare to take off from the roof of the Black Box while their craft circled half a block away, waiting for clearance.

"Thank you, Onesayer. But it is more than the text which interests me now."

"How so?"

"A story was told to me on Pleasant Reef ... by one of the child-bearing women ... that Uncle Rosy met with the Christian cardinals privately after the truce."

"What did you hear about that?" Onesayer snapped, realizing the emotion of his response was more automatic than real.

"That Uncle Rosy attempted to convince the cardinals to give up the cross symbol ... in favor of a human brain design. According to the story, Uncle Rosy felt the brain—as a miraculous and basically mysterious entity—was a more proper symbol of the universal God."

Onesayer scowled, glared out the window. Presently he said, "Uncle Rosy is a complex man, at once a great economist and a man of the cloth. What you heard is true, but this was not supposed to be mentioned on Pleasant Reef."

"I will give you the name of the woman."

"Good. The Master prefers to tell that story himself." *I don't really care about this,* Onesayer thought. *Let Uncle Rosy's whole damned system fall into disarray.*

"I did not know," Lastsayer said.

"Act as if you are not familiar with the story when the Master relates it to you."

"Yes, Onesayer."

"The cardinals were a stubborn lot, Lastsayer, and became extremely upset at Uncle Rosy's suggestion. Our Master decided to back down upon seeing their reaction, fearful that he might upset the delicate truce."

"Thank you for telling me this."

"You have an alert mind, Lastsayer. I like that."

Lastsayer Steven did not respond. He watched the other heliwagon take off. Their craft began to descend.

"Symbolism is very important, Lastsayer. Tragically, the cross Uncle Rosy's meckie holds may have led to the Holy War of twenty-three-twenty-six." *Another of the Master's errors,* Onesayer thought.

Lastsayer's green eyes flashed intently. "How is that?" he asked.

"As you know, the first Council of Ten was formed in the negotiations between Uncle Rosy, the scientists and the cardinals."

"I know: equal input from the cardinals and the scientists. But that was formed seven years before Uncle Rosy withdrew to the Black Box."

"Correct. After Uncle Rosy's withdrawal in twenty-three eighteen, a popular movement fanned by Cardinal John of Atlantic City and other Christian zealots demanded a holy war against all other religions. They said the cross held by Uncle Rosy was a sign of approval from the Master."

"I was not aware of that," Lastsayer said, watching the glassite roof of the Black Box grow closer while their craft descended. "Did Uncle Rosy approve, considering his feelings about a universal, rather than a Christian, God?"

"Uncle Rosy has always been torn between religious and economic issues. He likes to say economic considerations are more important ..."

"But you are not so certain?"

"I, too, have much to learn."

Lastsayer thought he heard bitterness in the other man's tone. He thought for a moment, then said: "Should Uncle Rosy have stepped in *before* the holy war started? I mean no disrespect."

"He wanted to give the AmFeds free reign, except in the case of a government overthrow attempt. He did not wish to meddle too much, but when he saw the destruction being caused by AmFed bombs ..." Onesayer fell silent. Dust swirled on the rooftop from the wind of the helirotors.

"He saw the economic futility of destroying foreign markets," Lastsayer said. "That would have put millions of AmFeds out of work!"

Onesayer sighed. "The AmFeds became so emotional over their holy war that they forgot about economics entirely."

"So the Master intervened, with you as emissary. Sayer Superior told me of your important role."

The heliwagon jolted as it landed.

A smile moved across Onesayer's large mouth. "I merely delivered a written bull to the Council of Ten reminding them of their economic responsibilities," he said. "I did not speak a word to them, of course. We are not permitted to address common people."

"The bull spoke of the Principle of Economic Captivity, I presume," Lastsayer said. He heard the heliwagon's engines begin to whine down.

"Yes," Onesayer said. Their safety harnesses snapped off automatically. He placed a hand on the front of each armrest. "The bull also specified that three nations would be established on Earth ... the American Federation of Freeness, Afrikari, and the Union of Atheist States. In its public version, this became known as the Treaty of Rabat. It survives to this day."

"Christian, pagan, and atheist." Lastsayer pursed his lips thoughtfully. He rose when Onesayer did, added, "What a great man the Master is! I look forward to my first session with him!"

Onesayer led the way down the aisle, said with a turn of his hooded head to throw words over one shoulder: "You will never see his face, of course. No one has, since he entered the Black Box."

"Oh, but just to be near him. The thrill of it!"

Onesayer nodded as he rolled onto an exit ramp, recalling a time long before when he had felt the same way.

O O O

Sidney turned sleepily in bed, throwing one arm over a rubber-skinned pleasie-meckie that lay beside him. "Carla," he whispered in an awakening haze, "I love you, Carla."

His eyes popped open, and when he became aware of reality, Sidney cursed at his misfortune. He pushed the meckie away.

The naked pleasie-meckie had fine-toned muscles like Carla's, with an aquiline nose and shoulder-length, golden-brown hair.

Sidney mentoed it to life. *Away,* he commanded tersely. *Return to your station.*

Obediently, the pleasie-meckie rose and dressed quickly in undergarments which lay in disarray on the floor. Then, as Sidney watched, it rolled into the closet and took a standing position to one side. He turned away, stared at the spray-textured ceiling. Sidney heard rustling in the closet for several moments. Then the meckie closed the closet door and Sidney was left alone.

He stretched and yawned. As usual, it was late morning when he awakened, and Sidney could see synthetic sunlight through the open doorway of the bathroom module. Moments later, he stood naked from the waist up at a grooming machine in the bathroom.

The tiny modular room was warm and cheerful, with a planter box of plastic marigolds along one wall beneath a sun-lite panel. White synthetic light from the panel warmed his left side.

Thinking about his strange space dream of the night before and of the haunting, recurring voices, Sidney waited while an electric shaver at the end of a right-handed meckie-arm trimmed the stubble off his face. The U-shaped grooming machine, Sidney's height overall, peered back at him with its mirror face between seeing-eye meckie-arms on each side. An array of brightly colored buttons above the machine's sink could be mento- or hand-activated. Gold lettering across the top of the mirror proclaimed: "UNCLE ROSY LOVES US."

Sidney turned his face to one side when the shave was finished, trying to find a better angle in the mirror. This made his ears seem to protrude less, but the pug nose looked worse. He sighed, wondered sadly, *Why can't I be better looking? I'm not even average!*

The meckie-arms took Lemon Delight Shaving Lotion from a dispenser next to the mirror and patted Sidney's face. The lotion stung; his eyes watered. Sidney always resented mechanical grooming, but held up his arms cooperatively while deodorant spray was pumped all over his pear-shaped torso.

In the next grooming maneuver, Sidney knew he had to be careful. He watched with trepidation as the left meckie-arm grasped a toothbrush and took on a load of Shiny Bright Toothpaste from a wall dispenser. A smiling picture of President Ogg looked back at Sidney from the dispenser with a message printed across perfectly even, sparkling white teeth: "VOTE FOR OGG."

The toothbrush darted into Sidney's open mouth and surge-scrubbed every tooth. Several times recently, not paying sufficient attention, Sidney had failed to open his mouth. The disastrous result: sticky white paste rubbed all over his nose and chin. *Not this time,* he told himself. The meckie finished with an automatic rinse, gargle, face wash, and set of Sidney's curly black hair, all accomplished without strangling, drenching, or costing him the loss of any hair.

After breakfast, Sidney moto-shoed across his small condominium unit to the living room module. This too was a cheerful room, despite the location of Sidney's unit at the building core where it could not receive natural light. Bright splashes of gold and orange washed furnishings and walls with color. An orange, plastic-encased videodome dominated the room's center, directly beneath a ceiling-mounted sun-lite panel.

He rolled past the videodome, pausing in front of a wall decorated with a gold and black checkerboard design. Concentrating upon one of the squares, he mentoed an unseen combination dial and heard the click of tumblers as he projected each number. The square slid away, revealing a lighted wallsafe filled with leatherbound scrapbooks and an assortment of personal treasures. He selected two volumes and an old-style pen, went with them to the couch.

Sidney sat down pensively, stacked both volumes on the coffee table and opened the cover of the top one slowly. A handwritten title had been scrawled across the yellowing first page in large, childish script:

**MY PILOT LOG, VOLUME ONE**
**Property of Captain Sidney Malloy American Federation Space Patrol**

He turned the page, read his fantasy: "I joined the Space Patrol as a lad of ten, assuming the duties of cabin boy on the Star Class Destroyer *AFSP Nathan Rogers.* Within six months, my leadership abilities became so apparent that I was promoted to Captain and given command of the ship."

He looked away, smiling as he thought, *Did I really write this?*

Sidney continued reading: "My first assignment: seek and recapture the escaped arch-criminal Jed Laredo. Laredo is wanted for detonating a powerful ice bomb following his escape from the asteroid colony at

LaGrange Six. Twelve-thousand inhabitants perished in the explosion. He is believed to be hiding near an abandoned mining base at Agarratown on the Celtian planet of Redondo...."

He flipped the ensuing pilot log pages, read the successful and heroic conclusion of his fantasy mission. Other fantasies followed, entered meticulously beside blueprints and specifications on a variety of spacecraft.

In one sense, the space scrapbooks seemed childish to him now, but still he felt the longings he had experienced as a youth. The exploits were not real ... he had always known this ... but the adventures contained a spirit of hope ... a certain innocence and naïveté concerning his future. This morning, as he prepared to write about his confused ego pleasure dream of the prior evening, Sidney still had hope ... but it was not so bright and untarnished as it once had been.

He sighed, placed Volume One to one side, and opened the next scrapbook, his fourteenth. Flipping to a blank page, he began writing: "While patrolling the Signus XX-4 Quadrant in the Summer of 2605, I received urgent word ..."

*How can I get this down?* he wondered, rubbing the pen thoughtfully against his lower lip. *Those strange, maddening voices....*

Interrupted by the doorchime, Sidney mentoed his new singing wrist digital. A sultry female voice sang to him cheerfully in a sing-song tone: "AM, ten-forty-one-point-three-four."

*Wonder who's there?* he thought, welcoming the interruption. He replaced the volumes in the wallsafe and reseated the panel.

As Sidney opened the hall door, Bob Hodges, his tall and thickly-muscled downstairs neighbor, rolled in without an invitation. "Hi Sid," he said cheerily. "How ya doin'?" Hodges was puppy-friendly, thoughtless but well-meaning.

Sidney regrouped his thoughts and returned the greeting. Then he led the way down a woodgrain linoleum hallway to the living room module.

"How about a little video?" Hodges asked, seeing the videodome as they entered the room.

Sidney grunted in affirmation, rolled directly into the videodome without another thought and sat in his favorite bucket seat, one of four inside. He sank into the videodome chair, consumed by the billowing softness of authentic Corinthian vinyl. Mentoing a channel selector to the left of his seat, Sidney watched a green button on the selector depress.

"Have to make sure you watch enough home video," Hodges said, laughing. "Hear you had a recent visit from those folks at the Anti-Cheapness League."

Sidney heard the videodome door slide shut. An overhead light dimmed. "It was nothing," he answered matter-of-factly. "They were investigating a faulty videodome report. Someone did a line test seconds after one of my dome circuits blew. With no repair order in on my set, they were concerned that it might have been down for several days."

"Oh," Hodges said. "No big deal."

"Naw. I gave them details on the video programs I'd been watching before the blowout, signed their form and they left." Sidney mentoed channel forty-seven on the selector.

Sidney watched three-dimensional screens all around light up, giving viewers the illusion of being seated in a crowded auditorium. People chattered at nearby seats, and Sidney made out details of their conversations.

"Jimmy Earl is next," a young man in the crowd said, "with the latest from Rok-More. Then the Mister Sugar Follies."

"How exciting!" a woman in a fur coat said.

Spotlighted at center stage, a man in a white sequin Western outfit spoke excitedly into a handheld microphone. "The latest from Rok-More Records!" he said, waving an arm to his rear toward a mini-stage containing a spotlighted record cube display. "Donna Butler's in the Happy Shopping Ground, folks, but her songs will never die! Supplies are limited, so order *Donna's Greatest Hits* now! As a bonus for those of you in our home video audience, I'll throw in this delightful little 'Heart of Gold' pendant." He held the pendant up, added in a voice grown suddenly tender, "Donna's signature is on the back, folks. Won't you pledge your undying love for Donna? Order now!"

The audience auto-clapped and cheered as a product number appeared on a sign above the record cube display. Sidney felt a chill in his spine from the patriotism of the moment, and mentoed the number into a Tele-Charge board that was connected to an arm of his chair. He signed the board with a transmitting pen, noting that Hodges was doing the same.

With glazed eyes, Sidney watched the Mister Sugar Follies now, a group of twelve men clad in blue-and-white soft drink cans. After an explanation by one that they were permitted to expend energy since it was Job-Supportive, the men danced stiffly in a row like tin dolls to a twangy tune. As they kicked their feet in near unison, Sidney noticed his throat gone dry. The subliminal receiver in his brain had been activated.

"You thirsty?" he asked, glancing at Hodges.

"And how!" came the reply. "Feel like I'm out in the desert!"

Sidney mentoed for drinks, and presently two frosty cans of Mr. Sugar popped out of a table compartment between their chairs.

As Sidney drank the icy cola, an unbearable itching sensation took over his body.

"Quickly!" Hodges said, feeling the same thing. "Mento for your Itcho-Spray! The commercial's on!"

Sidney had barely noticed the Itcho-Spray Man on stage, and he quickly mentoed for the product.

"You DO have some on hand?" Hodges asked, near panic.

"Certainly. But I think ... I'm going to have to scratch—"

"Don't do it! You have to use the product! Hang tough, man! Hang tough!"

"Aaaagh!" Sidney grunted, fighting an overwhelming urge to claw his back, chest, and legs.

A white ball of Itcho-Spray popped out of the table compartment and floated in the air above their heads. It exploded in a little "pop," showering them with clear liquid droplets.

They sighed in unison as the itching crisis subsided.

"Relief is just an Itcho-Spray away!" the Itcho-Spray Man said.

The spotlight shifted to a smiling President Ogg now, who stood at a podium bearing the Great Seal of the President of the American Federation of Freeness. Sidney felt the videodome vibrate as the crowd auto-clapped and roared its approval.

"Employment and consumption are at record levels under my administration!" the President boomed. "A vote for me is a vote for prosperity!" He delivered a short speech concerning his past accomplishments and promises for the future, then short-stepped to one side of the podium and bowed. He blew kisses and waved as the curtain closed.

"Who you gonna vote for?" Hodges asked, leaning toward Sidney to be heard over the crowd noise.

"I don't know," Sidney replied. "Probably Ogg again. Ben Morgan may be all right, but we don't know much about him."

"Better the evil that we do know?"

Sidney laughed.

"Think I'll go with a punch-in this time," Hodges said. "I like General Muñoz."

Hodges's last words seemed exceedingly loud to Sidney, as the crowd noises had subsided quickly. Another commercial was onstage now, a chorus line of dancing soap bubbles selling laundry detergent. "But I've heard he isn't interested," Sidney said.

"Maybe not," Hodges concurred, shrugging his shoulders. "But I have to vote my conscience. It came to me last night like an inspiration. I'm convinced he's the only man for the job."

Sidney glanced at his wrist digital, mentoed it to activate the sexy-voiced time singer. She reported that it was eleven twenty-nine. "Time to get ready for work," Sidney said.

* *

Another holy water break approached. Before dismissing the class, Sayer Superior Lin-Ti explained the mechanics of the subliminal transmitting device:

"Following Dr. Hudson's instructions, General Muñoz established the vote percentile he desired. One-hundred percent would be too obvious, of course, so he chose something more reasonable—around fifty-seven percent. Then he touched the cross with both hands instead of the one-hand method used for weather control. While touching the cross, Muñoz transmitted his auto-suggestion.

"This caused a powerful beam to enter the brains of millions of AmFed consumers, tapping their subliminal receivers and forcing them to vote as the General wished. To reinforce the auto-suggestion, he re-broadcast several times a day in the days preceding the election....

* *

"This is much more than a room," Onesayer Edward said as he and Lastsayer Steven rolled into the Bureau Monitoring Room at a little past one o'clock Friday afternoon. "Actually, it takes up the entire second floor of the Black Box."

"Most impressive," Lastsayer said. He looked around the room curiously, watched sayermen scurrying about with microcomputer printouts. Other sayermen sat on high stools at consoles along each wall, operating CRT screens, minicam receivers, and computerized memory terminals. A background hum of pink sound muffled most of the noises, making the room seem relatively quiet.

"You are versed in Rosetran, I presume?" Onesayer asked.

"I know fifteen computer languages," Lastsayer said, gazing up with light green eyes at a large "Keep the Faith" sign on one wall beneath a sun-lite panel.

"You will begin at Station Five," Onesayer said, nodding toward a workstation along the wall to their left. A large red Arabic numeral "5" on the wall marked the station. He looked down at the smaller Lastsayer, saw him nod.

"This is a highly efficient operation," Onesayer said as he led the way to Station Five. "We accomplish a great deal with very few sayermen. Sophisticated machines do most of the work. Sayermen scrutinize problem areas flagged by the machines."

Lastsayer noticed it was a bit warm in the room, and said, "I believe I am familiar with everything here. We had a mockup on Pleasant Reef."

One of two stools at Station Five was occupied by a hooded sayerman who sat with his back to them mentoing entries on a console keyboard. The keys moved up and down without being touched. Onesayer and Lastsayer stopped a meter behind the occupied stool, continuing their conversation.

"Every citizen of the American Federation works for the government," Onesayer said. "So they regularly pass through our electronic security monitors. There, cell readers pick up every memory in their lifetimes...." He paused at Lastsayer and smiled broadly. "I am sorry. You did mention being familiar with everything."

Lastsayer smiled in return, nodded confidently.

"You understand the drawback of the electronic monitors, do you not?" Onesayer asked.

"The delay factor. Citizens who do not pass through the cell reader for a time have a gap in their lifelog files."

"Right. This gap can range from a few hours to several days. Even today, people stay home sick with common colds."

Lastsayer looked at Onesayer closely, noted a red streak in the corner of one eye. "Odd is it not, Onesayer Edward? All the terrible diseases modern medicine can cure, but the common cold remains a mystery."

The sayerman on the stool turned abruptly at the mention of Onesayer's name, looked startled. "Oh!" he exclaimed, nearly falling off his stool in an effort to stand up. "I did not see you there, sir!"

"Quite all right, Ninesayer," Onesayer said.

Ninesayer stood up straight to face Onesayer and extended his left hand. Onesayer and Lastsayer extended their hands as well, and the three men touched class rings, murmuring in unison, "Peace be upon you."

Ninesayer had large, loose cheeks and tiny blue eyes which peered back at Lastsayer from beneath an oversized hood. He seemed a friendly sort, and smiled pleasantly while Onesayer introduced them.

"Lastsayer will be working with you," Onesayer said.

"I could use some assistance," Ninesayer said, glancing at his battery of electronic equipment. "We have two rather large problems at the moment."

"I had not heard," Lastsayer said, wrinkling his brow in concern. "Life on Pleasant Reef is rather sheltered."

Onesayer explained about the garbage comet and told of the plot to overthrow the AmFed government. Then he turned to Ninesayer and said, "Show us General Muñoz. He worries me."

Ninesayer nodded, mentoed Muñoz's consumer identification number. A darkened minicam screen on the wall flickered on, revealing General Muñoz seated alone at his desk. Muñoz rubbed the cross which dangled from his neck with both hands, smiled craftily.

"Run the tape back five minutes," Onesayer instructed. "Let us see what he has been up to."

Ninesayer mentoed the machine, causing the tape to roll back.

"All right," Onesayer said. "Hold it right there!"

The sayerman watched as General Muñoz closed his eyes and held both hands to the cross. An intense expression came over the General's mustachioed face, and he sat motionless for perhaps a minute.

"He is using the subliminal transmitter again!" Onesayer said excitedly, "making voters punch in his name for President!"

"We obtained details on its operation from CM … uh, from cell memory readings on his co-conspirator, Dr. Richard Hudson,"

Ninesayer explained, glancing at Lastsayer. "Muñoz's first broadcast occurred last night."

"You can use the term 'CMR' around me," Lastsayer said.

"Muñoz is power-mad," Onesayer said, "and has access to dangerous technology. According to his CMR, he intends to destroy Afrikari and the Union of Atheist States with earthquakes and other … 'natural' … disasters the minute he feels he can get away with it."

"Without regard for the economic havoc it will cause to the AmFeds?" Lastsayer exclaimed. "Hoovervilles will spring up all over the landscape!"

"The man is extremely dangerous," Onesayer said, closing his olive eyes momentarily in abhorrence. "Eighth generation radical Christian."

"A direct descendant of Cardinal John of Atlantic City," Ninesayer said.

"And the last in his line," Onesayer said. His words were measured and angry.

"Homosexual," Ninesayer explained, glancing at Lastsayer.

"Oh," Lastsayer said.

"And … he will he dead within seventy-two hours," Onesayer said. "Uncle Rosy has placed a contract on him. It will be a nasty accident."

"Product failure?" Lastsayer asked.

"Of course!" Onesayer said, smiling. "Uncle Rosy never misses an opportunity to help the economy!"

* *

It was early morning on Pleasant Reef, following the daily prayer to Uncle Rosy, and Sayer Superior Lin-Ti stood considering the lesson. A youngsayerman entered the ordinance room late, taking his seat sheepishly under the glare of Lin-Ti. It was the tall, fat one whose appearance was so reminiscent of Onesayer Edward. Lin-Ti scowled at the offender, then opened his history primer, removing a bookmark ribbon….

# Chapter Four

## BACKGROUND MATERIAL, FOR FURTHER READING AND DISCUSSION

*Dr. Hudson: "I started where Uncle Rosy left off, so the mento transmitter is as much a credit to him as it is to me. Uncle Rosy was a brilliant man of science, you know. He made many pioneering discoveries in the area of thought-transmission for the purpose of operating consumer products."*

*Student: "Uncle Rosy was motivated by economics, was he not, Doctor Hudson?"*

*Dr. Hudson: "Mentoing and increased consumption go hand in hand. But in reviewing copies of his lab diaries, I detected a reverence for the mysteries of the brain. Listen to this excerpt: [after pause] 'Our technology cannot begin to approach the beauty, the precision, the wonderful balance of the human brain.'"*

Minicam transcript from Dr. Hudson's Boston College classroom, October 8, 2587 (six months prior to Hudson's appointment as Bu-Tech Minister).

### *Saturday, August 26, 2605*

Garbage day minus six arrived without Sidney's knowledge. Understandably, this information was kept on a "need-to-know" basis.

Sidney awoke early in the morning to a jangling telephone next to his bed. When he opened his eyes sleepily, a cordless tele-cube floated in the air above his face. Carla was on the line, announcing she could not make it to the reunion. Her doctor had diagnosed a virus.

"Why don't you take two Happy Pills?" Sidney suggested as he stared up at the cube. He brushed a lock of hair out of his eyes. "Maybe you'll feel well enough to—"

"I don't want any more pills for a while," Carla's tele-cube voice said firmly. "I need rest."

"There are sleep-sub—"

"Real rest," she interjected.

This sounded strange to Sidney. He could not recall a day when she did not take a pill. But he decided not to argue.

"Goodbye," Carla said.

Sidney watched the tele-cube float back to its cradle on the phone, thought, *Our relationship stinks!*

He and Carla had known each other nearly all their lives. Their parents had been close friends, and he had been her datemate since high school. But Carla always seemed to treat him more like a brother than a boyfriend … and there had never been any physical intimacy. Sidney had been counting on the reunion to put their relationship on a new track. He had planned it all out. *I was going to be so suave and sophisticated,* Sidney thought.

He felt his entire body shaking. *I mustn't become upset,* he thought. Sidney closed his eyes and lay back on the bed, recalling his father's exact words, spoken so many years earlier.…

"… It is absolutely imperative that you remain calm. The incorto injector I have surgically implanted in your body is not available to the public."

"I have the only one?" the nine-year-old Sidney had asked.

His father had nodded. "Its development was ordered stopped many years ago as a Bu-Med Job-Support measure. The device has not been perfected."

"Why not?"

"The injector has a major deficiency. Its operation can be blocked if your adrenalin level rises too much. This would result in a massive breakdown of your nervous system.…"

Sidney sat up on one elbow and as he recalled the conversation he gazed at a picture of his father on the dresser. A glint of synthetic sunlight touched the shiny gold electroplate frame and reflected off the polished plastic surface of the dresser top. He saw the same eyes and nose as his own, but the features were not so soft as Sidney's. His father smiled faintly in the picture, but there was deep concern in the eyes … possibly a fear of what the world had in store for Sidney.

*I don't want a massive breakdown,* Sidney thought.

Unable to return to sleep, he lay back and watched artificial dawn sunlight filter into his bedroom module through a single overhead sun-lite panel. He longed for the mercy of slumber. How attractive to remain there and not face the world! Like a whirligig, this thought rotated in his mind. But then he recalled the strange voices which had interrupted his ego pleasure dream two nights before. *When will they come again?* he wondered.

Old thoughts mixed with new ones. *I wish I had a dashing career in the Space Patrol,* he thought. *Carla would be my permie then.* This brought on a disturbing realization, as it occurred to him that his latent disability was the key to all his problems. If not for the affliction, life could have been so perfect!

In his despondency and anger, Sidney mentoed for his pleasie-meckie. The closet door popped open, and the scantily-clad meckie began to roll forward. But Sidney felt an inexplicable surge of guilt and resolved to overcome his sexual cravings.

*Get back!* he mentoed angrily.

After the pleasie-meckie returned to its closet station, Sidney lay in bed thinking and wishing for the rest of the morning. During several moments, he even found himself questioning the AmFed Way … for the first time in his life. Maybe his disability was not to blame after all. Maybe it was the system.

*I can function in society!* he thought, tormented. *But the system won't allow it, won't give me the opportunity!*

Eventually he discarded such thoughts, trying to see the good side of things. For deep inside, Sidney Malloy believed in the AmFed Way. And in the Doctrine of Greatest Good.

When Sidney finally arose, he felt numb and more down than up. Thinking of the voices and of his depressed state, he considered going to a drive-in psychiatrist's window. But he discarded the idea in favor of a Happy Pill. There had been rumors that the psychiatric windows actually were fronts for therapy recruitment, that the resident analyst could declare anyone incompetent and have him sent to a therapy orbiter.

People had been known to disappear.

He felt better after the pill, and kept himself busy that afternoon inside the videodome. The dome was a room-within-a-room, a place where reality could be forgotten. Sidney Tele-Charged several products that were advertised on the screen. He felt better with each purchase.

O O O

Early in the evening of the same day, Sidney rolled off the elevator at Parking Level One wearing a black paper tuxedo with no hat. He unlocked the autosedan door with its plastikey and slid into a bucket seat which swiveled invitingly to meet him. The seat clicked into place as the door closed. A shoulder harness snapped shut across his body. Dashboard dials lit up … green, red, and blue.

Sidney mentoed a destination into the car's computer, felt cool vinyl against his paper clothing as he sat back in the soft seat. The vehicle's sexless computer voice blared, its tone high-pitched and irritating to him: "Destination … Sky Ballroom … thirty-nine twelve American Boulevard. Confirm please.…"

Sidney did not hear the instruction, was thinking about the reunion and about Carla.

"Confirm please.…" the computer insisted. "Confirm please.…"

"Yes, yes," Sidney said irritably, sitting forward and focusing his eyes on a red "CONFIRM" light that blinked rapidly on the dashboard. "Confirmed."

The autosedan began to move, and Sidney again sat back. It darted up a ramp to street level and surged unhesitatingly through automatic doors, its collision sensors probing the darkness ahead.

Minutes later, he moto-shoed off an elevator at the entrance to the Sky Ballroom. A gold and blue wall banner above a long reception table carried this announcement:

WELCOME NEW CITY HIGH GRADS! CLASS OF '85.

Sidney paused at the reception table, and in a moment was watching himself in the magik-mirror while a woman fastened a plastic nametag to his lapel. It was a full-length mirror, showing a reflection of the side of his body that was away from the glass. Sidney concealed his right hand from the mirror, held it behind his protruding stomach and wiggled the fingers. The image wiggled its fingers. When the woman finished fastening his nametag, Sidney faced the mirror and stuck out his tongue. It reflected only the back of his head and body, as if he were standing behind himself.

Sidney became aware of a fair-haired man in a Space Patrol uniform who stood along a side wall. The man seemed to be watching Sidney with pale, unfocused eyes, and Sidney recognized the eagle pin of a full colonel on his lapel. A nametag below that read: "PEEBLES."

*Is he really looking at me?* Sidney wondered. *Or at something else?* Sidney turned his head the other way, saw only a bare wall.

Sidney put the man out of his mind and rolled through double swinging doors into the main ballroom. There were happy crowd sounds in this room, and a band tuning its instruments. He searched for familiar faces.

It was a crystal clear night, with twinkling stars and a crescent sliver of moon which shone through an overhead glassplex dome. People played talking video games, electronic dice, and galactic pool along one wall. Sidney paused to watch as a man he did not recognize auto-shot a ball into one of the side pockets of the galactic pool table. A wallscreen above the table lit up with brilliant flashes and spades of orange and blue as the ball disappeared into the pocket.

"The synthetic black hole pockets are clever, don't you agree?" a man to Sidney's left asked. "They consume matter almost as voraciously as real ones."

Sidney turned toward the voice, nodded to a tall, amber-haired man in a white, long-sleeved Greco tunic. Trimmed in gold braid, the tunic had military epaulets and a Space Patrol crest on each sleeve. "Tried to bring back a real black hole one time," the man said, studying Sidney's round face closely. "Damn near killed me!"

"Is that right?' Sidney said, interested.

"Say," the man said, looking down at Sidney with an eyelid flicker of recognition, "aren't you Sidney Malloy?"

"Yeah. I am." Sidney noted the man had deeply-set blue eyes and a straight, sharp nose. The features were distantly familiar. Suddenly the identity jumped out at him. "Tom!" he said, half yelling with excitement. "You're Tom Javik!"

"How ya been, buddy?" Javik asked, embracing his old friend.

"All right," Sidney said as they pulled apart. "Who else is here tonight?'

"Just got in. Let's find a table."

They selected a window table. From his chair there, Sidney could see why this was called the Sky Ballroom. It "kissed the very boundary of the heavens," just as the advertisements had promised. New City stretched out below in all directions, "a sea of lights beneath a universe of stars."

A dance floor and slightly elevated stage occupied the center of the room. Above the floor a delicate aquamarine crystal chandelier seemed sky-suspended. Fifty-one musicians onstage tuned their guitars and practiced the hip gyrations they were allowed to perform.

"Whatcha been up to?" Javik asked. He rubbed an ingrown hair sore on the side of his neck.

"Not much. I'm a GW seven-five-oh in the Presidential Bureau. Central Forms. You're still in the Space Patrol, I see."

"Naw. I borrowed this tunic from a friend. I got in big trouble—had to take garbage shuttle duty in the Transport Corps." Javik wrinkled his nose angrily.

"At least you're flying," Sidney said, furrowing his dark eyebrows thoughtfully. "I'd trade places with you in a minute." Sidney studied a swiveling song request panel mounted at the table center. "They've got old tunes here," he said. "Remember the Space Boogie?"

"Hey hey!" Sidney detected sadness in Javik's tone. "How about the Gimme Gumbo Rock Waltz?" Javik asked.

Sidney searched the list, pointed. "Yeah. It's here."

Javik laughed and looked around. He squinted to look across the room, then pointed and said: "Near the wall. That guy in the blue tux is Jerry Sims!"

"Oh yeah," Sidney said, unenthused. "I didn't know him as well as you did." Sidney looked back at the song request panel, mentoed it to see another reader-card.

"Excuse me a minute, Sid," Javik said, rising to his feet. "I just want to say 'hello.'" He moto-shoed to the table and spoke with his friend for several minutes.

When Javik returned, he asked about Carla. Sidney thought of his pleasie-meckie which resembled Carla, and he smiled with some difficulty. "We're still datemates," he said. "She was supposed to be here tonight, but called and said she wasn't feeling well. Had a new dress picked out, too."

"Too bad." Javik's deeply-set blue eyes flashed mischievously. "Hey, we should have bought renta-dates for the night!"

"Naw," Sidney said, laughing. "Those girls giggle too much."

"Know what you mean."

Just then, a waitress in a striped black and yellow tigress outfit rolled over, flopping her pointed mechanical ears joyfully. "Good evening, gentlemen," she purred. "What would you like to have?"

Javik glanced at Sidney and winked, then replied, "Raspberry fizzle."

"Make it two," Sidney said. He studied her figure when she was not looking, then glanced at Javik and saw him wink back. They watched the waitress's long slinky tail drag behind her as she left.

"Know what I wanted to say to ask her for," Javik said, smiling as he locked gazes with Sidney.

Sidney smiled uneasily in return, watched Colonel Peebles slide into a seat several tables away. Peebles stared at Sidney with unfocused, glazed eyes.

"That guy over there," Sidney said, nodding his head to one side. "He seems to be staring at me."

Javik turned in the direction Sidney had designated, then quickly snapped back to look at Sidney. "Peebles," he hissed. "What's that bastard doing here? He wasn't in our class!"

Sidney shrugged, stared at the song request panel. "Where do you know him from?" he asked.

"The a-hole testified at my discharge proceedings. Made the Space Patrol toss me out on my butt. He's a fairy, you know, like the pretty-boy Major I punched out." Javik glanced around nervously.

Sidney did not ask for further details. The two men fell silent, then looked up at the stage where a man in a white tuxedo spoke into a microphone: "We are about to begin your program, grads! Make your song requests now. Keep in mind that musical performance is a Job-Support profession, and as such is exempt from the Conservation of Motion Doctrine. . . ."

O O O

As Sidney and Javik watched the program, Carla stood at her vanity mirror, thinking of Billie Birdbright.

Birdbright would arrive in a few minutes, and she pictured his handsome, bronzed face in her mind … the strong, dimpled chin and wavy, bright yellow hair … those playful, smoke-grey eyes. She used a small brush to paint a tiny black beauty mark on her left cheek, turned her face slightly to admire it from a different angle.

*I have a right to be happy,* Carla thought, thinking for a fleeting moment of Sidney as she placed the brush on her makeup table. *I couldn't be expected to pass this chance up.*

She sprayed perfume on her neck and practiced smiling in the vanity mirror. Carla saw moist lavender lips that matched the color of her eyes, bun-swirled golden-brown hair with a godiva fall and a black ruby clasp to one side. The evening dress was lavender mache, with the bodice cut in a long narrow vee, exposing portions of her bust and midriff. She pulled some of the fall hairs forward over each shoulder, and they cascaded over her breasts.

Carla moto-spun approvingly before the mirror. She knew she would be Birdbright's bedmate that evening just as the other girls had been. With this in mind, she selected every article of clothing and toiletry with care. A quiet time in the videodome watching a roller rock concert along with vi-do dinners and wine capsules would start the evening off well....

The doorchime rang.

*Oh!* Carla thought with a start. *I'd better start dinner!*

She moto-hurried into the kitchen module and took two ceramic vi-do trays of porkchops with applesauce and synthetic baby peas from the freezer. She popped them into the microwave oven.

O O O

Sidney mentoed nine song request buttons, with instructions to run a tab in his name. The bandmembers began to perform, gyrating their hips wildly as they did a hard-driving rock song with an oboe lead.

"It's Space Boogie time!" Sidney exclaimed, thinking of Peebles but forcing himself not to look in that direction.

"Wouldja look at that!" Javik said excitedly, pointing at a man with short-cropped saffron yellow hair who was moto-shoeing down a nearby aisle. "Hey Bob!" Javik called out, waving his hands. "Over here!"

Javik turned to Sidney. "It's Bob Maxwell!"

Maxwell smiled as he saw them and rolled to their table. "Well!" he said in the old familiar husky voice. "You fellows are a welcome sight!" He pulled a chair from an adjacent unoccupied table and sat down.

They stack-clasped hands like school chums. It came naturally, as if there had not been twenty intervening years.

Sidney looked at Maxwell, noted a big man with tiny metallic blue eyes, a small mouth and a weak chin. A few lines around the mouth, but otherwise he had not changed much. "You look to be in pretty fair shape, Bob," Sidney said. "Been working out?"

"Some. Maybe a couple of kilos heavier than in high school." Maxwell paused and touched a belt button to auto-clap with the crowd as they did a New City High yell. Sidney and Javik joined in, too.

"We are tops.... Class of eighty-five!" the partyers chanted. "We are tops...."

"Remember the pranks we used to pull?" Maxwell asked as the chanting died down. He looked across the table at Javik. "Like the time I dropped a dehydrated sponge in your glass of milk?"

Javik sat back and belly-laughed. "Scared the hell out of me when it puffed up! I was madder'n hell!"

Sidney laughed, too, adding, "And the time we went to Liberty High with buckets of Markesian slime...." He nudged the table in his mirth, causing it to rock.

"The funniest damn thing!" Javik said, beginning to gasp as he laughed. "We greased ... the hallways while they were in class, then ... ha! ... watched as they fell all over the place!" He broke down laughing.

"No way for 'em to catch us," Maxwell recalled, revealing small, even teeth as he smiled. "The harder those Liberty High punks tried, the more they fell! Your idea, wasn't it, Sid?"

"Guess it was," Sidney said.

"Sid always had the imagination," Javik recalled. "How about those stories he made up to scare the girls when we parked at Lookout Rim?"

Presently, the waitress arrived with a tray containing two red drinks in tall glasses. She placed the drinks in front of Sidney and Javik, then turned to Maxwell.

"Nothing for me," Maxwell said. He waved a hand to send her away.

They listened to wailing band music for several minutes while Javik and Sidney sipped their drinks. After a while, Sidney tapped his foot to the music unconsciously.

"What's that tapping noise?" Maxwell asked.

Sidney stopped tapping, felt hot in the face.

Maxwell leaned over to look under the table, then straightened and glared at Sidney with unfriendly little blue eyes. "Was that you?" he asked.

"Yeah," Sidney admitted sheepishly. "Guess it was."

"Energy conservation," Maxwell said officiously. "Do it in the gym, man, not here!"

Javik swallowed a sip of his drink, wrinkled his nose in anger. "Criminy," he said. "Ease up, Bob. We can relax the rules a little tonight!"

Maxwell flashed a cool look at Javik, then turned to watch the band as it began to play a rock waltz. The lights dimmed for the number, and couples took to the dance floor, where they short-stepped onto disco spinners. Each couple grabbed an invisible force field pole at the center of their spinner, causing the device to start slowly into motion … whirling one way and then the other in time to the music. Some dancers wore lighted disco shoes in various colors, and soon the floor became a blur of lights.

Javik asked a woman at another table to dance. Sidney watched Javik roll by Peebles's table, saw Peebles's expression turn to hatred as Javik passed. Then Peebles's cool, emotionless eyes took over once more as Javik and his partner reached the dance floor.

Sidney heard Maxwell say something, turned to face him. "What?"

"Tom's the same old operator," Maxwell said.

Sidney sipped his drink through a straw, tasted the sharp bite of iced raspberry liqueur. "Yeah," he said. "Say, what line of work you in?"

Maxwell stiffened. "Spent some time as a shredding machine operator in Bu-Cops. Then I volunteered for another assignment … in cooperation with Bu-Med."

"Oh yeah?" Sidney said casually, watching the disco dancers perform. "What's that?"

"Can't say, really. It's classified." Sidney noticed that Maxwell's facial muscles were tight.

"Sounds interesting, Bob."

Moments later, Javik returned to the table. It was break time for the band, and the ballroom lights brightened. "Nikki Johnson," Javik said. "Says she's been permied and divorced four times."

Sidney swallowed a sip of liqueur, looked over the top of his drink at Javik. "You got her life story in five minutes," he said, laughing. "See what you can get out of Bob here. Says his job is classified."

"Is that right?" Javik asked, his curiosity peaked. He reached across the table, patted Maxwell on the shoulder and said, "You can confide in us, Bob. We're old pals, remember?"

"Well," Maxwell said, wriggling uncomfortably. He chewed at his upper lip, looked around. "It's the reason I don't drink anymore." Maxwell thought for a moment, then removed a tiny brass-plated computer from his jacket pocket. "Carry this everywhere," he said nervously, leaning forward and dropping his voice to a whisper.

"What is it?" Javik asked, reaching out in an attempt to touch the unit.

Maxwell pulled it away, said flatly: "A bio-medical surveillance monitor."

Javik rested his hand for a moment on top of the song request panel at the center of the table, then pulled it back as he asked, "What the hell is that?"

"In fisherman's English, it's a cappy-finder."

Sidney swallowed hard, listened as Javik said, "A cappy-finder?"

"Yeah. I could turn it on right here and walk around until the yellow light starts blinking. That would indicate we have a shirker on our hands, someone with a medical problem he isn't revealing … or a person with a problem he doesn't know about himself."

Sidney's blood ran cold with fear. He coughed, felt a shiver run down the center of his back.

"You okay, Sid?' Javik asked.

"Yeah." Sidney coughed again. "Got a little swizzle down the wrong pipe."

"Turn it on," Javik urged, looking back at the little brass computer.

Sidney stood up hurriedly, felt himself becoming unglued. "Excuse me," he said, his voice faltering. "I'll be right back." He scurried away, consumed with the necessity to flee.

But Maxwell flipped the device on before Sidney got away. A yellow light on the unit blinked rapidly, then stopped as Sidney escaped down the aisle. Maxwell's gaze followed Sidney.

"What does it mean?" Javik asked.

"Our friend has a problem," Maxwell said, rising to his feet. "And he acts like he knows about it."

"Sid looks healthy enough to me. Maybe your monitor needs adjustment."

"Just calibrated it," Maxwell said, replacing the unit in his jacket pocket. "Can't let this rest, you know. The man needs therapy." He watched Sidney slip into the restroom.

Javik jumped to his feet, said in a low. angry tone: "Why? He's not hurting anyone!"

Maxwell rolled away from the table in the direction Sidney had taken. Javik was close behind. "He's hurting employment," Maxwell said, glancing over his shoulder. "Each therapy client supports seven point-three-two-five Bu-Med employees. I've seen the figures."

"Hang the figures!" Javik rasped in Maxwell's ear. "We're talking about Sid Malloy. He's a friend, not a god-damned statistic!"

"Friendship has nothing to do with it," Maxwell said coldly, turning a corner and rolling to a stop outside the restroom. "It's my sworn duty to take him in. Look, Tom, I had no idea this was going to happen."

"Then forget it."

"Can't. Rules are rules."

Presently, Sidney rolled out of the restroom. When he saw Maxwell waiting for him with an all-knowing expression, Sidney thought, *Now I've had it.* His legs began to shake. Quickly, the knees seemed ready to give way.

*An attack,* Sidney thought. *I'm having a breakdown!*

"Malloy," Maxwell said in an authoritative tone. "I'm going to have to …"

But Sidney grew woozy and did not hear the ensuing words. His knees folded, and he leaned against the wall for support.

Javik rolled to Sidney's side and held him up by the right arm. "You'll be all right," Javik said. He pulled at Sidney's arm. "C'mon, buddy. Let's get out—"

Maxwell pushed Javik in the shoulder. "Can't let you do that," he said.

Javik shook him off angrily, shoved past and went toward the elevator bank with Sidney.

Sidney felt his left arm shaking uncontrollably now, only half saw Javik and Maxwell through seizure-glazed, unfocused eyes. The Space Patrol crest on Javik's sleeve came into focus, then blurred.

Sidney saw the outlines of people as they turned their heads to watch, felt the prying press of eyes he could not actually see. Then Sidney's vision cleared momentarily, and he saw an angry Maxwell blocking the path, his arms folded across his chest and his face contorted in angry determination. Maxwell's lips moved, but Sidney swooned and the words sounded garbled to him, as if spoken underwater: "Hold … it … Tom … you're … not … go … ing … a … ny … far … ther!"

Upon hearing this, Javik's mind went blank with rage. He pushed Sidney to a sidechair. "Rules be damned!" Javik yelled, grabbing Maxwell by the collar. "I'll kill you, you rotten son-of-an-atheist!" He hit Maxwell in the face with a roundhouse right and fell to the floor pummeling his opponent with unanswered punches.

Sidney saw the unfocused images of people all around, pointing at him and turning their faces to the side in revulsion. "A cappy," one man said, his tone lilting and cruel. Sidney rolled his eyes in that direction, saw the lapel tag and shoulder epaulets of Colonel Peebles.

Sidney tried to control his left arm, but it flailed wildly. He glanced down at it, saw that it was contorted at the elbow and wrist joints, bent in a horrible manner like pictures he had seen of clients on therapy orbiters.

"Isn't it disgusting!" Peebles exclaimed.

"Let Bu-Cops through!" a woman said. "Make room!"

"How interesting," Peebles said. "Look at his face.... It's twisted on the same side as the arm!"

"We shouldn't have to look at this!" a woman said indignantly.

In his pain, the voices Sidney heard became increasingly distant, increasingly muddled. *"Don't fight it, fleshcarrier,"* he thought one said. *"This could save you!"*

O O O

When the police stormed in, Colonel Peebles rolled forward to guide them. "Over there," he said, motioning to Javik, who was rising to his feet, apparently tired of hitting the prone form of Maxwell. Bloody and bruised, Maxwell dragged himself along the floor to get away. Then he tried to stand, but slipped back to the floor.

Two policemen grabbed Javik, but he broke free, knocking both of them down. Three more cops rushed over now with electro-sticks, and they shock-pummeled Javik to semi-consciousness.

"Kill him!" Maxwell yelled from his position on the floor. "Kill the bastard!"

"This man is my prisoner," Peebles announced as Javik was subdued. Peebles flashed a red Bu-Mil priority card. "Take him to Compound Five at the Bu-Tech Space Center."

"Yes sir," a police corporal said.

"And put the cappy in Therapy Detention," Peebles ordered. "Don't lose track of him, corporal. General Muñoz wants to be kept advised of his whereabouts at all times...."

O O O

Later that evening, Carla stood in the bathroom doorway of her condominium in a lavender bathrobe with a white-and-gold rope sash. Fluttering false eyelashes at a bare-chested man who sat on her waterbed with covers drawn across his lap, she asked, "May I offer you a tintette?"

"Yes," Billie Birdbright said. He smiled. "Thank you."

Carla removed a packet from her robe pocket, lit a lime tintette and puffed on it for a moment. Then she moto-slippered to the bed, trailing pale green smoke behind her. Carla sat on the edge of the waterbed, placed the tintette in his mouth.

Only moments before, she had been consumed by animal passion, had known Birdbright's strong and tender embrace. *A fantastic bedmate,* she thought, kissing him on the cheek. She studied Birdbright's profile as he smoked. The high cheekbones, tan skin and firm jaw gave him a virile appearance. Birdbright was the handsomest man she had bedmated.

In her thoughts, she compared Birdbright with the male pleasie-meckie she kept in the closet. Birdbright was the first man she had known whose sexual abilities approached those of the machine. *Billie may even be a little better,* she thought.

The words of a girlfriend spoken ten years before came back to Carla as she recalled being self-conscious at first about the ownership of a pleasie-meckie: "Even permies have them," the friend had said. "It isn't discussed much, of course, and the meckies do arrive in plain unmarked boxes...."

Carla smiled at the recollection. Since that time, she had traded in her pleasie-meckies twice a year, always Tele-Charging the finest, strongest model available. *I owe it to myself,* she thought.

Birdbright tapped the tintette on a nightstand ashtray, looked at Carla inquisitively. "Whatcha thinkin' about?"

"That wouldn't interest you," Carla said with a smile. "Tell me what a Chief of Staff does. You're a GW three, aren't you?"

"Two." He set the tintette on the ashtray. "I assist the President in all areas. He likes me to delegate as much as possible, of course."

"Job-Support," she said.

"Precisely. But some matters are ... rather delicate in nature." He beamed.

"How exciting!"

"I can give you one example, I suppose, without revealing exact figures—Recently, I reviewed the forms budget for the year twenty-seven-sixty-two."

Carla did a quick mental calculation, then exclaimed, "A hundred fifty-seven years from now? But there must be a million variables between now and then! How can you account for every one of them?"

Birdbright smiled confidently as he explained: "Through charts and projections on the activity in every governmental office, we know exactly how many people will be employed in each bureau that year, what they will be doing, where they will live. . . ."

"And their names as well?" she remarked with a teasing smile and a toss of her golden-brown hair over one shoulder.

His smoke-grey eyes flashed, but he smiled quickly. "All except that," Birdbright said. "Names don't matter anyway."

"How can you be sure of the projections?"

"Bu-Tech's Stat Division provides us with mega-reams of data. I can tell you that the American Federation of Freeness controls its destiny very tightly. Technology has mastered everything imaginable!"

"Intriguing," Carla said. Recalling the pleasie-meckie in her closet, she thought, *Not quite everything . . . now that I've met you.*

"Freeness has been charted for the next thousand years," Birdbright said. "It can take only one path, the path chosen by Uncle Rosy."

O O O

As Birdbright spoke, Onesayer Edward stood in the dimly lit Central Chamber of the Black Box of Democracy. He gazed up at Uncle Rosy across the internally illuminated pages of an open book, saw a hulking shadow of a man in a hoodless robe seated upon the chamber's only chair. Onesayer had seen tuxedo meckies carrying the Master's laundry, so he knew the robe was white—but it was made to appear light yellow by a row of tiny soft yellow overhead bulbs which cast weak shadows around the room.

It was silent in the chamber, except for a soft, almost imperceptible humming sound which came from Uncle Rosy's lips. Onesayer recognized the melodic, lilting notes of the Hymn of Freeness. Uncle Rosy loved that tune. He had composed it himself.

Uncle Rosy's chair was immense, suitable for the size of its occupant, and rested upon a raised platform to one side of the room. Threesayer and Twosayer stood to each side of Onesayer, holding open volumes as well, dressed as he was in hooded dark brown friar robes without jewelry.

"There will be no further reading today," Uncle Rosy said in a kindly, resonant voice which echoed off the black glassite surrounding walls. "Onesayer, I will hear your report."

Onesayer closed his volume, slipped it into a robe pocket and moto-shoed forward. Looking at Uncle Rosy from this new position, he tried unsuccessfully to catch a glimpse of the Master's facial features. He had never seen the Master's face in person, remembered decades earlier when he used to imagine what a glorious countenance it must be. Lately Onesayer's thoughts had been altogether different. He had grown tired of waiting for the Master to step down and turn the holy duties over to him. It was cool and damp in the chamber. Onesayer shivered.

"Your report?" Uncle Rosy said, with the tiniest bit of impatience.

The corpulent Onesayer nodded, and with a graceful turn to one side extended an arm toward the center of the chamber. As he did this, a circular floor screen flickered on, revealing a view of galactic space. Uncle Rosy leaned forward, studied a fiery purple and yellow fireball which moved silently across the star-dusted expanse.

"The view from Drakus Ohm," Onesayer said, "one of AmFed's deep space observation stations."

"I know what Drakus Ohm is," Uncle Rosy said. This time Onesayer detected more than a hint of irritation in the tone. It surprised him. Never before had the Master displayed such an emotion.

Onesayer heard the whir of fast-approaching moto-shoes, watched a tuxedo meckie carry a tray of food up a ramp behind Uncle Rosy's chair. The meckie had six little blinking white lights down the front of a black headless metal body, with an oblong speaker box on each side. Its mechanical arms had a rim of white dress shirt at the wrists which appeared dirty yellow in the low light. The meckie placed the tray on a mini-table to one side of the great chair. It waited several seconds for further instructions. Not receiving any, it left the chamber.

"The comet continues to behave erratically, Learned One. It turns one way and then the other, always returning to a collision course with Earth."

"As if it had a life and brain of its own," Uncle Rosy said. He leaned to the right, resting an arm on one of three chrome handles beside the chair.

"Yes. It is strange indeed. Bu-Tech and Bu-Mil are combining in an effort to stop the comet, but ..." Onesayer fell silent, clasped his hands behind his back and gazed up at the distant row of yellow bulbs along the ceiling.

"But?" Uncle Rosy prodded.

Onesayer dropped his gaze, looked at the Master. "I have been in the Bureau Monitoring Room since midday, reviewing all the lifelog and minicam tapes on Dr. Hudson and General Muñoz."

"And?"

"I do not think much of their plan. No back-up provision or evacuation contingency. And now Muñoz has some wild idea that an office worker named Malloy—a man with absolutely no space experience—should pilot the ship. We have checked the lifelog tapes on Malloy, Master. The fellow is pathetic—a real loser."

"I see," Uncle Rosy said.

"They are sending along another man who has experience ... he's been doing garbage shuttle duty the past couple of years. So far, they can't locate him."

Uncle Rosy said nothing, sat leaning to one side.

Onesayer noticed the chrome handle moving down slowly beneath the weight of Uncle Rosy's arm. "Master!" he yelled. "The Zero Handle! You are leaning on it!"

"Oh," Uncle Rosy said absent-mindedly, pulling his arm away from the handle. "Suppose I was." Uncle Rosy pushed the handle back into place.

Onesayer took a deep breath, resisted an urge to shake his head in dismay.

"Foolish of me," Uncle Rosy said cheerfully. "Another five seconds and Earth would have gone boom!"

"Yes, Master. That reminds me.... What would you think of using the second handle at this time?"

"The Orbital Handle?" Uncle Rosy said, placing his hand on the central chrome handle. "You hope Earth can elude the comet by modifying its orbit?"

"That is the obvious benefit, Master. But there is another."

"Which is?"

"The AmFeds have always been pretentious, thinking that their technology can deal with any situation."

"It has worked well for them in the past," Uncle Rosy said in his resonant voice.

"And the past is always a precursor of what is to come?"

"Ah, Onesayer Edward," the Master said, pleased. "You are learning!"

*False encouragement,* Onesayer thought bitterly. "On this pretentiousness, Master, the AmFeds do not know of the existence of our Orbital Handle."

"Nor of the other handles. It would cause them to stop and think, eh, Onesayer?"

"It would be healthy if they were forced to re-evaluate assumptions."

"Under normal circumstances, I would agree, Onesayer." Uncle Rosy removed his hand from the Orbital Handle. "But this is quite a different situation."

"Then why did you install the handles? I understand number one, the Zero Handle. As Master, you may find it necessary to detonate the planet. And number three … our army of ten thousand armadillo meckies that can fly, swim, and break through walls. But number two, Master … I cannot think of a more opportune occasion to use it for the first time."

"Continue as I have instructed, Onesayer. Dr. Hudson and General Muñoz are to be eliminated."

"At least hear me on one point, Master. Hudson could improve the odds of stopping the comet. We should not kill him yet."

Onesayer saw the shadowy head of Uncle Rosy shake slowly from side to side. There was no other response.

Onesayer shifted nervously on his feet. "He is a genius, Master. You have often said this."

"He is dangerous, Onesayer. We cannot tolerate someone who reads the thoughts of the citizenry and forces them to vote as he wishes!"

"I see that, Master. But …"

"There are no buts to be considered. When I thought of mentoing, I saw it as an aid to the economy … making consumption easier …

more automatic. In my early lab work, I hoped thought transmission would make life more pleasurable for my people."

"Hudson IS evil, but we can get him later."

"No, Onesayer!" Uncle Rosy said angrily. "He has gone too far!"

"Learned One, you speak with anger. But the AmFeds can ill afford to lose him now … in the presence of such grave danger."

"No matter, Onesayer. I have given my orders."

"But Master—"

"You HAVE instructed our operatives to sabotage the products used by General Muñoz and Dr. Hudson?"

"Uh, the contract is out on Muñoz."

"And Hudson?"

"Uh, not yet, Master."

"I gave that order YESTERDAY, Onesayer. Why was it not completed yesterday?"

"I had hoped you might reconsider—"

"Onesayer Edward!"

"Forgive me for arguing, Learned One, but the Thousand Year Plan … the glory of Freeness and the AmFed Way … all could be destroyed! Surely *this* matters!"

"Much remains for you to learn, Onesayer," the hulking shape said. "Some things can be controlled. Others cannot."

Onesayer did not reply. He glanced at the two sayermen standing silently nearby in the hope that one would speak up on his behalf. But they said nothing, making Onesayer feel very much alone.

"They will stop this comet themselves," Uncle Rosy said, "or it was not meant to be done."

"I have never heard you speak this way, Master."

"And you are disturbed?"

"I am concerned. We are responsible for the work of many lifetimes … for tradition and honor … for dreams brought to reality."

"Well put, Onesayer. But there are forces at work here even I do not understand. I have never admitted such a thing before, and it is not to go beyond this chamber."

"Yes, Learned One. I will follow your wishes."

"One more thing, Onesayer. Tomorrow morning you are to notify President Ogg of the electoral conspiracy against him. Show him that they thought-speak, and assure him that we are in control of the situation. But say no more."

As the conversation ended and Onesayer rolled out of the chamber, he felt centuries of suppressed anger coming to a head. *I must kill the Master,* he thought bitterly. *He will never step down ... and besides, he has gone mad! If I can hide the body and take his place ... no one will know the difference!*

For a fleeting moment, it occurred to Onesayer that there might be no body. Uncle Rosy might be a projecto-image. *No,* he thought. *The Master leaned on one of the handles.... Still, it could be a meckie. The Master might be somewhere else, watching. Or he may be dead already, and another sayerman has taken his place....*

The range of possibilities nearly drove Onesayer mad.

O O O

It was late Saturday evening when Onesayer took the elevator to the top floor of the Black Box, rolled along a long hallway and entered his suite. As he rode the escalator to his prayer loft for the final daily prayer, Onesayer felt emotions different from any he had ever experienced before.

He reached the prayer loft landing and short-stepped off. *This has always been automatic for me,* he thought, *but I feel ...*

Onesayer could not form the feelings into coherent thoughts. He stood for a moment staring at the bust of Uncle Rosy which rested in its usual position on the leading edge of the prayer rug. An overhead mini-spot illuminated the bust, and Onesayer recalled feeling that this gave it an inspirational appearance in the surrounding shadows of night. But the bust did not look inspirational to him now. There was something insidious about it.

*I should be on that rug by now,* he thought, *pledging myself anew to the Master....*

Onesayer rolled slowly to the sculptured bust, felt hot with anger as he reached it. *I have prayed to this idol for the last time!* he thought, glaring down at a "Keep the Faith" inscription on the pedestal. His foot darted forward swiftly, dealing a powerful blow to the bust. The little sculpture flew a meter and a half into the air, crashed and shattered as it fell to the hardwood floor.

*Uncle Rosy's fate as well,* he thought, staring bleakly at the broken pieces. A portion of the bust's pedestal remained intact, along with its "Keep the Faith" inscription. Words echoed in his brain: *Keep the Faith ... Keep the Faith ... Keep the Faith....*

Onesayer lifted the pedestal piece angrily and hurled it to the floor. *There!* he thought as the piece shattered. *I am free of it!*

A shudder ran through his body.

* *

The youngsayermen were gathered in the high-ceilinged gallery of the Great Temple at Pleasant Reef. They stood around Sayer Superior Lin-Ti at a glass display case, watching intently as he unlocked the case.

"This is the actual cross worn by General Muñoz," Lin-Ti said, lifting out a burnished gold cross and chain.

"Does it still work?" a youngsayerman asked.

"Oh yes," Lin-Ti said. "Of course, we are too far from Earth to change their weather or votes. This is a mechanical device, you know. It is not spiritual. . . ."

# CHAPTER FIVE

## WHAT FREENESS MEANS TO THE AMFEDS: FOR FURTHER READING AND DISCUSSION

*"Something for nothing is perfectly acceptable. The most important people get ahead by luck, you know. They are in the right place at the right time. Once a person understands Freeness, there is no limit to how far he can go!"*

Remarks to a newsy reporter by Charley Chance, twelfth minister of Bu-Free

### *Sunday, August 27, 2605*

Garbage Day minus five began in the Black Box of Democracy with Onesayer Edward rising at his usual time before dawn. This morning, for the first time in more than three centuries, he would not perform the prayer ritual. *I will never return to the prayer loft!* he thought as he pulled a clean robe over his head. *It is finished!*

New thoughts whirled through Onesayer's brain as he rode the elevator to the second level and moto-shoed the short distance to the Bureau Monitoring Room. *I will disfigure his face after killing him. Then if I can get one of my robes on him …* Doubt returned to his consciousness, and Onesayer wondered if Uncle Rosy really occupied the Master's chair. *Whoever it is,* he thought. *I'll get him.*

"Peace be upon you, Onesayer," a sayerman said as Onesayer entered the room. Onesayer nodded without noticing who had spoken. He rolled directly to the broadcasting alcove located along a side wall. It was shift-change time, and sayermen arrived and left, exchanging blessings and touching together their class rings.

Oblivious to this activity, Onesayer mentoed the minicam broadcaster as he entered the alcove: *One-five-six-three-oh-nine-four-one-Ogg.* He glanced at a computer sheet on President Ogg, then took a seat on a high stool and stared intently at a round telescreen as it flickered to life.

Onesayer watched the screen as an immense black man wearing a bright green leisure suit short-stepped onto the running board of Autocopter One, then turned to retrieve a briefcase from the expando-cart which lifted it to his level.

President Ogg heard his satin suit rustle as he moved. He placed the case behind the single copter seat, short-stepped into the cockpit and sat down. From the helipad on top of his penthouse, the President could see the morning sun beginning to do its dawn-peek over a dusty horizon. Its golden-orange rays across New City gave a reddish silhouette to mountains in the distance. He enjoyed taking a heli-spin at this time of day, had often commented on it by saying, "The morning is as new and bright as the best products in our American Federation!"

Onesayer spoke from the Bureau Monitoring Room: "Good morning, President Ogg."

Ogg jumped. The voice seemed to come from somewhere inside the cockpit. "Who said that?" Ogg demanded, sitting straight up and looking around nervously. He saw no one.

"My name is not important," the voice said.

Onesayer smiled as he watched President Ogg reach for his radiophone. Onesayer mentoed a force-field gun, and Ogg felt invisible restraint against his forearm, preventing him from lifting the receiver.

"There is no need for that," the voice said.

"Great Suffering Depression!" Ogg cursed angrily. He took a deep breath, released his fingers from the receiver and pulled his arm back.

"Not to be alarmed, Mr. President," Onesayer said. "The Black Box of Democracy would have a word with you."

"The Black Box? What sort of prank is this?"

Ogg noted that the voice did not sound male or female. It could be a syntho-voiced meckie. Or someone speaking through a voice scrambler. He pinched the thin skin on the back of one hand to be certain he was awake. It hurt.

"There is an evil electoral conspiracy, Mr. President. In violation of the American Federation of Freeness Constitution."

"Oh?"

"An interesting dinner party will take place this evening, at the home of General Muñoz."

"Muñoz? What's he up to?"

"He is the leader of the conspiracy."

"I will need evidence," the President said, "enough to appoint an investigating committee." His gaze darted around the cockpit.

"You will have the evidence, Mr. President, because you should always be kept informed. But there will be no investigating committee."

"We MUST have a thorough investigation," Ogg insisted, his voice fervent, "with reports, meetings, and photographs." Ogg wiped perspiration from his brow. "We'll set up a crisis bureau, employing thousands of people!"

"No time for that! They plan to rig Tuesday's election! Muñoz will take power the same day!"

"But we can't take action without reports," Ogg lamented as he shifted in his seat. His satin suit rustled. "It's not possible!"

"Leave it to us, Mr. President. And do not be alarmed at what you see happening."

"What will that be?"

"Do not be impatient. First, there is a bit of evidence for you to observe, as required in the by-laws of the Black Box of Democracy."

Ogg rubbed the thumb and forefinger of one hand together nervously.

"The Muñoz dinner party," the voice said. "In the glovebox of your autocopter is a palm-held video receiver. Flip it on at six-thirty this evening."

President Ogg located the receiver, held it in one hand. It was blue plastic and chrome, had one red switch and a tiny darkened screen. "All right," he agreed. "I'll do that."

"They will say nothing incriminating at the table," the voice said. "But watch their gestures and expressions. Pay particular attention to their eyes."

"This doesn't sound like evidence to me!"

"They thought-speak, Mr. President, with the aid of brain-implanted transceivers."

"My Rosenbloom! I've never heard of such—"

"They also have a powerful subliminal transmitting device. At this moment, it is changing the voting preferences of a majority of the electorate."

"Muñoz as a punch-in victor?"

"Right. We have been on full alert for some time now. But we could not take action until they committed the overt act of changing votes. Just planning to do it was no crime."

"I see. No I don't! Muñoz isn't clever enough for this!"

"Dr. Hudson's doing. Remember last year in your office when he explained the subliminal receiving features of every consumer brain implant? They were to make Harmak and Home Video advertisements more effective, he said."

"I remember. But how did you …"

"They found another use for Hudson's discoveries. I must caution you not to tell anyone about our conversation, Mr. President." The voice fell silent.

Ogg listened to the quiet in the cockpit, and a feeling of urgency came over him. He watched the golden orange layers of dawn give way to pale blue daylight.

*Whose voice was that?* he thought. *God's?*

O O O

Dr. Hudson attended church services alone Sunday morning. Since the church building was overflowing, Hudson and hundreds of others sat in cars out in the parking lot, listening to the sermon through drive-in speakers.

"Uncle Rosy and God are side-by-side in the Happy Shopping Ground," the minister's metallic voice said.

Hudson turned a knob on the speaker to lower the volume, then glanced around nervously at the occupants of nearby cars. *Did anyone see me do that?* he thought.

O O O

Across town in Building B of the Bu-Tech Space Center, General Muñoz and Colonel Peebles stood in a sixth-floor briefing room. They squinted at one another against the glare of the midmorning sun which flashed through a nearby window. Peebles mentoed a window shade, watched it roll halfway down until the sun's rays were covered.

"Hudson's people did a nice job, wouldn't you say?" General Muñoz asked, looking through a clear glassplex barrier to admire a three-dimensional galactic model.

"Adequate," Colonel Peebles said, fingering a strand of gold braid which encircled one shoulder epaulet and hung at the side of his Space Patrol uniform.

"Adequate? It's identical to our real model next door, except in this case the planets and other heavenly bodies don't follow the impulses of parent bodies. These little spheres move in accordance with our fabricated control room instructions."

"Very nice," Peebles agreed. He smiled as he looked at the model. Miniature comets and meteors made their way along varying courses in slow motion, trailing emerald green, blue, or orange flames against a black, star-encrusted backdrop.

Muñoz glanced at the briefing room's digital wallclock, noted the time: AM 10:26:33. Below that, another digital reader showed the Estimated Time of Arrival of the garbage comet:

| DAYS | HOURS | MINS | SECS | D/SECS |
|---|---|---|---|---|
| 5 | 7 | 28 | 13 | 0.73 |

Looking back at the squeak of a door, they watched two dark blue-uniformed military policemen escort Tom Javik into the room. The MPs saluted, did a moto-boot about-face and left. Javik folded his arms across his chest, glanced around defiantly.

"Mr. Javik!" General Muñoz exclaimed, caressing his orange mustache. "So nice that you could make it!" The voice was honey-sweet but carried with it a threatening undertone.

"Our brawler has a cut over his eye," Peebles observed. An I-told-you-so smile touched his mouth as he added, "They had some difficulty restraining him last night at the Sky Ballroom."

General Muñoz rubbed his chin thoughtfully as he studied Javik. He noted a torn and wrinkled tunic, fearless and defiant deeply-set blue eyes. "We'll order you more suitable clothing," Muñoz said. "But then I'm getting ahead of myself. You know who I am?"

"Yes," Javik said, meeting the tiny General's gaze. "And I've ... met ... Major Peebles."

"It's *Colonel* now," Peebles said stiffly. Javik heard a familiar whine to the voice.

"Getting directly to the reason you are here," Muñoz said, "I am prepared to reinstate your commission in the American Federation Space Patrol. As a First Lieutenant. An Akron class cruiser is being prepared for the mission right now."

"Fast ship," Javik said. "And long-range." He narrowed his eyes warily, asked, "What's the catch?"

"No catch," Muñoz replied. "Your assignment is Project Romo."

"Who's heading up this mission?"

"Captain Sidney Malloy."

Javik's eyes opened wide. "Huh?... Not the same Sidney Malloy I know?"

"One and the same."

Javik laughed. "You've got to be kidding!"

"Your crippled little friend will be commander in name only. Operationally, you will be in charge." Muñoz touched the burnished gold cross which hung from his neck.

Peebles stared at the ceiling.

"I like Sid," Javik said, "but what in the hell is going on? The cockpit of an Akron cruiser is no place for him!"

"There are reasons," Muñoz said, staring at a trash can across the room. "Command reasons." He gestured toward the galactic model, adding, "You leave tomorrow. Malloy will meet—"

"I haven't accepted the assignment yet," Javik pointed out, smiling faintly.

"True enough," Muñoz said. "If you don't accept, we'll find someone to replace you."

Javik twisted his face, trying to think.

"Malloy goes in any event," Muñoz said. "He will go separately to Saint Elba, receiving therapy there before joining you ... or someone else. There are no therapy facilities here."

"This is crazy," Javik said.

"As if you're in a position to be choosy," Peebles sneered, staring disdainfully at Javik.

Muñoz glared at his adjutant, then motioned to the galactic model again and explained: "That is Earth," he said, pointing to a tiny sphere in the galactic model. The sphere began to pulsate with a white light at the General's mento-command. "And there, in orbit between the Earth and Moon at $L_5$, is the therapy habitat of Saint Elba." A pulsating blue light marked the orbiter's location.

"Saint Elba is the first recharging stop," Colonel Peebles explained. "It is there that Malloy will be picked up, along with two mass driver units and fire probes, all partially assembled."

"Partially assembled?" Javik said.

"Due to a shortage of time," Muñoz said, "assembly crews will accompany you on the journey, doing their work along the way."

"How many people?"

"Two hundred. All cappies. They'll be released to rescue craft when the mass drivers are complete."

"I see. Fire probes, huh? What am I supposed to hook onto?"

Muñoz activated a red blip adjacent to the Earth sphere "This represents your ship, the *Shamrock Five*," he explained. The blip moved to Saint Elba, then continued off into space. "From Saint Elba you and Malloy will proceed in the direction of the Ikor Constellation, along a heading of thirty-two-point-five degrees from the Columbarian Plane. Three additional recharging stops will be necessary before rendezvous. Charging stations are now being established along the route." Javik noted three pulsating yellow lights, watched the red blip pause at each.

Javik furrowed his brow. "I don't see what … I mean, it's clear space beyond that for millions of kilometers."

"You'll be changing course twenty-six thousand kilometers beyond the last recharging station, along a new heading of ninety-two-point-one degrees C.P. This will conserve the E-Cells by taking advantage of strong space currents in the region."

"I'm familiar with the area," Javik said, watching the red blip change direction along its new course.

Javik glanced at the impact countdown wallboard, asked, "What day will it be at the time of the last course change?"

"Thursday," Colonel Peebles said, glancing at a palm-held note screen. "Eighteen hundred thirty-six hours to be precise."

"The object of rendezvous is THERE!" Muñoz said, revealing excitement in his voice. The largest of several comets in the Columbarian Quadrant began to pulsate. "That celestial body is on a collision course with our mining base in the Romo asteroid group, threatening our principal source of Argonium One."

"E-Cell gas," Javik remarked.

"Argonium One's use is classified," Peebles said, officiously.

Javik narrowed his eyes and leaned closer to the galactic model. "That … celestial body, as you call it … looks like a comet to me."

Muñoz hesitated, then said: "Correct."

"There are rumors of a comet headed toward Earth, General. Some say it's our own garbage."

"Nonsense," Muñoz said firmly. "Utter nonsense." He mentoed a time-advance button to speed up the motions in the galactic model. "I'm eliminating your ship," he explained, "and doing a fast-forward on the celestial body. The blinking green light is our Romo mining base."

The comet sped across space in a blur and hit the Romo asteroids dead center. Javik shielded his eyes as a bright, silent explosion filled the model with tiny fragments of smoldering matter.

"Any questions?" Muñoz asked. He stared sidelong at Javik, noted Javik was staring down the bridge of his nose at the model.

Javik mumbled something.

"What was that?" Muñoz asked.

"Project Boomerang," Javik said. He smiled defiantly. "That's a better name for the project. After all, it is our own garbage coming back."

"Not true!" Muñoz huffed.

Colonel Peebles glanced at Javik haughtily and said, "Bu-Tech studied photographic plates taken by deep space gamma ray cameras. The celestial body's—"

"You mean the *comet's*?" Javik asked, glaring ferociously.

"Very well. The comet's composition is quite standard ... primordial noble gases and the like, with a fusion-hardened nucleus of—"

"Bull!" Javik said. The smile returned.

"Look," Peebles said, his voice trembling with anger. "Experts plotted its course with coordinate measurements of Right Ascension and Declination ... obtained by angular offsets to the adjacent field stars. That is the course you see here." Peebles nodded toward the galactic model.

"Do you really understand any of that?" Javik asked.

"Certainly!" Peebles's pale blue eyes peered icily at Javik.

"Well, your galactic model is wrong. I think it's intentionally wrong. And your impact board refers to the comet's ETA here, not at Romo."

"We don't have to listen to this!" Peebles huffed, glancing at Muñoz for support. Peebles mentoed the window shade, and it snapped up, throwing a flash of sunlight in Javik's eyes.

Squinting, Javik flushed with anger and said to Peebles, "Listen, you wet-behind-the-ears armchair ..."

"STOP THIS! BOTH OF YOU!" Muñoz thundered He glared at Peebles, then mentoed the window shade down, returning the coolness of shadow to Javik's face.

"I accept the assignment," Javik said, "with a couple of provisos."

Muñoz took a deep breath, tried to exude calmness. "Which are?"

"Firstly, two cases of Chambertin Clos de Bez wine pellets are to be placed aboard. … Vintage twenty-five-seventy-two."

"Done," Muñoz said.

"Rather expensive taste for a brawler," Peebles sniffed. "A jug of White Rippo sounds more suitable."

Javik disregarded the remark, said, "And I want Brent Stafford assigned to command his own ship … at least a destroyer."

"Who?" Muñoz asked.

"Our brawler's co-pilot during his garbage detail," Peebles said.

"And during the Atheist Wars," Javik said. "He deserves his own command, General … somewhere in the galaxy."

"All right," Muñoz agreed. "Take care of it, Allen." Muñoz furrowed his brow, faced Javik. "Keep your cappy friend out of the way during the flight. Give him innocuous little tasks …"

"He's in command, General," Javik said, smiling.

"You know what I mean. Common sense must prevail."

"Right, General. Boy, this is the damnedest mission I've ever seen!"

"We're depending on you, Lieutenant Javik. We can't use remote-control pilotry on a deep space mission of this importance. If we had an equipment malfunction, with a meteor storm in the way … why, remote repairs by signal from Earth would be impossible."

"I know," Javik said. "One more thing … I'll need papers to get Malloy free on Saint Elba."

"You'll have them," Muñoz said, glancing at his adjutant.

"I want them signed by you, General," Javik said. "Not by an *aide*." Javik smiled viciously in Peebles's direction and saw his comment hit home as Peebles's eyes flashed angrily.

Slipping into his unspoken conversation mode, Muñoz mentoed to Peebles: *We must cooperate, don't you see? I have to send Malloy, and this Javik knows him best…. THE MISSION MUST GO SMOOTHLY!* Muñoz sighed deeply. "Very well," he said. "Prepare the papers for my signature, Allen."

Peebles rolled to a corner desk and began to prepare the forms.

"And give me something to get into Therapy Detention right now," Javik said, throwing the words at Peebles as if they were a command. "I'm going over to see Sid. It's less than a block away."

Peebles's gaze met that of Muñoz.

Muñoz nodded. "Don't say anything to Malloy now about his captain's commission. Be discreet, Javik. We don't want word of this getting out." Muñoz pressed a set of Lieutenant's bars into Javik's palm.

"Yes sir."

Presently, the forms were prepared and signed. As Javik took them, Muñoz said: "Report to Conditioning by thirteen hundred hours, Lieutenant Javik. Room C five-thirty-four."

Javik saluted and rolled toward the door.

Looking at Peebles, General Muñoz mentoed: *Is the Madame ready?*

*Almost.* Peebles smiled his characteristically cruel smile. *Hudson told them to sharpen her knives.*

*Good. She will have two heads to sever!*

* *

"We must imagine now," Sayer Superior Lin-Ti said, "for we have no record of what happened in the Realm of Magic, except so far as they spoke to humans."

Lin-Ti closed his eyes. "Picture a realm far across the galaxy, with no land or water mass, populated by bodiless beings. They were at a party, and from all around came the sounds of laughter and merriment. For this was a comet party—a real event at which all the citizens of the realm watched while the fleshcarriers learned their lesson.

"'*Ha!*' one said. '*That fool Malloy is captain of their ship, He'll find a way to botch the mission. Mark my words!*'

"'*Right,*' another said. '*He'll take some 'heroic' action to blow their pitiful little plan. Ah, but we have chosen him well—a nobody with delusions of grandeur!*'"

"Other beings spoke of similar matters," Lin-Ti said, "and all agreed they had selected a delightful way to have fun. These beings were not malicious: they just wanted to have a good time...."

* *

Lastsayer Steven paced the hallway nervously outside Onesayer's suite. *Almost eleven,* he thought. *Could Onesayer have forgotten my first audience with the Master?*

He mentoed Onesayer's doorbuzzer, watched the button go in and then return as the chime sounded. There was no answer.

Lastsayer turned dejectedly to leave, considered going to the audience alone. *Dare I?* he wondered. He rolled partway down the hall toward the elevator bank.

"Lastsayer!" a boisterous voice called out. "Do come back!'

Lastsayer turned, saw Onesayer Edward peeking around the corner of the doorjamb with a silly leer on his face. He wore no hood, exposing the shaved head of the Sayerhood.

Lastsayer began rolling back. "Onesayer!" he said. "It is three minutes before the hour!"

"So it is. So it is." Onesayer motioned with one hand. "Come in for a moment. I must tidy up before we go."

Thinking that Onesayer's voice sounded odd, Lastsayer arrived at the doorway with an excited protest: "But we will be late!"

"Don't worry about it. The Master can't tell time."

"What?"

Onesayer smiled as he said, "I was just kidding. I'll explain our lateness to him. He won't blame you." Onesayer short-stepped to one side, motioned for the other man to enter.

Stunned, Lastsayer looked up at the taller Onesayer. "You used apostrophic words!" Lastsayer said.

"What? Oh yes. You're … uh … you are quite correct. Thank you for pointing that out to me."

Lastsayer touched his onyx ring to Onesayer's as he rolled into the suite. "Peace be upon you," Lastsayer said.

Onesayer returned the blessing, fumbled in his pocket for something.

"You look tired," Lastsayer said, noting faint lines around Onesayer's large olive eyes. "And you do not sound the same."

Onesayer laughed as he rolled through the foyer into the dining area. "I was doing my Uncle Rosy impressions before you arrived. Guess I lost track of my own voice."

"Is that permitted?" Lastsayer looked around the dining room module, noted Greek urns on a blue slate floor. A long marble dining table in the center of the room was bathed in sunlight from an overhead solar relay panel. Somewhere, in another room, a bird chirped.

"I found no specific rule prohibiting it in the Sayers' Manual," Onesayer said, using the full resonant tone of Uncle Rosy.

Frowning uneasily, Lastsayer said, "I feel out of place asking this, but are you well?"

"Of course I am well! A couple of Happy Pills, no more!"

"Forgive me for asking, Onesayer."

"All is forgiven! Now relax and listen to my impression. Fivesayer says it is very good."

"I do not believe we have time. The audience with …"

But Onesayer was not listening. He clasped both hands in front of his waist in a very dignified fashion and said in the tone of Uncle Rosy, "You have much to learn, Onesayer Edward. You understand it will be a while before I step down and allow you to become Master … all the details remaining to resolve.…" He paused and looked fully into the smooth face of the younger sayerman. Lastsayer stared back with a worried expression. "Pretty good, eh?" Onesayer asked, in his own voice.

"I have only heard tapes. I was hoping to meet the Master in person this morning."

Onesayer smiled. "A bit of sarcasm! I like the way you think, youngsayer! I like the way you think!"

"Thank you, Onesayer. Now can we—"

"Is something else bothering you, Lastsayer? Other than being a few minutes late?"

"Since you ask, I'm disturbed … better to say concerned … at the way you mimic the Master."

Onesayer's tone became decidedly hostile. "Oh you are, are you?" He moto-shoed toward a side doorway, paused to glare back at Lastsayer.

"It occurs to me that Uncle Rosy should be informed of this, Onesayer. A strict interpretation of the Sayerman's Code of Ethics.…"

"Hang the code!"

"This might be a test, Onesayer. A test of my loyalty. How am I to know?"

"Inform him, then!" Onesayer yelled. He rolled through the doorway to another room, calling back, "Inform away!"

Lastsayer followed and caught up with the elder sayerman in the living room module, a bright room with deep blue shag carpeting and throw pillow furniture. "Wait, Onesayer. I have not yet had my first audience with the Master! I will not say anything because I do not feel qualified to make judgments yet."

"You have much to learn, Lastsayer," Onesayer said in the voice of Uncle Rosy. He smiled wryly.

Lastsayer felt frightened, furrowed his brow. "You do appear tired, Onesayer," he said. "There are lines around your eyes. Possibly we could postpone the aud—"

"Lines you say?" Appearing startled, Onesayer rubbed a middle finger beneath his right eye and snapped: "I have no lines!"

"I would suggest rest, Onesayer. Things will appear better to you afterward."

"You SUGGEST rest, do you?" Onesayer's voice was high-pitched, near cracking. "A Lastsayer does not SUGGEST anything to a Onesayer!"

Lastsayer's jaw dropped. He rolled back half a meter. "Excuse me," he said. "I am very sorry."

"Wait here," Onesayer ordered angrily. He gathered his robe in a very dignified fashion and swept out of the room.

*I said too much,* Lastsayer thought dejectedly. Uneasily, he looked around the room, noting a brown-and-gold sayer's edition of *Quotations from Uncle Rosy* on a sidetable. He picked up the book and manually turned a sheet of rice paper to Uncle Rosy's picture.

Lastsayer nearly dropped the book in astonishment. The picture had been defaced! Someone had penned in lambchop sideburns and a short goatee on the Master's face! The sacrilege of such a thing! He closed the volume, returning it to its place on the table.

*Best not to say anything about this,* he thought, moving away from the table. *Such occurrences may be commonplace here.*

In the bathroom module, Onesayer peered into the grooming machine mirror. A terrified face looked back. *Lines,* he thought, rubbing the skin around his eyes. Shallow, barely discernible lines were to the sides and below each eye. They had not been there the day before. He was sure of it.

He recalled smashing the Uncle Rosy idol the evening before. *This was how it happened with Sixsayer Robert before he died,* Onesayer thought. *It started with a few lines. . . .*

Onesayer slammed his fist down on the sink, felt pain shoot through his hand. *So soon,* he thought. *How could it happen so soon?*

As he turned away from the mirror, a thought raced through his mind. Uncle Rosy knew of his disloyalty and was trying to kill him! *But I'll get him first!* Onesayer thought.

O O O

Sleep voices, at the edge of Sidney's consciousness:

*"Malloy doesn't know about the killer meckie yet."*

*"Ah, but he will learn of it soon enough … when the Montreal Slasher gives him a neck full of steel!"*

*"Ingenious, the way these fleshcarriers destroy one another.… Imagine that … an entity which is programmed to kill! It has no other function!"*

*"Their ingenuity … as you call it … is moronic in comparison with our garbage comet!"*

Sidney dreamed he and Javik were in the command cockpit of a space warship. Suddenly they turned and saw two long knives approaching through the hatchway. Swish … swish … swish-swish-swish! A faceless being controlled the weapons, and Sidney was terrified of the entity he could not see.

The dream-Javik drew his service revolver and fired. But the knives kept coming. Closer and closer. Swishing and darting through the air.

Fwoosh! A blade severed Javik's head. It fell to the floor with a dull, distant thud. With a twisted and unusable arm, Sidney could do little to defend himself. It would be over in seconds. Sidney sensed relief ahead … a nothingness beckoning to him across the cosmos.…

"Wake up, Malloy! The morning's almost gone!"

Sidney felt a strong arm shaking his shoulder. He opened one eye and turned his face up to see a ruddy-faced male attendant looking down at him. The white-smocked attendant was young and muscular, with tiny rat-like dark eyes.

"A lady's here to see you," the attendant said.

"What is this place?" Sidney asked. He used his good hand to brush tousled curls of black hair off his forehead.

"You're in the Hotel Ritz-Broadway," the attendant sneered. "And I'm your private manservant! WHERE DO YOU THINK YOU ARE? THIS IS THERAPY DETENTION, PAL! YOU'RE SCHEDULED TO LEAVE FOR THE ORBITER TOMORROW!" The attendant shook his head scornfully.

Sidney rolled over on the cot to turn his face away. He curled his legs into a fetal position. Every muscle ached, especially those in direct contact with the unsympathetic cot. The grand mal seizure of the previous evening had left him with the fatigue of a thousand sleepless nights. The left side of his face felt numb, and his left arm and left-hand fingers were contorted horribly. He saw bones almost popping out, stretching their skin to the limit. Taut muscles appeared ready to snap. He tried to straighten the fingers, could not.

"You guys that get special treatment really bum me," the attendant said. "All the other applicants have been to Sunday services this morning, but not you!"

"I don't know what you're talking about," Sidney mumbled.

"Somebody called in with a Presidential code … said you were to await a visitor. What are you, Malloy? A bigwig of some sort? Well it won't keep you off the orbiter, pal. Nothing will!"

*Leave me alone,* Sidney thought. *Just leave me alone.*

"Come on, fella," the attendant said, again shaking Sidney's shoulder.

"Go away. I don't want to see anybody." Sidney's deformed arm twitched as he spoke, then jerked violently. He grabbed it with his good hand, took a deep, determined breath.

"The lady's a looker," the attendant said, short-stepping around the cot to the side Sidney faced.

Sidney did not reply. He turned away from the attendant. *Carla,* he thought. *I can't let her see me like this.* Sidney recalled what Javik had done for him the night before, wondered if he was all right.

"Hey, maybe the lady CAN figure a way to keep you off the therapy orbiter," the attendant said. "You'd better smarten up and talk to her. Once they get you out there in space, you can forget about coming back."

*I'd rather face that than Carla,* Sidney thought. He turned away once more and closed his eyes.

"All right," the attendant said, weary of the argument. "Suit yourself."

Sidney heard the whir of departing moto-shoes. He opened his eyes and looked across rows of empty cots, then turned his head the other way to see additional rows. He was in the middle of a large sleeping room, and the surrounding sameness reminded him of his desk in Central Forms. Noticing a plastitag around his right wrist, he read it:

Malloy, S./Client No. 165632029

*Maybe Carla can get me out of here,* he thought. But he made no effort to get up or to cry out. A door slammed. Echoing quiet dominated the room.

O O O

After the meeting with General Muñoz, Javik changed to casual Space Patrol togs. A high overhead sun cast distorted, short shadows of Javik's body as he rolled up the long ramp to Bu-Med's Detention Center Building shortly before noon.

Carla was leaving the building as Javik entered. She smiled attentively, and to Javik she seemed particularly receptive to him.

*Attractive woman,* Javik thought. *And vaguely familiar....*

*Now there's the sort of man I should pursue,* Carla thought as she rolled down the ramp. *Instead of wasting my time with Sidney. This one's really in the Space Patrol.*

After presenting his pass at five checkstations inside the building, Javik found himself facing the rat-eyed attendant in charge of Sidney's sleeping room. The attendant was seated at a small desk at the end of an eighteenth floor hallway.

"Another one to see Malloy?" the attendant said as he examined the pass. "Forget it, mister. He won't see anybody."

"I'll go in and see for myself," Javik said, retrieving the pass.

"Not permitted. You can only see him in a glassplexed visiting area."

"Do you see the signature on this pass?" Javik said forcefully, holding the pass only centimeters from the attendant's face. "General Arturo Muñoz!"

"Uh, yes. I noticed that."

"And you know who he is, I presume?"

"Of course, but ..."

"Show me the way," Javik said. "Unless you want to explain to the General why you wouldn't let me through."

"No, of course not." The attendant was flustered. He thought for a moment, then rose and said, "This way, please."

Designating a room several moto-paces away, the attendant opened the door to it. He started to enter with Javik, but Javik told him to wait outside.

The attendant followed the instruction, although it obviously made him uncomfortable to do so.

Javik mentoed the door shut behind him.

The sleeping room was large, and at first scan appeared empty. Smelling woodsy sweetness, Javik looked up to see the fine mist of air freshener as it dropped from ceiling nozzles. Presently he made out a solitary form huddled fetally on a cot near the room's center.

"Sid," Javik called out as he rolled along an aisle between cots. "Hey, Sid. That you, buddy?"

The form stirred. It rolled over to face Javik, exposing a twisted, unrecognizable face.

"Oh, I'm sorry. . . ." Javik caught himself as he recognized half the face. "Hey, Sid," Javik said as he reached the cot. "How ya doin'?"

"Tom! You shouldn't be . . ." Sidney felt self-conscious under Javik's stare and turned away. "Leave me, Tom. *Please*."

"Good news, Sid. You're assigned to a space cruiser with me! I'm a First Louie now!" Javik sat on an adjacent cot, stared at Sidney's back.

"Don't humor me," Sidney whined. "I'm no kid."

"Honest, Sid. General Muñoz signed an authorization. After you're treated on Elba, he says I can pick you up. You'll be on Elba tomorrow. We blast off from there Tuesday."

"Really?" Sidney said, not turning around.

"I can't give you any mission details now, and you're not to mention it to anyone. But take my word. It's legit. Look at this pass here. See that signature?"

Sidney took the slip of paper with his good hand and read. "Hey!" he said. "This is signed by General Muñoz! Isn't he the Bu-Mil Min—"

"You got it, buddy." Javik retrieved the pass, then patted Sidney's back like an older brother. "You and me on a big mission, Sid! We used to dream this day would come!"

"What's the assignment?"

"Classified for now. Our ship's the *Shamrock Five*. It's a beauty, pal!"

"You asked for ME? Re-a-ll-y?"

"Yeah, sure. Listen, Sid, I gotta go. I'll see ya on Elba!"

"This is fantastic!" Sidney said, turning the good side of his face up to Javik, with the twisted part concealed beneath a forearm.

After Javik left, Sidney recalled the nightmare he had suffered that morning. The vision had prophesied correctly that he and Javik would be on the same ship. But those terrible knives . . . Sidney assured himself that this part of the vision would not happen.

O O O

*A nice way to spend Sunday evening,* General Muñoz thought *After dinner I'll call far a game of Knave Table. . . .*

Muñoz sat on a pillow at the head of a walnut-grained plastic banquet table with his eyes closed. One tiny hand rested on the burnished gold cross that dangled from his neck. He smiled serenely and listened while his dinner guests took their seats in the candlelit dining room module. On the inside of his eyelids, a video weather transmission revealed Afrikari blanketed by dark AmFed-made clouds. It had been this way since just after Friday's meeting with the Alafin, thus rendering their telescope useless. The General was pleased.

He opened his eyes, spread a white lace napkin across his lap. Looking around the table, he smiled and nodded to each of the eight men and four women as they placed napkins on their own laps. These were the hand-picked members of his inner circle, a group whose loyalty was unquestioned. Muñoz knew every thought they made in his presence. And they knew his, since each had been given the ultimate gift, an implanted mento transceiver.

Unknown to anyone at the table, President Ogg watched them intently at that moment from his study, using the palm-held video receiver given him by the Black Box of Democracy. *Thought-speak,* Ogg thought. *The voice said they thought-speak.*

"Good evening." Muñoz said. He raised one hand, causing meckie-arms in front of each plate to pour red wine into crystal goblets. The General glanced for a moment toward a great fireplace along one wall, studied a large gold cross which stretched from the mantle to the ceiling. Along the mantletop were his favorite war trophies, gold and silver mementos inlaid with precious stones. Candlelight flickered and danced on the cross and on the trophies. He considered mentoing the fireplace but decided against it. The evening was warm.

General Muñoz lifted his wine goblet, sloshed wine and peered through the crystal at the drip pattern made by the liquid as it ran down the inside of the goblet. He smelled the bouquet, tasted.

"Magnificent!" he said, watching the guests as they raised their goblets. He nodded to Dr. Hudson on his immediate right, mento-addressed the gathering: *Election programming has been initiated. I selected fifty-seven-point-three-six percent as my portion of the vote.*

*Good choice,* Hudson mentoed. He pushed his eyeglasses forward to scratch the bridge of his nose.

*Allen and I are going to my country condo tomorrow,* Muñoz mentoed. *An early celebration, you might say!*

"Excellent wine," a dark-haired woman at the other end of the table said. "A LaTour, I believe?"

"You are quite correct, Miss Stevens," Muñoz replied.

*Congratulations, General,* she mentoed while raising her glass in toast. *Soon you will be President of the American Federation of Freeness!* "A toast!" she said aloud. "I propose a toast to the general for his hospitality!"

"Thank you," Muñoz said, raising his glass. *And a toast to each of you,* he mentoed happily, *the future ministers in MY council!*

They drank and laughed and spoke of harmless things for several minutes. Then the center of the table opened up, with its walnut-grained plastic panels sliding down into the surface. An oblong-shaped conveyor track appeared, carrying a variety of dishes which moved slowly around the table. The conveyor stopped and started, following mento-commands given by the diners.

Colonel Peebles sat to the General's immediate left. He watched a meckie-arm as it piled honey-basted Peking Goose, Mandarin Pancakes and plum sauce on his plate. The meckie-arm spread plum sauce on Peebles' pancake with a scallion brush, then dropped bits of goose and scallion on the pancake and rolled it up.

*That will be enough for now,* the light-eating Peebles mentoed. The conveyor clicked into motion, stopping at the next diner.

General Muñoz nibbled on a piece of gooseskin, tasting the pungent bite of spices. Suddenly he dropped his gooseskin and stared wide-eyed at a trash can near the fireplace. A piece of paper fluttered in the air over the can!

"Leave me alone!" Muñoz yelled, putting his hands up and recoiling. "Leave me alone!"

"What's wrong, General?" Hudson asked.

"There!" Muñoz said, pointing at the trash can. "There!"

But before Hudson and the others could turn their heads, the piece of paper, had fallen back into the can. "Didn't anyone see it?" Muñoz wailed. Realizing they had not, Muñoz buried his face in his hands and felt his pulse thump wildly.

"What was it, General?" Colonel Peebles asked. He read General Muñoz's thoughts, saw the vision of a piece of paper fluttering over a trash can.

Picking up the same thought, Hudson asked: "Another fireball?"

Muñoz kept his face buried in his hands. "Get it out!" he yelled. "Get it out!"

Hudson barked a command, and a servant hurried over to the can, removing it to another room. "We'll have your disposatubes reconnected, Arturo," Hudson said.

Muñoz nodded, rested his forehead on the back of one hand and sat there breathing hard. Little droplets of perspiration were visible on his forehead. *Don't any of you think it,* Muñoz mentoed. *I am not mad!*

*"Why did you send Javik along?"* a distant, teasing voice said, speaking from inside General Muñoz's skull.

*There!* Muñoz mentoed to the gathering. *Did you hear that?*

*Hear what, General?* they mentoed. *We didn't hear anything.*

The voice returned: *"This is private conversation, General. We told you to send Malloy alone. But you got Javik involved."*

"I couldn't put a cappy on the ship by himself!" Muñoz yelled. "We can't rely on a god-damned cappy!"

Muñoz's guests sat at the table in shocked silence, afraid to do or think anything.

*"You should have listened, General,"* the voice said. *"You should have listened!"*

"Blast you!" Muñoz bellowed. "I'll do as I damn well please!"

The voice receded, and Muñoz closed his eyes tightly, his face contorted in pain and fury.

*What in the hell is going on?* President Ogg thought as he watched these events. *The man is mad … stark, raving mad!*

Attempting to change the subject, Colonel Peebles mentoed the gathering: *I almost wish military action had been necessary, just to see if the Black Box is what it's cracked up to be!*

Surprised, Hudson looked away from General Muñoz. *Huh?*

*What do you suppose is inside those shiny black walls, Doctor?* Peebles mentoed, looking with pale blue eyes across the table at Hudson. *A robot army? Or some terrible array of automatic weapons?*

Hudson made idle chatter, then mentoed: *Your guess is as good … or should I say as bad … as mine. We must be careful about undue curiosity, Allen. It could lead to our undoing!*

"I must have this recipe!" exclaimed a pudgy man seated halfway down the table. He wiped his chin with a napkin.

"Certainly, Brockman," Muñoz replied, straightening as he regained his composure. "Have your chef give mine a call." *You'll make a fine Bu-Cops Minister,* the General mentoed.

"Thanks, General," Brockman said with a wink to make it clear he was responding at once to the spoken and to the unspoken. *I'd like to investigate the possibility of giving thought-reading powers to my police detectives,* he mentoed. *Dr. Hudson tells me the Council Ministers' transceivers can be tuned to a private wavelength … making our thoughts unreadable by subordinates.*

*A simple modification,* Hudson mentoed. He sipped his wine and sloshed it in his mouth before swallowing it.

Muñoz nodded in affirmation, then mentoed angrily: *In two days that fool Ogg will be out of office! He doesn't know the first damned thing about technology, but loves to use it for his own purposes and take all the credit! Look at the beautiful weather he told Bu-Tech to create just before the election!*

"A toast!" Colonel Peebles exclaimed, lifting his wine goblet. "To President Ogg's re-election!"

"Yes!" everyone said, raising their glasses. "To President Ogg!"

"Good man," Muñoz said, drinking his last bit of wine. He touched his cross with one hand and closed his eyes to watch simultaneous cloudbursts dump on Afrikari and on the Union of Atheist States.

"That lying bastard!" Euripides Ogg raged as he watched the tiny video screen. "The way their eyelids flicker during long silences … they're making conversational gestures without speaking aloud! The Black Box …"

A chill ran down the President's torso as it occurred to him that someone might be eavesdropping on him at that moment. He fell silent, turned off the video screen and stared at his bookcase.

*I should do something,* he thought. *But what?*

* *

After collecting the homework assignments, Sayer Superior Lin-Ti stacked them neatly and slipped them into his briefcase.

"During the balance of the week," he announced to the class, "you will read Chapters Six through Eight on your own. I have been called away on urgent business.…"

# CHAPTER SIX

## HISTORICAL PERSPECTIVE, FOR FURTHER READING AND DISCUSSION

*August 6, 2326: The Last Holy War. "A great little war," in the words of colorful General William C. ("Bomber Bill") McKay, Bu-Mil's seventh minister. On that day, AmFed turbo bombers rained holy bombs on non-Christian enclaves around the world. The Treaty of Rabat followed, in which the planet was divided into three nations—the American Federation of Freeness (encompassing North and South America, India, the Middle East, Europe, Australia, and Southeast Asia); Afrikari (all of Africa except Egypt); and the Union of Atheist States (Soviet Union, China, and several minor nations).*

### *Monday, August 28, 2605*

It was the first morning coffee break, Garbage Day minus four.

Carla mentoed the galactic pool cue, watched her white cue ball carom off an obstacle post and enter a side pocket. A wallscreen over the table lit up with bright yellow and purple gamma flashes as the cue ball's matter was consumed by one of the game's synthetic black holes.

"Damn!" Carla said. She looked at her opponent, Samantha Petrie. Petrie was plump, perhaps three years Carla's junior, with saucer-like round eyes and a toothy smile.

"Too bad," Petrie said with an I-got-you smile. "That'll cost you another hundred bucks."

Carla nodded with resignation. "That's enough for me," she announced, reaching into her belt purse. Carla wore a tangerine orange business suit dress, with a ruffled white blouse and a narrow striped tie. A tiny painted orange beauty mark graced her left cheek.

"Three straight!" Petrie said. "I've never beaten you like that!"

"I beat myself. Too many things on my mind." Carla passed three crisp new hundred dollar bills to Petrie, then closed her belt purse.

They moto-shoed across the crowded Presidential Bureau Gameroom to a wallscreen on which President Ogg could be seen delivering a campaign speech. "Do you want to talk about it?" Petrie asked.

Carla thought for a moment, then: "Might help."

They sat on a couch in front of the wallscreen, listening while Ogg harangued about Hoovervilles and unemployment lines in the "bad old days." People on nearby lounge chairs and couches watched the screen or chatted in low tones. The President concluded by requesting that everyone punch Tele-Charge voting button number one on Tuesday. "A vote for me is a vote for prosperity," he promised. The screen went dark.

"Sidney has a terrible handicap," Carla began sadly. "He's being sent to a therapy orbiter."

"Oh," Petrie said, her tone sincere. "That's unfortunate."

Carla picked nervously at her cuticles. "I tried to visit him yesterday at the detention center, but he refused to see me."

"What does he have?"

"A nerve disorder. I've known about it for years, but he was always able to control it … until Saturday night. He had an attack at the reunion."

"How sad."

"I just wanted to give him some code information—a few numbers and names to drop in the right places. You know, to make life a little easier for him up there." Carla felt tears welling up in her eyes. "I also wanted to say goodbye."

"I wish there was something I could do."

"I know what you must be thinking," Carla said, glancing at Petrie. "He should have submitted himself for therapy long ago.

"I didn't think any such thing. I know how you feel about him."

"Do you? How?"

"It's been obvious to me for a long time that one of you had to have a problem … loving one another the way you do but never becoming permies."

"I suppose I do love Sidney, but I just never …" She cleared her throat, wiped tears from her cheeks. The orange beauty mark smeared. Petrie put an arm across Carla's shoulder.

Carla chewed at her upper lip. "It's been terribly difficult. And I hurt him by not going to the reunion."

"No one can blame you for that," Petrie said consolingly. "If that hunk Billie Birdbright had called ME at the last minute, I'd have found a way to go out with him, too."

"I couldn't turn Billie down. All the girls want to go out with him. Just think of it, Samantha—He's Chief of Staff!"

"You shouldn't feel ashamed. This may sound cold, but you have every right to be happy. It's Sidney's problem, not yours."

"I suppose."

"How was the date with Billie?"

"Fine."

"You can tell me, Carla. Did you?..."

Carla laughed and pushed her friend away. "You're a Nosy Nellie!"

"I hear a lot of good stuff that way!"

Carla's face grew sad again and she stared at the darkened wallscreen. "I've seen the statistics," she said. "One institutionalized cappy supports seven-point-three-two-five government employees. But … well, I don't know." She sighed.

"Cappy sounds so impersonal, doesn't it?" Petrie said.

"He's much more than a statistic," Carla said. "Sidney is flesh and blood, a warm, loving human being!"

"Yes, but maybe this is better for him. You know, being with his own kind. Everything in the American Federation is so perfect. Their kind is better off in a separate area, where people won't laugh and call them names."

"I suppose you're right." Carla rubbed her temple with the fingers of one hand and thought back over the years she had known Sidney—all the good times and special occasions.

*Will I ever see him again?* she wondered.

O O O

From the fifth floor conditioning room in Building C, Javik could see New City Field perhaps a thousand meters to the east. A mid-morning sun seemed to drift in a clear blue sky, casting the profile shadows of rockets and support aircraft across the asphalt of the field.

Javik smelled the acridity of his own perspiration, looked down at rings of sweat on his grey workout suit. The lung pump to which he was connected throbbed and surged, strengthening and cleansing his body's breathing system. He removed the mouthpiece, watched a large group of people in the distance who were gathered around an older model passenger rocket. Small guard contingents could be seen posted at other ships on the field, and Javik knew the reason: people trying to escape the comet had already stolen a number of small and medium sized rockets.

Javik looked to one side as he felt the pressure in the room change, saw Colonel Peebles moto-shoe in carrying his military cap in one hand. "Greetings," Peebles said.

The tone was sinister to Javik's ears, and he did not return the salutation.

"Getting in shape?" Peebles asked. His nose wrinkled. "Smells like it."

Javik smiled as he noted the lack of muscle tone on Peebles's emasculated body. This was Peebles's second visit of the day, and Javik saw no point in feigning civility. They had nothing to discuss.

"The general would like me to brief you on certain ship's functions," Peebles said, "and on the method of approach you will use in getting close to that streaking ball of fire."

"Ha!" Javik said. He lifted a dexterity amplification cube, held it between both palms and went through a series of joint and muscle tone exercises. "That'll be the day, Peebles … when I take instructions from you!"

"This mission is no simple exercise," Peebles said, glancing around the room irritably.

"There are message box briefing systems onboard ship, I presume?"

"Of course."

"I'll study inflight. You didn't tape them yourself, did you?"

"No. Job-Sharing wouldn't permit such a thing."

"Good. I don't want to listen to your whining voice in space." Javik smiled as he twisted his torso.

Peebles took a deep, exasperated breath, turned to leave.

"I do have one question for you," Javik said as he continued exercising. "I was grabbing a cup of coffee from the vending machine outside the briefing room … right after I talked with you and Muñoz."

"Oh?"

"The door was open, and I heard you say something about hoping for the best. What the hell kind of a comment was that?" Javik set the dexterity amplification cube on a bench. "All our technology, and you're hoping for the best?"

"I don't recall saying anything like that," Peebles said, lifting and dropping his eyebrows. "You must have misunderstood." He rolled out of the room hurriedly with this thought: *What I wouldn't give to watch the Madame do her slicing routine on that insolent bastard!*

*Peebles just retreated,* Javik thought. *Wonder how that weakling got to be an officer....*

O O O

Alone in his office, Dr. Hudson mulled over what he had to do. A half-eaten donut lay on a napkin at the right side of his green desk mat. He stared at the donut disconsolately.

*Muñoz has gone crazy,* he thought. *I've got to get off a message to Nancy. She can keep that blasted cappy off our ship....*

Hudson formulated the wording of an electronic letter in his mind. *I'll send it myself after hours,* he thought. *Then I can destroy all record of it on this end.*

But Hudson understood too well the hardest part: in his presence, Muñoz could read his thoughts. *I'll have to control every thought when he's around,* Hudson thought. *I'll clutter my head with other things. He'd kill me for this....*

* *

A slushpile of humanity was assembled in the cool morning shade of the passenger rocket. Sidney Malloy stood in their midst, wearing a light green hospital gown. He shivered at a gust of wind, squeezed the gown collar shut around his neck with his good hand. Having lost track of the shots given him by attendants since his capture, Sidney felt numb and wobbly.

For a moment, he wondered if Javik had really visited him in the sleeping room, or if it had been a drug-fogged dream. *It happened,* Sidney told himself. *It happened!*

Blind and crippled babies cried incessantly in the arms of white-uniformed Bu-Med attendants, next to people who had met similar fates by accident or disease in their later years. They leaned on moto-crutches and sat in wheelchairs, drooling, chewing, grimacing, having convulsions and throwing up. Sidney breathed through his mouth because of the stench, looked from face to face at forlorn eyes and hopeless expressions on all sides. These were the traditional clients of Bu-Med.

Another group of clients waited to be taken aboard for the trip to Saint Elba. These pale-skinned men and women stood apart in handcuffs and chains, surrounded by black-uniformed Security Brigade guards. Moments earlier, Sidney had heard an attendant explain that they were "doomies," the dangerously insane who demonstrated against Freeness and the AmFed Way. The attendant said this type always searched for causes, and now their cause was a comet which allegedly would destroy the planet. The doomies spoke in angry tones, lunging and pulling at their chains in great clatters and surges of fury. Some had rebellious, angry eyes that glared at anyone daring to look upon them. Others were heavily sedated, and their eyes rolled up and around, not focusing upon anything.

A sea of white-uniformed attendants surrounded and far outnumbered these groups of clients. Sidney overheard two female attendants talking nearby:

"You *volunteered?*" said one. "I was assigned to this rotten duty by the Job Board."

"I don't think it's rotten," the other said. "We can help these poor creatures."

"You've got a strange attitude, sweetie," the first said. Sidney detected cruelty in her voice.

A small boy with straw-yellow hair screamed suddenly and fell to the pavement at Sidney's feet, writhing and kicking spastically. Sidney started to reach down to him, when a female attendant rushed over and administered an injection in the boy's arm. Sidney felt a sharp pain in his own twisted left arm, as if the needle had punctured his skin too. He rubbed the arm. Feeling a little dizzy, he shook his head to clear it.

When Sidney's head cleared, he watched the boy's jerking motions gradually slow and subside. The boy lay there unconscious on his side, with a twisted, pained expression on his thin face. Two attendants placed him on a moto-cot and rolled him to one side.

"Is this craft spaceworthy?" an attendant asked. Sidney did not hear another attendant's reply. Voices were drowned in the whir and clank of an approaching entry lift.

Hearing a mumble to his left, Sidney looked down at a hunchbacked old man whose lips were moving slowly. The man had sparse grey hair, deeply creased skin and dark age splotches across his face and on the backs of his hands. A single black hair grew out of a mole on the old man's chin.

Forgetting his own situation momentarily, Sidney was repulsed by the sight of such a decrepit human specimen. *He's not far from the Happy Shopping Ground,* Sidney thought, dismayed that anyone had to reach such a loathsome state. Then Sidney asked, "What did you say?"

The old man cleared his throat, hawked, and swallowed. "This is a bunch of shit," he said in an angry, gravelly voice.

Sidney stared down at a broken front tooth as the man spoke, then asked, "What do you mean?"

"The good things in society are reserved for normal, youthful people." The voice was bitter. "They're throwing us away, like someone's garbage."

Sidney wanted to tell the man he was going to be in the Space Patrol with Tom Javik, but decided against it and said, "I'm sure they'll take good care of us." He watched the entry lift lock into place against the passenger rocket.

"My son hid me out for years," the old man said, rubbing the mole on his chin. "But finally his wife … the bitch … turned me in."

"You should be thankful for having such a wonderful son."

"Thankful? There's nothing to be thankful about! I couldn't go out in public! They don't want people like me around!" The old man started to lose his voice, coughed.

"There are a lot of good things about the American Federation," Sidney said.

The old man wiped saliva and phlegm from his chin with his gown collar, then glared up at Sidney and demanded, "Name just one."

"Freeness."

"Ha!"

"There were terrible depressions before Freeness," Sidney said, "with millions of people out of work. They stood in souplines and begged for survival."

"Employment for everyone isn't worth the price," the old man said, coughing and hawking again. "Now leave me be!"

Sidney stared at the old man in disbelief, for Sidney still believed in the AmFed Way. It was not a perfect society, he told himself, but it was the best ever devised. Then a distant, wafting voice in Sidney's brain said, *"The old man is right, fleshcarrier. The AmFeds don't give a damn about you! And they'll never let you near the cockpit of a Space Patrol ship!"*

"Tom promised me," Sidney said, aloud.

*"Sure, but the AmFeds will find a way to keep you in your place. You're worth more to them as a cappy."*

"You're wrong!"

*"Each institutionalized cappy supports seven-point-three-two-five government employees."*

"Who are you?" Sidney asked. "And why do you call me fleshcarrier?"

*"We live in the Realm of Magic,"* the voice said, *"where there is no flesh. You live in the Realm of Flesh … where there is no magic."*

"What do you mean?"

There was no further response from the voice, and Sidney noticed a paunchy male attendant looking at him strangely. "Mental case," the attendant said, glancing at a brunette female attendant next to him.

She nodded.

Sidney flushed red. He saw a white driverless limousine approach and pull to a stop near the passenger rocket. A tall, black-robed priest short-stepped out onto an expando-platform. As the platform rose straight up in the air, the priest stood with white-gloved hands clasped in front of his round belly. When the platform stopped just above the height of his limousine, he raised his arms and spoke in a tone that was at once powerful and soothing.

"Let us pray," the priest said.

Everyone except the doomies bowed their heads.

"We are gathered here to embark upon a great journey of mercy," the priest said. "May Uncle Rosy grant us the ability to heal these broken bodies, to calm these troubled spirits."

Then the priest said "Amen" and came down to moto-shoe through the group, laying gloved hands upon the clients' shoulders and heads.

"Oh thank you, father!" a leper woman cried out. "Thank you!"

Pausing in front of Sidney, the priest reached down with gloved hands to touch his shoulders and said, "May Uncle Rosy bless you and make you well, my son."

Sidney looked up into the holy man's clear brown eyes, saw sincerity and eyes that were close to tears. *I'm going to get on that ship,* Sidney thought. *The voice was wrong.*

O O O

Onesayer Edward grasped the edge of his Basin of Youth and peered down into the mirror-like surface of the holy water there. *Blast it to Hoover!* he thought, looking at the skin around both eyes. *The lines are deeper today!*

It was mid-morning Monday, and he stood at a greystone basin which had been designated with his name. The basin felt rough to his touch, was closest to an arched entrance to the central chamber, one of sixty-six basins along the same wall. Brown-robed sayermen stood silently at each basin with their hoods thrown back, revealing shaved heads. They splashed holy water on their faces and drank the sacred elixir from red plastic cups.

Onesayer dipped a hand into the warm water, rubbed liquid against the creases on his face. He waited for the water to grow calm, then again peered into the reflective surface. It was definite. The lines around his eyes had grown deeper. He shook his head sadly.

"What is it?" Twosayer William asked, looking over from the adjacent basin. A noticeably consumptive sayerman, his oval face was punctuated by a prominent hooked nose. Twosayer wiped holy water from his eyebrows with two fingers, awaited a reply.

"Nothing," Onesayer replied. He leaned over and threw holy water on his face.

Twosayer rolled closer, said, "You are certain?"

Onesayer flicked a quick glance up out of the corner of one eye, saw Twosayer standing erectly over him, looking down inquisitively with grey green eyes. Onesayer looked down quickly, closed his eyes and splashed holy water on his face. *Get away from me!* he thought.

Twosayer was the shorter of the two, by at least half a head, and to Onesayer seemed the sort who was always trying to gain advantage over the next sayerman. Twosayer looked for weaknesses in others or tried to position himself so that he appeared taller than he actually was … standing on the higher portions of sloping ground or floor whenever he had the opportunity.

Onesayer felt an open hand on his back. "You can confide in me," Twosayer said in a tone that seemed false to Onesayer's ears.

"I am fine," Onesayer said forcefully. Grasping the basin edge tightly, he stared angrily at the ripples of water. Onesayer was startled to see a tiny blotchy shadow on the back of one hand. He dipped the hand into the water quickly. *Did he see it?* Onesayer wondered. Then Onesayer spoke without looking up, "Please … I will talk with you later."

Onesayer felt the hand leave his back.

"All right," Twosayer said slowly. "But if I can …"

"Peace be upon you," Onesayer said irritably. He watched peripherally as Twosayer rolled back to his own basin after he returned the blessing. Twosayer drank holy water from a red cup and then threw the cup into a wall-mounted disposa-tube. Machinery inside the wall whirred.

Onesayer wiped his face dry with a towel, then straightened and turned away from Twosayer. Feeling warm under the presumed gaze of Twosayer, he rolled away hurriedly into the Central Chamber. The low light of the chamber felt refreshing to him. It protected him from enemies.

# Chapter Seven

## BASIC DISINTEGRATION THEORY, FOR FURTHER READING AND DISCUSSION

*1. Wherever possible, the product or a key component is constructed of a fragile material; 2. Ideally, the product should self-destruct, taking other products with it; 3. Never rely on one part to break down—systems should be designed so that several key components fall apart at once.*

### *Monday, August 28, 2605*

It took an hour for the priest to complete the blessings.

When Sidney rode an entry lift up the side of the HLLV passenger rocket with a group of clients and attendants, he thought about how old and dingy the rocket appeared. Dull silver flecks of EZ-plating hung from the great bird's skin, barely reflecting sunlight, and numerous dents gave the ship an anachronistic appearance. Some rivets were missing. Others hung loose, ready to fall at any moment.

"Why do you suppose this ship hasn't been replaced?" a man behind Sidney asked. Sidney turned his head to look at the speaker, a thin man in a green client's smock.

"I was just wondering the same thing," Sidney said, scratching one of his black, bushy eyebrows. "Something got bogged down in red tape, I guess."

The lift came to a stop, and the attendants escorted their clients through an oval doorway into the ship's worn interior. Like Sidney, some clients moto-shoed under their own power. Others had to be carried or pushed, and some rolled in shakily on moto-crutches.

As Sidney entered the rocket, an overwhelming stench burned his nostrils. The odors made him nauseous. They were an amplification of the unwashed crowd smells he had experienced since being taken into detention. Trying to breathe through his mouth, he glanced around the compartment while awaiting instructions.

All seats in the passenger module had been removed, and the grey creme painted walls had a wide, dark green stripe along the bottom. An attendant told Sidney to sit on the floor against one wall beneath a tiny porthole. Sidney brushed away rust flakes from the dirty metal floor, then sat down cross-legged. The floor was cool under his thin smock. His twisted left arm ached.

"Put her over there," a burly male attendant said. Sidney watched two white-uniformed attendants guide a saggingly heavy retardo client to her spot on the floor. Stringy brown hair almost covered her face. She sat facing Sidney with her knees hunched up, lolling her head from side to side and appearing to laugh uncontrollably without uttering a sound.

Sidney laughed, too, then looked away to watch the attendants leave. Presently, he looked back at the woman. The smiling mouth changed now, almost imperceptibly, to a grimace. She seemed to be screaming out in silent pain, and it was no longer funny.

"Is there anything I can do?" Sidney asked her.

The woman did not reply. She continued to smile and grimace. Then she rocked forward and back, her hands clasped together about bruised and scabby shins.

All the clients were told to take seats on the floor, and Sidney felt the suffocating press of humanity all around him. The doomies were pushed and dragged into the compartment. They sat in an area near the door, still chained together and accompanied by Security Brigade guards. Other clients were directed to an elevator for placement in upper and lower passenger compartments.

It took perhaps an hour and a half to load the ship. By the time the heavy metal door rang closed, Sidney was not feeling at all well. The air was close and hot. His deformed arm twitched spasmodically. Stinging sweat trickled down his brow and into his eyes.

As the rocket engines surged, Sidney detected the licorice odor of G-gas filtering into the compartment. The rocket rumbled into the blue, nearly cloudless morning sky, and Sidney watched the skyline of New City through a large porthole on the opposite side of the compartment.

"This ship is so slow!" someone said. "How could they be concerned about G-forces?" A tittering of laughter lasted several seconds, then subsided.

Sidney closed his eyes. He tried to calm himself by recalling his scrapbooks and dreams of space travel. Javik's words came back to him: *You and me on a big mission, Sid. We used to dream this day would come.*

As the ship settled into flight, some of the attendants tried to cheer their clients by organizing singing commercials, and Sidney participated in a mediocre round of the "Shiny New Song." It went:

*Our land is full of pretty things,*
*Cars and homes and plastic rings;*
*Shiny New! All Shiny New!*
*Happy times for me and you!*

The doomies refused to take part, and sat to one side talking in low, angry tones. Finally, the attendants gave up their effort, and the clients slipped into silent thought, each to his own remorseful, self-pitying corner of consciousness.

Sidney had such feelings as well, but felt better when he realized his days of boredom as a GW seven-five oh working five hundred floors underground were gone forever. *I'm going to a zero-gravity region!* he thought. Sidney's ill feelings and twitchings subsided now, and he told himself that a positive attitude would make him feel better.

The retardo woman facing Sidney dozed off and leaned her head against a large, ruddy-faced blind man who sat next to her. The sightless man wore dark wraparound sunglasses and had a tuft of unkempt dark brown hair that appeared not to have been combed for days. A small mouth and high cheekbones appeared oriental to Sidney, although he could not determine the shape of the man's eyes behind the sunglasses.

The blind man allowed the woman to slip her head onto his lap as she fell into a deeper sleep. Her grimace-smiles subsided in slumber, and soon she appeared more at peace. Sidney looked around to stare at the disjointed jerks and unusual mannerisms of crip-clients. And he listened to the haunting, guttural grunts of retardos. A tow-headed boy with only one arm sat to Sidney's left, staring straight ahead.

Sidney rose to his knees with a bit of difficulty. *Not so easy with only one good arm,* he thought. He peered through a tiny porthole on the wall. The HLLV was traveling through a region of sparse cirrus clouds, and Sidney saw a fleet of Atheist sky mining ships working the area. They looked like giant potbellied beetles, with scores of anteater-like vacuum snouts swishing the air on all sides.

Sidney had studied the ships as a boy. He knew the snouts collected recyclable minerals and chemicals which were in the atmosphere as pollutants. He had always wondered how such a resource retrieval system could be practical, considering the E-Cell fuel such ships must consume. *They must be spy ships,* he thought, *working busy AmFed shipping lanes.*

A great burst of noise and clatter came from the doomie area, and Sidney turned to see them jostling about, pulling and rattling their chains as they chanted rhythmically:

> *Crazy are we, no....*
> *The comet's in the sky!*
> *Fire will rain upon us....*
> *And surely we will die!*

"Get 'em!" a stocky Security Brigade sergeant yelled.

Black-uniformed guards and Bu-Med attendants rushed the doomies and overpowered them with numbers. Sedative injections were administered, and the doomies passed out in a heap on the floor.

Shortly afterward, the HLLV left Earth's atmosphere and Sidney felt a momentary weightless sensation. It excited him when he was lifted a few centimeters off the floor before dropping back gently as the ship's gravitational system began to whir.

His studies told him what would happen next. Soon they would reach the staging area for transfer to an Inter-Orbital Transport Vehicle. The HLLV would release its passenger module for pickup by the transport, a lighter craft that never touched planetary surfaces. It would take the group to the orbiting $L_5$ city and therapy habitat of Saint Elba.

O O O

That afternoon, Tom Javik stood alone in a gold and white Space Patrol uniform at the base of the *Shamrock Five.* He glanced up at the shimmering black-and-silver Akron class cruiser, thought how fortunate he was to be assigned to it.

He watched Colonel Peebles short-step out of a computer-operated limousine parked at the edge of the landing pad. A woman with hair cut boot-military length followed. The pair moto-shoed toward the waiting ship's captain.

"Jeez!" Javik said in a low tone out of the side of his mouth. "That woman is UG-LY!" He smiled, picked food out of his teeth from a just-completed afternoon meal.

"This is Madame Bernet," Colonel Peebles said as they arrived. "She will be Onboard Systems Coordinator for the mission." Javik detected a sneer in the colonel's expression.

"This wasn't mentioned previously," Javik said.

"Oh, wasn't it?" Peebles said, feigning innocence. "It's quite standard now. But then you wouldn't know that … having been out of touch for two years."

Disregarding the remark, Javik studied the Madame intently and saw a clear, lineless face with a sloping, weak chin and a bulbous nose. She was quite short, and seemed lost in a loose-fitting white-and-gold dress emblazoned with the Space Patrol crest. Her hands remained in pockets at each side, and her smile never touched her eyes.

*Glad I didn't stumble into this Madame's pleasure dome,* Javik thought, attempting humor to allay the inexplicable fear he felt.

Madame Bernet saluted crisply. "Request permission to board, Lieutenant Javik."

"Very military," Javik said. A gust of wind blew his amber hair across his eyes. He pushed the hair back.

A look which Javik could only describe as murderous flashed across the Madame's face. "Request permission …"

"Permission granted," Javik said, scowling at the Madame.

As Madame Bernet short-stepped onto a boarding elevator, Javik turned to Peebles and said, "She's a meckie. Nicely done, I might add."

Peebles lowered his eyelids and asked: "What makes you say that?"

"The eyes. They never lie. The eyes are not human."

"I see. And that is a professional opinion?" Peebles shifted uneasily on his feet as he watched the boarding elevator ascend.

"Yes. I assisted Bu-Industry several years ago in a meckie experiment where human-like meckies were given tasks onboard ship."

"Re-e-e-ally?" Peebles said, a strange grin on his face.

"No matter how they were programmed, there always seemed to be an emergency they could not handle. Your Madame Bernet is a meckie,"

Peebles's grin faded. "All right," he said, irritably. "It is a meckie. But that really doesn't make any difference on this mission. It will be coordinating the cappy workcrews, tending to them so that you can operate the ship without distraction."

"Show me the program trade," Javik said, looking up to watch Madame Bernet roll off the entry platform and enter the ship.

"There won't be time for that," Peebles said. "It's not accessible without special tools."

"How convenient," Javik said. He scowled as he moto-shoed around chrome thrust deflector fins to a spot beneath the *Shamrock Five*. There he inspected a trailer release mechanism.

*I don't like unknowns,* Javik thought, touching the cool metal surface. *But God I want to fly this gorgeous ship … and I promised Sidney….*

Something troubled Javik about the meckie. But he put all such thoughts out of his mind.

O O O

An hour later, a six-armed Union Maid meckie discovered the bodies of General Muñoz and Colonel Peebles at Muñoz's country condominium. Water covered the floor of the bedroom module, and the men were found in a lovers' embrace on top of the waterbed.

Finding no life signs, the meckie automatically went to Emergency Mode. "Rule one-one-nine," the meckie said in its halting tone while rolling into the hallway. "Report death of ministerial personnel directly to the President."

Nineteen minutes later, the meckie stood in President Ogg's sunny office giving its report. "Product failure," the meckie said, waving its six mechanical arms demonstrably. "Minister Muñoz died of electrocution when his water-filled mattress ruptured, causing liquid to come in contact with an electrical heating coil."

"Who programmed you?" Ogg demanded, his blue green eyes flashing angrily. "Report the ministerial death only! A forensic team will determine the cause of death!"

The oval office fell into shadow momentarily as a small cloud passed in front of the sun.

"I was programmed by Bu-Tech," the meckie said as the sun returned, "with input from Bu-Med enabling me to substantiate human death."

"Well they went too far! It's bad enough that they've got you cleaning AND playing doctor. Now you're an entire police team, too!"

The meckie did not respond. Its arms fell disconsolately to its sides.

"What else can you do?" Ogg asked angrily, rising out of his chair. His voice throbbed with emotion as he asked, "How many citizens are you putting out of work?"

"I am a complicated mechanism," the meckie replied.

"Meckies!" Ogg gruffed. He rolled to the meckie's side and mentoed to open the control box on its top. Scanning the switches inside he thought: *There it is.* He mentoed a combination of numbers to activate the meckie's selective memory erasure feature. *No memory of the Muñoz incident,* the President thought, wishing he could destroy the mechanical servant. He kicked it, causing a dull thud.

Billie Birdbright entered as the meckie left.

"I want a full confidential investigation into the cause of death of General Arturo Muñoz," Ogg said. "His body is at his country condominium … on Kingsgate Road near Lake Ovett."

Surprised, the dimple-chinned Birdbright said, "Yes, Mr. President."

"Send in an entire forensic team by autocopter fleet. I want a preliminary report before quitting time today!"

"Yes, Mr. President."

"Not a minute later, Birdbright! You know how I feel about working after five o'clock!"

O O O

The *Shamrock Five* cleared Earth's atmosphere minutes after takeoff. Javik checked the flight-clip and mentoed course coordinates to the ship's mother computer. The sleek space cruiser rolled gently to starboard and accelerated in the vacuum of space.

"What a beautiful bird!" Javik said.

"Handles sweet," Madame Bernet agreed. She sat in the copilot's seat, stared dispassionately at Javik.

"I'm at the controls of the finest ship ever built!" Javik exclaimed. "Had a couple of good ships before, but this baby tops 'em all!" But when Javik glanced to his right at Madame Bernet, his elation faded. *That damned meckie keeps staring at me,* he thought.

Madame Bernet grunted, did not take her eyes off Javik.

"*Shamrock Five,*" the radio blared. "This is HQ What are your coordinates?"

Javik looked at the gleaming control panel and responded: "Twenty-nine degrees, sixteen minutes, fourteen-point-seven AT. We've just set course for Saint Elba. Speed twenty-one thousand KPH and accelerating."

"Very good, *Shamrock Five*. Over and out."

Javik snapped his gaze toward the meckie. It was not staring at him now, seemed interested in a red plastic ball attached to the instrument panel. The meckie's fingers darted forward to touch the ball. A red sign below the device proclaimed: "LEAVE NO SECRETS—SQUEEZE TO DETONATE."

"HEY!" Javik barked. "Get away from that!"

The meckie withdrew its hand, then stared at Javik insolently with cold and inhuman eyes.

*Plasto-cyanide bomb,* Javik thought, recalling his military days. *Could blow this ship to powder!* "You're no co-pilot," he said tersely. "I want you out of here immediately. Get in the passenger cabin."

"As you wish, Lieutenant," the meckie said, rising to its feet.

After Madame Bernet left, Javik lit a chromium tintette and blew a thoughtful puff of silvery yellow smoke through his nostrils. *That thing gives me the creeps,* he thought.

He shivered.

"Don't think about it," Javik murmured to himself as he flipped on the auto-pilot. "They're not going to send someone ... or *something* ... along to screw up the mission."

But Javik wondered if the perfume of the new ship had blocked the stench of the mission. Something did not seem right.

# Chapter Eight

## UP CLOSE WITH THE MASTER, FOR FURTHER READING AND DISCUSSION

*April 8, 2299 through April 21, 2299: Uncle Rosy's famous "Long March," in which he led a moto-shoe procession from New City to Philadelphia for the cause of newness, collecting old consumer goods for disposal.*

### *Monday, August 28, 2605*

To President Ogg, quitting time was as sacred a moment as starting time. Glancing irritably at his watch, he thought, *Seven minutes past five. The preliminary forensic report on Muñoz should have been here twenty-two minutes ago!*

He rose angrily and rolled into the outer office. *Crisis or no crisis,* he thought, *I'm not staying any longer!*

Two minutes later, he rolled out of the elevator at the rooftop helipad. While crossing the pad to reach Autocopter One, Ogg heard the elevator doors open behind him. He turned to see Billie Birdbright rush out, face flushed, carrying a sheet of paper.

"Mr. President!" Birdbright gasped, holding the sheet up. "The report! It just came in!"

"And?" Ogg said, raising a bushy eyebrow impatiently.

"I glanced at it in the elevator. Product failure, sir. Muñoz was electrocuted when his waterbed sprung a leak. Apparently the water touched a hot wire."

"Just as the meckie said...."

"What was that, sir?" Birdbright rubbed a fat cheek nervously with one finger.

"Nothing, nothing. Get the committees set up first thing tomorrow. I want a full investigation into—"

"Mr. President, Muñoz was found in an embrace with Colonel Peebles."

"Dammit," President Ogg said, his enthusiasm deflated. "Can't afford a scandal. Not with the election tomorrow."

"What shall we do, Mr. President?"

"Keep the committees out of this one." Ogg scowled, hardly believing he had spoken these words. "We can't release this to the public. Don't mention it to anyone."

"It WAS a product failure, sir, and they are entitled to posthumous Purple Badges."

"I suppose that's true. Uncle Rosy wouldn't want them denied full honors."

"That's right, Mr. President."

"We'll set up a different scenario for their deaths," Ogg said, smiling as if a light had just gone on inside his head.

Birthright's smile reflected that of his superior. "Another product failure, sir?"

Ogg nodded. "Have the bodies placed in Muñoz's autolimo after dark tonight. The car is to be pushed off Saint Patrick's Bridge. That's on a little-used road near Lake Ovett."

"And the death certificates will be documented to show the story the way you want it told."

"Correct." Ogg turned toward the autocopter.

"Brilliant, Mr. President!"

"That's why I'm Head of State, Billie," Ogg said, beaming proudly. He short-stepped into Autocopter One. The machine's rotors whirred to life.

During the flight home, Ogg worried over the decision he had just made. *The Black Box couldn't have arranged the waterbed failure,* he thought, nervously. *Surely they would have made the deaths more palatable ... more readily acceptable to the public.*

But as the autocopter prepared to land at a private helipad on the landscaped roof of his condominium building, it occurred to Ogg that the Black Box of Democracy may have wished to discredit Bu-Mil, feeling too much power had gravitated to that arm of government.

*Did I interfere?* he thought. *Will I incur the wrath of the Black Box?*

Autocopter One made a crisp landing on top of the building.

O O O

It was late Monday afternoon when the Inter-Orbital Transport Vehicle picked up Sidney's passenger module.

"We're only a few hours from Saint Elba now," the blind man sitting across from Sidney said.

"That so?" The retardo woman seated next to the blind man smile-grimaced as she spoke.

"I remember not so awfully long ago," the blind man said, "when it took much longer … before G-gas allowed passengers to travel at high speeds."

Sidney leaned forward to touch the blind man on his bulky arm and asked: "Were you in the Space Patrol?"

"I sure was!" the blind man said, excitedly. His wraparound sunglasses slipped. He adjusted them. Then his voice slowed and the words slurred as he added, "Until we had an explosion. … I was checking an argonium gas leak in the E-Cell compartment of a turbo-bomber hangared at New City Field…."

"You were in maintenance?"

"Uh huh. Left pilotry to the glamour boys."

"You were lucky to survive an explosion."

"Funny thing," the blind man said. "I remember seeing a brilliant flash of orange light. They found me fifty meters away. Didn't have a scratch on me, but the eyes were gone."

Sidney stared at the blind man for several minutes without thinking of anything to say. He did not want to sound patronizing and was afraid Javik would not want him to mention the important mission they were going to share. *This is a stranger,* Sidney thought. *He may be a spy.*

The blind man kept his face pointed in Sidney's direction for a couple of minutes, and Sidney saw the man's lips quiver twice, as if he had a thought but then decided against saying anything. Presently, the blind man turned his face away from Sidney, and his features grew rigid.

Most of the passengers slept during the IOTV flight. They leaned on one another or against walls. A few found places on the floor to curl up in tight balls. Sidney dozed off, too, for short periods. Each time he woke up, he looked at the blind man.

The blind man continued to stare straight ahead, or Sidney assumed he was staring behind the dark wraparound sunglasses.

"No more bathroom privileges for clients!" a female attendant called out at one point. "All clients wait until Saint Elba!" Sidney recognized the voice. It was the same attendant he had heard earlier at the field … the one with the cruel voice.

"Our Johns are on the fritz and the lousy bastards don't wanna touch the same toilet seats we do!" the blind man yelled.

"How much longer?" clients called out.

"Three hours more," an attendant replied. Presently Sidney heard "two hours," then "one hour." The quarters began to smell of ammonia and excrement to Sidney, and in the close hotness he felt he might throw up at any moment. He too had to use the bathroom, but tried to think of other things.

The side porthole over his seating area occupied his attention almost totally during the last hour of flight. Sidney pressed his face against the glass, trying to get a first glorious glimpse of the habitat. The porthole was prismatic, allowing him to see forward along the ship's course by adjusting a wall-mounted lever.

In the blackness of space ahead, Sidney knew one of the bright stars was not really a star. He watched until one began to grow dramatically in brightness.

*The Saint Elba habitat!* he thought, realizing it was reflecting sunlight from its position between the orbits of the Earth aid the Moon. Gradually the habitat's brilliance far exceeded that of the stars beyond. Then it became a narrow band of reflected sunlight.

Within minutes, Sidney could make out identifying features. He recognized the burnished solar collector suspended above Saint Elba, and then the central hub, spokes, and tubular outer rim. Saint Elba appeared to be graceful and serene, at once in harmony with itself and with the heavens.

For a time, Sidney was surprised at how small Saint Elba appeared, but as the IOTV matched the habitat's orbit and approached, he began to realize the immensity of the structure. A thick glassplex and titanium outer rim resembled a balloon bicycle tire. He saw twinkling lights and buildings through glassplex on one side of the outer rim, then lost sight of the interior as the IOTV dipped to the habitat's south side.

"Note that the spokes are rotating about the central hub," an attendant said. "This creates pseudo-gravity in the outer rim."

The attendant spoke while looking through another porthole two meters to Sidney's left. Sidney looked at him, saw folds of pink flesh popping out of the man's smock and hanging over his belt.

"I don't see any movement in the outer rim," Sidney said raising his voice to be heard over the rustlings of people who were awakening.

"A thick cosmic shield is on this side," the attendant said, glancing at Sidney. "The habitat rotates inside it. That shield is made of millions of metric tons of compacted Moon slag and dust."

Sidney nodded appreciatively and peered out the porthole again. The IOTV moved to a position on the south side of the orbiter's sextagonal hub to wait with another ship that was about to dock.

Sidney barely made out the name of the other craft. *The* Shamrock Five, he read, recognizing it as an Akron class long-range space cruiser. *Hey! That's my ship!*

O O O

Being faster than standard transport craft, the *Shamrock Five* arrived at Saint Elba almost simultaneously with the IOTV carrying Sidney.

"You have priority, *Shamrock Five*," the radio on Javik's command console blared. "We'll bring you in."

Alone in the cockpit, Javik mentoed the Auto-Docking Mode, scanned the blinking lights and glowing dials of the instrument panel.

From the IOTV standing by several hundred meters away, Sidney watched Javik's ship enter the docking tunnel. *Just coax 'er in, Tom,* Sidney thought, seeing a tiny form in the cockpit of the sleek black and silver ship. *What a beauty!* Then Sidney recalled what Javik had done for him at the reunion and glanced down at his twisted arm.

It twitched.

*Why would Tom want ME?* Sidney wondered, feeling self-pity. *He said I'd be treated here first....* Sidney thought of Carla now, and of his former co-workers, neighbors and friends ... people he might never see again.

At the same instant, Javik thought of Sidney. Maybe Javik half-noticed a round-faced fellow with curly black hair peering out of a porthole on that IOTV, but surely it was too far away for recognition. Still, Javik too reflected upon the reunion, and looked forward to his rendezvous with Sidney on Saint Elba.

*They'd better turn him over to me without a runaround,* Javik thought, *or somebody's going to wish he didn't get in my way....*

The *Shamrock Five* was drawn by titanium magne-drive deep into Saint Elba's cavernous docking tunnel. Squinting under the glare of exterior docking spotlights, Javik said to himself, "So far so good."

He flipped on the console screen and checked four outside views of the docking operation. "No problems," he murmured.

"Docking five hundred meters," the onboard computer announced.

"Passenger cabin view," Javik instructed, leaning forward to speak into a speakercom.

The screen flickered and showed Madame Bernet seated alone in the ten-seat passenger cabin, eating a sandwich. *Nice feature,* he mused. *Wonder how the meckie processes the food.* As the meckie finished the sandwich, it licked its fingers.

Javik looked away for a moment to watch the dock come into view, a broad, dimly-lit platform with several ships tethered at the sides. *I'll take a trouble detector through the ship tomorrow before liftoff,* he thought. *I don't want to leave the cockpit with that sub-human wandering around.*

As his eyes darted back to the console screen, Javik saw Madame Bernet staring directly at the camera. *She seems to know I'm watching. How in the hell?...* He flipped off the screen, and it went dark.

*Maybe the damned thing IS human,* he thought, reflecting on the way the meckie continually stared at him. *And it has the hots for me.* Javik realized this was a feeble attempt at levity, and he felt uncomfortable.

"Docking two hundred fifty meters," the computer reported.

*Let's see,* he thought, planning his activities of the following day. *I'll look at the ejection pods and other safety equipment. That would be through hatch seventeen....*

Javik saw the docking platform clearly now. He watched dockworkers in white bubble suits as they scurried about on moto-boots.

Saint Elba's magne-drive turned the *Shamrock Five* to one side, and the ship began to approach the dock sideways. Presently the ship jerked, then rocked gently and settled into place in its padded docking slip.

O O O

As Javik and Madame Bernet rolled off the *Shamrock Five* onto Saint Elba's shadowy docking platform, Madame Bernet yawned. The meckie stretched, locked its fingers together and cracked the knuckles. "God, I'm drained," it said. "Took a couple of sleep-sub pills in flight, but now all I can think about is a nice soft bed."

*For Christ's sake,* Javik thought. *This meckie is overplaying its part!*

Low-wattage light standards dotted the platform, providing enough illumination to cast weak shadows of the two as they rolled side by side toward an arched doorway. As they rolled through the doorway into a more brightly lit area, a loudspeakered woman's voice announced: "Welcome, brave crewmen! I am Mayor Nancy Ogg."

Javik focused on an illuminated glassplex viewing area above them. "There," he said, nodding his head in the direction of the viewing area. "She's a looker, too!" Javik realized too late that this was the sort of sentiment he used to share with Brent Stafford. He missed Stafford.

"I see her," Madame Bernet said.

"Decontamination showers are directly ahead of you," Mayor Nancy Ogg said. "The inconvenience is necessary, since we must be concerned about the tiniest micro-organisms brought in from outside." She paused and added, "But you understand this."

"Yes, ma'am," Javik replied with a cordial grin. "I most certainly do." *They're worried about Zero-G Plague,* he thought. *No one dares speak of it because of space superstition.* He recalled that it had been almost three decades since the epidemic at Saint Michaels killed sixty-six thousand people.... Stringent decontamination procedures had been established after that.

Javik watched as Madame Bernet entered a women's shower room silently. *Wonder if she'll rust,* he thought.

After the showers, Javik and Madame Bernet dressed in fresh Space Patrol uniforms they found in the dressing areas.

A tweed-suited Mayor Nancy Ogg greeted them in the hallway, accompanied by Sergeant Rountree. Javik passed the release authorization to Mayor Nancy Ogg and asked her to locate Sidney immediately.

"A cappy?" she said. "What do you want with a miserable cappy?"

"He's to be captain of the ship," Javik said with a bit of irritation. He stared down the bridge of his nose at the Mayor.

"What?" she said. "A cappy?" Dr. Hudson's electronic letter was in the lapel pocket of her suit. *We'll lose Malloy for a couple of days,* she thought. *It won't be difficult.*

"You're to treat him quickly and release him to me."

Mayor Nancy Ogg studied the release form intently. "General Muñoz signed this?" She handed it to the security sergeant, adding, "We'll have to do some checking, of course."

"You weren't notified?"

"No."

"Christ! All right. Check all you want, but make it fast. If Malloy's not treated and ready to go tomorrow, the comet intercept mission is off. And you probably know it isn't headed toward any mining base."

The Mayor's dark brown eyes flashed angrily as if to say that Javik was acting impertinently to one of her status. *So you know that comet's coming down our throat,* she thought. *Well you'll go alone at the last minute—out of patriotic duty.*

Mayor Nancy Ogg said nothing further about the Malloy matter, and turned her attention to Madame Bernet. "Who might you be?" she asked, sweetly.

The meckie identified itself, after which Javik explained, "Madame Bernet is a meckie, our Onboard Systems Coordinator for the mission."

*So THIS is the killer meckie,* Mayor Nancy Ogg thought. *It looks human, except for the eyes.*

"This way, please," the Mayor said, motioning toward a nearby conveyor transporter. A strip which moved slowly and noisily, the transporter carried pop-up metal chairs.

Javik started to roll toward the conveyor, but stopped as he saw Madame Bernet and Mayor Nancy Ogg hold back.

"After you," the Mayor said to Madame Bernet in a syrupy, overly gracious tone. *I'm not going to turn my back on this ... monster!* she thought.

Madame Bernet's eyes flashed angry glances at the Mayor and at Sergeant Rountree. "Thank you," the meckie said, smiling warily. It rolled by Javik.

*Do they sense what I do about Madame Bernet?* Javik thought. *Or do they know something?*

"Step aboard," Mayor Nancy Ogg instructed as they all reached the transporter. "Disembark at Landing Platform One."

Mayor Nancy Ogg watched the meckie and Javik take seats. Then she and Sergeant Rountree sat behind them. Mayor Nancy Ogg recalled seeing a decommissioned Atheist killer meckie once in the War Museum. She felt fascination and fear.

After a short ride on the conveyor transporter, they transferred to a monorail car destined for the habitat's outer rim. They sat in triple-wide seats, with Mayor Nancy Ogg and her sergeant on one side, facing Javik and Madame Bernet.

"There aren't many people moving about at this time of night," the Mayor said, glancing around the car at four scattered attendants in other seats.

Javik smiled at her, caught her gaze.

She looked away.

*She carries herself with an air of superiority,* he thought, feeling captivated by the Mayor's almond-shaped brown eyes. *But I see a passionate woman beneath the facade.* Javik flicked a glance to his left, saw Madame Bernet staring bleakly out the window.

The monorail car jolted.

Sergeant Rountree looked across at Javik and said, "I'm sorry the ride is so rough. We're working on the tracks, you know."

Javik insisted it did not bother him. Then he looked at the Mayor and asked, "Forgive me for prying, Your Honor, but are you related to President Ogg?"

"My older brother," she said, pinning her gaze on Madame Bernet. The meckie stared out the window at the blackness of the tunnel's interior, apparently unaware of the Mayor's interest.

"Fine, man," Javik said.

"Yes," Mayor Nancy Ogg thought. *But a bigot?* she thought.

"I'd vote for him tomorrow," Javik said with a flirtatious smile in the Mayor's direction, "but there are other more pressing matters requiring my attention."

"I'm certain my brother understands," she said stiffly.

*Cool one,* Javik thought. *Too bad I don't have time to soften her with my charms.*

When the monorail car exited the spoke tube, it began to decelerate. Javik saw the lights of an arch-glass terminal building ahead, and beyond that the twinkling lights of a resting city.

They disembarked at the terminal. Sergeant Rountree led them along shadowy motopaths past a fruit tree orchard and into an area of apartment buildings surrounded by illuminated Japanese gardens.

"We're just outside the habitat's principal shopping district," Mayor Nancy Ogg said as they negotiated an arched bridge.

"Very nice," Javik said, noting carefully manicured dwarf shrubs and trees along each side of an illuminated stream.

"I'm terribly sorry about the temperature," Sergeant Rountree said as they reached the end of the bridge and entered a narrow motopath. "We've had trouble with the solar heating system. It's been four degrees on the cool side for a week."

"There's no need to apologize for everything," Mayor Nancy Ogg said sternly, flashing an angry glance at her sergeant.

Sergeant Rountree did not meet the Mayor's gaze; he mumbled something in an apologetic tone.

"Hardly noticed the temperature," Javik said, amused at the confrontation.

They stopped at a fourplex building, where Mayor Nancy Ogg handed Javik and the meckie plastikeys. "Separate apartments have been prepared for each of you," she said. "The apartment numbers are on the keys."

Then she turned to leave and remarked, "I'll send for you in the morning. We'll breakfast together. Your ship will be recharged and ready to go by tomorrow afternoon."

"I'd like to see Malloy right after breakfast," Javik said with a tone of authority.

"We'll see," Mayor Nancy Ogg said.

O O O

After decontamination showers in the Hub, Sidney and the other clients were allowed to use the bathrooms and were provided with fresh clothing. As the fatigued group boarded a monorail car for the trip to the habitat's outer rim, an attendant said, "Saint Elba's night barrier is in place now, shielding the reflected rays of the sun. The barrier moves back and forth automatically, creating day and night in the habitat. We even have seasons!"

They disembarked at the arch-glass terminal building, and from there were herded unceremoniously into the back of an autotruck. The truck moved quickly through shopping and residential areas. Presently, Sidney saw the lights of a massive building which stretched laterally as far as he could see. In height the structure was perhaps one hundred stories, limited as it was by the thickness of the outer rim.

"Elba House," an attendant said.

A few minutes later, the clients were lined up in the lobby of Elba House, awaiting admittance. Toward the front of one line, Sidney watched six desk attendants as they matched clients with counselors. Loudspeakered voices rang around the room as the attendants called for counselors. When Sidney's turn came, he rolled to the desk.

"I'm supposed to get rush treatment," Sidney said, leaning forward and speaking in a low tone to a beefy, flat-nosed male attendant. "I have a very important mission...." Sidney caught himself as he noticed the attendant sneering at him.

"Everybody here is on an important mission," the attendant said. "Especially the mental cases!"

Two attendants seated nearby tittered.

The attendant grabbed Sidney's right wrist and read the plasti-tag. "Malloy, S.," he said. "Client number one-six-five-six-three-two-oh-two-nine." The attendant checked his log-book, then spoke into a voice-amp: "Counselor, Ruth Bremer. Is Ruth Bremer present?"

A woman called out with military precision: "Present."

Sidney turned to watch a slender woman with neatly trimmed dark brown hair moto-shoe to his side. She wore a plain white Bu-Med dress emblazoned with a triangular Bu-Med lapel crest. "I am Bremer," she announced curtly.

Sidney studied his counselor as she leaned over the desk and mentoed an auto-pen to sign the custody form. The pen moved across the page without being held. Of a bit less than middling height, the counselor had hard features, with a protruding chin and a tiny nose. Sidney became conscious of how tired he felt. The excitement had begun to wear off.

"Take Malloy to one-four-six-five-eight in R Wing," the attendant instructed.

Bremer nodded and grasped Sidney by his good arm. "A maximum security wing," she confided as they rolled toward a double-wide door marked "SUBWAY."

"Maximum security?" Sidney almost spat the words out. "I'm not dangerous!"

"They know that," she said with a hint of condescension in her tone. "Anyone can see you're not in chains."

"Then why?"

"Orders, fellow," she said stiffly. "I just do what I'm told."

Pausing at a subway loading platform, they watched as a four-passenger mini-car approached. I'll complete the necessary forms to get you out of there as soon as possible," she promised.

"Thanks for that," Sidney said. "But I'm supposed to—"

"Don't thank me!" she scoffed. "That will cost you two work credits! I don't fill out forms for nothing!"

"A Lieutenant Javik of the Space Patrol is going to ask for me tomorrow," Sidney said, "I'll be going with him."

"Sure," the counselor said. "I'll put the whole staff on alert."

"Thanks," Sidney said. Then he caught her frigid gaze and realized she was insincere. Sidney fell into silent and troubled thought.

R Wing was a six-minute ride away. They took an elevator to the fourteenth floor and moto-shoed down a long, curving hall which was punctuated with signs. One sign appeared more frequently than others:

**THANK ROSENBLOOM**
**FOR**
**FULL EMPLOYMENT**

"This is it," Counselor Bremer finally announced, stopping at a maroon door. She read an attendance screen on the wall, added, "Your roommates are already in bed. Enter quietly and find a bunk. I'll set up your therapy schedule in the morning."

She mentoed the door. It slid open to one side, revealing a darkened room with bunk beds along the opposite wall and a table with two straight-backed chairs near the entry. A tiny barred window was high on one wall.

"I'll hold the door open for two minutes to give you more light," she said.

Sidney hesitated, then rolled across the threshold. But he felt a sudden wave of fear and turned to re-enter the hall. An unseen barrier in the doorway halted him abruptly.

"Ow!" he said, rubbing a bruised eyebrow. "What was that?"

"Thought barrier," she replied stiffly. "Get to bed. *Now.*"

"But why?…" Sidney remembered and said, "Oh. Maximum security."

Counselor Bremer did not respond, stared at him coolly.

Sidney looked down at his twisted left arm, noted sadly that the elbow, wrist, and fingers were lock-bent. Every muscle and tendon ached and appeared taut to the point of bursting. Angrily, he tried with all his energy to straighten the arm and hand. But it was to no avail. He stood there for a moment afterward breathing hard and glaring across the thought barrier at Counselor Bremer.

"You have forty-five seconds," she said.

Sidney turned like a whipped meckie-pup and found an unoccupied upper bunk. He unsnapped his moto-shoes quickly, then laid his weary body upon an electric lift which had dropped silently from above. His body weight activated the lift, and it carried him to an upper bunk.

Darkness fell across the room as Sidney rolled into bed, wearing a thin green Bu-Med smock like the one issued to him on Earth.

*How long will my treatment take?* he thought. *Will Tom find me here?*

"Bremer's a tough one," a husky voice whispered from below. "She'll chew ya up and spit ya out."

Sidney did not respond. He lay awake with his eyes open watching faint shadows cast upon the ceiling by the high wall window. Tired to the marrow, he tried to collect his thoughts. The room gradually filled with light snoring sounds. As Sidney's thoughts ran together in a blur, he too drifted off to sleep.

* *

Sayer Superior Lin-Ti resumed his place at the podium. Weary from three days away, he thought of the burdens of Ins position. *So much responsibility,* he thought. *I should delegate more….*

He flipped to Chapter Nine.

# Chapter Nine

## THE CAPPY PROBLEM, FOR FURTHER READING AND DISCUSSION

*February 16, 2341: Mandate of Retardation passed unanimously by the Council of Ten. The major tenets of this mandate held that "cappies" ("crips" and "retardos") were to be sterilized, could not own real property and were to be committed to therapy orbiters.*

### *Tuesday, August 29, 2605*

In the few minutes before Garbage Day minus three began on Saint Elba with the opening of the habitat's night shield, Sidney's room remained in darkness. A nightmare captured his mind with a sense of reality that drenched his bed in perspiration—Sidney was imprisoned on a planet which rotated freely in a round cage. Spaceships entered and left through iron gates which clanked noisily in airless space as they opened and closed. He knew this was impossible, but his dream permitted no questions.

It was an unhappy place. Desperate prisoners plotted escape…

"Escape … dawn … take the Hub…." Words echoed in Sidney's consciousness and vanished like fine sand through burlap. He squirmed in his slumber, pushing blankets away to cool his body. Half awake now, he began to realize that some of the dream voices were real.

"The snoring!" an urgent voice husked. "It's stopped!"

"Is he awake?' another asked.

Sidney froze. His heart pounded. He sensed someone very near, listening to his breathing. Sidney tried to feign sleep by taking loud, deep breaths.

Suddenly a strong hand grabbed his throat. "One squeal and you're dead!" a man rasped. He pulled Sidney to the floor and held Sidney's good right arm in a clamp grip.

"What did you hear?" another man asked. His voice was high-pitched, commanding.

"Nothing," Sidney gasped, flailing his deformed arm helplessly. "I heard nothing!" Sidney looked beyond a shadow which hulked over him and saw faces half-illuminated by low light entering the room through the barred high wall window.

"Let's tie and gag him," one suggested.

"Maybe he'd like to throw in with us," said another. It was the same husky voice that had spoken to Sidney in the darkness when he first arrived, warning him about Counselor Bremer. This was a potential friend.

"Don't chance it," the man with the high-pitched voice said.

"But he's no threat to us," the potential friend said. "This is so big no one can stop it." But Sidney felt the grip of the man who held him tighten around his neck.

"Stone's right," the man with the high-pitched voice said. "We have hundreds set to break! And thousands will follow!"

Sidney breathed an audible sigh of relief as the grip loosened. The man released him, pushing him to the floor. Sidney rose to lean on the elbow of his right arm and looked at the dark outline of the man they called Stone.

"You okay, fella?" Stone asked.

But before Sidney could answer, the man who had held him said. "He's a crip. Look at his arm."

"I can't go with you," Sidney said, thinking of his rendezvous with Javik. He counted five other men in the room, four kneeling around him and another standing near the door.

"Suit yourself," the man with the high-pitched voice said. Sidney noticed that the man's face seemed pale whenever he got a glimpse of a section of it, even in the low light. *These are doomies,* Sidney thought.

Before Sidney could gather the courage to phrase a question, a great clamor arose in the building. There was a loud thump in the room above, and from all around came the sounds of breaking glass and people shouting. The hall door slid open, casting bright light into the room. The noises grew closer now, and half-dressed men ran or moto-shoed by the door.

"It's started!!' Stone shouted, jumping to his feet. "The thought barriers are open!"

It was every man for himself. All except Sidney crowded to the door without another word, and then were gone.

Through the open door, Sidney watched with amazement as hordes of clients surged and pushed in their frantic flights to freedom. Sidney heard gunfire in the distance, and the incessant wail of sirens. He rose to his feet

A group of armed Security Brigade guards rolled by, followed by a cluster of Bu-Med attendants. "Halt!" the guards yelled. Gunfire rang through the hallway.

Then Sidney smelted smoke, and heard screams of panic from outside the door. "Fire!" someone called out. "Fire!" Sidney snapped on his moto-shoes, peeked into the hallway.

O O O

Mayor Nancy Ogg had not gone to bed after seeing Javik and Madame Bernet to their apartments for the night. Instead she returned to her own apartment and studied a checklist at the kitchen table. Gradually she fell asleep there, dropping her head to the tabletop.

When the night shield began to open at dawn, reflected sunlight filtered through the kitchen module's greenhouse roof. The Mayor stirred, knocking papers to the floor. She sat up, stretched and yawned.

*Busy day ahead,* she thought.

As the Mayor leaned over to retrieve her papers, she heard sirens whining in the distance.

O O O

As Sidney poked his head out of the doorway, he saw flames at both ends of the hall. Agonized screams filled the smoke-contaminated air. Several paces to his left on the floor, Sidney saw the bleeding bodies of two green-smocked clients. It was apparent that they had been shot.

Sidney coughed as he ventured a few meters into the hall. Common sense told him to go back in the room and close the door. At least that would delay the inevitable, and left open the possibility of rescue from a window.

*"Into the flames, fleshcarrier!"* a tenor voice inside his head commanded. *"Down the hallway to your right!"*

"To certain death?" Sidney asked, aloud.

*"To POSSIBLE death,"* the voice said, laughing.

"Possible?"

*"If you're lucky, you'll get out."* Again, laughter.

"Don't be ridiculous!" Sidney said. He watched as many clients, attendants, and guards gave up and sat in the middle of the floor to await death.

*"I will tell you this, curious fleshcarrier. It's a matter of simple odds ... as in a card game or at a roulette wheel."*

"How thick are the flames?"

*"I do not MEASURE flames,"* the voice said haughtily. *"How does one MEASURE flames?"*

Sidney shook his head negatively, but started to roll in the direction designated by the voice. Rolling slowly at first, he passed seated and standing people who cried out or prayed. Others were already dead, and lay in confused positions on the floor. Sidney picked up speed.

When he was only two meters from the dancing violet and orange flames, the heat had become almost unbearable. Suddenly the floor above the flames cracked and broke away. A great burst of cool white foam hit Sidney and the flames. He slipped and fell to the floor, his body and face covered in foam.

"This way!" a voice called from above.

Sidney wiped foam from his face and clothing. His eyes stung. He looked up to the floor above and saw a red-and-yellow-uniformed fireman drop a flexible metal ladder to him.

"Hurry!" the fireman urged.

Sidney struggled partway up the ladder, having difficulty on the flexible metal links due to his bad arm and slippery foam on his body. About halfway up, he stopped, breathing hard. "My arm!" Sidney gasped. "I can't climb any farther!"

Through blurry, watery eyes, Sidney saw three firemen lift the ladder. They helped him off at the top, then dropped the ladder back for more people.

"You're a lucky one," a fireman said. "Over there," he instructed, pointing toward a group of people who were gathered near a window, their shapes forming silhouettes against dawn light. "Get in the escape chute!"

*Luck?* Sidney thought as he followed the fireman's instructions. *Was it only a matter of odds?*

When Sidney's turn came, he slid down a spiraling escape chute to ground level.

O O O

Javik awoke to the piercing whine of sirens. From bed, he could see through the skylights of the bedroom module to the edge of the habitat's outer rim far above. Beyond that, the sun reflected off the solar collector and peeked around the night shield, bathing the room in yellow light.

He went to the balcony and looked across a terraced Japanese hillside garden to a large building in the distance. Flames licked from the windows of middle floors. Black smoke billowed in the air. Emergency vehicles screamed, rolling at high speed toward the conflagration.

"Remain in your homes!" a loudspeaker truck boomed. "Keep all doors and windows shut! Emergency oxygen systems will not function if doors and windows are open!"

Javik went into the living room module and scanned its contents. The room had bright green plastic tables and side-chairs, with a green paisley short couch that matched the curtains. He rolled to a wall-mounted telephone in a pool of sunlight near the couch, mentoed a tele-cube. It rose from its cradle on the phone, hovered in the air in front of his face.

"Number please," a pleasant female syntho-voice said.

"Get me Hub Control," Javik commanded. "Hurry!"

"Sorry, sir. Those circuits are busy. Please try back in—"

"Damn!" Javik cursed. "Then get me Elba House."

"Sorry, sir. Those circuits are busy too."

Javik mento-slammed the circuit shut. The tele-cube floated back to its cradle. *Sidney will have to fend for himself,* he thought. *Right now I've got to take care of my ship.*

Javik dressed quickly and met Madame Bernet in the hall. Fastening the top button of a white-and-gold uniform dress, Madame Bernet asked, "You saw the fire?"

"Yeah, and I can't reach Hub Control! We'd better get to the ship! This whole orbiter may go up!" Javik wiped a hand through an uncombed shock of amber hair. The sleep-tormented hair did not smooth out.

Reaching the street in seconds, Javik and the meckie rolled hurriedly along a motopath in the direction of the habitat's spoke tubes, hoping to catch a monorail for the Hub. He smelled smoke.

As they passed a small cluster of fruit trees, Javik stopped abruptly. "There!" he said excitedly, pointing toward the arch-glass monorail terminal building several hundred meters away. A mass of green-smocked clients, many of whom obviously had severe handicaps, streamed into the building. Some operated moto-crutches or rode in electric wheelchairs. Others ran or moto-shoed.

"A breakout!" Javik moaned. "How in the hell are we …"

Madame Bernet drew a long, gleaming knife from a concealed pocket in its dress, rasped: "We'll force our way through!"

"You're armed?" Javik short-stepped back several paces and pulled his own pistol.

"For *your* protection," the meckie replied, gluing its gaze on Javik's weapon.

"Sheathe that!" Javik barked, glancing at two clients who were picking pears on the opposite side of the grove. "I have a better idea!"

The meckie hesitated, then followed the command with obvious reluctance.

Javik bolstered his pistol and grabbed the meckie by one arm. "Come with me," he said.

Madame Bernet did not reply, seemed to think for a moment before accompanying Javik. As they approached the clients, Javik saw that both were men, and he recognized the puffy facial features and vacuous expressions of mongolism. One of the clients, who was quite tall and fat, smiled as he extended a pear to Madame Bernet.

Perplexed, Madame Bernet glanced at Javik.

"Take it," Javik said. "And smile."

Madame Bernet obeyed, then looked confused as she stood there with the piece of fruit in her mechanical grasp.

Javik addressed the shorter client: "We need your smocks," he said. "Okay?"

Unresponsive, the client stared back with wide open, childlike eyes. He extended a pear, which Javik accepted.

"They don't understand," Madame Bernet said, reaching into a deep pocket with her free hand. "My way now, Captain?"

"Wait," Javik said. "I'm going to try one more thing first." He removed a shiny coin from his tunic pocket and offered it to the shorter client. The mongoloid smiled, reached for the object. Javik pulled it back gently, touched the man's smock and said, "Trade." Then Javik offered him the coin again and pulled at the smock. "Trade," he repeated.

On the fourth attempt, the client understood. He removed his smock and handed it to Javik in exchange for the coin. Madame Bernet followed the same procedure to obtain the other smock. Entirely naked now, the mongoloids stood smiling as they examined their shiny new treasures.

"I don't see any guards yet," Javik said, "but you can bet they're around somewhere." They threw on the green smocks over their own uniforms.

"Hide in the crowd," Javik said. "We'll get the smocks off when the *Shamrock Five's* in sight."

But when they reached the monorail terminal, the meckie stopped abruptly. "Go no farther," it said tersely.

"What?" Javik said, turning to confront Madame Bernet.

"I sense … danger," Madame Bernet said.

"You have a short-circuit," Javik snapped. "This is the only way!"

But the meckie stood rigidly, with both hands thrust into the pockets of its smock.

"Do as you please," Javik said. "I'll go on without you!"

The meckie stared straight ahead at an indeterminate point in the distance. Its expression was resolute.

"Damned thing can't respond," Javik cursed as he rolled away. "Just like the Bu-Industry meckies. The minute an unusual situation arises …"

Javik reached the terminal building and pushed his way through a noisy crowd of clients. It smelled of human waste and perspiration inside, and Javik spent a long hour pressed against other bodies before he was able to board a railcar for a standing-room-only ride.

Minutes later, the car came to a stop in the Hub. To Javik's surprise, he saw hundreds of black-uniformed security men standing outside next to long, clear glassplex units. Javik did not see a single client in the bunch. As the car squeaked to a stop, he realized the reason for this. The security men manually connected glassplex hall-tubes to each door of the monorail car, thus forcing all clients to follow a controlled exit path.

"I'm trapped!" Javik yelled, hardly able to hear his own words in the din of humanity.

When the car doors opened, most of the clients realized they had been tricked. "Let us out!" they yelled, beating furiously on the glassplex windows of the monorail car.

Javik smelled tear gas in the car. He was forced into the hall-tube in a rush to escape the gas, and Javik saw some clients pushed back against the walls. He lost his own footing momentarily then, but eventually was able to regain control and began to move forward with the crowd.

*I've got to get back to the skip!* Javik thought, desperately.

He saw a large holding room ahead, filled with a mob of green-smocked, angry escapees. The surging crowd slowed and stopped before Javik reached the room. He stared at a clear glassplex side wall just an arm's length away, felt hot, perspiring bodies against his own.

*Maybe I can shoot holes in the glassplex,* he thought. *I could break off a piece and crawl through....*

Someone stuck an elbow in his ribs. It hurt. *No,* he thought. *There are armed guards everywhere out there! They'll kill me if they see my weapon!*

Javik ran through the options with military precision. Soon it became apparent to him that he could do but one thing. *I'll have to find someone to listen to me,* he thought.

O O O

The telephone rang during Hudson's Tuesday morning shower. Earlier than usual this day, he was anxious to watch the first election returns on home video. *It never fails,* he thought irritably, mentoing the water off. *The minute I step into the shower....*

Hudson stepped out onto a simulated marble tile floor and wrapped a towel around his waist as he counted the third ring of the phone. He heard a thump overhead. *That damned crazy woman upstairs,* he thought. *Doing unsanctioned exercises in her bathroom again. I'll make another complaint to the Anti-Cheapness League. They'll take her away this time!*

Hudson sat on the commode cover and mento-answered the call. A tele-cube flitted forth, pausing in front of his mouth.

A scramble code beeper went off as Mayor Nancy Ogg identified herself at the other end of the line. "Lieutenant Javik is missing!" she said, her voice faltering. "We're searching everywhere!"

"What do you mean? He arrived, didn't he?" Hudson scowled as he heard a loud thump upstairs.

"Yes. Last night. I saw him … and the meckie … to apartments for the night. Personally. But there's been a major breakout from Elba House since, and a terrible fire there!"

"Judas Priest!"

"Elba House is still burning! We've got mass confusion here, Dick!"

Hudson put his hand over the tele-cube as he heard another thump upstairs, yelled: "Keep quiet up there!"

"Are you there, Dick?" Mayor Nancy Ogg asked. "Are you there?'

"Yeah," Hudson snapped, releasing his hand from the tele-cube. "Listen, Nancy, can you control the fire?"

"We think so. I'm getting reports on it every half hour."

"Where is Madame Bernet?"

Detecting anger in Hudson's tone, she replied nervously: "The killer meckie? Why, my Security Brigade took it in. They're checking its memory circuits … to see if it might have disposed of Javik prematurely."

The telephone beeped.

"How the hell did this happen?" Hudson asked, unable to suppress his rage any longer.

"Well, it wasn't my fault!"

"Maybe if you'd been a little more dedicated to your job, instead of always trying to think of ways to get off Saint Elba …"

"I tried. Really I did. I even stayed up late last night, trying to make sure everything would go right today." She sobbed.

"Don't use tears on me!" Hudson said.

Mayor Nancy Ogg continued to cry.

"Look," Hudson said. "I shouldn't have been so quick to blame you. There's a lot of tension here over this comet thing."

Mayor Nancy Ogg wiped her eyes with a tissue. "Okay," she said. She blew her nose. "Dick, don't stay on Earth too long. If it looks like the comet can't be stopped …"

"Don't worry about that," Hudson said. "All the council ministers have escape rockets.…"

After the call, Hudson rang Muñoz's country condominium. It rang thirty times without an answer.

*Damn it,* Hudson thought. He placed the call again. Still no answer

Hudson cursed again, called President Ogg. A recorded voice answered: "Thank you for calling the White House Office Tower. Our hours are nine to five, Monday through Friday. At the tone, you may leave your name, number and a brief message."

Hudson heard a tone, said, "Emergency message for President Ogg." He gave his name, then changed his mind and hung up the telephone.

*I'll call during office hours,* he thought. *This is too important to leave on tape.*

O O O

Hudson flipped on the videodome at a little past seven AM The polls had just opened, and returns were beginning to stream in from electronic tabulating machines on the East Coast.

"This is unprecedented, ladies and gentlemen," an announcer said, with the soul-less smile of one having political aspirations of his own. "A punch-in candidate, General Arturo Muñoz, holds forty-six-point-three percent of the vote. President Ogg has a narrow lead with forty-nine-point-one percent, and Benjamin T. Morgan …"

Hudson smiled. *Precisely according to plan,* he thought. *The General will trail in a close race, then will vault to the front on the strength of late returns.*

A team of network news analysts was having a round-table discussion as the tabulated returns came in on a studio wall. Suddenly this picture disappeared and the sound went off. A message appeared on the screen:

**IMPORTANT BULLETIN**
**PLEASE STAND BY**

Then the videodome blared: "We interrupt this broadcast for a special announcement. General Arturo Muñoz, fourteenth minister of Bu-Mil, has been killed in an autocar accident. The mishap occurred sometime before dawn when the General's limousine plunged through a guardrail and went off the edge of a narrow bridge near Lake Ovett. Another body has been discovered in the wreckage, believed to be that of his adjutant, Colonel Allen Peebles. Preliminary investigation points to a malfunction of the car's electromagnetic circuitry. The state funeral celebration and posthumous Purple Badge ceremony will take place Thursday, beginning with …"

Dr. Hudson mentoed the set to silence. He sat staring at the darkened screen in disbelief. *How could this have happened?* he thought, frantically.

He left the videodome and moto-paced back and forth the length of the living room module. *What the hell should I do now?* he thought. *But Arturo was insane.... Maybe we're better off....*

Feeling hot and clammy, Hudson wiped perspiration from his brow with one hand. *Could he have left any evidence to incriminate the rest of us?*

Hudson paused, stared at his feet and thought: *Too risky to check Arturo' s office ... but maybe my own ...* It occurred to Hudson that something might remain to be cleaned up. A bit of paper, some item previously overlooked.

Hudson's autocar deposited him at the edge of Technology Square, then disappeared into an underground parking tube. The square was empty, recently cleaned. He moto-shoed across it and up the ramp to the Bu-Tech Office Tower. At the entrance, he placed his hand on the black glass of a security monitor identity plate. The vacuum went on, sucking at his palm. Suddenly he pulled the hand back, as if it had been burned.

*My God!* he thought. *The vacuum ... it's ... it's a cell reading mechanism!*

Dr. Hudson realized in that instant that the monitor had been reading all his memories, contained in the tiniest cell of his body. He cursed himself for being so stupid. He had even thought of the concept, but it had never occurred to him that his predecessors were so advanced!

A cold wave of fear spread over him, and a torrent of stinging sweat rolled over his eyebrows and into his eyes. Hudson turned quickly, nearly stumbling as he did so, and moto-sped down the ramp. The shoes accelerated quickly, and halfway down the ramp Hudson mentoed instructions for them to slow down. But they continued to accelerate!

*I'm going too fast!* he thought, panicky. The shoes were out of control, and raced across the square at full speed. *I can't turn!* he thought, frozen in fear.

The shoes carried him past the skatewalk and through a planting area, then barreled onto busy American Boulevard. He saw a streetcleaning truck heading directly toward him! *Oh no!* he thought. *It's going to hit me!* Hudson closed his eyes, put his hands over his face and prayed for mercy from a God he had never served.

"Eeeeyah!" Hudson screamed as the truck hit him, dragging him into the midst of its whirring brushes.

Moments later, Hudson's mangled body was thrust out of the back of the machine. The streetcleaner skidded to a stop, and its crew of orange-uniformed drivers and helpers got out.

A small crowd gathered around the crumpled, bleeding form. Billie Birdbright was one of the first to arrive. "What happened?" he asked.

"Product failure!" a man next to Birdbright said joyously. "He lost control of his moto-shoes!"

"Praise be to Uncle Rosy!" Birdbright exclaimed happily, not recognizing Hudson. "Another Purple Badge!"

"And another soul for the Happy Shopping Ground!" the man said.

Everyone in the crowd bowed their heads and murmured, "Truly we are blessed! All of us are employed!"

Birdbright heard the happy whine of approaching sirens, saw a white-and-red Product Failure van screech to a stop nearby. Six white-smocked team members rolled out, each with bold red lettering across his chest. The first man's chest read, "DOCTOR," and two other men and three women had signs reading, "INS. AGENT," "LAWYER," "MORTICIAN," "P.F. STAMPER" and "HELPER."

"He's dead!" the doctor announced, kneeling over the body and checking the pulse.

"Wonderful!" the mortician said, clapping her hands in joy.

The lawyer, doctor, and insurance agent mentoed auto-pens to scribble on clip-pads as the helper and mortician rolled the body over. "Stamp his forehead!" the doctor called out cheerily, glancing over the top of his clip-pad.

"I can't!" the P.F. Stamper called back. She smiled winsomely. "It's too mangled!"

"Oh my," the man next to Birdbright said. "His head's too mangled for a P.F. stamp!"

"Stamp him anywhere, then," the doctor said. "Just be sure it's on the skin and plainly visible. We want this brave fellow admitted to the Happy Shopping Ground!"

Birdbright watched the P.F. Stamper tear open the victim's shirt and lift a large chrome-plated auto-stamper over the body.

"KWAK!" the stamper went.

"Oh!" the crowd murmured, noting a large black "P.F." on the victim's bare chest. Below that the date of occurrence appeared, in smaller letters.

"A product failure!" Birdbright said, turning to a woman on his left. "Isn't it wonderful?"

The woman nodded, smiled, and murmured something,

"A bonus, ladies and gentlemen!" the insurance agent called out. "The streetcleaning machine is scratched and dented!"

The orange-uniformed streetcleaner crew auto-clapped and whistled at this news. "Scrap it!" they said in unison. "It's not fair to repair."

The Product Failure team loaded Hudson's body into the van, then ceremoniously radioed for a tow truck.

Moments later, feeling warmth in his stomach, Birdbright watched the van speed away. *It's all so wonderful!* he thought. *Praise be to Uncle Rosy!*

* *

Ordinance Room One, inside the Great Temple at Pleasant Reef:

"The beings from the Realm of Magic would have laughed their heads off at this point," Sayer Superior Lin-Ti said from the podium, recalling the previous day's lesson. "But you see, they had no heads."

The youngsayermen laughed politely.

"Just think of it, youngsayers!" Lin-Ti said, raising his hands to emphasize the point, "Malloy stumbling around in a cappy riot; Javik heading for who knows where; Muñoz, Hudson and Peebles all dead...."

Lin-Ti opened a discussion period, and the group agreed that these bodiless beings must have been terribly amused at the self-destruct capabilities of the fleshcarriers.

A youngsayerman asked if Malloy might have been insane ... and Muñoz too ... because of the voices they heard. "No normal person hears voices like that," he pointed out.

"But this was not a normal situation," Lin-Ti said.

"And our Master heard voices, too!" another youngsayerman said, blurting out the words.

Lin-Ti looked at the speaker. It was the tall one who resembled Onesayer Edward. "And how do you know this?" Lin-Ti asked, tersely.

"Uh ... er ..."

"You read ahead?'

The youngsayerman lowered his head in shame. "Yes, Sayer Superior," he said. "I am very sorry...."

# Chapter Ten

## THE CAPPY PROBLEM, FOR FURTHER READING AND DISCUSSION

*Mid-September, 2311: Bloody "Cappy Power" revolts on the therapy orbiters of Saint Joseph and Saint Michaels, in which cappies briefly took control. New security measures were established to prevent recurrence.*

### *Tuesday, August 29, 2605*

Sidney needed to catch his breath. He sat hunched forward on a plasti-marbo bench in the smoky morning shade of Elba House's rhododendron garden, a few meters off the motopath where hordes of clients rushed by heading toward the Hub. Sidney watched red and yellow helipumpers hovering over the burning R Wing as they sprayed long streams of white foam on the fire. It was warm in the garden, and the thin green smock clung to moisture on his body. He coughed sporadically in the contaminated air.

Sidney cupped his face in his hands, stared through his fingers at the ground. *I faced certain death up there,* he thought. *And yet … I got out! Was it merely luck, as the voice told me? Or …*

He took a deep breath, desperately attempting to collect his thoughts. He heard the throb and hum of oxygen pumps, felt a hot breeze across his hands. His nostrils burned.

"You!" a man called out from the motopath nearby.

Sidney looked up, saw a short, white-uniformed man standing at the edge of the motopath, staring back at him hostilely. The man held a clip-pad, had straight silver hair. A triangular Bu-Med crest adorned his left lapel. It read: "GW 500."

"Procedures Checker," the little man announced officiously. He rolled to Sidney and touched a button on his pad to auto-flip through several sheets of paper. "Name please," he said crisply.

After Sidney replied, "Sidney Malloy," the man scribbled something on his form and commented, "Odd first name."

"Sidney isn't so unusual. It was very popular when I was born."

The man scowled ferociously. "Last name first!" he strapped. "Always give your last name first!" Angrily, he tore out the partially completed form, crumpled it and tossed it to the ground. "Malloy, Sidney," the man said as his mentoed auto-pen danced across the page without being held. "Your client number?" he asked, not looking up.

Sidney glanced at his plastic wrist tag and provided the numbers, then watched the auto-pen move over the form.

"Now let me see your pass."

"My pass!" Sidney said. "What pass?" Sidney looked beyond the Procedures Checker to Elba House's burning section. He heard screams and felt empty in the pit of his stomach. The hot breeze carried smoke into Sidney's face. He coughed.

"Tut-tut, you must have a pass," the little man insisted, still not looking up. He wrote furiously with the auto-pen, shaking his head from side to side in disapproval the way Malcolm Penny used to do in Central Forms.

"What's this all about?' Sidney asked, growing alarmed.

"Clients who are out of the building must be escorted by an attendant or must have in their possession a valid and countersigned pass. Rule twenty-four, section nine hundred six-point-three."

"But the building's on fire!" Sidney snapped. "A fireman told me to take the escape chute!" Sidney watched a woman slide to safety out the end of a chute as he spoke, tried to point her out to the Procedures Checker.

"Tut-tut, no excuses," the Procedures Checker said. He entered something on a form, then touched a button to flip to another sheet.

"I'm not trying to run away," Sidney said angrily, hearing his voice grow loud. "I'm waiting here for someone to give me instructions."

Sidney heard terrible, agonized screams from Elba House, saw an elderly man and woman jump to their deaths. Sidney felt the emptiness in his stomach again, saw his deformed arm quiver. His face was hot, and stinging drops of perspiration drenched his eyes.

The little man coughed, then peered over the top of his clip-pad at Sidney, narrowed his eyes and chirped, "Procedures are for a purpose. You must ask permission, don't you see? Forms must be completed, then reviewed by higher authority and referred to a pass committee for evaluation…"

"A pass committee? I'd have died up there waiting!"

"I'll need your signature on this form," the Procedures Checker said, growing visibly nervous. Timidly, he extended the pad to Sidney, designating a signatory line on the form with his auto-pen.

Sidney grabbed the clip-pad violently, thundered, "PEOPLE ARE DYING UP THERE, AND YOU'RE TALKING ABOUT FORMS AND PROCEDURES?" Wedging the clip-pad between his chest and bad left arm, he tore off the completed forms, ripped them in half and scattered them in the hot breeze.

The Procedures Checker looked on in stunned terror, as if Sidney had committed a terrible sacrilege.

"GET AWAY FROM ME!" Sidney roared, lifting the clip-pad menacingly. "AWAY!"

The little man rolled backward over a bench. Mumbling something Sidney could not hear, he picked himself up and fled down the motopath.

Sidney hurled the clip-pad after the fleeing bureaucrat, then stood for several moments holding his quivering left arm against his chest in an effort to stop its shaking. His heart pounded so hard he felt it might break through bones and flesh. *I've got to find Tom,* he thought.

Sidney wiped perspiration from his eyelids with both forefingers, then rolled into smoke-filtered sunlight on the moto-path. *I've never been that angry before,* he thought. *That was a very bad energy leak.* He thought again of people dying in the fire, felt helpless and confused.

Thoughts went by in a blur as he rolled forward. Barely aware that he was coughing intermittently, it astounded Sidney that he did not really care about the energy leak, was not even concerned about rules. These were frightening new feelings, but they gave him a strangely euphoric sensation, and a new feeling of freeness. These emotions mingled with the deeply felt sense of loss in his soul over the Elba House tragedy.

Never before had he openly questioned the AmFed Way, but things appeared so wrong to him now ... paperwork and procedures having become more important than human lives.

Suddenly he realized that something was trying to enter his consciousness and crowd away his thoughts ... an immense force clawing and pounding at his brain. Screams of agony continued from the fire above. Peculiar, repulsive odors touched his nostrils. A fit of coughing took over his body, then subsided.

*"Burning flesh!"* a tenor voice inside his skull said.

*"Billions more fleshcarriers will burn when our garbage comet hits Earth!"* another, deeper voice said.

Cackling laughter echoed in Sidney's brain. *"Die, fleshcarriers, die!"* the voices said.

Sidney swooned dizzily and fell to his knees in the middle of the motopath. Above the top of Elba House, the reflected morning sun was almost fully visible on the burnished solar collector. Sidney looked up at Elba House, squinting in the glare. A puff of black smoke covered the sun, then dissipated.

Sidney raised his good arm toward the smoky holocaust, opening the hand as if to place it against another in prayer. Slowly, jerkily, his twisted left arm rose, its quivering fingers groping heavenward. In a great final burst of energy, Sidney brought the deformed hand up, and it grew straight with true, beautiful fingers that pressed reassuringly against the other hand.

"Oh please," Sidney murmured, closing his eyes tightly. "Please...." He fell silent and wished with all his being that the terrible conflagration would end. Believing he was making the greatest wish of all, the wish for someone else, his body trembled for a moment. When he opened his eyes, he saw no more flames, heard no more screams.

Soon he saw dozens of people sliding to safety through escape chutes. "It was miraculous," a Bu-Med attendant said as he reached the ground. "The flames were almost upon me.... I had given up hope." He wiped his face on the sleeve of a singed and dirty white uniform.

"They were spraying something on the fire," a woman said.

Sidney looked down at his left arm and hand. They had been healed! *A miracle!* he thought with rampant joy. *I've found God!* He extended his hand, flexing fingers which only minutes before had been twisted.

*Have I been chosen for something more?* Sidney wondered, watching puffs of grey smoke disappear through a hole in the habitat's glassplex skin. He thought of the doomies and what the voice had said about a garbage comet. *That's it!* he thought. *The mission I'm going on with Tom! My destiny!*

The voices in his brain returned, cackling with laughter. *"This one breaks me up!"* a tenor voice said. *"He thinks he's been chosen to save his world!"*

*"Isn't it hilarious?"* said the other.

"What the Hooverville?" Sidney said.

*"You WERE chosen, fool,"* the second, deeper voice said, *"but not to save anyone. We selected you because you're such a magnificent sap! It increases our fun, don't you see?"* The voices laughed uproariously. Sidney heard more laughter in the background—unmistakable party sounds.

"A sap? That's what you think I am? Someone to laugh at?"

*"Yes! And you're doing marvelously!"*

"I HAVE found God!" Sidney yelled. He waved his healed arm and hand in the air. "This didn't heal through *luck*!"

*"Your mind made the flesh sick,"* the first said. *"Then your mind healed it. . . . Flesh is like that, you know."*

Sidney shook his head in disbelief. "Oh come now. . . ."

*"It's quite simple, fleshcarrier. Really, it is."*

"Who are you?" Sidney demanded. "God? The Devil? And what do you mean by a garbage comet?"

The voices laughed in disturbing unison. Then the first said, in a tenor, lilting tone: *"As we told you, we occupy the Realm of Magic, and are unburdened with smelly, bulky bodies . . . with all their chronic pains, quirks, inefficiencies, and frailties."*

"You are more advanced than we?" Sidney asked.

*"Fleshcarriers are next to lowest in the Great Order,"* the deeper voice replied. *"Magicians are second highest."*

*"Only the Realm of the Unknown is higher,"* the other said.

"What are you, then?" Sidney asked, staring at a pebble on the motopath. "Concentrated energy?"

The voices laughed again. *"It is nearly impossible to explain in your terms, fleshcarrier,"* the deeper voice said. *"Energy is part of it, to be certain. But there is more, much more. Our existence is . . . essential . . . primordial, yet exalted. Words are inadequate."*

"But you are not God?"

*"No,"* the tenor voice said. *"Like you, we have no proof of God's existence."*

*"Or non-existence,"* said the other.

*"We are what we are not,"* the tenor voice said.

*"That is a good way to put it,"* the other agreed. *"We are what we are not. But come now—we can dispense with such serious talk. We're having a party!"* A wave of raucous laughter bounced around the inside of Sidney's skull.

Sidney stared at the pebble, wondering where it stood in the Great Order. "This is all very confusing," he said.

*"Don't look for profundities,"* the deeper voice said. *"Philosophy is no fun … philosophy is no fun … philosophy is no fun.…"*

Other voices picked up the chant: *"Philosophy is no fun … philosophy is no fun … philosophy is no fun.…"*

"Shuttup, for Christ's sake!" Sidney screeched. "Shuttup!" He cupped his hands over his ears, felt a migraine headache at each side of his temple. The smoke over Elba House was white and wispy now. Sidney saw helipumpers hovering over the smoldering structure, searching for flare-ups.

"Listen to me!" Sidney yelled. "Listen to me!"

*"Yes, fleshcarrier?"* a sophisticated voice unfamiliar to Sidney said. Then others piped in with irritating whines: *"Yes, fleshcarrier? What do you want?"*

"I asked about the garbage comet. You didn't answer."

*"You fleshcarriers didn't want all that garbage around,"* the sophisticated voice said. *"So you catapulted it … along with decaying, stinking bodies … all of it in flimsy, leaking containers. Well we're sending this muck back to you now in a massive garbage ball!"*

"My God!"

*"It will hit Earth Friday!"*

"My Rosenbloom! That's only three days away! No! It can't be!"

*"We couldn't send back the garbage without telling a few fleshcarriers what was going on! That would take all the fun out of it, don't you see?"*

"What'll I do, what'll I do, what'll I do?" Sidney lamented. "Carla will be killed, and these monsters are enjoying it!"

The tenor voice returned: *"We always have fun! The most complicated minds have the greatest need for play"*

*"And you tried to spoil our fun, don't you see?"* the deep voice said, *"by hurling all that nasty, smelly crud at us."*

*"What a rotten, terrible thing to do!"* exclaimed the other.

They cackled uproariously, then faded off into a cavern of Sidney's skull.

"Tom!" Sidney called out. "Where in the hell are you, Tom?"

O O O

"Is everything all right?"

Sidney looked up from his kneeling position, saw a white-uniformed little oriental woman staring down at him with her hands on her hips. She smiled softly, kept one eye closed against the sunlight on that side. "You were talking to yourself," she said. "Who is Tom?"

"Tom Javik. I'm supposed to operate a space cruiser with him. There's a terrible emergency...."

"I will help you."

"You will? How?"

"Say," she said, studying Sidney's soft-featured face. "You look like a fellow I saw yesterday, except half his face was distorted, and one arm ..."

"I've experienced a rather miraculous recovery," Sidney said. He heard oxygen pumps throb, noted the air around him no longer looked or smelted smoky. "Now how can you?..."

"How nice! I sat across from you on ..." She interrupted herself, laughing as she tossed a long ponytail of dark brown hair over one shoulder. "But then you wouldn't remember!"

"I believe I would," Sidney said, rising to his feet. Although the woman did not look at all like Carla, something about her reminded him of Carla. He looked away, watched distant patching ships at work outside the habitat as they repaired holes made by the fire in the habitat's glassplex skin.

"I mean, you couldn't possibly! You see, I'm a chameleperson, bred in the laboratories of Bu-Tech."

As Sidney was trying to comprehend that statement, he looked back at the little woman and saw her body become very large and masculine, clothed in a green client's smock. Clear facial features disappeared, being replaced by puffy-ruddiness. The dark brown hair changed to a matted tuft. Dark wraparound sunglasses appeared over the eyes.

"You're ..." Sidney said, pointing with a shaky forefinger, "... You're the blind man on the ship!"

"Quite so," a familiar masculine voice said. The chameleperson changed once more now, and presently it again was the oriental woman. "Very convenient for undercover work," she said.

"You must lead an extraordinarily interesting life," Sidney observed.

"Oh I do, I most certainly do! But now I'm concerned about you ... out here on the motopath, talking to yourself."

"I must find Tom Javik," Sidney said. He motioned toward Elba House. "So many things are happening to me."

"You escaped from the fire?"

"Yes," he said. Then, with sudden excitement: "I prayed just moments ago, and the fire went out!"

Their work completed, some of the helipumpers began to leave, whirring high over Sidney's head.

"I see," she said, shielding the reflected sun with one hand. Her light brown, almond-shaped eyes narrowed suspiciously.

He looked at her with sudden hostility. "You don't believe me?"

"Sure. I believe you. But you may have received some assistance from the fire brigades." The wind blew her hair forward. She pushed it back.

"Didn't you notice? The fire went out suddenly … as I knelt!"

"I'm sorry. I didn't see that."

"Who are you anyway?" Sidney demanded, noting a Bu-Med GW 500 badge on her lapel. "A Procedures Checker?"

"No," she replied calmly, again tossing her ponytail over one shoulder. She noted Sidney's black, scowling eyebrows and said, "I CAN help you, if you'll just—"

"How many forms will be required?"

"Why, none. I'd like to—"

"No forms?" Sidney gasped with mock incredulity. His voice whined sarcasm as he added, "But you can't do anything without forms!"

"Interesting, the way you put that," she observed, studying him intently. "Were you ever in mental therapy?"

"Why do you ask?" Sidney replied, glaring.

"The anti-establishment diatribe. We hear a lot of it from …" She paused, looked away uneasily.

"I see." Sidney turned abruptly, intending to leave. *Maybe I am going wacko,* he thought.

"Wait," she urged, taking him gently by the arm. A hypodermic ring on one of her fingers injected Sidney's arm with a concealed needle. He did not feel the pinprick. "I will take you to your friend."

"You know him?"

"No, but I have powerful friends of my own." Her voice was soothing.

"It's important, you know." The drug had begun to take effect. Quickly, Sidney was losing the ability to doubt anything this woman said.

"I understand," she said.

"A terrible comet . . ."

"Try to relax. We can speak of this later. . . ."

"Yes, later. Of course." It did not seem so urgent to Sidney now. His large round hazel eyes stared back as innocently as a sheep about to be butchered.

"Just come with me," she said sweetly. "My name is Cherry Blossom." *Another doomie mental case,* she thought. *There is no doubt.*

Sidney looked into her eyes, saw deep compassion and thought of Carla again. Maybe it was the way the woman tossed her hair over one shoulder as Carla did when she wore falls. Or maybe it was the way she looked at him. Carla had cared, too.

"Okay," he said. "I'll go with you."

O O O

Beyond the rhododendron garden, a small one-story moon-brick building stood in the shade of two elm trees. Cherry Blossom led Sidney through a revolving door in the building to a small lobby containing striped yellow-and-green lounge chairs, some of which were covered by glassplex smoking bubbles. A bank of elevators dominated one wall beneath a picture of Uncle Rosy. They took an elevator to the sub-eighty-one level.

"I noticed several missing floor numbers on the carscreen," Sidney commented as they rolled off the elevator. "Seventy-one through eighty."

"Off-limits areas," Cherry Blossom said matter-of-factly. "Management personnel reach those floors on private elevators," she explained, leading Sidney along a wide yellow corridor which was painted with a broad green stripe along the bottom of each wall. The brightly lit hallway was crowded with orange-and-green-uniformed employees and yellow-smocked clients.

"What is this place?" Sidney asked as they slowed to roll around a cluster of lethargically rolling people in orange smocks. "Something seems unusual here." He noted a silver-and-black scroll sign on one wall which read, "JOBS ARE SACRED."

"Bu-Prog," she replied flatly.

"Bu-Prog? I've never heard of that bureau."

"I will explain it to you presently," she said with a smile in his direction.

A door to Sidney's left was marked, "ARTHRITIS DIVISION—JOINT LUBRICATION BOOTHS." Beyond that, a series of doors had signs describing services for the aged, including sight recovery and aging reversal.

"Is this part of Bu-Med?" Sidney asked. Then he yelled, "Look out!" suddenly and pushed Cherry Blossom to one side. A blue-and-grey star-shaped creature hovered half a meter over her head. Perhaps the circumference of a human head, the creature had an eye at the tip of each scaly and pointed tentacle.

To Sidney's surprise, she looked up calmly and extended a hand to the creature. "Don't worry," she said, undulating her fingers in a graceful, welcoming gesture. "This is Henry, my Jupiter Airfish." Cherry Blossom's light brown eyes danced happily.

"A pet?"

She nodded. "He's entirely harmless. Did you miss me, Henry?"

The airfish lit on her hand, made a cooing sound as she petted its scaly back. "Found him dazed in Hub Warehouse Three one day," she said. "He'd come in as a hitchhiker on a cargo ship."

Sidney breathed an audible sigh of relief. "I've never seen anything like it," he said.

She tossed the airfish into the air, resumed moto-shoeing.

"We're in the moonslag radiation shield now, aren't we?" Sidney asked, glancing back to watch the Jupiter Airfish as it followed a few meters overhead. "I noticed that the elevator seemed to jump across a short gap. I assume that gap was the space between the habitat's rotating outer rim and the stationary radiation shield."

"Very observant," she said. *But not observant enough,* she thought. *Only three more applicants and I win the trip to …*

Sidney interrupted her thoughts. "This looks like quite a large facility," he said, glancing through an open double-doorway as he spoke. He saw endless rows of desk employees processing mounds of paperwork, heard the rhythmic tapping of rotatypers and the purr of Harmak.

"Yes," she replied, noting his interest in the room. "They are re-documenting identification papers for the cappies we process."

"This *is* part of Bu-Med then?"

"Oh no," she said. "Bu-Prog is a full-fledged bureau in its own right, voting by proxy in all votes taken by the Council of Ten." Cherry Blossom paused at a large imitation walnut door marked "ADMITTING" in bright gold letters. After touching a red wall button, she faced Sidney and folded open one of her lapels to reveal a green-and-yellow circular badge bearing the designation "GW 631."

Sidney furrowed his brow. "Bu-Prog?"

"Bureau of Progress. We have our own rehabilitation facilities. Our rehabilitation is not like Bu-Med's, however. Ours is very real, and includes relocation of the client in mainstream society."

"That sounds very nice." Sidney thought for a moment as he looked at the lettering on the door. He heard the Jupiter Airfish coo. "You're not planning to admit ME here, are you?"

She smiled as the Admitting Room door slid open. Two stocky attendants in green-and-yellow smocks rolled to Sidney's sides. "Hi, Cherry Blossom," one said as they took Sidney by each arm.

"Hey!" Sidney said, trying to pull away from their powerful grasps. "I can't go in there! You said you'd help me!" He glared at Cherry Blossom, his eyes wild with rage.

"This WILL help you," she said, smiling sweetly. "We'll cure your mental problems and then release you back to society. You'll be a contributing consumer again."

"I don't have time for that! A terrible comet—"

"Of course," Cherry Blossom said with a smile, "Bu-Med trackers may find you eventually. But we'll probably rescue you from them again.... The cycle goes on and on!"

The attendants dragged Sidney into the room. He pulled and kicked helplessly. "You lied to me!" Sidney yelled. "You lied!"

"This one said he stopped a fire through prayer," Cherry Blossom said as she followed them into the room. "And he keeps babbling about a comet."

"Another doomie!" one of the attendants exclaimed. "We get so many of them these days!"

O O O

The Admitting Room was long and narrow, with glassplex application booths along each wall. Perhaps half the booths were occupied when Sidney was dragged into the room, and outside each booth sat a Bu-Prog employee monitoring a CRT control panel.

"Brain scanners will take your application automatically," Cherry Blossom said, designating an application booth for Sidney. She lifted his right wrist as the attendants held him, read the plastic nametag. "After the app," she said, "you'll be issued a yellow smock and will receive a rehab itinerary."

Sidney was strapped to a white plastic chair in the booth. "Just sit there and relax," Cherry Blossom said. "This won't take long."

Sidney watched her mento-close the sliding door, made an unsuccessful attempt to calm himself as he felt his heart beating too rapidly. His skin was warm and clammy, making the Bu-Med smock he still wore cling to his body. Closing his eyes to relax, Sidney leaned forward and touched his temple with the hand of one strapped arm, feeling beads of browsweat there with his fingertips.

Cherry Blossom was at the control panel now, and as Sidney closed his eyes, he felt the vacuum surge of powerful electronic equipment probing his brain, attempting to tear away his thoughts, delving into private areas of consciousness and remembrance.

*"Don't let them do it, fleshcarrier!"* a voice said. It was the deeper of the two voices with whom he had grown familiar.

"The machine is too powerful," Sidney said. "I can't stop it!" He felt something tugging and tearing at the membranes holding his brain intact, and he wanted to scream out but knew that would do no good.

*"Does it anger you?"* the voice asked.

"Yes. Very much."

*"Then concentrate upon resisting it, fleshcarrier! Don't let it rape your brain!"*

Sidney concentrated, then became cognizant of a growing internal strength … and somewhere, beyond that, a vast and all-consuming nothingness. Words came back, dancing as thoughts upon an elusive consciousness: *We are what we are not.* From somewhere far away, he heard the metallic voice of Cherry Blossom screeching, "You're blocking, Malloy! You're blocking! Try to relax, damn you!"

Sidney felt his mind fighting, surging, dominating, pushing away the thought-probes of the brain scanner. A new serenity filled him. He saw his past and present self. All the motivations, hopes and desires of his lifetime were laid out in front of him. He was a child again, longing to join the Space Patrol, to explore uncharted and glamorous corners of the galaxy. Sidney felt pain returning as he re-experienced his first seizure at the age of nine. Years fled through his memory in seconds while Sidney relived the years of wishing as he worked in Central Forms … wasted time spent working and longing. Could it have been different? The fear of discovery returned. Again, Sidney kept his dreams alive in the pages of a scrapbook and in ego pleasure dreams.

"I've never seen such determined resistance," a man's voice said through the speaker.

"What does the manual prescribe, Dr. Arroyo?" Cherry Blossom asked.

Now Sidney was in pain, as he relived the grand mal seizure of that terrible evening in the Sky Ballroom. In his mind's eye, he writhed in the sidechair again, then slipped to the ballroom floor, screaming, twitching, and drooling as a horrified crowd looked down at him, their faces contorted in revulsion.

"Rule sixty-three, section twelve-point-six-two, paragraph three," Dr. Arroyo replied. "All clients must complete an application."

"He's refusing, then?"

"I would, say so, yes."

"What should we do?"

"All clients must complete an application."

"That's all it says?"

"I'm afraid so."

"Call in the advisers."

In a hushed conference held minutes later, the advisers determined that something might be faulty with the application equipment. So Sidney was placed in another application booth. But the same thing happened again. They tried yet another booth, and then another. All to no avail.

By this time, Mayor Nancy Ogg was made aware of the unusual situation, and she immediately recognized who Sidney was. She issued orders that he was to be sent to a holding room for the time being. The whole situation resulted in a very confused and upset group of Bu-Prog employees. They had never seen anything like it before, and were anxious not to displease the Mayor.

In a semi-conscious state in the holding room, Sidney wondered, *Why did the voices help me again? The fire, and now....* His own thoughts floated across his consciousness as if thought by someone else, and he almost felt able to answer them himself. The answers seemed on the very tip of his tongue, there but not there at the same instant.

O O O

It was warm that noonhour in the Spartan Cafeteria. Lastsayer Steven stood with his tray of bread and holy water, scanning the tables for a place to sit. The cafeteria was a glassplexed greenhouse at one side of the Black Box of Democracy's roof. He saw an autocopter landing on the rooftop helipad outside, heard the whine and thump of the engine and rotors. The cafeteria was beginning to fill, and sayermen spoke to one another in low, polite tones.

Seeing Twosayer William seated alone at a corner table, he rolled over and asked if he might join him.

"Why, certainly," Twosayer replied somberly. "Go right ahead." Twosayer thought of the comet, wondered if the intercept mission was proceeding smoothly.

Lastsayer noticed that all the sayermen threw their hoods back as they sat down. He did the same, and loosened a drawstring at his neck. "Frightfully hot," Lastsayer said. He smiled nervously, lifted a red cup of holy water to his lips and sipped.

"That it is," Twosayer said, shifting in his seat so that he sat higher than Lastsayer. "Sometimes it is a supreme test of our faith to keep the robes on."

Lastsayer laughed uneasily, then said in a low tone, "I have a problem, Twosayer. I need to confide in someone."

"Oh?" the elder sayerman said, touching one side of his hooked nose. Smiling compassionately, he asked, "How could someone with us only a few days have such an ominous problem?"

Lastsayer took a deep breath.

Twosayer tore a piece of white bread off the portion on his plate, added, "Surely it is not as earthshaking as all that!"

Lastsayer looked around as Twosayer ate the bread, watched sayermen at nearby tables to be certain they were not listening. "Could we speak somewhere privately, Twosayer? It is a most delicate matter."

"THERE ARE NO SECRETS IN THE SAYERHOOD, YOUNGSAYER! Speak up! I will listen!" Twosayer nibbled at another piece of bread, stared across the table with grey green eyes.

Lastsayer rubbed a finger nervously against his red paper cup of holy water. "I had my first audience with Uncle Rosy Sunday," he said.

"So I understand. A bit late, too, I hear."

"Onesayer was not prepared at the appointed time. I awaited him, but—"

"A sayerman does not cast aspersions upon one of his brothers!" Twosayer snapped. Lastsayer noted the voice was angry but the eyes seemed bright and alert, almost pleased.

"I was taught properly on Pleasant Reef," the younger devotee said. "Normally, I would not have said anything about it."

"Normally, I would not listen to such talk," Twosayer huffed. "Tell me why I should."

Lastsayer shook his head sadly. "Onesayer was in his suite, apparently high on Happy Pills."

"You are qualified to make such a judgment?"

"He told me had taken a couple."

"Continue."

"When I came upon him, he was behaving strangely."

"Be specific." Twosayer's eyes narrowed to intense slits as he stared across the table.

Lastsayer glanced around, met Twosayer's gaze and said, He did ... well ... um ... he did impressions of Uncle Rosy."

Lastsayer saw a smile glimmer at the corners of Twosayer's mouth, but it faded quickly. "Come now," Twosayer said. "I can hardly believe such a thing!" He took a drink of holy water, sloshed it casually in his mouth.

"It is true. I swear it! Could it have been a test, Twosayer William?"

"What do you mean?"

"To see if I am loyal to Uncle Rosy?"

"We do not use ... tests ... of that sort."

Twosayer finished his bread, took a gulp of water. "There are no secrets in the Sayerhood," he said.

"Does that mean I should inform the Master?"

Twosayer's eyes flared, and Lastsayer detected hostility in them. "That is all I wish to say on the matter," Twosayer said.

"As you wish." Lastsayer finished his bread and holy water hurriedly, then excused himself from the table.

O O O

At the same moment, Onesayer Edward stood done in his kitchen module, looking around. According to Uncle Rosy's rules, he was permitted to eat in his own kitchen every other day, and the fare there was not limited to bread and holy water. That was for the gathering places of the Sayerhood, where ceremony was essential. The vibrating sound of a circulating air fan touched Onesayer's consciousness, then receded. He felt dull. Something seemed to be blocking out a portion of his mind.

He rubbed a fat cheek thoughtfully with one hand, said, "What will I have for lunch today?" *I must be discreet,* he thought. *It would be too obvious to ask anyone for a weapon. Sayermen have no use for such things.* He stared at a built-in microwave oven, looked at the plastichrome food door above a countertop conveyor strip. *Shouldn't tear anything apart....*

*Atheists in Hell! he* thought, placing his hands on his hips. *Everything is automatic or built-in! I see no heavy objects which could be concealed beneath my robe....*

Onesayer mentoed a dispenser next to the food conveyor, watched a cellophane-wrapped package of eating utensils pop out. Removing the white plastic knife from the package, he fingered it. The blade was blunt, serrated. It chafed the tip of his finger a little bit. *This would not even penetrate Uncle Rosy's skin,* he thought.

Onesayer placed the knife on the counter, next examining the plastic fork. He pushed one of the tongs with his forefinger to test its strength, broke the tong. With a furious grimace, he slammed the fork to the counter, shattering the utensil into many pieces.

"Plastic is fantastic," he intoned. "Every break is a new task."

Whirling angrily, he left the penthouse suite and moto-shoed toward the elevator bank. Onesayer considered sneaking into the Master's suite to sabotage one of the consumer products there, but discarded the idea. *What if he has an armadillo meckie in there?*

Seeing Twosayer William approaching, Onesayer placed a hand over his eyes to make it appear he was scratching his forehead.

"Peace be upon you," Twosayer said cheerily, stopping as he neared Onesayer.

"Yes, yes," Onesayer replied hurriedly, rolling past the other sayerman with his hand still over his eyes. "Peace be upon you. Excuse me, please. I am very busy."

*He does act strangely,* Twosayer thought. *Hiding in the shadows ... covering his face.*

Onesayer reached the elevator bank, mentoed for an elevator. *I have never seen an armadillo meckie near the Master,* he thought. *Maybe I can rush him in the Central Chamber. There should be something lying around that I can use as a weapon ... something I did not notice before.* He decided to search every floor of the Black Box of Democracy.

A bell rang, signifying the elevator's arrival. *I will strangle him if necessary,* Onesayer thought.

When the elevator doors opened, one of Uncle Rosy's green-and-white delivery meckies rolled off, carrying a bundle wrapped in white cloth. "Master sent this for you," the meckie said, extending its mechanical arms with the bundle. "You are to open it when alone." A frosted white dome on top of the headless little mechanical servant pulsated with a dim light.

Onesayer felt his pulse quicken as he accepted the bundle. It was not heavy. Two flat cloth strips were wrapped around the girth. "Did he say what it is?" Onesayer asked.

"I know nothing about it." The meckie moto-whirled, returned to the elevator.

*A bomb,* Onesayer thought nervously as he rolled back to his suite. *Uncle Rosy plans to till me first!*

He set the bundle on the kitchen table, stood back and stared at it. *What if I do not open it?* he thought. *But surely the Master will ask me about it....*

Onesayer touched the bundle, thought: *He could order me killed at any moment anyway. If the Master knows my intentions, I might as well die this way as another.* Onesayer wiped perspiration from his brow, took a deep breath.

He removed the cloth straps slowly, pulled at an edge of the bundle. Expecting it to explode, he twisted his face as he unraveled. *Something hard inside,* he thought, feeling the remaining unwrapped portion. *It is long and thin....*

An object clattered to the table, ringing metallically. "A knife!" the startled Onesayer whispered, hardly able to believe what he saw. "And it is steel!"

Onesayer rubbed one finger across a flat side of the gleaming blade, watched moisture from his finger fog the surface and then disappear. The handle was black pearl, topped with delicate scroll work. He studied the scroll work, saw this: "For my good friend, Willard ... from Alafin Inaya."

*"Willard" expects me to kill myself,* Onesayer thought angrily. *Well, I won't do it!* Onesayer lifted the knife, rubbed a thumb against the lettering on the handle.

*I will get HIM with this. He knows I am desperate ... will be prepared. It might be suicidal for me....*

Onesayer looked at the reflection of his face in the gleaming blade. The image was distorted, but he saw deep lines framing his eyes and beginning to crease his cheeks. *I must hurry,* he thought. *There is not much time.*

O O O

At five minutes before two that afternoon, Mayor Nancy Ogg stood at the Hub Control Room viewing window, watching as two grey cylindrical mass driver shells were pulled by space tug to the waiting *Shamrock Five.* She held a lime tintette nervously in one hand, stared intently as the four-hundred-twenty-meter-long mass driver shells were connected behind the space cruiser like railroad cars behind an engine. She knew the fin-like chrome thrust deflectors at the rear of the *Shamrock Five* would keep rocket exhaust away from the trailers.

A computer printout slip lay on the counter to her left. It was the memory slip on Madame Bernet. *The last day and a half is blank,* she thought, taking a deep puff on the tintette. *What a time for an equipment breakdown!* She wondered if the meckie had killed Javik, and blew a thick cloud of green smoke through her mouth. *Where in the Hooverville is he?* she thought.

Her security personnel had been searching for Javik since midmorning. Now the ship was nearly ready to leave, exactly on schedule, and it had no captain! It occurred to her that Sidney Malloy was the titular captain. *He's an enigma,* she thought. *A milquetoast weakling, I've been told ... but we can't get an application out of him!*

*These problems aren't my fault. I can't be blamed for them!* But the Mayor had been associated with the government long enough to know how easily the blame could be pointed at her. After all, Javik had been on Saint Elba when he disappeared. And never before had a cappy defied an application machine.

She picked a bit of tobacco from the tip of her tongue with quivering fingers, glared down across the loading dock to the *Shamrock Five.* Madame Bernet stood inside the dock's glass-plex waiting area, talking with two black-uniformed security men.

Mayor Nancy Ogg turned at the hum of approaching moto-boots, watched the muscular Sergeant Rountree roll to a stop and deliver the rotating wrist salute of the Security Brigade.

"You've found Javik?" she asked nervously.

"No, Honorable Mayor," the sergeant replied. "I am here to report that the fire is under control. Patching ships are repairing holes in the radiation shield."

"And the escaped clients?"

"We believe all have been recaptured. They've been routed into the cargo holds of two surplus freight rockets, as you instructed."

"Good."

"Do you have transfer authorizations on them?"

"Yes," the Mayor said. "Saint Michaels will take all our overflow."

"I hate to see a reduction in your client count, Honorable Mayor. But we'll get more cappies when the burned-out wings have been rebuilt."

*I don't give a Hoover's dam about client counts!* she thought, raging inside. *I just want to get off this dismal orbiter!*

"Shall we run an identity scan on the escapees before shipping them out?" Rountree asked.

Mayor Nancy Ogg was deep in thought. "Eh? Oh ... I don't think that will be necessary. We have more important matters to consider." She lifted a shaking tintette to her lips, inhaled deeply. Cool nicotine entered her lungs, then surged out of her nostrils in a green puff. "Get the ID data from Saint Michaels," she said.

"Yes, Honorable Mayor."

"Put out the word, Sergeant Rountree.... Fifty thousand dollars to the man who finds Javik! I want him located ... NOW!"

The sergeant saluted brusquely, spun on his moto-boots and sped away.

Mayor Nancy Ogg glanced at a red console-mounted security phone, mentoed the receiver. "Get me Dr. Hudson," she said into a tele-cube which floated in front of her mouth. "Priority One."

O O O

By radio telephone from the Hub Control Room seconds later, Mayor Nancy Ogg reached Dr. Hudson's office.

"I'm terribly sorry," a receptionist at the other end of the line said. "Dr. Hudson is no longer with us."

"NO LONGER WITH YOU? WHAT DO YOU MEAN?"

"That is all I know," the receptionist said. "Shall I connect you with personnel?"

Seeing the conversation going nowhere, Mayor Nancy Ogg ended the call and rang President Ogg instead. Her brother took the call in his office.

"Sorry about Hudson," President Ogg said.

"He's been fired?"

"He's dead, Nancy. Product failure."

"Huh?" The Mayor leaned forward on her stool, felt numbness in her brain.

The line beeped. It was on scramble code.

"Moto-shoe fatality. Happened this morning, near Tech Square."

"Oh my God!" She coughed. Mayor Nancy Ogg knew she should be happy at the news of a product failure. There could be no finer way to die. But tears welled up in her eyes, overflowed her lower lids and poured down her cheeks.

"Nancy … are you all right?'

She cleared her throat, asked, "Have you ordered an investigation?"

"Not necessary, Sis. A Product Failure team has already stamped his body. It's all approved."

"Did they analyze his moto-shoes?"

"What on Earth for? No one wants to jeopardize Hudson's admission to the Happy Shopping Ground!"

"I WANT TO KNOW IF THE SHOES WERE SABOTAGED!" she blurted, unable to keep her composure.

"No one would want to harm Hudson," President Ogg said, trying not to betray uncertainty in his voice. *The Black Box did this one,* he thought, *and I'm not going to tamper with it!*

Mayor Nancy Ogg wiped tears from her face angrily, asked: "What about the comet intercept mission?"

"I'm not directly involved in that," President Ogg said. "But it's in competent hands."

"Didn't Dick discuss it with you this morning?"

"No. There was a recorded message that he called quite early. He started to say something, then said he'd call back."

"Lieutenant Javik is missing! That's what Dick wanted to tell you!"

"What? You mean the pilot?"

"I have the ship ready, Mr. President," she said in a sarcastic tone, "and there's no one here to operate it! Do you have any bright ideas?"

"Certainly," he said, presidentially. "I'll appoint a committee to look into it." He sat back in his chair, pleased with himself at seeing an opportunity for additional employment through committeeship.

"We're talking about a very large garbage comet, dear brother. This is Tuesday. It's due to hit Earth late Friday afternoon!"

"I know … I know… "

"Why don't you just send a substitute fly boy?"

"Without going through channels? I couldn't do that! Uncle Rosy would never have approved such a thing!" *The Black Box will stop the comet anyway,* he thought. *I can make myself look good on this one!*

Knowing her brother and seeing it was hopeless to argue the point, Mayor Nancy Ogg said, "I suppose you're right."

"Jobs are sacred, you know," he intoned.

*I'd better find Javik soon,* the Mayor thought as she hung up the telephone receiver. *Or we'll never stop that comet!* Mento-activating the speakercom on the Hub Control Room console, she said, "Sergeant Rountree, stake out all nightclubs and taverns on the habitat."

"Yes, Honorable Mayor," the speakercom blared.

"And round up everyone we have who might be able to operate the *Shamrock Five.*" *I'm not waiting for instructions on this baby,* she thought.

"Yes, Honorable Mayor," the Sergeant's speakercom voice said. "Does that include clients?"

"Yes, I suppose it does…."

"They may be our best hope. We have a couple of ex-pursuit craft pilots in the psycho ward."

"I recall. They went mad several weeks back and became doomies."

"Right, Honorable Mayor. They have Comet Fever."

"We'll use them if we have to, with mind control drugs. But that's the bottom of the barrel."

"I'll get right on it," Rountree said. "Maybe we can find someone else."

Mayor Nancy Ogg heard the line click shut.

O O O

Minutes after President Ogg completed his call with Saint Elba, Billie Birdbright rolled into the office ebulliently. "You've won, Mr. President! All the networks are projecting you a big winner!"

"That's wonderful," Ogg said, unenthusiastically because of the important duty on his mind.

"News of Muñoz's death broke before a lot of people voted. You really opened up a margin after that!"

"Get me the Manual on Committees," Ogg said. "We have something important to do, and I want it done correctly."

O O O

Later that afternoon, President Ogg stood near the head of a long simulated walnut table in Conference Room fifty-seven. Interim ministers Nigel Larsen of Bu-Tech and Meg Corrigon of Bu-Mil stood nearby in newly-donned white and gold ministerial robes. Standing off to one side, Chief of Staff Birdbright awaited instructions from the President.

The conference room occupied one-fourth of an entire floor of the White House Office Tower, along an exterior building wall which permitted illumination of the room by natural daylight. The windows were large, and the room radiated cheerfulness. President Ogg peered at chairs on the far end of the table. He envisioned all the chairs occupied, papers strewn across the table. This pleased him, and he smiled.

Ogg tapped a bulky forefinger on the table-mounted microphone in front of one chair, said, "I want to see this room full tomorrow morning, gentlemen!"

"Ahem!"

Ogg turned to see Lieutenant Colonel Meg Corrigon looking at him with a bemused expression. Corrigon was fiftyish, a career military woman whose neatly trimmed black hair came to a sharp widow's peak at the center of her forehead.

"I mean ladies … er, ah … lady and … well, you know what I mean!" Ogg smiled sheepishly.

Corrigon broke into a squeaky laugh.

"This committee will explore every angle of Lieutenant Javik's disappearance," Ogg continued. "It is an exciting opportunity for committeeship!"

"Excuse me, Mr. President," Nigel Larsen said, clearing his throat nervously.

"Yes?" Ogg turned a bit on his moto-shoes to get a better view of Larsen, looked upon a man with a very heavy face and an immense, pendulous triple chin. Curiously, Larsen's body was rather slender.

"Forgive me for asking," Larsen said, "but couldn't we simply send another ship's pilot now?" Noticing a scowl forming on Ogg's face, he added quickly: "Just this once, sir?"

"No!" Ogg said, glaring ferociously. "If we make an exception now, where will it stop?"

"But I don't think there are any other options, sir. And a pilot is needed up there quite desperately."

"WHO ARE WE TO DETERMINE OPTIONS?" Ogg thundered. "COMMITTEES DETERMINE OPTIONS!"

"Uh, sir...." Larsen's triple chin quivered.

"There are always options, Larsen! Options are the soul of committeeship!"

"Yes, Mr. President."

"It takes only one tiny break in the system, Larsen ... and then everything falls apart."

"Like a house of dominoes," Corrigon piped in.

"Well put, Corrigon!" the President said.

"Thank you, Mr. President." She placed both hands on the back of a chair, beamed proudly.

*This woman's not at all like her predecessor,* Ogg thought, comparing her with General Muñoz. *I can work with her!* Ogg extended his large hands to each side, palms up. "Can you imagine the destruction of everything we've built, Larsen?"

"No, Mr. President. I didn't think...."

"You didn't think!" Ogg said, pouncing on the miscue. "Well, snap out of it, man!" Ogg mentoed a microphone on the table, snapped his fingers against it. The sound echoed around the room. "Wake up!"

"Yes, Mr. President," Larsen said, afraid to meet Ogg's powerful gaze. "I see your point."

"By the book, ministers!" Ogg said. "Strictly by the book!"

"Yes, Mr. President," the interim ministers said in unison.

O O O

*The President wouldn't approve of me working late,* Chief of Staff Birdbright thought, glancing wearily at a digital cuckoo clock on the wall. A tiny cuckoo bird above the digital reader popped out upon Birdbright's mento command, chirped: "Tuesday PM, nine-fourteen and twelve seconds." The mechanical bird retracted with a crisp snap.

Birdbright stood at the telephone message board outside the Oval Office in a pool of white fluorescent light. The rest of the floor lay in night shadows. He mentoed for a transcript of the evening's messages, and a phone printer beneath the message board began to type, spewing out words and paper into a plastic tray. Birdbright sifted through the sheets, sorting them into two retained piles while tossing away a third category of junk messages.

*Here's something,* Birdbright thought, holding a sheet up. *From Larsen at Bu-Tech.... sent about an hour ago.* Birdbright read aloud: "Comp six-oh-two reports it is too late to divert comet to nitrogen-rich atmosphere of Kinshoto for burnout. *Shamrock Five* must take off before six PM tomorrow for Thursday rendezvous with comet. Still possible to divert fireball away from Earth."

Birdbright looked away, shook his head. *Larsen won't last long when the President sees this,* he thought. *Imagine that ... attempting to rush the work of a committee with a computer report!*

He looked down at the sheet again, squinted and pulled his head back to keep from throwing a shadow across the page. Birdbright blinked his eyes, read on: "If substitute crew cannot arrive before deadline, Comp six-oh-two recommends strategic placement of orbiting missile launchers around Earth for atomic assault on comet...."

Birdbright took this and several other messages into the Oval Office, mentoed on an overhead light and set them in the center of the President's desk. *I can see President Ogg's position,* he thought. *But Larsen may have a point too.* He grimaced, noting that Larsen had sent a copy of the report to Saint Elba's Mayor Nancy Ogg.

*Sparks are going to fly tomorrow!* he thought.

Birdbright noted two white plastic sacks bearing bureau ministerial crests on the desktop. He recalled receiving them from a courier just before quitting time that afternoon. President Ogg had left without examining them.

Birdbright knew these were the personal effects of Muñoz and Hudson. As President, it would be Ogg's sacred duty to review their contents and decide which items would go on display in the White House Tower Museum.

Birdbright poured out two neat piles on the desktop. He picked through Muñoz's effects first ... a gold wrist digital, gold and silver coins, a gold cross and chain. ...

*I recall him wearing this cross,* Birdbright thought, lifting the cross and dangling its chain across one hand. The metal was cool to his touch.

Wearily, he mentoed off the overhead light and sat in the President's chair, spinning it to gaze out the window. New City sparkled below like a freshly honed jewel, and above that a lazy quarter moon stood vigil. He held the cross up, rotating it to pick up glints of reflected light upon the cross's surface.

*Strange what I'm feeling now,* he thought. *Can't quite put my finger on it....*

Birdbright held the cross against his chest, scanned the heavens. Somewhere between the orbits of the Earth and the Moon was Saint Elba, and beyond that a great comet which threatened to destroy everything man's technology had built. He strained to see the tiniest speck of unusual activity in space, but nothing seemed out of the ordinary. Had he not been privy to information about the impending disaster and the uncoordinated efforts to stop it, Birdbright might have thought it was just another lovely summer night in God's chosen land.

* *

As Sayer Superior Lin-Ti rounded the top of the hill approaching the Great Temple, he thought of the day's lesson. *There is history and then again there is HISTORY,* he thought. *I fear the history writers may have included too much unsavory detail in this text. These are impressionable youngsayermen....*

The fog on the valley floor below was lifting early this morning, and he could see the upper half of the temple. Reaching a fork in the motopath, the Sayer Superior rolled over an arched bridge to the left.

*Ah well,* he thought. *There is always Selective Memory Erasure. I have ordered its application many times....*

# Chapter Eleven

## THE ECONOMICS OF FREENESS, FOR FURTHER READING AND DISCUSSION

*October 20, 2415: Council of Ten declare Tic-Tac-Toe, Hangman, Battleship, and dot-to-dot games to be against the public interest unless played on manufactured sets.*

### *Wednesday, August 30, 2605*

Garbage Day Countdown (Earth impact): Two days, eleven hours, fifty-four minutes....

Dawn formed reddish outlines across New City's skyline and around hills partially visible in the distance. Onesayer Edward was only dimly conscious of the view as he sat by the one-way window in his kitchen module. He had important matters on his mind this day.

Feeling tired, he swallowed a sleep-sub pill and followed that with a water capsule. It had been a fitful night of sleep, punctuated by periods in which he lay awake in darkness worrying about the distasteful task he would perform the following day. When the new day broke, he had no cohesive plan of action ... only the conviction that he would kill Uncle Rosy that day or would perish in the attempt.

*I'll cut up his face to erase the features,* Onesayer thought, staring disconsolately at an untouched plate of presto-eggs. *Then I can report that Onesayer died while attempting to kill the Master.*

Onesayer left the breakfast table without eating anything, took an elevator down to the Bureau Monitoring Room. *Act normally,* he told himself as he entered the room, touching a small bulge at his waist where the knife was concealed. The weapon was there, reassuringly, concealed beneath the folds of his robe and secured against his body by an extra robe belt.

Sayermen were busy at their posts, operating mento-activated keyboards and scanning video screens on the walls. The barely discernible hum of pink sound absorbed harsher machine noises, giving the room an air of smooth efficiency. Through a distant one-way window, morning sunlight filtered into the room, glinting off chrome trim on the machines.

"Great Suffering Souplines!" he heard Twosayer William exclaim. The hook-nosed Twosayer stood at a minicam screen near the entry, shaking his head from side to side in dismay.

Onesayer rolled to the station, asked: "What is it?"

"You are feeling better?" Twosayer asked, studying Onesayer closely. *He is aging!* Twosayer thought, elated at what he saw. But then Twosayer felt fear, as he saw Onesayer glare back at him disdainfully with crease-framed eyes.

Onesayer touched the bulge at his waist. His expression became menacing.

"Uh, take a look," Twosayer said, nodding nervously toward a cluster of six wallscreens.

Onesayer narrowed his eyes, glanced from screen to screen without comprehending what was happening.

"Javik ... the *Shamrock Five* pilot ... is on Saint Michaels!" Twosayer said disgustedly. "Instead of on Saint Elba!" He sneaked a glance at lines on Onesayer's cheeks as Onesayer concentrated upon a minicam screen. Twosayer suppressed a smile.

Onesayer saw Tom Javik at the head of a line of clients. Javik glared across a countertop at a Junior Therapist on the other side....

"You *must* complete these forms," the Junior Therapist insisted. He extended a packet of legal-sized forms and an auto-pen across the countertop. Fair-haired and with a light complexion, the Junior Therapist was vacuous-faced, with a slack jaw and unintelligent eyes. It was the same bureaucratic personality Javik had encountered so many times previously, and he felt rage building up inside.

"There's no form for what I'm trying to communicate to you," Javik said. "I was sent here in error, and it's imperative that I return to Saint Elba."

"Fill out the forms. I must have the forms!"

Onesayer shook his head in disbelief. The screen flickered off, went back on....

"Fill out the forms, please," the Junior Therapist said firmly.

Javik scowled ferociously across the counter, said in a threatening tone: "I'll give you thirty seconds to say something sensible. Then I'm coming after you!"

"You're forgetting your place!" the Junior Therapist huffed.

"Twenty-three seconds," Javik said, glancing at his wrist digital.

"I don't believe this is happening!" Onesayer said, gazing at the ceiling. He looked back at the screen....

"Guards!" the Junior Therapist screeched. "Guards!"

Javik reached for his concealed pistol, but had a second thought and relaxed his hand. "All right," he said. "Give me the damned forms."

The Junior Therapist took a deep breath and pushed the forms across the counter.

Javik glanced at two black-uniformed Security Brigade guards who had approached and were standing three meters away, watching intently. Javik looked down at the forms, took the auto-pen. "Where do I write 'help'?" he asked, without humor.

Onesayer looked away from the screen as it went dark, asked angrily: "Has a substitute pilot been dispatched to Saint Elba?"

"No," Twosayer said. He turned his oval face away, afraid to meet Onesayer's burning gaze. "There is still that cappy Malloy that Muñoz picked in a vision...."

"Aaay! Captain Cappy!"

"Now President Ogg has turned the whole matter over to an investigating committee. Ogg wants the committee to provide him with options."

"This is no time for committees!" Onesayer yelled.

"I know that, but...." Twosayer stared at the darkened screen.

"And you're just sitting here watching? That's all you're doing?" Onesayer was hurling apostrophes with reckless abandon.

"There is nothing we can do." Twosayer threw up his hands helplessly. "The Master has given us specific instructions not to—"

"We'll see about that!" Onesayer said. He stormed out of the room, intending to take a moto-stroll until his head cleared.

O O O

Forty-five minutes later, Onesayer Edward stood in the great central chamber, glaring up at the shadowy form of Uncle Rosy. Uncle

Rosy cleared his throat, shifted in his chair. Onesayer heard the iron door to the chamber slide shut behind him, and a rush of fear washed through him.

*Calmness,* Onesayer thought, attempting to mento-command himself. *Utter calmness. Then he dies.*

"I grow weary of all the monitoring and controls," Uncle Rosy said in a resonant, soothing tone which echoed softly off the black glassite walls of the chamber. "So much is required to support the AmFed system."

*We'll get to the point soon,* Onesayer thought, oblivious to his unspoken pun. He placed a hand against his robe over the knife.

Uncle Rosy cleared his throat again, and Onesayer heard the low strains of humming that came from the Master's lips. The notes were soft and lilting, unmistakably the Hymn of Freeness.

Feeling tears building up in his eyes, Onesayer blinked. "With the deaths of Muñoz and Hudson," he said slowly, trying to exude strength with each word, "all has fallen into bumbling disarray."

"It went bad before that," Uncle Rosy said. "General Muñoz chose the cappy last week."

"But Hudson might have taken corrective action after Muñoz's death—once he was free of the General's dominance."

"This is an I-told-you-so speech?"

Onesayer forced a smile, kept his hand over the knife as he asked: "Why did you send a knife to me yesterday, Master?"

"You wanted it, did you not?"

"I did, but not to take my own life." With these words, Onesayer took a deep breath and drew the knife. Locking his moto-shoes, he bounded up six steps to the level on which Uncle Rosy sat. He pointed the blade at Uncle Rosy, and it glinted in the low yellow light of overhead globes. Onesayer could see Uncle Rosy's features now less than a meter away, a cherubic face smiling back at him without the tiniest hint of fear.

"You hesitate, Onesayer. He who hesitates to take a thing is not yet ready for it."

"You *want* to die?'

"I feel … there are more perfect states than the sustenance of flesh." Uncle Rosy rubbed his chin thoughtfully, added, "I sense … serenity."

Onesayer switched the black pearl handled knife to the other hand. "You refer to the Happy Shopping Ground?"

Uncle Rosy laughed with a hint of derision. "I made that place up! I made everything up!" Noting a look of surprise on Onesayer's face, Uncle Rosy said: "The place to which I refer has no shopping centers, no products, no people, no machines...."

"You have found God, Master? Truly?"

"No, Onesayer Edward. Though I have tried. Voices have spoken to me recently ... since this garbage comet matter came up...."

"Voices, Master?"

"They speak of a Realm of the Unknown, say it is the highest state of existence. There are other ..." His voice trailed off.

"I hope you find serenity, Master."

Uncle Rosy smiled benignly, said, "Perhaps I have attempted to control too much, Onesayer. If not you at my throat now, eventually it would be someone else."

"You gave me the weapon, Master. Is that not controlling?"

Uncle Rosy raised one hand to support his chin. Nodding slowly, he said, "I merely sped the inevitable. Forces were already in motion." He laughed. "You argue with me to the end, eh, Onesayer?"

Onesayer smiled lovingly, said, "I feel ... closer to you than ever before."

"We are one," Uncle Rosy said. "You will find a clean robe on the ledge behind my chair. The wearer commands my meckies."

Onesayer felt the blade quiver in his grasp, asked, "How do I stop aging?"

"Look within yourself, Onesayer Edward. It is your second test."

"And the first ... is killing you?"

"That is correct."

"There will be other tests?"

"Always, Onesayer. There will be no end to them."

Onesayer closed his eyes and lunged forward, plunging the knife deep into Uncle Rosy's chest. Onesayer felt ribs cracking and flesh tearing away. He released his grip on the knife and pulled back in revulsion at what he had done.

Uncle Rosy's face was contorted in pain—holding both hands against his chest, he gasped "Finish it!"

Onesayer bit his upper lip hard, pulled the knife out. He held it with two hands now, samurai style, and plunged the blade again and again into Uncle Rosy's face and torso. Uncle Rosy gurgled as he swallowed his own blood, gasped and slumped dead over the Zero Handle.

"No!" Onesayer yelled, only half-conscious that he was speaking to a corpse. "Do not touch it!"

The Zero Handle began to move down toward contact under Uncle Rosy's enormous weight. Onesayer dropped the bloody knife and lunged for the handle. With both hands and all the power of his legs and back, he tried to stop the handle from proceeding farther. It slowed, but continued to drop. Releasing one hand from the Zero Handle, Onesayer tried to push the corpse away. But the weight was too great.

"I can't ... hold ... this ... much longer!" he gasped, seeing the point drawing dangerously near. "Earth is going to blow!"

In a desperation move, Onesayer released the handle entirely and knelt under the corpse's shoulder. With blood dripping on him, Onesayer mustered all his remaining strength and pushed the corpse up and off the Zero Handle.

THUD! Uncle Rosy's lifeless form slumped to the floor.

Then, afraid to breathe or make a move, Onesayer stared wide-eyed at the Zero Handle. It had stopped less than a centimeter above contact! He lifted the handle carefully, and this required all the strength he had left. Panting, he felt great gears in the mechanism move with painstaking slowness, like megalithic tumblers. Finally the Zero Handle was back in place, and he breathed a deep sigh.

*An unexpected test,* Onesayer thought. *And the Master's body is not yet cold,*

He glanced at the Orbital Handle, then back to Uncle Rosy's crumpled form, which lay in a pool of blood. Blood ran down the steps. *First things first,* he thought. *I must get him into my robe.*

Onesayer removed Uncle Rosy 's torn and blood-soaked robe, tossed it into a disposa-tube next to the chair. Then he pulled a black jade ring off Uncle Rosy's finger, replacing it with his own brown-and-black-striped onyx ring. Inside Uncle Rosy's ring; Onesayer read the gold scroll inscription: "For my good friend, Willard ... from Alafin Inaya."

*Identical to the knife inscription,* he thought. Onesayer tried the ring on several fingers, settled on the forefinger of his right hand.

*Wonder who Alafin Inaya was,* he thought, pulling off his own robe. He stood in his shorts now, still wearing about his belly the second sash he had used to secure the knife to himself. The ends of the sash dangled against one leg. Onesayer stared down at Uncle Rosy's body, then took a deep, agitated breath and set about performing the remaining distasteful task.

With great effort, he dressed Uncle Rosy's body in the brown sayerman's robe. When the garment was on, Onesayer slashed the front of it to make it appear the victim had been killed while wearing it. He considered throwing the black pearl handled knife into the disposa-tube, but instead wiped the blade on the sayerman's robe and slipped it into the sash about his waist.

By this time, Onesayer was hot and breathing heavily. After wiping his hands on a clean portion of the sayerman's robe worn by Uncle Rosy, Onesayer used both hands to wipe perspiration from his own forehead and eyebrows.

*It is done,* he thought, not feeling particularly proud of himself. *Now where is that Master's clean robe?*

He rolled around behind the chair, located the ledge Uncle Rosy had spoken of before he died. He selected one of three neatly stacked white robes, slipped it on.

Onesayer smoothed a wrinkle out of the robe and sat in the great chair. Continuing to perspire, he settled down into the chair's leather cushioning. Presently he began to cool down and to feel better. A sense of supreme satisfaction came over him.

*I am Master!* he thought, suddenly exhilarated. *Lord of all....*

He recalled the terrible peril of the comet now, stared down to his right at the middle chrome handle. *All things can be controlled,* he thought. *Even this.*

Onesayer pressed the handle all the way forward and down to its contact point, read a chart next to the handle and mentoed: *Orbital coordinates, B-six-seven-seven, normal ... planetary speed one-point-one-two-five ... rotation one-point-oh-oh, normal.*

Sitting back in the chair, he thought, *No one will feel that extra bit of speed. Just enough to get Earth out of the comet' s path.*

Onesayer mentoed for a meckie, recalling that the wearer of the Master's robe commanded Uncle Rosy's mechanical servants. Shortly, a black tuxedo meckie appeared at the base of the steps. Six tiny white lights down the front of its body blinked as it awaited instructions.

"Yes, Master?" the meckie queried.

*It calls me Master!* Onesayer thought. Speaking in the resonant voice of Uncle Rosy, Onesayer said, "Onesayer Edward tried to assassinate me. I killed him instead. Send the body to Astro Disposal and have it launched in an unmarked cylinder."

"Yes, Master."

"Tell no one of this disgraceful act."

The meckie wrapped the body in plastic and dragged it down the ramp and out of the chamber. Moments later, it returned to clean the blood that had spilled.

O O O

At the moment of Uncle Rosy's death, Sidney was seated in Admitting Room Two at an autopill dispensing application machine. An admitting clerk stood nearby, watching intently.

A woman approaching forty, the admitting clerk had frost blue hair and a matching, icicle-cool personality. Sidney glanced out of the corner of one eye at the scowling woman, then quickly looked back into the mechanical face of the application machine.

"Take two more capsules, dosage AA-nine," the machine instructed, pushing forth a tiny tray containing two yellow pills and a water tablet.

Sidney obeyed, felt a cool surge of water as the water tablet opened and expanded inside his stomach. Now Sidney felt the machine probing his thoughts again, heard it report in a hesitating, impersonal voice: "Con-readingO O O ninety-four-point three."

"May Hoover take you," the admitting clerk cursed. "Wait here," she instructed tersely. Then she spun and rolled through a double swinging door to the outer hallway. Fully conscious, Sidney watched her leave.

Moments later, Sidney heard low, anxious voices outside the door. He smiled to himself, pleased that he had been able to resist all attempts thus far to break down his will. Sidney closed his eyes, tried to connect with the voices in his brain. *You must help me find Tom,* he thought. *Please….* Getting no response, he thought: *They come and go as they please.*

"He'll fill out that blasted app!" a woman's voice boomed.

Sidney opened his eyes as the doors squeaked open, saw a black woman in a yellow tweed suit. The woman rolled toward him at a fast pace with an angry expression on her face.

The admitting room clerk was close behind. "Wait, Mayor Ogg," she urged. "Maybe we should try something else."

"*I'll* try something else," Mayor Nancy Ogg snapped, grabbing Sidney forcefully by the collar. Sidney felt sharp surges of pain as she backhanded him across the face four times.

"Wait, Mayor Ogg," the admitting clerk pleaded. I'm not sure we should—"

"Silence!" the Mayor rasped.

Sidney tried to grab Mayor Nancy Ogg's hand before she could strike again, but she was too strong for him. "You'll fill out the app, won't you, you weakling little creep," she demanded, slapping Sidney hard across both cheeks.

Sidney pulled his head back, tried to protect his stinging face with his hands. A crushing blow struck him on the temple, knocking him out of the chair and tearing his smock where the Mayor had been grasping it. As Sidney tumbled to the floor, he saw a hazy impression of the Mayor's and clerk's feet.

"Uhhh," Sidney groaned, half-conscious. He saw Mayor Nancy Ogg's foot lash out at him, but could not move out of the way. An excruciating pain cut through his rib cage. "Aaaagh...."

*"I'm rather enjoying this,"* a tenor voice in Sidney's brain said.

*"Malloy doesn't seem like such a clown anymore,"* the other, deeper voice said. *"Maybe we should give him half a chance...."*

Grimacing in pain, Sidney heard the voices argue heatedly. Then Sidney thought-said: *Help me out of here! We're running out of time!* But there was no response. He felt himself slipping off, into deep sleep.

"I think he's unconscious," a distant woman's voice said. It was the admitting clerk.

"Get a con-reading! Quickly!" a man yelled.

Sidney envisioned himself as the hero of a military-political movement, leading the twisted and pitiful slushpile of human garbage that Earth did not want. He controlled an immense army of cappies which threatened to attack Earth. The people of Earth begged for mercy, sent two emissaries from the Council of Ten to see Sidney.

*"I hate the way he plays hero"* the tenor voice said.

*"It is a bit irritating"* agreed the other. *"Still, I've grown rather attached to him."*

Sidney heard the voices argue again inside his skull, but they faded quickly. *Come back!* Sidney thought, finitely. *Come back!*

"Over a hundred! He buried the needle!"

"What the Hooverville? No one could have a con-reading that high! Check the equipment!"

Hearing these words in an awakening haze, Sidney knew they were not the voices he wanted to hear. Suddenly his awareness surged, and he almost felt able to stand up and moto-shoe around the admitting room. But the surge was short-lived, and soon he felt himself sinking once more. The evil thought-probing machine was at it again now, trying to tear away his innermost secrets.

*"Don't give in, fleshcarrier!"* the deeper voice in his brain said. *"This is making you stronger!"*

Sidney experienced another vision, imagined he was being given a private audience with Uncle Rosy. In a darkened chamber, Uncle Rosy sat upon a great chair, looking down at him with kindly, concerned eyes....

"You are the only one who can do it," Uncle Rosy said in the vision. "A holy mission lies ahead!"

"I'll do it!" Sidney said in the vision. "Thank you, Master! Thank you!..."

*"There he goes again,"* the tenor voice said, irritably. *"The Chosen One, the hero. Why, this fleshcarrier doesn't even understand his own motivations!"*

*"Give him a break,"* the deeper voice said. *"He's only a fleshcarrier. You're using OUR standards."*

*"True,"* the tenor voice said. *"But when will he realize he wants these things for himself, not for the good of others?"*

*"In time,"* the other voice said. *"In time...."*

Sidney heard the voices fade, saw himself as President of a bright AmFed nation, populated by contented, consumptive citizens. He felt the joys of Freeness, Job-Sharing, and Leisure Time. It was a brilliant society, showered with all the wonders of advanced technology.

"He has a nasty looking gash," a far off voice said. "We'd better get him into Emergency."

"But he hasn't been admitted to Bu-Prog yet! How can he be treated?"

"The equipment checks out."

"Put him on an autocart," Mayor Nancy Ogg instructed angrily, "and get him out of my sight!"

Sidney felt strong arms lifting him from the floor, heard a cacophony of voices. He struggled to open his eyelids, but they seemed weighted.

The cart was rolling now, and someone said, "What's the difference, anyway? He's only a cappy."

Managing to lift one eyelid, Sidney squinted angrily in the glare of bright hall lights. He tried to sit up, wanting to tell that person that cappies would get even someday. But a terrible pain in his ribcage kept him from rising. His head throbbed, and he cried out in agony before falling back on the cart.

"The client is awake," a woman said, her tone condescending

"Who cares? By all rights, Mayor Ogg should have killed him."

*I'll get them!* Sidney thought. He felt something warm and wet on the side of his head, touched a throbbing temple with one hand. Then he looked at the hand. It was bloody! He felt weak, closed his eyes.

"Put him in detention," one of the enemies said. "We'll hold him until he fills out the app. No medical treatment until he cooperates!"

"Each cappy supports seven-point-three-two-five government workers," another said, "and this doomie creep won't fill out the form!"

"It's positively un-AmFed!"

"I have a better idea," a female voice said. "A call just came in from Hub Assembly. They need a disposable cappy for an in-flight job."

"What's the job?"

"Who knows, but I hear they've been having problems keeping their cappies in line. Now they need a replacement."

"Sounds like a good chance to eliminate our little problem. I'll check with the Mayor."

*Disposable?* Sidney thought, his head throbbing. *What do they mean disposable?*

O O O

It was a busy morning.

Mayor Nancy Ogg moto-shoed wearily down the wide central area of Mass Driver One, craning her neck to watch green-and-yellow-smocked client workcrews on scaffolds. To Mayor Ogg, the clients looked like bees in a honeycomb, working two to a scaffold filling individual compartments of the massive E-Cell with Argonium gas and then setting exterior valves. Voices echoed around the walls, as did the metal-on-metal ring of tools.

*Odd, isn't it?* Mayor Nancy Ogg thought, *that most of an E-Cell has to be constructed by hand....*

She paused to watch a Bu-Tech foreman go over a set of computer-printed plans with two yellow-smocked client workmen. "Be sure to set the gas diffraction valve on each cell," she heard the foreman say.

Then the Mayor recognized one client as Sidney Malloy and thought angrily: *That weakling cappy! Now I'll get rid of him once and for all!*

The foreman smiled when he noticed the Mayor, said to her in a derisive tone, "Replacements." He flicked a sidelong glance at Sidney and the other client. Sidney heard contempt in the foreman's tone.

"It's looking good, foreman," Mayor Nancy Ogg said, glancing hostilely at Sidney. She resumed moto-shoeing, thought, *Jesus! I hate these stinkin' cappies! I hate everything about this place!*

Her thoughts were interrupted when a yellow-smocked girl rolled frantically toward the Mayor from a forward area. "We're not coming back!" the girl screamed. "They're going to eject us in space when the E-Cell is finished!"

*Disposable,* Sidney thought, recalling the words he had heard while lying on the autocart. *So that's what they meant....* He glanced around nervously, saw the foreman glaring at him.

"Pay attention!" the foreman snapped.

"Yes, sir," Sidney said.

Mayor Nancy Ogg short-stepped to one side as the girl rolled past, watched a Security Brigade officer capture the girl a short distance away and wrestle her to the ground.

"Another loony," the security officer gruffed, looking up at the Mayor as he knelt and handcuffed the girl.

Mayor Nancy Ogg nodded, said tersely: "Find out where the rumor started."

"Yes, Honorable Mayor," the officer said. "I know how to handle it."

Turning at the whir of fast-approaching moto-boots, the Mayor watched Sergeant Rountree roll to a crisp stop as he reached her. He snapped a rotating wrist salute, stood at attention.

"The ex-pursuit craft pilots are our best bet," Sergeant Rountree said. "That's not saying much, but with drug therapy we can alter their doomie mentalities."

"The killer meckie will keep them in line, too," she said.

As Mayor Nancy Ogg said this, Sidney and the other replacement were being led past her to a forward area of the mass driver. *Killer meckie?* Sidney thought, overhearing the remark. *What the hell are they talking about?*

"There are refresher tapes on mass driver mechanics aboard the *Shamrock Five*," Sergeant Rountree said, out of Sidney's hearing range. "They are rather technical, and we can only hope the pilots will understand them...."

"Have them start on the tapes now," Mayor Nancy Ogg said, pursing her lips thoughtfully. "But we'll wait until the last minute before committing ourselves."

"Right. I saw the letter from interim Minister Larsen. The *Shamrock Five* can leave as late as six o'clock tonight."

"It's *ex*-interim Minister Larsen now. My dear brother the President led a council recall move this morning. It just came in on my porta-receiver. Something about Larsen advocating anti-job measures."

"He was too pro-computer," Sergeant Rountree said.

"Now that Muñoz and Hudson are out of the picture, my brother can run the operation as he pleases." She bit at her upper lip, tried not to display emotion at the thought of Dr. Hudson. She glanced at the Sergeant's broad shoulders. Her gaze dropped, moving down along the center of his chest to his silver and black belt.

"I'm sure that's true, Honorable Mayor." Rountree caught her gaze, snapped his eyes back to attention. A little smile touched his mouth.

*That was a lightning stroke on Euripides's part!* she thought, looking away and rubbing her eyes. *No committees involved ... he had to justify it as a Job-Support measure.*

The central area Mayor Nancy Ogg stood upon was in the process of narrowing slowly as work progressed. After Sergeant Rountree left, she overheard another foreman say, "In the final construction stage, the mass driver core itself will be filled with gas compartments, leaving only a tiny corridor beneath."

Looking up at the silver-metallic curved ceiling, she thought: *The final construction stage will also involve ejection of the worker clients to their deaths in space, followed by automatic connection of the E-Cells to their mass driver engines.* It occurred to her that every "stinkin'" cappy should be ejected in space. She scratched the small of her back.

Mayor Nancy Ogg could see grey tubes and valves through an open forward firewall hatch, knew from a previous inspection that this was the base of a powerful mass driver engine that towered more than one-hundred meters above her.

Closing her tired eyes, she held the thumb and forefinger of one hand against her forehead. *Just a minute!* she thought, popping open her eyes. *The escapees that were shipped to Saint Michaels … could Javik be among them?*

Mayor Nancy Ogg started to roll at high speed toward the exit Sergeant Rountree had just taken, but had a second thought and slowed. *No,* she thought, answering her own question, *It's not possible.*

* *

"Was Onesayer Edward an evil man?" Sayer Superior Lin-Ti asked, gazing across the ordinance room at his group of youngsayermen.

"He became power-mad, Sayer Superior," a voice in the back of the room said. "And he murdered our beloved Master."

"Yes," Lin-Ti said, "but Uncle Rosy gave him the knife. And remember, Onesayer Edward waited patiently for nearly three centuries."

The youngsayerman did not respond. Lin-Ti saw troubled expressions on the faces of the group. Then Lin-Ti asked: "Would Uncle Rosy have entrusted the Sayerhood helm with an evil man? These are disturbing questions, youngsayers, many of which we cannot answer…."

# CHAPTER TWELVE

## UP CLOSE WITH PRESIDENT EURIPIDES OGG, FOR FURTHER READING AND DISCUSSION

*"There is no more certain way to reach the Happy Shopping Ground than to lose your life in the face of a disintegrating product."*

Remarks made by President Ogg at Astro-Burial Inc.'s No. 14 Launcher, November 18, 2603

### *Wednesday, August 30, 2605*

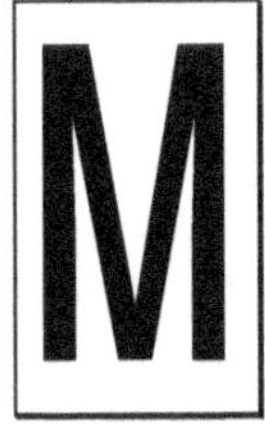

aster Edward sat on Uncle Rosy's chair for several hours after setting the Orbital Handle. He lost track of time, and just sat there reviewing three centuries of memories. It was late morning when he finally moto-shoed to the ramp at the rear of the platform and rolled down to a passageway he knew had to lead to the Master's private suite.

Master Edward heard only the whine of his own moto-shoes as he negotiated a sharp right turn in the arch-ceilinged black brick passageway. It was cool and damp in there, illuminated dimly by widely spaced yellow globes.

*I feel like an intruder,* he thought, shivering. *No one has....* He interrupted his thought at the sight of a tuxedo meckie a short distance ahead, standing off to one side of an ornate oak door. The meckie's button lights blinked rhythmically.

"Greetings, Master," the meckie said in a sophisticated but mechanical voice. The door slid open as the meckie spoke, and Master Edward saw Uncle Rosy's suite beyond, shimmering warmly.

*I am Master!* he thought happily. *Everything is at my command!*

His elation faded quickly, for as Master Edward entered the suite, he recalled his personal aging crisis. *Maybe there is something here to explain it,* he thought, recalling the terrible spectacle of Sixsayer Robert before he died … those deep, terrible wrinkles framing desperate, screaming eyes.

He paused to look around the suite, found himself in a large light wood paneled living area, with bookshelves on three walls. Reflective solar panels on the walls and ceiling provided the room with cheerful semi-natural light. The furnishings were beige fabrics and light wood, the carpeting soft driftwood grey.

*Nice,* Master Edward thought, fingering the smooth linen fabric of his Master's robe, *but simpler than I would have expected.*

An agatestone fireplace dominated one wall, and above the mantel hung a three-dimensional painting of a woman working in an old-style kitchen. Another tuxedo meckie stood near a raised panel door to one side of the fireplace, and the meckie began to blink its button lights when Master Edward looked at it.

"Greetings, Master," the meckie said in a voice identical to that of the first tuxedo meckie.

"And who are you?" Master Edward demanded, taking care to mimic the voice of Uncle Rosy.

"I have no name, Master."

"How do I tell you and the other meckie apart?"

"There are three of us, Master. You have never felt a need to tell us apart before."

Master Edward pursed his lips thoughtfully, said, "Hmmm." He rolled past a striped beige-and-grey couch at the center of the room, noted a blond wood coffee table in front of it with the words "Keep the Faith" inlaid on the tabletop in dark letters. The memory of Uncle Rosy's words danced across his consciousness, then flitted away: *Look within yourself.… There are things even I do not understand.…*

Master Edward took a deep, exasperated breath, tilted his head back and stared at the ceiling. The ceiling consisted of yellow and black mosaic tiles arranged in a stylized brain design. He chased an elusive thought through the alcoves of his mind, looked away.

Rolling to a bookcase, he scanned titles: *Journal of Holistic Medicine … The Einsteinian Phenomenon …* Another section contained religious books. Other sections were devoted to political, economic, and historic readings. He ran inquisitive fingers over the volume covers, glanced briefly through a volume entitled *Chairman Mao: His Life and Times.*

After replacing this volume, Master Edward was about to remove another book when his concentration was shattered by a piercing woman's scream: "Willard!" The voice seemed to come from somewhere near the fireplace, behind Master Edward and to the left. But he saw no one

"What the hell?" Master Edward cursed.

"Willard!" the voice screeched, a little louder this time.

"Who is that?" Master Edward asked, looking at the tuxedo meckie.

"Your wife, of course, Master," the mechanical servant responded, pointing at the picture over the fireplace. "On a simu-life projector."

Master Edward's eyes opened wide as he focused on the painting, because the three-dimensional woman in the picture was glaring directly at him with her hands on her hips. "Willard!" she howled, revealing a very large mouth. "Answer me!"

"What do I do now?" Master Edward inquired of the meckie

"Answer her, Master. You always say, 'Coming dear.'"

"Oh yes. It slipped my mind." Master Edward looked at the scowling woman. She seemed ready to leap out of the picture. "Coming dear!" he yelled. Lowering his voice, he looked at the meckie and asked, "Now what?"

"Nothing, Master. The simu-life projector yells at you during the day to keep your spirits up."

"Oh."

The miniature woman seemed placated now, as she turned her attention to a steaming pot of food on the range. As Master Edward continued to stare at the picture, the moving, lifelike portions stiffened subtly, and once again it appeared to be an ordinary three-dimensional painting.

"I do not know how that slipped my mind," Master Edward said, wondering why he needed to explain to a meckie. "Too much going on, I suppose." Delving into his knowledge of Uncle Rosy's past, he added: "Jennifer was killed in a rollercoaster accident more than three centuries ago … along with my children …"

"Yes, Master. At Glitterland. They are in the Happy Shopping Ground now."

*Uncle Rosy must have been terribly lonely,* Master Edward thought. *No one with whom to share his troubles....* Resuming his interest in the books, Master Edward reached for a weathered brown volume entitled *Laboratory Experiments of W. R. Rosenbloom, 2261-2266.* He blew dust from the top of the volume, opened it slowly. The book smelled of must. Its pages were yellow-edged and cracking.

Turning the pages carefully, he noticed each sheet was ruled in light green lines, with headings along the top and spaces below where Uncle

Rosy had entered dates, techniques, and comments concerning each experiment. He scanned the opening pages. All concerned a technique referred to as "S.M.E."

*I recall those initials,* Master Edward thought. *Selective Memory Erasure. Uncle Rosy used it on anyone who helped build or design the Black Box of Democracy.*

He read on, saw human subjects listed by consumer identification number on the pages, with a medical malady designated next to each. He located a guide in the back of the volume which connected names and numbers. *Where did he get all the volunteers?* Master Edward wondered.

Then he saw a penciled notation next to one name which read, "Returned to t-orbiter. Uncooperative." Several other names had notes which said, "Dec. Brain in jar 506" or "Dec. Brain in jar 712." Master Edward shuddered as he realized that "t-orbiter" referred to "therapy orbiter," and "Dec." meant "deceased."

*These were NOT volunteers!* he thought.

The middle section of the volume outlined a series of "placebo effect" experiments. Master Edward read that subjects given sugar pills were told these were "new cures" for their maladies. Locating a page outlining the results, he read aloud: 'The higher the suggestive force used by the controller, the more likely it was that a placebo would work. Subjects having the greatest faith in the placebo responded most favorably to treatment...."

*Faith,* Master Edward thought *Keep the Faith....*

Flipping through a number of experiments describing mentation for the purpose of operating consumer products, he found an entry near the end of the volume dated December 2, 2266: "I embarked upon these brain experiments with the intent of improving economic conditions through control of each consumer's buying impulses. This remains a valid concept, and I intend to leave copies of key experimental data where it can be utilized by future generations. I feel there is much more to discover concerning the brain, but I am somewhat fearful of proceeding."

Master Edward looked away from the book, gazed across the room at the painting over the fireplace. The three-dimensional woman was in motion again, and four children sat at the kitchen table eating cookies and drinking milk. *Faith,* Master Edward thought again, unsure of the reason for the returning thought. *Keep the Faith....*

He replaced the book on the shelf, turned forcefully to face the tuxedo meckie. "Tell me the secret of eternal youth," Master Edward demanded.

"Look to the holy water, Master. Then look within yourself. You have always said this."

"Elaborate."

"I cannot, Master," the meckie replied, raising its arms in helplessness. "That is all you have told me." The meckie's white button lights blinked. Curiously, it seemed nervous.

As Master Edward glared at the faceless mechanical servant, he felt a strong impulse to knock it over. "What is the source of our holy water?" he snapped.

The tuxedo meckie turned toward the raised panel door. The door slid open. "There is the source," the meckie replied. "Beyond the one-way glassite."

Master Edward moto-shoed to the open doorway, peered through it into a darkened room. He mentoed for light. Overhead fluorescent panels flickered on, flooding the room with harsh white light. A paper-littered desk stood to one side next to an electronic mail terminal. The opposite wall was clear one-way glassite, looking out upon a freestanding wall which contained instrument dials.

He rolled quickly to the glassite window, peered through it at the dials. There were six dials in all, each connected to an upside-down U-shaped black pipe which rose from and reentered the floor on the other side of the glassite.

Master Edward saw something written on each dial, squinted to make out the words. He mouthed them slowly as they became clear. "New City … Water District … Number one-oh-four."

He pulled his head back in surprise, said, "What the Hooverville? New City Water District? THAT is the source of our holy elixir? Ordinary tap water?"

Feeling shaky, Master Edward rolled the short distance to the desk and picked up a piece of electronic mail Printed on blue-bordered computer paper, he saw:

NEW CITY WATER DISTRICT NO. 104

PAST DUE ACCOUNT—NOTICE OF SERVICE TERMINATION

BLACK BOX OF DEMOCRACY

ACCT. #18DR-17654499Q

BALANCE DUE: $26,312.15

DEAR CUSTOMER:
THIS ACCOUNT IS SERIOUSLY PAST DUE, AND IT IS APPARENT THAT YOU HAVE CHOSEN TO IGNORE OUR CORDIAL REMINDERS. IF THE BALANCE IS NOT PAID BY AUGUST 31, 2605. YOUR WATER SERVICE WILL BE DISCONNECTED.
SINCERELY,
J.D. LAIRD
COLLECTION DEPARTMENT

Master Edward rolled out of the room in a state of shock, letting the slip of paper fall from his grasp as he passed beyond the doorway. *The secret was within my mind all the time!* he thought. *But now that I know …*

"Shall I pay this bill now, Master?" the tuxedo meckie asked, retrieving the paper. "Tomorrow is the thirty-first."

"What? Oh, yes. Go ahead and pay it."

The meckie rolled into the room with the slip of paper in its grasp. Moments later, Master Edward heard the whir and throb of the electronic mail terminal.

Master Edward glanced down at the inlaid coffee table with its familiar "Keep the Faith" message. *There can be no doubt,* he thought.

Stopping at the fireplace, he leaned both forearms on the mantel and stared down into the brick-lined pit where two wood logs rested on a grating. Master Edward mentoed the fireplace, watched orange and blue flames spring up instantly around the logs.

*And in what did Uncle Rosy believe?* he thought.

"Willard!" the woman's voice screeched. "Willard!"

"Yes, dear," Master Edward called back. "Coming, dear." *I should check to see if we are eluding the comet,* he thought. *But does it matter?*

O O O

It was early afternoon of Garbage Day minus two when President Ogg and Billie Birdbright looked into Conference Room fifty-seven through one-way glassplex. The two-hundred-twenty-meter-long room was full to bursting with committee-members, messengers, auditors, and an assortment of support personnel. Lieutenant Colonel Meg Corrigon stood at the head of the table, addressing the throng. To President Ogg's ears, her lips moved silently, for he had turned off the sound in the viewing room.

"Look at them!" President Ogg said, elated. "By tomorrow, they'll branch off into subcommittees, and the next day there will be sub-subcommittees!"

"It IS exciting, sir," Birdbright said.

"You're seeing government organization in its embryonic form," Ogg said, barely able to contain his excitement. "Why, who knows, Billie?... This could be the beginning of a new sub-bureau!"

"Marvelous, Mr. President," Birdbright said, trying to sound enthusiastic. "That would keep people occupied for years!"

"I can see it now," Ogg said, lowering his eyelids and gazing at an indeterminate, far-off point, "a new building, hundreds of construction workers ... required forms by the million!"

"Uncle Rosy would have been proud, Mr. President!" Bird-bright turned to look at the President, saw tears forming in his eyes.

President Ogg cleared his throat, then glanced quickly at his Chief of Staff to see if Birdbright had noticed his moment of emotional weakness. Birdbright had already turned away and was watching the committee meeting.

Ogg looked through the glassplex again, saw people streaming out the doors into adjacent conference rooms. "They're breaking off into splinter groups already!" he said. "My Rosenbloom, but this is exciting!"

"May I ask a rather pointed question, sir?' Birdbright queried, looking sideways at the President.

President Ogg lifted an eyebrow in surprise, replied, "Why, yes, feel free.... Always feel free to be direct with me."

"Sir, the crux of this comet matter is that Earth is going to be turned to garbage in fifty-one hours."

"And the necessary committee work will take much longer than that," Ogg said. "That concerns you, doesn't it, Billie?"

Noticing a twinkle in the President's eyes, Birdbright said, "Yes, Mr. President. To be quite honest, I don't see how you can possibly remain so calm."

"Consider the AmFed system, Billie!" Ogg said in a deep, presidential tone. "Upon what is it based?'

"Why ... upon the teachings of our Beloved Master, Uncle Rosy."

"That includes Job-Support, does it not?' Ogg's blue green eyes took on the omniscient expression of a Freeness Studies Instructor.

"It does," Birdbright said cautiously.

"And where is Uncle Rosy now?"

"He is presumed to have died … nearly three hundred years ago.

"But he lives on, Billie! … In our hearts and dreams … and, not unimportantly … in the Black Box of Democracy!"

Birdbright scowled, said: "I don't see what you're getting at."

"Do you think the Black Box would allow Earth to be destroyed?" Ogg removed a red-bordered priority letter from his pocket, unfolded it and passed it to his Chief of Staff.

"Uh, no," Birdbright said, accepting the sheet. "I suppose not."

"Read it, Billie. Came in on the mail terminal a few minutes ago."

"From Bu-Tech," Birdbright said, scanning the message. "Orbital speed of Earth up twelve-point-five percent … possibly due to pumping effect on the planet from rhythmic garbage shots … checking planet's reduction in mass from garbage shots…." He looked up. "Sounds pretty serious, Mr. President."

Ogg smiled. "The Black Box changed the orbital speed … to get us away from the comet!"

"How could they?…"

"Who knows, Billie. But I'm sure of it. We don't need to lift a finger! The Black Box is doing it for us!"

"Brilliant, Mr. President! Absolutely brilliant!" Birdbright wondered if his manner betrayed the doubts he felt. He handed the letter back to Ogg.

Ogg looked at his Chief of Staff askance while pocketing the message, said, "Don't repeat this to anyone, but I was contacted by the Black Box."

"Personally? When?"

"Sunday morning. I believe they arranged for the deaths of Muñoz and Hudson as punishment for a plot they had to take over our holy government by illegal means."

Birthright's jaw dropped. "How were they planning to—"

"I'll explain later, Billie. Rest assured the Black Box won't permit any harm to come to the AmFed system. I'm convinced of it."

"That makes me feel a little better, Mr. President," Birdbright said, still not feeling entirely at ease.

"All we need to do is what we've always done. That is to uphold the principles taught by Uncle Rosy. Without exception, Billie. Without exception."

Birdbright nodded in affirmation.

"Come along now, Billie," Ogg said, rolling toward the door. "I need to discuss the eulogy with you. Hudson and Muñoz are to be astro-disposed tomorrow."

O O O

On their second Wednesday afternoon coffee break in the Cave Coffee Shop, Birdbright and Carla sat at a window table overlooking the underground waterfall.

"Oh Billie, don't be silly!" Carla said with a soft smile. "We've only been out on one date. … and to coffee together a few times."

"I'm serious," Birdbright said, reaching into the vest pocket of his sportcoat to remove a pink and blue card. Smiling serenely, he reached across the tabletop to press the card into her palm.

Carla gazed into his smoke grey eyes adoringly, did not have to look at the card to know what it was. Her soft smile broadened as she looked down and read the card aloud: "Mr. William Birdbright requests the pleasure of your company for a Pre-Permie Counseling Session." She looked up to meet his gaze, beamed. "Oh, Billie!"

"Well?"

Their hands met at the center of the tabletop, and Carla felt the warmth and strength of Birdbright's grasp as he held her hands between his own. This was a table Carla had often occupied with Sidney. But Sidney seemed remote to her now, even though it had been only a few days since she had seen him.

Carla barely heard or saw the clamoring breaktime crowd at nearby tables. It was a private moment in an unprivate world, and even Harmak seemed to be playing her tune. She gazed deep into Birdbright's eyes, then looked away to watch the underground waterfall cascade over a stalagmite precipice. The water seemed to dance and sparkle with a magical quality. There could be but one answer.

"Yes!" she said, hearing her voice crack with excitement. "The answer is yes!"

Birdbright released her hands and jumped to his feet in an untypical burst of expended energy. "Did you hear that?" he yelled, looking from table to table. "She said yes!"

Several people laughed good-naturedly. "Congratulations!" said a blonde woman from the Sixteenth Request Department. "How wonderful!" exclaimed another. "When's the session?"

Birdbright beamed, reached down to pull Carla to her feet. "Right now!" he said, hugging Carla while the crowd auto-clapped and wished them well.

"Now?" Carla said, surprised.

"Why yes, of course. Our union contract says we can take off work for matters of permeage."

"I know!" she snapped. "But why did you make an appointment before receiving my answer?"

Birdbright winked. "I knew what you'd say," he said.

Carla's lavender eyes flared. She pulled away, said: "Why you egotistical, arrogant, self...." Her words trailed off as she detected a worried expression on Birdbright's face. "I love you," she said softly, kissing him on the cheek.

* *

Stork's Baby Bazaar was on the west side of the Bu-Permie Shopping Center, adjacent to a large bulletin board which proclaimed: LITTERING IS LAWFUL. Birdbright's bright blue autosport stopped several hundred meters away, and he and Carla short-stepped out onto a heart-shaped red platform. The platform was crowded and paper-littered, and they waited while other happy, laughing couples took turns rolling down to an eight-laned skatewalk. Carla turned to watch the autosport disappear into a parking tube.

Birdbright went first, followed by Carla. They rolled around an overpass and spiraled down to expressway level, taking the slow right-hand lane of the northbound side. They moved quickly from one lane to the other until they were in the fast lane, then zipped up an exit marked "STORK'S" onto another heart-shaped platform.

Holding Birdbright's hand tightly on the crowded platform, Carla looked up along the face of a three-hundred-story clear glassplex elevator structure which connected the platform with all floors of the building. The elevator cars were in the shape of babies wrapped in brightly colored swaddling blankets, seemed suspended from a massive ochre-colored stork's beak on top of the building. Carla could not see the entire stork now, but had seen it many times during helitours of New City. It was breathtaking.

The Stork Building looked like a baby shower gift, was covered with red, blue, green, and yellow animal designs on a silver-white background. A broad pink ribbon encircled the building and flapped in a gentle breeze above a flashing neon STORK'S sign. An elevator car arrived, and a concealed door in a blanket fold whooshed open.

They disembarked at the seventy-fourth floor, short-stepping into a wonderland of baby products. The store had been decorated gaily, had pink and blue ribbons, bright product signs and dozens of eager salesmen ready to smother their customers' inattention.

An exceedingly round salesman in a light blue bunting outfit moto-rushed over as Carla and Birdbright entered. He was propelled by white moto-baby shoes with bells across the top that jingled merrily when he moved. A teething ring necklace dangled from his neck, resting on top of a very firm and protruding tummy. His cheeks were bright pink, and a script nametag on his chest read "Jimmy."

"Oh goo!" Jimmy said, in the best jargon of the store. "We're so glad you're here! Do you have anything in mind?" He sucked on the teething ring, awaited a reply.

"We're looking for room seventy-four thirty-one," Birdbright replied.

"Ah!" the salesman said, oozing happiness. "Another Pre-Permie counseling session!" He waved an arm gracefully toward the rear of the store, flipping his palm to designate one of the side walls. "Right down that way, folks. Near the Ultra-Nu Combination Baby Set displays "

Birdbright and Carla moto-shoed in the direction designated, passed little bedroom sets, playpens, strollers, stuffed tigers, and elephants, mobiles and a whole host of other items. Colorful banners hung over the various displays to announce: "AS ADVERTISED ON NATIONAL HOME VIDEO."

Pausing to examine a lifetime photography contract, they overheard a salesgirl in a pink bunting outfit tell a couple that Stork's prices were competitive. "The Stork's label on a product will tell your friends that you paid the very highest price," the salesgirl said. The couple was visibly impressed, and the salesgirl added, "All our products carry the Goodie Homemaker's Seal of Approval!"

Room seventy-four thirty-one was two aisles away and had a bright yellow door encrusted with tiny red hearts. Birdbright mentoed a heart-shaped wall button, watched it go in as a buzzer rang. The door swung open, revealing a small office which had been made to look larger with mirrors on the floor, walls and ceiling. A rotund woman sat at a heart-shaped plastic desk in the center of the office. She smiled. "Come in, come in," she said in a friendly but hurried tone.

Carla glanced lovingly at Birdbright, smiled. They entered and took seats on a glassplex loveseat which had heart-shaped red throw pillows. Carla noted a sign on the front of the desk which read, "A HAPPY PERMEAGE IS A CONSUMPTIVE PERMEAGE." A pink-and-blue broach on the lapel of the woman's white dress identified her as a GW two-hundred.

"I am Wanda Sutter," the woman said, "your Pre-Permie Counselor." Glancing at an appointment telescreen to her left, she said, "You are William Birdbright and Carla Weaver?"

"Yes," Birdbright replied nervously.

Counselor Sutter reached into an automatically stocked desk drawer and removed a pink box which had a cameo baby picture on the cover. Opening the box, she took out several pamphlets and placed them reverently on her desktop. "This is a starter kit," she announced. "It contains government pamphlets on every conceivable subject, including that very popular publication, 'Consumption—How To Go On Full Automatic.'"

"Great!" Birdbright exclaimed.

"Wonderful!" Carla agreed, glancing up at the mirrored ceiling to watch the counselor from above.

"The kit also contains an instruction manual for conservation of energy during sexual intercourse," Counselor Sutter said, opening one of the pamphlets. "It's all arranged in a simple-to-understand step-by-step format."

Carla and Birdbright leaned forward to examine the pamphlet, nodded.

"Let me see now," the counselor said, reaching across her desk to pick up a computer sheet. "Mister Birdbright, you have a Consumption Quotient of eighty-three. Miss Weaver, you register eighty-seven. Now I would like each of you to hold hands and use your free hands to grasp the metal handles at your respective sides of the couch."

The lovers obeyed, and as they did so, the counselor mentoed a desk-mounted console. She studied the console screen for a moment, then exclaimed happily, "Marvelous! Your projected Combined Consumption Quotient is ninety-eight-point-three-seven! That's very high!"

"Oh!" Carla squealed, knowing the importance of this.

"A permeage made in the Happy Shopping Ground!" Counselor Sutter said, bubbling with delight. "Perfectly matched personalities! You will reinforce one another to buy, buy, buy!"

"Isn't it marvelous, honey?" Birdbright said, glancing at Carla.

"Oh yes!" she gushed.

Counselor Sutter stamped a duplicate form set, then placed the forms in a folder and handed it to Carla. "Now you must visit six more agencies to get their approval," she said, "after which you can obtain a permeage license at the courthouse. The addresses are listed on the inside cover."

Carla was so nervous that she dropped the folder. As she reached down to retrieve it, the counselor said, "Come back after the permeage and one of our salesmen will assist you in the selection of your first baby."

"We will," Carla said.

"Based upon the characteristics you want in the child," Counselor Sutter said, "each of you will be given specific birth pills which are guaranteed to produce a beautiful child from your union."

"Thank you," Carla said happily.

"Eye and hair color charts are on the wall outside my office," Counselor Sutter said, rising to her feet. "You may examine them as you leave. Now, if you folks will excuse me, I do have another appointment."

"I want a boy," Carla said as she and Birdbright rolled to the door, "with sandy brown hair with a touch of curl … and pastel blue eyes like the baby Becky got."

"Excellent selections," the counselor said. "And be sure to ask the salesman about baby's own cuteness machine. It will sleep-teach him to do the darnedest things!"

"Oh!" Carla said. "I can't wait!"

O O O

Uncle Rosy's suite contained four large modular rooms: living area, kitchen, bath, and bedroom. Additionally, there were a number of smaller adjoining rooms used for storage and offices. The suite was perhaps twice as spacious as a sayerman's quarters, and Master Edward had searched it rather completely by mid-afternoon, only a few short hours after the murder of Uncle Rosy.

He found nothing further of note, save for a large quantity of books. When the digital cuckoo clock on one wall struck four, Master Edward found himself seated on the carpet in a wash of reflected sunlight next to a bookcase, scanning volumes quickly. The sunlight warmed his head and shoulders but made it difficult to read the brightened pages.

*Religious books in this section,* he thought, closing a black leatherbound volume. *Buddhaic-Brahmanism, Judaism, Islamic-Taoism ... all religions destroyed in the Holy War of twenty-three twenty-six.*

He replaced the volume on the shelf, moved to another section and reached for a slender paperbound book, entitled *Franklin Roosevelt and the W.P.A.* As he opened it, a slip of white paper fell put upon his lap. Master Edward retrieved the paper and read these notes penned neatly in Uncle Rosy's handwriting:

**The Great Order of Existence**
**1. Realm of the Unknown. God?**
**2. Realm of Magic.**
**3. Realm of Inertia and Gas.**
**4. Realm of Flesh.**
**5. Realm of Plants and Lower Life Forms.**

At the bottom of the slip of paper, scrawled hastily, he read: "From voices in my brain, August 26, 2605. The voices returned two days later to say, 'The answer is not to be found within books. Important truths flow from the soul, like a primordial river.'"

*He wrote this only days ago!* Master Edward thought. *Voices? Muñoz and Malloy heard voices too—insanity! But all of them? Even Uncle Rosy?* He wadded the paper and hurled it, followed by the book, at a tuxedo meckie which stood motionless nearby.

"Yes, Master?" the meckie responded as the book thudded off its metal front. The meckie's lights blinked. "You desire something, Master?" To Master Edward's ears at that moment, the meckie's synthetically sophisticated voice sounded particularly irritating and inane.

Master Edward grunted something angry and guttural which was not intended to be discernible, then moto-shoed into the bathroom module. There, for the third time that afternoon, he glared dejectedly at the reflection of his face in the grooming machine mirror.

The aging had accelerated today, and now a grotesque mask looked back at him, its expression more sad than angry. Frustration and guilt were etched into the features, and he saw deep lines around the eyes, with shallower lines on the cheeks, on the forehead and around the neck. The backs of his hands had dark brown age splotches. The skin looked taut, drawn.

He smashed both hands against the mirror, watched spokes from a break in the glass spread across the mirror. A trickle of blood ran down the side of one hand, and he wiped it on his white robe.

*I feel so damned guilty!* he thought. *To have destroyed a great man, and now* ... Tears streamed down Master Edward's cheeks, running over his upper lip and into his mouth. He tasted salt.

Master Edward wiped his eyes and mouth with a hand towel, thought, *How can I step into the Master's moto-shoes? I am not as wise or as strong as he....*

Master Edward let the towel slip out of his grasp. It fell into the sink as he thought, *If only I could erase all memory of losing my faith, of killing Uncle Rosy and of the holy water source ... the meckies could pay the water bill without my knowledge....*

This thought started as a fantasy to him, but then something hit him with no less force than a Bu-Tech thunderbolt. *SME!* he thought, recalling the Selective Memory Erasure procedure.

Master Edward was yelling before he reached the living room module: "WHERE IS THE SME TERMINAL? WHERE IS THE SME TERMINAL?"

A tuxedo meckie blinked on its button lights as Master Edward roared into the room. "SME terminal, Master?" it said. "What is that?"

"Don't hold back on me, you little pile of gears!"

"Master, I know not of what you speak."

"Get the others, then!"

"The others, Master?"

"The other tuxedo meckies, you programmed fool! Get them!"

The meckie rolled out through the suite's main entrance, returned presently with two of its mechanical look-alikes. They formed a row on one side of the living room module, blinking busily. "Yes, Master?" they said in unison in their sophisticated, synthetic voices.

"Which of you took Onesayer's body?" Master Edward asked.

"I, Master," the centrally positioned meckie replied.

"And where is it now?"

"It, Master?"

Master Edward clenched his teeth, made fists. "The body, damn you! The body!"

"Onesayer's body, Master?"

"Yes, yes. Yes-yes-yes!"

"Onesayer's body was launched an hour ago, Master."

"Good." Master Edward unclenched his fists, relaxed his hands at his sides. "Now each of you pay close attention. I am looking for the SME terminal … the Selective Memory Erasure terminal."

"I do not know where the SME terminal is," they replied in unison.

"Why is the terminal not here?"

The meckies spoke at once, creating a jibberished sentence: "I do I not ordered know the terminal, Master."

"What?" Master Edward said.

The meckies repeated their jibberish.

"One at a time," Master Edward said, pointing to the centrally positioned tuxedo meckie. "You first."

"I do not know, Master," this meckie said.

"Now you." Master Edward pointed to the meckie on his left.

"I ordered the terminal, Master."

"Aha! Now we are getting somewhere!" Master Edward rolled very close to this meckie and demanded: "Where is it … uh, the terminal?"

"The terminal is on order, Master."

"Yes, but where is … Let me rephrase that. When did you order the terminal?"

"Thirty-one months ago."

"And why has the terminal not arrived?"

"This is a special order item, Master. One of a kind."

"Yes, but is it not important enough to rush through?"

"You have never said this in the past, Master. We have only made eleven requests so far. The Twelfth through Twentieth Request Departments have not been involved yet."

Master Edward took a deep, furious breath, put his hands on his hips and shot words at the meckie as if the words were bullets: "Send a request to all of the departments at once! Did that ever occur to you?"

"That has never been done before," the meckie said calmly. "Therefore it does not seem possible, Master."

Master Edward threw his arms up in exasperation and thundered: "LEAVE ME! LEAVE ME IMMEDIATELY. ALL OF YOU!"

The tuxedo meckies turned and scurried to the main doorway, but tried to exit simultaneously. The one in the center scraped through, but the other two bounced off the doorjambs on each side. This knocked something loose in their mechanisms, and the damaged meckies began to roll in circles, emitting high-pitched, whining sounds.

"Quiet!" Master Edward screeched, looking for something to throw.

The damaged meckies collided with one another head-on, tipped and fell to their sides. For several moments the whining continued, along with the whir and clank of gears. Finally the death knell ceased, and Master Edward stared at their fallen metal bodies. A moto-wheel on one meckie continued to roll silently for several seconds, but under his intense gaze this too came to a stop.

Master Edward looked around the room … at the simu-life painting, at the books, at the digital cuckoo, then back to the motionless tin can servants. All were silent. He felt alone, very much alone.

O O O

A half hour later, Master Edward looked up with one sleepy eye from the living room couch where he lay, saw the surviving tuxedo meckie standing in the doorway. In a voice devoid of emotion, the meckie said, "Master, it is time for the afternoon audience."

Master Edward scratched the back of one hand, said, "Cancel it!"

"But they ask of Onesayer, Master. What shall I tell them?"

"Tell them nothing."

"They wish to know when you will announce Onesayer's replacement."

Master Edward rose to rest on one elbow, glared. "You told them he is dead?"

"No, Master. They assumed it."

"How dare they demand this information? I will notify them when … and IF … there are to be promotions!"

"Yes, Master. They also say Earth's orbital speed is up twelve-point-five percent, and that—"

"I know that," Master Edward said angrily. "Who do they think did it?"

Continuing where its sentence had been interrupted, the meckie said, "—the comet changed course to match our adjustment."

Master Edward sat up, startled. "It remains on a collision course with Earth?"

"It does, Master."

"I feared as much! Go out and set the Orbital Handle at a one-point-five-three-seven factor." *The maximum,* he thought. *Any more and our solar system falls apart....*

"I will, Master."

"Then tell Twosayer and Threesayer I will see them promptly at nine AM tomorrow."

"I will, Master."

Master Edward recalled his training in the physics of orbital modification as he watched the tuxedo meckie roll away. He thought back to a more pleasant time many years before when he had stood at the tutelage console with Sayer Superior Lin-Ti....

Youngsayer Edward: "But what of the laws of physics, Sayer Superior? Will not the Orbital Handle cause havoc with the Moon and with the AmFed orbiters?"

Sayer Superior Lin-Ti: "No, youngsayer. The Orbital Handle's force field extends to the Moon and to the orbital positions at $L_4$ and at $L_5$. The system will make adjustments as a unit."

Youngsayer Edward: "Are there limits? Surely we cannot make radical adjustments without affecting other planetary systems!"

Sayer Superior Lin-Ti (laughing): "Be patient, youngsayer! You will learn such things in time...."

O O O

Working at deck level Wednesday afternoon in the forward E-Cell area of Mass Driver One, Sidney gave the Argonium gas handle a final spin. Workmen were busy all around. Their voices and the clanging ring of tools echoed off the walls.

"Now hand me the stitch-welder," another client workman instructed.

Sidney looked at the workman as he spoke, saw a young fleshy-faced man without apparent debility, his goggles pushed up out of the way over his forehead.

Sidney lifted the tubular brass stitch-welder, passed it to the other man. As Sidney bent over, a bolt of pain shot through his ribcage and his temple throbbed. These were the places Mayor Nancy Ogg had kicked him.

The man smiled slowly and guardedly, seeming to stare at the white bandage on Sidney's left temple. "You're learning fast," the man said.

"I've always had an interest in space mechanics," Sidney said. 'It's been a hobby with me since I was a kid."

Sidney had helped the man build two compartments since noon, but still did not know his name. Sidney recalled introducing himself earlier, but the man had simply grunted something in return.

Sidney flipped protective goggles over his own eyes, lifted a feather-light compartment assembly from the deck. He held it in place abutting the forward firewall next to the compartment they had just completed.

The man flipped his goggles down and began to stitch-weld the assemblies together. Sidney watched as the zig-zag weld took shape, then glanced back at the center of the mass driver shell, where Mayor Nancy Ogg and her security sergeant stood speaking with a strange-looking short-haired woman.

*I suppose it's a woman,* Sidney thought, noting a faint breast line. The woman was short, had a weak chin and a bulbous nose. Her hands were thrust deeply into the pockets of a loose-fitting white-and-silver dress. The expression was chilly, unsmiling.

"Okay," the man with the stitch-welder said. "It'll hold now."

Sidney let go, glanced through a hatch in the forward firewall where two men in green-and-gold space mechanic's coveralls were rolling aft. They passed a maze of grey tubes at the base of the mass driver engine, rolled by Sidney. "Did you lock the *Shamrock Five* entry hatch?" the taller of the men asked.

"Huh?" the other man said. "Yeah, I guess." To Sidney, the tone seemed disinterested.

*The* Shamrock Five*!* Sidney thought. *That's my ship!*

Sidney watched them roll aft down the center of the mass driver shell and recalled his arrival on Saint Elba less than two nights earlier. It seemed like a month before when he had peered through a porthole in the IOTV to watch the *Shamrock Five* dock.

Sidney pictured the sleek black and silver cruiser in his mind's eye. *It's nearby … and the hatch may be unlocked!* he thought, feeling his pulse quicken.

Impulsively, Sidney flipped off his goggles and moto-darted through the firewall hatch. He pressed himself against the firewall on the other side, breathing hard. *Don't stop now,* he thought, touching the bandaged bump at his temple. *You're disposable anyway….*

He looked up. The mass driver engine towered like a government office building, except it had tubes, valves, and ramps. Sidney's heart skipped a beat: a Security Brigade guard on a lower ramp had just spotted him!

"You!" the guard bellowed. "What are you doing in here?"

Sidney took off before the guard finished his question, sped around the base of the engine. He saw the *Shamrock Five* now through two glassplex portholes in the mass driver's forward-most wall. *There!* he thought, seeing a hatch between the portholes. *The hatch!*

He heard guards yelling from above and behind. "WHERE DID HE GO?" one asked.

"FORWARD!"

"THERE HE IS!"

"GET HIM!"

Sidney was at the hatch, expecting to feel the searing pain of bullets at any moment. *Will it open?* he thought. He mentoed the door, held his breath as he listened to tumblers rolling inside the door. He looked back, saw three guards speeding toward him.

"Pttting!" A bullet ricocheted off the wall near his head.

The door slid open!

Sidney rolled through quickly, mentoed the door shut. A red handle inside on the wall at one side had a sign below it which read: "DOUBLE LOCK—No Access From Rear."

He threw the handle down, looked forward.

Sidney stood on a short glassplex-sealed gangway, could barely see in the low light from one underfoot light panel. He heard distant, angry voices and pounding on the other side of the hatch. Another hatch was forward, and he rolled to it quickly.

Sidney mentoed this hatch. It opened. Just inside was another red double lock handle. He threw it on.

Sidney fell to his knees, still grasping the handle and breathing hard. He caught his breath, yelled: "Tom! You here, Tom?"

There was no response.

Sidney wondered why two trailers full of cappies were connected to the *Shamrock Five*. *Disposables,* he thought. *Did Tom know about that?*

O O O

Sidney rolled through the passenger compartment and peeked into the cockpit, still calling for Tom Javik. Then he searched two aft magnetic container storage rooms.

*He's not aboard,* Sidney thought, rolling back to the cockpit. *Where is he?*

Inside the cockpit, Sidney touched one of the white molded plastic command chairs. He looked around the dimly lit area, saw the faint twinklings of stars far out at the end of the docking tunnel. He slid into the seat.

An array of dials, levers, and handles confronted Sidney, and he studied them intently. He focused upon a brass plate marked "SHAMROCK FIVE—SP-1607" and next to that recognized a red ball plasto-cyanide bomb detonator from photographs he had once seen.

*Let's see here,* he thought, moving his fingers across a row of blue handles. *Direct Command Mode, Takeoff Mode, Docking Mode, Attack Mode....*

"Attack Mode!" Sidney whispered excitedly to himself, resting his hand on that handle. "My Rosenbloom! I can't believe it!" For a moment, he imagined being under Uncle Rosy's direct orders to save Earth ... Atheist fighter ships were attacking the *Shamrock Five* from all sides! ...

Returning to reality, Sidney retracted his hand. There was a slight throbbing at his bandaged temple where Mayor Nancy Ogg had kicked him. He touched the bandage, felt the bump.

*I've got to be realistic,* he thought. *I'll radio for Tom.* Sidney scanned the instruments, located the speakercom. He mentoed a switch to open the circuit, heard the crackle of static electricity. *Well get the ship out to where we can see the garbage comet.... I'll pray for it to go away. That's how I stopped the fire.... Garbage comets? Can it really be?*

Just then, laughter cackled distantly in Sidney's brain. It drew closer. *"Ha!"* a familiar tenor voice said. *"He's at it again—thinks he's a miracle worker!"*

*"It is pathetic,"* a second, deeper voice said. *"Now listen, fleshcarrier. You can't pray to God. God didn't send that comet! We did!"*

The voices cackled with laughter again. To Sidney, it sounded orchestrated.

"You listen to me!" Sidney said angrily. "I'm trying to help people! Millions will die if I don't try!" Sidney thought of Carla, felt tears coming on. He fought them back.

The voices receded, laughing merrily.

"Who's there?" a speakercom voice asked. "Who said that?"

"Get me Lieutenant Tom Javik," Sidney said, addressing the speakercom. "Tell him Sidney Malloy is aboard the *Shamrock Five*, ready for takeoff."

Presently a rasping voice came on the frequency. "Who?" the voice asked. "Who is this?'

"Sidney Malloy. I'm in command of the *Shamrock Five* until Lieutenant Javik takes over." Sidney was not aware of his appointment as titular captain by General Muñoz. "Get Javik for me!" Sidney rasped. "Now!" He rested his hand on the Takeoff Mode handle.

"Javik is missing, fella. You're that cappy he asked for, aren't you? Just open the hatches and give yourself up."

"No! What do you mean he's missing? You're lying!" But Sidney read a voice pitch meter on the dashboard. The meter dial was in the green zone.

*It's true,* Sidney thought, his spirits sinking. *Tom isn't here!*

Static crackled across the frequency.

"You're just making it hard on yourself," the voice said. "Be reasonable. No one's going to hurt …"

Sidney mentoed the frequency shut. *I'll have to fly this baby myself,* he thought, studying the instrument panel. *Now how do I cut the trailers loose? Maybe Direct Command Mode….*

He threw on the appropriate handle, saw the words "Direct Command Mode" illuminated in blue over the handle, and beneath the handle, in blinking red lights, the words "Standing By." The entire instrument panel blinked on with luminescent green, red and blue dials and blinking lights.

*Release trailers,* Sidney mentoed.

There was no response.

"Release trailers!" he yelled.

Still no response.

Sidney stared at the words "Standing By," drummed a finger on the instrument panel.

"Ship's computer," he said, speaking into a console-mounted microphone. "How do I release the trailers?"

"That is not in my program," the computer replied.

"Where would such a thing be programmed?"

"That is not in my program, either."

"Can't you even suggest where I might look?" Sidney asked, pleading.

"No."

Frustrated, Sidney shook his head. *A bureaucratic computer,* he thought.

* *

At the forwardmost hatch of Mass Driver One, Madame Bernet confronted five black-uniformed security guards, one of whom was Sergeant Rountree.

"Roll aside!" Madame Bernet commanded. I'm going through!" The meckie stood with both hands thrust into its pockets, glared menacingly.

"This hatch is double-locked," Sergeant Rountree said angrily, holding one hand on the handle of his bolstered pistol. "Stay the hell out of our way now, Madame!"

Without another word, Madame Bernet drew two long knives out of her pockets. The meckie crossed them in front ceremoniously, then swished them through the air, their steel blades glimmering brightly.

Sergeant Rountree and the other guards drew their pistols, commenced firing at the meckie.

"Pttting! Pttting! Thud!" Bullets ricocheted off walls and off Madame Bernet's plastic and metal body.

The killer meckie smiled, a death's head smile. Then, with five precise strokes, it decapitated the guards. Sergeant Rountree was first to die. The guards fell in blood-squirting heaps, their bodies separated from their heads.

Madame Bernet crossed the knives, then slid them into pocket-concealed sheaths while mentoing a code to break the hatch's double lock.

The hatch slid open.

The meckie passed through the door, double-locked it again.

Seconds later, Madame Bernet stood at the rear hatch of the *Shamrock Five*. The hatch slid open at a mento-command. As the killer meckie rolled in, the *Shamrock Five* shifted on its tether, causing a raised surface to appear underfoot. Madame Bernet's moto-shoes struck this bump, and the meckie fell violently to the floor, butting its forehead against a bulkhead.

The meckie jumped to its feet with knives drawn, rolled in a confused pattern. Something had been damaged in the fall, and a programmed track commanded: *Mission complete! It is time to kill!*

Madame Bernet rolled forward through the passenger compartment, paused uncertainly when she saw the seat upon which she had ridden from Earth to Saint Elba. *Mission complete!* the program repeated. *It is time to kill!*

The meckie restarted, rolled to the cockpit hatch.

Sidney turned at the sound of steel hitting the hatchjamb. "Who the hell are you?" he asked, recognizing the short-haired woman he had seen on the mass driver.

Madame Bernet did not respond, appeared disoriented to Sidney. With a gaze that rolled all over the cockpit, not focusing upon anything, the meckie began to swing its knives while rolling into the cockpit. The knives moved slowly at first, then faster and faster.

"Swish!... Swish!... Swish-swish-swish!"

The meckie closed in on Sidney, flailing wildly like a blind man fighting a burglar. Sidney fell against the instrument panel, accidentally tripping the "Takeoff Mode" handle. He ducked, climbed around the command chairs and rolled into the passenger compartment.

The ship's four Rolls Royce engines rumbled on, then smoothed out. Sidney lunged to the floor behind a double chair to hide, peered across the top of an armrest at the cockpit. The meckie was still in there, thrashing around and cutting everything to pieces. Sidney heard breaking glassite, thuds and crashes.

Sidney recalled the dream he had experienced in the detention center sleeping room on Earth ... the knives that approached inexorably.... Tom's head being severed horribly....

*He's dead,* Sidney thought, grimacing at the thought. *That monster killed him!*

The engines whined, and Sidney felt a surge of power. *Tethers are holding it back,* he thought. *This thing's trying to take off!*

The tethers snapped, and the ship lurched violently, throwing Sidney against the seat behind him.

O O O

Mayor Nancy Ogg stared impatiently in the direction of the forward firewall hatch Sergeant Rountree had gone through minutes before. Just as she started to roll forward, the mass driver shell lurched, and she rolled hard against a quarter bulkhead. Grabbing the bulkhead to stay on her feet, the Mayor read a Patterman Gravitonic Indicator dial mounted there. The reading: "1.027."

She saw other people sprawling upon the floor, heard confused yells and the clanging of unsecured metal tools. A scaffold fell to the deck just a meter away, sending its occupants flying and screaming in pain.

"Get medical attention for the injured!" Mayor Nancy Ogg yelled. *For cappies?* she thought. *Who cares about them?*

Acknowledging the command, a melon-shaped security corporal snapped a first aid kit off the bulkhead. But the mass driver lurched again, and the corporal went sliding across the floor.

"We're taking off!" someone yelled. "The tethers just broke!"

O O O

The *Shamrock Five* surged unhesitatingly through Saint Elba's main docking tunnel, probing the darkness ahead with its collision sensors. Still in the passenger compartment, Sidney lifted his head and peered out a porthole. Outside spotlights flashed on.

Presently, Sidney no longer heard Madame Bernet slashing about in the cockpit. Instead, he heard the radio blaring from that direction. *They've found an override frequency,* he thought, recalling when he had shut off communication.

"*Shamrock Five*!" a voice said over the radio speakercom. "You do not have takeoff clearance!"

Sidney rolled cautiously to the cockpit hatchway.

"*Shamrock Five*!" the radio blared. "Acknowledge!"

Sidney looked around the doorway with one eye, saw the meckie crouching in a corner, knives crossed in front of its body. A piece of plastic skin on the back of one of the meckie's hands had been peeled off, and Sidney saw metal gears and nylon tendons inside.

*A meckie!* he thought. *Is it out of power?* He recalled the comment he had overheard concerning a killer meckie, shivered with fear.

Sidney lifted a manual from the floor, hurled it at Madame Bernet. The meckie did not move.

"Shut down your engines!" the radio commanded, "or we will blast you away!"

Sidney lunged for the instrument panel, replied: "Accidental takeoff. Do not fire upon us! Your mayor is a passenger in one of the trailers!"

The line clicked on, then went off.

*They're checking,* Sidney thought. *She probably didn't have time to get off.*

Sidney cleared debris off the command chair and slid into the seat.

The *Shamrock Five* and its mass driver trailers cleared Saint Elba's docking tunnel and darted into open space. Sidney saw twinkling vastness ahead, flipped on the semi-automatic Direct Command Mode. A red "Standing By" light went on under the mode's handle.

Presently the voice returned to the radio, and it demanded, "Shut down your engines! Hit the master switch!"

"Request refused," Sidney said. "This ship is not turning back!"

"Why not, for Rosenbloom's sake?"

"Call it a holy mission."

There was a pause, followed by: "You're crazy!"

*I don't think so,* Sidney thought.

After another pause, the voice said, "Release the trailers."

*The Mayor IS aboard,* Sidney thought. "I'd be happy to," he said. "How is that accomplished?"

"We'll find out. Stand by, *Shamrock Five*."

"Standing by for course coordinates," the ship's computer said.

Sidney flipped through a console-mounted clip-file which miraculously had survived the meckie's onslaught. *Ah,* he thought. *Here it is!*

"Course eighty-four degrees, seventeen minutes, CP," Sidney said. "Fifty-eight…" He paused, adding, "Wait a minute, computer. This says takeoff was supposed to be yesterday! Won't that change the coordinates?"

"Give me the original figures," the computer said. "We are tracking the comet, and will correct."

*The comet?* Sidney thought. *If I'm nuts, so is this computer!* Sidney completed the entry of coordinates.

"Course received," the computer said. "Over and out."

Sidney felt acceleration in the gravitonically normal cockpit, was pushed back against his seat. *They'd better tell me how to release those....*

"*Shamrock Five*, this is Saint Elba. Locate a green panel box on the cockpit bulkhead, just behind the co-pilot's chair."

Sidney turned around, reported back: "I see it."

"Open the box. Push two green buttons inside. Hit them simultaneously."

"All right," Sidney said. "But no funny ideas about firing on me afterward. I'll have the rear guns trained on those trailers."

"No tricks," the radio voice agreed.

Within seconds, Sidney had cut the trailers loose. On the console screen, he watched two ships close in on the trailers. Sidney gave the command for maximum speed, and the *Shamrock Five* hyper-accelerated. The images on the screen became pinpricks, then disappeared entirely.

He glanced at the killer meckie out of the corner of one eye, thought he saw an eye open. Sidney did a double-take, but he saw nothing unusual the second time. He looked away, took a deep breath.

*I must have been seeing things,* he thought.

* *

On a page margin of the history primer, the tall, fat youngsayerman penned this note: "If there be a nerd Heaven, Sidney Malloy is there."

*Wait a minute,* the youngsayerman thought. *Did the cappy die?*

He flipped ahead to find out....

# CHAPTER THIRTEEN

## THE ECONOMICS OF FREENESS, FOR FURTHER READING AND DISCUSSION

*Patent Law 78 was an unwritten law mandated by the Council of Ten in 2366. It stipulated that the government would buy out and shelve any patent which threatened national economic security, and further that future patents were to be denied upon any such items.*

### *Thursday, August 31, 2605*

Master Edward sat alone in the Central Chamber, staring down from his perch at the round illuminated floor screen in the center of the room. Only half conscious that it was nearly two o'clock in the morning, he studied a video schematic of the Great Comet's trajectory.

"Blast!" he said in an angry undertone, noting that the future paths of Earth and the garbage comet continued to meet. A digital readout at the bottom of the screen described the comet's Estimated Time of Arrival:

**Impact Countdown:**

| DAYS | HOURS | MINS | SECS | D/SECS |
|---|---|---|---|---|
| 1 | 16 | 5 | 46 | 0.38 |

He watched desperately as the deciseconds and seconds flipped away, then mentoed for a videograph report.

*There,* he thought as the graph appeared on the screen, pointing in the low yellow light of the room. *That is where I altered Earth's orbital speed yesterday. And then the comet changed its own trajectory to remain on a collision course....*

His gaze moved to the point where the tuxedo meckie had increased the orbital speed again the prior evening. Master Edward shook his head sadly as he saw the comet had altered its own course to match that change.

At Master Edward's memo-command, the screen changed once more, and he watched the Great Comet as it flashed across space. The comet emitted bright blue and amber tones, illuminating the ceiling of the room. He felt fascination, fear, and awe.

He considered fleeing in an escape rocket but discarded the thought almost at the moment it came to him. *If I have any hope of reversing the aging process,* he thought, *I must remain here.*

Master Edward longed for a simpler time. His life had grown unbearably complex in a few short days. He touched the handle of the knife at his waist, thought, *I could end my misery in an instant.*

He gazed at the screen with unfocused eyes, reminding himself as he had several times since killing Uncle Rosy that he could never be as great a leader as the Master had been. *Uncle Rosy must have sensed I could not handle the job,* he thought. *That is why he delayed....*

An overwhelming feeling of loneliness came over him.

"Master!" a voice called from across the chamber. "Might I have a word with you?"

Master Edward saw a hood-robed figure standing in the doorway which led to the antechamber containing the Basins of Youth. Surprised, Master Edward called back: "Who is there?" He realized as the words came out that he had forgotten to speak in the tone of Uncle Rosy. *Did he notice?* Master Edward wondered.

"Lastsayer Steven."

"Enter," Master Edward said, remembering to use the resonant tone of Uncle Rosy.

The robed figure rolled forward to one side of the floor-screen, and Master Edward saw Lastsayer's smooth face in the illumination of the comet. *Too much light in here,* Master Edward thought nervously, pulling his robe over the lower part of his face and nose.

"Peace be upon you, Master," Lastsayer said.

"What is this about?' Master Edward asked without returning the blessing. He peered over the edge of his robe, heard his own words muffle in the robe and pulled it several centimeters out from his mouth.

"I heard of Onesayer's disappearance," Lastsayer said.

"And you are here about a promotion?" These words dripped with acidity. Master Edward looked for the tiniest indication that Lastsayer had noticed the earlier vocal faux pas, saw only fear and curiosity in Lastsayer's expression. *One of the others would have noticed immediately,* Master Edward thought, relieved. *This sayerman has not been here long enough.*

"No, Master. It is something far more important."

"And what is so important that you could not sleep?"

"Undoubtedly you already know of what I am about to tell you. . . ."

"I have no time for dilly-dallying, Lastsayer! Get straight to the point or get straight out of here!"

"I should have come to you sooner," Lastsayer said hurriedly. "Sunday morning, I saw Onesayer high on Happy Pills . . . and he performed disrespectful imitations of you."

"I can hardly believe that!" Master Edward exclaimed, showing false emotion.

"It is true, Master. Although I risk my position in the Sayerhood by speaking against him."

Master Edward smiled grimly to himself, and said in Uncle Rosy's voice, "Tell me more."

"Onesayer seemed bitter about you remaining as Master. I received the distinct impression he wanted to take your place."

"By force?"

"It did not seem so to me at first, but as I thought about it more . . ."

"You saw this nearly four days ago, and waited until now to inform me?"

"I was not certain if I had been here long enough to recognize improper behavior."

"You think disrespect for me is commonplace?" Master Edward snapped. He studied Lastsayer's smooth face in the comet's reflection, saw trembling fear. The lower lip quivered. *No hatred there,* Master Edward thought. *Not yet.*

"N-no," Lastsayer stammered, shifting uneasily on his feet.

"You WERE disciplined at Pleasant Reef, were you not?"

"Yes, Master. There is no excuse."

Master Edward pulled the robe tightly about his face, thought, *Maybe I should bring an armadillo meckie in here to guard me. One of the sayermen could kill me easily if my plan occurred to him. . . .*

Master Edward stopped at the thought, felt himself welcoming the serenity of death. *Twosayer would kill me for sure,* he thought with a macabre sense of humor. *I could force it by promoting Steven to Onesayer....*

Noting Lastsayer Steven awaiting further instructions, Master Edward pulled the robe out from his mouth and said, "Go now, Lastsayer. And say nothing of this matter. I will deal with it."

O O O

During the early morning hours according to New City time, Sidney remained attentive in the cockpit, scanning the sky for a first sign of the Great Comet. Presently, he grew weary of the unchanging scenery and began nodding off.

As he slipped into slumber, the command chair on which he sat began to straighten, forming a sleeping platform. A soft pillow popped out beneath his head, and Sidney rolled over on one side to get comfortable.

Nervously, he opened one sleepy eye to peer at the meckie. Something seemed different. The meckie remained rigid, knives crossed in front.

*It's turned a little!* he thought with a sinking feeling. *Toward me!*

Sidney sat straight up. *No,* he thought. *I imagined it. Or the motion of the ship did it....*

Sidney searched the cockpit for a weapon, opening compartments quietly and looking under chairs and behind instrument panels as he stayed out of range of the killer meckie. Nothing was found. Then he rolled into the passenger compartment, thinking, *I can't sleep in that cockpit!* The hatch shut behind him upon his memo-command.

*The ship's flying smoothly,* Sidney thought, staring at an oxygen cart which was secured to the forward bulkhead. *And with gravitonics near Earth normal ...*

Sidney released the oxy-cart, rolled it in front of the cockpit hatchway. *There,* he thought, mento-locking the cart's wheels. *At least I'll hear the damned thing coming.*

He found a passenger seat, and it folded flat invitingly as he lay upon it, accepting the weary frame of the inexperienced space traveler. Soon Sidney was fast asleep, dreaming of magical things and wondrous places.

Sidney pictured himself in full dress Space Patrol uniform, riding in an open limousine down American Boulevard. Cheering throngs of people lined the street, and they waved national banners while calling out to him: "Captain Malloy! Captain Malloy!"

In the dream, a pretty girl threw flowers to him and blew kisses. It was Carla, his darling Carla! He reached out to her. She smiled, and her image faded into a crowd of smiling faces.

Suddenly, his pleasant dream became a terrible nightmare. Where Carla had been, he saw Madame Bernet, slashing spectators with both knives. Then the killer meckie leaped into Sidney's limousine, swinging its knives viciously.

"You did it for yourself, didn't you, fleshcarrier?" the meckie screeched in a familiar tenor voice as it cut Sidney's face and chest. "You don't care about other people!"

Sidney sat bolt upright on the sleeping platform, found himself drenched in perspiration. Wide-eyed, he stared across the shadowy passenger compartment at the cockpit hatch. The hatch remained closed as he had left it, with the oxy-cart in front of it.

Gradually, fitfully, Sidney fell asleep again.

O O O

The morning of the state funeral celebration was grey and cloudy. President Euripides Ogg stood regally on a red-and-yellow gazebo trailer parked at the base of Astro-Burial Inc.'s number three launcher. He shivered as a cool gust of wind blew in from the east.

"Tell Bu-Tech to warm this weather up," Ogg snapped to Billie Birdbright, who rolled up a ramp onto the trailer. "This is supposed to be a celebration!"

"They need clouds for the special effects," Birdbright said as he rolled to a stop. "The sun will pop out when—"

"I know, I know. But they could have made it a little warmer. . . ." Ogg brushed a lock of hair away from his eyes and surveyed the crowd which stood silently below, waiting for the eulogy to begin. An ocean of faces looked back at him, and for the first time in many years, Ogg was struck by the sameness of their features and dress.

Birdbright leaned close to President Ogg and whispered in his ear: "It's all set, Mr. President. We're locked in on the comet's trajectory. These caskets are going right down the maw of the comet!"

"Very good, Billie," Ogg said, unsmiling.

As Birdbright left, the President shifted his gaze, looking to his right at two astro-disposal casket capsules which rested side-by-side on the launch track. The capsules were draped with white-and-gold ministerial cloths, weighted at the ends and emblazoned with large star-shaped purple badges signifying that the men inside had been killed by malfunctioning products. Ogg suppressed a smile at the thought of Muñoz actually being killed by a faulty waterbed during a homosexual encounter instead of in the auto accident the government said had occurred.

President Ogg cleared his throat and mentoed his auto-speech implant. He began to speak at the direction of the programmed track. "This is both a sad occasion and a happy occasion," he began in a hesitating, remorseful tone. "We are saddened at the passing of General Muñoz and Dr. Hudson … two great leaders who guided their respective bureaus through the challenges of our age." Ogg smiled on cue, adding, "But heartened we are at the thought of these men buying eternally in the Happy Shopping Ground!"

"May Rosenbloom bless them!" the crowd thundered in a tremendous outpouring of emotion.

Ogg reached into one of two urns which rested on a ledge at his side, removing a handful of white confetti, then dipped into the second urn with his other hand and brought forth strands of multi-colored plastic streamers. He opened both hands, casting their contents out upon the casket capsules with these words:

*Paper to paper,*
*Plastic to plastic;*
*Take them, Uncle Rosy,*
*On a journey fantastic!*

A gust of Bu-Tech-made wind picked up the confetti and streamers, carrying them up into the air and away over the heads of the crowd. As this occurred, the sun broke through a cloud layer, casting warm golden rays upon the casket capsules. The crowd oohed and aahed at this, for indeed it had to be a message from Uncle Rosy.

Ebullient now, President Ogg said happily, "To your bosom, Uncle Rosy, take them today!" Then he mentoed the magne-launcher, catapulting the capsules out along the length of the nine-thousand-five-hundred-meter-long launch track into a patch of blue sky. The crowd turned their heads in unison to watch the path of the capsules, cheered moments later when they heard a sonic thump.

President Ogg thought of the garbage comet traveling toward Earth along the same trajectory. "There, you bastards," he cursed bitterly under his breath. "Stop the comet yourselves!"

* *

"In this chapter," Sayer Superior Lin-Ti said, "you will see why our modern social hierarchy was developed. Uncle Rosy set up a wondrous AmFed society … but ultimately it relied upon the control of the Sayerhood … and the Sayerhood relied upon Uncle Rosy. Everything hinged upon one man, you see, and when he died, chaos reigned.

"But this should not be interpreted as a failure of the Master. For he advanced humankind, hoping it ultimately could stand on its own. Today we are closer to that goal, much closer indeed…."

# Chapter Fourteen

## UP CLOSE WITH THE MASTER, FOR FURTHER READING AND DISCUSSION

*"Do not shoot at something until you know what it is. It may shoot back."*

Admonition from Alafin Inaya to Uncle Rosy during a hunting trip they took together in the Kenyatta Highlands, September, 2312. (As related in Emmanuel Dade's unpublished notes.)

## SHIPLOG OF THE AMFED SPACE CRUISER *SHAMROCK FIVE*, SP4607

### Date: Thursday, August 31, 2605—early afternoon
### Garbage Day Countdown: 1 day, 5 hours, 17 minutes

When Sidney awoke, he felt a dull pain in his ribcage where Mayor Nancy Ogg had kicked him. He touched the bandage at his temple and was pleased to find that the swelling had subsided. Sidney sat up, stretched, and looked across the shadowy room at the cockpit hatch. The hatch door remained closed, and in front of that stood the oxy-cart precisely where he had left it.

His chairback rose automatically seconds later, and as it did the passenger compartment lights brightened. Sidney looked up upon hearing a whir of gears, and watched a tray of food drop slowly from a ceiling-mounted levitator onto his lap. *I AM hungry,* he thought, studying a synthetic egg on bagel sandwich with interest. He stuck his finger in a bowl of reconstituted tomato soup. It was tepid. Sidney wolfed down the sandwich, gulped the soup. As he set the empty bowl back on the tray, the tray returned to its ceiling compartment.

Sidney considered ordering more food, but decided instead to roll across the room. After re-securing the oxy-cart to the bulkhead, he mentoed the cockpit door. As it slid open, he heard the sexless voice of the ship's computer. "Re-charging stop, twenty-three minutes," the computer reported.

*Re-charging stop!* Sidney thought. *If it's not completely automated, and there are people there, I could be in trouble....*

Sidney flicked a nervous glance at the still motionless Madame Bernet. *Don't see any further movement,* he thought, rolling to the instrument panel. Without sitting down, he spoke into the command speakercom, asking, "Can re-charging stop be avoided?"

"Remaining charge two-point-seven-four times greater than anticipated," the computer reported. "Unexpected beneficial space currents account for increased efficiency, and ..."

"Answer the question," Sidney said, slipping into the command chair.

"Answer depends upon variables."

"What variables?" Sidney drummed a finger impatiently on the instrument panel.

"Comet behaving erratically. It has accelerated and changed course in the past twenty-nine hours."

"Explain."

"Orbital speed of Earth has increased twice, to its present factor of one-point-five-three-seven normal. Cause unknown. Comet matched each change, is in apparent pursuit of Earth."

"So we need less E-Cell charge to rendezvous with the comet?"

"Assuming comet continues at present speed ... and assuming a rendezvous in deep space is required ... that is correct."

"Returning to my original question, do we have adequate charge onboard?"

"Answer depends upon variables."

"We've already been over that!"

"There are other variables."

Sidney sighed. "Be specific," he said.

"Comet's speed and course may change. Space currents are subject to variation. Earth—"

"Assuming an average condition for all such variables, do we have an adequate E-Cell charge to reach the comet?"

"This computer does not deal in probabilities. It deals in facts."

Sidney slammed the butt of his hand on the instrument panel. "Do not stop for recharging," he said tersely.

O O O

An hour later, Sidney felt bored. He glanced around the cockpit at the white plastic walls and at the still rigid Madame Bernet. *This isn't what I imagined,* he thought sadly. *The ship is flying itself!*

He touched the Manual Mode handle, felt a rush of excitement as he considered taking the ship off its semi-automatic Direct Command Mode. *Should I do it?* he thought.

He threw the handle down in answer to the question and grasped a gleaming tita-steel-plated control stick at his right side. The stick was cool to his touch. Sidney moved the stick halfway to starboard, and the *Shamrock Five* banked gracefully to the right.

*This is more like it!* he thought, suddenly exhilarated.

Sidney pressed a black button in the stick, causing the ship's twin Rolls Royce engines to blast. *It's so simple,* he thought, feeling acceleration in the gravitonically normal cabin. *Just as I imagined....*

Sidney pushed the stick to port, giving another blast to the rockets. The *Shamrock Five* responded quickly, and Sidney leaned into the turn, just as he had done so many times in dreams.

It seemed too good to be true.... Sidney at the command of a Space Patrol cruiser, flashing commands to powerful rockets! *I'm the only one who can do it!* he thought, *the only person who can save Earth!*

He reached to his uniform tunic with his left hand to feel the medals he had been awarded for past missions, patted his chest where they should have been. "What the?..." he grunted.

Sidney looked down at his chest, saw only a thin green smock that had been issued to him on Saint Elba. "Oh," he sighed. "For a moment ..."

*"Ha-ha-ha!"* Distant laughter echoed through his brain, grew louder quickly. *"Ha-ha-ha!"*

*"Enjoying yourself, fleshcarrier?"* a familiar deep voice asked.

Sidney felt warm now, embarrassed at the daydream. *You're alone out here!* he thought. *Get ahold of yourself!*

The cockpit was silent. He looked across the starboard bow at a distant shooting star streaking to his left. The shooting star angled off into the starcloth beyond, then flashed brilliantly, followed by a wisp of white light as it turned toward Sidney.

*Wait a minute!* Sidney thought. *That's no shooting star!*

Inadvertently, Sidney pulled the stick back sharply, and the ship's nose tilted up. He pushed the stick forward to compensate, and the *Shamrock Five* dropped its nose.

*It's the Great Comet!* he thought. A wave of euphoria passed through his body.

The comet veered heavenward for an instant, and this time its color and configuration changed so that it was a pale blue iceball trailing six silvery jet-ray tails from its nuclear region. The tails were magnificent plumes of gas which swept across millions of kilometers of space, as delicate and translucent as spun glass against sunlight. The midnight blue backcloth of space gave definition to the comet's icy nucleus, and it occurred to Sidney that he was witnessing the most beautiful spectacle in all of creation.

Now the comet swooped back, much as his ship had done moments before, returning to its original course. As the comet swooped, its silvery plumes turned to fiery yellow, while the pale blue nucleus became soft lavender. As Sidney thought about the comet's complexity, another thought hit him: *Did it mimic my ship's motion?*

Thinking the comet might follow him away from Earth, Sidney mentoed a directional computer button. The ship turned around one hundred twenty degrees. Nudging the speed toggle to decelerate, he watched the Great Comet on a video console screen.

But the comet remained on course, not flinching an eyelash. Sidney brought the ship around again and resumed acceleration. Then he moved the control stick. First one way, then the other. The comet refused to follow.

Now Sidney closed his eyes and clasped his hands together in prayer. *Please,* he thought, recalling his prayer when the Elba House fire was raging, *swerve and go in another direction. Please don't hit Earth!*

He opened his eyes. The comet had not changed course. Sidney repeated the prayer four more times, but nothing happened.

*Elba House was on fire,* he thought, trying to sort out events that had become a blur in his mind. *And the comet is fire....*

He tugged at his upper lip pensively, then moved his head from side to side. *Maybe the comet's too big,* he thought. *Too free....* Sidney hit a red super accelerator toggle on the console, felt G-forces push him against the chair back.

The comet grew visibly larger as the distance between it and Sidney narrowed. He saw its nucleus flare bright red. Then the misty tail plumes changed to emerald and gold. It was a spectacular display of raw primordial power, at once terrifying and delicately beautiful.

*I feel ... strangely compelled ... to continue this journey,* Sidney thought, *as if some immense presence is beckoning to me across the heavens....*

Sidney heard faint laughter in a distant cavern of his skull. He rubbed his temples with the thumb and two fingers of one hand. Gradually his head cleared, leaving him with a mixture of intense and conflicting emotions.

O O O

The black pearl handled knife lay on Master Edward's dining module table, and he leaned over the table with both hands on its cool marble edge, staring at the weapon despondently. He felt tired and dispirited. Although it was long past lunchtime of Garbage Day minus one, he had not looked in the mirror at all that day.

*No use looking at my face,* he thought, noting deep creases and brown age blotches on his hands. *I know what it looks like.* He sighed. *I am so weary!*

Master Edward straightened, lifted the knife. He pricked the tip of one finger intentionally, watched blood squirt out and drip to the table. The blood seemed impersonal, somehow not his own.

"Willard!" the simu-life picture screamed from another room. "Willard!"

"Yes, dear," Master Edward called back. "Coming, dear."

*I am going to join her ... and the Master,* he thought. *In death.*

He glanced to the doorway at the sound of rolling machinery, saw the remaining tuxedo meckie enter. "You did not call for lunch, Master," the meckie said. "You are not hungry today?"

Master Edward did not respond.

"Can I get you anything, Master?"

Master Edward stared at the knife, replied: "Serenity."

"What did you say, Master?"

"I want you to kill me."

"But no one can kill you, Master. You are the most perfect creation."

"I am re-programming you," Master Edward said, extending the knife to the meckie. "What was said before is not true. I *can* die. I *want* to die."

"As you wish, Master," the meckie said in its sophisticated, emotionless voice. Its button lights blinked uncertainly.

"Take the knife," Master Edward instructed.

The tuxedo meckie complied, stood motionless with the knife blade in its mechanical grasp.

"Kill me," Master Edward said, extending his arms to each side as he recalled Uncle Rosy's similar words the day before.

The meckie rolled forward quickly and slammed the knife handle into Master Edward's midsection.

Master Edward grunted and grabbed his stomach. But the injury was limited: his wind had been knocked out. "You tin can fool!" Master Edward gasped. "Turn the knife around!"

"This way, Master?" the tuxedo meckie asked, grasping the black pearl handle.

"Yes," Master Edward said impatiently. "Now hurry, blast you! Hurry!"

O O O

It was Thursday afternoon. Mayor Nancy Ogg had been brought back to Saint Elba three hours earlier.

She passed a stack of telebeam memos across her desktop to Sergeant Keefer. This was Rountree's replacement, a man whose appearance very much resembled that of his predecessor tall and muscular, just the sort of man with whom she would like to share a bed. Dr. Hudson had been a brain, and that had attracted her to him physically. It certainly had not been Hudson's appearance. She thought of her longings to be held by Sergeant Rountree. Now he, too, was gone....

The Mayor sighed, recalling the crisis she faced. She lit a lemon tintette and sat back in her chair with an intense expression. She heard the chair squeak, studied the black-uniformed man who stood in front of her desk. "Beams have been arriving all night," she said.

Sergeant Keefer flipped through the memos, appeared to be ill at ease.

"Sit," Mayor Nancy Ogg commanded.

Sergeant Keefer took a seat in a lattice glass suspensor chair, continued to flip through the slips of paper. "News travels fast," he said. "I see the psychotherapeutic community wants video-film and brain scan reports on Mister Malloy. Requests from San Dimitrio, Mariana City … every quadrant of the galaxy …" He paused upon seeing Mayor Nancy Ogg shake her head from side to side, an unspoken comment that she was not interested in such information.

"This Malloy; I've never seen anything like him," Mayor Nancy Ogg said, taking a puff on her tintette. She blew bright yellow smoke through her nostrils, peered through the smoke at Sergeant Keefer.

"Most unusual, Honorable Mayor. Most unusual."

"Where did Malloy learn to operate an Akron class cruiser?"

"We're checking his dossier file now, Honorable Mayor. We show him as a GW seven-five-oh, Presidential Bureau, Central Forms."

The Mayor scowled, flipped ashes into an ashtray. "Muñoz chose him to command the ship. Why?'

Sergeant Keefer leaned forward to return the telebeam slips to Mayor Nancy Ogg's desk, remained on the forward edge of his chair and said, "I don't know."

"Come now, Sergeant. Surely you can think more clearly than that. General Muñoz was drugged—or hypnotized!"

Sergeant Keefer remained leaning forward, looked confused.

Mayor Nancy Ogg snuffed out her tintette in the ashtray, stared at the wall. "Another problem," she muttered.

"What did you say, Honorable Mayor?'

"Nothing, nothing," she replied irritably, still staring at the wall. Then, turning to glare at Keefer with angry, smoldering eyes, she announced: "I'm putting the orbiter on immediate Evacuation Alert. Malloy duped Javik and then killed him. Malloy is a saboteur!"

"He c-couldn't have p-planted bombs," Sergeant Keefer stammered. "He looked so harmless …"

"And that would make him the perfect saboteur!" Mayor Nancy Ogg boomed. "Surely, even you can see that, Sergeant."

"Yes, of course." Sergeant Keefer hung his head.

"Speed up your background investigation," the Mayor commanded. "I want a full report on this man in one hour!"

O O O

From the couch of her living room module, Carla heard the chimes of a neighbor's digital cuckoo, counted six chirps. *Supper time*, she thought, infuriated.

She wiped tears from her face, took a deep breath and mentoed her telephone to call Samantha Petrie. A tele-cube rose from the phone's cradle. The cube floated through the air, paused in front of Carla's mouth.

"Billie hasn't called all day," Carla said, trying to regain her composure.

"You were going to get some of your permeage license forms filled out today, weren't you?" Petrie asked. "Why didn't you call me earlier?"

"I took the whole day off," Carla said, oblivious to the question. "He should have been here this morning." She sobbed, put her hand over the tele-cube, then released it. "That dirty …"

"Maybe something came up," Petrie said, trying to reassure her friend.

"Yeah. About five-ten, blue eyes, a good—"

"No, I mean at work. Did you try there?"

"Several times. I tried his home too."

"That IS strange."

"I don't know whether to be angry or worried."

"Get some sleep, Carla. I'll see you at work tomorrow. If he's not there, we'll call Bu-Cops."

Carla hung up the telephone, watched disconsolately as the tele-cube flitted back to its place. She curled up on the couch, and presently great sobs came upon her, reverberating through her body.

"Damn him!" she cursed as her anger and suspicion took control. "I thought he would change…." At long last she fell into a troubled slumber, resolving never to speak with Birdbright again.

O O O

Twosayer William stood on the lowest step of the platform which supported Uncle Rosy's great chair, looking across the chamber at a full assemblage of hooded sayermen. They looked back in the low light with sorrowful eyes, their mouths partly open in shock and turned down at the corners. It was nearly time to retire for the night, but no one thought of sleep. Rumors of murder and intrigue had been in the air since mid-afternoon.

"The memory circuits of Uncle Rosy's tuxedo meckie have been checked," Twosayer said, raising his voice so that all could hear. "Onesayer died yesterday in an attempt to take our Master's life."

The sayermen gasped.

Twosayer continued: "This morning, for reasons unknown, Uncle Rosy instructed the meckie to take his own sacred life as well."

A whispering and moaning swept over the group. Some sayermen fell to their knees, crying and wailing. Twosayer heard their swellings of despondency: "It cannot be true!" they said. "What are we to do now?" "All is lost!"

"Peace be upon you, brothers!" Twosayer called out. "Calm yourselves!"

"Did you see the Master's body?' Threesayer asked from the front of the assemblage.

"I saw His Holiness," Twosayer replied sadly. "But his features had so aged I could not recognize him."

"We wish to see him," another sayerman called out, 'To pay our final respects."

"I thought it best to send him directly to Astro-Disposal," Twosayer said, narrowing his eyes and glancing around the chamber. "I expect he is being catapulted now."

"That is best," Foursayer said.

Then others agreed. "Yes," they said. "That is best."

"Our Master would not have wanted the sayermen to see him like that," Twosayer said. "Let us remember him as he was."

"Yes," most of the assemblage agreed. "Let us remember him as he was."

"After a suitable period," Twosayer said, pushing out his chest a bit in pride, "I shall assume the duties of Master."

"Do we have time to wait?" a sayerman asked, his voice reflecting panic, "with the garbage comet due to hit tomorrow?"

"There is no stopping it!" someone said. "A cappy has stolen the space cruiser … the comet follows each change in Earth's orbit!"

Twosayer did not reply, considered the crisis.

"Take the holy duty now," a sayerman in the back urged.

"We need you now!" another said. "The AmFed people need you now!"

A murmuring rolled across the chamber, and generally it was agreed that Twosayer should not delay in donning the Master's robes.

But then Lastsayer rolled to the front, holding a copy of the Sayer's Guide high over his head. "It is not so easy!" he announced, yelling to be heard over the multitude

"Who is that?" someone asked.

"What did he say?"

"Who is he?'

"It is Lastsayer Steven! He holds a Sayer's Guide!"

"What is it, Lastsayer?" Twosayer asked nervously.

Lastsayer opened the volume, auto-flipped to a page near the back and read aloud from an internally-illuminated page: "If the Beloved Master dies or falls so gravely ill that he cannot conduct the responsibilities of his holy chair, that person holding the position of Onesayer will assume the holy chair." Lastsayer looked up from the book and gazed around the room. "We have no Onesayer," he said somberly.

"I am the senior sayerman!" Twosayer exclaimed, wrinkling his hooked nose angrily. "I am first in line to assume the holy chair!"

"But it does not say so in the guide," Lastsayer said. "A strict interpretation ..."

"But surely we can discern Uncle Rosy's intent," Eightsayer said, rolling forward.

"Yes," agreed another.

Threesayer rolled to the front, short-stepped to the stair level on which Twosayer stood. He was taller than Twosayer, and Twosayer moved to the next higher step. "Our newest sayerman is correct," Threesayer said. "Who are we to speculate upon Uncle Rosy's intentions? He often skipped one sayerman over another. For all we know, he intended to advance any one of us to the position vacated by Onesayer Edward."

Now the assemblage swung another way. "That is right," they said. "Threesayer is right."

"Uncle Rosy always had a special liking for me," remarked one.

"I disagree. He favored me!"

"He called me exceptionally bright."

"I was skipped twice."

"Maybe *I* am the Chosen One."

"It could just as easily be *me*!"

Twosayer became increasingly angry as the sayermen continued to argue, and he pushed Threesayer off the step. "You and Lastsayer plotted this to take away what is rightfully mine!" Twosayer screamed.

Threesayer fell to one knee, then recovered his footing and shot back: "Not true!" Turning to the assemblage, he said in a loud, clear tone: "Uncle Rosy would never have made such a sayerman our Master! A sayerman does not push his brother!"

"That is right!" the assemblage called out. "That is right!"

A murmuring rolled across the group, and this gradually increased in intensity. The consensus was that Twosayer should not have done what he did.

After that, a wave of sentiment went in favor of Threesayer becoming the new Master. But this succumbed when Foursayer and Ninesayer rolled forward to cite a host of apparently logical reasons why Threesayer should not assume the chair.

So it went into the wee hours of the morning, with all the sayermen arguing heatedly over the matter. Everyone had a favorite, be it himself or another, and there was a good deal of shouting back and forth. Finally, they grew tired of battling, and the sayermen retired for the evening without having decided upon a leader. They would pray for divine intervention to stop the comet.

* *

In Ordinance Room Six, the youngsayermen were seated on the floor in a half circle around Sayer Superior Lin-Ti:

"What sort of force was the comet?" Lin-Ti asked. "Was it a godlike thing?"

"In a sense, yes," a youngsayerman to Lin-Ti's right said. "For all things contain an element of God. But it was not sent by God ... not directly, anyway. God gave all the life forces in the universe free will, and those from the Realm of Magic...."

"What do you mean by God?"

"It is a convenient term, Sayer Superior ... for the being which resides in the Realm of the Unknown."

"Think on this, youngsayers: ask yourselves if each layer of existence might not have another layer beyond it ... supervising ... or perhaps just watching ... the layer below. We know that there is a Realm of Inertia and Gas which is higher than the Realm of Flesh ... and beyond Inertia and Gas is the Realm of Magic."

"And beyond that ... the Realm of the Unknown!" a youngsayer said.

Lin-Ti lifted one hand, pointing his forefinger upward. "But what if this 'unknown' is really many realms ... a succession of realms going ever higher?"

The youngsayerman thought for a moment, then said: "And what if the realms are not hierarchical? What if they are all at the same level?"

Lin-Ti smiled as he watched the youngsayerman think.

Excitedly, the youngsayerman said: "What if we are at the same level with God?"

"You mean we are God?" Lin-Ti asked.

"Yes. And no. We are magical, too … all these things could be part of the truth … of one existence…."

"It is a circle, is it not?" Lin-Ti said. "We are what we are not … ever-changing but ever the same…."

# CHAPTER FIFTEEN

## SHARING FOR PROSPERITY, FOR FURTHER READING AND DISCUSSION

*Labor Intensity Code (LI Code): Established by the Council of Ten in 2518, in honor of the two-hundredth anniversary of Uncle Rosy's disappearance. The key tenet of the code held as follows: "If two people can perform a given task, that is better than one."*

### *Friday, September 1, 2605*

A digital reader on the *Shamrock Five* instrument panel indicated it was nearly four AM by New City time, and Sidney gave this a fleeting thought as he unclasped his hands.

*Prayer isn't working,* he thought. His eyes and bones ached. His brain was unsupportive. *How many times did I pray during the night? he* wondered, wearily. *I called out to God AND to Uncle Rosy....* For a moment, Sidney attempted a count, but quickly gave up the effort.

Sidney stretched and yawned as he stared across the dashboard at the Great Comet. It loomed so large now that he imagined reaching out of the cockpit to touch it. An immense sweeping fountain of luminous lavender and green dust flowed from the comet's flaming orange nucleus, forming a single tail. Only moments before, there had been six distinct yellow tails and an icy blue nucleus, but the comet had changed as it was wont to do.

Sidney smiled and spoke in a tone reserved for the endeared: "You're a vain one, aren't you? like a fine lady, you are ... changing outfits all the time...."

The comet veered off against the midnight blue starcloth of space, then returned to its original course. It drew closer, ever closer.

"You heard me, didn't you? We're friends now, Great Comet—but why don't you do as I ask?"

The comet was unresponsive, and Sidney thought, *Friends, hell. I love that mass of fire and gas … as much as … no, more than … I love Carla.*

Sidney turned his head to the right at a metallic clang, saw Madame Bernet stirring to life. The meckie rattled its knives against a wall as it struggled to get up, its eyes open wide and flashing crazily.

Sidney half surprised himself by remaining calm. *I had hoped the comet would get me instead,* he thought.

But now he entertained no thoughts of fleeing. Instead, he watched the killer meckie rise to its feet with its razor-sharp knives slashing at the air.

"Die, fleshcarrier!" the meckie screeched as it rolled toward him slowly, smiling evilly.

Sidney's brain went numb. *Fleshcarrier?* he thought. *Am I having another nightmare? Things are getting mixed up!*

The killer meckie continued to close in on him, repeating the epithet: "Die, fleshcarrier, die!"

Sidney's gaze fixed on the blades. He saw glimmering red and orange reflections from the comet on the shiny steel surfaces. *Any second now,* he thought. *The first cut …*

He closed his eyes and grimaced from the expected pain. But it did not arrive, and at the sound of gears grinding, Sidney opened his eyes slit-wide. The blades were poised there, only centimeters from his face!

Then the blades receded, and as Sidney opened his eyes all the way, he saw the meckie tip backward and fall to its back. Within seconds, the cockpit was silent, and all Sidney sensed was the pounding of his own pulse.

*"Was it luck again, fleshcarrier?"* a tenor voice in his brain asked.

*"Don't tease him anymore,"* the other, deeper voice said. *"We've had our fun."* The voice paused, then said: *"We activated the meckie, fleshcarrier … through magic."*

*"Just wanted to have a little fun with you,"* the tenor voice said. *"But you're a fuddy-duddy of the first order!"*

*"I have to agree,"* said the other. *"At the very least he could have tried to get away!"*

"I imagined the whole thing," Sidney said, staring at the comet. "The meckie, the comet, voices in my brain … this whole adventure." He smiled, threw both hands up in the air. "Actually, I'm in a Bu-Med psycho ward somewhere having part of my brain cut out."

A staccato peppering of laughter riddled his brain. *"Heh-heh-heh-heh-heh-*

*heh....*"

"Emergency!" the ship computer reported. "Ship's E-Cell charge almost consumed! Begin throwing loose articles into the emergency fuel hopper!"

Before Sidney could react, the speakercom blared: "We have you in sight, *Shamrock Five*! Heave-to and prepare for boarding!"

Sidney's heart jumped. In the video console he saw two long-range gunships approaching from the rear and closing fast.

*"Don't listen to them, fleshcarrier!"* the voices in Sidney's brain said. *"Try to get away! You must get away!"*

"More of your blasted party games?" Sidney asked.

There was no response.

"Heave-to, *Shamrock Five*!" the speakercom repeated.

"Aw, what the hell!" Sidney said. He tore a biomedical support pack off the wall and tossed it into the emergency fuel hopper. Flipping to manual mode, he grabbed the control stick. His palm was warm and moist against the cool tita-steel plated surface.

Now the Shamrock Five seemed only minutes from a collision with the comet. *I've got to get away from these guys,* Sidney thought. *Maybe I can still....* He grimaced.

"Okay, Captain Malloy," Sidney whispered. "Here we go!"

He hit the red super-accelerator toggle, watched his console as the gunships disappeared in the distance. *They'll punch-out too,* he thought, his gaze glued upon the screen. *And that was my last bit of energy.*

The two gunships were back now, and Sidney saw brilliant lances of weapons fire cutting toward him. "Damn!" he cursed. "Just give me a little more time!" He felt there was no use trying to escape, but leaned on the control stick anyway. The *Shamrock Five* responded quickly, darting ahead, still closer to the comet.

"Veer away!" Sidney yelled, glaring at the comet's flaming orange nucleus. "Veer away, damn you! Don't hit Earth!"

But the comet continued to bear down on him.

The console screen showed the gunships changing course, then went black. *What a time for my equipment to go gunnysack!* he thought. The screen flickered back on, and he saw lances of weapons fire again. The *Shamrock Five* cut to starboard.

When Sidney next looked in the console screen, he saw only one pursuer. The other gunship had either fallen back or was taking a different attack course. Sidney mentoed for another view, but the screen went dark again. He hit the butt of his hand against the set. The screen remained black.

"Charge zero," the computer reported.

A silent explosion tore through the cockpit, throwing glass-plex and plastic in every direction. Sidney felt the screaming pain of torn flesh and broken bones. *My right leg!* He thought. *So hot! It's burning!*

"Emergency!... Emergency!..." the computer blared.

Sidney felt faint, then something cool bathed his leg. He looked down to see it immersed in blue foam. None of the instruments were working now. The ship was not moving.

He took a deep breath, waited for the next hit. *Either that or the comet,* he thought. *It's almost over now.*

But as Sidney looked in his console, he saw the pursuing gunships veer off and speed away in the other direction. They became pinpricks, then disappeared.

Sidney bit his lower lip hard, braced for more pain. *I'm ready,* he thought. *Ready to die.* This was the way Captain Malloy would have gone ... risking his life for mankind.

A tear ran down his cheek. More followed. *Who will know?* he thought. *No parade, no words spoken in praise ... no thought whatsoever of Sidney Malloy.*

"It doesn't matter!" he yelled. "It doesn't matter!" But then he grimaced and thought: *It matters. I can't lie to myself.*

The Great Comet was icy blue and flaming red now, from its head to its misty toe. Eccentrically placed within the burning nucleus, Sidney saw the first appearance of a miniature comet having a head and tail of its own. This tiny comet flared white hot and expanded quickly until it consumed the entire mother comet, then faded into a nebulous haze and disappeared into the womb of the mother. Sidney thought of the comet's complexity, wished that he could become a part of it, to roam forever through the heavens.

*Oh, what an exalted existence that would be!*

As Sidney thought this, the comet flared white hot again, but this time the tail was pulled into the nucleus and the comet appeared as a star. Although it was exceedingly bright, Sidney did not shield his eyes. This comet was not garbage to him ... it was the most beautiful primordial state in the universe, a delicate but powerful combination of all elements.

*"That trash IS rather pretty now, isn't it?"* one of the voices said.

*"This fleshcarrier appreciates beauty, I'll say that for him,"* remarked

another.

*"Rather an appealing fellow, but slothlike...."*

"Turn the comet away!" Sidney screamed. "Turn it away!"

*"We won't,"* a tenor voice said. *"But you can."*

*"Flesh be gone!"* a deep voice exclaimed.

Now the comet was a glowing, jagged ball of red fire, growing larger as it bore down on Sidney's motionless ship. He felt it reaching across the icy darkness to him with an awesome, unstoppable power. For the first time in his life, Sidney felt very special. He shivered, then felt wonderfully warm and calm as the Great Comet consumed him in a cosmic whirlwind. As this happened, Sidney had a vision of a magical land in which suffering and pain were nonexistent.

*"An idealist,"* the tenor voice said, scornfully.

*"He'll learn,"* said the other. *"Give him time."*

*"Had a lot of fun with this one, didn't we?"* the tenor voice said.

*"Oh my, yes! Maybe we should keep the fleshcarriers around for a while. There seems no end to their foolish predicaments!"*

*I'll give the fleshcarriers your message,* Sidney thought. *You can trust me....*

The jagged fireball turned to gold, and a hundred violet plumes surged across the heavens to form a new tail. Men on the deep space observation station Drakus Ohm reported that the comet hung in the sky for several seconds like a giant scimitar. Then it began to move, slowly at first, like a pony trying out its legs for the first time. Soon the comet was frisky and lively, streaking one way and then the other across the great expanse of space.

O O O

Carla opened one eye, peered drowsily across the top of a tiny package wrapped in silver paper which sat on her coffee table. She was in the living room module of her condominium, and as she rose to rest on one elbow, a shooting pain from having slept on the couch all night shot through her lower back. Golden streaks of artificial dawn light washed across the room from a sun-lite panel along one wall, glinting off the shiny wrapping paper of the package.

*Friday morning,* she thought. *I should call Samantha.*

She shook her head briskly, swung both stockinged feet onto the carpet and stared at the neatly wrapped parcel. Leaning forward, she looked down to examine a tiny white scroll card which read, "For

Carla." That was all it said.

"From Billie," she murmured angrily, grasping the parcel and lifting it to hurl it across the room. "If he thinks he can sweeten me …"

But something told her it was not from Billie, and she lowered her arm to hold the object in one open palm. Then Carla rolled it over and over, searching for a place to tear away the wrapping. But there was no edge to the paper, making it appear that it had been molded onto a box beneath.

Perplexed, the set the package back on the coffee table. As Carla pulled her hand away, the paper folded open along invisible seams, revealing a black velvet box. A hinged lid swung open automatically, and Carla's astonished eyes beheld a star-shaped mother of pearl and burnished gold brooch inside.

"Oh!" she squealed, reached for the treasure. "It's beauti …"

She caught herself, withdrew the hand. But she reached back quickly and lifted out the brooch. Seeing a hinge along one edge, she used her fingernail to open the brooch along the opposite side. Inside, a shimmering black surface filled the right side of the brooch as it lay open. On the left interior surface, a scroll inscription read: "Dearest Carla—This star will keep you safe."

Carla flipped the brooch over several times, tried to find something more, a clue as to who might have given it to her. She examined the velvet box and the paper wrapping as well, but there was nothing whatsoever to indicate its source. She held the brooch open in both palms, stared into the black glass star inside.

Presently, Carla saw tiny twinkling silver stars in the blackness, as if she was looking into a window upon the universe. Away off in the distance, she saw a bright star approaching rapidly, blocking out the blackness around as it grew in size. Soon the star became too bright to behold, and Carla dropped the brooch to shield her eyes.

When she peeked through her fingers to look at the brooch where it rested open upon the carpet, she saw the brightness fade away to a white mist. Then the mist cleared and the saw an image taking form. It showed a man and a woman asleep on their sides in a round bed.

*Why,* Carla thought. *It's Samantha Petrie.... Who's she with?...* The man had covers over all but his forehead and hair. He stirred and rolled to his back, causing the covers to slip a little.

Carla recoiled in shock. *My Rosenbloom!* she thought. *Its Billie!* She reached down to pick up the brooch, watched Birdbright shift again, throwing one arm over Petrie's shoulder.

Tears streamed down Carla's cheeks and fell on the brooch, giving the image in the black glass a distorted appearance. She wiped her face with the back of one hand, snapped the brooch shut angrily.

*I knew he was this way,* she thought, forcing the tears to stop. *I shouldn't take it so hard. But I had so hoped …*

The tears came anew now, and much harder than before. She sobbed and fell back on the couch in a fetal position with the brooch clutched tightly between her hands.

* *

"I do not understand something," a youngsayerman in the first row said.

Lin-Ti gazed down at him from the podium. It was the youngsayerman with the long body and fat features … the one who looked so much like Onesayer Edward.

"How did the history writers obtain details on the lives of the sayermen and of Sidney Malloy?" the youngsayerman asked. "The sayers never touch identity plates … and Malloy did not come in contact with one after losing his position in Central Forms."

Lin-Ti smiled. "As we so often discover," he said, "the words of Uncle Rosy hold true today, as they did centuries ago: 'Much remains for you to learn, youngsayer. Much remains for you to learn….'"

# Chapter Sixteen

## UP CLOSE WITH THE MASTER, FOR FURTHER READING AND DISCUSSION

*"The facts with which we operate are not all the facts, but are merely all the facts available to us at a particular time."*

Spoken by Uncle Rosy
(excerpt from E. Dade's unpublished notes)

### *Friday, September 1, 2695*

President Ogg used an automatic thumb to flip through a pile of papers on his desk, pausing to scan a bureau employment summary sheet. The report pleased him. Ogg glanced at his wrist digital and mentoed the desk intercom to call for his first afternoon coffee.

In the outer office, Carla Weaver looked up from her rota-typer screen to watch a pamphlet meckie roll toward her with its purple "TAKE SEVERAL" signs flashing. She thought of the brooch she had found on her coffee table that morning, smiled. *Someone really cares about me,* she thought, still feeling the effects of a Happy Pill she had taken half an hour earlier. *Wonder who it is.* Assuming the powers of the brooch to be technological in nature, she surmised that her benefactor might work in Bu-Tech.

"Hi, Wordie," Carla said cheerily as the pamphlet meckie arrived and waited patiently. She short-stepped down from the rotatyper platform, took five pamphlets and placed them in her purse.

"Ringgg!" A bell sounded across the office. It was time for the first afternoon coffee break.

Billie Birdbright rolled by in a big hurry, dodging the workers who had begun to fill the aisles. "Excuse me! Excuse me, please!"

Birdbright said nervously as he pushed his way through. He caught Carla's pill-glossed gaze for a moment. She watched him disappear into the President's office.

"Mr. President!" Birdbright exclaimed breathlessly as he rolled into the oval office. "Have you seen?"

President Ogg looked up calmly and replied, "This is my coffee break, Billie. Can't it wait?"

"No, Mr. President! Look out your window!" Birdbright pointed.

Ogg spun his chair, saw a distant streaking emerald-green-and-red comet moving across the southeastern horizon. His jaw dropped. "Is that IT? I thought Drakus Ohm reported it was going off in another direction!"

"It changed, Mr. President … and came out of nowhere!"

Ogg moto-paced around his desk, then stopped and shot a terse command to his Chief of Staff: "Get me a trajectory report on it!"

"Just got it minutes ago, sir. Bu-Tech says the comet came in on us fast, then veered off. It's in a holding pattern now."

"A holding pattern? How can a comet be in a holding pattern?"

"That's what the report said, sir."

Ogg glared at the comet, saw it flash brilliantly, followed by a wisp of white light. Birdbright moved to the President's side, and together they watched in astonishment as the comet began a most unusual series of maneuvers. It moved up and around, then back down and in zig-zags, trailing white smoke as it went.

"It's writing something, Mister President!" Birdbright said.

Ogg did not reply, leaned close to the window to peer at the horizon. "WE … ARE … NOT …" he said, reading the skywriting, "… YOUR … GARBAGE … DUMP!" A muscle on the President's cheek twitched.

Birdbright furrowed his brow. "What the hell does that mean, Mr. President?"

"How the hell do I know?" Ogg thought for a moment, then said, "Tell Bu-Tech to lay out a thick blanket of clouds until we can find out what's going on. We can't have consumers getting upset!"

"Yes, Mr. President," Birdbright said, rolling quickly to the door.

Euripides Ogg shook his head sadly, muttered: "And I told everyone there was nothing to worry about."

"What was that, sir?" Birdbright asked, pausing at the door.

"Nothing, Billie," Ogg said, glaring at his Chief of Staff. "Now get it in gear, man! Get it in gear!"

Birdbright scurried out of the office.

President Ogg watched Birdbright go, then fixed his gaze on the "Faith, Consumption, Freeness" sign over the door. *I have a feeling things aren't going to be the same around here after this,* he thought.

**The End**

# The Garbage Chronicles

# Introduction

During most of the previous decade, Winston Abercrombie was Garbage Thrust Commandant for the American Federation of Freeness. It was a crowded world, with no room for graveyards or garbage dumps, so the AmFeds used electromagnetic catapults to hurl bodies and trash into deep space. But Abercrombie did not follow the prescribed program.

He catapulted hundreds of thousands of full garbage canisters to the remote planet of Guna One, secretly intending to retrieve them for the creation of a massive and illegal recycling industry. This glut of merchandise would have destroyed the new-product-based AmFed economy, setting Uncle Rosy's Thousand Year Plan on its ear. Fortunately, Abercrombie's diabolical plan was discovered in time by the Black Box of Democracy, Uncle Rosy's watchdog agency. Abercrombie fled before apprehension, presumably to Guna One.

Captain Tom Javik has been assigned to scout Guna One and report on any unusual activities there, bringing back Abercrombie if he can be found. Javik would prefer another assignment—investigating a mysterious, comet-like body which has been skywriting over New City for the past eight months. But Javik is in no position to argue.

Just before leaving on his mission, Javik is joined by a miniature talking comet who calls himself Wizzy. Wizzy claims to have magical powers, and indicates that he is the offspring of the skywriter.

As Javik's ship hurtles across space at hyper-light speed, he finds himself attracted to a female member of his crew, the transsexual, Marta Evans. Repulsed at the thought of such a tryst, Javik gulps a sexual sublimation pill. But Evans pursues him aggressively. Her principal weapon of seduction is a mento-activated brassiere, a device she can snap open by sending a thought command from her brain-implanted mento8 transmitter to a sensor in the bra.

Poor Javik. Even with all of his pills, he is no match for this....

# Chapter One

*My observation is that there are two sorts of comets: one wandering, the other magical. None of the accepted scientific premises can be applied with respect to the behavior or physical makeup of a magical comet. Let those little minds obsessed with rules and categories stew over this one!*

Scrawled note found on Uncle Rosy's bedstand after his death

On the afternoon before the birth of the new magical comet, Tom Javik was escorted down a brightly painted sixth-floor corridor in Building B of the Bu-Tech Space Center. All the latest promotional colors were represented here in bright geometric shapes on the walls, ceilings, doors, and floor. The corridor was awhir with moto-shoes, as silver-uniformed government workers bustled to and fro.

"This has been redecorated since I was here last year," Javik said, smelling fresh paint. He glanced down at the oriental man rolling at his side. The small man wore silver-colored nylon pants and a matching top, with canary yellow stripes down his sleeves and legs. An octagonal blue lapel tag indicated rank: "GW 1000." This meant he held one one-thousandth of a job. He rustled as he moved.

"Haven't you heard?" the GW said, not looking at Javik. "Bu-Free came in this week and redid the whole wing."

"Bu-Free? What the hell are Freeness people doing in Bu-Tech? Are they setting up a giveaway?"

"Who knows? Here's your briefing room." He stopped at a purple and gold door and mentoed it, sending a thought command from his brain-implanted transmitter to a receiving unit in the door. The door slid open without having been touched.

As Javik rolled into the room, he was forced to narrow his eyes in sunlight which slanted across the floor. "Say," he said, "this looks like the same briefing …" Javik fell silent when he noticed the GW guide was leaving. The door slid shut behind the guide.

Javik was certain it was the same briefing room he had been in the year before. But it had been painted more brightly, with colorful geometric shapes like those in the corridor. And the galactic model was gone, having been replaced by a floor-to-ceiling CRT screen. The screen was dark, save for the words "Faith, Consumption, Freeness," in white letters at the center.

*Wonder what they've got in mind for me this time?* Javik thought, noticing a GW standing by the wall to his left.

The GW rolled forward to greet Javik; he was so similar in appearance to the guide that he might have been his clone. "Good afternoon, Captain," he said crisply. "I am Leonard Nakato." He touched hands limply with Javik in a Bu-Health-approved method of handshake. As much as practical, the expenditure of calories was to be confined to Bu-Health gyms. It was another Job-Support policy, based upon the centuries-old teachings of Uncle Rosy, founder of the American Federation of Freeness.

Javik returned the salutation. Then: "I was told to report for a presidential assignment. Is this the right room?"

"Yes," Nakato said, revealing a slight oriental accent. "Come with me, please." He pulled Javik's white-uniformed arm gently, then released it when the men began to roll side by side toward the CRT screen.

When they stopped in front of the screen, Javik saw his own reflection in the dark glassplex: tall, muscular, and in his late thirties, with gold captain's epaulets on the shoulders of his Space Patrol uniform. "Is the president going to speak with me by video hookup?" he asked.

Nakato mentoed the screen, causing the words "Faith, Consumption, Freeness" to fade. A large roulette wheel appeared on the screen, surrounded by what looked like green felt.

Deciding that this was the aerial view of a gaming table, Javik felt his lips mouth the word "What?" without making a sound.

"Mento the wheel," Nakato said. The window shade on Javik's left snapped down, making the screen image clearer.

"I'm not here to play games," Javik said. "Who's going to brief me?"

Nakato nodded at the CRT screen. "This is an assignment wheel," he said.

*"What?"*

"Bu-Free's idea. Some of their people were looking for things to do, so they got permission to set this thing up. You are to mento-spin it. The wheel will stop at the number indicating your assignment."

"I should be talking with a general," Javik said, "or at least a presidential aide." He turned to leave. "I must have the wrong briefing room."

Nakato checked a small clip pad that had been in his tunic pocket. "You *are* Captain Thomas P. Javik?" he asked.

"I am."

"Then this is the right place. You are to mento the wheel."

Javik turned slowly to face the screen. He closed his eyes and rubbed the fingers and thumb of one hand across his cheekbones.

"Captain Javik?" The voice was impatient.

Javik opened his eyes and mentoed the wheel. He felt a click in the back of his brain as his thought command was accepted by the CRT roulette wheel.

The wheel spun in a silent blur.

"Round and round she goes," Nakato said, "and where she stops …"

The wheel slowed, then stopped. A red pointer was over the number fifteen.

Nakato mentoed a pen to make an entry on his clip pad. The clear plastic pen floated out of his tunic pocket and moved across the paper without being touched. Then the pen floated back into the pocket.

The wheel faded, being replaced by white letters and numbers against a carmine red background:

**ASSIGNMENT 15**
**GUNA ONE**

"This is a search and scout expedition to Guna One," a pleasant woman's voice said, "largest planet in the Aluminum Starfield. It was the landing region used by the arch recycling criminal, Winston Abercrombie. When he was Garbage Thrust Commandant for the Federation in the nineties, Abercrombie catapulted hundreds of thousands of full garbage canisters to the region, intending to retrieve them for his own diabolical scheme. If successful, he would have undermined the AmFed economy with a glut of recycled goods, thus putting millions of manufacturing people out of work."

"Public enemy number one," Nakato said. "He's never been apprehended."

"Abercrombie may be on Guna One," the woman's voice said. "No one is certain. Your assignment is twofold: First, see if there is any unusual activity in the region. Second, locate Abercrombie and bring him back for trial. More details are provided in a briefing tape on board your ship."

The screen darkened. Then the original white-lettered message reappeared. The window shade snapped open, filling the room with sunlight.

"I'd rather go to the Columbarian Quadrant," Javik said. "That's where the garbage comet originated."

"The what?"

"The garbage comet." Javik's voice reflected irritation. "It's been writing the same sky message for more than eight months: 'We are not your garbage dump!'"

"Oh?" Nakato looked up at Javik with a blank expression.

"It's only the biggest cosmic mystery ever," Javik said. "And you don't know anything about it?"

Nakato shook his head.

"Look, I deserve the Columbarian assignment … if there is one. I was the one sent to stop the comet last year, you know. I feel … well … responsible for it being here."

Nakato was unresponsive.

"Maybe I could find out what caused it," Javik said. "I hear a hundred missiles have been fired at the thing, from behind Bu-Tech-made clouds. But the comet's too quick. Hell, it has the capability of moving five, maybe six times the speed of light!"

"Your assignment cannot be changed," Nakato said. He slipped the tiny clip pad back into his pocket.

"*Is* anyone going to the Columbarian Quadrant?" Javik asked.

"I don't know."

"What *do* you know?" Javik asked. His deeply set blue eyes flashed angrily.

"You leave tomorrow," Nakato said, unruffled. "Report to Robespierre at nine AM. Field sixteen."

Javik seethed, but he held his tongue. He recalled the many quarrels in his career and all the hot water into which they had gotten him. He was on the comeback trail now, fortunate to hold the rank of captain. The fights flashed across Javik's brain in a blur of fists and faces.

"I'll be there," he said.

O O O

At shortly past midnight, two magical comets hung in the ionosphere over New City, trailing delicate jet-ray tails of light across the deep blue starcloth of space. These were especially fiery comets, one large and brilliant blue, the other much smaller and cosmic pink. As the larger magical comet watched proudly, a tiny white nucleus with no visible tail emerged from the pink nucleus of its mother. The baby comet gasped for air and cried.

Anxious glances were exchanged between mother and father.

Reluctantly, the mother passed her newborn child to its father. Now the tiny white nucleus burned next to the father's brilliant blue fireball.

Words drifted across rarefied air as the cosmic pink comet spoke. "I wish he didn't have to go so young," she said.

"You know it's necessary," said the blue, his tone deep and mellifluous. "We've discussed it thoroughly."

"*We've* discussed nothing! You did all the talking—and the deciding!"

"Now, dear …"

"Don't you 'now dear' me!" the cosmic pink comet snapped, flaring an angry, hot shade. "I should have as much to say in this matter as you!"

The blue comet began to flash electrically. "There are laws," he said, his voice reaching a crescendo. *"Now go, woman! We will speak of this later!"*

Dutifully, the smaller comet bowed her nucleus. "Yes, Sidney," she said, trying very hard not to show the sarcasm which often irritated him. Demurely, she turned ninety degrees and sped off into deep space, trailing six magnificent plumes of cosmic pink gas.

*I've never seen her more lovely,* Sidney thought.

O O O

Any Earth inhabitant watching the sky at that hour would have seen a great blue comet dropping toward Earth, with a tiny white flame burning next to its nucleus. And had this observer been outside, oddly enough he would have felt cool. For the Great Comet was an electric fireball now, so cold that it left a layer of frost on the building tops below.

"Papa!" the baby comet cried out. "Papa Sidney!"

Sidney spoke tenderly to his child: "You are a new life force, son, with emotions much like those of a fleshcarrier. Physically, however, you resemble no other creature in the universe."

The baby comet cried softly.

"For the present, you have lungs, a heart, and other organs. Gradually, however, these will evolve into higher states. The emotions are different: They will stay with you always. There will be problems, but you will grow much wiser in only a few days."

"What are emotions, Papa?"

The Great Comet stopped its descent now, dimming and hovering a few kilometers above the surface. Below, New City twinkled like a distorted reflection of the universe.

"They are strong feelings, son, which will cause you to behave in certain ways. You must learn to control your emotions, but do not become callous in the process. Retain some vulnerability. This is perhaps the most important part of being alive."

"I do not understand."

"You will have to discover such things for yourself. Find the fleshcarrier Tom Javik. He will help you. And you will help him." The Great Comet glowed orange now, imparting warmth to the baby.

"I don't want to go, Papa! I'd rather stay with you, roaming the universe!" The little comet felt himself shaking all over. Mercuric perspiration ran down the sides of his molten rock body. He felt weak. "I have so many questions to ask you! Where did you and Mama meet?"

"On a singles flight to the Jahuvian mountain planets—one of the most romantic places in the universe."

"And she ensnared you?"

"I was a willing captive. There's one more thing you should know: Avoid water on your outside surface. Too much of it neutralizes your magical powers."

A great gust of wind blew all the mercuric perspiration from the little comet's body. Then the caressing warmth of his papa soothed him. The little comet wished he could stay in this place forever. It was so secure, so peaceful. He narrowly opened the yellow cat's eye on top of his body, trying to see his papa. But he saw only a warm orange glow.

"I will not dry you again," the deep, mellifluous voice said. "Go forth now, and do what is meant for you."

An irregularly shaped piece of molten material fell from the Great Comet's nucleus. It tumbled toward Earth.

"Don't leave me here, Papa!" the little comet cried out.

"Remember my words, son!"

"But Papa!"

"Become a Great Comet yourself! Make all creatures love and fear you! Place them in awe!"

The magical comet Sidney pulled away now, rising quickly toward the heavens. Soon he was out of Earth's atmosphere and traveling away at many times the speed of light. He became a speck in the distance, blending with the background of space.

The dense chunk of material comprising the little comet's body glowed bright red as it spiraled swiftly toward New City. Then it dimmed to a flicker and hardened, floating down on a cushion of magical air. With a dull thud, the piece fell to the skatewalk just outside the entrance to Javik's condominium building.

O O O

Tom Javik padded out of the bathroom module in his robe and slippers, crossing his unit to the kitchen module. He wore unmotorized slippers, the illegal type frowned upon by Bu-Health. The kitchen module was small, with black and gold foil-fleck walls, a mirrored floor, and a black plastic table by the window. A conveyor counter still had the dirty plastic dishes from dinner on it. Javik mentoed the conveyor, causing it to squeak noisily as it carried the dishes into a disposa-tube on one end. Machinery inside the wall whirred.

As he paused to examine an electronic letter on the table, the faint notes of a rock waltz reminded Javik of an old tune he and Sidney Malloy knew. For a moment, he thought of the way sounds and smells could bring back old memories.

The stereo system fell silent at his mento command. He looked out the window. From the 261st floor Javik could see the sparkling lights of downtown New City on the other side of the lake. Somewhere beyond the opposite shore in that cluster of government office buildings was the White House office tower.

*Sid used to work there,* Javik thought.

He looked down at the text of the blue-bordered letter with unfocused, bleary eyes. He closed his eyes and rubbed them, then looked back at the letter:

> RE: MALLOY, SIDNEY
> YOUR INQUIRY OF 18 OCTOBER, 2605
> REGRET TO INFORM THAT MALLOY HAS NOT BEEN SEEN SINCE 30 AUGUST LAST YEAR. IS PRESUMED LOST IN DEEP SPACE. KNOWN TO HAVE COMMANDEERED THE SHAMROCK V.

*Eight months ago!* Javik thought, staring at the cottage-cheese-sprayed ceiling. He let out a deep, exasperated breath. *Sid's gone for good.*

Javik pictured his sleek black and silver space cruiser, smiling softly as he thought of Sidney at the controls. *Didn't realize Sid had it in him,* he thought.

An overwhelming sensation of guilt hit Javik. He dropped his head and stared down along the blue and white striped front of his robe. "Poor little fellow," he whispered. A haunting, recurring feeling hit Javik that it was his fault for not reaching the cruiser in time to accompany Sidney.

*If only I'd made it,* he thought. *But Sid died well. That's some consolation.*

Javik shook his head, still staring down. *Nine hours to blastoff,* he thought, reading the illuminated green face of his wrist digital. *I should try to sleep.*

He pulled at the little pouch of fat under his chin, then leaned on the table and stretched his long frame. His muscles ached. In the window reflection he saw that his hair was tousled. He knew it was overdue for a trim and would be much worse after the mission.

"Wonder how much extra weight's in my hair," he mused.

Javik straightened and thrust both hands in his robe pockets. Staring at the floor all the while, he shuffled his way to the videodome in the living-room module.

The dome was orbit orange plastic, with a sliding black door that opened at his mento-command. He slid into one of two soft bucket seats inside, mento-flipping on the set.

The screen lit up all around, giving Javik the illusion that he was seated in a racing car barreling down a straightaway.

*Too hectic,* he thought, changing the channel.

Javik finally settled on *The Yippee Hour*, a rockem-sockem game show. Javik became a member of the studio audience now, seated between two immense fat ladies.

Contestants came and went with astonishing speed, all departing with their arms full of bright, shiny consumer products. One man with a stick-on blond mustache became so ecstatic at his winnings that he knocked his mustache off his lip. Undaunted, he left it on the floor.

A volley of commercials accompanied each new contestant. Javik dozed off and blinked awake several times. Once, with heavy-lidded eyes, he watched seven chubby men in pineapple suits do a modern dance step while singing the virtues of Piney Pops fruit tarts.

"Cute little fellows," Javik muttered. "Cute little fellows." he dozed off again.

O O O

On the skatewalk outside, the little comet righted himself and used the yellow cat's eye on top of his body to look around. "Gracious!" he said, in a squeaky voice. "Now let me get my bearings." He felt an unidentifiable emotional rush which made him shake.

It was shadowy on the skatewalk, illuminated faintly by a street lamp. A midnight moto-shoer whisked by, oblivious to the little coal-shaped visitor who lay below.

The comet flickered, then whirled around in several complete circles. When the moto-shoer had disappeared into the dark distance, the comet brightened, flickering bright red for a moment to call upon his imprinted data banks.

"There!" he exclaimed, pulsating light as he focused his cat's eye on the synthetic marble face of Javik's building. He scooted partway up the building's entrance ramp, traveling only a hair's breadth above the surface. An undersized, barely discernible red tail flashed like sputtering rocket exhaust from his rear end.

Being young and undeveloped, the little comet had to stop only halfway up the ramp, panting heavily. "Uh oh!" he squealed, out of breath. He tumbled down the ramp, arriving in roughly the same spot from which he had begun.

After several deep breaths, the neophyte comet was ready to try again. "Up we go!" he said, taking a deep breath. "Up we go!" He scooted up the ramp, and this time nearly reached the top. But once again he tumbled back to the skatewalk, where he lay for several minutes, wheezing and coughing.

"Oh dear! Oh my! What a terrible thing!" The little comet was quite upset. "Papa Sidney flies across the heavens, but I'm stymied at the tiniest slope."

A brilliant blue light flashed overhead. The little comet focused his gaze upward and saw his papa streak by, alternating his mighty nucleus between blue and white. The Great Comet made a graceful turn, then zipped away, disappearing beyond the building tops. The buildings were silhouetted for a moment in the waning light of the comet. Then it became dark again.

*He really is leaving me here,* the little comet thought. *All alone.*

On the next try, he struggled to the top of the ramp. Then he scooted along a slick marbleite surface to double sliding doors. Through the glassplex of the doors a faintly illuminated lobby could be seen. The lobby had a red plastic and chrome couch, with a matching side chair and table. Pictures of flesh-carriers and government buildings were arranged on two walls.

The entrance doors were electric-eye-activated, and this presented no small problem for the comet. He saw how to activate the system, but noted to his chagrin that the seeing eyes were a full meter and a half above him. So he hopped as high as he could. That was all he could think to do. He jumped perhaps half a meter on the first try and three-quarters of a meter by the fourth attempt. After that, however, the height of each effort decreased. He grew very weary.

The little lump of stone took a deep breath and spun around several times. "So weak," he said sadly. "So weak." He looked up at the night sky, still half expecting assistance to arrive from that direction. But all he saw over the building tops was a twinkling, unconcerned night blanket, dotted with silvery stars.

Without warning, a moto-shoer bore down on him from less than a meter away. A skate wheel hit rudely, knocking him through the building entrance just as the electric eye doors swished open.

"Son of a slut!" the fleshcarrier man who was moto-shoeing said, falling to one knee. "What the Hooverville was that?"

The comet scurried behind a planter, then peeked around to watch as an angry, wavy-haired man searched the entrance area. Finding nothing, the man soon abandoned his effort.

As the moto-shoer rolled to the elevator bank, the comet flew along behind, ever so silently. Presently the man and his stealthy pursuer boarded an elevator.

*Two-sixty-one,* the comet mentoed as the doors closed, using a knowledge of elevators imparted to him magically by his fireball father. Feeling no click in his brain, the comet quickly realized why. *I have no mento transmitter!* he thought. *Papa Sidney had one when he was human.*

The elevator rose swiftly.

*Only fourteen minutes, thirty-one seconds old,* the comet thought. *And already I'm facing another crisis!*

The comet was very upset at this latest development. He had no idea which floor the man had selected. Faint, incomplete thoughts touched the comet's consciousness. Something about a new autocar, cheerful thoughts.

*What is this?* the comet thought. Then he realized with a rush of excitement that the thoughts were not his own. They came from the fleshcarrier standing next to him! The comet's pulse quickened.

*What floor did you order?* the comet wondered. *What floor?*

But this thought was nowhere in the man's mind now. Other thoughts became more clear, however. All concerned new consumer goods purchases the man and his permie were contemplating.

Time was running out quickly. The elevator rose rapidly through the building's core, completely oblivious to the pressing concern of the little visitor from another realm.

*Ah, here we are,* the man thought, transmitting brain waves to the comet. *Floor two-sixty-one*

The elevator doors whooshed open.

*Now what am I doing here? the* man wondered. He mentoed the correct floor into the elevator's computer, unaware of the little magical comet at his shoe tops who was scooting out at floor 261.

*That was a stroke of luck,* the comet thought as the doors shut behind him.

It may very well have been more than that, although no concrete evidence has been found to support such an assertion. This was a building of 450 floors. Even the most foolhardy gamesman would not have bet upon such an occurrence.

Still, it happened.

The little comet scooted along a beige-walled corridor decorated with pictures of fleshcarriers and government buildings. He rounded a corner. Through a large window at the end of the hallway he saw something bright and pink flash in the sky over the city. Whatever it was disappeared in the blink of a cat's eye.

The little comet found himself at Javik's synthetic walnut door. *Maybe I can squeeze under,* he thought, seeing a slender band of light beneath the door.

In an attempt to get through the crack, he reached about halfway. But he was irregularly shaped, like a lump of coal, with a big bump on his back that held his eye. The bump would not pass through.

*Darn,* he thought, wishing he could think of a stronger word. He flipped over and over, trying different angles of entry. Then he looked for wide spots under the door. He squeezed and squeezed and squeezed some more. But he could not get through.

*"Dad blast it!"* he said, feeling better about this selection of words. He began to glow bright orange. Then he whirled and hopped about angrily, throwing a first-rate tantrum. At the height of his rage, he smashed headlong into Javik's door. Then he hit it again. And again.

*Crash! Thud! Kaboom!*

This caused a good deal of racket in the hallway, despite the comet's very small size.

A brunette woman in the unit next door opened her door to peer out. "What's going on?" she asked. She cinched the belt of her bathrobe and ventured into the hall on moto-slippers.

*Crash! Kathump! Thud!* The little comet continued to pummel Javik's door.

The woman jumped back, startled. The comet was flashing a brilliant rainbow array of colors.

"What's this?" the woman asked. She ventured closer. Then a little closer. All the while, the angry comet continued his onslaught against the door, falling back intermittently for wild, whirling spins.

Now the woman was only a few centimeters from the curious little creature. With a tentative smile, she reached down, saying, "A toy?"

The comet smashed into her shinbone.

"Ow!" the woman yelled. "Ow! Ow!... Harold!" She hobbled and rolled back to her condominium, squealing in pain and calling for her permie.

Javik's door opened. A sleepy, robed Tom Javik stood with one unmotorized slipper off, looking down at the whirling little fireball.

Before Javik could react, the comet darted through his legs and into the condominium.

"Hey!" Javik yelled.

Turning his head, he saw an orange light flash through his arch-ceilinged entry hall. The intruder disappeared into Javik's living-room module.

Fully awake now, Javik mento-slammed the door and ran for his bedroom module. "Service pistol," he mumbled.

Seconds later; holding his automatic pistol, Javik tiptoed into the living-room module. This room had champagne-colored carpeting, with specks of orbit orange in it, matching the orange of the centrally positioned videodome. The walls matched the floor, and this often made Javik lose his sense of perspective. He looked under two padded chairs and the couch. Then he tiptoed toward the videodome, feeling deep pile carpeting with his bare foot.

"I am not a threat to you," a tiny voice said.

Javik whirled in the direction of the sound. He saw what looked like a lumpy, dark blue stone hovering in the arched doorway. The stone's surface was rough and irregular, with the exception of a clear agate dome crystal that jutted out of its top. Javik heard buzzing and saw a faint, exhaust-like glimmer of blue light on the other side of the stone.

"My name is Wizzy," the stone said. "I came up with that name just now, sensing your fleshcarrier need for such a reference."

Javik glowered.

"Papa sent me to see you. I'd rather be somewhere else, though."

"Papa?"

"Papa Sidney. He says you and I should help one another.... Oops!" Wizzy fell to the carpet with a dull thump. Then he glowed red and let fly a barrage of curses that would have made any nonsynthetic flower wilt. The expletives made him feel better.

"Where'd you learn to swear like that?" Javik asked. "That was good. Damned good."

"The words just came to me. Like an inspiration."

Javik smiled. "A real religious experience, eh?"

"My data banks use a rare red star crystal … embedded in my nucleus … to absorb energy waves from every source." Wizzy continued to glow dimly red. "I am receiving your data at this moment. You are an expert in foul language, I presume?"

"Kind of. Yeah, I guess I am."

"Perhaps you would prefer that I leave?" Wizzy changed to dark blue and scooted a meter down the hallway toward the front door.

"Hold on a sec," Javik said. "What the Hooverville is going on?" He pointed his pistol down at Wizzy.

Wizzy settled to the floor, where he rocked back and forth. "Guess I need more strength to hover like that," he said. "I'm just a baby, you know."

"No, I don't know! Is this a gag?" Javik looked around warily, sighting around his apartment along the barrel of his gun.

Wizzy laughed nervously. For the first time, Javik noticed a dimly glowing yellow cat's eye in the agate dome on Wizzy's topside. There seemed to be no mouth on the device. "This is difficult for me," Wizzy said. "I have not yet acquired social graces."

"I'll say! Barging in like that!"

"You're supposed to instruct me, I believe."

"In social graces? *Me? Ha!* What a laugh. You and I should go to the same school, pal."

"Uh, I think Papa also wants you to explain my emotions to me. He says they are very important."

Javik continued to glance around warily. "I don't like this," he said. "Smells like a Colonel Peebles trick … but he's dead."

"You want me to leave, then?" The little comet moved farther down the hallway. "I shouldn't bother you."

"Hold on," Javik said. He walked past Wizzy and knelt beside him. "You look like a Bu-Tech surveillance unit," he mumbled, studying Wizzy's irregular surface.

"Oh no! Nothing of the sort!"

"A final security check before my ship takes off?" Javik touched Wizzy's surface. It was lumpy and cool.

"No."

"It *is* a classified mission."

"I said *no*. That's not it at all." Spying a chunk of aquamarine crystal on a charcoal-tinted glassplex hall table, Wizzy flew over for a closer look.

Javik shivered. He drew his robe shut at the neck.

"Pretty one," Wizzy said to the crystal. "Do you have a boyfriend?"

The crystal remained silent and motionless.

"So you're a male meckie, eh?" Javik said. "Well forget it, pal. That's just a meteor fragment I picked up in the Hepfer Droids."

"Speak!" Wizzy demanded.

There was no response from the crystal.

"Hmmmph!" Wizzy said haughtily. "Just another pretty face." He focused his cat's eye on Javik.

Javik leveled his pistol at Wizzy, saying, "You wanna know about emotions, eh? Let's start with fear, then. You got any of that?'

"I presume so. What is fear?"

"It's when you worry about your own skin."

"Skin." Wizzy glowed red again, calling upon his data banks. "Ah … epidermis. But I have nothing like that."

"You try to act smart, but you know what I think? I think you're dumb."

"I am not! I am wise now, with the inherited data banks of my parents. Papa Sidney says I will grow wiser each day!"

"Shit! What in the hell are you?"

Wizzy nudged the piece of crystal and dropped to the tabletop for a rest. "You remember Sidney Malloy?" he asked.

"Sure. But what—"

"That's my papa."

Javik's head snapped back in surprise. "Your *papa*? *Ha!*"

"He is! Papa Sidney's in deep space."

Javik lowered the gun. "Sid died last year … never returned from our mission."

"Oh, he's very much alive. Let me assure you of that. And I sense Papa wants to see you again someday. But he's quite busy now with assignments from the Council of Magic."

"Magic, huh," Javik said, scratching his head. "Where do you fit in?"

"I've already told you that. You and I are supposed to help one another. I would prefer not being here, but Papa said—"

"Papa said, Papa said! I don't care what your goddamned papa said!"

Wizzy flashed an angry shade of orange. "Now look here, Thomas Patrick Javik!"

Javik became introspective. He laid the gun on the floor. "I was thinking of Sid before falling asleep," he mumbled. "Is this a dream?"

"I sense an answer to that question," Wizzy said.

"And that is?"

Wizzy buzzed across the hallway and slammed into the knuckle of Javik's hand.

"Ow!" Javik groped for the pistol with his other hand.

Wizzy knocked it beyond Javik's reach. "Does that answer your question about a dream?"

"Yes!" Javik said. "Yes!" He shook his wounded hand, wondering if he should lunge for the gun.

Wizzy laughed mischievously. Then his yellow cat's eye darted around in surprise. "That sound I just made," he said. "What was it?"

"What?" Javik snapped. "What-what-what?" His hand throbbed.

"The odd noise I made. Ha-ha-ha! Like that."

"Laughter," Javik said with a sneer. "You were laughing, idiot!"

"This laughter—it has a purpose?"

"It makes a person feel good, you little SOB.!"

"SOB.?"

"Son of a bitch. You're a son of a bitch!"

"That would be SOAB. No, SOB. must be something entirely different. Like 'Sweet Old Boy.' But I'm not old, not at all old."

Javik fumed.

"You seem very confused. I think I'll laugh again. A ha-ha-ha! That feels very good, indeed. Ha-ha-ha!"

Javik shook his sore hand. The pain was subsiding. "Damn, but that hurt," he said. Out of the corner of one eye he looked at the automatic pistol. It lay several centimeters away, just beyond his grasp. *Maybe if I lunged …*

"Don't even think about it," Wizzy said.

The pain was almost gone now. Javik shook his hand and flexed the fingers, still eyeing the gun.

"Your weapon probably couldn't harm me, anyway," Wizzy said. "I am young, though, and uncertain of my powers."

*Should I go for the gun?* Javik wondered. *Could be an Atheist trick. Spying on my mission …*

"You still don't trust me," Wizzy said. "Now you think the Atheists sent me."

Startled, Javik blurted, "How did you…? Oh, my energy waves … from my brain?"

"Uh huh," Wizzy said. "I know all about your mission: You're to scout Guna One, checking for unusual activity in the landing region of garbage catapulted there by Winston Abercrombie. You're to bring him back, too, if you can find him."

Javik felt that his jaw must be scraping the floor.

"It's the Abercrombie recycling crime you're investigating. Isn't that right, Captain Tom?"

Javik stared at the table legs and chewed at his lower lip. "That doesn't prove anything," he said. "Atheist operatives are everywhere."

"What about this? You remember the big reunion at the Sky Ballroom … where they discovered Papa Sidney was a cappy? And the time you went to see him in therapy detention?"

Javik's sea blue eyes opened wide. "I remember those things," he said. He looked at Wizzy and nodded like an old man, with his chin continuing to bob up and down.

"'You and me on an important mission together'—that's what you said to Papa."

"Sure, I said that. But you could have gotten it from my thoughts."

"You weren't thinking about it in my presence, Captain Tom. Not reasoning this out too well, are you?"

"It's not up to me whether you can go. You'll have to be cleared with mission control."

"Impossible. They'd think you were nuts. Just for checking. It might cost you the mission."

Javik pursed his lips. "I need this assignment. It's the comeback trail for me."

"Then believe what I said. I *can* help you."

"I don't know."

"Don't believe me, then. I could care less. I'm just here because Papa—" Wizzy saw Javik's eyes flash angrily.

"All right," Javik said. "You're coming along." *I don't like this creep's personality,* he thought. *But something tells me—*

"Maybe I don't like you either."

"Huh? Oh."

"You've made a wise decision," Wizzy said. He yawned, using unseen mouth muscles.

"What did you say your name was?" Javik asked. He opened his hand and extended it.

"Wizzy. Wizzy Malloy." The little comet hopped on Javik's open hand.

Javik felt a tingle in his palm and heard a barely audible hum. It resembled the purr of a meckie cat. Wizzy was heavy —far heavier than he appeared to be. "Wizzy, eh?" Javik said with a smile. "Is that because you're a wise stone?"

"It's a name. That's all."

Javik wondered how the dark blue stone on his palm could be Sidney's son but not human. And he did not understand where Sidney was at that moment.

"Papa Sidney is flying," Wizzy said, referring to one of Javik's unspoken questions.

"He has a ship?" Frustrated at the lack of privacy, Javik felt his heart skip a beat.

"In a sense, yes. A very large ship. But I'm too weary to explain now." The cat's eye dimmed and closed. Soon Wizzy was breathing deeply, expanding and contracting on Javik's hand. The rolling rumble of snores followed;

"Well I'll be," Javik said, rubbing an itchy eyelid with his free hand. He placed Wizzy on the couch. Obtaining a hand towel from the linen-closet module, he laid it gently over Wizzy's clear agate top.

"Concentrate on happiness," Javik said softly. "That's the biggy—the emotion that's eluded me."

O O O

It was an overcast morning at the northeast corner of Robespierre Field, with a thick layer of Bu-Tech-made clouds overhead. Javik stood with his two crewmen beside other clusters of crewmen near their cream-colored, AmFed-marked ships. Gray-uniformed ground crews were making final adjustments to the ships, chattering back and forth as they worked.

Javik felt in the side pocket of his Space Patrol jumpsuit. Wizzy buzzed contentedly in there, and felt warm to his touch. Javik considered the reason for the Bu-Tech clouds: placed there at President Ogg's orders to conceal the sky writing comet's embarrassing activity from AmFed citizens. *We AmFeds like to think we can control everything,*

Javik thought, bemused. *But here's something beyond the power of our technology.*

Javik felt a chill wind as he removed his hand from his pocket. He mento-zipped his jumpsuit all the way to his neck. Glancing to his left, he focused on the buxom figure of copilot Marta Evans. Clad in a white and gold Space Patrol jumpsuit like his with ribbons across the chest, Evans had short yellow hair with big Venusian curls. She held her helmet with both hands in front of her waist.

He stared at her chest. *Amazing, the things surgeons can do,* he thought.

She caught his gaze, smiled.

Javik looked away and grimaced. *Stinking transsexual,* he thought. *Why couldn't they have sent along a real woman, or even a meckie, instead of this … thing?* Recalling the killer meckie that had been sent with him on the last mission, he shuddered.

Beside Evans stood the other crewman, the freckle-faced, red-haired science officer, Vince Blanquie. Blanquie was fat and soft. He shook noticeably.

Evans whispered in Javik's ear, "He's on withdrawal."

"Huh?"

"Video games. He's hooked. They made him cold turkey it, I hear."

"No mention of that in his dossier," Javik husked.

Evans shrugged. "My source is unimpeachable," she said. *I hope they left the sex-change operation out of my file,* she thought.

A meckie buzzed nearby. Javik turned to see it service the cluster of crewmen who stood at the base of an adjacent space cruiser. *Rings and necklaces,* Javik thought.

Moments later, the meckie stood in front of Javik, fitting a two-jeweled ring on the third finger of his right hand. "These were rush-packed," the meckie said, showing synthetic nervousness. "Hope they work okay." The meckie draped a language-mixer pendant around Javik's neck, then moved on to Evans.

Javik studied the ring. It was tita-gold, bearing two rectangular stones, one white and one turquoise.

"White for shower, turquoise for change of clothes," the meckie said to Evans. "It's called a wardrobe ring."

Evans grunted.

While attending to Blanquie, the meckie said, "Your necklaces are more powerful than older models. They can locate a common language denominator for up to five hundred beings within a fifty-meter radius. Less people, more radius—and vice versa."

After the meckie moved on to another crew, Javik lifted the necklace pendant. It was octagonal and ruby red, with four rainbow-hue stylized faces on it: one round, one square, one triangular, one rectangular. Javik knew they were representative of different cultures and races that might be encountered in deep space. He touched a button on one side, causing the faces to spin in a blur. The mechanism beeped and flashed a green light, indicating it was operating properly. Javik shut it off and tucked it beneath his shirt.

"The president!" Evans said excitedly.

Javik glanced quickly at Evans, then followed the gaze of her large olive green eyes to the west. Autocopter One banked over the General Oxygen Factory, then began its descent toward Robespierre Field.

The craft was white, with the red, yellow, and blue markings of the American Federation of Freeness. Javik saw a large presidential seal on the underside and smaller ones on each side of the cabin. The copter descended rapidly and set down in a cloud of dust. As it had dark-tinted windows, Javik could not see the president. Javik smelled dust and rubbed a speck out of one eye.

Presently, President Euripides Ogg short-stepped from the copter to a lift, followed by two aides. The lift dropped slowly.

President Ogg was an immense, hulking black man in a bright yellow leisure suit with green lapels. He brushed his hand through a wave of long, golden hair that he combed straight back from a widow's peak. The aides spoke to him nervously and constantly, one in each ear. The president and his aides moved quickly to a stage that had been erected for the occasion.

"He looks tired," Evans said.

Javik heard low tones from the clusters of crewmen nearby.

As President Ogg reached the top of the stage, Javik watched the aides brush dust from the President's suit. Then Ogg rolled to the microphone.

The crews fell silent.

"I'll make this short and sweet," Ogg said, addressing the crewmen. "Get out there and find where our catapulted garbage went!"

"Yes, sir!" the crewmen responded. Javik felt the patriotism of the moment as he spoke in unison with the others.

"And when you find it," President Ogg continued, "see if the garbage can do us any goddamned harm!" He coughed.

"Yes, sir!"

One of the aides was a tail blond man whom Javik recognized as Chief of Staff Billie Birdbright. Birdbright leaned close to Ogg's ear and whispered something.

Ogg nodded, looked flustered. "Uh," Ogg said, returning to the microphone. "I mean, report back any unusual activity."

"Yes, sir!"

Without warning, a great wind swept across the field. Javik shuddered and closed his eyes as dust blew in his face and filled his nostrils. He smelled grit and sulfur. He tried to open his eyes, but a blinding flash covered the sky.

"The comet!" someone yelled.

Javik opened his eyes to slits and held his hands over them. Through his fingers, he saw an immense blue and orange fireball streaking horizontally across the sky, disrespectfully shoving aside the Bu-Tech clouds.

"Be careful, Papa!" Wizzy squealed, peeking his head out of Javik's pocket. "There's water in those clouds!"

"What are you talking about?" Javik asked.

"Water can be terrible for a comet," Wizzy said. "Papa is taking a big risk!" After a moment's thought, he added, "Papa Sidney is very large, however. Perhaps a few clouds are of no concern to him."

Javik pushed Wizzy back in the pocket and zipped it shut. A muffled cry came from the pocket. *Sid's a comet?* Javik thought.

On the stage, President Ogg was very agitated. "Get away!" he screamed at the comet, jumping up and down and waving his arms wildly. "Get away!"

Without Javik noticing it, his pocket zipped open. Little Wizzy leaped out and dashed across the asphalt landing field in the same direction taken by the Great Comet. "Wait, Papa Sidney!" he called out. "Take me with you!"

Javik slapped his hand against his pocket. It was flat empty. "Uh oh," he muttered. *Wizzy's a comet too?* he thought.

Wizzy tried to fly high, but kept falling back to Earth. This made him look like a rock skipping across the landing strip. Soon Javik could not see or hear him.

"What came out of your pocket?" Evans asked, looking at Javik.

Javik did not respond. He watched the tail of the Great Comet disappear, leaving a gaping hole in the cloud cover. The sun appeared, pushing the long shadows of the scout ships across the field. Javik felt warmth on his cheeks.

*Wizzy mentioned a Council of Magic,* Javik thought. *So that's it? Magic?*

President Ogg continued to wave his arms until the Great Comet had gone. Then he turned to face the crewmen, saying angrily, "That will be all, gentlemen." He turned hastily and left the stage with his aides.

Javik saw Chief of Staff Birdbright break away from the president. Birdbright rolled toward the clusters of crewmen. "Which crew is going to Guna One?" he called out.

"Here, sir!" Javik yelled, raising his hand.

Birdbright was all business as he approached Javik, leaning forward and carrying a very stern expression.

When the chief of staff arrived, he and Javik exchanged salutes. Then Javik compared their heights. *He's a bit taller than I am,* Javik thought.

Birdbright's smoke gray eyes met Javik's gaze. "You are in charge?" Birdbright asked.

Javik straightened. "Yes, sir."

"As you must be aware, Captain, your mission is unique. The other crews are on random searches, but you …" Bird-bright paused and rubbed his dimpled chin thoughtfully.

"I understand, sir. The arch criminal Abercrombie catapulted garbage to Guna One intentionally—planning to set up a recycling station there."

"Lower your voice!" Birdbright rasped, "We do not appreciate that word!"

Javik lowered his eyelids in shame, cursing himself inwardly for his faux pas.

"The 'r' word!" Birdbright whispered, nearly touching noses with Javik.

*It doesn't seem so horrible to me,* Javik thought. *I'm tired of being beaten to death with this Job-Support thing!*

"'It's not fair to repair,'" Birdbright intoned. "'It's not nice to use twice.'" Javik saw Birdbright's eyes glaze over from the profound truth of the mantras.

Nodding dutifully, Javik thought, Anyone *who thinks 'Jobs Are Sacred' never pulled garbage-shuttle duty!*

"Abercrombie may be on Guna One," Birdbright said. "He's never been apprehended, you know."

"We'll be alert, sir."

Birdbright stared at Javik with the overbearing scrutiny of one knowing he is in a superior position. "Very well, Captain," he said.

They exchanged salutes again.

Moments later, as Autocopter One lifted and sped away, Javik wondered what lay in store for him. *Gawd,* he thought. The immensity of his assignment hit him. *This is big stuff!*

"What jumped out of your pocket?" Evans asked.

"A meckie toy," Javik said. "Sent by a friend to amuse me."

"Well, here it is back," Blanquie said.

Javik barely had time to cup his hands before Wizzy leaped onto them. Wizzy's dark blue body felt cool.

"Papa's gone," Wizzy said dejectedly. "I'm on my own."

"Aw Cha-rist," Javik said, seeing crewmen from other ships approaching.

"I'm sorry," Wizzy said. "My emotions …"

Javik stuffed Wizzy in his pocket and zipped it shut.

"What you got there, Tom?" one asked.

"Cute little gadget," another said. "Bring it out, Tom."

"It talks?"

"Leave me alone, guys," Javik said. "It's nothing. Nothing at all."

Gradually the crewmen dispersed.

Javik looked up at the patch of blue sky. The Great Comet came into sight for a moment, a far-off orange fireball heading out to deep space. Soon it became a tiny dot of orange light.

Javik felt something rustle at his side. Looking down, he saw Wizzy peeking out of the top of the pocket, watching the comet. Wizzy's cat's eye was bright orange now, as was the rest of his lumpy body. Javik felt Wizzy's warmth against his side.

*The same shade of orange as the comet,* Javik thought. *Wizzy could be a chunk of it.* Electrodes flashed wildly in Javik's brain. *Sid? Was that you out there, Sid?*

O O O

Far across the galaxy, in a cavern beneath the surface of Guna One, a blue female meckie studied symbols and cartoon pictures that had been scratched on a recently discovered limestone wall. This was an unnamed Earth-catapulted meckie, like all others on the planet, with a brass "REBUILT" plaque on her torso. Being rather standard in appearance, she had no head and a flashing blue dome light on top. Numerous dents and abrasions marred her rivet-covered surface.

Lord Abercrombie stood in the doorway of the cavern, looking in. "Anything more?" he asked, his bearded half face wrinkled inquisitively beneath a thistle half crown. "It's been two weeks now since we found these drawings." Lord Abercrombie's half body, split from his forehead to the ground, was draped in a floor-length, rust-colored caftan. The caftan hung oddly at the split, in a straight dropoff due to his left side having disappeared entirely into the Realm of Magic. Abercrombie knew it had not really disappeared. It was there but not there at the same moment. It was chilly in the cavern, and he inserted his only hand in his pocket.

"It's history," the meckie said in a voice that sounded like a gargle, evidence of an unsolvable mechanical defect. She half turned toward Abercrombie while pointing at a series of six cartoon squares on the wall. "There were three magicians here before you. One was a giant amoeba, and another a plant creature with wide philodendron leaves. The third was human-like, but with a duck-billed face."

"Really!" Lord Abercrombie said. His eye flashed intently as he glided to the wall. Rubbing his fingers over the carved pictures and symbols, he asked, "All became soil-immersed?"

"Yes. That is what it means to be a magician here—becoming one with the soil, one with the planet."

"But they're all gone. Where did they go?"

"I haven't been able to figure that out. Most of the symbols are strange."

"But you were a linguistics assistant," Lord Abercrombie said. "You, of all meckies, should be able to interpret such things!" He scratched his nearly bald half pate, feeling a few strands of baby soft hair there.

"Earth linguistics is a different thing," the meckie gargled. "I did find one familiar symbol, however. Here." She touched the wall.

Lord Abercrombie leaned close to study the symbol. It was a circle with four tangential triangles spaced evenly outside the circumferential line. Jagged lines inside the circle touched each triangle, looking like bolts of lightning between the triangles. "What is it?" he asked.

"Well, without the circle it's the symbol of magnetics." She moved her hand along the wall. "See here? It's beneath each of the three magicians."

"Hmmm. Yeah. Magnetics, huh? Maybe they used magnetics somehow in their magic."

"Could be."

"What about the circle? What does it mean?"

"I don't know."

"And the cartoons?"

"Maybe something funny was going on," the meckie said.

"Well, nothing seems very funny around here to me. Any incantations there, or magical potion recipes?"

"None that I've been able to figure out yet."

Lord Abercrombie put his hand on his hip. "Some kinda history here, eh? Well, add my story to it."

"That's a good idea, Lord. There are sharp pieces of obsidian on the floor here, evidently used by others to carve on the wall."

"Good."

"I don't draw very well, Lord. I will need artistic programming."

"Report to Servicing for that."

"Yes, Lord Abercrombie." The meckie paused for a moment, then said, "If I'm to portray you accurately, however, I will need to know more about you."

"Such as?"

"You're kind of a confusing personality, Lord. You wanted to set up a recycling base here, using the Earth-catapulted gar-bahge as raw material. Then you were going to ship the recycled products back to Earth."

"That's right."

"But you had all that trouble with Uncle Rosy and his sayermen. You were forced to hide here, beneath the surface. You managed to set up a system of getting gar-bahge down here to your recycling facility, and now you've got caverns full of recycled products—so much stuff you hardly have room to move around."

"So?"

"What are you going to do with all the stuff? Is it supposed to stay here forever, proof to yourself and to no other human that recycled goods could be manufactured?"

"Yeah, I guess that's right." Lord Abercrombie's eye stared at the dirt floor. He focused on a piece of obsidian. "The work kept me busy, I suppose. Maybe I held out a hope that some big shot from Earth would come here and beg me to go back, saying Earth needed my expertise to set up a recycling industry there."

"All right. But what about your obsession with creating planetary disasters? You spend half your time in the Realm of Flesh, and half soil-immersed in the Realm of Magic. In flesh, most of your time is spent with that old Earthian disaster control equipment, trying to create earthquakes, floods, hurricanes, and the like. In magic, that's all you do: Every waking instant is spent trying to impose your will upon the elements."

"Well, it's been something to do. It can get kinda dull around here. Haven't I told you that before?"

"It's power, isn't it? You want to feel absolute, dominating power over the planet and all its inhabitants."

"Could be. I don't know. Say, I don't need to be psychoanalyzed by a meckie! Just put what I tell you on the wall!"

"Yes, Lord."

"Tell how Uncle Rosy's evil sayermen came after me, and how I was fortunate enough to find the Sacred Scroll of Cork. Show that the scroll led me to this place and instructed me in the ancient methods of soil immersion."

"Okay, Lord. Shall I also relate your difficulties in magically inducing disasters? After all, you have only come up with one magically willed rockslide in four years of soil immersion."

"I've been *here* four years," Abercrombie said, irritated. "Only half of that time was spent immersed."

"Pardon me, Lord."

"Give me a break, historian."

The meckie picked up a piece of obsidian and placed it on a wall ledge. "What about your fleshy half, Lord? Should I show you and those old rebuilt meckies working with patched-together Earthian disaster control equipment?"

"I don't know."

"You *have* created some dust storms with the equipment, Lord. An earthquake, too. And three floods."

"Yeah, but the atmosphere goes haywire each time I get something going real good. That damned reverse rain, coming right up out of the planet!"

"That *is* a big problem," the meckie said. "We shouldn't dwell on the, negative, I suppose."

"Make it heroic," Abercrombie said. His brow furrowed.

"Guess I'd better not depict your indecision, either, Lord. You know, the way you're halfway between the realms of Flesh and Magic, afraid to commit yourself to either one."

"Leave all that out, too."

"There isn't much you're permitting me to say about you, Lord," the meckie gargled.

"Just show me getting here," Lord Abercrombie snapped. "Then leave a lot of blank space. My story isn't over yet."

# Chapter Two

*Cork: Called Guna One by the AmFeds. A planet abandoned by soil-immersing magicians aeons ago. Declared unfit by the Council of Mages for the safe and efficient practice of magic. Unusual magnetic and ionic conditions encountered there.*

From the *Encyclopaedia of Magic,* one of the microdata books kept in Stone 31-12

"S*ee if the garbage can do us any goddamned harm!"*

With these urgent words from President Ogg on his mind just minutes after takeoff, Captain Tom Javik mentoed the speed toggle on the chrome and white plastic dashboard. The scout ship *Amanda Marie* accelerated through the stratosphere, stretching to reach the limits of Earth's atmosphere. The licorice smell of G-gas wafted under Javik's nose.

"We're clear," Evans said moments later as they reached space. She glanced to her left at Javik.

"Speed twenty-seven thousand kph and beginning hyper-acceleration," Blanquie reported. He sat behind Javik and Evans at a midships science officer's console.

Javik mentoed course coordinates into the ship's mother computer—simply "Mother" to the crew—causing the ship to bank gracefully. The *Amanda Marie's* E-cell-powered ion engines emitted quiet blue flames, which Javik saw on the console screen between him and Evans. Looking at Earth, he saw that the hole in the gray cloud cover below was sealed now, evidence of the continuing tug of war between Bu-Tech and the Great Comet. The idea of Sidney as a comet seemed ludicrous to Javik. At the same time, it frightened the hell out of him. Gyros whirred as the ship's gravitonics system kicked on.

Wizzy buzzed out of Javik's pocket and flew around the cabin, examining each article of equipment with a child's fascination.

"That's Wizzy," Javik said, with a nod over his shoulder. "A newfangled flying meckie." Javik retreated inwardly to his thoughts: *If Wizzy is Sid's boy, and Sid is a comet …*

"Hi, Wizzy!" Evans said, cheerily.

Spotting a mirror on a half bulkhead behind Javik, Wizzy hovered in front of it to admire himself. "Does my tail look longer today?" he asked, directing his cat's eye gaze at the back of Javik's head.

Javik shot Wizzy a quick backward glance. "I dunno," he responded, noting that Wizzy's tail was silvery and translucent, his rock body pale and golden. *Wizzy is a friggin' comet!* Javik thought, as he faced forward. *I'd better take him aside … keep it from the crew.*

"Hmmm," Wizzy said. "The silver is nice."

"I'd like a word with you, Wizzy," Javik said, mento-unsnapping his safety harness.

"It is a beautiful tail, Wizzy," Evans said. "Kinda like on that big comet."

*Gotta move quickly,* Javik thought.

"Ain't like no meckie I ever seen," Blanquie drawled.

Javik swung his long legs out from under the instrument panel. "Did you hear me, Wizzy?" he snapped.

"Watch me change colors," Wizzy said, paying no attention to Javik.

Javik chewed nervously on his lower lip as Wizzy's tail and body switched colors. Now the tail became a sputter of gold light, with a lumpy, silver body. Wizzy's yellow cat's eye darkened, matching his tail.

A brilliant flash of orange light off the starboard bow diverted Javik's attention. A fraction of a second later, Wizzy was perched on the dashboard beneath the curved windshield, looking out at the return of the Great Comet. Wizzy did not speak this time. He, like the others, watched in awe.

The Great Comet approached fast, causing Javik to squint in the increasing orange-hot glare. He mentoed for a collision report.

"Comet-like body at fifteen thousand three hundred kilometers," Mother said, using a mellow, computer-synthesized voice. "Not on a collision course with this ship."

Spinning on his chair to look out his side window, Javik saw the comet swoop below them to the Earth, pushing away part of the cloud cover and creating another opening. Through the new hole, Javik saw the soft brown and green tones of Earth. Feeling his pulse quicken, he wondered, *Will it hit Earth this time?*

Wizzy let out a little squeal of excitement. He was on the sill of a side porthole now.

Suddenly the Great Comet rose and veered off, beginning a series of loops and swirls as it trailed a stream of white smoke.

*"W,"* Javik thought. *It made a "W"!*

"A message!" Evans said.

Javik glanced to his side at the co-pilot's seat, focusing for a moment on Evans's robust chest. It seemed automatic to look there, with the eyes homing in like smart missiles on their target. This time, however, Javik looked away quickly before she caught him.

He heard Evans rustle, and sensed her looking at him.

Javik's face felt hot. He fumbled in his jumpsuit for the titanium pillbox. Leaning away to conceal the box, he selected a brown sex-sub pill and a clear water capsule. Hurriedly, he swallowed the pills and replaced the tin. Cool water molecules expanded in his stomach. He waited for the sexual sublimation to take hold.

"What'd ya take there?" Evans asked.

Javik did not answer or meet her gaze. Closing his eyes, he felt a warm, satisfied feeling soak into his bones. Inaudibly, he sighed.

Evans snickered. It was not a loud snicker. But Javik heard it just the same.

He wiped beads of perspiration from his brow.

"Warm, Captain?" she asked, noting a scar on the bridge of Javik's aquiline nose. His deeply set blue eyes darted around like those of a cornered animal.

Feigning interest in a digital weather screen, Javik cursed himself for the continuing moments of weakness. *Evans is a transsexual!* he thought. *If the guys ever heard I dabbled like that, I'd be the laughingstock of the …*

Evans rolled to a midships porthole to get a better view of the comet. Javik pictured her attractive features in his mind's eye: soft, creamy skin, with smooth, rounded cheeks, and a small nose that turned up slightly at the tip. Long black lashes and dark eyebrows overhung the eyes.

"We are … not … your … garbage dump!" Evans read, squinting to read the skywriting. "That same message for more than eight months! What does it mean?" She turned to look at Blanquie.

Blanquie winked at her.

The gaze of Evans's large olive green eyes darted away like a timid fawn under pursuit by a buck.

"I think I know!" Wizzy said, in a tiny voice. "I think I know!"

"Shutup, Wizzy," Javik snapped.

"Well!" Wizzy huffed.

Javik watched the Great Comet speed off into deep space. A parallel with guerrilla warfare struck him: This comet was employing hit and run tactics. But Javik sensed the comet did not have to flee. It was playing games with the AmFeds.

*If that is Sid,* Javik thought, bemused, *he's getting even with the bureaucrats now … making them run around … embarrassing the bastards.*

"Damn, that thing's fast!" Blanquie said. "Just a pinprick of orange light now!"

Rolling to Wizzy's side, Javik spit out a terse command: "Come with me."

But Wizzy remained on the sill of the porthole. "Just a minute," he said, glowing red. His voice became hollow and faltering: "I sense trouble ahead … Davis Droids … signal intermittent."

"Davis Droids," Blanquie said. He flipped the selector on his CRT screen. "Here it is," he said. "Directly in the target of Abercrombie's garbage shots. Not much land mass there. Twenty million kilometers this side of Guna One, in the same Aluminum Starfield with the Guna planets."

"Wizzy," Javik said. "I want you—"

"Begin searching for garbage in the droids," Wizzy said.

"Is that meckie an official part of this crew?" Blanquie asked.

Irked, Javik snatched Wizzy from the sill and moto-shoed aft.

"See here!" Wizzy protested. "Put me down!"

"Shush!" Javik said. He rolled into the bathroom and slammed the door. "Keep it down," Javik husked, "Or by God, I'll flush you into outer space!" He held Wizzy over the unlidded toilet.

The gravitonics system whirred noisily here. A wall plaque beneath a Patterman gravitonics indicator read:

**CAUTION!**<br>**Do not use bathroom**<br>**if gravitonics**<br>**inoperable**

Seeing the toilet, Wizzy understood Javik's threat. He almost told Javik to go ahead, but reconsidered. It was cold out there. And a long way from Papa Sidney. "But the signals I'm receiving," Wizzy said. "We must heed them!"

"I'll be the judge of that," Javik said, smelling a chemical odor from the toilet. "You're comets, aren't you? You and Sid …"

"There's no secret about that."

"Some kinda magic? I mean, comets with personalities aren't your everyday sort of thing."

"You've got it."

"Good magic? I mean, uh …"

Wizzy laughed. "It's not Witchcraft. Trust me."

Javik's expression was very intense. "I don't want my crew disrupted with this sort of information. They're flaky enough as it is, and I need their undivided attention to duty."

"All right."

"Keep it between you and me. As far as everyone else is concerned, you're a meckie. A comet-like device some Bu-Tech pal of mine thought up to be cute. You got it?"

"Sure. No problem."

"It's yessir from now on," Javik said, holding Wizzy close to the toilet bowl. "That or I flush you,"

"I understand!" Wizzy snapped. He glowed orange-hot.

"Ow!" Javik yelled. He dropped Wizzy and blew on his hand. "Why, you little …"

Wizzy hovered in the air. "Let's get something straight, shall we?" he said. "Don't play big-time operator with me, fella. I know your background—the girls, the fights, the whole bit."

Javik continued to blow on his hand.

"You're a trash man."

Javik's eyes flashed angrily. "This assignment isn't like garbage shuttle duty. This is important. *Really* important."

"You're still chasing trash."

"Yes, but on a larger scale." Javik rubbed the palm of his burned hand. "You saw the President back there."

Wizzy laughed. "Large-scale trash? Trash is trash in my data banks." He had become dark blue again, with a short green tail.

"Just remember what I told you," Javik said tersely. He jerked open the door and rolled into the cabin. Mother's computer voice was completing a course projection for Evans. Then it fell silent.

"Check those droids," Wizzy shouted. He flew by Javik, alighting on a wall-mounted oxygen tank behind the captain's chair.

Javik seethed as he rolled forward.

"Sounded like a fight back there," Evans said, watching Javik slide into his chair. "Amazing, the way they can build personalities into meckies now."

Javik glowered as he stared out the windshield. His hand still hurt.

"Ogg's cloud cover isn't working worth a damn," Blanquie said.

Mento-swiveling her chair, Evans looked aft. Blanquie's freckled face was pressed against one of the portholes. His soft, round body seemed inappropriate for the rigors of Space Patrol duty. "Sure isn't," she agreed.

"Maybe the comet is God," Blanquie said, "just cruisin' around tryin' to decide if Earth is worth savin'."

"Yeah," Evans said. "Like Sodom and Gomorrah."

Blanquie laughed nervously. Then he coughed. "Maybe it's Uncle Rosy," he said, "angry because the AmFeds are off schedule on his Thousand Year Plan."

Javik watched another scout ship speed into space along a different course. Bullet-shaped and cream-colored, with AmFed markings, the other ship was moving faster than the *Amanda Marie.* Javik mentoed a speed increase and felt his ship respond instantly.

"Confirmed," Mother said. "Will accelerate to seventy-five thousand kph and hold."

"Hey, Cap'n," Blanquie drawled. "What them boys gonna do about the comet?"

"Haven't been invited to any ministerial sessions lately," Javik said acidly. "You can bet they're fuming about it, though. I hear a hundred missiles have been fired at it already. Maybe they're assembling a super-missile right now. Who knows?"

Blanquie giggled. "What if it *is* God?" he asked, looking at Javik's back with a silly leer on his face.

Javik looked around to see the silly expression, then turned forward, shaking his head in dismay. *At least the video gameaholic isn't shaking now,* Javik thought.

Blanquie concentrated on the back of Javik's jumpsuit. Gold captain's epaulets rested regally on the shoulders, with thin, stitched-on gold braids encircling the armpits. Javik's smooth, amber hair gave off a soft sheen.

"Just think on it!" Blanquie gushed. "If we blasted God with a missile!"

Javik saw Evans crack a smile. Out of the corner of his eye, Javik also saw Wizzy, on the oxygen tank behind his chair. "Pay attention to your duties!" Javik howled. "Evans! Blanquie! Think about the mission, damn it!"

Evans straightened, and Javik heard the whir of Blanquie's moto-boots as he returned to his station.

"Looks good so far," Evans said, reading a digital trouble scanner. She thought of the way Captain Javik often stared at her laboratory-shaped breasts.

"Now listen to me, crew," Javik said, his tone terse. "You risk your lives—and mine—every time you forget about duty!"

Blanquie gave an astrogational reading.

*I sounded pretty good,* Javik thought. *Strange, coming from me.* He stared at his instruments with unfocused eyes. *What sort of assignment do I have here? Is Wizzy going to get in my way?*

"No," Wizzy said in Javik's ear.

Javik started. He snapped his head forward.

"Thoughts create energy waves," Wizzy said. He flew aft.

Javik gazed into space in the direction taken by the Great Comet It was out of sight now, having blended with the stars and shining planets in the distance. *Damn, Sid!* he thought. *You're big time now!*

Oblivious to the businesslike chatter of the crew, Javik felt a rash of envy for the Great Comet. And he recalled his meeting with Sidney at the Sky Ballroom the year before.

*Sid was envious of me, then,* Javik thought. Those days seemed like long ago. They were simpler, more innocent days. But Javik did not want them back.

O O O

An hour later, from a dark resting place in an aft cupboard, Wizzy surveyed the thoughts of the crew. In the darkness, thoughts inundated him like sounds to a blind man. He practiced identifying them.

*This one's from Javik,* Wizzy thought. *He feels both attraction and repulsion for Evans. That's interesting.*

Wizzy concentrated on Evans's thoughts now. *Ah,* Wizzy thought. *She wants to hit the sack with our friend Captain Tom.*

Blanquie's thoughts crowded in: *I could turn this console into a video game. With a maze here, and sixteen laser-fired squibs …*

Wizzy laughed aloud when he heard this.

"Shutup back there!" Javik barked. He mentoed the mission briefing tape.

"Assignment fifteen," a woman's voice said over a dashboard speaker. "Guna One."

# Chapter Three

*No one has ever seen proof of the Happy Shopping Ground. I wonder if our Product Failure did really go to such a place!*

Whispered words picked up by a Black Box of Democracy detector

It was evening by New City time.

Leaving Mother in charge of all ship's functions, Javik yawned while rolling by Blanquie toward the captain's sleeping compartment. "Fifteen minutes to clothing destruct," Javik said, glancing at his wrist digital. "Has everyone changed?"

"I have," Evans said in a sultry voice. She popped her head out of the hatch of her sleeping compartment, on the deck to Javik's left.

Javik gave her a cursory glance downward. She was staring hard at him. Feeling the effects of his sex-sub pill wearing off, he mentoed his own sleeping compartment hatch hurriedly. Tumblers sounded as the lock was released. He leaned down and pulled open the hatch that was just forward of hers. It squeaked.

"Is Captain Daddy reminding us to change our clothes?" Blanquie drawled. He slouched at his console, a sneer on his freckled face. "Now we have a mother and a daddy on this ship."

"All right!" Javik snapped. "Just forget the automatic destruct time once. That's all. Just *once*. You'll be standing there in nothing but your moto-boots."

"Now that would be interesting," Evans said, examining her wardrobe ring closely. "Clever little gadget. All the problems of reducing weight in space, and they've still got a device that gives you a regular change of clothes!"

"You're too easily impressed," Javik said. He mento-locked his boots, then stepped on the top rung of the ladder inside his compartment.

"Night, Captain Daddy," Blanquie said.

Javik scowled at him.

"Did you brush your teeth, Blanquie?" Evans asked.

"How about a little co-hab tonight, Evans?" Blanquie asked.

She laughed. "Not tonight," she said.

Javik shook his head in dismay as he stepped down the ladder, pulling the hatch shut behind him. Reaching the corrugated metal floor of his compartment, Javik removed his pillbox from his pocket and slipped it into a wall-hung stuff pocket. It was a tiny room, with barely any walking space around the bed. Mirrored walls and a reflecting, gold-foil ceiling made it seem larger. A single porthole on the outside wall displayed a distant blue nebula with veinlike streaks of pink and green. Corner ceiling fixtures lit the room evenly.

He mentoed a nightshade over the porthole. It snapped over the glassplex.

Feeling a dull, low-level throb of pain in the back of his head around the implanted mento unit, Javik gave it a brief thought. The pain subsided.

Javik stood next to the bed, there being nowhere else to stand in a room of this size. Staring at his wardrobe ring, he mento-concentrated on the rectangular turquoise stone. The stone glowed.

A happy tune sounded from the ring, with a tiny computer voice that sang: "It's fresh-up time! It's fresh-up time!"

Javik hated that tune.

Now his Space Patrol jumpsuit disappeared in a puff of white smoke, leaving him wearing nothing but his moto-boots and his ring. A black thread shot out of the ring, followed by a thread of gold. For a moment, they hung poised in the air, like tiny cobras about to strike.

*Checking my size,* Javik thought, recalling the demonstration class he had taken.

Now the threads darted around Javik's wrist and up his arm, covering the arm with finely woven black and gold cloth. Over his shoulders and around his neck the threads flowed, forming a braided collar. Then down the other arm, back up the arm and down the torso. He felt the warmth of the pajama cloth take hold.

A white strand darted out of the ring next, and this encircled his waist and thighs to form a fresh pair of underwear. Then two new black and gold threads covered that and his legs, forming pajama bottoms.

*It is kinda clever,* Javik thought. He sat on the bed, sinking into its synthetic softness. Soon the moto-boots were off and he was under the covers.

"Captain Daddy," he muttered, just before falling asleep. "I'll have to speak with Blanquie about his attitude."

O O O

The wall-mounted transcriber worked while Javik slept below decks, making ship-log tapes from his resting brain. In the cabin above, Wizzy sat on the dashboard, rolling the gaze of his cat's eye aft. The chrome and white plastic cabin was empty, with captain and crew belowdecks in sleeping compartments. With his sensitive tympanic sensors, Wizzy heard the low hum of the transcribing machine, despite it being in another compartment.

Through the curving windshield he watched two closely aligned planets come into view, covered by a continuous system of swirling, mysterious clouds. Both planets were mountainous, plunging to high plains of green and thence to wide blue seas. Being so close to the twin spheres, Wizzy absorbed a torrent of animal and geological history from their energy waves, more than enough to whet his appetite for knowledge. But too soon *the Amanda Marie* had sped by and the planets were receding into the distance.

*I'll return to explore someday,* he thought, feeling the energy waves subside.

Now the faint twinklings of stars, red quasars, and bright planets beckoned to him from far off. He felt a weak signal trying to find its way into the atoms and molecules of his brain. Something about a solar system with three suns, a planet with disturbing activity.

*From Cork,* Wizzy realized. *The planet Javik calls Guna One.*

Static crackled in his brain, blocking out the Corkian signal. He surmised a meteor storm had intervened, or perhaps a solar flare. Feeling weary, he let his cat's eye lid droop.

Wizzy called upon his cometary data banks, drawing forth information imprinted in him at birth. Papa Sidney's deep, mellifluous voice spoke to him: "Energy waves take a variety of forms, including simple heat waves, radio signals, and microwaves. Your red star crystal sensor is highly adaptable, permitting you to learn from all things. The most ordinary-looking piece of plastic and the most brilliant nova in the universe have something to offer."

He tried for the Corkian signals again, but received no further messages. Staring out the windshield with a bleary, stinging eye, he tried to focus on a cluster of stars dead ahead. *That planet is out there somewhere,* he thought.

Wizzy's gaze wandered sleepily around the cabin, from the blinking instrument panels to the tan gortex, wall-hung survival packs. His eyelid drooped heavily, then opened once, seeing only unfocused images. He dozed off.

Moments later, a loud *clunk* and the rustle of clothing awakened him. Looking groggily toward the sleeping compartment hatches along the floor, he saw that one of them was open.

Marta Evans popped her curly blond head out and looked around. Then she lifted the adjacent hatch. It squeaked open. Wizzy heard voices after she entered that compartment.

O O O

Javik turned to one side, scrunching the air pillow between his shoulder and head. Hearing the hatch squeal, he opened one eye in the half-light of his sleeping compartment. A woman's foot was on the bottom ladder rung.

He sat bolt upright.

Evans short-stepped to the floor, looking down over her bare right shoulder at him. She wore a black lace blouse, low-cut, with black bikini panties.

"You!" he husked angrily, smelling lilac perfume. "Get out!" His tone was low and menacing.

Smiling softly, Evans knelt next to him on the mattress. He felt the bed move.

Javik moved away. "I told you to get out," he said. But his voice was not firm, and Javik knew Evans had noticed this. *Where are my sex-sub pills?* Javik wondered, his gaze fleeing frantically.

Kneeling on the mattress with her gaze locked on Javik, Evans mentoed the zipper on the front of her blouse.

*Ziippp!* Each side of the blouse parted.

*My God!* Javik thought, seeing her well-shaped bust, Evans wore a scanty yellow brassiere with tiny black buttons down the front. He looked into her olive green eyes.

She smiled. "Shall I get the buttons?" she asked. "Or would you prefer—"

"Uh, I don't think ..." Javik coughed. He felt weak.

She mentoed the buttons. Her breasts virtually exploded out of the brassiere as the garment flew open. The breasts were exquisitely formed and impressive. Javik saw no surgical scars.

Javik's gaze locked on hers. He felt his eyes burning with desire. He looked away and felt the tempo of his breathing increase.

"I've seen you watching me," she said.

Javik scowled. Another time he might have laughed at the situation. He had known many women, some as aggressive as Marta Evans. All the aggressive women had mento-activated bras.

Evans removed her blouse and brassiere. Then she leaned close to Javik and pressed her lips against his. Her mouth was soft and warm. She pulled back and said, "I thought you might like some company. It can get lonely in deep space." She brushed a yellow curl out of her eyes.

*Transsexual!* Javik thought, pulling away in revulsion. "I'm doing fine without you," he said. He reached around her to the wall-hung stuff pocket and located his tin of sex-sub pills. He noticed the pocket floated a little against the wall. "I'll have to adjust the gyros," he muttered, fumbling to open the tin.

She knocked the tin away. It clattered against the wall.

"Hey!" Javik said, leaning across the bed to retrieve the tin. "My ulcer pills!"

She lay next to him and nibbled at his ear. "What sign are you?" she asked. "Pisces?"

"Sparky the Hormone," he said, irritated that the tin was beyond his reach. His glands were beginning to go wild.

"I've never heard of that one," she said.

"Thirteenth sign of the Zodiac," he explained sarcastically. "The sign of natural craving."

"Oh."

*Stupid transy broad,* he thought. *Won't admit she's confused.* He butted the palm of one of his large hands against her shoulder and pushed her away firmly. Then he glared at her. Evans's green eyes were soft and feverish, reminding him of a girl he had once datemated in an astro-port—the one he almost permied. *What was her name?* he wondered.

Their lips drew close, then touched. Javik pulled her body against his. His lips ran down along her neck to her bust. Her lilac perfume smelled inviting and exotic.

Evans was beginning to breathe hard. She ran her hands through his hair.

Javik moved his hand along the curvatures of her body, from the soft skin of her bust along her waist to her hips. A shudder coursed through his body.

She sighed.

*How did they do it?* Javik thought. *No surgical scars. Anyone else would think this is a real woman. But I read her dossier.*

He massaged her stomach and pressed his hands against the underside of her breasts. Javik felt curiosity over how a transsexual made love. He knew he had reached the point of no return.

A loud *thump* sounded around the ship.

"What was that?" Javik asked, staring at the black nightshade over the compartment porthole.

"I didn't hear anything," she said.

*Thump!* the sound was right next to them.

"I heard *that*," she said, sitting up on one elbow.

*Crash!* This came from somewhere else on the ship.

Javik mentoed the porthole nightshade. It snapped open, revealing a clear view of deep space. A red quasar burned brightly to one side of his framed view. Suddenly a mangled, semihuman face appeared in the porthole, staring in with bulbous, bloodshot eyes. The eyes were unfocused, with death's disorientation. The head was oversized and entirely hairless, having no eyebrows or eyelashes.

Javik felt his heart beat irregularly. He reached for his service pistol, which hung in a holster on the wall. "The engines aren't on," Javik said, just realizing it then. "We aren't moving!"

Evans screamed.

"Topside!" Javik barked, pressing his feet against the moto-boot rack at the foot of his bed. He felt the boots snap on over his ankles.

Evans fumbled around, trying to find her clothes.

Javik scrambled up the ladder and opened the hatch. Looking into the cabin, he saw clusters of the strange creatures against the outside of the windshield and portholes, knocking against the ship. "Hurry!" Javik yelled to Evans. "They're trying to get in!"

Javik felt his hand quiver on the automatic pistol's handle as he short-stepped out of the compartment to the deck. He rolled forward to the command chair. Wizzy was on the dashboard, snoring heavily. Javik knocked him away with the gun barrel and fell into the seat. He heard Wizzy hit the floor and roll. There was a fit of breathing for a moment from the baby comet. Then the snoring resumed.

With bulbous-headed humanoids only centimeters away outside the windshield, Javik mentoed the engines. There was no response. He felt a sharp pain in the back of his skull around the implanted mento transmitter.

"Nine hundred thirty-three possible causes," the ship's mother computer reported. "Complex circuitry. Search commencing."

Switching the pistol to his left hand, Javik slammed down the black manual START toggle in the center of the instrument panel. Still no response from the engines. "Shit," he said. His head ached. *Something's terribly wrong with my mento unit, too,* he thought. *What a place for it to go gunnysack!*

Glancing aft, Javik saw Evans scurry half-dressed to her own sleeping compartment. He was about to yell for her when she hustled out with her service pistol and used it to pound on Blanquie's hatch. "Stations!" Evans yelled. "Blanquie!" Then she rolled forward.

Javik waved his gun menacingly at the creatures on the other side of the windshield. But they didn't react, and continued to pummel the ship with their mangled heads, legs, arms, and bodies. Their unfocused, bloodshot eyes stared beyond Javik. "Where's Blanquie?" Javik asked.

"I called him. Do you think they can get in?" She stood beside her chair.

"Zip that," Javik said, glancing at her blouse.

She mentoed it.

As Javik heard the zipper rise, he wondered how the mento-zipper system worked. He knew from experience that another person could not mento your zipper, but did not understand the technology. He scowled. *I am really low, he* thought, scolding himself. *On a critical presidential mission, and I'm in the sack with a goddamned transsexual.*

Evans pressed a red alarm button on her console. "Blanquie!" she yelled as the siren screamed. "Get out here!"

"Where *is* he?" Javik snapped.

At Javik's memo-command, Mother reported on the ship's mechanical problem: "Still searching. Maximum search duration three minutes, fourteen seconds."

"There's something strange about these creatures," Evans said. She shut off the siren.

"That's news?"

"I mean, they look like dead humans, with terrible wounds. Oh! That one has no arms!"

A hideous, deformed creature with open wounds at its torn and empty armpits pounded its body against the windshield. Javik grimaced as the glassplex flexed.

"His forehead!" Evans said. "What's that on his forehead?"

"I don't know," Javik said, glaring at the instrument panel. "Damn these engines!" He rubbed the back and one side of his head. The mento unit pain had become dull and had traveled around the outside of his skull.

"PF," she said, reading the creature's forehead. "Product Failure!" She felt a chill. "Catapulted bodies from Earth!"

Javik heard Wizzy snore fitfully from somewhere on the floor.

"I think we're in the Davis Droids," Javik said. "Asteroids to port and starboard."

"How could they be alive out here?" she asked.

"Forget 'em!" Javik yelled. "And help me get the friggin' engines started! Blanquie! Where the hell are you, Blanquie?" Javik flipped the starter toggle on and off, with no result. "Go back and check Blanquie. Get him out here. Now!"

Evans rolled aft rapidly. She opened the hatch to Blanquie's sleeping compartment and looked in. She screamed. Then she coughed as a rush of icy, rarefied air hit her face.

Whirling around on his chair, Javik saw Evans recoil from the hatch in shock.

Evans slammed the hatch shut and mento-locked it. "The compartment is full of monsters!" she said. "I saw Blanquie lying on the bed with blood all over him." She looked at Javik with terror-stricken eyes. "I think he's dead."

"Jeheezus!" Javik said.

"Could this be the Happy Shopping Ground?" Evans asked, rolling forward. "Are they Product Failure victims?"

"Do you wanna die, Evans?" Javik said. His voice became loud and high-pitched: *"You wanna die?"*

"No sir. I don't." She slid into her chair

"Then get a hold on yourself. I might as well be alone out here, for all the help you're giving." He mentoed Mother again.

"Three hundred sixty-two possible causes remain," Mother said. "Maximum search duration one minute, twenty-eight seconds."

"Sorry, sir," Evans said. "What should we do, Captain Javik?"

"What's all the commotion?" Wizzy asked in a little voice. He scooted out from under Evans's chair and hopped on the dashboard.

"So you're awake," Javik said. "Finally."

"I was tired," Wizzy said, studying the humanoids with his yellow cat's eye. Wizzy glowed red, calling upon his data banks. "Davis Droids," he said. "I warned you about this place. Nurinium here."

"What the hell is nurinium?" Javik asked.

"An element sprinkled around the universe by magicians," Wizzy said. "It gives inanimate objects life."

Javik shook his head. "Don't believe a word of it," he said, to Evans.

*Thud! Barump!* The creatures pummeled the ship with extra intensity. The windshield flexed again.

"Show me some of your wondrous powers, Wizzy," Javik said sarcastically. "Or would you rather sleep?"

"Well!" Wizzy huffed. "I'm not perfect? I told you that. And I am only nineteen hours, fifty-six minutes old!"

"All right, all right," Javik said. "Any idea why the engines won't start?"

Wizzy's cat's eye slanted toward Javik. "Creatures in the exhaust tubes," he replied, glowing red again. "Tubes are plugged."

"How the hell could they do that, with the ship going in excess of three hundred thousand kilometers per hour?"

Wizzy laughed, rocking for a moment on the dashboard. He glowed red-orange this time, although his eye remained yellow. "From your energy waves, and those of the ship, I see precisely what happened: One of the ship's E-cells was consumed sixteen minutes ago. There was a delay in switching to a new fuel cell—"

"Shit," Javik said. "And that shut off the engines. I could have solved it easily. Hell, Mother should have—"

"But you were preoccupied," Wizzy said, "and didn't realize the ship had stopped. It shut down in a very bad place."

"Never heard of a Mother failing before," Evans said gloomily.

Javik glared at her. "Thanks for the analysis," he said. "Both of you. Now what?"

"Something plugging the exhaust tubes," Mother reported. "Manual correction required."

*Thump! Kathud!* The pummeling continued.

"You're the captain," Wizzy said.

"Don't be rude," Evans said to Wizzy.

"The word is insubordinate," Javik said. He waved his gun at the humanoids. They paid him no heed.

Disconsolate, Javik stared down at the deck. Wearily, he set his pistol on his lap. The headache was subsiding. He sighed at the small relief of that.

An aft hatch clanked open.

"They're getting in!" Evans shouted.

Javik looked aft. A creature floated in, then fell to the cabin floor in the pseudo-gravity of the ship.

Evans rolled aft. She skirted the creature, which lay on the deck in apparent disorientation. Gasping in rarefied air over the hatch, she slammed it shut. Then she mento-spun the locking device while creatures in Blanquie's sleeping compartment thumped against the underside of the deck.

"I'm mento-holding it locked," Evans said. "They're trying to force it open again." She heard the ship's oxygen system hum loudly, replenishing the air supply.

Smelling the odor of decaying flesh, Javik studied the creature that had entered the cabin. It was male, wearing a torn Earth T-shirt and blue jeans. An electroplated purple badge was attached to the shirt, dangling next to a rip that exposed a black "PF" stamp on the chest. Seeing a deep gash on the face, Javik decided this must have been the cause of death. The creature staggered to its feet, waving its arms wildly as it took a step toward Javik. Then it took another step, hesitating and unsteady, like someone who was either afraid or not practiced in walking.

*It's not dead now,* Javik thought. He aimed and fired the gun.

There was a pistol crack and a flash of orange. The laser bullet missed, ricocheting around the cabin and whistling by Evans's ear. She dropped to the deck, continuing to mento-hold the hatch-locking mechanism.

A volley of subsequent shots from the automatic weapon were on target, tearing gaping, bloody holes in the creature's flesh. It continued to stumble ahead, its bloodshot eyes vacuous and long dead. Curiously, the open wounds did not drip blood.

Javik emptied his gun into the creature. But it continued to advance, slowly and inexorably. He looked for another clip. "Shoot it, Evans!" he shouted. "Hurry!"

Before Evans could take aim, the creature was lunging for Javik. Javik repelled it with a swift karate kick to the torso, causing the assailant to fall back on the deck. Slowly, however, the creature sat up and rose to its feet.

Without warning, Wizzy glowed bright orange and flashed across the cabin, slamming into the tattered humanoid. This had more effect than all of Javik's firepower, for the creature slipped and tried to go the other way. Its purple badge clattered to the deck. Cringing at the sight of Wizzy, the creature tried to get away.

Wizzy attacked again.

The creature fell over itself trying to escape. It crawled aft, in full and terrified retreat.

"Over here!" Evans said. "I'll open the hatch!"

Wizzy forced the intruder into Blanquie's sleeping compartment. "I'm going in, too!" Wizzy announced. "Close the hatch after me!"

"Right!" Evans said.

"He's afraid of me!" Wizzy said, pausing at the open hatch and displaying obvious pride. "Probably a primordial fear of comets."

"Who cares why!" Javik said, shaking his head. "Just do it!"

"You don't care to understand these things?" Wizzy asked, surprised. "With so much to learn, you would bury your head in the sand?"

"This is no time for philosophy!" Javik snapped.

"Fleshcarriers!" Wizzy huffed. Haughtily, he flew into the compartment.

Evans slammed the hatch shut.

Now there was a ferocious commotion below decks. Javik felt the ship shake and heard shattering glassplex, probably from the compartment's mirrors. Wizzy squealed down there, with all the zeal of an attacking samu-rani warrior.

"He's doing it!" Evans reported, looking along the side of the ship with a prismatic porthole. Creatures poured from the broken porthole of Blanquie's compartment, tumbling in the vacuum of space. Gradually they regained their equilibriums and made their way back to the ship, half swimming, half walking on air.

"Good work, Wizzy!" Javik said.

Evans screamed.

Javik hurried to the porthole with her and saw the reason: Outside, the bloody and battered corpse of Vince Blanquie tumbled in freefall.

Then it began to move, swimmingly and dreamlike with its humanoid brethren.

"Blanquie's one of them," Javik said. A chill cut through his shoulder blades.

"Open up!" Wizzy squealed from below decks.

Evans lifted the hatch, allowing Wizzy back in. Then she reseated it.

Wizzy hovered breathlessly in midair. "A … burst … of strength," he said proudly.

"Not a minute too early," Javik said. "Say, you sound done in." He opened his palm, and Wizzy landed there.

Wizzy breathed rapidly. "I fused a cover … over the porthole," he said. "Using titanium … from the compartment deck."

Javik felt him breathing, expanding and contracting like any human. "Good," Javik said. "Now I have one more assignment for you."

"Name it," Wizzy said, full of himself.

"The exhaust tubes. Can you clear them?"

"Just command it."

"I command it," Javik said. He tossed Wizzy in the air.

Wizzy clunked ungracefully to the floor. "Hey!" he yelled, surprised. "Give me a moment to get my stuff together!"

"Sorry," Javik said.

Presently, Wizzy entered an airlock on the starboard side of the *Amanda Marie*. Within seconds, he darted into space.

The creatures continued to pummel the ship.

Javik took his command chair and mento-held on the ship's starter button. With the mento transmission, a sharp pain returned to the back of his skull. Releasing the mento hold, Javik swore and slammed down the black START toggle.

Moments later, he felt the ship rumble as twin ion engines roared to life. He breathed deeply.

"Thank God!" Evans said.

Outside the ship, Wizzy was just exiting the last exhaust tube when the engines turned over. Had the engines started just a fraction of a second earlier, Wizzy might have been blown away into deep space and lost forever. As it was, he had to cling to a deflector fin with magic suction while the ship accelerated.

Some of the humanoid creatures clung to the ship, too. But they soon lost their grips and fell back as the *Amanda Marie* picked up speed.

Wizzy saw them float aimlessly in the asteroid belt behind the ship.

Inside, Javik was beginning to think of Wizzy. He flipped a dashboard toggle to reverse-thrust the engines. When the ship stopped, he threw the Hi-Tech gearbox into neutral.

Wizzy reentered the airlock, then was admitted to the cabin. He flew in, angry as a Jahuvian hornet. "Hey!" he squealed. "Remember me? I coulda been lost out there!"

Javik apologized, then pushed the toggle to resume acceleration. The *Amanda Marie* surged ahead.

"I'm just the guy who saved your butt," Wizzy said, glowing an angry shade of bright orange. He dropped to the corrugated metal deck, breathing hard.

"I would have gone back for you if you'd fallen off," Javik said. "I just wanted to be sure the engines were running okay."

"Hrrumph!" Wizzy said.

Javik laughed. "In case you're wondering, Wizzy—wanting to learn things as you do—you just displayed the emotion of anger."

"Anger? That is good?"

"Sometimes," Javik mused, glancing back at Wizzy and noting he was still bright orange. "It's gotten me into a lot of trouble, though."

"Is that what I am now?" Wizzy screamed. "Angry? Well, it feels good! Damned good!"

Javik tossed a disdainful look over his shoulder.

"Hrrumph!" Wizzy said again. He scooted aft along the cabin floor. "Must learn more about this anger," he said. Evans watched him disappear into Blanquie's sleeping compartment without another word.

"Some meckie you've got there," Evans said. She tossed the humanoid's purple badge in a disposa-tube. Then she moto-shoed forward, grabbing a half-bulkhead for support as Javik turned the ship.

"Mother, why did you delay in switching to a new fuel cell?" Javik asked, speaking into his dash microphone.

"Unknown," Mother said. "Better have me checked over in the next astro-port."

"That's a long way off," Javik said. "We alternate rest times from now on, Evans. Can't leave Mother alone." He watched Evans slide into the co-pilot's seat.

*I'll never go near her again,* he told himself, arching his eyebrows thoughtfully. *Never again.*

# Chapter Four

*When God created life on Cork, he must have been in a whimsical mood.*

Report of the sayerman team sent in pursuit of Winston Abercrombie

Sixty-six hours later, the *Amanda Marie* entered orbit just outside the atmosphere of Guna One. Javik scanned a clip chart on the wall to his left. "Should be Garbage Central down there," he said.

The ship's engines rumbled for a moment, bouncing Javik's long legs together under the instrument panel.

"You've hardly spoken to me since the Davis Droids," Evans said, squinting in the light of three synchronized Guna suns. She studied a planet file on the CRT screen, noting that the combined energy produced by this solar triumvirate was little more than the output of Earth's single sun.

"That hydraulic line fixed?" Javik asked tersely.

"Mother took care of it," Evans said.

"Took care of it, 'sir,' to you, Evans!" Javik snapped. "Don't forget it!"

She paused for a moment, then: "Yes, sir." Javik heard anger in her tone.

Evans clamped an Ego Booster headset over her ears and mentoed it on. Javik overheard portions of the recorded message as it played in her ears: "You are important and incredibly talented. You have many unique qualities."

"Turn that thing down!" Javik said.

She did as he instructed without looking at him.

Javik mento-banked the ship, giving him a clear view of Guna One. This time there was no pain around the mento transmitter, and he hoped it wouldn't bother him again. As he looked through the glassplex side window, he saw that the planet had flowing greens of varying shades, along with browns and blues, much like the colors of Earth. Quite a number of moonlike craters dotted the landscape, apparent evidence of meteor activity. Swirling, misty gray clouds moved rapidly across the surface, providing different views through cloud clearings every few seconds. Feeling the engines vibrate again, Javik glared at his instruments.

Evans removed her headset and stared at Javik. His features were drawn and tired, with hair matted on one side of his head from sleeping against that spot and not combing it out afterward. She took a deep breath, then said, "You might at least be civil."

"Shut up," Javik blurted. He paused. Evans saw his deeply set blue eyes half turn in her direction, seeming to stick their gaze in the vicinity of the windshield's center. His lips moved angrily as he muttered something under his breath.

"You're being rude."

"Just follow orders. Why is this damned thing running rough?"

"I'll ask Mother," Evans said.

"Adjust the engine polarity," Wizzy said.

Looking aft, Javik saw Wizzy resting on the back of Blanquie's chair. "What?" Javik asked.

"Increase engine polarity seven point three two percent," Wizzy said. "Shall I make the adjustment, Captain?"

"No. Where do you get that?"

"Unusual planetary magnetics here," Wizzy said, "caused by rare subatomic monopoles. See those craters down there? This place attracts junk from all over the universe."

"Your meckie is playing science officer," Evans said. Then she spoke into her dash mike: "Mother, what's wrong with the engines?"

"Unable to determine," Mother said, using a mellow computer voice.

"Should program a survival instinct into Mother," Javik said. "She sounds too calm, no matter what's going on in the cabin." He glanced back at Wizzy.

"The magnetics problem is not revealed by your instruments," Wizzy said. "But I know it to be true."

The ship rumbled again. This time the vibration was worse and continuous.

Javik cursed.

"My teeth are knocking together," Evans said.

"Just try the engine adjustment," Wizzy said. "If I'm wrong, you'll know soon enough."

"Make it!" Javik said.

Wizzy tapped a computer keyboard on the science officer's console. Then he returned to the chair back.

Javik felt the engines smooth out. He nodded with resignation and turned forward. *Is everything Wizzy says right?* Javik wondered. *Even that story of magical nurinium being sprinkled around the universe?*

"This ship needs a science officer," Wizzy. said.

"We can get along," Javik said.

"I know the inadequacies of the Theory of Relativity," Wizzy said, "and what happens when G-gas mixes with—"

"Okay!" Javik said. "You've got the job!"

"Science officer, *first* class?" Wizzy asked.

"All right, damn it!"

Wizzy squealed with excitement.

Javik ordered an atmospheric readout from the ship's mother computer.

"Like Earth in many ways," Mother reported, "with nitrogen, oxygen, argon, carbon dioxide …" The computer read off other elements, then said, "There are four unknown elements."

Wizzy glowed red to utilize his data banks. "The key unknown is nurinium," he said. "The same stuff I told you about in the droids."

Javik rolled aft and mentoed the science officer's CRT screen. It confirmed Mother's report, listing four unknown elements. Javik tugged at an eyelash and pursed his lips thoughtfully.

"I know what I'm talking about, Captain," Wizzy said. "Trust me."

"Magic?" Evans said. "You're talking about magic?"

"That's right," Wizzy said.

"Assuming you're correct about the atmosphere," Javik said, "and it sounds pretty improbable to me, is it breathable?"

"For some beings."

"Be specific," Javik said. "For humans?"

"Yes. But be prepared for surprises." Wizzy glowed faintly orange, and Javik thought he detected a teasing tone in Wizzy's voice.

"I'm waiting, Wizzy," Javik said.

"As I hinted, odd creatures live down here, Captain." Wizzy chuckled softly.

"Specifically?"

"Let me have a little fun with this. I am only three days, fifteen hours old, after all. Children need their fun."

Javik seethed. "Are they dangerous?"

"Would it matter if they were? You'd land anyway, looking for unusual activities. Could you return to Earth and tell them you were afraid to land?"

"More humanoids?" Javik asked, his breathing labored from anger. He scratched his forehead.

"Some are like that. A minority, however."

"I'm not going to play Twenty Questions with you. If you want to keep your position …"

"Be rational, Captain Tom," Wizzy said calmly. "I have bad points, admittedly. But on the whole, you need me."

"Aaargh!" Javik said. Furious, he spun Wizzy's chair.

Resting on the spinning chair back, Wizzy glowed bright yellow. Suddenly the chair stopped rotating.

Javik tried to spin the chair again. It wouldn't move.

Wizzy chuckled. Then he became dark blue again.

"I wonder if Abercrombie is down there," Evans said. "What a dirty guy. He could have ruined the AmFed economy with his recycling. Think of it! Millions of manufacturing and distribution people in souplines."

"Who cares?" Javik said.

"But isn't that why you're here?" Evans asked. "To promote the AmFed Way? The greatest good for the greatest number?"

"Naw," Javik said. He popped a red tintette out of a dispenser on the science officer's console. He lit the tintette and blew a puff of red smoke at Wizzy.

"I didn't know you smoked," Evans said.

"He's nervous," Wizzy said.

Javik laughed uneasily. He thought about flushing Wizzy into deep space, but knew Wizzy was reading this thought. It was a frustrating situation.

"Our Captain Tom is here for personal reasons," Wizzy said. "Promote Number One and to hell with everybody else. Right, sir?"

"Can it!" Javik said. He tossed the tintette in a wall-mounted disposa-tube. Machinery inside the wall whirred. "Punch down to Guna One, Evans," he said.

Evans acknowledged the command and mentoed the blue, T-shaped DIVE lever. The lever flipped down without being touched.

The *Amanda Marie* dropped its nose abruptly toward Guna One and accelerated. As Javik hurried back to his seat, he saw an orange glow in front of the ship. Remembering his mento transmitter headaches, he secured his safety harness manually.

"Entering the atmosphere," the mother computer reported.

Javik monitored the interior and exterior heat gauges. He punched a button to freeze the cooling tiles. A gauge told him that the ship's outside temperature had dropped.

Wizzy fluttered in the air during the descent, then landed on Javik's chair back. Javik heard a buzz in his ears. The buzzing was erratic: first loud, then low, first long, then short.

Wizzy grew very quiet. Then, suddenly, he shrieked in Javik's ear: "Wait, Captain Tom!"

Javik slammed against his shoulder harness trying to get away from the noise. Angrily, he snatched Wizzy off the chair back and held the little fellow in front of his face. The comet was cool but bright red. "Don't ever yell in my ear again, damn it!" Javik barked, setting his jaw. His ears rang.

"Sorry, Captain," Wizzy said. "Stop your descent. I am picking up disturbing/mysterious signals from the planet."

"You didn't care about danger before."

"I understood the other danger. Or thought I did. This is an unknown."

Mother reported the altitude at twenty-nine thousand, five hundred meters.

"Look at all those pockmarks on the surface," Evans said.

Javik placed Wizzy on the dashboard, saying, "I can't make heads or tails out of you, Wizzy."

"A life force," Wizzy said. "Very large, I think. I picked up similar, weaker signals from deep space. But they didn't repeat, so I forgot about them." Wizzy flew in a confused pattern around the cabin, then landed on the deck.

"We have to disregard everything he's saying," Javik said, to Evans. "He's out of his meckie mind."

Evans nodded.

"My metamorphosis is proceeding," Wizzy said, shaking. "I don't understand the changes." He scooted for cover under the science officer's console and remained there, whimpering.

"You're feeling fear, Wizzy," Javik yelled. "That's another emotion!"

"I want my papa!" Wizzy squealed. He sobbed.

The *Amanda Marie* continued its descent.

O O O

Below, in a gray-rock control room cave beneath the surface of the planet, a crew of dented and chipped meckies stood at computer terminals, punching entries into keyboards. The computer hardware looked long in the tooth, having been catapulted from Earth as garbage and salvaged by Lord Abercrombie.

"We've got it going!" a dented red meckie said. She, like the others, carried a brass "REBUILT" plaque on her torso. "Tell Lord Abercrombie we're making a big wind!" she exclaimed. "Hurricane strength!"

"But Lord Abercrombie is soil-immersed now," a silver meckie said.

"Oh, that's right," the red meckie said. "We'll tell him later, then. He'll be very pleased!"

O O O

Lord Abercrombie lay buried in the soil, deep in an underground chamber. This was how he spent half of each day, totally immersed in the Realm of Magic. The half of his body that remained human went into dormancy at these times, with no breathing and no fleshcarrier sensations whatsoever.

Abercrombie's head was the planet now. He looked out upon the universe with a billion porous visual sensors, reflecting the stars across the panorama of his magical soul.

*The universe is calling to me,* he thought, *telling me to join it.*

A torrent of rain poured up out of the ground, filling the atmosphere with water. Clouds formed quickly from this upside-down rain, followed by thunder and lightning. Within seconds a full-blown electrical storm was in progress, with clouds dumping rain back on the planet. When this subsided, more rain rose from the surface, restarting the cycle.

*That odd reverse rain again,* Lord Abercrombie thought helplessly. *What causes it?*

Thunder boomed across the sky.

O O O

At the same time, in the control room....

"Reverse rain in Sector Seventy-four," the red meckie said. "And one hell of a dust storm just ten kilometers south of that!" "Now our equipment is shorting out," another meckie said. "Not again!" the meckies wailed in unison. "Not again!"

O O O

"I see buildings down there," Javik said. He was looking through the midships magna-scope, manually adjusting it to focus. "One looks like a large stone castle ... and a number of smaller structures. Long gray strips, too."

"I'm picking up signals again," Wizzy said, glowing bright red. "Different this time." He sat on top of the science officer's console. "Messages from the planet's history. An expedition six hundred years ago led by someone named Yammarian. These were not humans. The expedition found evidence of Yanni tribesmen and Bolo herdsmen who once populated the planet. Found cliff habitats, too, and the skeletons of long goats. There was an upheaval here. Can't tell what sort. An earthquake, maybe—or a war."

"Anything else?" Evans asked.

"Don't listen to that stuff," Javik said.

"Not much," Wizzy said. "The Yannis are gone. They left or died during the upheaval."

"Well, they're back," Evans said. "Or someone is."

Wizzy's bright red color faded, then flickered. "I'm losing the signal," he said.

"Look, Captain!" Evans said, pointing across the dashboard to port. "Looks like a big storm heading right toward us! It's coming outta nowhere,"

Javik saw swirling, rust-colored particles only a few meters off the side of the ship, along with rain that seemed to be going up. It seemed impossible. The cabin darkened. "See if we can outrun it," Javik barked, trying to get back to his chair. The cabin lights brightened, compensating for the storm's darkness.

The storm hit before evasive action was possible. The *Amanda Marie* rocked violently, forcing Javik to hold a half-bulkhead with both hands. The cabin lights flickered off, leaving them in semidarkness. Then the lights danced back on.

"How odd," Wizzy squealed. "I saw rain going up—coming from the planet's surface."

"I saw it, too," Javik said. He crawled to his command chair as the ship rocked. Pulling himself up to the seat, Javik snapped on his safety harness. "Hit the thrusters!" he yelled.

"Nothing, Captain," Evans said. She was holding tight to her chair with both hands, trying to mento the thruster rockets. "No response at all."

"I'll bet there's dust in the thruster tubes," Wizzy said. "Now the main engines are sputtering, too."

The ship vibrated badly. It rocked to port, dipped its nose, and plunged.

"Going down fast, Captain Tom," Wizzy said.

"I can see that, for Atheist's sake," Javik snapped.

"Altitude fourteen thousand, two hundred meters," Mother reported. "Thruster tubes blocked. Manual correction required."

"Can't tell up from down," Javik said. "Too much damned dust."

"It's a magnetic storm," Wizzy said, glowing red from the red star crystal in his nucleus. "A remarkable battle between the planet and its atmosphere."

"Wonderful," Javik said. He grimaced. "Now we know what it is."

"Eleven thousand, six-fifty," Mother said.

Seeing that the rusty dust particles were thinning out, Evans said, "I think we're dropping below the storm."

"It's moving overhead," Wizzy said, looking through a porthole.

"Checking ship's functions," Mother said. "Still no thruster power. One main engine out."

The *Amanda Marie* rumbled roughly, then fell silent.

"Damn!" Javik cursed. "There went the remaining engine."

Mother confirmed this, then gave the altitude: "Seventy-two hundred meters."

Evans pounded on the instrument panel. "No CRT, accelerometer, or artificial horizon."

"And the para-flaps didn't go out," Javik said. "Aren't they automatic on this ship?"

"I think so," Evans said. She mentoed the flaps.

"Manual operation required," Mother said.

"I'll try 'em," Javik said, releasing his safety harness. He crawled aft along the corrugated metal deck to midships. There he grabbed a large black plastic wheel which was supported by an oblong pedestal. The surface of the wheel was abrasive to provide a gripping surface. Javik horsed with it, but it didn't budge. He cursed.

"Can you get it?" Evans asked.

"No."

"Thirty-nine fifty," Mother said.

"Get over here, Wizzy," Javik yelled. "Can you help me with this goddamned thing?"

"I'll try," Wizzy said. He alighted on one side of the wheel and clamped on with magic suction. With the two of them straining at it, the wheel finally broke free and moved. Then it stuck again.

"Where are all your wonderful powers now?" Javik asked, wiping his brow.

"Three thousand," Mother said.

"Unfortunately, they are inconsistent," Wizzy said. "One moment I feel super, and the next ... well, quite weak."

"What about now?" Javik asked. They resumed pushing and pulling.

"Not good," Wizzy said. He fell to the deck, short of breath.

"Get up," Javik said. He gave the wheel an angry, mighty push. It moved. He pushed it again, and it moved freely. Now Javik spun the wheel.

"Starboard flap's out, Captain," Evans said, sighting along the prismatic porthole at her side. Glancing at the porthole on Javik's side, she added, "Port flap's out, too."

Javik felt the *Amanda Marie's* nose rise as the para-flaps took hold. The ship continued its descent, but much less steeply.

"Eighteen hundred," Mother said.

Javik looked out a midships porthole and saw a para-flap undulating gracefully outside, like the wing of a great bird. He checked the other flap. It was functioning perfectly, too. Para-flaps were massive and white, with scalloped arches on the trailing edges and flotation cups on the undersides. They were awe-inspiring when viewed from the ground, and Javik recalled seeing a sky full of them once, with the sun setting beyond the Rosenbloom Mountains.

*Those were good days,* he thought, recalling the camaraderie of the corps.

"Fourteen hundred," Mother said.

Javik snapped to awareness. He returned to the command chair, asking, "What do you see, Evans?"

"Long gray strips," she said. "Maybe an airfield. We don't have a heck of a lot of choice." She pressed a yellow lever on her console to drop the landing gear.

Javik breathed a sigh of relief as he heard the gear pop down and lock into place. A green landing light flashed on at the center of the instrument panel. *Thank God,* he thought.

"Looks peculiar down there," Wizzy said. "Don't see any planes or rockets."

"Below a thousand," Mother said. "Final descent."

"I see ground vehicles," Javik said, watching streams of blue and pink flame streak along the gray ground strips.

"Primitive jets, sir," Wizzy said. "Jet-powered cars, to be precise."

"They're staying on the gray strips," Javik said. "So we'll land off to one side."

The *Amanda Marie* vibrated.

"Encountering turbulence," Evans said. "Rough glide."

"I know, I know," Javik said. He guided the steering toggle with one finger, hesitant to mento it.

The *Amanda Marie* hit an updraft, carrying it hundreds of meters from the gray ground strips. They crossed a heavily cratered area and approached a lightly wooded section where Javik saw pale green trees that resembled Sumerian pines.

"Up, baby," Evans coaxed, mento-adjusting the para-flaps.

The para-flaps fluttered desperately, carrying the ship just over the treetops. Now Javik could see a group of colorfully dressed people in a clearing. When the *Amanda Marie* was less than a hundred meters above the clearing, Javik noticed that the people below appeared to be wearing odd costumes—some were dressed like apples, others like oranges, bananas, watermelons.

"They're all dressed like fruit," Javik said.

"Not the bananas," Wizzy said. "Technically, the banana is neither fruit nor vegetable. More accurately, it can be categorized as cereal."

"Useless information," Javik said.

"Not to a nutritionist," Wizzy said.

Javik scowled.

The ship caught an updraft and rose momentarily. Then it dropped again.

"Hold on!" Javik yelled.

Javik and Evans braced themselves as the *Amanda Marie* bumped to the ground rather ungracefully. Javik felt a compression pain in his lower back. He rubbed it.

The ship rocked to one side on the ground, falling against one of the para-flaps. Then it righted itself. Javik heard the drone of electric motors as the para-flaps returned to their compartments.

Evans breathed a sigh of relief. "We're down," she said. "In one piece."

"I sense that our troubles have just begun," Wizzy said.

Javik mentoed the circular exit hatch without feeling any pain. The hatch unfolded from the center out like a camera orifice, revealing distant pine trees seen through dusty air. He smelled grit.

"Hmmm," Wizzy said as dust enveloped him. "Fine dry particles from a complex topsoil sediment, variable in texture … part crystalline, part disintegrated planetary mantle."

Javik shook his head as Wizzy went on to analyze the dust in its most minute detail.

A cacophony of cheers arose from outside, followed by the excited, unintelligible voices of many people. Rolling to the open hatchway, Javik commented, "They're dressed like trick-or-treaters." He felt the ship rock.

"What was that?" Evans asked.

Wizzy could be heard in the background, analyzing the entire climatological history of the planet, based upon the particles of dust adhering to the clear agate dome over his eye.

The *Amanda Marie* rocked again, then went back the other way. Leaning out of the circular hatch and looking to one side, Javik saw the edge of a mound of the colorfully dressed natives. *Now, why would they climb on top of one another like that?* he wondered.

The ship rocked once more, and this time it continued going over, in the direction away from the mound of natives. Javik had the answer to his unspoken question: They were toppling the ship!

"Going over!" Javik yelled. "Hold on!"

Wizzy buzzed by Javik and flew out the open hatchway.

The *Amanda Marie* fell on its side in a thunderous crash, slamming Javik and Evans against the interior walls. Then the ship began to roll over and over, gradually picking up speed. This created pandemonium inside, as Javik and Evans tried to get handholds on wall brackets, console bases, chairs, and anything else that was bolted down.

"Why are they doing this?" Evans wailed. She clung to the magnascope base.

With considerable difficulty, Javik crawled to his command chair and tried to pull himself into it. *If I could just strap myself in,* he thought. But he was not able to get off the deck. Hanging on to the chair, he heard laughter outside and strange words which almost sounded Latin. He decided the language mixer pendant around his neck was not working properly.

O O O

Outside, in the afternoon light of three synchronized suns, Wizzy flew unsteadily over the *Amanda Marie.* He was much like a tiny bird who had not yet perfected the art of flying. Below, people dressed in tattered fruit costumes pushed the ship, causing it to roll along a dusty, bumpy surface. Chanting phrases which Wizzy identified from his data banks as Corkian legalese, they guided the ship to a wide path, lined along each side with red, yellow, and blue cylinders which had been partially buried and propped upright.

*AmFed garbage cannisters,* Wizzy thought, glowing red as he continued to use his data banks.

Through the windshield and portholes of the *Amanda Marie*, Wizzy got glimpses of Javik and Evans clinging for their lives inside. Over and over the ship rolled, down the center of the path.

"Only one thing to do," Wizzy said to himself. He dived toward the people.

As Wizzy neared the throng, he realized they were not humans, and they were not wearing costumes. They were Fruit people, men and women, dressed in shabby, ill-fitting three-piece suits and suit dresses of varying colors and patterns. Each sported a tarnished gold chain across his waistcoated belly, and carried a worn briefcase in the hand which was not being used to push the ship. They looked distinguished to Wizzy, in a peculiar sort of way. He veered off just before hitting them.

The creatures swatted at Wizzy with their briefcases and ducked out of the way. Some yelled ferocious epithets in legalese. They continued pushing the ship.

"This is our chance, lawyers!" Wizzy heard one yell in a high-pitched, squealy voice. "Lord Abercrombie will favor us after such a large offering!"

From his ever-handy data banks, Wizzy pinpointed the language as one of seventeen Corker dialects, a variety which had been sprinkled generously with Aluminum Starfield Latin.

*Offering?* Wizzy thought. *What terrible rite is this?* He tried to pick up energy waves from the lawyer creatures' brains, but got nothing.

Wizzy dived at the creatures again. Again, they swatted at him and yelled epithets. After seven passes like this, all without success, Wizzy felt extremely tired. In a last-ditch burst of energy, he placed himself on the opposite side of the *Amanda Marie* from the creatures. Using all his strength against that side of the ship, he attempted to stop the crowd from rolling the ship any further.

For a fraction of a second, Wizzy thought he felt the ship hold. But then he realized he was slipping down along the riveted skin of the craft. It rolled over him, followed by hundreds of thunderous, trampling feet. Wizzy was kicked to one side of the path.

By the time Wizzy had picked himself up from the dust, he was behind the mob of Fruits and quite out of breath. Above him on each side towered the red, yellow, and blue garbage cannisters. He tried to fly, but did not have sufficient energy. So he scooted as quickly as he could off the path and up a little knoll overlooking the action.

Upon seeing where the ship was headed, Wizzy squealed, "Oh no!" Below him and perhaps a hundred meters ahead of the tumbling ship, Wizzy saw a huge, gaping hole in the ground.

"Wait!" Wizzy screamed. Panic-stricken, he scooted and fell down the knoll. "I've got to stop them!" he exclaimed.

The *Amanda Marie* hit a smooth downslope and picked up speed, leaving the Fruit lawyers running along behind. Some fell in their anxiety and were trampled by their cohorts.

"No!" Wizzy yelled. "Stop!" He scurried as fast as he could, but this was not nearly fast enough. He knew it was too late. The ship was outrunning everyone.

The *Amanda Marie hit* a bump at the edge of the precipice, then tumbled into the black, cavernous hole and disappeared. Wizzy felt an empty pang in the center of his nucleus.

Ahead, Wizzy saw the lawyers reach the edge of the precipice. The thunder of their feet subsided. They encircled the hole, looking down into it. As Wizzy caught up, he heard them chatter excitedly.

"Favor us, Lord Abercrombie!" they wailed. "Favor us, oh mighty Lord!"

Wizzy darted between the Fruit-lawyers' stubby legs and around their briefcases, soon reaching the edge of the hole! Looking down, he saw only blackness. It made him sad, extremely sad. This was a new emotion to Wizzy, and he did not understand it.

*I want to feel better,* Wizzy thought. So he laughed boisterously for several seconds. This did not help.

"End our suffering, Lord!" the Fruit lawyers moaned.

Wizzy leaned over the edge to get a better view, clinging there with all his remaining strength. *It worked the last time I laughed,* he thought. *Why don't I feel better now?*

He felt himself shaking, and wondered if this was caused by yet another emotion. Then he realized it was the ground that was moving, not him. He jumped away from the hole.

The Fruit lawyers cried out in terror, bemoaning the fact that Lord Abercrombie still was not pleased with them. Earthquakes were a bad sign. They ran for cover in the nearby piney woods, leaving Wizzy alone by the hole.

O O O

Shortly before this, Lord Abercrombie lay far below, immersed in the soil. It was nearly time for him to leave the Realm of Magic once again, returning to his half existence in the Realm of Flesh. Fear tore through him. He wanted completeness, either in magic or flesh. But he could not decide between the realms.

If he chose magic, the planet Cork would be his. *Chief Magician of Cork,* Abercrombie thought, letting the words roll across his pleasure sensors. *Has a nice sound to it. And no fleshcarrier can invade my private place from the surface, not as long as I remain soil-immersed.*

Cork was a planet waiting to be taken. But it seemed too easy, and this troubled him. *Why did the other magicians leave?* he wondered. There seemed no answer to such a question. Perhaps he could learn the answer—if he committed himself this time, not returning to flesh.

He wondered if he needed to commit himself entirely to the Realm of Magic before he would be able to use magic efficiently for the creation of disasters. In theory, that made a certain amount of sense. He was only pecking away at magic now, on the outskirts of something big. But could he return to flesh if he made such a commitment?

*What if being the planet is all there is here?* he thought. *A philosophical niche in which I can contemplate my navel … vegetating.*

Abercrombie stirred angrily. *God, but I hate vegetables!* he thought. He recalled a recurring nightmare in which his Earthian mother forced him to eat Brussels sprouts, those horrid little leafy balls. In the nightmare, his mother smiled in that falsely sweet way—the "It's good for you, dear" smile that he detested.

Cataloguing his enemies, past and present, Lord Abercrombie recalled when the villainous Uncle Rosy had sent six white-robed sayermen to take him back as a recycling criminal. But Abercrombie had stumbled across the Sacred Scroll of Cork, which led him to the Magician's Chamber: his private place. He was relatively safe here.

*But I was powerless to prevent the scroll's flight back to Sacred Pond,* he thought. *It is vulnerable there. And that makes me vulnerable—unless I choose to seal the surface entrance by remaining soil-immersed.*

He wondered if there might not be better planets. Why should he settle for a third-rate place?

Lord Abercrombie became aware of hordes of little feet scurrying across his surface. They were pushing something along the ground to the sacrifice hole his meckies had dug—a long, cream-colored canister with red, yellow, and blue markings—

*AmFed markings!* he thought. His visual sensors probed the canister as it tumbled across his planetary crust. *An AmFed ship! But what are those stupid lawyers doing? This is not gar-bahge, you fools!*

Lord Abercrombie felt himself returning to the Realm of Flesh as he thought of the ship. Maybe he could commandeer it to escape in his fleshy form, finding a better fleshcarrier life somewhere else, a life without Earthians pursuing him. But where would he go? On the other hand, he might still function as a magician, despite his frustrations to date. He was learning more about magic each day. Only the day before, he had magically induced a small rockslide. That was progress, his first magically created disaster in four years of trying.

But being a planet seemed so boring most of the time, just staring out on an unchanging universe, with occasional novas, comets, and shooting stars. He longed for action, for the excitement of change. This seemed possible only in the Realm of Flesh. And he longed for conversation with a real person. It had been four years....

His reasoning went in circles, touching each side of the argument over and over, and always returning to the starting point. It was frustrating.

As the AmFed ship tumbled into Abercrombie's maw, he wondered if he could put its computer hardware to use; maybe his meckies could adapt it to improve his outdated Earthian disaster control machinery. He needed to solve the reverse rain problem. At times, the patched-together disaster control equipment seemed to function well, producing nice phenomena, but then the rain would pour from the planet, and everything would short out.

*It's got to be in my equipment,* he thought. *Some misfunction I haven't discovered yet.*

Then Lord Abercrombie worried about the AmFeds sending warships to investigate the disappearance of an AmFed ship. He knew his magic was as undependable as his technology. He would be no match for sophisticated AmFed weaponry. They could destroy the entire planet.

*No,* he decided. *I can't keep the ship.*

The *Amanda Marie* hurtled deeper into the sacrifice hole, bouncing off dirt and rocks on the sides. Something fell out of the ship, but Lord Abercrombie did not focus on what it was.

*Magnetics,* he thought, recalling the symbols on the history wall. He pictured one of the symbols in his mind now: a circle intertwined with the symbol for magnetics. *Circle,* he thought. *Circle...*

Lord Abercrombie recalled that the symbols were beneath the pictures of his magician predecessors. *Circle,* he thought. *Could that represent a planet? Maybe the whole symbol refers to planetary magnetics.*

He wanted to consider this further, but began to feel ill, sick to his pleasure sensors. His fleshy hand clutched fitfully out of the dirt, reaching for its survival. He swooned. Suddenly, a monstrous burp echoed through the passageways and caverns of the Magician's Chamber. Lord Abercrombie jumped out of the hole, throwing dirt everywhere.

O O O

In sunlight on the planet's surface, Wizzy smelled a peculiar, sulfurous gas which nauseated him. He took refuge behind one of the upright garbage canisters.

*Burr … rupp!* An echoing regurgitation sound came from the hole, followed by the *Amanda Marie*. A deep voice thundered from the hole: "You stupid lawyers! Incompetent fools! Can't you do anything right?"

The ship was hurled high in the air over Wizzy, along with fragments of dirt and rock. Something white hurtled by too, causing Wizzy's magical heart to sink. *A body?* he thought.

Whatever it was sped away before he could identify it. The ship itself went so high that Wizzy almost lost sight of it. Then, from a distant, tiny speck, it began to grow larger. It was falling back to Cork.

Most of the Fruit lawyers managed to dodge rocks and other debris that pelted the area, but Wizzy saw one hapless banana man squashed flat by a large stone. It was horrible. Other Fruits nursed wounds and looked for their missing property. Briefcases and business cards lay on the ground in disarray.

"Lord Abercrombie refused our offering!" a bottom-heavy pear woman lamented. "Now the curse will be worse! He is furious with us!"

None could dispute this statement. There was a general condition of extreme unhappiness.

Soon Wizzy saw the *Amanda Marie's* para-flaps go out. *Someone's inside,* he thought, recalling that the automatic system had not functioned earlier. *At least one.*

The ship drifted down gracefully, landing almost without flaw at one side of the clearing. It was badly dented, with portions of riveted skin hanging loose like bloodless wounds.

"Oh my!" Wizzy exclaimed in a voice drowned out in the surrounding commotion. "I hope everyone's all right!"

The crowd ran toward the ship, yelling angry and confused epithets. Wizzy followed, scooting in short bursts and stopping frequently to catch his breath.

A tall pineapple man with scaly brown skin ran past Wizzy at one of these rest stops. This fellow looked quite silly to Wizzy in comparison with the others. He wore bright purple and black checkered shorts that were torn on one side and a faded, royal purple tunic. An immense, leafy green headdress grew from his head, on top of which he held on a misshapen helicopter beanie with one hand. "Be calm, my friends!" the pineapple man called out as he ran. "Calm yourselves!"

Ahead, Wizzy could see the open hatch on the *Amanda Marie. Pop your head out. Captain Tom,* he thought, staring anxiously at the open hatch. But there was no sign of movement on the ship.

# Chapter Five

*The effects of ultra technology often seem identical to those of magic. This is the point at which the Realm of Flesh approaches a more perfect, magical state. Only a knowledgeable observer can spot the difference.*

A Timeless Truth

"We're down!" Evans said, clinging with both hands to the midships para-flaps wheel. She released her grip. Her palms were moist.

"Ow," Javik said. A sharp pain shot through his shoulder. He had been holding fast to his command chair. Now he rose to survey the cabin. It was in disarray, with clip files, medical packs, and other items of equipment scattered about. Sunlight slanted through the portholes on one side. Javik rubbed his sore shoulder.

Evans rolled to the open circular hatch and looked out. "Lucky we didn't fall out," she said, watching the crowd of oddly dressed natives approach.

Javik was at her side a moment later. "Still no response from the engines," he said, holding his hand on his holstered service pistol.

"God, it stinks in here!" Evans said. "Some kinda gas in that hole."

"Sounded like a big burp to me," Javik said.

As the crowd approached, Evans speculated that they looked like a bunch of costume-party goers. "Maybe they're drunk," she said.

"They look like offbeat lawyers," Javik said. "Look at the three-piece suits, briefcases, and gold watch chains." He squinted. "Wait a minute," he said.

"Are those costumes?" Evans asked.

"Exactly what I was wondering. I can't tell."

The crowd became excited upon seeing Javik and Evans. They ran faster, pointing and waving white cards. As they neared, Javik realized they were business cards. And he realized something else.

"They're Fruit people!" Javik exclaimed.

"Frumba hallinon?" an orange woman asked, looking up and extending a business card. She was the first to arrive. Javik noticed a small folding shovel on her hip, secured to her belt.

Others arrived now, an endless variety of Fruit people, all dressed similarly and all waving business cards. "Frumba hallinon?" they asked. "Frumba hallinon?"

"What the…?"

Javik fumbled with his language mixer pendant. It showed a red light. Then it beeped and the light became green.

"Do you want legal advice?" the Fruit creatures asked. They still spoke in their native tongue, but now Javik understood.

"Where are we?" Evans asked. "In Glitterland?"

Soon the Fruits were clamoring to reach the visitors from Earth. Since the open hatch was high off the ground at midships, the Fruits had to pile on top of one another, just as they had done earlier to topple the ship. They fought to be first, pushing and kicking their brethren with complete abandon.

One watermelon man reached the top, where he hung desperately to the hatchway deck. Stretching to reach up, he pressed a business card into Javik's palm. Javik used his mixer to read it as the fellow was dragged down the heap to the ground. The pile fell now, and the Fruits scrambled to rebuild it.

Wily Watermelon
Attorney at Law,
non compos mentis

Javik flipped the card away, and watched the wind take it. Below, the Fruit people were clearing their ranks, allowing a tall pineapple man through. Obviously, he was someone in authority. Dressed differently from the others but carrying a similar folding shovel on his hip, the pineapple man's most distinctive article of attire was a red helicopter beanie with a bright yellow plastic rotor that spun as he walked.

A murmuring passed through the crowd. The Fruit lawyers who had been piling up retreated, nursing their wounds.

When he reached the front of the multitude, the pineapple man extended his arms to each side, gazing up at Javik and Evans. "You there!" he called out in a loud, syrupy voice. "Identify yourselves!" *Drat!* he thought. *This had better not interrupt my plans for tonight!*

Javik gave names, then said, "We are in the American Federation of Freeness Space Patrol. From Earth." He wrinkled his brow, recalling the dancing pineapple man he had seen when he was half asleep in the videodome—just before Wizzy's entrance. Every event after the time Wizzy appeared seemed unreal to Javik. But then he recalled Wizzy slamming into his hand to prove he was awake. *That hurt like hell,* Javik thought.

"I am Prince Peter Pineapple," the pineapple man announced proudly. "Of the Royal Family of Cork." He squinted in the light of three suns which were low in the sky to the west.

"This place is called Cork?" Javik asked. He saw Wizzy scoot up at the prince's feet, panting heavily. Wizzy was dark blue with a thin layer of dust on his body.

"It is our planet's name," Prince Pineapple explained. "Sixth planet in the Triad Solar System."

"We call it the Aluminum Starfield," Javik said.

Prince Pineapple smoothed his elegant leaf headless with one hand. "We know of Earth, you know," he said.

"You do?" Javik said. "How?"

"You sent us gar-bahge."

"I know," Javik said nervously, taking note of the affected pronunciation. "I have been sent to discuss that with you."

"We know you by your gar-bahge, Earthian. And I can't tell you how happy we are to see you."

"Uh ... we will straighten everything out. I promise you that."

"Wonderful!" the pineapple prince said. "Come down now, Earthians. King Corker would hear of your gar-bahge!"

"Why did your people push my ship in a hole?" Javik asked.

"Those foolish lawyers," Prince Pineapple said, glowering around. "Our lowest social strata. And there are so many of them! They tried to gain favor with Lord Abercrombie by offering you."

"*Offering* us? To what?"

"To our planetary God, Lord Abercrombie. It was a mistake, for which I apologize profusely."

The Fruit lawyers hung their heads in shame.

Evans leaned close to Javik's ear and whispered, "Could it be the same Abercrombie, with a new scam?"

"We'll find but," Javik whispered. Then: "We'd better do as they say. Too many of them." He removed the ship's black and white striped

Tasnard rope from its wall hook. At his mento-command, the rope secured itself to the base of the science officer's console. A small pang of pain struck at the rear of his head, then subsided.

Evans wrapped the Tasnard rope around her chest and under her armpits. At her mento-command, the rope dropped her gently to the ground.

Javik followed.

"Honored to meet you," Prince Pineapple said, bowing graciously as Javik reached the ground. The prince straightened to face Javik, and his black button eyes wavered nervously. He was a towering Fruit, fully half a head taller than Javik.

"Thank you," Javik said, bowing in return. *Don't trust anyone who won't look you in the eye,* he thought, recalling his commanders' Psych 101 course.

On the ground at Prince Pineapple's feet, Wizzy breathed deeply and loudly. Javik noticed this and saw that Wizzy was accumulating more dust from the motion of feet around him.

Prince Pineapple smiled, revealing puffy white teeth which resembled kernels of white corn. Looking past Javik at the *Amanda Marie*, he said, "You must understand our unfortunate lawyers. Since Decision Coins were implemented for virtually all matters, we have little need of legal advice."

"Seedy-looking bunch," Javik muttered.

"Lawyers hang around this clearing looking for clients," the prince explained. "Rumor has it one attorney found a client here two years ago. It became hallowed ground for them after that."

"I see," Javik said, shuffling his feet impatiently.

Prince Pineapple felt obliged to explain further: "The canister-lined pathway and sacrifice hole are hallowed for all Fruits," he said. "It looks like our local dimwits saw your ship and mistook it for a giant gar-bahge canister. We toss most of our gar-bahge in the sacrifice hole for Lord Abercrombie."

Javik fingered a pimple on the side of his neck.

"They are desperate to win Lord Abercrombie's favor. Poor creatures think they've been cursed." After reflecting for a second, Prince Pineapple added, "Maybe it's true."

"What an odd place this is," Evans said.

"Don't impose Earth standards," Wizzy said from the ground, using an instructor's tone. Breathing loudly, Wizzy glowed softly orange. The dust particles on his surface melted and disappeared. He became dark blue again.

"None of us have been ourselves lately," Prince Pineapple said. "It's this infernal gar-bahge thing, you know. Tremendous pressure over it. The Planet God has been troubled." *To hell with Lord Abercrombie!* he thought. *The foolishness he condones!*

Javik smiled uneasily. He looked back at his ship, noting many dents, torn pieces of skin, and numerous abrasions. It would require a major overhaul to make it spaceworthy again. "How were we blown back out of the hole?" he asked, turning to face the pineapple prince.

"Don't step on me!" Wizzy squealed. A prune man stood on him.

Prince Pineapple hesitated as he focused on Fruit people who were pressing in around them, listening to every word. Some took notes on long clip pads or whispered back and forth excitedly, using their Corkian legalese.

"Move along now!" Prince Pineapple commanded. "Make way!" He waved his arms demonstratively.

Javik noticed now that the prince and all the Fruits had four fingers and a thumb on each hand like any human, except the thumb was on the outside of the hand.

Slowly, the throng moved back.

"Come with me," Prince Pineapple said to Javik and Evans. He guided them toward an opening in the crowd. "It will be dusk soon."

"I'll join you later," Wizzy said. "I need a breather."

Javik held back. "My ship will be safe here?" he asked.

"Your ship is nearly new. New things have no value to our people."

Javik scratched his head thoughtfully. "Is that so? Well, it's received quite a bit of damage. Doesn't look so new to me anymore."

"Hmmm," Prince Pineapple said, studying the *Amanda Marie*, "The damage helps a little. Still, I do not find it very appealing. Perhaps with a few more dents and abrasions …"

"I can't leave my ship with this mob," Javik said.

The prince shrugged. "Very well," he said. "I'll post guards, then. Will that make you feel better?"

"It will."

Prince Pineapple spoke with a cluster of banana man lawyers, instructing them to stand guard over the craft. Then he drew forth a purple and black checkered wallet, removing several creased pieces of paper which looked to Javik like old Earth candy bar and gum wrappers.

Leaning close, Javik verified this. He recognized wrappers from a Big Hunk, a Hershey's plain, and a Juicy Fruit.

Solemnly, Prince Pineapple handed a creased wrapper to each of the banana men. They nodded and stuffed the wrappers in their pockets.

"Juicy Fruits are the most valuable," the prince said to Javik. He slipped the wallet back into his pants pocket.

"I see," Javik said.

When they were out of earshot of the lawyers, Prince Pineapple said: "Poor devils. Our law schools still pump out so many of them."

Evans caught Javik's gaze. She raised her eyebrows.

Prince Pineapple led the way along a rough path which skirted the piney woods: "The sacrifice hole appeared several years back," he said as they reached late afternoon shade. "Lord Abercrombie's metal men dug it. I saw them."

"Metal men?" Evans said. "You mean meckies?"

"I don't know what they're called," Prince Pineapple said. The prince's cadence changed now as they continued along the path. His steps became staccato-quick and inefficient. The big pineapple man was expending a lot of energy but not moving commensurately fast.

Javik and Evans rolled as best as they could on the uneven surface, but tripped several times as their moto-boot wheels encountered stones, twigs, and tufts of dirt. At one point, Javik fell to his knees.

"Hurry now," the prince said, looking back. "The king is waiting." *I must act as though I care,* he thought. *Or the king will suspect …*

Javik touched a button on his moto-boots to eject the wheels and wheel frames. He tossed them aside.

Evans did the same, leaving both of them wearing unmotorized service boots. "That's better," she said, testing them on the ground.

"Unusual shoes you Earthians wear," Prince Pineapple said. "Hurry now!"

"More suited to Earth, it seems," Javik said as they resumed their course. He added: "This Planet God, Lord Abercrombie. He is terribly upset at the gar-bahge situation?"

"Oh yes! Indeed he is! And so is King Corker, It is a good thing you arrived now. We could not have survived much longer." *Odd that Earthians would appear just now,* he thought. *By morning, I will be gone, scroll or no scroll.*

"I can imagine," Javik said, scanning the terrain. "You've certainly managed to keep the planet clean," he added. "In view of our garbage, I mean." *I expected to see junk strewn all over hell,* he thought.

Prince Pineapple led them over a sturdy wooden bridge which traversed a dry creek bed. "What wonderful gar-bahge you Earthians have!" he exclaimed. *Oh, the foolishness I must endure!* he thought. *There is more to life than gar-bahge. There must be!*

*Wonderful?* Javik thought. *Is he being sarcastic?* "They tried landfills on Earth many years ago," he said. "But we ran out of space and had to catapult the stuff." A little light went on in Javik's head now as he put Abercrombie, the sacrifice hole, and the garbage together. *The same guy!* he thought. *What's he up to here?*

Facing a fork in the path just after they left the bridge, Prince Pineapple selected the left path, which led them into the forest. This was a narrow neck of woods, and through streaks of sunlight Javik could see a clearing not far ahead. Beyond that loomed a large gray structure. He heard crowd noises and the roar of powerful engines.

Presently they left the woods, stepping into full sunlight. The terrain was flat here, with a town of low buildings visible beyond the gray structure.

"Wait!" a little voice squealed from somewhere behind them.

"It's your little meckie," Evans said. "Welcome back, Wizzy."

Wizzy came out of the woods, moving along the ground in staggering spurts, resting and then scooting for very short distances. He glowed a dim, sickly yellow which appeared on the verge of extinction. When he arrived, Evans reached down and lifted him to her eye level. He felt warm and wet.

"The little guy's panting!" Evans said. "This is one complex meckie!"

"I have emotions too," Wizzy said proudly. "I am similar to you in many ways."

"Sometimes he forgets he's a meckie," Javik said, scowling at Wizzy. Javik's sea blue eyes flashed angrily.

"You take him," Evans said, handing Wizzy to Javik. "He's all sweaty." She wiped her hands on her jumpsuit.

As Javik accepted Wizzy, a strong gust of wind blew, drying the baby comet's surface. Surprised at how heavy Wizzy was, Javik noticed that his surface felt sandpaper-rough and lumpy. On closer inspection, he noticed little stones, pieces of dirt, and twigs embedded in Wizzy's stony skin. He brushed Wizzy's back, but the debris remained.

"A natural process," Wizzy explained. "I am beginning to accumulate material as my system feels able to assimilate it. That is how I grow in the physical sense." He glowed orange-hot, forcing Javik to let go quickly. Wizzy hovered in midair where Javik's hand had left him. His lumpy body became smooth and molten. Then he cooled, returning to dark blue.

Hesitantly, Javik retrieved him.

"We must hurry," Prince Pineapple said. "The king does not like to be kept waiting … waiting … waiting …" His voice slowed, and his black button eyes rolled upward. Desperately, he dropped to the ground on the seat of his checkered pants. He unsnapped the small folding shovel from his belt. His motions were painstakingly slow.

Three times Javik reached out with the hand that did not hold Wizzy, offering to help. Each time, Prince Pineapple shook his head negatively.

From his vantage point on Javik's hand, Wizzy watched the prince unwrap a slender barbed cord from the shovel handle. Then he removed one shoe and sock and wrapped the cord around his bare foot.

Catching Evans's gaze, Javik shrugged.

By now, Prince Pineapple was quite run down and an unhealthy shade of pale brown. He unfolded the shovel and dug in the soil between his outstretched legs. The ground was hard here, permitting the prince only slow progress.

"Let me help," Javik said, touching the shovel handle.

Weakly, Prince Pineapple pushed him away.

"He is like me," Wizzy said. "I get awfully tired too."

The pineapple prince was leaning on the shovel now, breathing very slowly.

"He's more than just tired," Javik said. "It's like he has a run-down battery."

"My foot," Prince Pineapple said, looking at Javik. "Help me get it in the hole."

Javik set Wizzy on the ground and pushed the prince's stubby leg until his wrapped foot was in the hole. As the foot touched the freshly dug soil, Javik saw sharp barbs spring out from the cord, stabbing into the ground like hungry roots.

Presently, the prince's breathing became more rapid. The rich golden color returned to his face. "I shouldn't have tried to go so long on my morning charge," he said with a deep sigh. "Not on such an active day."

"You were right, Captain Tom," Wizzy said, hopping on the palm of Javik s hand.

"We are Fruits of the soil," Prince Pineapple said with a serene expression. "Children of Lord Abercrombie."

"That name again," Evans said.

Minutes later, Prince Pineapple's expression became angry as he pulled his foot from the ground and unwrapped it. "I hate myself for needing Lord Abercrombie," he said. "We are his captives, you know, unable to lead our own lives." He wiped his foot with a moist-pak towelette, then replaced his sock and shoe.

"What do you mean?" Wizzy asked, jumping to Javik's shoulder.

Prince Pineapple rose and wrapped the barbed cord around the handle of his folding shovel. Then he replaced the items on his belt clip. "Lord Abercrombie does not just give us nutrition," he said. "With that comes the worst sort of dogma … little statements from him to mold our opinions, to make us revere him. He even comes to us in dreams! No rest! He gives us no rest!" The prince grew silent, disturbed with himself for saying too much.

When they resumed their course on the path, Javik noticed that Prince Pineapple's cadence had improved, having eliminated the wasted motions. One of the three synchronized suns was partially obscured now, having dropped below the horizon formed by the buildings ahead.

Catching up with the prince, Javik held Wizzy out for him to see. "This little lump of stone is Wizzy," Javik said, revealing only a little derision in his tone. "A mechanical unit."

Prince Pineapple glanced back at Wizzy only briefly, for he had more important matters on his mind. *King Corker is already unhappy with me,* he thought. *I must try to please him, just for tonight. Can't have him ordering me into detention. Not when I am so close.*

"I'm science officer on the ship," Wizzy said.

"Oh?" Prince Pineapple said. "That's very nice."

Javik smiled as he followed the prince. "Wizzy thinks he fulfills an important role on the ship."

"Can't you say anything nice about me?" Wizzy asked.

"Well," Javik said with a sneer. "I'll think very hard about that. Maybe I can come up with something, if I take long enough." He placed Wizzy back on his shoulder.

"Hrrrumph!" Wizzy said.

To their left beyond a small meteor crater Evans saw a throng of carrot men and women being led out of cattle chutes. Fruit guards prodded the carrot people with electric sticks, using the power of blue shocks to herd them toward a ramp. At the top of the ramp was an elongated piece of machinery with what appeared to be conveyor strips.

"What's that?" she asked.

"A power plant," Prince Pineapple said. "It's nearly dusk, and extra power is required to run the lights. The Vegetable slaves jog on a treadmill to generate electricity."

"What about solar power?" Javik asked. "With three suns, I would have thought—"

"No need for that," Prince Pineapple said. "This keeps the Vegetables busy … and in their places." *It might have been much worse for me,* he thought. *At least I'm a Fruit.*

Javik grunted. He heard boisterous crowd noises and the roar of engines clearly now. The sounds came from the vicinity of the towering gray structure, which was perhaps five hundred meters ahead. Seeing colorfully dressed spectators on top, Javik realized it was the back of an immense grandstand. To one side of the grandstand he saw blue and pink streaks and balls of flame, and heard the *pop-pop* of what sounded like gunfire.

"Many Earthians used to arrive in your gar-bahge canisters, you know," the prince said.

"I know," Javik responded. "We ran out of burial space on Earth. I will apologize to your king, of course."

"No need for that. We have put the Earthians to good use."

"Oh?"

"I will show you," Prince Pineapple said. "Just ahead."

The path turned toward the grandstand. It was a wood frame thing, with horizontal rows of weathered, rough-hewn boards. In sunlight to one side, Javik focused on a group of male Earth humanoids with the same oversized heads as those in the Davis Droids. They wore glossy blue and pink uniforms and were gathered around unusual-looking land vehicles.

"The atmosphere here," Evans said to Javik, hearing her own words crackle nervously in the air. "Wizzy said it was different."

"Nurinium did it," Wizzy said from Javik's shoulder.

Javik scowled as they walked by. "Looks like they used old Earth parts to assemble these cars," he said. "That one has a DeMartini front end, but the rest looks like shop work."

Evans studied one vehicle as they passed close. It was Wind-sea blue and white, covered with dents, with mismatched body parts that had undergone extensive welding. The windshield glassplex was cracked, and none of the other windows had any glassplex at all. A large-caliber gun was turret-mounted on the roof, with smaller machine guns on each fender, two guns at the front and two at the rear. Three humanoids were looking in the engine compartment, speaking to one another in loud monotones.

A crowd roar drowned put the voices.

The three bulbous-headed humanoids paused to watch Javik and Evans with bloodshot eyes. Javik noticed they had yellow-stained teeth, like the "before" segment of a videodome toothpaste commercial. Grape-men guards rushed over and prodded them with electric sticks. Blue lances sprung from the tips of the sticks, jolting the humanoids to return to work.

"Those guards are Corkers," Prince Pineapple said. "Highest of the Fruit castes."

Javik counted six legs on each Corker. Grenache purple and rotund, they had plastic containers strapped to their backs.

One humanoid who had just been shocked into action donned a blue and black helmet and strapped it tight around his chin. Then he climbed through the window of the car and slid into the driver's seat. Seconds later, the vehicle roared to life, sending a huge streak of bright blue flame out of the tail.

This caught an inattentive Corker dead center, sending him rolling away. Singed and angry, he sprang to his feet and ran after the car. Another ball of flame sent him reeling.

"Damn fool Corker," Prince Pineapple muttered, watching the car speed away, heading for one of the drag strips. "Those fellows haven't got a lick of sense. Half the time they're out on their feet, drunk on the grain alcohol they carry in their packs. They're born tipsy, you know. I hear fermented grape juice runs through their veins."

"Your king is a Corker too?" Javik asked.

"We call these Earth Games," Prince Pineapple said, disregarding the query. He hurried along the path, adding, "Conceived in one of Lord Abercrombie's dream messages."

They rounded a corner of the grandstand, placing them out of view of the action. On this side the ground was littered with Corker backpacks and other debris. The prince kept looking up nervously at the grandstand. Then he yelled, "Look out!" and pushed Javik and Evans off the path.

A large bottle crashed to-the ground where they had been, followed by two plastic backpacks, partially full. Wizzy scurried away from a big splash of dirty-colored grain alcohol.

"It gets a bit rough back here during the games," Prince Pineapple said.

An inebriated Corker approached, weaving from side to side on the path. Short and round with a plastic grain alcohol pack strapped to her back, the grenache purple Corker had peculiar, scaly skin with bumps on it like flattened grapes. As she neared, Javik heard odd sucking sounds. Looking closely, he noticed she was sucking at a tube that led from the backpack to her mouth. Black, brackish liquid dripped down her chin.

Prince Pineapple nodded dutifully to the Corker as they passed. She did not acknowledge the gesture, and instead coughed, hawked, and spit a ball of black phlegm on the ground.

Javik wrinkled his face in revulsion as the Corker passed. "Smelly little brute," he whispered to Wizzy.

Still on Javik's shoulder, Wizzy went into a discourse on the smelliest, most vile things in the universe. After less than a minute of this, Javik stuffed the little comet in his jumpsuit pocket and zipped it shut. From the pocket, Javik still heard Wizzy's muffled voice, saying something about the slime in which Esterian pigs liked to root.

"We must go faster," Prince Pineapple said, seeing shadows lengthen across the path.

They moved more quickly now, crossing a footbridge over a highway of vehicles that were pulled by carrot people. Each vehicle carried a different variety of Fruit person. Javik noticed that some of the carriages were a good deal more extravagant than others, with longer cabs, more silver or gold trim, and longer teams of carrot people.

Wizzy fell silent in Javik's pocket, realizing just then what had been done to him.

Javik asked about the vehicles.

"They reflect status in the Royal Family," Prince Pineapple said. "Every Fruit is a member of the Royal Family. The king has a carriage pulled by one hundred carrot men. No one is permitted to have more."

"I see," Javik said. *I wonder if they call it carrot power,* he thought.

"Carrot people are strongest of the Vegetables," the prince said. "Health fanatics. They make ferocious warriors for the enemy, excellent slaves for us."

"Who are your enemies?" Evans asked.

"The Vegetable Underground," Prince Pineapple said.

"Fruits against Vegetables?" Javik asked, bemused but trying not to show it.

"Since time immemorial," came the reply. "But it is not a perfect system. Even drunkard lowlifes such as the Corker we passed at the grandstand have a good deal of status … simply by virtue of their close juice relationship to our king."

They could see the castle now, at the crest of a Vegetable garden terraced hill. "We grow our own slaves," the prince explained.

The Corker castle was massive, constructed of native charcoal stones in the Earthian medieval manner. Imposing ramparts of dirt and stone surrounded the structure, and Javik counted eight guard towers on this side alone, each flying a triangular purple banner.

"What is your position?" Evans asked of the prince.

"Number One Adviser to King Corker. We Pineapples are extremely intelligent—but not entirely appreciated, I fear."

"How so?" Evans asked, catching up with the prince and walking at his side.

"Important matters do not require brains here. Decision Coins are flipped. Whenever the king asks me for my opinion, I am expected to flip a coin."

"That sounds dumb."

"You think so, too?" Prince Pineapple asked, pleased.

"Definitely."

"We pineapples might have taken control of the planet on the First Day … if the blight had not hit us. Things would be different today if only …" He hesitated.

"What happened?" Javik asked, catching up and walking on the prince's other side. *Planet of the Grapes,* Javik thought, making a play on an ancient, tattered paperback book Sidney once had shown him. It was one of the illegal things Sidney kept hidden in his safe.

"A strange malady," Prince Pineapple said. "Only affecting pineapples. Some say the Corkers …" He sighed.

"The blight was intentionally inflicted?" Evans asked. "A power grab?"

"I have said too much," Prince Pineapple said. *And I am supposed to be so intelligent!* he thought, raging inside.

"We will not repeat it," Javik said.

The prince's gaze flitted all over the place, like a moth near light. "I have been fortunate personally," he said, "though recently in disfavor with the king. That's why I'm so anxious to take you straight to his court. He has been most unhappy with me of late." *A half-truth,* he thought, recalling his clandestine plans for that evening.

They reached a section of uphill straightaway lined with high English hedges. Ahead, Javik saw a wide moat and the castle's main drawbridge.

"The Corkers were destined for power anyway," Prince Pineapple said, attempting to change his image to the Earthian visitors. "They are our best fighters, having six legs instead of two like the rest of us. This gives them great individual speed and mobility on the battlefield."

"The ones I've seen don't look so ferocious," Javik said. Glancing through an opening in the hedge, Javik saw a wrinkled old prune woman sitting on a wooden bench. She smiled softly at him. It was an all-knowing smile, a haunting smile, the sort of smile that numbed you with its intensity.

They crossed a drawbridge over a wide, murky moat, then stood at the castle gates. Javik saw watermelon men guards along the wall above. Looking back, Javik was disturbed to see the old Fruit woman staring at them from across the moat. "Who is that?" he asked.

"Just a prunesayer," Prince Pineapple said. "I think you would call her a soothsayer, I've heard the word in the Earthian vocabulary."

# Chapter Six

*Morovia: A planet dominated by the police magician Lancaster IX. Linked through Dimensional Tunnels 901 and 902 across the universe to the planets Cork and Agrippa.*

From *A Magician's History of the Universe*

Standing naked next to the dirt hole in his Soil Immersion Cavern, Lord Abercrombie mentoed the white rectangle on his wardrobe ring, activating a dry shower. The rectangular white stone on his AmFed ring glowed, giving him a low-level electrical tingle through the epidermis of his fleshy half. He watched dirt fall from his body.

*Wait a minute,* he thought, looking at the back of his hand. *A freckle just fell off too!*

He soon forgot about this and mentoed the ring's turquoise stone. A blue, yellow, and white striped caftan with gold scroll sleeves stitched itself over his half body. Following his form, the caftan covered only his right side. Extending his single foot, he watched a white crew sock and brown patent leather shoe appear there. Then he felt a crown of thistle circumnavigate the outer portion of his nearly bald half skull.

Lord Abercrombie glided regally across the cavern floor, passing cardboard boxes and plastic crates of recycled products, so numerous that he had only a narrow pathway through them. In the rock-lined passageway outside, it was the same, with finished products stacked to the ceiling on each side. He entered a complicated maze of rocky tunnels which he had committed to memory. This led to glassplex tunnels which his meckies had constructed for him. Through the clear glassplex, he could see ancient underground firebat caves and iridescent, multi-tiered waterfalls.

He floated by a wall sign that read "DON'T ABUSE IT! REUSE IT!" In a moment of sadness, he considered how tarnished was his success, limited only to making recycled goods. He had no distribution system. No other human in the universe knew the goods were there.

"I'm not a Job Support criminal!" he yelled into the empty glassplex tunnel. "It *is* fair to repair!" His words echoed down the passageway, heard by no human except himself.

Now he floated by caverns filled with robotics-operated machinery—hundreds of recycling machines forming the heart of his enterprise, each with a hopper on top. He paused to watch a yellow meckie load old clothing into a hopper. Behind the machine a noisy, loose-belted conveyor carried freshly wound spools of recycled thread to the boxing room meckies. Meckies in other rooms recycled plastics, metals, glass, and paper.

But it was quieter now than it had been, with many machines idle. He was running out of raw material.

Presently he entered a wide cavern which had three walls of mirror glassplex. The side opposite the doorway was a black abyss, the opening to the Dimensional Tunnel. Fifteen large trunks on wheels were chained together in a train at the center of the cavern, with a rock-filled dummy chained at the rear of that. A frigid galactic wind howled through this room, causing Lord Abercrombie's fleshy half to shiver.

Pausing to light a lavender tintette in front of the mirror, he used his human eye and the bank of visual sensors on his magical side to study the reflected inner workings of his head and neck: an exposed pink cerebrum and a cerebellum that throbbed as his arm moved with the tintette. There was a clear, glossy surface over the exposed inner parts, through which he saw his open nasal cavity, his half tongue and half mouthful of teeth surrounded on the fleshy outside by an ebony beard. Below that was a split windpipe with a pink, lumpy thyroid gland next to it.

*I look like someone sliced me down the middle,* he thought. *From my head all the way to the ground.* Lifting his robe with his single hand, he saw one leg hanging oddly by itself, just centimeters off the ground.

Trailing lavender tintette smoke, he glided past the trunks to the edge of the black abyss. Here the wind flapped his robe and howled with an eerie, hostile loudness. He saw the blackest black imaginable from this spot, so dark that Abercrombie knew no artist could ever match its pigmentation. The Dimensional Tunnel was a powerful thing, an awesome thing. Lavender smoke disappeared into the abyss. He tossed the tintette in too.

*So many tests!* he thought. *And what do I learn from them?*

He considered throwing himself into the Dimensional Tunnel at that very instant. In a wild flight of fancy, he imagined finding the tintette again and smoking it in some strange and distant place.

*Surely I would land in a place where my enemies could not find me,* he thought. *But what new dangers await me out there?* Throwing himself in the Dimensional Tunnel was but one of his options if he decided to remain a fleshcarrier. In another scenario, he would remain on Cork in his fleshy form, using salvaged Earthian disaster control equipment to impose his will on the planet and its inhabitants. But that reverse rain problem … and planetary magnetics. What did it all mean?

Wearily, Lord Abercrombie trudged to the lead trunk in the train. Grabbing a side handle on this trunk, he used it to pull all fifteen trunks and the dummy toward the Dimensional Tunnel. They rolled effortlessly.

Reaching the edge, he glided to the rear of the procession of trunks and gave them a mighty push. Sidestepping the dummy, he watched the lead trunk disappear into blackness, followed quickly by the others and the dummy.

*Fwoosh!* They were gone.

He thought of the option being tested here, a scenario whereby the trunks could be filled with recycled goods and a meckie, just enough trinkets and a helper to get him started comfortably in a new place. If he chose flesh. That was a very large "if."

Now he wondered, *Should I ride in front of the trunks? Or at the rear? How about inside one?* He knew there was no way to answer this question with such a limited experiment. He could not see the other end of the Dimensional Tunnel: His laboratory was universe-size. But the experiments gave him time to think. He was considering all the possibilities he could, preparing a mental balance sheet of flesh versus magic.

With his caftan flapping in the wind, he shouted into the blackness of the Dimensional Tunnel, "Is there another place for me out there?" The words barely touched his ears and tympanic sensors before they were gone, sucked into the howling abyss.

He worried about missing a greater opportunity, a higher calling. Maybe there was a beautiful planet waiting for him out there in the Great Beyond.

*But what if every other place is taken?* he thought. *I might be murdered as an intruder.*

The unknown terror nearly overwhelmed him.

"Why wasn't Cork taken?" he yelled. "Why was this place left for me?"

There was no answer, only the ceaseless, eternal howl of galactic winds.

His human side felt lonely. It was an intense loneliness, as deep and black as the universe itself.

O O O

In the box-lined passageway outside, Lord Abercrombie was stopped by a silver and black female meckie.

"Would you answer a question for me, please?" the meckie asked. A white dome light on its top pulsed.

"What is it?" Abercrombie snapped. He was irritated, for there were important matters on his mind.

"You are always speaking of the great joys and benefits of recycling," the meckie said. "But isn't that a new outfit you're wearing? Shouldn't you be wearing recycled clothes?"

"Report to Servicing!" Abercrombie commanded. "A meckie cannot be expected to understand such things!"

The meckie rolled backward, shocked at the outburst. Gears ground. Then, dutifully, the meckie retreated under the weight of Abercrombie's ferocious glare.

O O O

Moments later, Lord Abercrombie was in the history wall cavern, watching the blue linguistics meckie carve Abercrombie's story in the limestone with a sharp piece of obsidian.

"I didn't use cartoons, Lord," the meckie gargled. "That is in my artistic program, but I didn't think you wanted humor."

"This is fine," Abercrombie said, studying a straightforward pictorial depiction of him under pursuit by evil, white-robed sayermen.

"I'm getting to the time you found the Sacred Scroll of Cork."

"Good." Lord Abercrombie glided to another section of wall and studied the circle/magnetics symbol which was beneath a cartoon of a plant being. "This circle," he said. "Could it represent Cork?"

"A planet? Sure."

"And the magnetics part … Couldn't the whole symbol refer to planetary magnetics?"

"Hmmm … Yes. Very possible. Maybe that's what defeated the other magicians. An imbalance in planetary magnetics which prevented their magic from operating efficiently. Come to think of it, that could account for your problems with disaster control equipment, too. Your laser shots can't get around the magnetic disturbances."

"Where do you come off saying such things? You're just an artistically programmed linguistics meckie."

"Uh," the meckie gargled with synthetic nervousness. "I saw a math and science program lying on a table in Servicing —quantum mechanics, geology, advanced math. Kind of a shotgun tape on a lot of things."

Lord Abercrombie glared at the meckie.

"I asked for it, Lord."

"You asked for a program without checking with me first?"

"Yes, Lord," the meckie said timidly. "I'm sorry, Lord."

"Get your metal ass into Servicing," Lord Abercrombie said, shaking his head. "Then get back here and finish this project."

"Yes, Lord." The meckie placed its piece of obsidian on a wall ledge, then turned and whirred out of the cavern.

O O O

Rebo had only one name. This was the way it was far across the universe on the dimensionally connected planet of Morovia. One person, one name.

With his head bobbing, he loped on three legs in front of his small band of black-jacketed cutthroats. Dark brown hair covered his bulky body, with one stocky leg at the front and two at the rear—a tricycle arrangement of calloused paws instead of wheels, with a large oval head that jutted forward on a mane-covered neck, a knotlike, knurled chin, and wide, cuplike ears. An arm to each side of the front leg had six slender fingers, which he used on one hand to grasp a long knife. The polished steel blade glinted in low light from the street lamps which burned wearily overhead. This was a tired neighborhood on the Southside of Moro City.

Scraps of paper and a piece of yellow cloth swirled in a warm breeze at Rebo's feet. It was the height of the Morovian summer. He felt beads of perspiration all over his body, culminating in sticky pools of moisture at his arm and leg pits.

Pausing at a street corner, he glanced up to see a curtain move in a third-floor tenement window across the street. Someone was pulling it shut. Rebo dropped his gaze to the main level of the tenement, to Marnus's Flower Shop, one of many tiny mercantile businesses huddling side by side in the tattered block. The flower shop was dark, save for one light at the rear.

"Old Marnus can't hurt us," a woman's voice husked from behind Rebo. "Let's leave him alone." The only female in the gang moved to Rebo's side, brushing against him.

Glancing at Namaba in the low light, he saw her rest on her haunches. With soft, golden-brown hair and a long golden mane, Namaba wore the scaly black obbo skin jacket of the club, with its wide-winged grapple bird insignia across the back. A yellow ribbon with black polka dots adorned her mane.

"Blades!" Rebo said, disregarding her appeal.

With the exception of Namaba, the gang members drew knives and popped them open. Their red eyes reflected on the shiny steel.

Rebo glared at Namaba.

Reluctantly, she slipped a hand into her jacket pocket, bringing forth a pearl-handled switchblade.

Rebo gazed at her with the disdainful, detached stare favored by Southsiders. Impatiently, he grabbed her knife and snapped it open. "It's no good to you closed," he said. His lips parted into a cruel smile, revealing iridescent blue teeth that illuminated the shadows.

"He's just an old man," she said softly.

"He told the other shopkeepers not to pay our standard protection fee." Rebo's voice was cultured. "For that, he dies."

"We don't need to kill him. Why not just rough him up?"

"I need an example. One our people won't forget." The tone was resolute, indicating to her that his mind would not be changed easily.

Namaba knew she was in no position to question Rebo. He had saved her from the laboratory fire, and by Morovian tradition this made him her lifelong master. There was no formal law decreeing such a thing; it was a matter of maintaining self-respect. Still, killing an old man did not seem the sort of activity conducive to nurturing self-respect. Her conscience would bother her long afterward, perhaps for the rest of her life. Rebo had told her often that a conscience was nothing for a Southsider to have. It was a meddling, unnecessary thing. Maybe he was right.

Rebo's red-eyed gaze moved around the group, and he spoke the club members' names in his thoughts: Kaff, the big one; Yott, the lover; Howack, the small one with blond hair covering his body; Namaba, the sensitive one; and Durl, the crazy one who never knew when to stop hurting people.

"We rule the night!" Durl exclaimed. His glowing eyes flashed crazily. He lunged and slammed a heavy chain into the lamppost.

Rebo laughed. Durl always made him laugh.

Copycat laughter rolled through the group—except for Namaba. Rebo heard the chugging of their steam engine hearts and heavy, matching breathing. He felt his own cardiopulmonary system running roughly from the high excitement.

Now Rebo turned his head and bounded across the street. As the others followed, he heard the clatter of their heavy chains. He smelled familiar street odors here: raw sewage in the gutter as he leaped over it, and the garbage of ripe fruit and meats from a cluster of overflowing trash cans on the sidewalk. A dog had its head buried in one of the cans.

Rebo kicked this can over for effect, spilling garbage across the sidewalk and sending the dog fleeing. Rebo liked making noise, and Namaba had once offered a plausible explanation: It made others fear him.

Rebo used his calloused front foot to kick in the glass storefront door, then glanced around as his gang fell in around him, awaiting instructions. Their iridescent blue teeth and red-pupiled eyes reflected readiness. The big one known as Kaff swung his chain and broke away the remaining spires of glass. Then Kaff stepped to one side.

Rebo coiled on his haunches, then sprang through the doorway, making a beeline for the back office. Reaching the office, he found himself in a small room full of books and papers, with a wide, leafy potted plant in the corner to the right of the door. It was a Parduvian flytrap plant. The old man had threatened him with it once. *Imagine that!* Rebo thought at the memory. *Threatening me with a plant!* The room reeked of alcohol.

Old Marnus sat at a paper-littered dark mahogany desk in the light of a suspensor lamp, resting his front leg on the desktop. His calloused toes were twisted and yellow, possible evidence of martial arts training.

Rebo had learned to look for such things.

Looking in from the doorway behind Rebo, Namaba saw that one of Marnus's hands held a pen, which the old Morovian had been using to make entries on a faded yellow ledger sheet. His body and facial hairs were silver-gray, except the scraggly beard had streaks of black in it which seemed curious to Namaba, like paint drippings on the old flower vendor's face. She touched Rebo's forearm.

Rebo pulled away to swat at a fly that buzzed in his face.

The insect flew away, settling on the large plant in the corner. *Whahoosha!* The plant made a powerful sucking noise, drawing the hapless fly into its center. Rebo felt cool air from somewhere.

"I have been expecting you," old Marnus said. The voice was throaty, with a chronic wheeze. He set down the pen with a note of finality, then reached for a brass alcohol flask. After taking a big gulp, he smiled, as though having won a bet with himself that he could swallow the liquid before Rebo made his move. It was common knowledge around the Southside that old Marnus loved to drink. Calmly, he replaced the flask on the desk.

Rebo felt his face flush with anger at the old Moravian's apparent unconcern in the face of obvious peril. His heart did not even seem to be chugging. But Rebo's was. He met old Marnus's defiant stare, then lunged across the room menacingly with his knife extended.

"Rebo!" Namaba yelled. "Please, Rebo!"

The old flower vendor did not flinch.

Rebo paused at the desk's leading edge, still staring. *Have to admire you, you old fool,* he thought. Smiling, he dug the knife into the desktop, flicking off a piece of dark wood. *Must have been a tough one in your day.*

For a fleeting moment old Marnus smiled in a kindly way, and Rebo felt himself returning the kindness with his own expression. They understood one another.

"Can I have him, Mr. President?" Durl asked, moving to Rebo's side. Durl fingered his chain.

"You popped the last one," Rebo said, leaning close to old Marnus and smiling cruelly. "This one's mine." He used the blade of his long knife to sweep the papers off the desk.

Marnus salvaged his flask.

Looking back, Rebo caught Namaba's anxious gaze. She shook her head. Her eyes begged Rebo not to kill. But he knew she would stay with him no matter what he did. It was her Moravian obligation.

Marnus raised the alcohol flask to his lips. But if he made a second bet with himself, he lost this one. Rebo's razor-sharp blade sliced open the front of his neck. The flask clattered to the floor.

The sound of releasing steam filled the room. Everyone ducked as old Marnus's body flew around the room like a discharging balloon, bouncing off walls and furniture. There was no blood, for no blood coursed through Moravian veins. Only air and water.

Presently old Marnus's limp and shriveled form landed on the floor by the desk in a gray woolly bag. His foreleg twitched.

"Search for cash and securities," Rebo barked. He did not know what the word "securities" meant. It was one of those words buried in his brain on this high vocabulary planet.

While the gang pulled open drawers and ransacked file cabinets for hiding places, Namaba knelt over Marnus's lifeless form. The odor of death permeated the room. It made her gag. Tearfully, she rose to her feet.

Rebo focused on the large potted plant in the corner. Namaba saw him staring at it. He moved toward it cautiously, saying, "Maybe the old buzzard hid his valuables in the plant."

A brass plaque on the plant's red brick pot read: "PARDUVIAN FLYTRAP." Crouching, Rebo dug in the dirt with his fingers, stepping around the plant as he did so. He tried to move the plant away from the wall, but it was too heavy to budge. So he reached to the back of the pot and dug there.

"Nothing here," he said, rising to his feet. He studied the central leaves, then inserted his knife blade between them.

The plant *whooshed* ferociously. Angrily, it seemed to Rebo. And cold air came from somewhere. He pulled his knife away just before the jaws snapped shut.

"Ha!" Rebo exclaimed.

"What are you doing?" Namaba asked, loping to his side. Wiping tears from her face, she said, "You think there's money in this thing?"

"Could be." He slashed at the base of the plant, but was unable to cut through its tough, fibrous skin.

Namaba tried to cut the leaves, also without success. Then she and Rebo tried to rock the pot. It did not move.

"Kaff!" Rebo yelled. "Yott! Give us a hand!"

They all tried to rock the pot, but still it did not budge. Kaff had the idea of pulling open the plant's jaws. Three large leaves comprised the jaws, and they opened easily. While the others held the leaves open, Rebo reached inside.

"It's cold in here," Rebo said. "And I can't find a bottom."

"Try a little deeper," Kaff said.

Rebo climbed up on the edge of the pot and reached way inside. "It oughtta be here somewhere, but I still don't feel it." So he stuck his head in and groped deeper. "It's cold in here!"

Seeing that Rebo's feet were in midair now, Namaba urged him to be careful,

Without warning, there was a loud *Wha-hoosha!* and the plant's jaws snapped shut around Rebo. This clamped the hands of Namaba, Yott, and Kaff between powerful leaves.

"Hey!" Rebo yelled, his voice hollow and distant. "Get me out of here!"

With great effort, Namaba and the others were able to pull their hands free. Then they tugged at Rebo's ankles, trying to free him. He screamed in terror. Namaba tried setting her paws against the pot for traction, but this did not help. Slowly, Rebo was being pulled deeper inside.

"Help me!" Rebo screamed.

"It's dragging him in!" Namaba said, panicky.

Now the rest of the gang joined in the desperate effort to save their club president. But with all their grunting and tugging, it did no apparent good. Rebo continued to disappear, a little bit at a time.

All gave up except Namaba. They told her it was no use. But she held Rebo's ankles, closing her eyes and steeling herself mentally and physically. It may have been her Moravian sense of obligation which provided such determination. But Namaba was the sort who might have done this for anyone.

"Give it up!" Kaff yelled. "He's lost!"

Opening her eyes, Namaba saw that only Rebo's ankles remained visible. Suddenly, the plant made a loud *Wha-hoosha!* sound and pulled Rebo and Namaba inside. The leaves snapped shut.

"They're gone!" Yott said.

"Let's go!" Durl yelled. "We gotta get outta here!"

Stumbling over one another, the survivors of Rebo's cutthroat gang ran away, leaving a ransacked office, the woolly remains of old Mamus, and a mysterious potted plant.

O O O

With his eyes closed, Rebo whirled through the bottomless vacuum of the Parduvian flytrap at hyper-light speed. He knew he was moving fast, perhaps too fast for Morovian flesh to survive. Cold air swirled past him, running along his face and down his neck, then along the bumpy length of his body, cutting through the thick hair that covered him. Knives of freezing cold cut into the skin, blades of air so frigid that they seemed hot. It was burning, searing cold. Unbearable cold.

Plates and lances of shadowy blue color raged across his brain, and he absorbed them like metal against ice. Short stretches of blackness followed, and then the frozen storms of shadowy blue returned. He felt the temperature dropping, until it seemed to Rebo that it could not possibly get any colder.

He wanted to shiver. But Rebo had no control over any of his bodily functions. Something pulled or pushed him along a great freezing tunnel. He sensed twinkling vastness all around. Or perhaps he saw dancing lights far ahead in the shadowy blue distance. He was not certain. Although his eyes were closed, he felt able to see something out there, at the dim reaches of his consciousness.

Rebo screamed but heard no sound. His brain fogged over, then contracted and swelled like a great undulating ocean wave. Something held fast to his ankles in a clawlike grip. He tried to shake free but could not. A smell of cleanness snapped his nostrils alive, then faded, leaving him with memories of the stinking filth back home in Moro City.

Now the twinkling vastness ahead focused into distant stars in the shape of old Marnus's face, laughing at him and drawing him inexorably forward. Through closed eyelids, Rebo saw bright green and blue planets in the foreground. Inexplicably, he passed through some of them. Suns flared white-hot like great growling beasts on each side. Worlds and their suns approached quickly and faded. Now the image of old Marnus's face neared, still laughing. Rebo passed right through the image, and then it was gone,

Rebo's body rolled into the shape of a three-legged fetus, then straightened for a time. Soon it resumed spinning, carrying him headlong through aeons or perhaps only seconds. He had no sense of time or space, only the sensation of eternity and vastness all around, pressing in on him and releasing him at the same moment.

Namaba released her grip on his ankles, and for a time they walked together in the vacuum place without touching ground. Then they ran and skipped, frolicking through the universe like young lovers. Presently she took hold of his ankles again and they spiraled over and over into the bottomless maw of the Parduvian flytrap.

*A fly?* Rebo thought, feeling Namaba's strong grip. *Is that all I am? A miserable speck of an insect?*

Strange, deep thoughts of life, love, and the meaning of existence touched him, but he forced them back. Gang leaders did not need to consider such matters. They were better left to Morovian philosophers, that odd breed who lived in another part of his world.

Before Rebo could sort out these disturbing new thoughts he sensed the warmth of soft yellow and orange colors in place of the harsh, shadowy blue storms. He began to feel warmer, sleepier. Then a tremendous red flash blasted across his eyelids, making him terribly hot, as hot now as he had been cold before. He knew he could not stand more heat. Even so, the temperature rose. To unimagined limits.

With Namaba still hanging tight, they spun at tremendous speed in a huge, clear tube. They spiraled from the center out, ending up in the outer ring. Here their speed slowed, and gradually Rebo was able to see objects outside the ring through the clear tube walls. It looked like a cave out there—an immense underground area with translucent spires and steeples of ice rock.

In slow motion, they passed a great stone chair upon which sat a bearded creature with a split head and body. On each side of the creature art objects were displayed that looked as though they had been fashioned from pieces of scrap: great hunks of iron and ragged, broken slabs of plastic tied together by wire. The creature's half face was contorted in anger, and he screamed at them as they passed.

"Intruders!" the creature bellowed. Rebo did not understand this word.

Soon they had passed the creature. They picked up speed again, remaining in the outer tube. Objects in the caverns outside became a blur. Moments later they slowed again. Rebo recognized the surroundings, for they were back in front of the half-faced one, passing in slow motion while he yelled at them in a language Rebo did not understand.

"Intruders!" Lord Abercrombie screeched. "No one will steal my domain!" Then he laughed, and his laughter seemed to echo across the universe. Rebo wanted to plug his ears, but could not move his arms.

This recurred perhaps thirty times. Each time the creature laughed, and each time he hurled a menacing epithet at them. Rebo had never seen anything like this in the Southside. Nor had he imagined what the universe outside his world was like. He was not surprised at what he saw, for he held no preconceived notions about how such things were supposed to be.

He became aware of a change. Cool air rushed across his body, and he was no longer in the clear outer ring of the great spiral. Now he flew headfirst through a wide, black tunnel, with Namaba still holding fast. *Up,* he thought, judging from the pressures on his body.

A blinding flash of light forced his eyes shut. He lapsed into unconsciousness. When he awoke moments later, Rebo found himself face down on a dirt surface with his front leg bent to one side. Namaba lay behind him, still grasping his ankles. From the aches in his body, it seemed to Rebo that he and Namaba had been through an eternity together.

Namaba let loose her grip on Rebo and pulled herself up. When Rebo saw her terrified expression, he felt it must be a reflection of his own: a grimace with wide-open, burning eyes that flitted nervous glances in all directions. She was breathing hard, with intermittent gasps. He heard her steam engine heart chug, and felt his own doing the same.

Rebo felt his chest swell and drop irregularly. A great tenseness climaxed inside him and released, leaving him limp and drained—a deep weariness such as none he had ever before experienced. It was worse than the time he had run from the police for two hours with no opportunity to catch his breath.

Steam came out of Namaba's ears.

*That was a faraway place,* Rebo thought, looking around at the terrain, they were on a wide, dusty path, with the marks of many feet on the powdery surface. Lining the path were cream-colored upright canisters which had red, yellow, and blue markings. He remembered seeing canisters like them before. Two had landed in Moro City the year before, right in the middle of Nelson Park. The police had arrived quickly to take the cannisters away, and Rebo had never heard of them again.

In the low light of dusk, the gaze of her red eyes met his. He followed her gaze to the edge of a cavernous black hole that was around twenty meters to Rebo's left. He surmised that they must have traveled through it to reach this place.

"Where do you think we are?" Namaba asked. The question seemed ridiculous to Rebo. How could either of them know?

Rebo felt perspiration forming on his hair-covered body. Rising to all threes, he removed his club jacket. He became conscious of a stream of opposites during the moments of his journey: freezing and heat, cleanness and filth, seconds like aeons, speed and tremendous, painstaking slowness. As he set the jacket on the ground, he felt his breathing become slower and more even.

Namaba's terrified expression changed to one of curiosity. Beyond the canisters she saw that they were in a large clearing, surrounded by a thick forest of pine trees.

Their jutting heads moved in unison to watch a white glider plane fly gracefully over the opposite side of the clearing. The plane disappeared below the treetops for a time. Then it rose once and dropped again, not reappearing.

Rebo focused on a tall metallic cylinder on the opposite side of the clearing below the last sighting point of the glider. At the *coo-roo-coo* of a bird, he turned his head. In the piney woods behind them, a big-beaked green bird was perched on a tree branch. The bird flapped its wings rhythmically.

*I am a murderer,* Rebo thought. He became angry at the thought. *I don't need to think of such things! They are of no consequence to me!* He recalled chiding Namaba often for letting her conscience get in her way.

Namaba was saying something, but Rebo did not hear the words. When he became aware of her, she was pointing across the clearing at the big cylinder. "Let's see what it is," she said.

Minutes later, in fast approaching darkness, they were ransacking the *Amanda Marie,* tossing gear and supplies all over the cabin and out the open hatch.

"Odd food," Rebo said, biting into a chocolate bar, wrapper and all. "I don't like the covering."

"I don't either," Namaba said. She removed the wrapper from her candy bar and discarded it. "Better this way," she said.

As they reached a frenzy of consumption, fine, steamy mist poured from their noses and ears and their steam engine hearts purred at peak efficiency. Soon particles of food were escaping from the pores of their skin in the form of dark brown, powdery waste products. It was so dark now that they could barely see their way around the cabin, even with the aid of their glowing red eyes. They lay their bloated bodies down on the corrugated metal deck and went to sleep.

# Chapter Seven

*One of my great disappointments lay in the decadence of the Corker ruling class. Debauchery seemed imprinted in their Fruity souls.*

Comments made by Felix the Magician after abandoning Cork

While waiting for the castle's main gate to open, Javik looked beyond the old prunesayer to the Corkian sunset. The sky along the horizon was color-splashed, with a craggy ridge of clouds resembling mountains. They glowed pastel pink, imitation mountains with dirty blue bases. Seconds later, like a chameleon, the range had become dirty white and silver. As voices called out from the guardwalk above, the sky and its clouds changed to dark gray.

"Who goes there?" a guard asked.

Prince Pineapple identified himself, then said to Javik with a smirk, "They can see me clearly, but always call out like that anyway. Consummate idiots!"

The heavy wooden gate cranked up, creaking and straining as it went. When it was fully open, Javik saw the mechanism behind the gate: large stone gears and ropes pulled by zucchini men slaves turning a wheel on the walkway above.

As the prince strode briskly into the castle, two Corker guards greeted him, saluting with a touch of their right thumbs to the center of their foreheads. Prince Pineapple duplicated the gesture.

"This way," Prince Pineapple said, looking down at his smaller Earthian companions. He hurried them across a gold-inlaid, white slate courtyard. The courtyard had a well in the configuration of a six-pointed star at the center, with a star-shaped frame of tomato and green bean vines surrounding it.

A marble-floored corridor beyond that had, at every doorway, two Corker guards holding electric sticks. They stood nearly motionless, moving their moist purple mouths only a little to suck at grain alcohol tubes.

Rounding a corner with the prince, Javik focused on elegant carved double doors directly ahead.

"The king's court," Prince Pineapple said.

The doors swung open as they neared, activated by rubber supermarket-door pressure pads at their feet. The court was full of Fruit people of every variety, chattering idly in a crescendo of idiocy. These people were dressed gaudily, with ornate pompadour leaf wigs in all the pastel colors. All sported white gloves, and many peered haughtily through monocles. To Javik, they looked like overdressed characters from an AmFed cartoon movie.

When the prince and his guests entered the room, the court grew quiet, with the members moving to the walls and talking in hushed tones. This exposed a purple and gold strip of synthetic Persian carpet at the center of the room. Puffing his chest out theatrically, Prince Pineapple strutted down the center of the carpet toward an unoccupied, gilded throne which rested on a wide platform.

A tinny bell rang from somewhere in the room.

"King Corker has been notified," Prince Pineapple said, stopping in front of the throne. He removed his helicopter beanie.

Two scantily clad peach girls pranced out from side doorways at each side of the throne. They pranced on tiptoes to the front of the throne, then began an undulating belly dance. It was an exotic display of potbellies and synchronized, pulsating folds of fat.

"Delectables from the king's harem," Prince Pineapple said.

The peach girls circled one another, trailing sheer black veils from their fingertips. Then they spread their pudgy legs and stretched back, swaying their arms gracefully. One of the girls had difficulty with this maneuver. Struggling to bend her back and touch her forehead to the floor behind her, she lost her balance and tumbled over.

Javik suppressed a smile as the peach girl staggered clumsily to her feet. The performance was bad, so bad in fact that he wanted to turn off the videodome switch. If only one had been handy!

"Yay mish-mish!" a Corker guard yelled, raising his electric stick high in the air exuberantly.

"Yay mish-mish!" all the men in the court yelled. Prince Pineapple joined in halfheartedly.

"What does that mean?" Javik asked. He shook his language mixer pendant. It seemed to be operating, but was not translating these words.

"Oh, what a peach!" Prince Pineapple said, surprised at the question. "I think it's one of your Earthian languages."

"Mmmm!" another Corker guard yelled. "Juicy Fruities!"

"Mmmm!" all the court's men yelled. "Juicy Fruities!"

Looking around, Javik noted-that all the men in the court except Prince Pineapple were watching the peach girls with lust-inflamed eyes. The prince seemed almost not to notice them, and to Javik he had the appearance of one deep in thought, shouldering some great burden.

*What foolishness,* Prince Pineapple thought. *What a complete and utter sham!* He glared at the base of the throne.

"All kneel!" a casaba melon doorwoman called out.

The peach girls stopped dancing abruptly and fell to their knees at each side of the throne.

Following the others in the court, Javik and Evans knelt. Javik watched out of the corner of his eye as the king entered through one of the side doors.

Just then, Wizzy flew out of Javik's pocket and alighted on Javik's shoulder. "Took a little snooze," Wizzy announced too loudly. The words echoed around the room. He yawned in a loud, mouthy moan, stretching his lumpy body.

"Shhhh!" Javik whispered.

King Corker was a very large grape man in a ruffled white blouse and tight red pants, with scaly, grenache purple skin and six stubby legs like the other Corkers. But King Corker was much larger than other Corkers, perhaps twice their size. He wore an oversized grain alcohol backpack, and with one pudgy hand pulled the pack's plastic tube out of his mouth. Syrupy black liquid dripped from the tube down the front of his ruffled blouse. He appeared unconcerned about this.

As the peach girls undulated their thick arms in welcoming gestures, King Corker padded across the platform on red slippers. When the king hopped on his throne, Javik was intrigued at how neatly his six legs stacked on top of one another as he sat. The king sucked on his alcohol tube and stared down dispassionately with his black button eyes at Javik.

Prince Pineapple rose, pulling Javik and Evans up with him. "Visitors from Earth, Sire," he said, staring at the floor.

*He doesn't even meet the king's gaze,* Javik thought. *This prince is not to be trusted.*

"From Earth? From Earth?" King Corker said. "There is mirth from Earth?"

Prince Pineapple did a high backflip at the royal rhyme, clicking his heels as he went over. Everyone in court followed suit, even ladies in petticoats, like a mass automatic reaction—with the exception of Javik, Evans, and the king.

"Tell me a story," King Corker said petulantly, looking at Javik with a pouting smile across his wide mouth.

"You mean about why we're here?" Javik asked.

"Suffering souplines!" King Corker exclaimed angrily. He glowered at Prince Pineapple. "You didn't inform them that I like stories?"

"Uh, sorry, Your Majesty," Prince Pineapple said, obviously flustered. "I … uh … was overly concerned about the gar-bahge." Under King Corker's increasingly ferocious glare, Prince Pineapple leaned close to Javik and said in a cracking voice, "Tell him your funniest story. King Corker loves to laugh."

"Oh!" Wizzy squealed, jumping high in the air over Javik's shoulder and then landing back on the shoulder. "I like to laugh, too! Ha-ha-ha! A-ha-ha-ha-ha-hee!"

Javik winced.

"Shush, Wizzy!" Evans whispered. "Not now!"

King Corker appeared on the verge of exploding into anger. He drummed a forefinger impatiently on the arm of his throne.

"Does he mean a joke?" Javik asked, looking sidelong at Prince Pineapple.

"Anything. But make it quick. It's rude to keep funny things from our king."

"Well," Javik said, scratching the back of his neck, "here's one I heard a few weeks back. Once during the Atheist Wars, General Ishmael Roberts … he was the founder of our American Federation Space Patrol, Your Majesty." Javik paused, expecting a nod from the king.

King Corker scowled. He sucked at his alcohol pack.

"Hurry!" Prince Pineapple whispered. "Get to the punch liner

"I was just giving him a little background. Aw, Cha-rist!" Javik sighed, then resumed his story: "General Roberts was asked by a neighbor in his condominium building about the placement of key AmFed warships in deep space. It was a thoughtless question, touching upon highly classified information. Anyway, General Roberts leaned close to the questioner's ear and asked, 'Can you keep a secret?'"

Javik glanced around the court, assuring himself that all ears were tuned in, hanging on his every word.

"Yes?" King Corker said, pursing his moist lips like a spoiled child about to receive another gift.

"Hurry," Prince Pineapple said nervously.

"You can't hurry a story," Javik snapped. "Timing is the whole thing. Anyway, Your Majesty, this neighbor was very eager, and he said, 'I sure can, General.' So General Roberts smiled and said, 'Well, so can I.'" Javik studied the king's face.

King Corker did not crack a smile. He sat motionless, appearing confused at the tale.

The silence of death permeated the court.

Javik shuffled his feet.

"I warned you, get to the punch line," Prince Pineapple said in a desperate tone. "Please!"

"That was it," Javik said. He shrugged, then glanced at Evans.

She shook her head and rolled her eyes upward.

Prince Pineapple covered his face with his hands. Cautiously, he peered through stubby fingers at the king.

King Corker's jaw had fallen in incredulity.

"Try another one," Evans urged. "One of those bawdy barroom stories."

"I thought the king might prefer something more highbrow," Javik muttered.

"That was an awful story," King Corker said. He thought for a moment. "So awful that it was funny." He laughed uproariously.

A floodgate of laughter broke loose across the court. This became a tittering of glee that died down when the king stopped for a breath and then started to roll again when the king resumed laughing.

*Such fools,* Prince Pineapple thought. *This court is full of mindless puppets.*

"Ho!" King Corker said. "Very clever, Earthian. And now I will tell *you* a story."

The court fell silent. Everyone leaned forward so as not to miss a word of the king's tale.

"Shall I tell a riddle or a joke?" King Corker mused, gazing playfully at the ceiling.

A watermelon man in a bright gold buttonless suit hurried to the king's side. The watermelon man flipped a large gold coin in the air, caught it in one hand, and pressed it against the back of the other hand.

"A riddle, Sire," he reported. "Lord Abercrombie wants a riddle."

"Our planet God has spoken!" the court intoned. Javik saw Prince Pineapple's lips move, but no sound came from them.

*I have a good pineapple brain,* the prince thought. *We have no need for Decision Coins. Look at our pitiful king, consulting with a melonhead.*

"Very well," King Corker said, watching the watermelon man hustle to a position along the wall. "A riddle: Why can't Vegetable Underground troops go on a break for longer than five minutes?" He chuckled.

*I have heard this story so many times,* Prince Pineapple thought wearily. *And we're always expected to laugh.*

Javik looked around, then back to the king. King Corker looked like a fat, purple man about to burst with mirth.

A wave of tittering rolled through the court.

"Gosh," Javik said with a silly grin. "I don't know that one.

"Any longer," King Corker said "and they'd have to be completely retrained!" He spit the words out with an exploding laugh, then howled with glee to the point where tears ran down his scaly cheeks. The peach girls dabbed his face with tissues. This must have been very cheap tissue, for little pieces of it stuck to the king's skin.

As Javik looked on in amazement, the entire court fell into a pandemonium of laughter. Fruits held one another up and repeated the punch line endlessly. "Did you hear that?" they asked. "The V-U's would have to be completely retrained!

"Ah, ha-ha! Oh boy!" they said.

"That was a good one!"

"Those stupid Vegetables!"

After the peach girls stepped away from King Corker, he looked at Javik and asked, "Did you like my story, Earthian?"

Javik laughed halfheartedly and heard Evans do the same. "Very much, Your Majesty," he said. "It was hilarious."

"We hate Vegetables here, Earthian," the king said. "They are stupid, foolish creatures."

"Vegetables are dumb," the court chanted.

"And bitter, bitter, bitter," the men of the court yelled with deep voices.

"But Fruits are sweet," the ladies responded.

"Fruits are neat," everyone said.

The court grew silent. Then the peach girls fluttered out a side door, trailing their black veils.

"We have a saying here," King Corker said. Raising a forefinger in the manner of a Freedom Studies instructor, he added, "And it is very important." His head bobbed from the profound truth of this as he said, "'Once a Vegetable, always a Vegetable.' There is no hope for them, Earthian, except as servants."

Javik nodded.

King Corker sucked on his grain alcohol tube, dripping blackish ooze down his chin. A glazed, drunken look came over him. "I watched your ship come down," he said. He raised a hand, then dropped it.

Two watermelon men moved quickly from their wall positions to the sides of the king's throne. Upon reaching the throne, one of them flipped a Decision Coin, then whispered in the king's ear. Then the other watermelon man flipped a different coin, and he too leaned over to pass along a bit of wisdom to the king.

King Corker nodded, then waved both of them away.

"Our planet God has spoken!" the court intoned.

"Curious-looking creatures, these Earthians," King Corker said, looking from Javik and Evans to the prince. "Suppose I shouldn't say that. They do resemble the way Lord Abercrombie looked before his transformation."

"That wouldn't be *Winston* Abercrombie?" Javik asked, looking into the king's black button eyes.

"One and the same," King Corker replied irritably.

"Earth criminal!" Wizzy exclaimed.

"What is that on your shoulder?" King Corker asked. He spit a ball of phlegm into a brass spittoon. The spittoon rang.

"An embarrassment," Javik said, reaching for Wizzy.

Wizzy jumped away, hovering in the air. Javik grabbed for him, but the little comet flew just beyond his reach.

"Abercrombie came here to recycle," Wizzy said, glowing red. "A terrible crime. The Sayerhood came to return him for justice, you know. But they never found him."

"Wizzy, we don't care about all that!" Javik barked. "Now come back here!"

But Wizzy flitted away, just beyond Javik's grasping fingers.

Javik glanced at the king nervously. King Corker's face was a dark shade of angry reddish purple. He leaned forward on the throne, apparently having difficulty formulating a sentence. Little sentence bursts came out: "That thing … is not …" He tugged at the tube of his grain alcohol pack. The tube came off, squirting dark liquid all over him. "Get this off me!" he thundered.

The watermelon men moved quickly to his aid, pulling the backpack off their foundering king. His white lace shirt was a mess, completely soaked in black ooze. Under different circumstances, Javik might have thought this a comical sight. But there was nothing funny about the moment.

"I sense danger from Abercrombie," Wizzy announced, oblivious to the king's discomfort and rage. "He hates Earthians now, especially Uncle Rosy. And wants revenge for his failure."

"Silence!" Javik said.

"But isn't this your assignment, Captain Tom?" Wizzy asked, his voice an intolerable singsong. "To find any dangerous conditions and report them to Mission Control?"

"This is not the time or the place," Javik said. He lunged unsuccessfully at Wizzy.

"Enough!" King Corker thundered. "I will not tolerate disruptions!"

"You'd better control that thing," Prince Pineapple whispered to Javik.

Javik nodded. He inched toward Wizzy.

Undeterred, Wizzy said, "Winston Abercrombie was the AmFed Garbage Thrust Commandant. More than a decade ago—"

"You asked me about emotions," Javik said in a gentle tone, inching closer to Wizzy. The court was ominously silent, making Javik's words seem loud. "I want you to feel one now,". he said. "That emotion is *fear.*"

"Fear?" Wizzy said, moving out of Javik's range. "What is that?" He glowed red as he searched his memory banks. "Ah, here it is: 'apprehension concerning one's physical well-being.'"

Javik lunged for Wizzy while he was thus occupied and caught him. Feeling the intensity of all eyes in the court, Javik said, "I'm sorry." He stuffed Wizzy into his jacket pocket. "We obtain data from the device ... but it's not functioning properly now." He felt his face flush hot with blood.

Wizzy became silent as Javik zipped his pocket shut.

"Check that thing out," King Corker said to Prince Pineapple.

"Yes, Your Majesty." Prince Pineapple extended his hand to Javik, "Give it to me," he said.

"Gladly," Javik said. He unzipped the pocket and handed Wizzy over. "This thing's more trouble than it's worth."

While Prince Pineapple studied Wizzy, Wizzy glowed bright orange, becoming too hot for the prince's sensitive fingers.

"Ow!" Prince Pineapple said angrily, letting go of Wizzy. "It's hot!"

Javik shook his head in dismay.

Wizzy flew around the king's throne, then became dark blue and returned to alight on Prince Pineapple's shoulder.

"It's okay," Javik said. "He's not hot now."

Prince Pineapple looked warily out the side of one eye at the lumpy object on his shoulder. It was rather heavy.

Wizzy did not move or make a sound.

"Now," King Corker said, looking first at Javik, then at Evans. His eyes flared. "You are here about the gar-bahge, I presume." Javik noticed the affected pronunciation again. Apparently it was done to make trash sound cultured.

"Yes, Your Majesty," Javik said. "We're very sorry about it. The President of our American Federation of Freeness has asked me to extend his personal apology."

"Yes, yes," the king said impatiently.

"He has authorized me to send cleanup crews."

"Cleanup crews?" King Corker said, surprised. His eyebrows lifted in astonishment. "What on Cork for?"

"Why, to clean up the garbage … to take it away."

"We don't want it cleaned up!" the king said, glaring at Prince Pineapple. "Didn't you explain anything to him?"

"We didn't discuss the crisis in great detail, Sire. I thought you might prefer—"

"We want more gar-bahge, Earthian!" King Corker howled, directing a scalding glare at Javik. "Is that clear?" He thumped a clenched fist on the arm of his throne. "We want *more*!"

"I—I didn't expect …" Javik was stammering. "No one thought … I mean …" He looked desperately at Evans for support.

She looked away.

"We have a serious shortage of gar-bahge," Prince Pineapple said, looking at Javik. "In the past there was always enough for all. Our stores were full. There was plenty for Lord Abercrombie. But now, even the royal gar-bahge is threatened."

"How terrible," someone in the court said. Then a murmuring followed: "How terrible. How terrible."

"When can we have more gar-bahge, Earthian?" King Corker asked.

"Uh, I wasn't authorized to … uh, I mean …"

"An *underling*," King Corker muttered. "I do not deal with *underlings*."

"I have an idea," Javik said. "Why don't you manufacture new things, then smash the stuff around? You know, make dents, scratches, mangles, and rips."

King Corker's eyes widened. "You must be daft, Earthian. Imported gar-bahge is the only thing to have. Can't you see that?"

"Uh, sure. Then maybe I could arrange for more garbage. I'll go back to Earth and see."

"Go back?" King Corker smiled cruelly. "You aren't going *back*, Earthian. I know of such tricks, you see. You would bring warships."

"Oh no," Evans said hurriedly. "We wouldn't think of that!"

"No," Javik said. "We're from the government, and we're here to help you."

"One of the three biggest lies in the universe," King Corker said, recalling a sheet of paper in his royal funny file.

Javik's mouth opened in shock. He shuffled his feet.

"Your Decision Coin," King Corker said, looking at Prince Pineapple.

With Wizzy still on his shoulder, the prince fumbled in his pockets. Eventually he produced a large golden coin like the ones used by the watermelon men.

"Give it to the Earthian captain," King Corker instructed.

Prince Pineapple obeyed, then glanced sidelong at Wizzy.

Wizzy's cat's eye dimmed drowsily, so that it was only halfway open.

Javik studied the coin. Despite its size, it was very light in weight. Probably made of an alloy, he surmised. On one side was the bust of a human man's face bearing a stern, fatherly expression. Javik recognized it as Winston Abercrombie. Around Abercrombie were the smiling faces of Fruit people. The word "YES" was engraved in Corkian below the bust.

"Lord Abercrombie," Prince Pineapple said in a low tone.

Javik turned the coin over. The other side depicted a cluster of Vegetable faces surrounding a carrot man in a baseball cap. Below that was engraved the word "NO."

"And Brother Carrot," Prince Pineapple whispered. "The Evil One."

"Flip it," King Corker said.

Javik hesitated. "But what…?"

"Flip it!"

Javik shrugged and tossed the coin high in the air. It clanged to the floor and rolled around at his feet.

Prince Pineapple looked at the coin. Then he retrieved it, while Wizzy used magic suction to cling to his shoulder. "Yes, Your Majesty," he said, stuffing the coin in his pants pocket. "It decided yes."

"Our Planet God has spoken," King Corker said reverently.

Then the court intoned, "Our Planet God has spoken."

It was a wondrous, charmed moment for everyone except Prince Pineapple and the visitors from afar.

"To the games!" King Corker shouted. Smiling, he looked at Javik and Evans, adding, "One Manno, one Wommo."

Prince Pineapple looked sadly at the watermelon advisers who stood nearby, recalling a time not so long before when King Corker had listened more to him. Until court politics turned against the prince. *Now I am Number One Adviser in title only,* he thought. *And soon he will take the title. What do I care anyway? This foolishness is not for me.*

"Did you hear me, Prince Pineapple?" the king asked.

"Yes, Sire. But I wonder if …" Prince Pineapple stared at the ground, then looked past the king at the wall.

"What are you trying to say?"

"I just wonder if another course of action might not be appropriate."

King Corker was displeased. He balled both hands into tight, pudgy fists. "Another course of action?" he said. "You question the Decision Coin?"

"No, but perhaps we did not need to flip it."

Wizzy released a loud snort. He was sleeping fitfully on Prince Pineapple's shoulder.

Prince Pineapple hesitated, then said, "The Earthians are our guests, Sire. Emissaries from another planet."

"So what?"

"I'm not sure they should be enslaved, Your Majesty. There might be repercussions."

*Enslaved?* Javik thought. *In this place?* He sneaked a glance at his service pistol, bolstered on his hip.

"Such as?" King Corker asked. "We already have a shortage of gar-bahge. What could be worse than that?"

Wizzy snorted again then fell into a buzz saw of snoring. He tipped a little on the prince's shoulder.

Javik shook his head. "That damned Wizzy," he muttered.

"Stop it!" Prince Pineapple said to Wizzy, giving Wizzy a shove.

Wizzy clung to his perch and snorted again. Then he grew silent.

Prince Pineapple looked at the king, saying, "Enslaving them might destroy our last hopes of getting more gar-bahge. It could *force* Earth to send warships."

"You argue with me? And with the coin?"

Prince Pineapple bowed nervously. "No, Sire. I am merely advising you. I thought that was my function here." *I'm pushing it,* he thought. *Shouldn't do that, especially in public.*

"The decision has already been made. There is a declining Earthian population here, with no means of reproduction. We once had eight hundred and fifty thousand of them. How many remain?"

"Less than fifteen thousand, I believe."

"Closer to ten. The games take their toll. How will we be entertained when the games are over? Answer that one, *Adviser.*"

Prince Pineapple hung his head.

"Take them!" King Corker ordered. "Now!"

"Yes, Your Majesty," Prince Pineapple said. He bowed obediently. This time, Wizzy fell off the shoulder.

"Aargh!" Wizzy grunted as he hit the floor. "Can't anyone take a nap around this place?"

Prince Pineapple retrieved Wizzy, then grabbed Javik's arm. "Come with me," he said.

"Like hell!" Javik said. He placed a hand on his holstered service pistol.

"You will be given an opportunity to survive, Earthian," King Corker said. "They are games of skill."

"And what are these games?" Javik asked, keeping his hand against his gun handle.

"You will learn soon enough," King Corker said. He motioned, and six bulky pear man guards surrounded Javik and Evans. A pear man put his hand on Javik's pistol, but Javik pushed the hand away.

"We'll take that," the pear man said. Then two pear men held Javik's arm while another reached for his gun.

Javik fought back, but was pushed to the floor. "Evans!" he yelled.

But Evans remained motionless. "It's no use," she said.

Javik was nearly squashed under a mass of Fruit flesh. He lost the gun. Struggling to his feet afterward, Javik glared around. King Corker was staring at him with cold, black button eyes.

"They are Earth games," the king said. "You should find them familiar."

O O O

Lord Abercrombie's fleshy half was tired, and he decided to go to bed early. Wearily, he rose from the black satin cushions of his throne and floated out of the main chamber.

He went down one box-lined passageway, made a left, then took another left. Soon he stood in the doorway of the Servicing cavern. He saw the blue linguistics meckie being worked on by two black and white repair technician meckies.

"I want that science program and anything else you have on geology, magnetics, astronomy, and disaster control," Lord Abercrombie said in a loud voice.

The repair technicians stopped working and listened while Lord Abercrombie spoke.

He continued, "Program the whole works into that yellow meckie in the corner."

"Yes, Lord," one of the repair technicians said.

"And tell it to report to me first thing in the morning."

Lord Abercrombie turned and went to his bedroom chamber.

# Chapter Eight

*Some thoughts are never spoken. These are among the most important*

*Quotations from Uncle Rosy*, page 18

Javik and Evans were separated when they left the king's court. Four pear men pushed and dragged Javik down a long, dimly lit corridor. The walls, ceiling, and floor were polished agate stone in varying shades of amber and brown. Javik slipped twice on the smooth floor, then took shorter, more careful steps. A hunger pang shot through his midsection.

Reaching a wide spot in the corridor, they stopped. One of the pear men slid open a rectangular metal lid on the floor, revealing a dark compartment below. Javik heard the dull whir and thud of machinery. He smelled rubber.

"In here," the pear man said.

Javik struggled, but the bottom-heavy Fruits were stronger than they looked. They forced him through the opening.

Javik fell a short distance after they let go, slamming his head and shoulder against a hard rubber surface. Realizing that the surface was moving slowly, he guessed he was on a conveyor. Machinery whirred loudly, and now the rubber smell was very strong. Faint illumination from the hatch opening faded. Looking up, Javik saw the lid slide back over the opening, leaving only a thin halo of light there. Soon he lost sight of the halo as the conveyor carried him away.

Another odor touched his nostrils next, a repulsive odor. "It stinks in here!" he mumbled. He shuddered at the realization of what it was. *Decaying flesh,* he thought, recalling a number of burial details on which he had served. And he recalled the odor of the creature in the Davis Droids.

Crouching in the darkness, Javik tried to think of his next move. The holster on his hip was light, evidence that it was empty. The rubber floor stopped now, falling silent. He heard a thunderous crowd roar above, and felt the floor shake.

Something rustled nearby, behind and to the left.

Javik whirled to face that direction, clenching his fists and extending them.

Then he heard other rustlings, from other directions. "Manno," he thought someone said, from his left.

Then he heard it again, a clear monotone: "Manno."

Javik recalled the King's words: *"One Manno, one Wommo."*

The sounds drew closer, and the disgusting odors became intolerably strong.

Javik crawled to his right, then sensed breathing on that side. They were all around him. Terrified, Javik curled into a defensive, fetal ball.

"Manno!" they yelled in monotones.

"Manno!"

"Kill the Wommos!"

Javik twitched at each utterance, expecting to feel humanoid hands on him at any moment. His body was rigid, and he felt the tautness of his arm, leg, and chest muscles. His heart was like a sledge inside: Boom-da-dee-boom! Boom-da-dee-boom!

"Get back!" Javik yelled. "Stay away from me!"

"Manno?" a raspy voice asked. "You are Manno?"

Slimy hands pawed at Javik in the darkness. He pushed them away, but they returned: wet fingers caressing his face and body. The fingers of many creatures, pressing all around.

Javik lashed out with his feet and felt his boots strike home against flesh and bones. The creatures fell back but returned, like an encroaching sea which could be stalled but never defeated.

A narrow band of light hit the side of Javik's face from above. Then the band of light widened. Looking up, Javik squinted as a lid slid open, clanging metallically. He heard thunderous crowd noises outside.

"One more pilot," a tenor voice said from above. Faces covered the opening. "Get the new Earthian. The one with no wounds."

Before Javik could react, a lariat snapped down and slipped expertly under his armpits. The lariat tightened around his body and pulled him to the surface. Javik thrashed at the rope as he was pulled up and out of the hole. He felt a sharp shoulder pain as he was dumped roughly on the ground.

A Corker removed the lariat, smiling at Javik with moist, purple lips.

Rising to one knee, Javik found himself on one end of a great stadium filled with cheering Fruit people. It was night, and the stadium was ringed with bright floodlights. The other end of the stadium was open, with two parallel strips of floodlighted gray concrete extending into the distance. Far down the track, Javik noticed that the lanes narrowed to one. The Fruit spectators were colorful and demonstrative, waving their arms excitedly and hurling empty grain alcohol packs in all directions. Vendors hawking new packs worked the aisles.

Javik took a deep breath. He was hungry and tired, with the burning eyes and drifting consciousness of a person in need of sleep. A fine, stinging dust blew across his face. He felt a sneeze coming on. "Ah … ah …" It did not come. Having no tissue handy, Javik depressed one nostril to blow phlegm on the ground. He repeated the procedure with the other nostril.

"I think it's an Earthian," a Corker on his left said. Javik did not look in that direction.

"Different from the others," observed another.

"Cleaner looking."

Javik focused on two large auto carriers parked in pools of light at the near end of each concrete strip. One carrier was pink and black, the other blue and black. Cars painted in the same manner as their respective carriers roared down ramps from each carrier simultaneously, one from each carrier, then streaked side by side along the track—a pink and black car on one strip, a blue and black car on the other. He saw the cars vie for position as the lanes merged to one. The blue car shot in front at the junction, then went into a weaving pattern. Lances of flame shot from the front of the trailing pink car. Gunfire peppered the air.

"Damn," someone said.

The blue car exploded in a high ball of blue flame. Javik stood up to see the car crash off the track against a low rock wall. A glowing orange capsule shot straight up from the crash scene. Then a white parachute opened over the capsule, guiding it back to Cork. Still glowing orange, the capsule drifted closer to Javik. He saw that it was a cage, with shimmering, orange-hot bars. Inside, the dead Manno pilot was stretched straight out and spinning slowly, like a pig on a spit.

*What the hell?* Javik thought.

"You saw it folks!" the public address man announced. "Another Manno loss!"

Pink balloons fluttered over the Wommo auto carrier to celebrate the victory. The Wommo fighter car pilot slowed her car at the other end of the track, then took an exit ramp to the left into a pink and black pit area.

"Never get in front," a Corker guard said to Javik. "You've gotta lay back."

"Listen to him good, Manno," an avocado man said, looking at Javik with seedy, dark green eyes. He nudged Javik's sore shoulder, causing Javik to grimace.

"He'll learn fast," the Corker said. "If he doesn't want to be a toastie."

*Jeheezus!* Javik thought.

"Who cares?" someone behind Javik said. "Let him roast."

*I care,* Javik thought. *But should I? Maybe this is as good a way to go as any.*

He watched the giant auto carriers exchange places, rolling by one another efficiently and rapidly. Javik was surprised at how mobile the big units were. Within moments each carrier was set up at the opposite track. Two cars rocketed down the ramps now, hitting the tracks side by side.

"You see that, Earthian?" the avocado man asked. "You can't go too fast or too slow. Too fast and the parallel car nails you from behind. Even if you get away, there's no glory in it. Too slow and another enemy car is on your track, coming right up your ass."

"Over here," a Corker said. "We need another pilot. He'd better …" The ensuing words were drowned out in crowd noises and an explosion on the track.

"Darn!" someone said. "There went another one."

"They're beating the hell out of us today."

"Glad I don't have to go out there."

Two beefy Corkers pulled and pushed Javik to a table attended by a very round orange man. Without a word, the orange man pushed a blue and black jumpsuit and a helmet across the table toward Javik.

Javik slipped the suit on over his Space Patrol outfit. The suit was a couple of sizes too big. The helmet fit poorly too, being designed for bulbous-headed humanoids. He heard radio chatter across built-in earphones.

He was about to ask for better-fitting headgear when a Corker shoved him roughly, saying, "This way." Javik was escorted to the

Manno auto carrier, a massive warship standing in a bright pool of light. The blue and black carrier was long and three-tiered, with a hodgepodge of fighter cars on all levels. Each car had a large-caliber gun mounted on the roof, with machine guns on the front and rear fenders.

Javik was taken up a side walkway and assigned to a dented and bullet-riddled squareback on the lower level. A large black Corkian numeral "5" was on the door. Since the door was welded shut, Javik had to remove his helmet and pull himself in through the open driver's window. He slid into a torn black vinyl bucket seat. The seat squeaked as his weight settled into it. This placed him in a black-barred cage. Javik knew he would roast there if he lost. Nervously, he fingered the strap of the helmet on his lap.

Outside, a cheerful public address announcer called out action for the spectators. His voice was throaty.

It smelled of oil in the car. The instrumentation looked primitive to Javik, with rudimentary gauges for speed, tach, and other mechanical functions. A black pole suspended from the roof to his right had three white buttons on it, marked clearly: "TOP," "REAR" and "FRONT." *The guns,* he thought.

Locating the fuel gauge, he saw it waver. *What does this thing run on?* he wondered. *Probably alcohol of some sort.* He did not detect a telltale odor. After figuring out the braking and acceleration system, he rested his foot on the accelerator pedal.

A Corker leaned in the window and told Javik to press the "START" button. Javik moved away to keep dark fluid on the fellow's mouth and chin from dripping on him. "Watch for the green light on the track," the Corker said. "Then hit 'TAKEOFF.'"

Javik touched the starter button and heard the engine roar to life like a rudely awakened beast. The headlights flashed on automatically. The car rumbled roughly and hesitatingly at first, then began to smooth out. As Javik looked down the black stripe on the car's hood, he felt the change in the engine's rhythm. Another car was in front of him, and beyond that a traffic signal flashed red.

"You're coming up, Manno," a weak voice reported from Javik's left. Glancing in that direction, Javik saw an old and wrinkled lettuce man slave. The man's, body was light green and white, with white eyebrows and a crown of white fuzz. There was no neck: the body was the head and vice versa.

Javik nodded. He gunned the engine. Noticing a shoulder harness for the first time, he pulled it across his chest and snapped it into place.

"They race and fight on Earth highways like this?" the old slave asked. "Just like the promoters say?"

"I guess so. This sure as hell is exaggerated, though. We don't mount guns on cars back home. They're carried in glove compartments." He thought of the autocar signboards by which Earth drivers could exchange epithets. Feeling tense, Javik decided not to mention this. He used a sleeve to wipe perspiration from his forehead.

The slave grunted.

A Corker guard on the ground below yelled at them: "Cut the chatter! Pay attention to the games!" The guard purchased a new alcohol backpack from a passing vendor, paying for it with discarded Earth candy bar wrappers.

"It's Manno against Wommo!" the public address man announced. Javik heard sucking sounds over the speaker system and surmised the announcer was a Corker.

Waves of ovation, roars, and catcalls rolled through the stands.

Javik touched an unmarked console button to see what it was. Nothing happened. He checked several other buttons with the same result.

"Disconnected," the old slave said.

"What a heap," Javik said. He smelled exhaust from the car just ahead. Then the other car roared down the ramp and into combat, leaving a puff of black smoke across Javik's vision. When the smoke began to clear, Javik saw the car explode in a distant ball of blue flame. An orange capsule shot up, then sprouted a parachute.

"Haven't seen a Manno victory all day," the slave said.

*Inhuman games,* Javik thought, seeing the traffic signal flash red. *Men against women, playing on the conditioned rivalries between Earth sexes.*

He snapped on his loose-fitting plastic crash helmet. Over the built-in earphones he heard nervous chatter as the Manno fighter car pilots communicated with the carrier's control tower.

"Okay, Ladykiller Five," the control tower said. "You're up next."

Javik was daydreaming, recalling some of his more memorable pleasure dome visits.

"Ladykiller Five, you there?"

*Five,* Javik thought, drifting back to awareness." *That's me.* "Here," he said into a microphone in front of his mouth.

"Blow that Wommo fighter car away, buddy."

"Right," Javik shook his head in disgust. *This is an important mission?* he thought. *I'd rather be ridin' a garbage shuttle.*

"Watch your blind spots, Ladykiller Five," the tower said. "Keep the other car in front of you all the time. Or rocket ahead to a Manno safe zone. That's a blue and black wall at the side. You can hide behind it, then pop out and blast the Wommo car when it passes."

"Don't we get any practice?" Javik asked.

Sardonic laughter filled the earphones. Then: "You've discovered the gun buttons?"

"Yeah." Seeing the traffic signal flash yellow, Javik held a finger close to the "TAKEOFF" button. *Not too fast,* he thought. His heart began to beat faster.

"You aim the gun bar by rotating, pushing, and pulling it."

The traffic signal flashed green.

Javik hit the "TAKEOFF" button and felt the accelerator under his foot depress. The car roared ahead, thumping as it bounced off the ramp to the pavement. G-forces threw him against the bucket seat. The helmet strap pulled at his chin. He grimaced from the stress.

*This piece of shit moves out!* he thought. But the car felt loose under him. Something rattled in the rear.

Peripherally, he watched a pink and black Wommo car on the track to his left. It dropped back.

Javik tapped the accelerator to free it from takeoff mode. His car slowed, drawing even with the other car. He could see the pilot, a bulbous-headed Wommo humanoid in a pink and black jumpsuit. She glanced at him nervously. *Very young,* he thought. *Maybe only a kid.* He adjusted his helmet with one hand.

Machine-gun fire peppered the hood and broke his windshield.

*No more lapses,* he thought, grabbing the gun bar. It was cool. *She means business.*

A voice crackled across his earphones. "Fire on her, Ladykiller Five. What are you waiting for?"

He pulled all three triggers at once, and saw the red and yellow flash of his guns on the front fenders. *Wrong way,* he thought, turning the bar. He saw the fender guns turn toward the Wommo car. Noticing the guns on his car's right side raising higher than his car body, Javik felt a small sense of relief. The maneuver permitted his guns to fire over the car without the embarrassment of self-destruction.

The lanes were merging into one, and Javik hit the brake pedal. A bullet whistled by his nose, lodging with a thud in the parachute pack overhead. His fighter car slowed, but not enough. *I'm ahead of her,* he thought. *She's experienced!*

Javik's car hit the single lane first. Turning the wheel, his car spun into gravel on the shoulder. Then he swung across the lane and went into a weaving, elusive pattern. He heard the staccato rat-a-tat rhythm of machine-gun fire from the pursuing fighter car. At the loud boom of a big gun, he felt numb. Nothing hit.

Looking in his rearview mirror, Javik turned his guns and tried to zero in on the other car. A bazooka shot from his big gun hit the track to one side of the enemy car, not close enough to do any damage. He moved the bar a little and fired the big gun again. This one was a direct hit.

In his mirror he saw the Wommo car explode in a pink ball of flame. He heard the whoosh of the pilot's cage as it ejected. A distant, throaty voice announced the event over the loudspeaker.

Javik breathed a sigh of relief.

But then an urgent voice crackled across his earphones: "Get out of there, Ladykiller Five! Punch it!"

In his rearview mirror, Javik saw another Wommo fighter car approaching fast. Its headlights grew larger and brighter as it neared.

He floored the accelerator pedal. His car jumped ahead. Then he pressed the bazooka button. The shot missed, exploding off the track.

A blue and black Manno pit area came into view on his left. He took the exit at full speed, then hit the brakes. The car squealed and shimmied. Then a deceleration hook beneath Javik's fighter car grabbed catchers on the pavement, throwing him against his shoulder harness. The car slowed and stopped.

Dozens of smiling humanoid Mannos ran to Javik's car and pulled him out.

"Nice going!" they said in their monotone voices, patting him on the back. "You kept us from being shut out today!"

Javik was speechless. He wanted to be far away from there.

They lifted him and carried him on their shoulders, chattering all the while in their dull voices about it being party time. The stench of unwashed, decaying bodies was almost unbearable to Javik. Cold night air blew across his face, and for the first time he realized he had been perspiring.

*I'm a hero,* Javik thought, unenthused. *Whoopee.*

# Chapter Nine

*Two objects can be the same and different at the same moment. If you doubt this, compare an apple and an orange.*

One of the Timeless Truths

Earlier, after Prince Pineapple watched the pear men guards escort Javik and Evans out of the king's court, he turned to face King Corker.

"That will be all," King Corker said. He rose and padded out via his side door.

Prince Pineapple remained where he was. Holding Wizzy up to eye level, he said, "I hope your captain does well."

"Eh?" Wizzy said, lifting the lid of his cat's eye to peer through the clear agate dome on top of his body.

"I was hoping that your captain does well. Tonight. In the games."

"What do I care?"

"I just thought—"

"Pipe down, will ya? I'm so tired I can hardly keep my peeper open! A growing comet needs his rest, you know."

This remark surprised the prince, for he had no idea up to that time that Wizzy was anything other than a talking mechanical device. But the prince said nothing of this, remarking instead in a gracious tone, "Of course. You can explain all that to me later in my apartment. It is quiet there, a place where you can rest."

Wizzy did not respond.

Prince Pineapple felt Wizzy shudder on his palm. Then Wizzy emitted a gentle snort. Soon he was fast asleep, snoring and wheezing.

Prince Pineapple snuggled Wizzy against his belly and thought of the day's strange events. He considered discarding Wizzy somewhere outside, but decided against this. *The king must not be alerted in any way,* he thought. *I make my move tonight—Wizzy or no Wizzy.*

Deep in thought, the prince carried Wizzy out of the castle and along the narrow trail that led to his apartment near Sacred Pond. Low Vesuvius shrubs lined the trail, with occasional roots across the path that he had to step over. Cork's three synchronized suns were dropping quickly below the level of the horizon, casting yellow-orange tones against a swirling cloud layer to the west.

He climbed a low hill, from the top of which he could see Sacred Pond. The scroll bubble was barely visible, giving off low light in a fog mist at the center of the pond. Giraffe-necked trail lights flickered on as the suns disappeared from view. Prince Pineapple shivered, and for the first time became aware of Wizzy's warmth against his stomach. Wizzy glowed faintly red in the diminishing daylight. Unknown to the prince, Wizzy was in the midst of a data retrieving dream.

*Wizzy's an odd gadget,* Prince Pineapple thought.

Wizzy whistled like a teapot, then chuckled in his sleep.

*The Sacred Scroll of Cork,* Prince Pineapple thought, watching the bubble appear brighter as the abyss of night enveloped it. *I must try for it tonight. While Wizzy is asleep.*

It occurred to the prince that Wizzy might be dangerous to him, sent by Lord Abercrombie to prevent him from learning the secrets of the Magician's Chamber. Abercrombie had the secret and wanted to keep it for himself. Or Wizzy might be an agent of the king: an elaborate setup.

*I must be on guard,* he thought.

O O O

Later that evening, Prince Pineapple sat in a rocking chair in the darkened bay window of his apartment, looking down on the black murkiness of Sacred Pond. The scroll bubble was not visible from here, being completely enshrouded by fog. In the yellow light of a giraffe-necked trail light below, he saw sheets of wind-driven rain pounding the waters along the shore. At the edges of the lamp's upside-down bowl of light, curls of thick fog drifted like ghosts agitated by the light.

He glanced at a gold and brown pillow which lay on the floor in a slice of light coming in from the bedroom. The pillow was imitation Persian, with just the proper combination of rips and worn threads to make it very valuable. Wizzy was asleep there, his lumpy body swelling and subsiding with each breath he took.

Prince Pineapple turned to look back out the window. *Like a blanket over the pond,* he thought. *The fog rolls in each night like a blanket.*

He envisioned the Sacred Scroll of Cork sleeping peacefully at the center of the pond, untouched by Fruit hands. His pulse quickened, and he felt hot pineapple juice rushing through the veins of his neck. His head throbbed.

He closed his eyes in an attempt to reduce his juice pressure. *This is not the way I want to go,* Prince Pineapple thought, thinking of the recurring nightmares he had of dying from a burst juice vein. *"Keep calm," Lord Abercrombie tells us in our dreams. "Let a Decision Coin reduce the pressure … reduce the pressure … reduce the pressure …"*

Touching a finger to one side of his temple, he felt the throbbing subside. He grew calmer, dropping his arm to his lap.

*I'd better go now,* he thought, watching the rain. *Doesn't look like the weather will break.*

The prince rose and tiptoed past Wizzy. But in his haste, one of Prince Pineapple's feet caught on a tuft of carpet. He fell roughly, causing a lot of noise. He swore under his breath.

Wizzy stirred. His lumpy body stretched one way, then the other. This was a molecular transformation possible only in the Realm of Magic. Any scientist will tell you that cold stone is not pliable.

"Can't you keep quiet?" Wizzy asked angrily. He tipped his cat's eye toward Prince Pineapple.

The prince was struggling to his feet, cursing himself for his stupidity. "A thousand pardons," he said.

"None of which are accepted," Wizzy said. "I feel terrible … aches in every chem-bond of my body." He sniffled, then felt something strange taking over his respiratory system. "Ahh!" he said, breathing in deeply. "Ahh … ahh … ahh-choo!"

Shaking his head sadly, Prince Pineapple muttered, "He'll never go back to sleep now."

"What did I just do?' Wizzy asked.

"Huh? Oh. You sneezed."

"Sneezed?" Wizzy glowed red, searching his data banks. "I have a cold?"

"Perhaps." The prince leaned against a wall.

"Do you have anything to treat such a condition?"

"Aspirin. But you have no mouth. Besides, you're a mechanical being, not at all similar to me or to a human being."

"You're laboring under a misapprehension," Wizzy said, changing to a deep shade of blue. "Use a knife to scrape powder from the aspirin tablet. Sprinkle me with it."

Prince Pineapple left the room for a moment, returning with a knife and an aspirin tablet. He did as Wizzy requested, kneeling over him and scraping fine white powder over his dome.

Wizzy glowed orange and became molten, thus absorbing the aspirin into his magical system. "Thank you," he said, cooling down and changing color again.

"Go back to sleep," Prince Pineapple said.

"With all the commotion around here? Are you kidding?"

"I'll be quiet. I think the sleep would do you good." He straightened and folded his arms across his chest, looking down at Wizzy.

"Since when are *you* my guardian? Everyone's always telling me what to do."

"I was only . . ." Prince Pineapple paused in mid-sentence. He sighed. "Well, I think *I'll* take a nap anyway." He returned to the bay window rocker, pulled a knitted blanket off the chair back, and slid into the chair. He covered himself and closed his eyes.

"Hrrmph!" Wizzy groused. He buzzed halfheartedly around the room. Then, as Prince Pineapple watched with one narrowly opened eye, he settled back on the pillow.

Prince Pineapple shifted to get more comfortable.

"You want to hear about me?" Wizzy asked. "I'm a baby comet, you know."

"Some other time. Let me rest." He kept one eye open narrowly, trying to conceal it at the edge of the blanket.

"First you wake me up and then you want *me* to be quiet while *you* sleep? That's a fine thing to do."

Peripherally, Prince Pineapple looked out the window at the diagonal sheets of wind-driven rain. He heard trees squeak together from the force of the storm. *Sacred Pond will be rough,* he thought. *Maybe the wind will subside.*

"Funny thing about you," Wizzy said. "I pick up thought waves from humans. But from you, nothing."

"You can read thoughts? Unspoken thoughts?" He sat up in the rocker, staring full-faced at Wizzy.

"Not yours, dear Prince. Nor those of your brethren. Perhaps you have no brains."

"No brains?"

"Well, not much in the way of brains anyway."

Prince Pineapple leaned forward, dropping the blanket to the floor. His eyes were bird alert. "Not much in the way of brains, you say? That may be true of the others, but I'll have you know I am in possession of a marvelous brain."

"I wouldn't be so sure about that. My red star crystal sensors" are quite sensitive—although not yet fully developed. You'd think I would receive something from you if you had a decent brain. Just a hum, mind you … or a few garbled thoughts."

"I am capable of more than garbled thoughts!" Prince Pineapple jumped up and paced the room. Presently: "Lord Abercrombie tells us to use Decision Coins for all matters. If my brain is damaged, it is from disuse."

"That is possible. Entirely possible. Now why don't you relax? I'll tell you a little about how I came to be here."

Prince Pineapple, sat on a shabby brown and yellow couch against one wall. "And how will I comprehend such things?" he asked "Not having a decent brain and all."

"You do sound rather intelligent. Perhaps my sensors need adjustment. I'm sorry if I offended you."

The prince glowered, thinking, *Maybe he'll talk himself to sleep. I have a good brain. I use it all the time.*

O O O

The Orgy Building comprised one large, rectangular room with bead curtain doorways at each end. The room was full of partying humanoids when Javik was shown in by a Manno teammate. Nearly everyone in the room wore an electroplated purple badge, signifying conspicuous bravery back on Earth in the face of a disintegrating product. The bulbous-headed Mannos and Wommos swarmed around drunkenly, filling up nearly every square centimeter of space available. There was no music. Despite this, many partyers twisted their hips, swaying to unheard tunes while clutching drinks in tall glasses. It was like an Earth party in some ways, but distorted.

"After you've eaten from the kill," the Manno at his side said in a characteristic monotone, "find a Wommo bitch and take her in one of the fornication rooms along the wall." He pointed through the crowd at a row of red doors set very close together along the opposite wall. As Javik gazed across the room, he became aware of movement overhead.

The ceiling of the room was tinted glassplex or heavy glass, substantial enough to support a throng of Corkers and other Fruits above. They kneeled and peered down at the Earthian party, their eyes open fully in frenzied fascination. Most of them were gathered over the fornication rooms, where they pushed and fought for better views.

"They enjoy watching all our Earth games," the Manno said. "Fruits don't engage in our form of sex, you know. They grow in orchards and vineyards. When they're ripe, they simply fall off."

"No fun in that," Javik said, smelling what he thought was roast pig. If spoken to an old acquaintance, these words might have given the impression that Javik was his old womanizing self. But Javik did not feel the words he uttered. They came automatically, as if from a politician's voice tape. He was hungry and angry, hopelessly out of synch with his surroundings.

"Excuse me," the Manno said. "I just spied a delectable, if you get my drift." He sauntered off, wading into the crowd like a bee going for pollen. Soon Javik lost sight of him.

The room was divided into Manno and Wommo sides, with blue and pink banners designating each camp. On each side were banquet tables covered with red and white checkered picnic cloths. The tables held barred cages from the fallen fighter cars of the day, with the dead and unfortunate pilots spinning inside on spits. The cage bars were black now, having cooled. As Javik watched, tackle sets over each table lifted off the tops of the cages, exposing the humanoid roasts. The spits stopped turning.

To Javik's horror, the throngs moved in on the humanoid food, tearing off jagged hunks of cooked flesh which they stuffed in their mouths. Animal sounds shook the room: growls and snarls, sighs and grunts of satisfaction. The tables rocked as hungry humanoids pulled at the roasts from all sides.

"You'd better hurry," a Manno at Javik's side said. "We only got one kill today."

Javik only stared. Hunger pangs tore at his stomach. Cannibalism. It was beyond belief.

"Say," the Manno said, moving in front of Javik to look at his face. "You got our kill!" The Manno limped as he moved, and carried a deep gash across his abdomen. Black letters stamped on his forehead indicated that he was a Product Failure victim.

Javik looked away.

The Manno grabbed his arm, pulling Javik toward the Manno banquet table.

"Wait," Javik said, his voice feeble. He offered little resistance.

"Hey, guys!" the Manno yelled as they neared the swarm at the table. "Save a piece for this guy. He got our kill."

Stepping to one side so that Javik could get through, the Mannos greeted him with smiles that dripped meat juice. They patted him on the back and pushed him forward. Javik's hunger-starved nostrils tried to convince his brain that the strong aroma was roast pork. Then he saw it close up: a shredded female body with great pieces of cooked brown flesh torn away. The body was more dead than the dead, for it had died twice: once on Earth and again on Cork. Javik told himself that it should never have lived, if this was to be the end of it all.

"Eat," someone said, thrusting a piece of breast meat into Javik's quivering hands.

Javik held the meat unsteadily, staring at it in horror. This was being forced on him. He had to eat it. That made it all right, he told himself. A dull hunger pang tugged at his midsection.

The Mannos turned their attention away from Javik now, resuming their demonic gluttony. The animal sounds increased.

Javik's mouth was filling with saliva. The fluid gushed in, anticipating his first bite. He wanted that meat. He needed it. He lifted the succulent piece close to his lips, nearly touching them.

"Go ahead," a familiar female voice said.

Looking to his left, Javik saw Evans smiling at him. In one hand she held a bone with shredded meat hanging from it. Dark red meat juice ran down her chin and over the front of her Wommo jumpsuit. She chewed and swallowed, smiling and staring at Javik all the while. Her smile fit the occasion. It was satanic and all-knowing, seeing every frailty Javik had. Evans did not need eyes. Her smile saw it all.

"Eat," she said.

Javik heard a *clunk* overhead. Glancing up, he saw a cluster of Corkers looking down at him from the level above. "I'm like a zoo animal," he said.

"Don't be silly," Evans said. She nibbled at the bone.

Javik gagged. Looking down at the meat in his hand, his eyes widened at the realization of what he had almost done. He hurled the meat to the floor. "You think you know me, Evans?" he said, confronting her. "You filthy transsexual!"

Mannos scrambled on the floor to recover Javik's meat. Someone scolded him for wasting food. But he scarcely heard the words.

Evans's eyes narrowed to slits. The smile disappeared. "That was in my dossier?" she asked. "I had hoped they might leave it—"

"Get away from me!" Javik said.

Her all-knowing smile returned. "I know what you want," she said. "Let me demonstrate a fornication room for you." She nodded in the direction of the red doors.

"Shove off! Do you hear me, Evans? Shove off!" He felt his glands trying to convince him to accompany her. He seemed to be battling the inevitable. He craved Evans. He wanted to throw her down right there and enjoy her. His body screamed for her.

*"No!"* a voice thundered inside his skull. *"Not a transsexual!"*

*"But who would know?"* another interior voice asked.

"Give in," Evans said. Her voice seemed to come from Javik's own brain.

*"Give in,"* another voice in his head whispered.

Javik steeled himself against the onslaught. "I'm not religious," he said, staring at meat juice drippings on one of his boots. His words were measured. "Never have been. But this seems … so evil to me."

Evans moved close to him. She pressed her short, buxom body against his. Her breasts were soft and inviting against his stomach.

He took a deep breath and moved away from her, bumping into a Manno behind him. "You fit this garbage dump real well," he told her.

Her facial muscles slackened. Javik saw fear in her eyes.

"You're warped!" Javik screeched. "Everything here is warped! A cracked reflection of Earth!"

She laughed derisively. But it was a forced laugh.

*Those Corkers are getting a good show,* he thought. *Wait'll I start busting faces.*

"Hey, Manno!" a partyer shouted from the other side of the table. "Take it easy, teammate. We're here to have a good time."

Javik wished he had lost on the track that day. It might have been easier that way.

"Give in," Evans said. The smile was gone now, and she looked confused. Her gaze moved around nervously. Beads of perspiration clung to her forehead.

His body screamed for satisfaction. But now the scream met the high wall of Javik's innermost determination, his last line of defense. It had to hold and did. He felt the craving for Evans subsiding. Now, he went to the attack and smiled, enjoying the look of hurt it caused on Evans's face.

"You got the kill today," she said. "The *only* Manno kill …" She was struggling to keep him in line. Her demonic smile returned for a moment.

He felt the corners of his mouth sag.

The hated smile took over her face again. It was a battle of words and expressions, with each side searching for the winning combination.

*Another Earth game,* he thought.

"You might as well enjoy yourself," she said. "While you can."

He wanted to knock that smile off her face. He wanted to see her dead. He wanted to throw her down and enjoy her. His glands screamed. He licked his lips.

"You can have some of our meat," she said, extending the bone to him. "We have plenty."

"I don't …" he said. He felt a torrent of angry words inside. He just shook his head.

She withdrew the meat. "We Wommos are good," she said, setting her jaw. "Better than Mannos. I'm glad I changed sexes!"

Javik's glare of hatred met a like glare from Evans. In that instant, he knew Evans would try to kill him if she went up against him on the track. She was no longer Co-Pilot Marta Evans. She was someone—or some*thing*—else. It scared him. It scared the living hell out of him.

She chewed at her upper lip while watching his every move.

Javik thought she was sizing him up for a fight. He had been in enough brawls to know the signs.

"Maybe I'll see you around," she said stiffly. She turned and walked away. Javik knew what "around" meant. It meant tomorrow, on the fighter car track.

He thought he heard the anger of more than one woman in her words. He was not even certain he heard anger. It was more a threatening undertone which made him realize what a remarkable source of competition the Corkers had tapped for their deadly games.

He watched Evans push her way through the crowd, moving into her netherworld, a place reserved for the unholiest of beings. Taking a drunken Manno by the arm, she pulled him toward the bank of fornication rooms. Overhead, Corkers scrambled to follow her.

*I'm getting' out of this zoo,* Javik thought. *I'm gonna die as far away from here as possible. Someplace they can't use me.*

He battered his way through the drunken throng, feeling himself being drawn away by a welcome burst of inner morality. But he knew even that reservoir of strength would be short-lived without food. He told himself nothing would get in his way, and scarcely heard the Corkers overhead who scrambled to follow him.

At the Wommo banquet table, an ecstatic Wommo popped the eyeball out of a humanoid toastie. Tossing the eye high in the air, she caught it in her mouth. The Wommos cheered as she gulped.

Misshapen faces appeared and receded, gawking, smiling, and leering at him drunkenly. He called upon his last vestiges of pride to keep moving him forward.

"I've tasted Manno and I've tasted Wommo," a shrill-voiced Wommo said, singsonging the words. "The Wommo is sweeter, not nearly so chew-y."

Javik cursed softly, stumbling as he approached a bead curtain doorway. He readied himself for guards on the other side. *Lightning strokes,* he thought. *Short and fierce. Ten of those purple pudgies couldn't take me down.*

The bead curtain came into focus, swaying gently. The beads knocked together with a dull, hollow sound. Javik took a deep breath.

Suddenly, three Corker guards spread the curtain, filling the doorway with their bodies. They pointed metal lances at Javik, but his trained eye saw the tips waver. And he noticed the drunken, rolling gaze of the big Corker in the middle. This one swayed way back. He had corporal stripes on his sleeves.

"Return to the party!" the corpulent corporal commanded. His voice was loose and throaty. He coughed and spit purple, bubbly phlegm on the floor.

Javik felt the blood drain from his face. *I'll kill these …* he thought. In the midst of the thought, Javik ducked under the corporal's lance and kicked him hard against the soft underside of his belly. The Corker grunted, tumbling over on his alcohol backpack with his lance pointed straight up in the air.

Seizing the vertical lance before the other guards could attack, Javik ran outside. A cool night breeze washed through his hair. The sting of a lance pricked the calf of his left leg. Jumping to one side, Javik swung back with his own weapon, knocking the guard's lance away.

The guard quick-footed backward, stopping when his alcohol backpack bumped the building.

"How about you?" Javik barked, lunging at the third guard.

This guard must have had more than the minimum issue of sense, for he dropped his lance and ran into the night as fast as his six stubby legs could carry him.

The big Corker corporal fought his way to his feet, with help from the other remaining guard. "Have you gone mad, Earthian?" the corporal asked. "Go back inside."

A droplet of rain hit Javik's cheek as he surveyed the area. He felt the night wind pick up. He was on the opposite end of the Orgy Building from the entrance he had taken. The building was one of three similar buildings fronting a dimly lit dirt carriage road. Across the road was a thick, dark section of piney woods.

"Did you hear me, Earthian?"

Javik's consciousness focused on the inverted bowl of stars over his head. He longed for his ship. Maybe he could clear the thruster tubes and fly it to a safe place on Cork for further repairs.

Excited voices snapped him to awareness. "Over there!" a guard yelled. Javik saw two squads of Corker guards running toward him, one from each end of the road. They moved drunkenly, throwing yellow light on the ground with the lanterns they carried.

O O O

In the shadows of Prince Pineapple's apartment, Wizzy told of being dropped to Earth by his Papa Sidney. He described the subsequent adventures with Captain Tom Javik as well, and commented on their dislike for one another. Resting on a white coffee table doily, Wizzy tilted his cat's eye toward Prince Pineapple and said,

"I wish I could be somewhere of my own choosing … streaking across the galaxy like Papa. I do not belong here."

Prince Pineapple leaned forward on the couch, resting his elbows on his lap and cradling his chin on his hands. This placed half of his face in the slice of light coming in from the bedroom. The wind howled outside. "Nor do I," he said. "I too am forced to do objectionable things."

"You have a papa?"

"There is but one papa on this planet: Lord Abercrombie. He leaves us virtually no free will. From ripening, we are trained to relegate even the simplest matters to Decision Coins." His voice grew bitter. "Our lives are but a series of coin tosses. I see no sense in it."

"Nice pun," Wizzy said.

Deep in his problem, Prince Pineapple was all seriousness. "As I told you," he said, "I have brains."

"I can see that," Wizzy said, wondering if pun recognition might constitute a valid intelligence test.

"We are told not to get too upset. Or we might burst a juice vessel. I'm angry enough now to let one blow wide open." The prince's face glowed crimson. He felt his juice pressure rising.

"Don't be silly," Wizzy said.

"I want to learn so many things," Prince Pineapple lamented.

"And I, too," Wizzy said. He rose half a meter above the doily, giving off a faint hum as he held position. "Is there no solution to your problem?"

"If only I had the Sacred Scroll," Prince Pineapple said. He worried for a moment, wondering if he should have revealed this. Then he sighed deeply, and his face grew a paler shade of red. He felt his juice pressure dropping.

"And what is that?" Wizzy asked, unable to read the prince's thoughts.

"Every magical planet has a Sacred Scroll. They were created thousands of years ago, describing the locations of all Dimensional Tunnels connecting the magical planets." He sat back, resting his hands on his lap. "On Cork, the scroll is protected by a magician's bubble at the center of Sacred Pond."

"Dimensional Tunnels," Wizzy said, glowing red as he searched his memory banks. "Also known as warples. Synthetic in nature. They crisscross the universe invisibly, permitting rapid travel between certain planets."

Prince Pineapple lifted his eyebrows in astonishment. *A most peculiar device, this Wizzy.* Then: "I need Cork's scroll," he said. "Do you suppose you might help me?"

"I would like to help you. I could check in on Captain Tom afterward, I suppose."

"Then row with me to the center of Sacred Pond. Help me pop the magician's bubble."

"That may not be so easy."

"We must go tonight. Already the other advisers are whispering against me."

"Do you know of anyone else who has tried to pop this bubble? Have *you* tried?"

"King Corker has blocked all attempts. He requires so much paperwork that no one has been able to obtain permission. I'm sure he wants the scroll for himself."

"I see." Wizzy settled back on the doily.

"Legend has it that the bubble can be popped only at night. And only with a dull instrument."

"Do you think the king has tried?"

"Of course. He would like to replace Lord Abercrombie. But I say we don't need a lord. Cork is a very ancient planet. According to legend, nutrients flowed from the soil before any lord appeared. That means they will continue to flow after the lord is gone."

"You want to throw Abercrombie out?"

"Yes, and then seal the entrance to his chamber, preventing anyone from getting in again."

Wizzy glowed red. "You might seal the chamber from the surface," he said. "But you can never seal the other side, the Dimensional Tunnel side."

"That is true. But at least I would accomplish something."

Wizzy flickered. "I'm losing my data base," he said. "Do you know how to get in?"

"No," Prince Pineapple looked away. A saying of unknown origin wafted across his consciousness: *"When you see what it is all about, there will be nothing left to do except to have a good laugh."* The thought puzzled him.

"Why do you expect to succeed when the king has failed?"

"It is only a feeling I have. That I am chosen, I suppose. Undoubtedly this is a common enough thought. But I must try anyway."

"And if you fail?"

"I will defect. This very night. Brother Carrot's Vegetable Underground could learn much from me. I hear he treats some Fruits rather well. I know all about Corker defenses."

"You have a boat to cross this pond?"

"Of course. Quite a sturdy little craft."

"I just thought of something. It's a rainy night. That's not a good time to venture out."

"But I have no choice. King Corker will order me into oblivion soon. Perhaps tomorrow."

"I do have certain magical powers," Wizzy said. "Though rather limited and unperfected. I could perish if I ever became very wet."

"Then stay in the apartment. It is yours. I have no further need of it."

"If I went with you, could you promise to keep me dry?"

"I would try. I could wrap you in plastic and keep you under my coat."

"But in a boat," Wizzy said, having second thoughts. He heard the wind and looked at the rain slanting against the window. "On a stormy night."

Prince Pineapple placed his palms on the couch, preparing to rise. "I should go," he said. "Make up your mind."

"We are alike, you and I," Wizzy said. "Controlled by others, sent off in circles to do inane things … as if we had no brains or wills of our own."

"Yes!" Prince Pineapple exclaimed, smiling as he locked gazes with Wizzy's cat's eye. "That's exactly right. Let's do this together. It will be a marvelous adventure."

"But some things confuse me," Wizzy said. "According to Papa Sidney, I'm supposed to help Captain Tom correct the damage caused by the evil anti-jobs criminal, Abercrombie. But Papa was hurt by Job Support. They sent him to a therapy orbiter because that sustained more jobs than rehabilitation. Shouldn't my Papa have opposed Job Support? It hurt him terribly. Why did he continue to love the AmFed Way? Will I ever understand why?"

"That does sound peculiar," Prince Pineapple said. He settled back on the couch for a moment.

"Maybe Papa isn't so bright."

"But he has deep feelings. A wonderful sense of devotion. I can tell that from listening to you. He loves Earth and you."

"And he loves that idiot Captain Tom!" Wizzy exclaimed. "This love … You can help me to understand it?"

"Love is not something I can explain. It is something which comes over you, causing you to do strange things."

"Papa said that, too."

"It is not a reasoning thing."

"Then how am I to know it?"

"It will affect you when you least expect it."

"I'm so confused."

"I felt love once," Prince Pineapple said. "For a lush young pineapple girl." He sighed. "But that was long ago. So very long ago."

Wizzy recalled the words of his papa just before dropping Wizzy to Earth: *"You must learn to control your emotions, but do not become callous in the process. Retain some vulnerability. This is perhaps the most important part of being alive."*

Prince Pineapple moved across the room. He flipped on a lamp. The room's darkness retreated, hiding in safe corners and under furniture. "I suppose I can wait a while longer," he said. "It can't get any worse outside."

A tree rubbed against the side of the building, followed by the crack of a branch. The branch thumped as it fell to the roof.

Wizzy alighted on the pineapple prince's shoulder. They went together to the couch. "I want to learn everything in the universe!" Wizzy exclaimed. "I want to experience everything in the universe!"

Prince Pineapple laughed as he made himself comfortable on the couch. "And I would settle for the knowledge of Cork."

"Maybe all the universe's secrets are here," Wizzy said, surprising himself with the statement. "Your goal and my goal may take us to the very same place."

"What do you mean?" Prince Pineapple asked, watching rain batter the bay window.

Wizzy shifted on the prince's shoulder. "I don't know," he said. "The words came out before I had a chance to think about them."

"You asked about love," Prince Pineapple said.

"I want to understand all my emotions," Wizzy said. "They seem to exert a great deal of control over me." His tone became excited. "Maybe that's what the words meant. Understanding my feelings may be a universal thing. I may not need to look elsewhere." The words floated across Wizzy's consciousness as if spoken by someone else.

"Could be. Be cautious of what you seek, however. Certain things are better left undiscovered."

"Such as?

"Sadness. You won't want any of that. It's such a tragic thing. You don't want the death of a loved one, or loneliness." Prince Pineapple recalled his lost love. "These are not good feelings."

"I want them anyway."

"I don't think so." Prince Pineapple stroked Wizzy's back gently.

"But how will I ever know unless I try them?"

"Take my word for it. That should be enough."

Wizzy thought about this while wind-driven rain beat against the outside of the building.

They talked for hours like this, a pineapple prince conversing with a lump of stone on his shoulder. When the cracked plastic clock over the fireplace struck three, Prince Pineapple said they had to go.

"There is a break in the rain," the prince said. "We must hurry. It may not last."

As Prince Pineapple covered Wizzy with plastic wrap, Wizzy thought: *Plastic Is Fantastic.* The thought came to him involuntarily, a mantra from his father's life. "Don't wrap it too tightly," Wizzy said. "I need to breathe, you know."

It occurred to Wizzy that he had not actually agreed to accompany Prince Pineapple in pursuit of the Sacred Scroll. Not in so many words. Nevertheless, the decision had been made.

O O O

With guards approaching him from each end of the road, Javik's choices were limited. He dashed across the road into the woods, stumbling in darkness as the woods tangled him. Branches scratched his arms and face. Roots hooked his feet, sending him crashing to the ground. He closed his eyes and plunged forward, not knowing or caring where he was going. Just as long as he escaped.

Angry voices followed, calling out warnings and Corker curses. "You will starve, Earthian! Earthians need Earthians!"

"Death awaits you out there!"

"May the Lord God Abercrombie swallow you whole!"

This imprecation stuck in Javik's brain. *Abercrombie's a god here?* he thought. *Truly?* He pressed on, with more than a few misgivings.

Gradually the voices receded into the abyss of darkness in his wake. He slowed to a walk, holding his hands out in front of his face to warn of impending obstacles. A root caught his foot, but he pulled free without falling. Shallow scratches stung his face and arms. A shinbone throbbed. Pausing to reach down, he felt a flap of skin there. The pants were torn and wet with blood. It was not raining, but the waterlogged trees overhead dripped overflow on the back of his neck.

The ground was spongy here. He walked across stretches of clearing that lulled him into false security. Without warning, a branch would slap him rudely, or a root that apparently had life of its own would attempt to throw him down.

He could see very little, but had the impression that everything was purple: the trees, the ground, the air. Even the sky. He looked up often, occasionally catching a glimpse of a tiny star way out yonder twinkling faintly against a purple universe. He wondered if the color sensation was only in his mind, if it had something to do with the throbbing of his leg.

Javik felt sleepy. His footsteps grew labored. A hunger pang gnawed at his stomach. He envisioned millions of grenache purple Corkers jumping over a fence of exaggerated height. Slowly and gracefully their chubby bodies floated in the stratosphere to clear the fence. He yawned.

*I've got to stop somewhere,* he thought. *Sleep. I need sleep.*

But a misty rain pelted his face, appearing suddenly like a cold slap. Now Javik was really miserable. He could not lie down in the rain. If only he could find an overhanging rock or log for shelter.

A branch scratched across his face. He cursed. His cheeks and forehead burned.

Pushing another countless branch out of the way, he stepped up a little incline, unable to see anything but a great wash of purple across his brain. The ground changed. It became smoother underfoot, like compact dirt instead of the mottled forest floor. The misty rain had become a hard drizzle. He rubbed his eyes.

Off to the right and left, he saw flickering yellow lights. They didn't look like Corker lanterns. More like trail lights. He was on a trail.

"Which way?" he asked. These words were the first spoken in quite a while, and seemed to rush out of his stomach like bad food. He tasted acid. Javik had lost his bearings, with no idea which way to turn. It occurred to him that a Decision Coin would be handy. This was no time to have to think. He wanted to lie down.

A mixture of euphoria and fear struck him at finding the trail. What if he turned the wrong way and it led him back to the Corkers? What if both ways led to the Corkers?

Following his instincts, he turned right. Presently he walked under the yellow light of a giraffe-necked trail light. Beyond that he passed into purple blackness, with another speck of yellow light visible in the distance ahead. Soon he was past this lamp and in purple blackness again. This pattern continued until he reached an illuminated clearing.

The clearing seemed to be illuminated by a glow from the sky. The sky here was not purple. It was luminescent and pale white, far less intense than daylight. The faint shadow of his body stretched across tall grass on the ground.

The clearing grew lighter, and Javik began to distinguish terrain colors: pale green grass stalks dotted with tall-stemmed white flowers that had bright red centers. A powerful gust of wind shoved the flowers over in unison, like rows of cheerleaders. The rain stopped.

A blinding flash of green light filled the sky. Javik slammed his eyes shut. They ached. He felt his pulse quicken. The wind blew harder and louder, nearly toppling him.

Then the noise, wind, and light subsided, allowing Javik to open his eyes narrowly. High in the sky, an emerald green fireball veered heavenward, trailing three misty golden plumes. The plumes changed to silver.

Javik gasped. "A comet!" he husked, feeling the words rasp like sandpaper against his throat.

The Great Comet flashed high over Javik's head, staying so far away that he could keep his eyes open narrowly.

He smelted sulfur, reminding him of the terrible fire the year before on the therapy orbiter of St. Elba. He thought of Sidney Malloy.

The comet circled and repeated its maneuver. This time Javik noticed it was heading in a ten o'clock direction from the way he was facing.

*A sign?* he thought. *It went the same direction twice.*

The comet hovered overhead now, just low enough to illuminate the clearing.

Javik ran across the clearing in the direction the comet seemed to have indicated. Reaching the woods, he found an unlighted trail. As he walked briskly along the trail, he found that it had trail lights but they weren't operating. The pine tree tops made eerie profiles against green light from the sky.

The light moved with Javik, keeping his way dimly lit.

Feeling a rush of strength and excitement, he broke into a full run. Presently, Javik reached another clearing. The comet was still high overhead, hovering there like an emerald green personal sun.

Squinting to look into the Great Comet's brightness, Javik thought he saw the faint outline of a round face in the nucleus. The outline was gray, like that of a light charcoal sketch. Then it gained definition. It was a distantly familiar face. Javik was not certain. He rubbed his eyes and shook his head. He closed his eyes.

"Sid!" he yelled before opening his eyes. The realization hit him like a Bu-Tech thunderbolt. "Sid! Sid Malloy!" His eyelids snapped open as if mento-controlled.

Javik ran out in the clearing with his hands stretched to the heavens. Beyond the face in the comet, the stars seemed to burn brighter now, like reflected bits of silver on a black velvet cloth.

The face in the nucleus smiled, exposing a row of bright white teeth. It gave Javik the impression of an epic scale videodome toothpaste commercial. He didn't wonder how a comet could have teeth. He accepted it. This was not a moment to question such things.

As Javik stood in awe with his face turned to the eerie light above, he thought of Wizzy. *He spoke truth to me,* Javik thought. *Everything Wizzy said was true!*

"Sid!" Javik yelled. "Speak to me, Sid!"

There was no response. The gray lines of the face became black, and the face took on a kindly, cherubic-cheeked expression.

"Skywrite something!" Javik pleaded. "Like you did over Earth! Come on, Sid! Say something to me!"

The Great Comet moved laterally. Javik ran to follow it. He reached the crest of a little hill, giving him a view of the entire clearing. He saw a wide path framed with AmFed garbage canisters. Several hundred meters from that, a familiar profile jutted into the air.

"My ship!" he said. "The *Amanda Marie*!"

Javik watched the comet. It became bright orange, from its flaming nucleus to the tip of its misty tail. The face remained visible in the nucleus, but it was less defined now, a faint circle of cadmium yellow. The comet rose gracefully, then dipped like a hawk diving for its prey.

*My God,* Javik thought. *So this is where Sid went.* He shielded his eyes from the light. The backs of his hands became warm as the comet neared. Then they grew cooler and the light receded.

Through his fingers, Javik saw the Great Comet hovering high overhead, still orange but with a scolding expression on its face

"Sid!" Javik yelled. "What's the matter, Sid?"

The face faded. The comet rose steeply in the sky, blowing a great wind across the clearing. It took a lateral course now, moving close to the horizon of the planet. The clearing grew darker.

Javik shivered.

Soon the comet was a distant speck. Then it dropped out of sight below the horizon. For several moments, glowing orange particles from its tail remained in the sky. They sparkled like the dying embers of a fireworks rocket. Then it was dark. Purple dark.

O O O

Wizzy was at the window of Prince Pineapple's apartment. "There!" he exclaimed. "Did you see the comet? Going away fast?"

"That was your papa?" Prince Pineapple asked, pressing his face against the glassplex. "I can hardly believe it!"

The Great Comet became a speck of orange light, then disappeared below the horizon.

Minutes later, Prince Pineapple ran into the Stygian blackness outside, carrying Wizzy under his coat against his belly. Although Wizzy was loosely wrapped in plastic, the prince leaned forward as an extra measure to keep rain from hitting him. In his haste, Prince Pineapple nearly slipped and fell.

"Careful!" Wizzy squealed as he was jiggled about. "I could fall and roll into the pond!"

A trail light at Sacred Pond's edge provided enough illumination for the prince to locate a shelter for Wizzy. Selecting a thick shrub next to the path, he leaned over and placed Wizzy under it.

A cool, wet breeze blew across Prince Pineapple's face as he straightened and surveyed the area. Curls of fog shifted on the surface of the water. He felt the wind shift on his face and saw the change in the curls of fog. Water lapped against the shore. *The rain's holding back,* he thought. *Maybe luck will be with me,*

He stepped off the path into shadows, clearing brush away where he had hidden the pram. It was a small craft, but rather heavy for its size. He dragged it to the shore, then returned for the oars.

As he passed Wizzy, the little comet squealed, "I felt a drop of rain! Check my wrap!"

"Impossible," Prince Pineapple said. "It's not raining at all." He tossed the oars in the pram, then went for Wizzy.

"You took your time," Wizzy gruffed as the prince lifted him. "Each drop takes a portion of my strength. Oh, to be in deep space, where there is no atmosphere and no water!"

*Wizzy had better help me,* Prince Pineapple thought as he stepped in the pram, *or I'll drop him in the deepest part of Sacred Pond.* He placed Wizzy beneath the aft bench.

Moments later the little boat was cutting slowly across the pond's choppy, foggy surface. Wizzy heard the dipping of the oars in water and the thump of waves against the hull. And he heard the dull clunk of wood against wood whenever an oar slipped from its oarlock; Prince Pineapple would curse whenever this happened, but soon would be back at his task. In a distorted vision through the plastic wrap, Wizzy could see Prince Pineapple from the belly down, leaning forward and back as he pulled at the oars.

"Whatever you do," Prince Pineapple said, "don't say anything that rhymes. It would force me to flip backward, head over heels. That would capsize this little boat."

"Like you did in court?" Wizzy asked, choosing his words carefully.

"Exactly like that."

"You can't control it?"

"I have tried. Dear me, but I've tried! It's instinctual with us. Our muscles pull us right over."

"You might have warned me about that earlier."

The pineapple prince disregarded this remark. Soon he was grunting with each pull at the oars and panting heavily. After a while he had to ship the oars in order to take a rest. He wiped his brow, just then the boat rocked violently.

"What's going on?" Wizzy squealed.

"It's getting rough out here."

"I can tell that."

A wave washed over the gunwale, splashing cold water on the plastic wrap over Wizzy. Some leaked through and touched him. This sent the little comet into a state of panic. “Save me!” he cried out. “Save me!” Wizzy glowed bright orange now and scooted through Prince Pineapple’s legs to a dry forward portion of the deck.

The prince turned to watch Wizzy. “The plastic wrap!” Prince Pineapple said. “You’re glowing like a coal! It’s melting all over you!”

Wizzy paled to yellow. “That burst of heat dried me off,” he said. “But there’s a limit. Bursts like that use a lot of energy. I presume you brought more plastic wrap?”

“I did not.”

“I wish I hadn’t come on your ridiculous voyage!”

“Remember all those things we have in common,” Prince Pineapple said. Angrily, he resumed his struggle with the oars. 2He was fighting a strong current now, and had to row just to remain in one place. A floating log bounced off the side of the pram’s hull, sending a dull, disturbing shudder through the boat.

Prince Pineapple watched the log disappear in the current aft of his boat. He was straining to the breaking point; his hands were burning from his effort.

A light rain started. This caused Wizzy to cry out in terror and seek the farthest reaches of shelter under the forward bench.

Rain mixed with perspiration ran down Prince Pineapple’s face. Because of the current, he took quick breaks of only a few seconds to wipe his face.

All the while, Wizzy complained with each wave that washed aboard and with each increase in the intensity of precipitation. It was raining steadily now, and the prince turned to see Wizzy glow bright orange, drying himself. Finally, in desperation, Wizzy suction-perched on the underside of the forward bench, clinging there like a fat fly on a ceiling.

“I feel dizzy,” Prince Pineapple said.

“Then turn back!” Wizzy said.

“Never!” Prince Pineapple rowed harder now, drawing strength from his deepest reservoir of energy. Images of the Sacred Scroll of Cork danced across his half-closed eyes.

Something heavy landed on his belly, then pushed its way under his coat. “I’m losing strength,” Wizzy said. “Keep me in here. Keep me dry....” The voice faded.

Prince Pineapple considered returning to shore for Wizzy’s sake. “Do you still want me to take you back?” he asked.

Wizzy did not respond.

Now Prince Pineapple thought of the perspiration on his underclothes. Soon this wetness would soak through and meet the encroaching outside moisture from waves and rain. There would be no dryness then. He reminded himself of his priorities. Wizzy was expendable. The scroll was not.

Just at the moment when Prince Pineapple felt he could row no more, the waves subsided and the rain stopped. He shipped his oars and took deep breaths to restore himself. An eerie low light radiated across the surface of the water. The pond was like glassplex here, and there was a purple luminescence just below the surface.

"What's going on?" Wizzy asked. He poked his nucleus out from under the coat.

"I don't know. It's different here. And I feel the boat moving forward, as if it's being pulled by something. It's not an opposing current now."

"The rain is gone!" Wizzy said happily. He ventured into the night air for a little spin, being careful only to fly above the boat. His tail was yellow orange as he flew, and it cast a sparkling reflection on the water that had accumulated in the boat bottom. Soon Wizzy alighted on Prince Pineapple's shoulder. There he glowed orange for a moment to dry the fabric of the coat.

Overhead, Prince Pineapple saw stars burning more clearly than he could ever recall having seen them. Two synchronized Corkian moons passed over them quickly, momentarily casting their warm glow across the water. Then the moons disappeared beyond the horizon of fog.

"I have seen the magician's bubble out here," Prince Pineapple said. "On clear days. According to legend, my scroll is trapped in the bubble."

"*Your* scroll?"

"A slip of the tongue."

Squinting his cat's eye, Wizzy saw a yellow glow in the fog off their starboard bow. "I see something out there," he said.

"Where?"

"Off the starboard bow."

"Where? Where?"

"It's impossible to miss!"

"I don't see it!"

"Well I see it clearly," Wizzy said. "The fog's clearing. We're drawing nearer. Yes! It's a bubble—floating just above the surface of the pond."

"Must be a spell on me," Prince Pineapple muttered thoughtfully, "caused by Lord Abercrombie's soil nutrients every time I recharge. I am permitted to see the bubble from afar, but once I draw near …"

"Could be a magician's trick, all right."

"We're going directly toward the bubble?"

"Yes. And I see something inside. A rolled parchment."

"The Sacred Scroll!" Prince Pineapple said. "How far?"

"Less than fifty meters."

"Tell me when we're close enough to hit it with the oar handle. Something dull will pop the bubble, according to legend."

"Don't rely on that legend. It may have been planted in your pineapple brain by Lord Abercrombie."

"There's nothing wrong with having a pineapple brain."

"I didn't say there was. But your legend smacks of trickery to me."

"Then forget the oar. Do it your way. You with all the knowledge of the universe."

"We'd better stop bickering," Wizzy said. "It's just ahead now."

Prince Pineapple felt the boat slow.

"Almost there," Wizzy reported, perching himself on the bow seat. "We'll go right under it."

The bubble-was bright yellow and perhaps half as big in circumference as the length of the pram. Inside the bubble, floating freely, Wizzy saw an old-looking rolled parchment tied with brown cord.

When the bow of the pram slipped beneath the bubble, Wizzy glowed the hottest white-orange he could and smashed against the underside of the bubble. He bounced off a soft surface. Then he tried again, bouncing off again.

Seeing where Wizzy was attacking, Prince Pineapple thrust forth his oar handle. He felt it strike something soft. Then there was a loud clap of thunder. A lightning bolt in front of Wizzy's eye sent him scurrying for cover beneath the prince's coat. The oar clattered to the deck of the boat.

Prince Pineapple began to see something where the oar had struck: the broken image of a rolled, yellowing parchment, bound with brown leather cord … unidentifiable letters on the parchment with an "X" over them. The image faded to invisibility.

"I saw it!" Prince Pineapple said. "But now it's gone!"

Venturing out on the prince's lap, Wizzy said, "We're dead in the water. You just have to reach out and take it. Would you look at that! It says 'Torah' on the scroll, but that's been crossed out. The bubble's gone now. You blasted it with the oar.

Prince Pineapple reached for the place he had seen the scroll. He felt something there: stiff paper. But he withdrew his hand suspiciously without grabbing hold. "Too easy," he said.

"Probably a discarded religious document from Earth," Wizzy said. "Torah … that was sacred to one of their religions."

"This cannot be," Prince Pineapple said. "The Sacred Scroll of Cork predates the arrival of Earthian gar-bahge."

Wizzy glowed red, calling upon his data banks for assistance. "I think it's the original scroll, all right," he said. "With fake markings added by Abercrombie to confuse anyone finding it."

Prince Pineapple extended both hands, wrapping his fingers around the parchment. The paper was rough to his touch and cool. He pulled it to him, pressing it against his belly. "I have it!" he said. "I have it."

Wizzy flew to one side of the prince and watched him bend over the scroll, like a fleshcarrier parent sheltering its child.

A bright vision flashed across Prince Pineapple's brain. He saw Lord Abercrombie clutching the scroll in much the same way. In fast forward, he watched Abercrombie cross a series of obstacles: desert … ice … swamp.… It went too fast for further details. In his vision, the prince saw Abercrombie immerse his entire body in the soil—in a rock-walled cavern somewhere beneath the planet's surface. Then he saw the scroll fly back on its own, returning to Sacred Pond. Distantly, Prince Pineapple heard a voice. The image faded.

"Snap out of it," Wizzy said. "Let's get this boat moving."

Prince Pineapple tucked the unseen scroll inside his coat and buttoned the coat all the way up. In a daze, he located the oars. Soon he was guiding the pram back the way they had come. "That sure was easy," he said.

"Your troubles have just begun," Wizzy said.

# Chapter Ten

*The females of every fleshcarrier planet claim to have special powers. On Earth, it is known as "woman's intuition." Morovians call it "yenta." Universally, it causes females to nag.*

Excerpt from the expeditionary notes of Sevensayer Arnold

Javik made his way across the purple-dark clearing carefully, trying to recall his ship's location from the momentary flash of the comet. His belly ached with hunger, a gnawing sensation that increased with each passing moment. There was food on the ship. He looked forward to it.

After a good deal of probing with his hands and with the tips of his boots, he encountered something on the ground which rustled like gortex. He knelt and picked it up, recognizing it by touch as a survival pack. All the pack's normally full pockets were open and empty.

He muttered a curse. His foot came in contact with a cello-wrapper, then another. Then a small pile of them. All were empty.

"Someone's been here, damn it. And I'm hungrier than hell!"

Bemoaning his misfortune, Javik located the Tasnard rope he had left dangling from the side of the ship. He wrapped the rope around his chest and under his armpits, then mento-commanded it. The rope lifted him gently up to the corrugated metal surface of the entry platform. The hatch was open.

He smelled something peculiar as he entered the cabin, something unlike any odor he had ever before encountered. It struck him that it was a dull odor, if an odor could be dull. His nostrils flared as he sniffed the air. He still could not see anything, but the sensation of purpleness was gone.

*An animal?* he wondered. *It's not an offensive odor.*

Javik stood motionless for a moment, listening to night sounds. The mournful howl of a wolf drifted across the clearing, followed by what sounded like an owl's hoot. Then he became aware of something alive on board, breathing deeply and roughly, as a large man or animal might do. He detected separate sounds.

*There's two of them in here,* he thought. *Asleep with full bellies.*

Cork's two synchronized moons moved overhead in their rapid night passage, lighting the clearing with a cool harvest glow. Feeling exposed in the doorway, Javik dropped silently to the deck. When the moons had passed, he rose and crept stealthily across the cabin.

*Can't risk a light,* he thought, pushing debris on the deck away carefully with his foot. *Maybe I can find Blanquie's automatic pistol.*

The rumbling breathing changed in cadence. Javik froze. Only one of them was breathing deeply now. The other was chugging rapidly, like a steam engine. Presently, the rapid breather joined the other in a symphony of deep breathing.

Javik emitted a sigh of relief, then tiptoed aft. He dropped to all fours, feeling along the corrugated metal floor for the sleeping compartment hatches. Feeling a fine powder on the surface, he paused to lift some to his nose. It smelled dull.

Now his groping fingers touched one hatch cover and, just aft of that, another. Still farther aft, he touched a third. This was Blanquie's, the one he wanted. Javik mento-spun the little wheel that controlled the hatch, and heard the wheel's metal parts grind too loudly.

A sleeper stirred, causing the ship to move.

*Something heavy,* Javik thought.

The deep breathing resumed its cadence.

Carefully, Javik lifted the hatch. It creaked, but did not disturb the sleepers. Then he dropped his legs over the edge into the compartment, probing down for the first rung of the ladder. He reached up and dropped the hatch cover without locking it, then descended to the floor of the compartment. A loose object was on the floor. His foot found it, sending him down with a thud that shook the ship.

He took a deep breath, listening with every pore and nerve of his body.

"Ahunga!" a deep, loud voice said from above. This translated across Javik's language mixer pendant as: "What in the MoroHell?"

Javik tried to mento-lock the hatch, but felt no click in the back of his brain. *That gun had better be in here,* he thought. He mentoed on the light, feeling the brain click that told him his implanted mento unit was functioning. Corner ceiling lights flashed on, casting stark white shadows around the compartment. He tried mentoing the hatch lock again, but got no response.

While Javik searched the compartment, he heard an angry voice and a good deal of commotion in the cabin above.

*Crash!* Something fell up there. The shattering of glassplex followed.

"Over there!" another voice said from above. This voice was not nearly so deep as the other, and sounded female to Javik. "A light!" the voice said.

They spoke in a peculiar language, translated to Javik by the language mixer pendant around his neck. He touched the pendant for a moment, then mentoed off the compartment lights.

*They saw a ring of light around the hatch,* he thought.

"Now it's gone!" the female voice said.

Javik groped in the darkness, opening cupboards and drawers. Finally, he located the service pistol in a drawer, wrapped in a cotton shirt

The voices and movements were directly overhead now. "I saw it here someplace," the female voice said.

Javik checked the clip of the automatic pistol. It was loaded. He crouched in a corner, staring up at the pitch-black ceiling of the sleeping compartment.

"This thing opens," the deep voice said. Javik heard the hatch mechanism turn.

*If only I could mento the main cabin lights from here,* Javik thought. *Then I could see them when the hatch opens.*

The hatch creaked open. The voices were near now. Javik saw four eyes above, glowing in the dark like red coals.

*Not human,* Javik thought. *That's for sure.* His pulse quickened.

"In here," the deep voice said.

"You're going in?" the other asked.

Javik felt the floor shake as one of the intruders descended the ladder. Whatever it was moved athletically and heavily, with no hint of clumsiness. The odd, dull smell touched Javik's nostrils again.

"Here somewhere," the deep voice said from inside the compartment with Javik.

Javik held his breath for a moment that seemed like an eternity. Then he mentoed on the compartment lights. "Freeze!" Javik shouted as the lights went on. He trained his gun on the intruder.

Rebo coiled back on his haunches, staring at Javik with smoldering, startled eyes.

Javik was equally startled upon seeing a three-legged, hairy creature wearing a black leather jacket. Rebo held his long knife in one hand. He shifted it to the other menacingly, staring all the while at Javik with red, pupilless eyes. He took a step in Javik's direction.

"Back!" Javik ordered.

Rebo took another step forward.

Javik aimed the gun at the pillow on Blanquie's bed and fired. An orange flash shot out of the barrel, whacking a laser bullet into the pillow. The pistol crack was deafening.

Terrified, Rebo dropped his knife and leaped for the hatch ladder. He pulled himself up smoothly to the cabin level, then reached back to close the hatch.

Seeing what the creature had in mind, Javik fired again. A bullet grazed Rebo's fingers, creasing and stinging them. He cried out in pain, then withdrew his hand. Javik heard him lumbering away.

Javik climbed out of the sleeping compartment and mentoed on the main cabin lights. He saw two of the three-legged creatures standing near the open main hatchway. The creatures froze where they were as Javik leveled his gun on them. Near them, a layer of light brown powder covered the deck.

Following Javik's gaze, Namaba glanced down at the powder.

"What is that stuff ?" Javik asked.

"Our bodily wastes," she replied. "Excreted through our pores after we ate."

"Powdered shit," Javik said, angrily. "On *my* ship!"

"Who are you?" she asked.

"I'll ask the questions here," Javik said. He touched a deep scratch on his forehead.

"Very well," Namaba said.

"Quiet," Rebo snapped, turning his jutting head to glare at her.

"It looks like you ate everything I had," Javik said, looking at the one he judged to be female. "Two months' rations!"

"Our boilers were low," Rebo said, answering for her.

Javik motioned aft with his pistol. "Move back there," he said. "Sit on the floor so I can think."

Namaba and Rebo followed the command, loping past Javik warily. Javik noted that the larger creature kept eyeing the open sleeping compartment hatch.

"Try for that knife and it'll be the last move you make," Javik said. "This thing packs a big wallop."

"Do as he says," Namaba said. "Your knife is no match for his thunder piece."

Rebo glared at Javik.

"We are Moravians," Namaba explained. "I am Namaba, daughter of Heroista the Alchemist."

"And I am Rebo, son of Montenegro the Prisoner." His eyes flashed defiantly.

"What are your last names?" Javik asked.

"Last names?" Rebo said. "What is a last name?"

"Well, my name is Tomas Patrick Javik. That's a first name, a middle name, and a last name."

"Three names for one person?" Rebo exclaimed, "How curious!"

"It helps to distinguish me from everyone else. There are only so many names to go around."

"Your people have little imagination," Namaba said. "We have thirty-two billion inhabitants on the planet of Morovia. Every one with a different name."

"Sometimes a duplication occurs," Rebo said. "By accident. But the Name Bureau always finds it and issues a decision concerning who gets to keep the name."

Javik located an empty survival pack and began scouring the cabin for food and survival gear. He found a box of space matches, a half-eaten bio bar, and a penlight. Kneeling, he searched a pile of rubbish on the deck. "Ah," he said, locating a tiny tube the size of a roll of candy. "The lightweight tent." He tossed it in the pack. Questioning Namaba and Rebo as he searched, Javik learned of their remarkable journey to Cork.

Javik stuffed a package of dehydrated apples and two bio bars in his pack. "What were you on Morovia?" he asked.

"I was a very important leader," Rebo said, "in charge of an entire territory of inhabitants."

"That doesn't explain much," Javik said. "What's the emblem on the backs of your jackets?"

"The Southside Hawks," Namaba said. "Our club."

"I'm club president," Rebo said.

"Punks," Javik said. "We've got punks on Earth, too."

"We're not punks!" Rebo said, bristling.

Javik swore at each empty food wrapper he found. He kicked the base of the magna-scope console, glaring at the Moravians. They sat motionless. "Did you guys have enough to eat?" Javik asked with a sarcastic whine. "I oughtta kill you."

"We're very sorry," Namaba said. "We thought your ship was abandoned."

"That's quite correct," Rebo said. "How were we expected to know? There was equipment all over the place, you know."

"Funny," Javik said. "Both of you speak kinda elegantly—not with big words, but not like gang members either."

"Everyone on Morovia speaks this way," Namaba said. "We are renowned for having large vocabularies. That has no bearing on intelligence, of course. We use many words we don't understand."

Javik located a leaking, smashed container of water capsules. "Shit," he said. Only two of the clear little capsules were undamaged, so he placed them carefully in his titanium pillbox, returning the box to his pocket.

"What do you plan to do with us?" Rebo asked.

"I'm going to try to get this ship going," Javik said angrily. He eyed a shattered land compass on the floor. "And you're getting off." He found two collapsible plastic water pods, ten-liter size, and stuffed them in the pack. *I'll need these,* he thought.

"Take us with you," Namaba said. "Take us back to Moro City."

"Yeah," Rebo said. "There's an airfield just outside—"

Javik laughed boisterously. Seeing a holster on the deck, he retrieved it and strapped it on. "If this ship takes off," he said, "and that's a mighty big 'if' with all the hull damage, it's not going very far. I just want to get it to a safe place where I can work on it." He holstered the pistol, gazing at Namaba's eyes. They burned soft red, with no pupils. He looked away.

*Chee-rist!* Javik thought. *I'm attracted to her! Why? First a transsexual and now a three-legged beast! I've been away too long!*

"Why do you look at me so?" Namaba asked.

After a moment of silence, Javik's gaze flitted to Rebo. Rebo was giving him a hard stare, possibly because of Javik's interest in Namaba. *This one could be dangerous,* Javik thought. He dropped the survival pack on the science officer's chair.

"Can you go to Moro City after repairing your ship?" Namaba asked.

"This ship isn't going anywhere near Moro City," Javik said, rummaging in the pack. The salivary glands in his mouth gushed as he found a bio bar. He tore the cello-wrap off and bit away a corner of the bar. It was honey sweet, and he savored it.

Four red eyes watched as Javik ate. Rebo licked his lips.

Sternly, Javik motioned toward the open main hatch. "Get out," he said in a low, even tone. "And make it fast."

Rebo and Namaba scrambled for the circular hatchway. Namaba let herself down the Tasnard rope hand over hand, followed by Rebo.

As Javik watched, the Morovians lumbered across the clearing. Soon they were out of range of the light cast by the *Amanda Marie's* open hatch.

Javik mento-flipped on a spotlight to watch them. He followed their path by mento-directing the light, dogging their every move. The Morovians glanced back nervously as they ran, continually trying to elude the beam of light. But Javik kept it on them until he saw them enter the woods.

Javik ate half of the bio bar, then wrapped the rest hurriedly. He knew he should not have eaten even that much, despite the gnawing ache of hunger across his midsection. There was no telling when he would find more food.

After switching off the spotlight, Javik noticed four red eyes looking toward him from the woods, burning in the darkness like hot embers in a firepit.

O O O

"We should have rushed him," Rebo said. From his crouched position with Namaba just inside the woods, he glared across the clearing at the *Amanda Marie.* The ship's spotlight flashed off. Rebo pushed a small pine tree branch out of his way. It cracked.

"But the thunder stick," Namaba said, her voice a nervous, shivering whisper. "We could have been killed!"

"A bluff," Rebo said. "It just made noise."

"And your yenta tells you that?" Her tone was sarcastic.

"I have no yenta," he said, irritably. "And neither do you."

"All Morovian women have yenta," she said. "And mine tells me he would have killed us. He is very intense."

"Pshaw!"

"But I sense goodness in him—a potential friend."

"I don't know …"

"I'll tell you something else, Rebo. You're different here—not the same ruthless gang leader I knew on Morovia. My yenta tells me this, too. You know it to be true."

There was no response. Rebo shifted on his haunches.

"It's true, isn't it?" she prodded.

"Yes," Rebo said. "I am different, and it confuses me."

O O O

A giraffe-necked light cast the short shadows of Prince Pineapple and Wizzy as they disembarked from the pram at the edge of Sacred Pond. Prince Pineapple kick-shoved the boat out onto the water, clutching the scroll under his coat with one hand.

From his perch on the prince's shoulder, Wizzy said, "The rain has stopped. Let's have a look at the scroll."

As Wizzy glowed white to provide light, Prince Pineapple pulled the scroll out and unfurled it, holding one hand at the bottom edge and the other at the top. This seemed peculiar to the prince, for while he felt the stiff parchment paper between his fingers, he could not see it.

"Wrong side," Wizzy said, seeing a heavy "X" across the sheet. "Rather a poor job of Torah fakery on Abercrombie's part," he muttered.

Prince Pineapple flipped the scroll over, pulling it close so that Wizzy could read it more easily. The paper crackled.

"It's a map," Wizzy said. "It says in one corner to look for three-dot trail markers."

"Three dots," Prince Pineapple said. "Magical signs. Yes, I have seen such markings."

"We're to take Baker Road from Sacred Pond, to Avenida Five. Thence to All Souls Hill and across Dusty Desert."

"The Badlands," Prince Pineapple said, his tone reflecting disappointment. "I feared as much."

"There's a Bottomless Bog shown here," Wizzy said. "And a place called Moha. Are you familiar with those?"

"Moha sounds familiar. Can't quite place it. There's a shortcut to All Souls Hill. We will pass your ship." He rerolled the scroll and secured it with the cord. Removing his coat, he placed the scroll and the coat on the ground. "I should recharge now," he said. "A long journey awaits us."

Wizzy did not comment on this. *I haven't actually agreed to remain with the prince,* he thought. *But he does need me to read the scroll, and Captain Tom doesn't want me around....*

* *

Twenty-five minutes later....

Prince Pineapple leaned forward with a newfound sense of purpose as he walked, for now he had the Sacred Scroll of Cork. Wizzy was on his shoulder, brightly lit to show the way. They were crossing through the carriage parking lot of the shopping center, passing dimly lit stores whose windows displayed discarded Earth household gadgets. Prince Pineapple-knew the stores would be bare soon. Lord Abercrombie would demand all gar-bahge for himself. It was inevitable.

Pausing at the corner of the center's largest building, the prince whispered, "Dim your light. I hear something."

Wizzy darkened.

Prince Pineapple looked around the corner, then scampered back to a dark doorway. "Corker security patrol," he whispered.

Two guards walked past, making loud sucking sounds as they worked at their grain alcohol backpack tubes. Had the guards been attentive, they would have seen and apprehended Prince Pineapple. Fortunately, they did not turn their heads.

Five minutes later, Prince Pineapple and Wizzy had reached the safety of a shortcut path through the woods. It was a little-used way without lighting, so Wizzy glowed brightly again, concentrating his light forward.

Many roots and stones were embedded in the ground, and in places the path was difficult to locate because of the lack of traffic. Prince Pineapple took the wrong way once, and it was nearly ten minutes before he realized his mistake. He backtracked, finding the correct path.

"We're going around Corker Stadium," the prince said. "Can't risk going out there. Too many guards."

Presently they reached a wider path, with trail lights glowing yellow. Wizzy dimmed to conserve his energy.

"We were on this trail yesterday," Prince Pineapple said. "Your ship is just ahead."

Wizzy recalled his papa's instructions concerning remaining with Captain Tom. But Javik had been cruel to him. *He doesn't want anything to do with me,* Wizzy thought. *Surely Papa will understand.*

Prince Pineapple took a fork in the path, stepping onto a wooden bridge. Wizzy heard the cadence of the prince's feet on wood boards and the squeal of a raccoon.

Returning to his thoughts as they left the bridge, Wizzy wondered if he might have been more pleasant, despite Captain Tom's attitude. He turned this over in his mind several times. No answer leaped out to salvage him from the dilemma. At times, Prince Pineapple would say something to jar Wizzy's concentration. And Wizzy tried to think of other things. But each time a nagging question returned: *Should I go back for Captain Tom?"*

"Light!" Prince Pineapple said. "Give me light!"

"Huh?" Wizzy said. "Oh." He glowed brightly.

They had reached the end of the trail, arriving at a wide clearing. The cool gray light of dawn washed across the sky, showing distant treetops on the other side of the clearing.

Wizzy recognized this place. The ship was here somewhere. He slanted his cat's eye, gazing in all directions. The beam of his light moved as he scanned.

"That way," Prince Pineapple said, pointing ahead and to the right.

*Now this guy's giving me orders,* Wizzy thought. *First, Papa, then everyone else.*

Wizzy was directing the light beam the wrong way, causing Prince Pineapple to trip. "Pay attention!" the prince snapped, stumbling over something.

Wizzy directed his beam ahead of Prince Pineapple. They made their way to the center of the clearing.

Suddenly, Prince Pineapple dropped to a prone position on the ground. Wizzy fell from his shoulder, tumbling in cool, damp grass. "Dim it," Prince Pineapple said.

Intent on escaping the dampness of the grass, Wizzy did not respond. He found a dry area of dirt on which to sit.

"Dim it, I said!"

"Oh," Wizzy said, darkening. "I thought you said, 'Damn it.'"

"Someone's on your ship," Prince Pineapple said, pointing across the gray light of the clearing.

Now Wizzy saw it too—the *Amanda Marie* with its cabin lights blazing. And someone standing in the lighted hatchway. "One of the guards you posted?" Wizzy asked.

"I doubt it. They wouldn't stay all night."

"A scavenger, then?"

"Nothing of value there yet. The ship is far too new."

"Maybe it's Captain Tom!" Wizzy said, surprised at the excitement in his voice.

"Could be," Prince Pineapple said, rising to his feet. "We'll give it a wide berth to play it safe." He skirted the ship now, angling toward a craggy hill across the clearing with Wizzy dark on his shoulder.

Wizzy saw the profiles of mountains against the dawn sky. Deep grays in the sky were giving way to pastel pinks and blues, like an artist mixing colors on his palette. "We're going up there?" he asked.

"Right. We'll have to scramble through the woods with no trail for a while. The trailhead's too close to the ship.

Wizzy was curious about who was on the ship. "But what if it *is* Captain Tom?" he asked.

"And what if it is?" Prince Pineapple said, his tone worried. "Remember how he treated you, Wizzy. He doesn't want to see you."

"I suppose you're right."

A distant, brilliant flash of orange in the sky caught Wizzy's attention. A Great Comet swooped down gracefully, then veered up and away. Within seconds it was a far-off speck, no more noticeable than a bright star. "Oh!" Wizzy exclaimed.

"What's the matter?" Prince Pineapple asked.

"There!" Wizzy said, casting his gaze toward the retreating comet. "It's Papa Sidney!"

"I don't see anything."

"It's almost out of sight now. But it *was* Papa! I know it!" Wizzy thought for a moment, then: "He was telling me to stay with Captain Tom."

"Don't be ridiculous."

Wizzy lifted off from the prince's shoulder, flying in a holding pattern there.

Prince Pineapple continued on for several steps, then turned. "Come on, Wizzy. We've a long way to go."

"I have to find Captain Tom;" Wizzy glowed orange. A bright yellow tail flared from his nucleus.

"But the scroll! I can't read it without you. I can't even see the damned thing."

"I'm sorry, but I must do as Papa says."

Prince Pineapple hung his head dejectedly, sensing there was no way to change the little comet's mind. Removing his beanie, he gave the helicopter rotor a spin. When he looked up, Wizzy was gone, streaking across the clearing toward the ship.

Wizzy changed course once to look back at Prince Pineapple. The prince was barely visible in the low light, a solitary, shadowy figure standing there. Then the prince replaced his helicopter beanie on his head, taking a few hesitating steps toward the craggy hills. He picked up his pace and began to walk briskly.

*He's going anyway,* Wizzy thought. *The fool!*

Wizzy thought he saw Prince Pineapple wave to him. But the visibility was not good, and Wizzy thought it might even have been an obscene gesture.

O O O

When Wizzy reached the ship, Javik was standing in the circular hatchway with his hands on his hips. Javik's legs were spread, and the position of his body gave the impression of a person blocking the entrance. His head moved from side to side in negative fashion. He was not glad to see Wizzy. "What do you want?" Javik asked.

"I came to help." Wizzy noticed scratches on Javik's face.

"You can help by staying the hell out of my way!"

Wizzy bristled at the remark. Perching on a large rock near the base of the *Amanda Marie*, Wizzy saw the sky open up with pale blue color as the new day arrived.

"Even if you were worth a damn," Javik said, "which you definitely are not, there would be nothing for you to do here. The ship has big problems."

"How bad?"

"I just checked all systems. The ailerons are heavily damaged, with two flaps totally useless. Most of the rocket tubes are plugged. Hell, this thing went through a bad dust storm, then was rolled on the ground and tossed in a hole."

"Couldn't we make the parts with the metalworking equipment onboard? We could shape wall and floor pieces into ailerons."

"I'm surprised you understand that," Javik said. "We'd need too much time. Corkers will be here soon, looking to take me back."

"Why don't we go with Prince Pineapple?" Wizzy asked. He told of the prince's quest for the Magician's Chamber occupied by Abercrombie. Javik listened intently, and Wizzy thought he saw his expression brighten for a time. "It's supposed to be a rough journey," Wizzy said. "Rougher than a cob, from the looks of the scroll map."

Javik turned and went in the cabin. Wizzy followed, and watched Javik's angular form slump into the captain's chair. Through the windshield beyond Javik, Wizzy saw the tangerine orange ball of a Corkian sun just above the treetops.

Wizzy flew to the dashboard and set down there. "Why don't we go with the prince?" he asked.

"And what will you do if I don't?" Javik asked, smiling thinly.

"I'll stay with you, of course."

"Because Papa said? Is that why?"

Wizzy's yellow cat's eye looked perplexed and angry at the same instant.

"I saw the comet," Javik said. "It passed overhead just before you arrived." The cabin grew quiet for nearly a minute. Then Javik kicked the base of the instrument panel. "Damn this ship!" he said.

"Remember your mission," Wizzy said. "Find anything unusual and report back. Wouldn't that be something if you could learn more about the arch-criminal, Abercrombie?"

"I know enough about this friggin' planet! All I want now is a couple of pleasure dome maidens, a table full of food, and at least three days of uninterrupted sleep."

"But Abercrombie is nuts. Prince Pineapple says so, anyway. Abercrombie must hate Earth because of what Uncle Rosy did to him. What if he tries to break this planet out of orbit?"

"And send it toward Earth?"

"Right."

"Too farfetched. It'll never happen." Javik kicked the instrument panel base again.

"Maybe not. But you can't stay here."

"You're right about that, Wizzy. And I'm not going back to those games."

"Then you'll go with Prince Pineapple?"

"'These are not problems,'" Javik muttered, recalling a schoolboy mantra. "'They are opportunities.'"

"What?"

"Nothing. Yeah. I'll go." With a rush of energy, Javik lunged to his feet. Locating the survival pack he had filled, he glanced around the cabin for anything he might have missed.

"Do you have a tent in there?" Wizzy asked, recalling the dangers of water for him.

"You think I'm stupid or somethin'?" Javik barked. He unsnapped a gortex bag from the wall and stuffed the bag in his pack. "Stay outta my way as much as possible. You got that, Wizzy?"

Wizzy burned orange with anger, becoming so hot that Javik saw smoke under him on the plastic dashboard. Wizzy smelled the burning plastic and cooled down. Had Wizzy been human, he might have bitten his lip at that moment. For he did not say anything in response.

O O O

When Javik and Wizzy reached the hatchway, they saw Prince Pineapple standing below, looking up at them. "I had a thought," the prince said excitedly. "Maybe we could all go together—on your ship."

"Everyone wants my ship," Javik said. "But it's a no-go. If I could get it running, I'd blast outta here so fast it would ..." He sighed, adding: "I'll go with you, Prince. On foot."

"Wonderful!" Prince Pineapple exclaimed.

Javik wrapped the black and white Tasnard rope around his chest and under his armpits, then mentoed it.

"You won't regret this," Prince Pineapple said.

The Tasnard rope carried Javik gently to ground level. Wizzy flew down in a streak of yellow light.

"I already do," Javik said, looking at Wizzy. Javik mentoed the Tasnard rope. It curled neatly into his open palms. He put the rope in his survival pack.

Wizzy flew in a short, angry circle.

"Let's see your scroll," Javik said, looking at Prince Pineapple.

The tall pineapple man unbuttoned his coat and handed the parchment to Javik.

"You can't see this?" Javik asked, accepting the scroll. "Not at all?"

"No." Prince Pineapple's tone was tense. He did not like having to depend upon anyone. "Lord Abercrombie placed a spell on me," he said. "I'm sure of it."

"Well, I can sure see it," Javik said. "It shows a steep path, gaining thirty-three hundred meters in elevation over a distance of nine kilometers. Water at two points, one near the top. Then a high desert, fifty-two kilometers across. Icy Valley on the other side."

"Icy Valley," Prince Pineapple said. "I have heard of it. Magicians created it, according to legend." He looked past Javik, not meeting his gaze.

After looking over the prince's rather thin and worn coat, Javik removed his wardrobe ring and handed it to him, saying, "Put this on."

Prince Pineapple tried the ring on each of his stubby fingers, finally settling on the pinky of his left hand. That was the smallest of the lot.

"Now remove your coat," Javik said.

"What on Cork for?"

"Just do it," Javik said, looking nervously across the clearing. All three Corker suns were above the treetops now, filling the clearing with light.

Prince Pineapple dropped his coat to the ground, placing the scroll on top of it.

Javik held the prince's hand and stared at the rectangular turquoise stone on the wardrobe ring. He mentoed it. The stone glowed bright turquoise blue. Then an orange thread darted out of the ring, pausing in midair for a moment like a snake about to strike.

Prince Pineapple jerked his hand.

"Just stay still," Javik said. He gripped the prince's hand tightly. "This won't hurt a bit."

The orange thread sped up, down, and around Prince Pineapple's left arm, then did the same on the other arm, went around the neck and around the torso. A closed plastic zipper appeared down the front. Within seconds, Prince Pineapple was wearing an orange vari-temp coat. Through a similar procedure, he received a pair of matching pants, which stitched their way over his purple and black checkered shorts.

"That outfit will work better in all temperatures than what you had," Javik said. He retrieved the wardrobe ring and used it to obtain his own similar outfit.

"Magic?" Prince Pineapple asked, touching the sleeve of his new coat in awe.

"Naw," Javik said, lifting his survival pack from the ground. "Just Bu-Tech."

Prince Pineapple removed his red helicopter beanie with its bright yellow plastic rotor. He held it against the coat. "Are you sure this doesn't clash?" he asked.

"Oh no," Javik said, recalling the bright purple outfit the coat and pants covered. "You look great, Prince."

Prince Pineapple pursed his lips in a serious manner and looked at Javik. Then the prince donned his beanie and turned toward the trailhead. Soon he was leading the way up a rugged path that skirted a rockslide.

"Watch your step," Prince Pineapple said. "I have been to the top once, and there are perilous places—narrow stretches of mountain goat trail with steep dropoffs."

Wizzy flew at the rear, flaring a bright green tail which intermittently changed color as he gained control over it. A thick mist rolled down from the gnarled, gnome's-cap rocks above. Soon they entered the mist. The trail became steeper, putting a noticeable strain on Javik's Achilles tendons. He stopped to stretch the tendons, jogger-style, then caught up with the others.

O O O

Lord Abercrombie rolled over on his narrow four-poster bed, pulling the imitation down blankets over his face. Reflected morning sunlight had traveled to his bedroom via an elaborate network of mirrors, throwing the room into cheerful white light.

He was on his flat side now, with his invisible magical side penetrating the mattress and bedsprings. At the whir of an approaching meckie, Lord Abercrombie looked through the mattress and bed frame with his magical visual sensors.

It was the yellow meckie, the one Abercrombie had ordered programmed with scientific data. It was dented, stocky, and rivet-covered, with a yellow light pulsating on top. It had no face, and one arm dangled at its side in disrepair. "Are you awake, Lord?" the meckie asked. His voice was deep and metallic.

"I am now," Lord Abercrombie said grumpily.

"I was told to report to you first thing in the morning, sir."

"That didn't mean in my bedroom," He peeked out from under the covers with his human eye. "I meant in the main chamber."

"Oh. Excuse me, Lord." The meckie turned to leave.

"As long as you're here, tell me about planetary magnetics. Can that be spoiling my magic, and my other disaster control efforts?"

"Definitely, sir. The linguistics meckie was in Servicing when I received my program, and she filled me in on your concerns."

"Oh? Well, I suppose that's all right."

"I went to the surface last night and did a little homework on planetary magnetics. While you slept."

Lord Abercrombie sat up and put his pillow between the small of his back and the headboard. Reflected sunlight slanted across his covers from a ceiling mirror. He didn't say anything.

"I spoke with a magical tree up there, Lord. It's an old oak, about five hundred meters east of the entrance slab."

"I know the tree. It's one of the history-keeping places of the Council of Magic. But it would not tell me anything—other than its age and galactic serial number."

"Maybe it let its guard down a little for me," the meckie said. "It was a beautiful evening last night, with harvest moons making their passage every hour. I spoke with the tree about the weather. You know, sir—small talk."

"You're here to describe chitchat with a tree?"

"There's more than that. He's not a bad sort, actually. Just following orders. He's tens of thousands of years old, you know."

"I can imagine."

"Anyway, he said the weather used to be more stable—less stormy. Then the magicians came around and started stirring things up."

"The others tried disaster control, too?"

"Apparently. I didn't ask for details. Anyway, the tree mentioned something about Cork being out of whack magnetically. Everything is okay until somebody tries to fool with Mother Nature. Then the monopoles go crazy."

"Monopoles?"

"Subatomic particles, Lord. Responsible for magnetism."

Lord Abercrombie's human eye became bird alert. "The reverse rain—it's caused by a magnetic imbalance in the planet?"

"Uh huh. The planet and its atmosphere function as a single unit."

"Did the tree say anything else?"

"No. I tried a number of direct questions after that, but it closed up the trunk hole it had been using as a mouth and wouldn't say another word."

"Good work. Now what? How can I be more effective?"

"Well, Lord … Do you mind if I sit down?"

"No. Go ahead."

The meckie hopped on a side chair, retracting its wheels to form a flat surface under its body. Its defective arm hung loosely at its side. "I've been thinking about this planet, Lord. I think the magnetics are shifting all the time. Pulling one way, then another. Those little monopoles travel in packs, kinda like schools of fish."

"You mean through the dirt?"

"Mostly through iron and other elements in rock."

"Oh."

"You moved a couple of rocks with magic, didn't you, Lord?"

"You *have* done your homework."

"My theory is that you moved them when the monopoles were somewhere else, or at least when they weren't present at full strength."

"So I should strike when the little buggers aren't around."

"Precisely." The meckie's dome light pulsed erratically, then resumed its regular pattern.

"And how do we determine where the little bastards are?"

"No way of telling that. They're not detectable by any equipment I know of."

"What do they look like?"

"Invisible."

"That's just great. So we keep trying, eh? And if we're lucky …" Lord Abercrombie paused reflectively.

"That's about it, Lord."

"Thank you. You may leave now. And get your arm fixed."

After the meckie left, Lord Abercrombie lay back in bed and pulled the covers over his half head. *Maybe I can find some of those monopoles when I'm soil-immersed,* he thought. *I'll wipe 'em out.*

O O O

Rebo and Namaba shivered as they crept out of their hiding place in the woods. They moved a few steps into the clearing toward the *Amanda Marie*, then stopped and looked around, their red eyes darting nervously. Over the craggy hills to their left, a thick, dirty white mist rolled toward them.

"The creature with the thunder piece went that way," Namaba said, pointing.

Rebo did not say anything.

They took a few more steps, then stopped again to check for danger. All seemed clear, and Rebo nodded to her that it was safe. He bolted for the ship, with Namaba in close pursuit.

Reaching the ship, they found that the rope no longer dangled over the side. So Namaba positioned herself near the base, leaning forward and exposing her backside to Rebo in leapfrog fashion. It was a maneuver they had practiced often in Moro City.

Rebo took a long, loping run for her back, then used her as a springboard to leap to the deck level of the ship. Finding another rope in the cabin, he secured it and dropped it down for her

The cabin was in disarray, with scraps of cello-wrap and equipment strewn everywhere. Sunlight slanted in through the open hatch, sending the cabin's night shadows retreating for their secret day places.

Namaba began searching for food.

Rebo climbed down into the sleeping compartment hatch and found the knife he had left there. His feet were cold on the metal floor. He stood looking at the shiny knife blade for a while, recalling the previous evening's confrontation with the two-legged creature.

*I ran away,* he thought. *In Mow City, I would have fought to the death. But he did have a powerful weapon....*

While Namaba moved around noisily on the upper deck, Rebo continued his thoughts. *I didn't want to kill!* he thought. *It wasn't fear that stopped me.* But Rebo was not certain of this, unaccustomed as he was to reasoning things out.

He slipped the knife into its sheath on his coat, then noticed a ruby-red, octagonal pendant on the floor. Picking it up, he saw that it was multicolored, with geometric-shaped faces on it. The mechanism beeped and flashed a green light. Rebo kept the device and took it with him to the main deck level. It was bright in the cabin now, forcing him to squint.

"No food," Namaba said, approaching him. "It's all gone." She stood with her back to the sunlight, casting a hulking shadow at Rebo's feet.

"I found a nice necklace for you," Rebo said, placing the pendant and chain around her neck. It beeped.

"Pretty," she said, watching the device's light flash from green to red, then back to green.

Rebo rummaged in a pile near one corner, locating a handful of dried pear pieces. They searched together for a while, not finding anything more. "You take this," he said, extending his paltry bit of food to her.

She looked surprised at this, but accepted his offer.

"What's wrong?" Rebo asked.

"Nothing," she said, chewing the dried pears in one mouthful. "Only …"

"Only what?"

"You've never been this thoughtful," she said. She swallowed.

"Whattaya mean? I pulled you outta that laboratory fire and took you under my wing in the Southside Hawks. Wasn't that *thoughtful*?"

"You needed a woman," she said. "It was a prestige thing."

"Aw, get off that, will ya?"

"Just forget I tried to compliment you," she snapped.

"Listen," Rebo whispered. "Did you hear that?"

Looking across the clearing, they saw hundreds of Fruit people approaching. All were wearing three-piece suits and suit dresses. All carried briefcases.

Rebo was first to the rope, but he stepped aside and helped Namaba down.

"Hurry," she said, waiting for him at the bottom.

Two Fruit men were only a few meters away now, running at breakneck speed. As Rebo and Namaba fled, one of the Fruits, a kiwi man with fuzz all over his round little body, yelled, "Wait! We want to speak with you about your legal needs!"

Rebo and Namaba hurried toward the hill trail they had seen the creature with the thunder piece take. But the kiwi man was very fast and caught up, running alongside Rebo. The big Moravian gave the fuzzy fellow a stiff cuff, sending him rolling away. Business cards flew out of the kiwi man's pockets.

Now the other fast Fruit caught the Moravians. This fellow was a very speedy and especially seedy variety of lemon. He too ran alongside Rebo. "We are lawyers!" the lemon man yelled. "Here to represent the Earthian slave, Javik! The police are not far behind!"

The pendant hanging from Namaba's neck beeped.

Rebo heard the distant, mournful wail of sirens. Looking back, he saw four police chariots with bright silver badges on the sides being pulled across the clearing by teams of carrot men.

"Police?" Rebo said, alarmed. He slapped a business card out of his face.

The lemon lawyer clutched at Rebo's fur. "Maybe you need a lawyer, too," he said. "I could use the work."

Rebo gave the sticky yellow fellow a massive cuff, sending him spinning and reeling away. Then the Moravians picked up their loping pace. Four other lawyers caught them anyway and clutched at them, pulling their fur so hard that it hurt. One tore the pendant off Namaba's neck. The pendant beeped, then was trampled underfoot.

Rebo and Namaba used their forelegs as weapons now, laying waste to the quartet of clamoring lawyers. "Faster!" Namaba said. "We've got to get away!"

Although he had no idea what lay ahead on the steep trail into the hills, Rebo knew he had to go that way. Visions of police chases in Mora City flashed across his mind as he and Namaba reached the trailhead.

Their feet struck a rocky surface. The trail became steep quickly, skirting a rockslide. Ahead, Rebo saw a bend in the trail with a large rock outcropping over that point. Beyond the bend, wisps of fog curled invitingly, offering security for the pursued.

"Adarka!" a police bullhorn blared.

Rebo did not understand the word, and did not realize the function of the pretty pendant which lay on the trail far behind them. But the authoritative sound was enough to make him pick up his pace. Glancing back, he saw thousands of lawyers at the trailhead, falling behind as they fought, with one another for position.

"Adarka!" the police repeated.

When the fleeing Moravians reached the trail bend, Rebo looked back again and saw purple-uniformed police officers struggling to get past the clog of lawyers.

Rebo and Namaba rounded the bend, stretching their legs to climb a steep, rugged trail. The trail moved into thin fog now, skirting a dry creek bed. Then it leveled out for a time. But soon it rose steeply once more, cutting around gnarled trees that clung to the rocky hillside. Soon the din of police and lawyers could be heard no longer.

They galloped more slowly now. "We've got to find food soon," Namaba said, glancing back at Rebo. "Our boiler pressures will be low after all that exertion."

O O O

Prince Pineapple, Javik, and Wizzy were traversing a narrow switchback trail, still going up sharply. The path was hard and rocky at this point, but curiously enough there was soft forest soil only a few steps to one side. It appeared as though someone had intentionally selected the most difficult route. Ahead of Javik, Prince Pineapple's stubby legs moved rapidly, pulling him forward with unaltering, powerful steps.

Feeling warm and drained from the exertion and only half a bio bar back at the ship, Javik wondered how the soft-looking pineapple man could keep up such a pace. And only the day before, the prince had been so weak … *He's had another recharge,* Javik thought.

The rugged path seemed to grow steeper and more rocky with each step. Javik saw no end to it. Gnarled pine trees along the trail sparkled in streaks of sunlight that filtered through the fog.

"You won't believe what's on top," Prince Pineapple said as he stepped over a jagged, fallen rock. "A high desert, with no way around it. There's sheer cliffs all around, making this the only approach."

The trail cut into woods now, offering some shade. The ground beneath their feet was softer here, with more moisture and less rocks.

"We'll need to find water soon," Javik said. "I finished the only water capsules I could find. Brought along a couple of collapsible plastic containers we could fill."

"I remember a creek along here somewhere," Prince Pineapple said. No sooner were these words spoken when he stopped and pointed a quivering finger at a tree. "Three dots!" he exclaimed. "Sign of the magicians!"

"We're on the right trail," Wizzy said, inspecting the dots closely. They were raised and white, in the form of a triangle. The dots don't actually touch the tree," Wizzy said. "They float just off the surface. Portable dots, I guess."

"No time to concern ourselves with that," Prince Pineapple said.

They continued on the trail, and presently Javik heard running water. At first it was only a distant, welcome murmur. Then it became louder, sounding like the flow of autocars on a New City expressway.

"Strange how it's so green and wet here," Prince Pineapple said, stopping at a viewpoint and looking at the ridge ahead. "But just beyond that ridge …"

Javik looked back. There was no movement downtrail. Much of the mist had burned off now, condensing in the rays of the Corkian suns. The clearing from which they had started was visible far below, with the *Amanda Marie* glinting in sunlight.

Wizzy flew by him.

Squinting, Javik made out movement around the ship: thousands of tiny, shifting specks that had to be Fruit people. *Got out of there just in time,* he thought.

"It's like another world on top," Prince Pineapple said, continuing on and leaving Javik behind. The prince's words became more distant. "I was there once, you know, but turned back. It's so desolate. This time there'll be no turning back."

Javik quick-stepped to catch up with the others.

Wizzy circled Javik as he arrived, then flew at Javik's side.

"Why does Sid want us together so badly?" Javik asked, turning his head toward Wizzy. "For your good, or for mine?"

"For both, I'm certain," Wizzy said. "I as his son and you as his closest friend."

"His *closest* friend?" Javik's blue eyes opened saucer wide. "But I didn't even see the guy for twenty years before our reunion!"

"Time doesn't always erase deep feelings," Wizzy said. "Besides, Papa Sidney sees things on a universal scale now. Twenty years is but a moment to him."

"I think you're starting to understand love, Wizzy," Prince Pineapple said.

After a while they reached a place where a narrow band of running water crossed the trail. Stopping here, Prince Pineapple removed his helicopter beanie and said, "I'm going to recharge. There's a good spot for you to get water off the trail." He set his cap on a rock and trudged off.

Javik removed his survival pack, feeling a twinge from his shoulder. He knelt on the ground and searched in the pack, pulling out two collapsible water pods. Afraid he might get his automatic pistol wet, he unsnapped the holster from his belt and placed it on top of the pack.

Prince Pineapple was seated on the ground now, opening his folding shovel. Javik passed him, reaching a little waterfall that cascaded down the hillside into a pool. After splashing water on his face and drinking, he began filling one of the pods.

Wizzy circled over the prince's head, looking down on his leafy green headdress. Ceremoniously, Prince Pineapple wrapped one bare foot with the barbed nutrient-transmitting cord. Soon the foot was inside a little hole he had dug.

Javik watched Prince Pineapple, too, while filling the second water pod. He saw contentment on the prince's face now as nutrients from the rich soil flowed into his pineapple body. Prince Pineapple had a dreamy far-off expression, with half his face in sun and half in shade. Javik thought again of the videodome commercial. This prince was another distortion in this garbage-distorted world, like an Earth videodome fantasy come to life.

O O O

With the three travelers thus engrossed, and with the camouflage sound of running water, none of them noticed two hairy, black-jacketed creatures approaching from below. Talking as they rounded a switchback in the trail, Rebo and Namaba did not see Javik's survival pack until Namaba nearly stumbled over it.

"The thunder piece!" she said, seeing the gun.

Javik and Rebo saw one another at the same instant. Javik dropped the water pod in the pool and ran for his pack, thinking he might be able to frighten the creatures by running directly toward them.

Instinctively, Rebo grabbed the service pistol. Remembering how Javik had held it, he gripped the handle, pointing the barrel at Javik.

Javik stopped cold. "Be careful with that thing," he said, hearing strange but understandable words cross his lips as the language mixer did its job. He was less than a meter from the business end of the barrel. It looked very large.

*I see how to use this,* Rebo thought, eyeing the trigger. His forefinger inched toward it. Then he stopped. For the first time in his life, he consciously questioned ways which once had been automatic for him. He felt guilt for past killings, especially for the old flower vendor

Wizzy was in action now. He streaked toward Rebo in a blur of orange light.

Javik was a little quicker. Seeing Rebo hesitate, he slapped the gun away.

Then Wizzy hit Rebo hard on the side of the head, knocking the bulky three-legger hard to the ground. Rebo rolled on his stomach with a moan, exposing the grapple bird insignia on the back of his coat.

Javik retrieved the gun, noticing that Namaba was making no effort to get it. "Over there," he said to her, motioning toward Rebo with the pistol barrel.

Namaba moved to Rebo's side.

Rebo sat up, rubbing the side of his head with one hand. His head moved slowly in a circle, with his eyes clamped shut. His hair-framed face was contorted in pain. Then his eyelids lifted slowly, revealing dazed, dull-red eyes.

"Lucky for you I was here," Wizzy said. He was dark blue now, hovering in midair at Javik's eye level.

"Whattaya mean?" Javik snapped. "*I* knocked the gun away!"

"That guy's a lot bigger than you. He would have smashed the hell out of you before you got to the gun."

Javik pursed his lips thoughtfully. "Maybe," he said grudgingly.

"Look at my body!" Wizzy exclaimed. "I've grown since yesterday. I feel it. Do you see any difference?" Wizzy stretched his yellow cat's eyeball, trying to get a glimpse of himself. But he couldn't even see his tail.

"You look lumpy again," Javik said, smiling thinly as he studied Wizzy. "Pebbles and dirt are stuck all over you."

"Always critical, aren't you!" Wizzy snapped. "For your information, Captain Tom, the dirt and pebbles make me stronger. I'm gaining strength every day."

"Sure, sure." Javik looked away, seeing that Prince Pineapple was finishing his recharge.

Wizzy glowed bright, molten orange. The lumps on his body became smooth and liquid, sparkling in the sunlight. Then he cooled to a glistening hue of dark blue.

Prince Pineapple walked up, buttoning his shovel to his belt. "Had a little trouble, I see," he said.

"Thanks for helping, Your Highness," Javik said, sneering,

"I only just noticed," Prince Pineapple said, sputtering with surprise at the remark.

"Finish filling those water pods, will ya?" Javik said to the prince. "I need to think about our guests for a moment."

"I am a prince of Cork," Prince Pineapple announced haughtily. "I do not fetch water."

"Now look," Javik said, turning his gun halfway toward Prince Pineapple. "I don't have time to …"

Wizzy flew to Prince Pineapple's side, saying, "Captain Tom is throwing his weight around. Let me help you with the water, Prince."

"Maybe just this once," Prince Pineapple said, reassessing the situation. Scowling, he turned and went with Wizzy toward the little waterfall.

Javik watched Namaba as she knelt and cradled Rebo's head on her lap. Her red eyes had an intriguing softness to them. The light brown face was delicate and hair-framed, remotely simian, with light brown hair on her body that glistened golden in the places where sunlight touched it. Although she wore a black jacket matching Rebo's, the only other article of clothing was a yellow ribbon with black polka dots secured to the mane of her long neck. Catching Javik's intense gaze, she looked away shyly.

As Javik had nearly finished filling the pods before the interruption, it did not take Wizzy and the prince long to complete the task. Prince Pineapple filled the second pod, and Wizzy capped it, sticking the cap to his underside with suction and then spinning it securely over the pod opening.

"Whee!" Wizzy said as he spun.

When they returned, Javik was still looking at Namaba. Glancing up at Prince Pineapple as the prince brought back one of the pods, Javik said, "They're going with us. I don't want to lug that water and a survival pack across the desert."

"No argument by me," Prince Pineapple said. "That water's heavy." He went for the other pod.

"But what will they eat?" Wizzy asked, hovering at Javik's side.

"I'm not sure we need to be concerned with that," Javik said. He secured his holster to his belt and slipped the gun into it. Then he fumbled in the survival pack. Locating a roll of nylon cord, he said, "Maybe we'll use 'em till they drop."

Namaba looked at Javik in a way that made him regret the statement. It was a scolding expression, the reproachful look a child might receive from its mother.

Javik looked away uneasily, wishing he had not snapped at everyone. He was tired and in a mean mood, feeling that events were slipping from his control, and with a hunger pang gnawing incessantly at his belly. He cut off a length of cord. "This will secure our water pods to that big guy," he said.

As Prince Pineapple returned with the other pod, Javik focused on the shovel and nutrient cord attached to the prince's belt. *Maybe,* Javik thought. *Maybe I could* … Javik resolved to wait until the last possible moment before making such a radical decision—the moment when there were no more scraps of food in the pack.

O O O

Early that afternoon the travelers reached a high wall of closely fitted granite stones. Prince Pineapple said this comprised a portion of the rock bowl holding Dusty Desert. A howling wind blew on the other side of the wall, filling the air above them with particles of grit.

"According to legend," Prince Pineapple said, "this was once a great high lake. But it dried up long ago, leaving only sand and dust."

"Dust?" Wizzy said. "I understand the sand, but the dust—that is another matter, beyond my geologic knowledge."

"Don't worry your lumpy nucleus about it," Javik said. "We have to cross this thing, whether you understand its origin or not."

"One must seek to comprehend," Wizzy said. "One must always seek to comprehend."

Prince Pineapple found a way of scaling the wall, stepping in narrow rock chinks with the sides of his shoes. Reaching the top, he removed his beanie and knelt to protect himself from the wind.

Javik followed, then dropped his Tasnard rope over the edge to bring up the water pods. After this, he dropped the rope back, mentoing it to help Namaba and Rebo up. Javik kept his distance from the Moravians, and always held one hand near his holstered pistol.

The howling wind subsided now. Javik looked out on the desert, watching dry, powdery dust and sand swirl in little whirlpools. A number of red, yellow, and blue AmFed garbage canisters were scattered about, half buried.

Prince Pineapple walked the wall to Javik's left, searching for a way down to the desert floor. A mottled black and gray rat dashed across the top of one of the prince's shoes. It paused nearby, staring up at him with beady, bulbous little eyes. Then it scampered down the wall to the desert, disappearing in a mound of dusty soil.

Prince Pineapple knelt and looked over the edge where the rodent had descended. "Here's a good place," he said, stuffing his helicopter beanie in his back pocket. Finding a foothold, he lowered the other leg carefully, locating a second chink to support his weight. Soon his leafy headdress was below the top of the wall.

The wind picked up again as Javik descended.

When all were gathered at the bottom, Wizzy surveyed the great expanse of Dusty Desert, rolling his cat's eye gaze around in awe. "We have to cross *that*?" he asked.

"Only an early obstacle," Prince Pineapple said. "There will be others. Some may not be shown on the scroll." *Moha,* he thought. *Now, what is that?*

They brought forth the Sacred Scroll and studied it.

"No headings shown here," Javik said. "We'll have to guess on a course." Glancing at the map and getting his bearings as best he could, Javik sighted across the desert along his outstretched arm. "Off that way, I'd say."

While Prince Pineapple put the scroll away, Javik mentoed his wrist digital to activate the land compass feature. "Three-five-two," Javik said. "That's our course."

Prince Pineapple kicked at a clump of sandy dirt.

"I'll carry your shovel and barbed cord now," Javik said, touching the prince's arm.

"Wha-what?" Prince Pineapple's scaly brown face took on the twisted countenance of surprised rage.

"I'm in charge of this mission, and I've just given you an order."

The prince glared down at Javik. "*You're* in charge? Wherever did you get that idea?"

"You question my authority?" Javik asked, his tone menacing. He placed one hand on the handle of his automatic pistol and looked up at the prince with his best icy stare. Javik knew the stare was fear-inspiring. Once, someone had called it a "death stare." It was the sort of thing that could send women and small children scurrying for safety.

Prince Pineapple was no match for the death stare. His gaze flitted away nervously. "But why must you have my nutrient kit?" he asked. "Surely you don't intend to attempt a charge on yourself?"

"It has occurred to me. But I'm not ready to take that risk. Not until the food's gone."

"You feel this will control me in some way, then?" Prince Pineapple stared at the ground as he spoke. He sniffed the warm odor of sun-drenched dust.

Javik smiled stiffly. As Wizzy and the Moravians watched, Javik gripped Prince Pineapple's arm.

"Ow!" Prince Pineapple said. Angrily, he pulled away and removed the shovel, cord, and sheath.

Javik secured them to his own belt.

They covered their mouths and noses with scarves, then ventured out on the desert, with everyone walking ahead of Javik. This was at his command, for he was feeling increasingly alienated from everyone in the group. Javik's feet slipped often in the mixture of sand and dirt. He wondered why. It should be less slippery than sand alone.

*Aw, to hell with the answer,* Javik thought. *I'm getting like Wizzy.*

Hearing Javik's thoughts with the red star crystal embedded in his nucleus, Wizzy studied a bit of gritty sand adhering to the agate dome over his eye. *Let me see,* Wizzy thought. *Intermingled face-centered cubic crystals and young, rich latosol … an odd combination of old and new geology.*

Wizzy's thoughts were interrupted when a cloud of gritty sand enveloped the group, blocking out all three suns. Soon they were a struggling column, with Prince Pineapple pushing ahead and the others lagging behind.

Javik began to fall back more than the others, owing to his hunger-weakened state and to second thoughts he was having concerning the wisdom of what they were doing. Soon he stopped and waved his arms. "We'll have to go back!" he yelled. "We can't cross this wasteland on foot."

"Press on!" Prince Pineapple screamed over his shoulder.

Javik tasted dusty dryness through the scarf. His lips were parched,

Rebo and Namaba fell back, joining Javik. Then, reluctantly, Wizzy abandoned the prince, too. "I'm having trouble flying in this stuff," Wizzy said to Javik.

Now the pineapple prince turned angrily, glaring back at the others across the top of the dirty scarf covering his nose and mouth. "Leave me my nutrient kit, then," he demanded.

"Not a chance," Javik yelled. He glanced at his wrist compass, turning his body until he faced the return course. The wind blew a flap of his scarf open, exposing his mouth. He resecured it.

Rebo shifted the water pods on his back. Namaba pulled one of them lower to distribute the weight more evenly.

They started back, leaving Prince Pineapple alone and angry. The prince remained steadfast, and soon Javik could not see him any longer. Then the prince emerged from a swirling, dark cloud, trudging angrily and kicking up a lot of his own dust. He caught Javik and the others just as they reached the desert edge, at approximately the same place from which they had begun.

Prince Pineapple's eyes were aflame with anger. For the first time, he stared Javik down. "Why did you…?" he sputtered.

"I don't know if we should go on," Javik said, reactivating his blue-eyed death stare to win the battle of glares. "I mean, is it really worth it?"

"How can you ask such a thing? With so much at stake?"

Rebo set the water pods on the ground thoughtfully. "Prince Pineapple," he said. "Why do you want this Abercrombie so badly?"

"Someone has explained the Magician's Chamber to you?" Prince Pineapple asked, surprised.

"Yes." Rebo nodded in Wizzy's direction.

"Then you know I must rid Cork of the devil Abercrombie. He is evil."

"And replace him with yourself?" Rebo asked.

"Certainly not! We'll throw him out together and seal the entrance."

"We have no stake in your planet," Rebo said. "None of us do, except you."

"That's not entirely true," Javik said, recalling his mission. "You've got some points, though, Rebo."

Rebo motioned Javik to one side and then whispered, "This prince is a bad one. Too haughty. And he has shifty eyes."

"He's not so bad," Wizzy said, flying up and overhearing the remark.

Javik remained away from Rebo and kept one hand near his holstered pistol. "What makes you think I trust *you*?" Javik asked, looking at Rebo.

"That pineapple guy is just using you," Rebo said. "He needs you and Wizzy to read his damned scroll. You have no use for him."

"You're a smart one, eh?" Javik said. "Used your brains back in Moro City, did you?"

"Had to," Rebo said. "Or I'd have been dead a long time ago."

Glaring at Javik and Rebo, Prince Pineapple started to say something. His lips parted. But he decided not to speak. Seeing a shady spot next to a curving protrusion on the rock wall, he retreated to be by himself.

Namaba moved in to eavesdrop on Javik's conversation with Rebo. She picked pieces of grit out of Rebo's fur with her long fingers. After a while she said, "My yenta tells me we should continue. We must cross this desert."

"How?" Rebo asked.

She shrugged.

"Yenta?" Javik said. "What's that?"

"A very powerful form of intuition," Wizzy said, glowing red to retrieve the answer from his storehouse of knowledge. "Morovia is one of the planets where a more refined form of this phenomenon can be found."

"We don't need a galactic travel commentary," Javik said.

"Wizzy is correct," Namaba said, looking at the little comet "My mother once explained it to me in much the same words. How did you know?"

"I, too, have yenta," Wizzy said. "A variation on yours."

"But aren't you male?" she asked.

"That is my hormonal inclination."

"The guy can't even say yes or no," Javik gruffed. "He's worse than a New City bureaucrat."

"Moravian men have no yenta," Namaba said.

"Forget this yenta stuff," Rebo said. "I think we should go back. Call it common sense. That desert is too much for us."

"My yenta tells me there is a way back to Morovia on the other side of the desert."

"Do tell," Rebo said.

Namaba looked at Wizzy, asking, "Do you know of any basis for my feeling?"

Wizzy glowed red. "Hmmm," he said. "Well, here's a little something. The entrance to the Corkian Magician's Chamber is adjacent to this end of the Dimensional Tunnel. Offhand, I'd say you got here through the Dimensional Tunnel."

"But we landed far from that," Rebo said. "Near Captain Tom's ship."

"Abercrombie used meckie-dug tunnels and a sacrifice hole to divert you," Wizzy said. "There's a labyrinth of passageways beneath us."

"I saw his metal men digging the sacrifice hole," Prince Pineapple said.

"They're called meckies," Javik said.

"There you have it," Wizzy said. "The lady with the yenta is correct. The way back to Morovia is across this desert."

"I don't know," Rebo said. He brushed dirt off the thigh of his foreleg. "Why do you oppose me now, woman? Have you forgotten your obligation to me?"

"A yenta cannot be denied," she said softly.

"You're ungrateful!"

"I have repaid you many times over, Rebo. And don't forget about the reward. I could have turned you in to the police."

"You considered that?"

"Everyone in your precious club did. Don't kid yourself."

Javik looked back across Dusty Desert, thinking how similar it was to a sea—so treacherous and storm-tossed, with ripples of gritty sand like dehydrated, time-frozen waves.

The argument subsided.

As if in answer to Javik's thoughts, a great desert sailing ship emerged from the dust, showing its prow and forward mast. Three gray sails were puffed full with air.

Namaba yelled something. Javik did not make out the words. Soon all of them, including Prince Pineapple, were standing beside one another, looking out at what they presumed to be an apparition.

But if it was an apparition, Javik found it to be extremely detailed, with three masts of billowing sails, full rigging, and bright orange banners on top of each mast. Men scurried about on the deck and clung to the rigging.

Fruit men, Javik thought as the ship neared. Then he saw a massive carrot man in a baseball cap and a number of smaller carrot men.

Struts on each side of the ship had been fitted with balloon tires to roll the craft along the desert, and Javik counted the struts: eight to a side. As the ship drew closer, Javik heard it creak, and he picked up the wind-tossed shouts of the crew. Dust-encased lettering on the bow spelled out the Corkian equivalent of *Freedom One.* Javik read this easily, using the language mixer pendant hanging from his neck.

"A schooner," Wizzy said, glowing red. "Rather ancient by Earthian standards."

The crew released lines to slacken the sails, and the *Freedom One* slowed, drawing up parallel with the wall. Four apple men dropped a wooden gangway. Unfortunately, they forgot to secure the upper end, and it clattered to the ground.

"Idiots!" the big carrot man yelled. "Can't find decent slaves anymore!"

Prince Pineapple stepped back, showing fear on his face. "Brother Carrot!" he husked. "With *Fruit* slaves!"

Another gangway was located and let down properly. Brother Carrot loomed at the top of the gangway. "You folks need a ride?" he asked boisterously, tugging at the brim of his cap. Javik saw that it was not a baseball cap after all, but was instead a black captain's cap with gold braid on the brim. He towered over the surrounding Fruits and Vegetables. An oversized folding shovel and nutrient cord were strapped to his waist.

Prince Pineapple tried to conceal himself behind Rebo, but was spotted.

"I see one of you knows me," Brother Carrot said with a broad smile. "And who are you, Mr. Pineapple?"

"Prince Peter Pineapple," the prince answered, showing his face. He straightened and stepped out from behind Rebo.

"Ah," Brother Carrot said, walking slowly down the gangway. "So you're the one. The missing adviser."

"News travels fast," Prince Pineapple said.

"An army does not progress without intelligence," Brother Carrot said. The wooden gangway shook under the weight of each step he took.

"You plan to attack King Corker?" Prince Pineapple asked.

"I am like you," Brother Carrot said, reaching the ground. "An enemy of the Fruit king."

*We are not alike!* Prince Pineapple thought, using good judgment to curb his tongue. *No Vegetable is the equal of a Fruit!* "These are … uh … my friends," he said. He introduced Javik and the others to the Vegetable Underground leader, giving a brief summary of their backgrounds. He did not give any details on Wizzy other than his name, being uncertain as to how the Vegetable leader would respond.

Rebo loped close to Brother Carrot and looked directly into his black button eyes. They were about the same height. "You have a gang, pal?" Rebo asked.

"A gang? Well, a very large gang, you might say. It's called an army."

"Same thing," Rebo said. He leaned close to Brother Carrot, speaking in a low tone. "I can be of use to you, pal. And Namaba, too. We know about fighting."

"That so?" Brother Carrot said, showing mock interest.

"We could use a ride across the desert," Javik said. "Isn't that right, Prince?" he added, looking at Prince Pineapple with a teasing smile.

"Uh, yes," Prince Pineapple said uneasily.

"You want to be in my army, too?" Brother Carrot asked, looking at Javik.

"Thanks, but no. I've had my share of combat." He rubbed the scar on the bridge of his nose.

"I don't need volunteers anyway," Brother Carrot said. He looked at Rebo. "Thanks for the offer."

"Sure," Rebo said.

"The ride is yours," Brother Carrot said. He turned and stepped up the ramp, adding, "Umfira ti-ta."

The language mixer on Javik's pendant beeped. He shook it, scowling at a red trouble light on the device. The light blinked green. "What did you say, Brother Carrot?" Javik asked.

"Come aboard," Brother Carrot said, waving expansively with one arm;

The language mixer was working now.

As Brother Carrot led them up the gangway, Javik held back and said to Wizzy in a low tone, "What do you read on this carrot guy? Is he a friend?"

"No signal received," Wizzy replied. "I tried, but there don't seem to be any brain waves."

"Vegetables have no brains," Prince Pineapple muttered out of Brother Carrot's hearing range.

"There was no signal from you, either, Prince Pineapple," Wizzy whispered.

"There's something wrong with your apparatus, then," Prince Pineapple huffed.

Javik suppressed laughter.

"Enemies of the king!" Brother Carrot said as he reached the deck of the ship. "So many enemies!" He broke into singsong: "A foe of King Corker is a foe of . . . Oops! That didn't work, did it?"

O O O

In the captain's cabin, Brother Carrot introduced the group to Captain Cucumber, an amiable dark green chap who didn't say much. The captain smiled a lot, deferring often to Brother Carrot when questions were asked.

Javik watched Rebo and Namaba move to a corner at one end of the long cabin. There they rested on their haunches and listened intently while the others talked.

Brother Carrot was a dominating figure. When he rested his frame on a spindly-legged sea couch, the couch's legs bent. "We have thirty freedom ships like this," he said proudly.

"Imagine that!" Prince Pineapple said.

Javik thought the prince's tone was patronizing, but Brother Carrot seemed not to notice.

"For the past week," Brother Carrot said, "we have sailed the desert sea, learning its treacherous ways, charting deadheads and the like." He smiled, and his black button eyes glowed as he looked at Javik. "Quite a few of your Earthian gar-bahge canisters are buried in the sand out there. They make navigation tricky."

"I can imagine," Javik said humbly. He and Prince Pineapple were seated on oak side chairs.

"My army of thirty thousand men crosses Dusty Desert tomorrow," Brother Carrot exclaimed.

"But King Corker has no idea," Prince Pineapple said, leaning forward with his eyes open wide in astonishment.

Brother Carrot laughed, and his laugh filled every corner of the room. It was boisterous and surprisingly good-natured for a man having his extensive responsibilities. "Your King Corker has never had any sort of an idea." he quipped.

Prince Pineapple smiled. "True," he said. "Oh, so true! Decision Coins are his crutch."

Brother Carrot removed his cap and brushed dust from it. "Prince Pineapple," he said. "My sources tell me you have been in disfavor with the king for several months now."

Prince Pineapple scowled. "Your sources are correct," he said. "But should you divulge military secrets to me? The disfavor story might be a ruse."

"King Corker can do nothing now, even if he knows. Events have been set in motion. Big events. My carrot men are fierce fighters, you know. Each is better than twenty-five of the king's royal guardsmen … those fat, drunken slobs."

"Your brethren are well known for their strength," Prince Pineapple said. Suddenly he raised his rear end and reached in his back pocket, pulling out a rather mangled helicopter beanie. "Thought I'd lost this for a moment," he said, noting that the yellow plastic rotor had been broken from his sitting on it.

"Too bad," Javik said. "You broke it."

"This just adds to its value," Prince Pineapple said. "Honor prevented me from breaking it intentionally, of course. But the way it happened was quite acceptable."

Javik watched the prince don his beanie.

Brother Carrot's eyes flashed ferociously in Prince Pineapple's direction. "You think of my carrot people as good slaves," he said. "But I'll free them. I'll free every last Vegetable in captivity."

"Good luck to you, sir," Javik said.

Brother Carrot ranted for several minutes now, saying something about a powerful Fruit Doom bomb that he was going to use against King Corker. Javik tried to ask him about the bomb on two occasions, but each time was unable to get in a word. Presently, Brother Carrot looked at Javik and asked, "Where are you folks going?"

"Can you drop us off at the edge of Icy Valley?" Javik asked.

"I'd be happy to," Brother Carrot said. His eyes continued to flash from his anger over the Vegetable enslavement. "But I don't recommend that way. Go farther west, to the meadow-lands. The way is much easier there, and there are many quaint Vegetable villages."

"Uh," Prince Pineapple said, groping for words. "The Earthian here wants to go a different way. He has been sent to check on the garbahge situation."

"I see," Brother Carrot said. "Very well, then. I will take you to Icy Valley."

"This Fruit Doom bomb," Javik said. "What is it?"

Brother Carrot darkened. "A terrible thing," he said. "But I must use it to prevent further battle casualties, you see. It will shorten the war."

"How does it work?" Javik asked.

"Classified," Brother Carrot said, smiling thinly. He sat back and focused his eyes on Javik.

*This is not a suitable occasion to use my death stare,* Javik thought. He looked away.

# Chapter Eleven

*Nothing worth attaining is ever easy. If it seemed easy to you, you're not there yet.*

One of the heretic, anti-Job Support thoughts banned by Uncle Rosy

Get under way!" Captain Cucumber shouted, speaking into a brass, wall-mounted tube near Javik. The captain read from a chart spread across a dark-stained table: "Heading, forty-eight degrees, twenty-six point seven minutes north latitude, one hundred five degrees, fifteen point four minutes west longitude."

Javik heard running feet on the deck overhead, and the voices of mates barking instructions to the crew. Soon the schooner began to move. Then it picked up speed, and wind could be heard howling through the rigging. It was a creaky ship, and it built up a cadence of noises as its balloon tires carried it across the dusty wasteland.

"Your Fruits call my people the Vegetable Underground," Brother Carrot said, looking at Prince Pineapple with a bemused smile. "But that's a misnomer. We are not underground. Nor are we rebels. The Vegetables are a different people, a sovereign nation. We would live in peace with King Corker, but he insists on enslaving my people."

Prince Pineapple rose nervously and walked with some difficulty to a porthole, holding on to bolted-down furniture and handrails as the ship pitched. Through a haze of dust and sand he saw that they were riding the face of a dune, rising along the sandy giant at a sharp angle.

"Hold on!" Captain Cucumber yelled.

The *Freedom One* powered over the top of the dune and headed down the other side. Prince Pineapple felt acceleration.

"Quite a ride, eh?" Brother Carrot said.

The dunes in the distance looked like great ocean waves to the prince. He recalled a trip across the Purple Sea when he was a child, a vacation cruise with the most important pineapples of the day. Those were better days.

Seated on the floor in the corner, Rebo was watching a fly crawl along the floor. It jumped over a ridge in the pegged wood, then took a big hop toward Prince Pineapple.

Seeing the fly out of the corner of one eye, Prince Pineapple smashed it with one foot. "Miserable fruit fly!" he cursed.

Brother Carrot snickered.

"Now why'd you have to do that?" Rebo asked.

"Because I hate fruit flies!" the prince thundered. "That's why!"

"Poor little fellow," Rebo said. "He couldn't have harmed you. Not a big strong pineapple man like you."

Prince Pineapple looked away haughtily, peering out the porthole again.

"It's a survival thing with him," Brother Carrot explained. "Fruits are trained from infancy to kill fruit flies. Slaves are always leaving them on my ship."

Wizzy flew to the couch and set down on a cushion next to Brother Carrot. "I see you keep many Fruit slaves," Wizzy observed, looking up at the carrot man's ruddy, orange face. "Only moments ago, however, you were criticizing King Corker for the same practice."

"This thing you introduced as Wizzy," Brother Carrot said, looking calmly at Prince Pineapple. "What is it, precisely?"

Before Prince Pineapple could answer, Wizzy piped up, "I'm a little comet, Your Excellency, from far across the universe."

"I know nothing of comets!" Brother Carrot exclaimed, proud of his ignorance. "You are strange creatures … all of you."

"Come here, Wizzy," Javik said. "Leave Brother Carrot alone."

Brother Carrot placed a large hand on Wizzy, saying, "I've decided to answer your question, little fellow. The Fruits took the first slave. We merely retaliated."

"But where does it stop?" Wizzy asked. "And who can be sure which side took the first slave? You have firsthand knowledge of this?"

"Really!" Brother Carrot said haughtily. "This is a truth which my people have always known. How dare you question our ways?"

Javik snatched Wizzy away before the argument worsened. "My apologies, sir," Javik said. "The little fellow here is not overly bright. We'll explain it to him later."

"Put me down!" Wizzy said.

"Okay," Javik said, placing Wizzy on a side table. "But don't ask any more questions."

"That's right," Brother Carrot said, glaring at Wizzy. "You've got a lot to learn." Brother Carrot sat back, seeming to realize for the first time how angry he had become. His face broke into a wide smile. The boisterous, friendly laugh returned.

"I'm going topside," Javik announced, stepping cautiously across the deck as the ship rocked. "Is that okay, Brother Carrot?" he asked, lunging for a dark-stained railing on the two-step staircase leading to the door.

"It's a mite dusty up there," Brother Carrot said. "But go ahead."

"I'll be back soon," Javik said. "I want to see how this ship works." As his foot touched the first step, he caught Namaba's gaze. He heard the wind outside. The ship creaked.

While Javik watched, Namaba rose from her haunches and loped to his side. She kept the gaze of her soft red eyes on him as she moved.

Javik stepped back and drew his service pistol. "Get back over there," he snapped.

"I want to talk with you," she said. "Alone."

Looking beyond her to the corner, Javik saw Rebo sitting on his haunches there. Rebo's expression was troubled. "All right," Javik said to her. He motioned her ahead of him.

In the corridor outside, Javik slid the cabin door shut. With the pistol, he motioned to the right.

Namaba led the way down the long, dark-stained corridor, loping on three legs in the Morovian way. Bright brass light standards clung to the walls, casting yellow light on Namaba as she passed. Javik smelled linseed oil.

At the end of the corridor, Javik motioned Namaba aside and swung open a heavy door leading to the deck. The door squeaked noisily. Hesitating, he watched dust swirl along the deck and heard the crewmen and their overseers shouting back and forth. The ship attacked the face of a fresh dune, throwing a thick cloud of dust and sand across the deck toward Javik. He slammed the door shut.

"We'd better stay in here," Javik yelled, raising his voice to be heard over the noise outside. Feeling something in his eye he tugged at the eyelid.

Namaba looked at him with sparkling, innocent eyes. "I don't care where we go," she yelled. "But I need to talk with you."

They moved down the corridor to a quieter place. With his gun still drawn, Javik looked intently at her. She was taller than he, and easily twice his weight, with light brown hair around her face that shone golden in the light of a nearby light standard.

"What is it you want?" Javik asked, blinking to clear his eye.

"Why did you bring us?" she asked. "Just to have Rebo carry your water? Is that all? We can't survive without food."

"Maybe I didn't think it out too clearly," he said, his voice wavering. He stared at the floor.

"Well it's high time you did," she snapped. "Our lives are at stake."

Javik stared past his pistol barrel at the pegged oak deck. He heard Namaba chug-breathing, and saw the base of her hairy forepaw on the deck. He did not look up, feeling unable to meet her gaze.

"We have to eat," she said. "You can't leave us to die somewhere along the trail."

Slowly, Javik raised his gaze to meet hers. "I haven't done you any harm," he said. "There was no food for you back there."

She looked away. Then: "There are animals in the woods of this planet. We could hunt."

"You mean kill something and cook it?" Javik asked, his face twisted at the revolting thought.

"You have a thunder piece. I assume it kills."

"'I couldn't eat that sort of food," he exclaimed. "It would have to be processed, blended, strained, and stabilized first."

"You'd eat it," she said, "if you had no choice."

"I'll share what little food I have with you," Javik said.

"The contents of your pack are but a snack to us," she said, glaring at him. "You're just stumbling around, aren't you? Do you expect to find a restaurant out here, with nice clean plates and tablecloths?"

Javik considered gaining the offensive by criticizing her for stealing his food from the ship. But that was history and unchangeable. Her voice carried an unmistakable scolding tone, but had an underlying softness that intrigued him.

*God help me,* Javik thought, *but, I think she's attracted to me.* It was inevitable. Women just had to get close to him.

O O O

In the captain's cabin, Prince Pineapple stood at a porthole with Wizzy hovering at his side. The ship was surfing across the face of a dune wave, pitched at such an angle that the prince had to hold a brass wall handle.

"Your Captain Tom doesn't trust me," Prince Pineapple said. "That's why he took my nutrient kit."

"It does give him a degree of control," Wizzy said.

"You agree with what he did?" The words were clipped, angry.

"Not necessarily. But I can see why he feels as he does. I have read his thoughts. He believes you want the Magician's Chamber for yourself, that you will do anything to gain power."

"How preposterous! Wherever did he get such an idea?"

"He saw something he didn't like in your eyes. You rarely meet his gaze. And he heard the wrong inflection to your voice. Insincerity was the word he used in thought."

"What sort of evidence is this?" Prince Pineapple gazed at Wizzy until Wizzy's cat's eye focused on him. Then the prince looked away.

"A commander needs no evidence. He is responsible for his mission and for the welfare of his party. He makes decisions."

"That sounds like an army training manual excerpt," Prince Pineapple observed tersely.

"Not entirely," Wizzy said. "I've seen something of this as well. Any observant being can see the nervousness or guilt in your eyes. It's in your mannerisms, too. You seem … uncertain."

Prince Pineapple shook his head in dismay. *Can it be?* he wondered. *Do others see something I'm not aware of myself? No. I can't believe it.*

While the prince thought, Wizzy gave advice on what he should do to get back in Javik's good graces. This struck Prince Pineapple as peculiar, considering Wizzy's own shaky status with the leader of their expedition. The drone of Wizzy's voice was starting to give Prince Pineapple a headache.

"Leave me alone," Prince Pineapple said, pushing Wizzy away from the window.

O O O

During his next soil-immersion period, Lord Abercrombie searched for monopoles diligently, trying to find the subatomic particles that allegedly were causing him so much trouble. They were nowhere to be found. But Lord Abercrombie knew they were there. He tried magically inducing two rockslides, a flood, and a forest fire, all without the tiniest hint of success.

*If I ever find a pack of those little buggers,* Lord Abercrombie thought, *God help them!*

After a while, he turned his attention to activity on the planet's surface, using his billions of visual and auditory sensors. He saw the *Freedom One* crossing Dusty Desert. It made him angry.

*Prince Pineapple wants to replace me,* Lord Abercrombie thought. *Add him to my list of enemies. Right up at the top with the monopoles. And Brother Carrot with his army of blithering Vegetables. I've always worried about him. Can't forget Javik, either. He's Uncle Rosy's emissary.*

Furiously, Lord Abercrombie pulled himself out of the hole. "They're all against me!" he muttered, blowing dirt off his wardrobe ring. After mentoing the white stone on the ring, a dry shower cleaned every pore on his fleshy half. Using the turquoise stone next, he watched and felt a white caftan with a blue scroll sleeve thread its way over his half body. A black satin slipper wrapped itself around his foot, and a thistle half crown attached itself to his skull.

"I can see some of my enemies," he said. "I hear them, too—plotting against me and against my Corker allies. But what can I do? Hardly anything while buried. One tiny rockslide is the grand total of my magic." He kicked a tuft of dirt. The dirt crumbled. Moments later he stood before an instrument panel in the Disaster Control Room. "Three of the bastards on one ship!" he said, his voice reflecting fury and frustration. "Maybe I can get all of them at once this way ... if those monopoles stay out of my way."

He touched a green console button, then slammed down three adjacent brown toggles. "Sector one-one-six," he said, speaking into a microphone. "Three hundred kph winds ... from the southwest, heading two-eight four."

"Confirmed," a computer voice reported.

Meckies at stations around the room tapped keyboards to coordinate the attack.

"Don't fail me," Lord Abercrombie said, coaxing the old equipment.

"Two fifty," a meckie reported.

Lord Abercrombie closed his eye and prayed softly.

"Three hundred, sir," came the next report. "Approaching the desert sailing ship. Impact estimated at four minutes."

"Hot damn!" Lord Abercrombie exclaimed.

"All systems working," another meckie said.

"I'm going into soil immersion," Lord Abercrombie said, turning to leave. "I want to enjoy this firsthand."

"Trouble, sir," a meckie said. "That reverse rain again."

Lord Abercrombie leaned over and moaned, "Oh no!"

"Equipment shorting out, sir."

Sparks flashed from all the consoles in the room.

"So close," Lord Abercrombie said, feeling ready to cry. He straightened and barked a command: "Shut down all systems!"

Hurriedly, the meckies did as they were told.

Abercrombie stepped back as the console near him continued to spark. At times like this he felt like giving up on the Realm of Flesh. But Magic offered no more prospect of success.

The rolling whine of an emergency siren sounded from the tunnel outside their door, along with the loud whirs and clanks of approaching meckies. Soon the room was full of meckie technicians, searching for a loose piece, a pulled wire, or anything else that might have caused yet another failure.

But Lord Abercrombie sensed this search would do no good. *This planet is cursed,* he thought. *Someone has made it uninhabitable for beings like me.*

"Hit 'em with anything we've got left!" Lord Abercrombie shouted. "Try wind, earthquakes, anything!"

O O O

It was midday, with three synchronized Corkian suns blazing overhead. As Javik stood with his companions at the edge of Dusty Desert, he felt cool in his vari-temp coat. The coat fluttered in a light wind. Behind them loomed the wall of closely fitted granite stones that formed this far side of the bowl holding the desert.

"That rain was really something," Rebo said. "Came right up out of the desert. Damndest thing I ever saw."

"I've seen it before," Prince Pineapple said. "It's become rather commonplace on Cork."

"We've seen it, too," Wizzy said, hovering nearby. "When our ship was approaching the planet."

Brother Carrot waved from the deck of his desert schooner as it pulled away. "Good luck, my friends!" he yelled. Javik heard him say something after that, but the words were lost in the wind. The *Freedom One* picked up speed, cutting through rapidly moving clouds of surface grit.

"Nice fellow," Namaba said.

Prince Pineapple searched the wall for a place to climb.

"I don't think Fruits and Vegetables are so different," Wizzy said, perching on a wall stone near Prince Pineapple. "Brother Carrot carried a folding shovel on his belt, just like yours. He had a barbed cord, too."

"Pshaw!" Prince Pineapple said, finding a foothold to begin his ascent. "Fruits are superior. Everyone knows that. We grow on trees and high vines, while Vegetables grow next to the dirty ground." He climbed partway up the wall.

Wizzy glowed red as he retrieved data from his internal storehouse.

Prince Pineapple neared the top of the wall. "There is no comparison," he said. He lifted himself to the top of the wall and stood with his hands on his hips, looking down at the others with an air of superiority.

Wizzy flew up to hover in the prince's face, "What about strawberries?" Wizzy asked. "They're Fruit, and they grow along the ground."

"A strawberry is *not* Fruit!" Prince Pineapple exclaimed. "What an odd notion!"

"Enough of this," Javik said, climbing the wall by the same route Prince Pineapple had taken.

"You're wrong, Prince!" Wizzy said. "Extremely wrong! And what about green beans? They grow on high vines, which would make them as good as any Fruit."

"Preposterous!" Prince Pineapple thundered.

Reaching the top of the wall, Javik stepped between them. "Stop this!" he snapped. "Some of us do not have time to stand around arguing. Unlike his Royal Hind Ass here, my food source is not unlimited."

Prince Pineapple scowled ferociously.

Wizzy added Javik's expletive to his own stored arsenal.

Namaba and Rebo scaled the wall without help from Javik's Tasnard rope. As Namaba reached the top, she gave Javik a scolding smile.

He looked away. "All right," he said. "Let's find the trail and get a move on."

When they had descended the other side of the wall, Javik told Prince Pineapple to bring out the scroll.

"Idiots," the prince muttered as he handed over the scroll he still could not see. "I am surrounded by idiots."

Javik knelt on the ground, where he spread open the scroll. "We're here," he said, pointing to one side of the Dusty Desert.

To Prince Pineapple's eyes, it looked as though Javik were pointing at the ground. "Draw me a map in the dirt," the prince demanded, "so that I may see, too."

Hurriedly, Javik used a stick to scratch out a portion of the scroll map on the ground. "Here's the Dusty Desert," he explained as he drew. "And Icy Valley. Just beyond that is a forest. We'll camp there."

"The valley must be behind us," Prince Pineapple said, turning and pointing at a misty area between two snow-covered hills.

"Tomorrow we cross Bottomless Bog," Javik said. "If these distances are correct."

"Where's that Moha shown?" the prince asked. "Something disturbingly familiar about that name."

"Here," Javik said, making a mark in the dirt.

Just then, a ferocious wind roared across their position, obliterating the dirt scratchings and nearly tearing the parchment from Javik's grasp.

"Lord Abercrombie is angry," Prince Pineapple said. "He will not let us pass without a fight."

"You think he caused that wind?" Javik asked. "Naw. There's no weather control here."

"We will see," Prince Pineapple said, groping for the scroll he could not see.

Javik released the scroll and watched the prince roll it carefully. Namaba tied it with the piece of leather cord. When the Sacred Scroll of Cork was safely secure beneath his coat, Prince Pineapple turned away from the wind, taking the path that led toward the misty valley.

Javik removed his vari-temp coat and stuffed it in the pack. He felt the warmth of three suns on the back of his neck as he followed the others. Javik imagined tiny solar nutrients entering his body, and tried to convince himself that his strength was returning. But this was a ruse. He knew he was declining, and had a frightening thought: What if the whole planet was against him?

*Can such a thing be?* he wondered. Javik felt that forces were whipsawing him—doing with him whatever they wished.

He felt the suns cool, and looked back. Clouds were moving in from behind. Ahead, curls of fog were approaching, running out of the valley to greet them. A shiver ran down the back of his neck and through his shoulder blades. He stopped to put the coat back on.

When Javik caught up with the others, Rebo and Namaba were zipping up their heavy club jackets and pulling the collars around the lower parts of their long necks. Prince Pineapple stood to one side of the trail, apparently expecting Javik to assume the lead. Wizzy hovered nearby.

"You lead," Javik said to the prince. "Then the Moravians."

Prince Pineapple frowned and stomped ahead, negotiating a narrow, rocky path that sloped gently downward from the desert plateau. They passed a number of AmFed garbage canisters here, and at Javik's suggestion these were given a wide berth.

"Many are radioactive," he told them.

Swirls of fine, light gray mist curled ahead of them like a graceful, supernatural life form that was beckoning to the travelers. What was in the valley beyond? "Come see for yourself," the mist seemed to say.

From the rear, Wizzy saw Prince Pineapple disappear into the mist, followed by the others.

"The ground's frozen," Javik said, feeling his footsteps crunch. A dull, aching pain pulled at his belly. *Gotta find more food,* he thought, glancing at the folding shovel which rode on his hip. Gastric juices filled his mouth as he focused on the nutrient cord wrapped around the shovel handle. He swallowed.

"Something strange about this mist," Wizzy said.

*I agree with that,* Javik thought. *But there's also something strange about Wizzy … and the others.* The recurring video-dome commercial flashed across his weary mind. He saw ten pineapple men dancing in a chorus line, then ten Wizzies, then ten three-legged Morovians.

"Can't see two meters ahead," Prince Pineapple said, walking very slowly. His foot slipped on a pebble, causing him to fall against a rock wall he had not noticed in the fog. He stumbled, trying to regain his footing.

"Watch it!" Rebo said, catching Prince Pineapple by the arm. "There's a dropoff on your right."

Prince Pineapple leaned against the wall, breathing deeply from the sudden fright. "Wonder how far down," he said.

"Just be glad you can't see it," Javik said, catching up with the others.

The trail dropped steeply now. Soon the prince slipped again and came very close to going over the edge.

"I'll lead," Javik said. "And if any of you have any funny ideas about hitting me over the head, remember this: I have the nutrient kit, which may be our only hope for food. I'll fall over the edge. You can count on it. And in this fog, who knows if you'll ever find me?"

"We get the message," Namaba said.

Javik used his wardrobe ring to fit himself with a pair of brown ski gloves. Then he did the same for Prince Pineapple and the Morovians.

"You oughtta toss those jackets over the edge," Javik said to Rebo and Namaba, seeing that they were shivering. "Let me fit you with something functional."

"We'll manage," Rebo said.

"I'll take you up on that," Namaba said. She tossed her black club jacket over the edge of the cliff. Rebo glared at her.

Javik fitted her with a lemon yellow ski outfit. It surprised him more than a little to see the clothing follow her irregular form perfectly, giving her pants, a jacket, and a hooded top.

Resuming their course, Javik guided a gloved hand along the rock wall and probed ahead with one cautious step at a time, not committing the weight of his body until he was sure of his footing.

After an hour that seemed much longer, Javik felt run-down. Stopping on the narrow trail, he shared a bio bar and dried apple pieces with Rebo and Namaba. "Maybe we'll find food after we get out of this valley," Javik told them.

"He expects to find a restaurant out here," Namaba said. "I think we'd better learn to hunt."

"I haven't seen that many wild animals around," Rebo said.

"There are very few animals on Cork," Prince Pineapple said. "This is explained in one of our legends, which says that—"

"Hang your legends!" Javik snapped.

"We'd better figure something out soon," Namaba said, looking at Javik, "or that shovel on your hip will be used to bury us."

Javik closed his pack and put his arms through the straps to pull it on his back.

A short distance down the trail, they dropped underneath the fog. Now, less than thirty meters below, they could see the snow-and ice-covered valley floor, stretching into the distance like a placid white lake.

"It's clearing," Javik said, glancing warily at the others. The trail became less rugged, dropping gradually. As Javik negotiated this section, he looked back often and remained well ahead of the others, fearful that he might catch a heavy rock on the back of the head.

Reaching the valley floor, Javik saw that the foggy mist formed a rather uniform ceiling all the way across the valley. The terrain was almost perfectly flat, permitting him to see a distant rock wall. It struck him as unusual that snow and ice would be on the valley floor but not on the trail they had just traversed.

When the balance of the party caught up, Javik scrutinized the scroll again. "We're here," he said, pointing to a spot on the parchment. "At the base of the cliff trail. Another trail should be somewhere over there." He pointed across the valley to his right, approximately along the line of a nearby path formed by small animal tracks. Javik counted four sharp toes on each track. He wondered what sort of an animal it was, and if he had the nerve to kill one and eat it. Looking up, he saw Namaba staring at him.

Wizzy flew in the direction Javik had designated. "There's a pretty good trail here," he called out, hovering over a slight rise in the terrain.

When Javik and the others reached the trail, Javik found it to be a trough of ice, perhaps a meter below the level of the surrounding terrain. Fresh, powdery snow lay on the ground all around, but there was none in the trough. Here the brown earth was visible beneath a thin layer of ice. As Javik stepped down to the trail, he felt the ice crackle under his feet. He kicked at the ice, lifting a slab and exposing a section of ground.

"Can you explain this, Wizzy?" Prince Pineapple said, stepping into the trough next to Javik.

Wizzy glowed red, but came up with no answer. "I'm sorry," he said. "It's a mystery to me."

Javik knelt, removing one glove. He dug in the soil with his bare hand. "Ground's warm," he said.

"Magicians have passed this way," Prince Pineapple said.

The travelers set out single file on the trough trail, led by Wizzy and Prince Pineapple. "Kinda pretty here," Wizzy said, tilting his yellow cat's eye toward the prince.

Prince Pineapple did not respond.

"I said—"

"I heard you," Prince Pineapple said curtly. "Just keep your distance."

"You still sore at me?" Wizzy asked, hovering near the prince's face.

Prince Pineapple pushed Wizzy out of the way and trudged past him.

"I'll find a friend somewhere else," Wizzy said.

"I'm hungry," Namaba said, looking back at Javik.

"There isn't much food left," Javik said.

"We've got to eat," she said. "It's that or die."

"I'm hungry, too," Javik said.

"Then let's finish off what's left," Rebo said, loping along the trail and looking back at Javik.

"There's two bio bars left," Javik said. "And some dried apples. I'll split it all up now. You can do what you want with yours."

This was agreeable with the Moravians, so Javik stopped and opened his pack. The remaining food was divided. Then Javik wrapped his portion and returned it to the pack, while the Moravians gulped theirs.

"Don't ask for any of mine," Javik said.

Noticing some crumbs on the trail, Namaba fell to her knees and pressed her face against the ice. She scoured the trail with her tongue until all the stray crumbs had been retrieved.

Javik watched her intently as he pulled on his pack. Glancing up the trail, he saw Prince Pineapple and Wizzy waiting.

"Thank you," Namaba said as she stood up.

Javik nodded. "Water anyone?" he asked. He held his mouth under the spigot of one of the water pods on Rebo's back, filling his mouth. He shut off the spigot and straightened, holding some of the water in his mouth.

He swallowed slowly, watching the Moravians drink. Seeing Rebo take too much, Javik stopped him.

"But all the snow around," Rebo said. "We could melt it and drink it."

"Might be contaminated," Javik said.

Rebo put his mouth to the spigot again, disregarding Javik's instructions.

"Enough!" Javik barked, giving Rebo's large head a stiff shove.

Rebo straightened and met Javik's gaze. They stood two meters apart, with their gazes locked, portending mortal combat. Rebo was first to look away. Then he looked back at Javik, saying, "l could take you now, before you had a chance to pull that thunder piece near your hand."

"I doubt it," Javik said. The fingers of his gun hand twitched.

"I'm very fast for my size," Rebo said.

"He's telling you the truth," Namaba said.

Javik's mouth became a thin, steely line. His lips parted, and terse words crossed them: "We're in this together, Rebo. You understand that, or you would have tried to take me earlier."

Rebo smiled, revealing iridescent blue teeth. He extended his forepaw to Javik. "You're a pretty tough little guy," Rebo said as they clasped hands.

Javik knew he was taking a chance. But he couldn't keep looking over his shoulder. He would have to sleep sometime. Studying Rebo's face, he saw deep lines framing the undersides of the eyes, lines formed in the worries and battles of another world.

"I was a killer once," Rebo said as their hands separated.

"That was on a different world," Namaba said. "And besides, those times are dead." She looked at Javik. "Rebo is not the same here."

Javik looked at Rebo again, noticing a scar on the side of his head and a nick out of one of his wide, cuplike ears. This was not a killer. Not any longer. He was a potential friend. Javik was sure of it.

"Hurry up!" Prince Pineapple yelled, glowering.

Javik caught Namaba's gaze before they resumed their course. "Those morsels of food won't last us long," she said.

Thirty minutes later they reached the rock wall at the opposite side of Icy Valley. A short search produced two trails within a hundred meters of one another, each taking a different route up the rock face.

Javik studied the Sacred Scroll of Cork. "I only see one trail here," he said.

"Maybe it doesn't matter," Prince Pineapple said. He took several steps up the nearest trail, then stopped and screamed.

Javik dropped the scroll and drew his service pistol. "What is it?" he yelled, running toward the prince.

Prince Pineapple was roaring back down the trail. "Look behind me!" he squealed. "On the trail!"

"Where?" Javik said. "I don't see anything!"

"Paula!" Prince Pineapple said, near hysterics as he reached Javik. He buried his face in his hands.

"What are you talking about?" Wizzy asked, joining them at the trailhead.

"Paula Pineapple," the prince said. "The girl I almost permied. She's on the trail holding a huge cleaver. She threatened to cut me up into little pineapple squares."

"But there's no one there," Wizzy said.

"That's right," Javik said. "Take a look for yourself."

Prince Pineapple pulled one hand away from his face and looked back up the trail. "I still see her," he insisted. "She's going to kill me if I take that trail."

"Nonsense!" Javik said. "I'll show you." He holstered his gun and hiked up the trail, taking big, confident steps.

As Prince Pineapple watched in terror the image of the pineapple girl faded. Then the image disappeared in a puff of mist. Suddenly, Javik stopped and drew his gun again. He backed down the trail.

"What is it?" Prince Pineapple called out. "I don't see her anymore."

As Javik retreated, he kept his eyes glued on a beautiful dark-skinned girl who stood in the center of the trail, holding an automatic rifle. The barrel was pointed directly at Javik. He knew the girl. It was the one he had almost permied—the one from the astro-port so long ago. He had left her because of the uncertainties of war.

Reaching the trailhead, Javik explained what he saw, stuttering. Then he asked, "How? H-how could she be here? We're on the opposite side of the universe from Port Saint Clemente."

"We don't see anything," Namaba said.

"I'll try it," Rebo said. While Javik watched, Rebo loped up the trail, approaching the dark-skinned girl who still stood on the trail holding a rifle. As Rebo neared her, the girl's image faded and disappeared in a puff of mist.

When this happened, Rebo stopped in his tracks. Then he turned and loped down the trail.

"What happened?" Javik asked.

"I saw Namaba," Rebo said. "She was blocking the trail, holding a long switchblade in each hand." He looked back. "She's still up there."

Namaba's dark eyebrows arched in surprise. "Me?" she asked. "How could that be? I'm here."

"Magicians at work," Prince Pineapple said. "Or Lord Abercrombie."

"Do you see the pattern?" Rebo asked, looking at Javik.

"You love Namaba, don't you, Rebo?" Javik asked.

Rebo nodded, catching Namaba's troubled gaze.

She looked away.

"In each case," Javik said, "we are threatened by the one we love most in the entire universe."

"Exactly," Rebo said. "The image of Namaba on the trail is fading now."

"Let's try the other trail," Prince Pineapple suggested.

The others agreed. Prince Pineapple led the way up the second trail, stepping slowly and cautiously at first. The trail became steep and narrow. Soon they were in mist again, on a cliff trail similar to the one that had led them into Icy Valley. With each step, Prince Pineapple expected to confront Paula Pineapple again. But she did not appear. They increased their pace and began to make good progress.

But then Wizzy flew to the front and squealed, "Wait! I think we're going the wrong way!"

"What?" Prince Pineapple said, stopping.

Javik and the others made similar surprised comments as they stopped.

"Someone wants us to go this way," Wizzy said, "It's too easy."

They talked it over. Generally, it was conceded that Wizzy might be right. But Javik was less convinced than the others. "Maybe it's just the opposite," he said. "Whoever is orchestrating this knew we would have doubts. Maybe we were expected to stop and turn back."

"How do we decide?" Prince Pineapple asked.

"Your Decision Coin," Javik said.

"Don't be silly. Abercrombie controls that."

"I don't agree," Javik said. "I'm in charge here, and I say flip it."

Prince Pineapple shrugged and produced his large gold coin.

"The 'yes' side and we take this trail," Javik said. "The 'no' side and we take the other."

Prince Pineapple flipped the coin, being careful to keep it from falling over the cliff. It rolled a little ways and lodged against the rock wall at one side of the trail.

"It's 'no,'" Javik said, retrieving the coin. He handed it to the prince.

"Then we take the other trail," Prince Pineapple said.

Javik smiled. "Wrong," he said. "We do the opposite. Abercrombie does control that coin. He wants us on the other trail."

Prince Pineapple shook his head in confusion. "I don't know," he said, stuffing the coin in his pants pocket.

"I'm sure of it," Javik said. "Let's go."

O O O

Lord Abercrombie was soil-immersed, permitting him to see and hear the activity on the trail. *I don't control Decision Coins,* he thought. *They're strictly chance.*

He concentrated on breaking a large rock outcropping just over the heads of the travelers. It was already cracked from natural conditions, and should not require that much effort. But no incantation, prayer, or command could convince even the smallest chunk to break away.

*Two days ago I induced a small rockslide,* he thought, frustrated. *Now, whenever my enemies are vulnerable, I can do nothing.*

Lord Abercrombie was more dismayed than angry. He had experienced so many failures that the latest installment came as no surprise. He felt this attitude probably contributed to his failings. The magnetic imbalance of Cork could not be responsible for everything. But he was helpless to change, and felt himself falling into the great cosmic crevasse populated by losers. He wondered why attitude suddenly seemed so essential to magical success. Attitude was supposed to be a psyche thing, a concern for super-achiever fleshcarriers. It should not belong in a magical situation. Maybe it had something to do with his being caught between realms: Things were getting muddled from his indecision. Or maybe it was something deeper, an overlapping between the realms of Flesh and Magic.

Lord Abercrombie's tympanic sensors picked up a cracking sound. A tiny piece of rock broke free from the outcropping and bounced down the cliff face, falling harmlessly on the trail next to Javik. It was such a small piece that none of the intended victims noticed it.

*Oh, well,* Lord Abercrombie thought. *It was something, anyway.* Helplessly, he watched Prince Pineapple lead the way up the correct trail.

O O O

As the travelers resumed their journey, the ground began to shake. Javik heard a low rumble, which grew louder.

"Run for it!" Wizzy squealed, looking up the cliff with his cat's eye. He could not see very far in the thick mist. "I hear a rockslide."

"Uptrail," Javik yelled, seeing a domed rock shelter just ahead. "Under that big rock."

They ran and flew for their lives, taking shelter under the domed rock. An avalanche of jagged rock thundered by them, bouncing off the side of the cliff. From the safety of their shelter, they heard the rocks land angrily on the valley floor.

When the noise subsided, Javik ventured out cautiously. The mist was becoming dark gray now, and he knew why. "We must hurry," he said. "It will be nightfall soon."

O O O

Still soil-immersed, Lord Abercrombie was raging at the latest turn of events. *So close!* he thought. *I almost had them!* Then he wondered if he had caused the slide or if the rocks would have fallen anyway. After all, the outcropping had been cracked long before he took notice of it.

*I have to assume I did it,* he thought. *I can't give up now.*

O O O

Javik led the way up the trail, sidestepping a number of small rocks in the way. "Don't step on any of this loose stuff," he said.

Beyond the slide area, the travelers began to move quickly, trying to reach a suitable campsite before dark. They glanced up often, fearing the mountain would cut loose again.

*We're moving deeper into Lord Abercrombie's web,* Prince Pineapple thought. *He is all around us, ready to swallow us at any moment.*

Night was descending rapidly, spreading its purple-black Corkian mantle across the cliff trail. It took away what little visibility the fog had left for them, forcing them to travel slower and slower. Wizzy's white glow worked as a fairly decent light for a while, but he had trouble keeping it lit. Perhaps it was due to the full day he had already had, with many occasions to call upon his data banks. Finally, he asked to be carried. Grudgingly, Javik placed him in a pocket of his vari-temp coat.

The intense darkness made the prospect of another rockslide terrifying to Javik. If he heard it coming, where would he flee? Surely such a catastrophe would send some and perhaps all hurtling over the edge.

It was dark and windy when Prince Pineapple insisted on a break. For some time before that, Javik had noticed that the prince had been dragging his steps. By the time he called out, Prince Pineapple had slipped to last in line.

"Tell him to be careful with this," Javik said, passing the folding shovel and nutrient cord to Namaba. As she passed it on down the line, Prince Pineapple said he had heard the command, and that it was an unnecessary thing to say.

Every muscle in Javik's body wanted to sleep. But this was no place to pitch a tent. An icy wind cut across his legs. He considered donning a pair of vari-temp pants with the aid of his wardrobe ring, but decided against it. Too much energy required to mento it. He probed with his gloved hands for a place to sit. The ground was cold under his bottom.

Javik heard Namaba and Rebo find their own places to rest. Their breathing was labored, coming in short, staccato bursts, like steam engines with just enough poop left to go straight to the garbage launch facility.

The clunk and clang of Prince Pineapple's shovel rang out from downtrail.

"Maybe we can sleep here," Namaba suggested. "Right on the trail."

The idea had some appeal to Javik, and even made a certain amount of sense. It might be safer than stumbling around in the dark. But no one seconded the motion.

She did not repeat her suggestion.

Soon they were back at it, straining their muscles nearly to the breaking point. Prince Pineapple was a hot dog now with the fresh charge. Generously, he offered to carry the water pods and the survival pack. These were turned over to him. Even with this added weight, the prince surged far ahead of the others, often going so fast that he had to stop and wait for them to catch up.

It was a night of nights, the sort of monumental struggle one never forgets. With each step, Javik thought the trail grew steeper and more rocky. The wind bore down on them from uptrail, the worst possible direction, often forcing backward steps. If only it would blow from behind! Such a wind would help them to the top.

But the wind god, or whoever was in control of such matters, was not on their side.

Javik did not mention his thoughts. They only brought to mind Lord Abercrombie and the suggestion that he might be working against every move they made. Javik tried to convince himself that Abercrombie did not exist, and that even if he did exist, he could not control the wind or rockslides. But with each attempted step, Javik grew less confident of this.

Sometime in the early morning hours they stumbled onto a high plateau. The mist disappeared here, and Javik saw two harvest moons dropping below the horizon. A blanket of stars twinkled overhead, a cool blanket which offered welcome psychological warmth. Javik felt physically warmer here as well, as the wind had died down, going to one of the hiding places for such phenomena.

"You wanna camp here?" Prince Pineapple asked, coming back down the trail. With the moons behind him, Javik could not see his face.

"Yeah," Javik said.

In waning moonlight ahead, Javik saw the ghostlike outlines of treetops, framed majestically against the Corkian sky. Somewhere nearby a river ran, making its night journey with the moons. They were on soft soil now, at the edge of a forest. The moons disappeared below the horizon.

Javik took Wizzy out of his pocket and awakened him. "Give me some light," Javik said.

Wizzy did not complain, despite being so tired that he could barely keep his peeper open. He glowed bright white.

Prince Pineapple moved in close to watch. He moved around to stay warm.

Javik searched in the pack until he found the tent tube, a tiny roll no larger than a package of Lifesaver candies. Locating a flat spot on the ground, he set the tube down. "Stand back," he warned.

Everyone moved away from the tube.

Javik mentoed it. *Come on, brain,* he thought, knowing there was no manual way to pitch the specially packed, lightweight tent. *My mento unit had better be operable.* He felt no pain around the implanted mento unit.

The gortex tent popped open like fast-forward photography on an inverted, ugly flower.

Prince Pineapple gasped and stepped back. "Oh!" he said.

The tent stood taller than Javik and was at least four meters square. In Wizzy's flickering light, four curved, interlocking corner poles of expandable titanium appeared and stabbed through eyelets at each corner of the tent fabric. Then eight stakes hammered into the ground all around like a short burst of machine-gun fire. The door flap unzipped and flopped open, a final indication that the unit was ready for occupancy.

"Amazing," Prince Pineapple said. A light went on inside as he poked his head in. "It even has beds!" he exclaimed, seeing three single beds, completely made up. He heard a fan whirring.

"This is nothing," Javik said, his voice weary. "The Earth-use models have full appliances, even videodome units. That makes for a heavier package, of course—nearly a quarter of a kilo instead of this little one-hecto baby."

"Sure looks like magic to me," Prince Pineapple said.

A short distance away, Rebo and Namaba found a place on the ground where they cleared away the rocks, twigs, and pinecones. "Do you have enough space?" Rebo asked, selecting a spot for himself. The river was loud here.

"I'm fine," she said. Namaba lay on her side, with her head on one arm. In the light cast through the open tent doorway, she watched Javik enter the tent.

"Where did Rebo and Namaba go?" she heard Javik ask.

"I think they're over toward the river," Prince Pineapple said.

Rebo lay down on the ground where he could see Namaba's glowing red eyes. "You said I was different," he said. "And I agree.

There have been great changes in my brain. With this yenta you say you have, Namaba, can you explain it?"

"Your words are not so harsh," she said. "And they are slower, evidently spoken from a calm soul! I see it in your eyes, too, Rebo. They are softer and more compassionate."

"Softer? You mean I am no longer a man?"

"No, silly! I just mean that you're nicer now. More considerate."

"Then let's get married," he said. "When we return to Moro City."

"A meteor shower!" Javik yelled, poking his head out of the tent.

Namaba and Rebo sat up and watched a sky full of burning embers plummet to Cork. One large chunk caught Namaba's attention. It disappeared below the treetops, and she heard it hit the ground.

"Only about fifty kilometers off," Javik said.

The sky grew dark again, revealing the backdrop of stars.

"You might return to your old self back home," Namaba said, lying back down beside Rebo. "Your gang was always first, and I was just a possession."

"I've given that a lot of thought;" Rebo said. "I'll be leaving the Southside, finding honest work."

"I like the sound of that," she said. "But I can't forget the way you were. If only I had met you now."

"I can't forget my other self, either," he said, showing sorrow in his tone. "The image of that old flower vendor still haunts me."

"Yeah. That was a terrible thing."

"Rebo! Namaba!" Javik yelled. "You guys okay over there?"

"We're fine," Rebo said. But he did not feel fine. The tank in his steam boiler stomach was in a knot.

"I'm afraid it's too late for us," she said. "I've known the other Rebo."

"But I won't ever see the Hawks again! I promise," Namaba saw his eyes narrow to dim slits. Then they closed, evidently in prayer.

"No," she said. "I'm sorry, but no."

Presently, Rebo heard rumbling slumber from the other side of the camp. He wished he could fall asleep so easily. But his mind churned. It was the new mind in the new Rebo, carrying thoughts that seemed never to have existed before.

He heard Namaba turn to her other side. During the next hour, Namaba turned over many more times while Rebo lay awake. But this was no consolation to him. He wanted to share happiness with her, not turmoil.

# Chapter Twelve

*The planet naturally attracts space debris, much of it radioactively and ionically charged. When this is combined with a basic magnetic imbalance, the place becomes inhospitable to the pure energy waves required by a magician. Magic still works there, but only erratically.*

Conclusion of the magicians' task force assigned to Cork, sixty-seven centuries before Abercrombie's arrival

As Javik slept, Lord Abercrombie left his soil-immersion chamber and floated just above the surface to the Disaster Control Room. There he supervised work on the old earthquake and flood machine. This was comprised of a long bank of cracked CRT screens and discolored computer keyboards along one wall, manned by six dented meckies. As he entered the room, he heard squeaking, whirring, and synchronized rattles as the meckies tried to get the equipment going.

"Anything?" Lord Abercrombie asked, expecting to receive the usual long list of problems.

"We're flooding the ancient riverbed on the east edge of Dusty Desert," a soprano-voiced silver meckie reported.

"Eh?" Lord Abercrombie said, moving to the meckie's side. He rubbed his human eye and then studied the water table gauges to one side of the CRT screen. Not believing the readings, he slammed the butt of his hand against them. The needles jumped only a little, returning to their original position. "I don't believe it," he mumbled. "How long has this been working?"

"Three and a half hours, Lord," the silver meckie said.

"And no sign of the monopoles?"

"Not so far. We're concentrating all the spring waters for thousands of square kilometers—raising them to the level of the desert plateau."

"How long before we get a rip-roaring flood?" Lord Abercrombie asked.

"Just a few hours, if everything holds together."

Still not believing his good fortune, Lord Abercrombie said, "Be careful not to get the flood going too soon. We want to catch Brother Carrot's entire fleet when they're in the middle of the desert."

"Yes, Lord."

Lord Abercrombie felt like jumping up and clicking his heels. There had been so many misfortunes, so many dashed hopes. Then he remembered that he only had one heel left. It didn't matter, anyway. He needed to keep a more even temperament, not becoming too euphoric during good times or too depressed during the bad.

*It's not a loser's mentality,* he told himself. *I'm just being sensible.*

"What about the monopoles?" the silver meckie asked. "They could get in our way if we wait for Brother Carrot. How about a hurricane where the army is now?"

"We'd have to shut down the flood to do that," Lord Abercrombie said. "Better not risk it. Let's keep what we have going."

O O O

Three midmorning suns cast their rays around the campsite as Javik opened the tent flap and stepped out. His feet and hands were cold. He wiped his nose with one sleeve, then stared at the bio bar in his hand. With gnawing, screaming hunger at his midsection, he lifted the high-energy bar to his lips. Slowly he nibbled at it, tasting the sweetness of honey and feeling the texture of reprocessed oat flakes on his tongue. When he was halfway through the bar, he considered saving a portion for Rebo and Namaba. Then he ate Rebo's allocation, following that with Namaba's.

*I warned them,* Javik thought, licking the corners of his mouth to retrieve the last molecules of sweetness there. Hearing running water, he walked past the sleeping form of Rebo and looked over the edge of a low embankment.

A small stream ran below his vantage point, sparkling cheerily in sunlight. On the ground nearby, Rebo stirred and stretched. Javik wondered where Namaba had gone. Then he saw her, in shade at the base of the embankment, leaning over the water. The stream was not as large as Javik had imagined it to be the night before. And it seemed quieter now. Oddly, the banks were wet by each side a good ten meters above the water level.

Rebo loped to his side, yawning.

"Look at that water level," Javik said. "It's dropped a lot recently. I'd say overnight."

"Huh," Rebo said, not showing interest. "Boy, am I hungry!" he said. "You got anything left in your pack?"

"No. You finished your share yesterday." Javik was still hungry, even hungrier than he had been before eating the bio bar. The bit of food had activated his appetite. In a big way.

Prince Pineapple walked up, asking for his nutrient kit. Javik gave it to him, then watched the prince nudge away sleepily, looking for a spot to recharge.

"We've gotta figure something out," Rebo said. "Can't go on without nourishment."

"Don't imagine you have many streams in Moro City," Javik said, returning to his own subject. "But they aren't supposed to drop like that. Not in such a short period of time."

Rebo was watching Prince Pineapple recharge himself on a patch of dark ground at the edge of the forest. The prince had one foot immersed in a freshly dug hole and his eyes were closed. In ecstasy, he leaned back on both elbows.

Javik looked too, wondering if the nutrient kit would work for him and the Moravians. To Javik it looked as though Prince Pineapple was receiving a form of sexual gratification. It was the way he leaned back, and the look of sublime pleasure on his pineapple face.

"Why couldn't we do that?" Rebo asked.

"I was just thinking the same thing."

They watched Prince Pineapple remove his bare foot from the hole and wipe it with a moist-pak towelette. Glancing at Javik and Rebo nervously, he found his sock and slipped it on.

"I'm pretty damned hungry," Javik said.

"Same here."

Without another word, they walked toward Prince Pineapple, reaching him just as he was refilling his hole.

"We'll take that," Javik said, grabbing the shovel and barbed nutrient cord.

"You first?" Javik asked, extending the items to Rebo.

"Go ahead," Rebo said. "I'm not afraid, even if it kills you, I'd have to give it a try. We're different, you know, and it might only work for one of us."

Javik looked around for a place to dig.

"It won't work for either of you," Prince Pineapple said. He stomped on the loose dirt from his hole, packing it flat.

Javik dug at a furious pace, clanging the shovel on stones and throwing loose dirt in all directions. Some dirt landed on the prince's shoes.

"Watch it," Prince Pineapple said haughtily. "And don't damage my shovel."

"Get rid of him," Javik said. "Before I lose my temper."

"Beat it," Rebo said, showing no respect for the prince's royal status. He gave Prince Pineapple a mighty shove, causing him to stumble backward.

"Ruffian!" Prince Pineapple said.

Wizzy flew up just then. "You shouldn't do that," he said. "A prince of Cork deserves our respect."

"I can take care of myself," Prince Pineapple huffed. He stalked off in the direction of the tent.

"Wait!" Wizzy squealed, flying behind the angry prince.

Prince Pineapple paid no heed to Wizzy.

"I'd like us to be friends again," Wizzy said. "We have too much in common to be at one another's throats."

"You have no throat," Prince Pineapple said coolly.

"It was a figure of speech."

"But I have shifty eyes," Prince Pineapple snapped, still stalking away. "You can't be friends with someone like that."

"Let's talk about it," Wizzy said.

"There's nothing to discuss," the prince said, raging. "And I don't need any friends."

Wizzy stopped following, and let the angry prince go his own way. Prince Pineapple found a log on which to sit and sulk.

Sadly, Wizzy flew off to be by himself. He missed his friend and thought back upon their wonderful conversation in the prince's apartment. *My first friendship,* Wizzy thought, alighting on a tree branch. *It didn't last very long.*

A chubby yellow bird chirped cheerily on a nearby branch.

"You wanna be my friend?" Wizzy asked.

The bird had a short beak, with nervous, beady eyes. It looked at Wizzy curiously, then chirped again and flew away.

"Guess not," Wizzy said. He tried to cheer himself by remembering his Papa Sidney's strong friendship with Captain Tom. *I'll find a friend,* he thought. *Somewhere in this great big universe, there's a friend ... just waiting for me to find him.*

Wizzy circled the campsite. Spotting a worm crawling along the ground, he landed in its path and glowed a friendly shade of lavender. Unimpressed, the worm crawled around him.

"Oh, well," Wizzy said.

Just then the chubby yellow bird dived at the worm, snatching it in its beak. A startled Wizzy watched the bird fly off and disappear in the woods.

"Maybe that's the way to get a friend," Wizzy said. "Just swoop down and carry one away." Resolving to give this more thought, Wizzy flew down to the creek, hovering over Namaba as she washed.

O O O

"That was great!" Javik said after his recharge, leaping up from the hole. He felt nourished and sexually gratified at the same time, a wonderful completeness he had not experienced in recent memory.

"Pretty good, huh?" Rebo asked.

"*Pretty* good? It made the whole trip to Cork worthwhile, that's all!" Javik knelt and removed the barbed cord from his foot.

"Say," Rebo said, looking at Javik closely. "The scratches are gone from your face. So's the scar you had on your nose."

"That so?" Javik said. He rubbed his forehead, the bridge of his nose, and his cheeks. They were smooth.

Rebo was hesitant to attempt the charge. "I'm not like you," he said. "This could still kill me." He took the cord from Javik and wrapped it around one paw. Timidly, he extended the paw toward the hole Javik had used. It touched dirt. He put his weight on the paw. There was a slight tingling. Rebo's red eyes flashed around nervously.

"Anything?" Javik asked. He brushed off his own foot and put on his sock and boot.

Rebo shifted his paw around in the hole. "My skin's kinda thick," he said. "So I barely feel the barbs." He shifted his foot again. There was no change in the sensation.

"Try a new hole," Javik suggested. "Maybe that one's used up for a while."

"Huh?" Rebo said, glancing at Javik. "Oh, yeah. Thanks." He stepped out of the hole and used the shovel to dig a fresh one. Soon he was recharging, too. It worked so well that steam shot out of his ears in frosty puffs against the cool morning air.

"That *was* good," Rebo said as he finished. "What a meal!"

"Did you feel anything else?" Javik asked, keeping his voice down.

Rebo thought for a moment. "Yeah," he said. "Now that you mention it. Kind of a noppi noppi feeling."

Javik's language mixer pendant did not translate this expression, but no explanation was required. "A guy could set up one hell of a resort here," Javik said. "Folks would cross the universe to enjoy some of this. It even heals cuts and scars."

Javik noticed brown powder forming all over Rebo's body, blowing-off in the wind and getting on his black club jacket. *Bodily waste,* Javik thought, picking up the dull odor again. *Not so distasteful as human wastes.*

Rebo smiled broadly. "Ah!" he exclaimed.

"I'd better fill the water pods," Javik said. He retrieved the nutrient kit and connected it to his belt.

Recalling that Namaba was at the creek, Rebo's smile faded. "I can get it. Wait. Do we even need water now? With the nutrient kit working for us?"

"The charge might wear off quickly," Javik said. "And what if something went wrong with the nutrient kit?"

"Yeah, I guess."

"Stay here and fill those holes," Javik said. "You can push the dirt back with your paws."

Rebo did as he was told.

Javik returned to the camp and lifted the partially full water pods and the survival pack out of the tent. Stepping safely away, he mentoed the habitat into a tight little ball.

*What a terrible death,* he thought, *if I ever mentoed this thing shut while still inside.* Javik had heard of a camper getting squeezed into a tight little roll, but wondered if it was just another folktale.

Moments later, Javik put the tent roll in the pack. Leaving the pack there on the ground, he took the water pods and trudged down a short bank to the river.

Namaba smiled when she saw him. "I was waiting for you," she said, securing the yellow and black polka dot ribbon to her mane.

Javik told her the marvelous news about their new source of nutrition, omitting the prurient details.

Namaba wiped cool water across her face. "That *is* good news," she said. "I'll recharge, too, when we return to camp." She noticed Javik's scratches were gone, and commented on this.

"The recharge," Javik said. "Some kinda wonder cure."

Standing at the top of the embankment, Rebo watched Javik and Namaba. He heard their muted words and saw them smiling at one another. Namaba's laughter cut through the chill morning air like a knife piercing the center of Rebo's steam engine heart. He focused on the bolstered thunder piece worn by Javik. But his thoughts of harming Javik were short-lived. Rebo felt ashamed for having them.

Namaba watched Javik as he knelt on a flat stone and filled the pod. He capped it and reached for the other pod.

"Do you remember the two trails?" she asked. "Back at Icy Valley?"

"Yes." Javik suppressed a burp from the recharge.

"If I had gone up the first trail," she said, "I know whose image I would have seen there."

"Sure. Rebo's."

As Javik looked at her, a soft smile formed on her lips. "I would have seen *you*," she said.

*"Me?"* Javik fumbled with the second pod's lid. He noticed the river level was still dropping, leaving only a few centimeters of water in some places.

"I love you," she said.

Javik forgot about the water level. Feeling his heart kick, he set the full plastic pod on a rock and stood up. Taking a deep breath, he gazed downstream. The river, which was now a creek, reached a bend several hundred meters away, a place where sunlight sparkled cheerily on the water. Two ruby red birds flew close to the water at the bend. Their wingtips touched the water, spraying mist.

"How can you be so sure?" he asked. "We've hardly spoken."

"Moravian women know such things instantly," she said. "We feel love this way. It only takes a glance to know. Or a touch. She moved close to Javik and clasped one of his hands in hers. "We have yenta, you know."

Namaba's grasp was firm. She had light brown hair on the back of her hand. Her palm and fingers were cool from the stream, but Javik felt them warm quickly in his grasp.

Javik compared Namaba's feelings with what Wizzy had told him about Sidney Malloy. *Sid considers me his best friend,* Javik thought, *though I've only seen him twice in twenty years. Now this. These things don't fit the normal pattern. You can't have a friend you hardly ever see, or a lover you barely know.*

"I will tell you a love poem," she said, looking into his deeply set blue eyes. "One my mother taught me...."

Javik did not remember the words. It was something about a Morovian maiden whose soldier went off to battle far away. He died on a far-off battlefield while she waited in Moro City, pining away beneath a flashing VD clinic sign. It was a sad poem, with words that lilted and drifted across the sun-sparkled water.

He felt her grip tighten.

Javik looked up at her. She was a head taller and much heavier, but Javik did not give this much of a thought now. He saw a tear roll down her cheek.

"I always cry at that story," she said, brushing the tear away with her free hand. Then she pressed her lips against Javik's, rubbing gently from side to side.

Her lips were surprisingly soft to him. He kissed her in the Earth human way that he knew.

The ways of Earth and Morovia were different, so they took turns trying the new techniques. It was a union across the heavens, two different life forms finding common ground. Javik felt it was an important moment. Not just for himself and Namaba, but in a larger, cosmic sense.

"You have been with many women," she said. Javik did not hear jealousy or anger in her tone. It was simply an undeniable statement of fact.

Javik's entire love life flashed across his eyes. The old life of pleasure-dome maidens and girls in every astro-port had died. He would never return to it. He knew Namaba should seem even more unusual to him than the transsexual, Evans. By all rights, he should be repulsed by Namaba. But his feelings were far from revulsion. He needed constancy, someone on whom he could rely. He wondered how Moravians made love.

"Do you think we might share a child?" she asked, apparently sensing his unspoken thought.

Javik smiled. "We will see," he said.

They walked hand in hand up the embankment, each cradling a full water pod in one arm. As they entered the campsite, Javik thought Rebo was going out of his way to avoid them.

Rebo rested on his haunches off to one side, busying himself by picking things out of his fur. He seemed preoccupied and sad.

Peripherally, Javik saw Namaba as she looked at Rebo. She used to go to him at times like this, helping him to clean himself in the Moravian way. But Rebo was on his own now. Javik knew she had decided this. The touch of her lips and the grip of her hand had told him so.

O O O

Far across Dusty Desert from Javik and his party an ancient riverbed was full. Moments later, from his soil-immersed position, Lord Abercrombie watched the waters roll across the desert, over ridges of pebble and sand, returning the place to its former watery state. Desert palms were uprooted or immersed in a high wall of water.

"Heh, heh, heh!" Lord Abercrombie's laugh reflected the turn in his fortunes.

*Nothing can stop a flood,* he thought. *It's on the way.* He wondered if monopoles could swim.

O O O

"What was that?" Brother Carrot asked. "A low roar? Do you hear it?" He stood at the bow of the *Freedom One* as the big desert schooner crossed the face of a dune. Twenty-nine other ships laden with eager Vegetable troops followed Brother Carrot's lead craft.

Captain Cucumber stood next to him. "I hear something, too." He peered across the desert.

"It's getting louder," Brother Carrot said. "Must be the wind."

Suddenly a wall of water appeared, bearing down on them at high speed. Brother Carrot and the captain ran for the passageway. Just as they closed the door behind them, the water hit.

The *Freedom* rolled to one side. It became dark in the passageway.

"We're going over!" Brother Carrot said, scrambling to find a handhold in the passageway. He grabbed a hand railing. "My beautiful fleet!" he moaned. "My beautiful army!" He heard his men belowdecks as they clamored in confusion.

The cucumber captain was not so fortunate. Unable to find a handhold, he slid on the pegged floor the full length of the passageway. This left him in a jumbled position on the other end, against a cabin door. "My ship!" he moaned. "My beautiful ship!"

Water seeped in as the ship was consumed, getting Brother Carrot's shoes wet. The ship began to rock gently now, and the din of rushing water quieted. Brother Carrot felt the ship right itself and float upward.

"We're floating!" Brother Carrot exclaimed.

At the other end of the passageway, the captain was struggling to his feet. Holding the handrail, he sloshed his way slowly back to Brother Carrot. "You're right' he said, a hesitant smile on his cucumber face.

"You mean this thing was designed to float?" Brother Carrot asked.

"Sure. We took extra time and sealed the hulls."

"Idiot! We could have launched our attack earlier!"

"But this flood, sir."

"We would have missed the flood. Can't you understand that?"

"Yes, sir."

Sunlight streamed in the passageway portholes as the *Freedom One* bobbed to the surface. Brother Carrot peered out a porthole and was overjoyed to see other ships bob up. Some had broken spreaders or masts. All had torn sails and rigging in disarray. Two AmFed gar-bahge canisters popped to the surface below his porthole.

"Nine, ten …" Brother said. "There's eleven, twelve … I count fifteen ships on this side."

He ran to the hatch and slid it open. Knee-deep water rushed in. He waded out, reaching the gunwale on the ship's starboard side.

Men were streaming across the decks of the *Freedom One* now, lining the rails on each side of Brother Carrot. Hearing the chatter of his crew around him, Brother Carrot watched men filling the decks of the other ships in his battered fleet.

Dusty Desert was gone now, having been replaced by a lake that stretched across the entire rock-lined bowl. Waves lapped gently at the hull of the *Freedom One*. The ship rocked.

Brother Carrot removed his familiar black and gold cap, waving it in the air. Boisterous cheers rang across the water as the soldiers on each ship saw him. The men on his own ship cheered too, and patted their leader on the back.

"All accounted for," Captain Cucumber shouted. "I count twenty-nine other ships."

"Signal each of them," Brother Carrot said, replacing his cap on top of his leafy head. "Have the rigging repaired in breakneck time. That means I'll break the captains' necks if it isn't done. We'll float across now."

"But none of us have necks, sir," Captain Cucumber said;

"Eh?"

"Our heads and bodies are one, sir."

"Then I'll find a way to separate them. Hop to it!"

O O O

Using sensors in each grain of sand, piece of dirt, and drop of water on the planet's surface, Lord Abercrombie saw and heard this activity. *Damnit!* he thought. *I didn't expect this at all. Who'd have imagined it? Those blasted ships float!*

Lord Abercrombie knew he could not remain halfway between realms any longer. It was becoming too much of a strain. *I must commit myself,* he thought. *But to what? A coin flip. That's what I need. I'll find someone on the surface who is flipping a coin.*

Using his visual sensors in a patch of grass, Lord Abercrombie found King Corker standing there, trying to decide whether or not to attend the games at Corker Stadium. This was a small grassy area on one side of King Corker's courtyard. Bending his blades of grass to look upward, Lord Abercrombie saw a castle guard tower silhouetted against a cloudless sky. A purple Corker banner on the tower fluttered in a light breeze.

"Bring me a Decision Coin!" King Corker thundered.

A watermelon man aide scurried up.

*Okay,* Lord Abercrombie thought. *Here's my question: Do I commit myself to the Realm of Magic?*

"Should I go to the games?" King Corker said to the aide. "Or should I languish in my harem?"

"You must select a yes or no question, Your Majesty," the watermelon man said.

"Oh, King Corker said. "You're quite correct. Very well, then. You pick one."

*Fools!* Lord Abercrombie thought. *Hurry up!*

"Should King Corker go to the games?" the watermelon man said. He flipped the coin, then caught it on one palm and slapped it to the back of his other hand. "It says yes, Your Majesty."

"I would have preferred the harem," King Corker said, "but bring me my carriage."

*I have a trip to make, too,* Lord Abercrombie thought.

But he was not anxious to make the commitment to magic. He would do it the following day, after trying a few more events with the disaster control machinery. The monopoles were staying away, Abercrombie reasoned, and he could have a last fling in his fleshy form.

O O O

The path through the forest was easy to follow, with three-dot magical markings on a number of ancient trees and rocks. Prince Pineapple walked briskly ahead, almost out of sight of the others. The continuing confrontation between him and the rest of the party was leaving scars.

Sunlight filtered through high pine boughs, making intricate webs of light over Javik's head. Walking beside Namaba that morning, Javik watched Wizzy spend his time flying through the high, sunny boughs. The little comet's body and tail sparkled in the slender strands of light that touched them.

Spending a good portion of the morning up there, Wizzy would yell such things as, "It's incredible up here! The rays are so symmetrical, so delicate!" Then he would streak along the beams of light, forming parallel streaks of light with his tail.

"I'm seven days old today!" Wizzy squealed at one point. "And I feel great!"

Once, Javik scolded Wizzy for being light-headed. "Don't be so silly," Javik shouted. "We have important problems, such as figuring out how to get back to Earth. You're not helping at all."

"Can't one be happy and have problems?" Wizzy replied, alighting on a high branch.

"No!" Javik yelled.

This activated the soap box orator in Wizzy's personality. While a bird warbled sadly in the background, Wizzy gushed philosophy, saying he was starting to understand happiness at long last, that it was to be found wherever you were, despite any problems you faced. "Every situation has bits of happiness," Wizzy said. "They should be discovered wherever they are hiding and nurtured."

"I wish I'd never brought him," Javik said, leaving Wizzy behind, still discoursing. "He's out of his mind."

"It's beautiful here," Namaba said. "Like pictures I have seen of places on Morovia. Country places."

"You've never been outside the city?"

"Never before."

"I'm looking forward to seeing Morovia with you," Javik said. "I hope the Dimensional Tunnel will take us there, and not somewhere else."

"We'll have a wonderful life there."

"First I have to check on Abercrombie," Javik said.

"What do you mean?"

"If he's a threat to Earth, I've got to get him out of the Magician's Chamber. That may mean killing him. If he's no threat, I'll leave him there."

"You didn't mention that before. I thought Abercrombie was the prince's concern."

"I've been thinking about it. I'll probably never see my ship again, meaning there's no way to return to Earth. I was called a patriot once. That's what some folks said, anyway. There was a Colonel Peebles, though. He criticized me for making independent decisions. So I hit him in the face. I hit a lot of people in the face."

"And you want the honor back?"

"Sure. Wouldn't anyone?"

"I wonder if it's worth the danger," she said.

"I don't know," Javik said. "All I know is I have to do it."

They fell silent.

Presently the ground became soft and moist, and the travelers made impressions in the soil as they walked. Javik heard and felt the suction of his heels as he lifted them to make each step. The red top of an AmFed garbage canister was visible in deep mud off the trail to their left.

Wizzy dropped from the treetops now, gliding gracefully across the path in front of Javik. "End of the forest," Wizzy called out. Then he raced ahead along the path, disappearing over the crest of a little hill.

Prince Pineapple followed Wizzy, showing his broken helicopter beanie last as he too disappeared over the hill.

Javik was next to reach the crest. Here the sunlight was much stronger, with only a few slender trees on each side. At the bottom of a little hill a great swampy area stretched as far as he could see. He smelled decaying vegetation. Patches of brackish, green moss and other plants floated in the dark water. Skirting the edge of the water, tangled bushes seemed shadowy and threatening, even in full sunlight.

"Bottomless Bog," Prince Pineapple said, looking back at Javik.

As Namaba and Rebo caught up, a mosquito buzzed in Javik's ear. He swatted it away.

Bottomless Bog was a stupefying thing, appearing every bit as wide as the great Dusty Desert. But the bog seemed even more foreboding. It was dark, dank, and mysterious.

Wizzy flew back and buzzed nervously near Javik's ear. Thinking he was another mosquito, Javik nearly cuffed him, withdrawing his hand just in time.

A slender, straight line ran down the center of the bog. Prince Pineapple identified this, saying, "According to legend, that is a single log. In ancient times, trees grew in the area now comprising the bog, trees which were as high as these cliffs." He looked up.

High, polished cliffs stood on two sides of the bog, reflecting the bog's dark surface on their mirror faces. The cliff tops were immersed in clouds, extending so far up that Javik could not see how high they were.

"And how deep is the bog?" Wizzy asked:

"Bottomless," Prince Pineapple said.

Wizzy cast a fearful cat's eye gaze at the bog. "Bottomless?" he said. "But it looks shallow."

"It isn't," Prince Pineapple said.

"Just a minor obstacle, Wizzy," Javik said, sneering. "Remember your philosophy. Find happiness in each situation."

Wizzy glowed an embarrassed shade of red.

"I wonder if we could go around," Javik said, swatting another mosquito. He looked at Wizzy, adding, "You're energetic today. Fly around those cliffs and see if there's a way for us."

"Are you kidding?" Wizzy said. "I'm beat now. Maybe tomorrow."

Scowling, Javik said, "If you hadn't played in the forest all day, you might be able to make yourself useful."

"I'm not at your bidding!"

*That's telling him!* Prince Pineapple thought.

"Let's have a look at that scroll," Javik snapped, glancing at the prince.

Slowly, Prince Pineapple brought forth the Sacred Scroll of Cork from under his coat. He extended it to Javik.

"Come on," Javik said. "Don't play games with me."

"Games?" Prince Pineapple asked.

"Reach back in your coat and get me the scroll."

"It's here. In my hands."

Javik's eyes flared angrily. Then a look of shock crossed his face. "I don't see it," he said. His fingers darted forward and touched an unseen parchment held by the prince. "I can't see the damned thing anymore!"

"Nor can I," Namaba said. She looked at Rebo.

"Nothing there," Rebo said.

Prince Pineapple thought for a moment, then said, "We have all recharged now. Lord Abercrombie's spell is on each of us."

"I can see the scroll," Wizzy said sassily. "And I'll read it to you, Captain Tom … if I so choose."

"You'll read it," Javik said. "Remember what papa said."

"Spread it open," Wizzy snapped.

Javik and Prince Pineapple held the scroll open, deciding not to place it on the moist ground. Wizzy hovered in front of it, his yellow cat's eye slanted at something no one else could see. "Uh huh," Wizzy said. "Uh *huh*."

"What does it say?" Prince Pineapple asked anxiously.

"We have to cross the log. No way around, according to a specific notation. An unnamed meadow is shown on the other side. Then we must pass between two white cliffs. At this point the scroll is marked 'Moha.'"

"Nothing on what Moha is?" Prince Pineapple asked.

"I looked for that when I could see the scroll," Javik said. "There's no detail at all."

"Beyond Moha," Wizzy said, "it's only a short distance to the Dimensional Tunnel. It's adjacent to the Magician's Chamber entrance."

"We'd better start across," Prince Pineapple said. He tugged at the scroll.

Javik considered keeping it, but had another thought and released it. *No sense antagonizing him unnecessarily,* Javik thought.

"Be careful with my nutrient kit as you cross the log, Captain Javik," Prince Pineapple said. He placed the scroll back in its carrying place beneath his orange vari-temp coat. "If you lose it, all of us except for Wizzy will perish. That includes your girlfriend."

Javik nodded, pursing his lips. "Lead on," he said, pointing toward the log.

Prince Pineapple reached a flat-stone-covered path leading down to the point where the log touched the shore. Decaying moss clung to the sides of the log and floated in the water. Jumping on the log, Prince Pineapple looked back and said, "No rhymes, please! Can't afford a backflip here." He started across the log, unable to see the opposite shore.

Just as Javik reached the log, a thick swarm of mosquitoes surrounded him. He fought them off, but they were persistent. He felt his skin swell on the back of his neck and on his forehead.

"Goddamn bugs," Javik said. He fumbled in his pack. "And no repellent here!"

"They don't seem to bother Rebo or me," Namaba said. She was just behind Javik, and helped him swat the mosquitoes. "Our skin is pretty tough."

When the mosquitoes had eaten their fill of Javik, they flew off, skipping across the murky water. To Javik, they seemed gleeful as they left, frolicking away on full stomachs.

Namaba tested the log with her forepaw. The log didn't move.

Behind her on the shore, Rebo asked, "You okay?"

"I think so," she said. "It seems sturdy enough." She stepped on it carefully, balancing her two rear paws on the wide surface of the log. Then she took a little hop forward, pulling with her forepaw and pushing with both hindpaws.

"Watch for patches of moss," Prince Pineapple said, glancing back. "The wet stuff is slick." He was several meters ahead, moving cautiously.

Wizzy waited until last. Hesitantly he scooted along the log behind Rebo, just millimeters above the surface.

"Whatsamatter, Wizzy?" Javik called back, seeing Wizzy's trepidation. "You don't seem so chipper anymore."

"Don't tease him," Namaba said. She smelled stagnant water.

"Mind your own business!" Wizzy screeched. He had a funny feeling as he followed the others. Something was wrong in this place. Terribly wrong.

O O O

"Perfect!" Lord Abercrombie said, brushing dirt off his half body as he left the Soil Immersion Chamber. "Now let's try a nice little earthquake in Sector 114!"

Not taking time to dry-shower, Lord Abercrombie used his wardrobe ring to dress while he floated on air through the labyrinth of passageways. Following the circuitous route known only to him, he arrived presently in the Disaster Control Room. There he saw meckies working on one of the computer terminals. Parts were strewn on the floor.

"Just needs a minor adjustment," a silver meckie reported, his voice a less-than-reassuring mechanical whine. "Nothing to worry about."

"Hurry," Lord Abercrombie said. "They're crossing Bottomless Bog. *The end of my fleshy self is near,* he thought. *This would be a nice way to go out.*

"Another hour at most," a gold-plated female meckie said. "We'll finish in plenty of time."

Lord Abercrombie floated around the room nervously while the meckies continued their work. He knew it would take all the remaining hours of daylight for Prince Pineapple and his group to cross the bog—at least five to six hours. *I'll drown that motley bunch in the bog,* he thought. *Then tomorrow, before my permanent soil-immersion, a nice quake-induced rockslide to bury the Vegetable army on the trail.*

O O O

King Corker's open French brocade carriage sped along Avenida Seven in bright afternoon sunlight, pulled by one hundred of the strongest carrot men in the realm. The king was late for the games. He sucked impatiently on his grain alcohol tube.

"Faster!" the king yelled, his voice a drunken gargle.

The white-suited cantaloupe coachman cracked his whip over the blinder-fitted carrot man team, urging them to greater speed.

*Snap! Snap!*

Now the coachman brought his whip arm way back to get a good lick at the team. The tip of the whip caught King Corker's backpack tube as he sat in the rear, pulling the tube right out of his mouth.

"Fool!" King Corker yelled.

The coachman glanced back nervously as the coach took an exit leading to Corker Stadium. "Sorry, Your Majesty," he said.

King Corker rubbed a sore upper lip. He muttered angrily, glaring at the crowd as his coach entered the stadium. The crowd roared their support for his royal personage.

"Whoah!" the coachman bellowed, hauling back on the reins. The coach screeched to a stop in front of the flag-draped royal box.

Two watermelon man aides ran forward. They helped King Corker down.

"Damn fool driver!" King Corker said as he was escorted to his box seat. He pulled his backpack tube forward to look at it. The tube was bent. "Get this pack off me," he ordered, refusing to sit down. "And bring me another." One aide removed the royal alcohol pack while the other ran for a new one. "My driver did it," King Corker fumed. "With his infernal whip."

"Shall we tweak his nose, Sire?" the aide asked.

King Corker considered this while the other aide fitted him with a replacement pack. "Yes," the king said. "Then twist his ears. And don't forget to cut five centimeters off his nutrient cord. He won't be so careless again."

As the king took his seat, he saw a bright flash on the horizon, beyond the gray concrete fighter car track. Realizing it was a comet, King Corker felt his heart palpitate. His breath became short. He took a deep breath, feeling his heart pounding wildly.

The comet's nucleus was bright red, the color of Earthian blood. It had a threadlike, golden tail that stretched across the sky.

"Bad omen," a woman said behind King Corker. She was a member of the royal court.

Others in the stands whispered nervously, concealing their words from the king's ears.

King Corker knew what they were saying. A comet like that always brought evil tidings, often portending the death of a king. He watched the comet swing wide and then speed away. It disappeared below the horizon.

King Corker lifted one arm weakly, signifying that the games were to begin. A bright blue starter flare flashed over the track, in line with the last sighted position of the comet's nucleus.

O O O

Seeing the flare, Marta Evans hit the red super-accelerator toggle on her dashboard. Her pink and black fighter car sped down the ramp of the Wommo auto carrier, bumping as it hit the pavement. It was a hot afternoon.

Out of the corner of her eye she saw a blue and black enemy fighter car running with her on the parallel track. Two hundred fifty meters ahead, the simmering tracks merged. She had played this Earth game six times now, with six enemy kills.

*I'm good,* she thought. *Damned good!* She licked her lips, anticipating how good the toasties would taste at their evening orgy. She tasted perspiration salt on her lips.

Her car shook.

"Piece of crap car," she muttered. "It's not steering right."

She noticed ripples in the pavement ahead. Her car dipped and rose, screeching as its underside slammed into each peak and valley.

*Earthquake!* she thought. Instinctively, she hit the brakes.

But before her car could slow appreciably, she and the parallel car arrived at the merge point simultaneously. They exploded in pink and blue balls of flame. Two glowing toasties shot skyward. Then white parachutes flowered, supporting the toasties as they dropped to Cork.

O O O

In his earthquake-damaged royal box, King Corker pulled himself out of a heap of rubble. Large portions of the grandstand had been destroyed, and his subjects cried out in pain from wherever they lay. One of the king's watermelon man aides lay on his face nearby, mortally wounded. He had been split asunder, and his black seeds were all over the place. The other aide was nowhere in sight. Survivors streamed out of the stands, running wildly to get away from the stadium.

Having remained in the Disaster Control Room for the earthquake, Lord Abercrombie saw the results flash across a digital CRT screen. "Oh, no!" he moaned. "We hit the wrong sector! We're wiping out our allies!"

"We're sorry, Lord Abercrombie," the meckies said in unison. They milled around nervously, awaiting an outburst from their lord.

"It's not entirely your fault," Lord Abercrombie said, feeling compassion for the dented and scratched meckies who had tried so hard for him. "If only I had decent equipment!"

"Do you think the monopoles did it?" one of the meckies asked.

"How the hell do I know?" Lord Abercrombie said. He bemoaned his misfortunes for a full five minutes, then recalled his decision to soil-immerse himself in the Realm of Magic the following day. It was beginning to look like a very wise decision.

Wanting a last fling in the Realm of Flesh, Lord Abercrombie set his loyal meckies to work yet another time. They worked feverishly, searching for that precise combination of tachyon laser signals that would shake Bottomless Bog.

Fifteen minutes later a meckie reported a tremor in Sector 221, a region five hundred kilometers from the bog. "Strength zero point two three, Sandlin scale," the meckie said.

"That's closer," Lord Abercrombie said, heartened. "Not very large, though. Try again. Stronger and closer."

The next quake was ten times as powerful. Unfortunately, it was also ten times as far away.

"Keep trying," Lord Abercrombie urged. "We've got it going now, and I'll shake the whole planet if I have to." He wondered how long the aging equipment would hold together—machinery that had been knocked down on Earth, containerized, and catapulted across an entire universe.

But fortune smiled on Lord Abercrombie this time. A sizable tremor shook Bottomless Bog. Prince Pineapple was less than fifty meters from shore when he felt the log move. Looking back, he saw ripples rolling across the dark water, hurling themselves against the log. The log was quite narrow at this point, having tapered significantly.

"Look out!" Wizzy squealed. "Waves!" Feeling too weary to fly, he dropped to the surface of the log and held on with magic suction.

Frantically, Prince Pineapple motivated his stubby legs and scrambled for the shore. He made it.

Javik and Namaba fell to their knees on the log and tried to hold on. The log began to whip, first one way, then the other. They crawled to safety with no time to spare.

Rebo was not so lucky. He was on a more slippery section and was having trouble keeping his balance. From the shore, Javik saw that the water pods on Rebo's back were getting in his way.

"Dump the pods!" Javik yelled.

Rebo pulled off the roped-together plastic containers and dropped them in the bog. They floated. Then, on all three knees, he started to crawl for shore.

Suddenly the log snapped just behind Rebo, sending him and Wizzy in opposite directions on different pieces of wood. Rebo began to lose his balance. He held on precariously for a moment, then fell in the water with a splash.

"Help!" Rebo yelled. Slimy, decaying vegetation filled his mouth. His voice gurgled, "Hellup!"

Javik found the black and white striped Tasnard rope in the survival pack. "Swim!" he yelled. "Swim for shore!"

"I don't know how!" Rebo yelled, floundering in the water. Steam shot out of his ears from the exertion.

"Help him!" Namaba said. "Oh, Tom, help him!"

Javik mentoed the Tasnard rope. It flew toward Rebo, but fell far short, plopping in the thick water. "Not enough line," Javik said.

"Oh God!" Namaba said.

O O O

Wizzy had been carried quite far away on the other section of the log. He glowed orange-hot, attempting to dry away any water that touched him. Swampy water ran across the surface of the log, hissing when it hit Wizzy's superheated surface.

Feeling a survival-inspired burst of energy, Wizzy rose straight up in the air, hovering above the log like an autocopter. Bright silvery-purple particles shot out of his rear, forming a short tail of intense light. Far across the water, Wizzy saw Rebo drowning. And he saw the unsuccessful shoreside effort to save him.

Wizzy's first instinct told him to fly for shore. Already he had been weakened by the water, and he was not certain how much strength he had left. His strength had shown a troublesome proclivity for appearing and disappearing without warning.

But he recalled Javik referring to him as useless. This haunted him. Without further ado, Wizzy streaked toward Rebo.

"Look!" Namaba said, pointing at the ball of light speeding across the surface of Bottomless Bog. "It's Wizzy!"

Javik stood motionless, watching.

Wizzy made a soft landing on top of Rebo's head, which was the only dry spot he could see. "Stay calm," Wizzy said. "I'll try dragging you to shore."

Wizzy used magic suction to grab hold of Rebo's fur. "This may hurt a little," he said, tugging at the fur on top of Rebo's head.

"That's all right," Rebo said, grimacing from the pain. "Go ahead."

Wizzy pulled hard. Rebo began to move through the muck, but thick patches of dead plant life in the water made the going difficult.

"He's doing it!" Namaba said.

"Good going, Wizzy!" Javik yelled.

But Rebo thrashed his arms and forepaw, splashing slimy water all over Wizzy. This sapped the little comet's energy in a matter of seconds. Soon he could not glow orange-hot to dry himself and could not pull any more.

Javik mentoed the Tasnard rope and it plopped in the water, just short of Rebo. "Try to reach it!" Javik yelled.

Rebo thrashed more now, trying to reach the rope. This covered poor Wizzy with more water.

"I can't … hold on!" Wizzy screamed. He let go of the fur on Rebo's head and rolled down Rebo's neck into the water. He sank out of sight.

Rebo managed to grab hold of the rope. It was slippery with slime, so he wrapped it around one arm. "I've got it!" he said.

Javik mentoed the Tasnard mechanism, ordering it to bring Rebo in. But it only responded weakly, not enough to move the big Moravian. "Too much goo on it," Javik said. "Help me pull."

Prince Pineapple, Namaba, and Javik pulled the line in. Moments later, Rebo crawled ashore. On his knees in soft ground and gasping for breath, Rebo looked up at Javik gratefully. "I am your servant now," Rebo said. "Moravian honor dictates it."

"Wizzy!" Prince Pineapple bellowed, looking out on Bottomless Bog. "Wizzy!"

Thinking about what Rebo had said, Javik unwrapped the Tasnard rope from him and mentoed it to locate Wizzy. The tip of the rope flew lethargically out to the place where Wizzy had disappeared and sank in the bog. Javik felt it go limp in his hands. Slowly he pulled the rope back. Wizzy was not attached to it. Javik repeated this procedure a number of times. It became apparent that the effort was useless.

"Wizzy's gone," Prince Pineapple said. "The water …" His voice trailed off in sadness.

"I know," Javik said. He felt disheartened too, and this surprised him. He wished Wizzy would pop out of the water and say something annoying. In his mind's eye, Javik saw Wizzy again in the treetops, chasing streaks of sunlight. And he recalled their angry words. This had occurred only hours before.

Javik turned his back on Bottomless Bog. Ahead stretched a gentle flowered upslope, with jagged white cliffs in the distance. The shadows of approaching night stabbed across the cliff faces.

He heard a rustling noise at his side. Then he felt Namaba's hand in his. She squeezed him reassuringly. "I love you," she said.

# Chapter Thirteen

*When you see what it is all about, there will be nothing left to do except to have a good laugh.*

Quotation from Judao-Buddhic novel (22nd Century Earth)

Wizzy tumbled through murky green water that was faintly illuminated by daylight above. After several seconds in the water, he became aware of the fact that he was not lung breathing any longer, having discarded that antiquated system of oxygenation in favor of a higher physical state. His papa had told him this would happen. Wizzy was not sure when the transition had occurred, but knew it was a good sign. It meant he was becoming more like Papa Sidney every day. But this was only a tiny bit of cheer in Wizzy's great chasm of gloom.

The daylight overhead dimmed as he dropped deeper into Bottomless Bog. The water grew cooler. Most of Wizzy's. strength was gone now, having dissipated soon after the water completely enveloped him. He knew there was no fighting back. He might as well conserve his remaining energy.

*But for what?* he thought.

A net of vegetation on the bog lake's false bottom supported him for a second. Then it tore away, and Wizzy resumed his descent.

Wizzy closed his cat's eye, with the dim hope that this might conserve a small bit of strength that would be useful later. But he knew the bog was too deep. Even with that extra dab of energy, it was foolishness to imagine ever pulling himself out.

The water became pitch black now. He despaired. Wizzy felt the entire universe crushing in around him, forcing him down and pressing him into a deep, permanent sleep.

*I'm only seven days old,* he thought. *It isn't fair.*

Wizzy wondered if he would become a simple, ordinary rock, undistinguishable from any other. Or would he retain his precious consciousness? He knew most, if not all, of his remaining strength would dissipate in the continued exposure to water. But how fast would it occur? Would it be only seconds from now? Was this his final thought? Perhaps he would become a storehouse of cosmic information, keeping all the data he had accumulated as a growing comet and adding to that all the information from sitting on the bottom of a bog for millions of years. A multitude of questions raced across his brain as he tumbled deeper into Bottomless Bog.

It occurred to him now that the bog might really have no bottom, as its name suggested. Perhaps he would tumble forever, with unanswered thoughts such as these continually cropping up.

*It has to have a bottom,* he thought. *This is a planet. The bog can't be deeper than … but it is a magical planet.*

His thoughts warped now, reaching beyond the limit of his young brain's capacity. He pictured a bog passing through the entire diameter of the planet: two bogs on opposite ends of the globe, connected at their deepest points. He might tumble to the center of the planet—and then? Would he continue up and out the other side?

*No,* he thought. *Gravity would pull me back to the center. I don't have enough momentum.*

If the bog was magical, this line of reasoning had no merit. Magical things did not follow any of the accepted laws of physics.

Wizzy felt a crosscurrent move him. He thudded against a rock wall, then dropped again. *The shoreline,* he thought. *I was close when I slipped and fell. Must be a straight dropoff.*

With a distinct *plop* that sounded clearly in Wizzy's tympanic sensors, he landed on a soft bed of decaying plant life. He sank slowly. Finally, he reached a muddy bottom where his descent stopped.

*I'm on the bottom,* he thought, feeling an undefined emotion. *There is a bottom!* He felt mud oozing over him, covering him entirely.

Wizzy returned to the thought of resting for millions of years on the bottom. He pictured it all in his mind: Someday in the far future the bog would dry out. The once muddy bottom would become parched and cracked. Snows would come and go. Seasons would change. Winds would blow across the land, ultimately turning the mud to a fine powder that would blow away. Layer after layer would erode, finally exposing Wizzy.

His mind rolled at such a thought. It was a pleasing thought. Three suns would warm him once again. Stars and harvest moons would grace his evening. Comets and shooting stars would flash overhead.

Would his magical powers of flight return then, once he had dried out? Or had they been lost forever? He assumed the powers would return. After all, a few million years meant nothing in terms of the universe. He knew Papa Sidney would not pull him out, for Wizzy would not learn anything that way. Patience. That was what Wizzy needed. He would wait for the inevitable drying out.

He felt better in his world of thought until a troubling realization struck him: What if his magical flying power never returned?

Now he envisioned Cork shifting on its axis. Heavy rains would come, drenching the once parched soil. Trees and other green plants would spring from the ground, spreading their seeds in the wind to form duplicates of themselves. Ultimately a period of decay would return. The water table would rise. Many of the plants would die. Once again the area would become a bog.

If all this occurred, would Wizzy be able to escape before the water descended upon him? Or would he be paralyzed, condemned through all eternity to be buffeted by the elements?

*Maybe I'm dying here in obscurity,* Wizzy thought. *Becoming part of the planet.* He knew it was this way with other life forms: In death, their remains became one with the soil, one with the cosmos.

O O O

Namaba scrambled up a little hill to a knoll. Nightfall was approaching fast, with gray light turning to deeper, darker shades.

"We can camp up here," she said. "The ground is firm, and we can watch for Wizzy."

When Javik and the others reached the knoll, they agreed that it was a suitable place. A meadow of scarlet flowers extended up a gradual rise above them. In the distance, the hulking shadow of a cliff wall rose. It appeared impregnable to Javik. He searched in the fading light for the crack in the cliff that marked the pass they would have to find. He couldn't see it.

"What a beautiful meadow!" Namaba exclaimed.

"Quite a contrast to the bog," Rebo said.

Namaba looked at Rebo and smiled. "Yes," she said. "Quite a contrast. The bog is how you used to be, Rebo. Dark, murky, and treacherous."

"And the flowers? That is how you see me now?"

Namaba smiled softly. "No, you macho Moravian," she said. "But you're closer to them than the bog."

Rebo looked perplexed.

Javik took Prince Pineapple aside and said, "Listen, Prince. I'm going to have to ask you to sleep outside the tent tonight. I'll bring your bed out." Javik scratched the mosquito bites on his forehead.

"I have seen Earthian fornication rooms," Prince Pineapple said with a huff. "I know what you and Namaba have in mind."

"You don't understand at all," Javik said. "All you've seen is the physical side. It is more than a mere game."

"I doubt that."

"I need the time with Namaba," Javik said. His voice was firm. "We don't know what will happen tomorrow. That beautiful meadow may be treacherous. And who knows where it leads?"

Prince Pineapple set his jaw and stared up the hill. Two synchronized moons were making their first nightly pass over the cliffs, rising rapidly into the sky. Stars rushed out now, as if switched on by a planetarium master.

"I'll put your bed out," Javik said.

Prince Pineapple did not respond.

Javik turned and walked away. The issue was settled. Prince Pineapple would sleep outside, whether he liked it or not.

"Let's put the tent here," Namaba said. She cleared away rocks with her forepaw,

Rebo was nearby, clearing a place on the ground to sleep. She saw him look at her sadly. Then he looked away.

As Javik mentoed the tent, he thought of Wizzy's disappearance. Now no one could read the scroll. *Things are not going well,* he thought.

Then he caught Namaba's tender gaze and recalled Wizzy's philosophy of finding happiness in unlikely places. The red glow of her eyes intensified. She smiled, revealing iridescent blue teeth.

"Maybe Wizzy wasn't such a bad guy," Javik said, watching the tent stake itself.

"You're sorry you didn't get along with him better, aren't you?" she said, noticing puffy mosquito bites on Javik's face and neck.

The tent flaps opened.

"In a way," Javik said. He dragged out a bed for Prince Pineapple, placing it well away from the tent. When Javik returned, he brought his survival pack with him. "I can feel sorry about Wizzy now," he said, "when he isn't here. But his blasted personality …"

"We all wish some things could be changed," Namaba said. "But we can't dwell on them."

"I know." Javik stepped into the tent and mentoed on the overhead lights. As they filled the enclosure with white light, a ceiling heater fan began to whir.

Hesitantly, she followed.

Javik arranged his orange vari-temp coat, gun, and other gear on a pop-up table in one corner. When this was finished, he looked at Namaba. She was just inside the doorway but looking out, apparently not certain what she wanted to do.

"It is pleasant in here," she said, feeling warm air from the heater fan.

Javik mentoed the tent door. It zipped shut with a noise that startled Namaba.

She moved away from the door.

Looking at Javik uneasily, she removed her yellow vari-temp coat and pants. "There are things I wish could be changed, too," she said. "I didn't stop Rebo from killing an old man back in Moro City. Rebo feels terrible about it now, too. It was senseless." Moisture glazed over her soft red eyes and filled her eyewells.

"I thought you said not to dwell on unchangeable things," Javik said, moving close to her.

"That is true," she said. "But some things should not be forgotten."

"Let's live for now," Javik said. He took her hand and led her to one of the beds, where they sat down.

"I will try," Namaba said.

"I don't know how Moravians make love," Javik said. He half stood to reach her mouth and rubbed her lips with his, the way she had shown him. "But I'm willing to learn."

Namaba kissed Javik in the Earthian way. Then she pulled away. "There has to be a way to do it," she said. "Maybe your method and mine are not so different."

"I want you to carry my child," Javik said. "Don't laugh at me." He kicked off his boots.

"I'm not laughing." She gazed at him tenderly. "Children are the common ground of two souls, however different they may be."

Javik smiled impishly. "You're as bad as Wizzy," he said. "Spouting philosophy."

She laughed. "I suppose you're right."

Javik thought about Namaba's laugh. It was rich, warm, and honest. A spontaneous thing. He wished he could hear it more, that they might enjoy a lifetime together. There were so many things he wanted for the future. He mentoed off the lights, leaving the heater fan on.

Namaba's red eyes and iridescent blue teeth formed purple spectrums on the tent walls, reminding Javik of the purple darkness of the Corkian night. He glanced quickly at his digital watch, then pressed his mouth against hers. *I couldn't have timed this more perfectly if I'd tried,* he thought. *Only five more seconds.*

Javik's clothing disintegrated in a puff of dark smoke, leaving him wearing nothing but his wrist digital and his wardrobe ring.

O O O

From his position on the ground outside, Rebo heard them making love.

"I didn't know there was a position like this," Namaba said.

"Three legs do have an advantage!" Javik exclaimed.

Rebo heard Namaba's steam engine heart chugging loudly. He moved out of hearing range and cleared a new place to sleep.

O O O

After Javik and Namaba made love, he donned pajamas and fell asleep on his own bed. He slept for less than an hour, however, before stirring and half opening his eyes. An eerie red glow illuminated the interior of the tent.

Javik sat straight up and snapped open his eyes. The first thought in his sleep-addled brain was fire. Then he saw that the glow came from Namaba's eyes, which were wide open. She was lying face up on her bed. The heat fan whirred.

"Namaba," Javik whispered. Then, a little louder: "Namaba!"

She did not move or say anything.

"You awake?"

Still no response.

Namaba's breathing sounded deep and regular to Javik. He wondered if that was the way all Moravians slept. But her eyes gave off a glow that disturbed him, preventing him from returning to sleep.

Javik swung his feet off the bed and crept through red light to the door. He mentoed the door, causing a mosquito net to unzip. The outside tent flaps flopped open, letting in cool air. He flipped on a penlight and tiptoed barefoot across the campground, intending to see if Rebo slept the same way.

"Ow!" Javik whispered, stubbing his toe on a rock or a twig. Pain surged through his foot, then subsided as he neared Rebo.

Rebo was asleep on his side, snoring deeply. Javik moved around to see his face. Rebo's eyes were closed.

Perplexed, Javik returned to the tent. He lay awake for a while, finally drifting into troubled slumber. He dreamed of a black widow spider. In his dream the spider's face was Namaba's, and it had her same soft voice and pleasant ways. He and the spider made love, after which Javik fell asleep. While he was asleep in the dream, the spider hovered over him. Suddenly, as he lay helpless, the dream spider sprayed paralyzing gas on him. Then the spider's jaws opened wide. It was going to devour him!

Javik tried to wake up. But he could not move, could not breathe. A great weight was on his chest. He smelled a dull odor.

Javik sat bolt upright for the second time that night. Perspiration stuck to his clothing and poured down his brow. He wiped his face on a sheet and threw all the bedding off.

He swung out of bed, removed his service automatic from the corner table, and placed the gun next to his pillow. He did not sleep again that night.

O O O

At dawn Javik dressed and left the tent. He stood looking uphill at the first stretch of meadow they would cross that day. Dew-kissed scarlet flowers sparkled as the first bits of daylight touched them.

Entranced, Javik walked past Prince Pineapple's bed and selected a rock. There he sat and watched as Cork's three suns began their daily march across the sky. A wash of red against the distant white cliffs became orange, then gold with streaks of pale blue. The colors reminded him of Sidney's comet. They were pure and changed in the blink of an eye.

Feeling tired, Javik slid the shovel and nutrient cord out of the belt carrier. Then he set about digging in the soft, loamy soil. The shovel clanged against a rock. This caused Prince Pineapple to stir and turn the other way on his bed.

Soon Javik's bare right foot was wrapped in the barbed cord and immersed in cool, moist soil. His foot tingled. Juices flowed up his leg to the rest of the body. Thinking of Wizzy as he recharged, he gazed dreamily across the camp toward the glistening, dark bog. There was no sign of life there. He could see one part of the log where it had split and recalled poor Wizzy there, clinging for his life.

*I miss the little fellow,* Javik thought. *I'd like to give him a swift kick, but damnit, I miss him.*

Javik spent extra time recharging, and this helped make up for some of the sleep he had lost. Afterward he noticed the mosquito-bite bumps on his face and neck were gone.

He left the shovel and cord on the ground and walked down to Bottomless Bog. Javik looked out at the split log ends and across the murky, vegetation-soaked water. There were no ripples, no mosquitoes, no signs of life whatsoever.

When Javik arrived back in camp, he saw Prince Pineapple swinging grumpily out of bed. "Damned lumpy mattress," the prince said. He stretched, then rubbed a crick in the back of his neck. "Bedding's damp too."

"Did His Royal Hind Ass wet the bed?" Javik asked.

Nearby, Rebo opened one eye. He sat up on the ground and rubbed his hands through the fur on top of his head.

"Certainly not!" Prince Pineapple huffed. "I was referring to dew upon my covers."

"I'm sure Rebo would trade his spot for your comfortable bed," Javik said. "He slept on the ground last night."

"Ruffians belong on the ground," Prince Pineapple said, casting a wary, disdainful glance at Rebo.

Rebo lunged playfully at Prince Pineapple, stopping short.

Prince Pineapple jumped back, then realized that Rebo was only kidding around. "Hrrumph!" the prince said.

Javik laughed, forgetting for a moment about his problems and aches.

Namaba emerged from the tent. Smiling at Javik, she said, "New day, old day. Gone is gone." Seeing a surprised look on Javik's face, she explained quickly: "Traditional Morovian greeting."

"Oh," Javik said. "I thought you were talking about my mosquito bites."

"Gone after a recharge?" she asked.

"Uh huh. I went down to the bog afterward. No sign of Wizzy."

Namaba detected hostility in Javik's eyes as he looked at her. She moved close to him and asked, "You are angry with me?"

"You did keep me awake last night," he said. "Your eyes …"

"Their glow disturbed you? I'm sorry, Tom. I was awake all night, you know."

"But I spoke to you. There was no answer."

Nearby, Rebo was winning an argument with Prince Pineapple over who would recharge first.

"I was deep in thought," Namaba said. "Thinking of this new land and of our new love. A Morovian in a thought trance cannot hear anything. It is when all of our physical senses are shut off."

Javik rubbed the bridge of his nose where the scar used to be. It was smooth.

"This place!" Namaba exclaimed, gazing out at the meadow that sloped above them. "It's so beautiful!"

Javik agreed.

"If only we could stay here," she said.

"You mean, just pitch a tent and live in the meadow?"

"Sure. Why not? We could use the nutrient cord for food."

"But what if Rebo and Prince Pineapple don't want to stay? We're all on one cord."

"Couldn't we divide it?"

"I don't know," Javik said. "Wouldn't want to chance it."

After everyone had recharged, Javik was packing his gear for the day's journey. He heard Rebo call his name from somewhere in the meadow. "Captain Tom! Come look at this!"

Javik walked briskly, following the sound of Rebo's voice. Over a little hill he found Rebo standing in the midst of flowers and scattered rubble. An AmFed garbage canister lay nearby on its side, split open from head to tail.

"Is this from Earth?" Rebo asked. He stood with his hands on his broad hips, looking up at Javik.

Javik nodded.

"Ooh!" Prince Pineapple said, coming up behind Javik. "What beautiful gar-bahge!"

"I think it's a goddamn mess," Javik said, sniffing a peculiar, metallic odor. "We'd better be careful. I don't see any nuclear material down there at first glance, though."

Javik made his way down the hill of scarlet flowers, followed by Prince Pineapple.

As they arrived, Rebo held up a blue tintette. "What's this?" he asked.

"Put it in your mouth," Javik said. "See if you can find a match and light it."

"It's a bomb? An Earthian suicide technique?"

Javik laughed. Looking up the hill, he saw Namaba loping toward them. "You smoke it," Javik said, looking back at Rebo. "Here, give it to me."

"Nice selection of imported gar-bahge here," Prince Pineapple said, picking through the rubble. "Here's a clock, a Charlie Choo-Choo lamp, and a couple of Batman comics."

"What's going on here?" Namaba asked.

Javik placed Rebo's tintette in his own mouth. "Anyone got a light?" he asked.

No one stepped forward.

"Well, I wanna do this right," Javik said with a bemused expression. "I'll be right back." He ran up the hill.

"How strange," Namaba said. She picked up three tintettes from the ground—one blue, one yellow, and one red.

"Put them in your mouth," Prince Pineapple said.

Presently, Javik returned with a tin of lightweight matches. "That's the way," he said, seeing Namaba with three tintettes in her mouth. "You'd be a super consumer on Earth."

"I'm doing it right?" she asked.

"Pick one," Javik said. "It will be easier."

She kept the red tintette, discarding the others.

"I'm gonna take some of this stuff with me," Prince Pineapple said, loading his arms with junk.

"Put that down for a minute," Javik said. "Prince, you and Rebo put tintettes in your mouths, too. We're all gonna have a smoke."

When all had tintettes firmly grasped between their lips, Javik told them to gather in a close circle. "You've done this before, haven't you, Prince?" Javik asked, as he struck a match,

"Oh, sure," Prince Pineapple said.

Javik lit the tintettes, then doused the match. "Watch me," he said, taking a deep puff. He let out a big puff of bright blue smoke.

Rebo took a shallow puff. "Ugh!" he said, coughing. "I'm your servant now, Captain Tom, but this is asking too much!" he discarded the tintette.

Prince Pineapple puffed and coughed, too.

Seeing red smoke curl out of Namaba's nostrils, Javik said, "That's it! I think she's got it!"

"What's the purpose of this?" she asked, gagging. She had an aghast expression. Her eyes rolled upward.

"I'm not much of a smoker myself," Javik said. "It's not a good habit to have in the cockpit."

"Earthians enjoy this?" she asked, picking a piece of tobacco out of her teeth.

"It's a leading pastime," Javik said.

Namaba shook her head in disbelief.

"Look, Namaba," Javik said, taking her arm and leading her up the hill. "There's something I've always wanted to try. We see it on home video all the time."

She looked at him inquisitively.

"Bring your tintette," he said.

They walked up the hill of scarlet flowers. The sky was blue and young, an intense, vibrant blue that has been known to grace the skies over lovers. The sweet, delicate aroma of mint touched Javik's nostrils whenever he kept the tintette away from his nose. He felt sublime.

Reaching a flat section of meadow at the top of the hill, Javik began to skip, sort of a jerky slow motion.

Namaba let go of his hand and laughed. "You look so silly!" she said. "What are you doing?"

"I've seen it on home video," Javik said. "It's in magazines, too, and on billboards. We're lovers, don't you see? Frolicking in a meadow with tintettes dangling from our mouths. It's the AmFed Dream. And we found it clear on the other side of the goddamn universe!"

Namaba took a puff of her tintette and tried to skip. But this turned out to be more of a jerk-hop, owing to her third leg. She coughed, puffed, and laughed, trailing red smoke behind her.

"Slower," Javik said. "Do it slower."

"But why?" Namaba asked, stopping and looking at him curiously.

"Because that's the way it's done on home video."

She skipped in slow motion, with movements that alternated between near grace and total clumsiness.

"Better," Javik exclaimed. He caught up with her and blew smoke in her face.

Namaba took this as a challenge. Gleefully, she inundated his face in smoke.

They had a short battle like this, then held hands and were off together, slowly skipping and jerk-hopping across the meadow.

"Hey!" Prince Pineapple yelled to them. "What are you doing?"

Javik envisioned a camera panning in on them as they frolicked in the flowers. He and Namaba were the stars of a videodome commercial, watched in more than three hundred million homes.

"What a commercial it would be," Javik exclaimed. "Me and a three-legger!"

Namaba stopped and looked at him with a hurt expression. "You're making fun of me?" she asked. She was breathing hard, with little puffs of steam coming from her ears and nostrils.

Javik smiled. He stretched up and gave her a little peck on the lips. "I was just being silly," he said.

They walked back toward Rebo and Prince Pineapple. At the sight of the prince, Javik was reminded of his recurring thought. Prince Pineapple so resembled a videodome cartoon character, and now the tintettes.... Javik discarded his tintette.

"Hurry!" Prince Pineapple yelled. "We've a long way to go today." His arms were full of salvaged garbage.

"Hey," Javik said turning to Namaba. "Remember how silly Wizzy was yesterday in the woods?"

"We've found our moment of happiness," she said, flipping her tintette away with surprising expertness. Namaba looked down at Javik. Her eyes sparkled.

*This is no goddamn dream,* Javik thought. *And I'm glad it isn't.*

They stopped, and their lips touched in the Earth way. Javik hardly heard Prince Pineapple as he continued to yell at them. Javik and Namaba were in their own little world. He wanted it to last forever.

O O O

Brother Carrot stood in morning sunlight on the foredeck of the *Freedom One*, watching his troops disembark. His fleet bobbed in gentle waves next to the granite wall that comprised the limits of the new lake. Carrot soldiers clattered down wooden gangways to the top of the wall. From there they climbed freestyle to the ground.

"Kill the Fruits!" Brother Carrot bellowed, using a megaphone.

His men cheered.

When the *Freedom One* had been unloaded, Brother Carrot strode triumphantly down the gangway, waving his black and gold cap.

His troops shouted and cheered their adulation.

O O O

Lord Abercrombie watched helplessly while the Vegetable army marched on the Corker stronghold. After causing so much earthquake damage with his disaster machine, Lord Abercrombie was disaster-shy, afraid to make things worse.

It was mid-morning when Brother Carrot led his men past Javik's ship. Rays of sunlight glinted off the undented portions of the ship's titanium body. Brother Carrot felt warm from the exertion of the brisk march down from what had once been Dusty Desert. He loosened his collar.

"To victory, lads!" he yelled in the megaphone. "Send the Fruits to their gory, juicy beds!" Looking back, he saw six black and gold uniformed carrot colonels who marched in front of six columns of rifle-carrying carrot men. Each colonel sported a black and gold cap like Brother Carrot's, except the colonel's caps had much thinner strands of gold braid on the brims.

The colonels passed Brother Carrot's message on down the lines, using their own, smaller power megaphones.

Boisterous hurrahs rose from the ranks.

Between Brother Carrot and the colonels, fifteen of the strongest, meanest carrot men in the Vegetable army pulled a towering wood and plastic catapult. Beside that rolled the Fruit Doom bomb trailer, pulled by six carrot men. The Fruit Doom bomb was big, round, and black—a deadly sphere that Brother Carrot knew would annihilate his enemies. Being a live bomb, it buzzed loudly.

Brother Carrot smiled at the thought of King Corker's demise. Then he turned and thundered, "There is plunder ahead, lads! Plunder for all!"

"Plunder!" the colonels announced to the majors, not quite as loudly as Brother Carrot.

"Plunder!" the majors yelled in unison, their megaphoned voices not as loud as those of their superiors.

And so the message went down the lines, until the corporals had their opportunities, too. "Plunder!" they squealed gleefully.

Bawdy cheers ran through the ranks.

The army narrowed to double file, negotiating a trail through the woods. Then it widened to six columns again as it emerged on the other side.

The earthquake-ravaged remains of Corker Stadium loomed ahead beneath a cerulean blue sky. Corkers and other Fruits in their path fled the advancing juggernaut. Some of the more foolish Fruits sat regally in their carriages, commanding carrot man slaves to pull them to safety. A dark cloud passed in front of the suns, throwing Corker Stadium into shadow.

A hundred meters to his left, Brother Carrot watched a team of six carrot man slaves unharness themselves, leaving a pudgy casaba man stranded in his carriage. The casaba man was furious, and he shook his fist at them, shrieking, "Back to your stations! Back to your stations!"

Brother Carrot waved his cap triumphantly.

His troops cheered.

The six freed slaves waved to Brother Carrot and shouted their support. Then they overturned the carriage, sending their pudgy former master fleeing for his life. Shouting boisterously and waving clenched fists, they ran to join their brethren in the Vegetable army.

More slave teams joined Brother Carrot as he marched through the Corker shopping district. The slaves brought stones, clubs, and anything else on which they could lay their hands.

The burgeoning army entered the expressway now, marching by abandoned Fruit carriages and the bodies of Fruits who had been killed by their slaves. Brother Carrot pushed down the brim of his cap, shielding his eyes from the suns.

They rounded a turn, bringing the rocky fortress of Corker Castle into view. Brother Carrot saw Fruits streaming across a drawbridge, entering the castle through the main gate. Purple Corkers lined the walkways and ramparts, their weapons glinting in the sunlight.

"There it is, lads!" Brother Carrot yelled, waving his cap once more.

His men cheered again, and a thunderous cheer it was. For now the ranks were swelled with thousands of freed slaves.

They passed a green expressway sign that read "CORKER CASTLE—NEXT EXIT."

Now Brother Carrot increased the marching tempo, and his men quick-stepped up the exit ramp. Ahead, the castle drawbridge was being closed. Those Fruits who were not able to get sanctuary fled in all directions.

"Onward, lads!" Brother Carrot urged.

Rifle shots rang out from the castle and echoed down the valley. Then a Corker cannon roared. The cannonball arched and landed short of Brother Carrot, off to his right in a banana grove.

A gunnery officer caught up with Brother Carrot, saying, "We should set up here, sir. We're just out of range of their guns."

"Halt!" Brother Carrot boomed to his colonels.

The command echoed down the columns, and finally the army ground to a halt.

"Over here!" the gunnery officer barked, motioning to the carrot men in charge of the catapult.

The catapult squadron positioned the big wooden siege machine on a flat parking strip. Outriggers were cranked down. Then the Fruit Doom bomb was wheeled over and loaded onto the catapult's sling.

"Carefully, men," Brother Carrot said. "Load it carefully!"

Rifle and cannon shots continued to ring out from the castle. One cannon ball rolled close to the empty bomb trailer and bounced off a fir tree.

"Hurry men," Brother Carrot yelled. "That was too close."

"Ready, sir," the gunnery officer reported.

"Aim carefully," Brother Carrot said to the gunnery officer. "We'll only get one shot."

"Better move it a quarter of a degree left," the gunnery officer said, standing next to the siege machine and eyeballing the target. "And raise it just a hair."

Carrot men spun positioning dials as the gunnery officer spoke. A platform holding the catapult arm shifted.

"There!" the gunnery officer shouted.

"That's it?" Brother Carrot asked. He heard the bomb buzzing.

"Yes, sir."

"Then let 'er go!" Brother Carrot shouted.

The gunnery officer moved a toggle on the side of the catapult, causing the long mechanical arm to snap forward. The Fruit Doom bomb arched toward Corker Castle, spinning slowly in the air. To Brother Carrot, the projectile seemed to travel in slow motion. He knew it was a terrible weapon to use. But it would prevent Fruit and Vegetable deaths in the field.

"Oh, no!" someone said. "It's going in too low!"

"No," the gunnery officer said, stretching and using body motions to urge the bomb a little higher. "I think it'll just barely …"

Brother Carrot covered his face with his hands.

The Fruit Doom bomb arched just over the castle wall, landing in the courtyard. A mushroom-shaped black cloud rose over the doomed castle.

This brought a tremendous cheer from the Vegetable troops.

Brother Carrot peeked between his fingers.

"On target, sir," the gunnery officer reported.

O O O

When the bomb hit, King Corker was standing on a balcony overlooking the courtyard of his castle. He was in the middle of shouting a command to the captain of the Corker guards when a warning trumpet sounded.

Before anyone could react, the courtyard was swarming with voracious, razor-toothed fruit flies. King Corker had only half turned toward his room when the flies caught him. He died a terrible death, his flesh consumed in a horde of frenzied attackers.

The screams of dying Fruits filled the air.

O O O

From the other side of the moat, Brother Carrot heard the screams. Five minutes later, a pervasive, deathly silence settled over Corker Castle. Brother Carrot knew it was over. He felt bad about it, but knew it was something that had to be done.

After another five minutes, Brother Carrot gave the Command to turn on the Mother Hummer. When his men were slow to react, he snapped angrily, "Faster, men. We don't want flies killing all the Fruits in the valley. Who would do our work for us?"

Two soldiers jumped now, flipping switches on the sides of the bomb trailer. A large, clear plastic funnel rose out of the trailer bed. A loud drone-whir filled the air, throbbing and pulsating with that one sound no tiger fruit fly could ignore.

A steady stream of flies left Corker Castle now, making a straight course for the trailer. They disappeared into the funnel.

"Beastly little creatures," Brother Carrot said to his gunnery officer.

"Yes, but cross-bred with herpes stock to perfection!"

"War is hell," Brother Carrot said, watching the last flies enter the funnel. Looking up with moist eyes, he saw slaves all along the castle walkways. Some lowered the purple Corker banner. Most of the slaves were carrot men, but Brother Carrot spotted occasional cucumber, lettuce, and cabbage people.

Five plump tomato girls from King Corker's harem appeared on one wall now, waving white lace and squealing so loudly that Brother Carrot could hear their words from across the moat. "Long live Brother Carrot!" they said. "Long live Brother Carrot!"

While Brother Carrot watched, the drawbridge was lowered. Then he brushed dust off his uniform and called all the officers forward. "This is our moment in history, lads!" he told them.

O O O

Soon after that, Brother Carrot led a company of men along the short, curving section of road that led to Corker Castle. The men had grown quiet, and Brother Carrot knew why. Each of them had imagined this moment for so long, in so many waking and sleeping dreams, that now they could only savor it with their eyes.

Layers of puffy white clouds moved rapidly across the sky. To Brother Carrot they looked like the fleeing ghosts of fat little Corkers. He smiled.

The smile hardened when three dead banana men came into view. They were laying face up in a grassy planting area at the center of the road. Most of their flesh had been torn away by the savage fruit flies.

"See that?" Brother Carrot said to the company colonel as they passed. "Good slaves. We could have called the flies back a little earlier."

The colonel nodded and murmured in solemn agreement.

They reached an uphill straightaway now, with high English hedges on each side, the last stretch before reaching the castle. Brother Carrot felt his pace quicken. The men chatted excitedly in low tones. Freed Vegetable slaves cheered wildly and waved brightly colored cloths from the castle walls above.

The drawbridge was only a few steps away when a wrinkled old prune woman in a frumpy brown dress stepped through an opening in the hedge. Stopping at the side of the road, she leaned her chin on a carved wood cane and stared up at Brother Carrot. She had a most curious expression on her face. Brother Carrot judged it to be a combination of sadness and bemused tolerance. He wondered how she had survived the Fruit Doom bomb.

"Greetings, Brother Carrot," the old woman said in a throaty voice. "And greetings to your lean, hungry warriors." She used one hand to smooth her dress.

Brother Carrot raised his right arm, causing the procession to stop. The old woman was terribly wrinkled, and her skin was a pale plum shade. The eyes were unmistakably sad, Brother Carrot decided. And the mouth was mildly amused. "How long have you been here?" he asked.

"All the time," she rasped.

"Why didn't the flies get you. Are you a magician? Or a witch?"

The old woman laughed. It was a wheezing, choppy laugh, like the strainings of an engine that didn't have long to run. "What would flies want with an old prune lady?" she asked. "My skin has lost its sweet bloom. It is old and leathery."

Brother Carrot stared at her.

"I am Priscilla the Prunesayer," she said. "Once I was a lovely young plum, easily the fairest in the land."

"And now you tell fortunes?"

She straightened for a moment, then leaned on the cane again. "That is correct."

"And what is mine, old woman?"

"Why, the same as King Corker's, naturally."

"You mean I will die?" he asked.

"We all die sometime," Priscilla the Prunesayer said.

"That wasn't what I meant," Brother Carrot said. He stepped close to her, intending to grill her militarily with questions.

The old prune woman closed her eyes, and a serene expression crossed her face. Then she tottered for a moment.

Brother Carrot reached out to steady her, but she slumped to the ground.

"I think she's dead, sir," the company colonel said.

O O O

As Brother Carrot looked down on the prunesayer's body, thousands of Fruits fled the area. Many ran up the trail toward the lake that covered Dusty Desert. Others crossed the western grasslands. Still more reached the eastern seashore and took to boats.

Two who escaped by boat were Matteo and Nacho Pear. They used their own sailboat, not at all a large craft—less than eight meters in length and sloop rigged. Matteo and Nacho had sailed it often to the small unnamed island they saw now across the strait, on picnics and other happy occasions. This island was the first in a necklace of isles that stretched across the sea. Legend told them this. The brothers planned to hop from one landfall to the next, seeking refuge as far away as possible.

But never before had they sailed beyond the first island.

Feeling a strong wind against his face, Matteo pulled the mainsail halyard. He thought of the good times he and Nacho had enjoyed on this boat. A dark cloud structure bore down on them from the sea, bringing with it a chill wind and a misty rain. He secured the mainsail, then raised the jib.

The little boat began to pick up speed.

"I'll get even with those rotten Vegetables!" Nacho yelled. He stood at the tiller, finding the best angle on the wind.

Matteo heard these words as he knelt in the bow, securing the bowline on a cleat. He saw the dark outline of the unnamed island on the horizon. "Death to the Vegetables!" he bellowed.

O O O

In less than a day Lord Abercrombie would soil-immerse himself permanently. There would be enough time to look over his recycling facility and meckies one last time.

For now, he was soil-immersed in the usual half-committed way, knowing he would be back in Flesh in a matter of hours. With the visual and auditory sensors in each droplet of seawater, Lord Abercrombie heard the angry words of the pear brothers. He saw the lumpy form of Matteo as Matteo fine-tuned the rigging to get the most speed out of the boat. And he saw Nacho at the tiller, trying to steer a straight course in changing winds.

With countless sensors all over the planet, Lord Abercrombie eavesdropped on other Fruits as they vowed eternal revenge. All this triggered a moment of introspection in Lord Abercrombie. The past and future of his planet appeared before him like a magnificent, fluxing historical tapestry.

Vagabond Fruit armies made thrust after thrust against a fat and sedentary Vegetable kingdom. The Fruits were lean and oppressed, with all the power and fury of righteousness on their side. In fast forward across the tapestry, he saw the Fruits in power again, with wronged Vegetables hiding in the hinterlands plotting revolution. These Vegetables were led by Brother Carrot. The cycle repeated itself over and over in much the same pattern. Different faces appeared and disappeared. But the words and deeds were much the same.

Lord Abercrombie laughed at the timeless folly of the situation. Every pore of the planet echoed his laughter. Then the laughter became a storm of embarrassed rage, for Abercrombie came to understand the foolishness of his own paranoid fears. His laughing rage blew across the surface of Cork in a powerful, howling wind.

O O O

It was late morning, and Prince Pineapple walked briskly along the dirt meadow trail, well ahead of the others. Over one shoulder he carried a dark green gortex stuff sack Javik had let him use. The sack rattled, being full of treasures from the AmFed garbage canister. The jagged white cliffs ahead seemed just as far away now as when they broke camp. He quickened his step.

He became aware of distant laughter. It seemed to bounce off the white cliffs, traveling on an angry wind across the scarlet flower petals of the meadow. He felt the wind pick up now, pressing the flowers around him against the ground. The laughter became loud. Menacingly loud.

Frightened, he turned and bolted back down the trail.

Javik saw Prince Pineapple running back at full speed, with his bag bouncing on his back and his pineapple face contorted in terror. "Run!" Prince Pineapple yelled. His black button eyes were wild.

Javik heard the laughter now. It grew louder as Prince Pineapple approached, becoming a thunderous, booming cacophany as the prince ran screaming by. Javik covered his ears. He and the Moravians fell to the ground.

Looking back, Javik saw Prince Pineapple trip and fall.

The laughter grew fainter now. Soon it was gone.

"What the hell was that?" Javik asked. He became aware of a pain in his right hand. Namaba had been squeezing it too tightly. She was wearing the lemon yellow vari-temp coat and pants he had given her.

Namaba released her grip. "I don't know," she said.

Prince Pineapple crawled back with his bag, joining the others. "Is it gone?" he asked.

O O O

They increased their pace after that, walking so hard toward the cliffs that Javik felt a muscle pain in the front of one thigh. Late morning became midday, then mid-afternoon. Three Corkian suns baked the travelers and withered the flowers along the trail. Perspiration covered Javik's body. He wiped his brow often with moist-pak towelettes.

Heat waves simmered in the distance. Javik shielded his eyes with one hand to look at the white cliffs ahead. "That bog has to be way behind us," he said. "But I'd swear those cliffs were not one step closer than this morning."

Prince Pineapple fell to the ground in a heap. "Let's rest," he said. "A little nap … a recharge …" He was lying in a bed of flowers asleep as the last word crossed his lips.

"Sounds good to me," Javik said.

"Hand me that shovel and cord," Rebo said. "I'd like to recharge and go on ahead a ways."

Javik unhooked the nutrient kit from his belt and handed it to Rebo. "You think something's just ahead?" Javik asked.

"It's his yenta," Namaba said acidly.

"I just feel a little restless," Rebo said, smiling crisply at Namaba.

"And I don't claim to have any damned yenta."

Namaba sat back on her haunches and smiled apologetically. "Sorry I picked at you," she said. "I'm tired."

Rebo took the shovel and cord a few paces off the path and went through the now familiar recharging ritual.

Moments later, Javik saw Rebo's tripod form loping away on the trail ahead, framed against the distant white cliffs. Javik watched him for a while, then removed a tiny yellow plastic square from a side pocket of his survival pack. The square was smaller than a sugar cube. At Javik's mento-command, it flowered into a white sheet lean-to with three foam pads on the ground.

Manually, Javik moved the lean-to so that it afforded shade for Prince Pineapple. "Don't want any cooked pineapple," Javik said, winking at Namaba.

She smiled.

Javik and Namaba settled down for a nap on two of the pads, using the remaining shade of the lean-to. Before falling asleep, Javik asked Namaba about her mother. "She was an alchemist, wasn't she?" he said.

"Uh huh. I used to help her with her experiments. I caused the fire that nearly killed both of us, you know. If it hadn't been for Rebo happening along."

"I'll have to thank Rebo for that sometime," Javik said. "No. That might be rubbing it in. Do you think he's jealous?"

"Yeah. But he likes you."

Javik grunted.

"My mother used to call me Nama," she said.

Javik was tired and silly. "Your mama called you Nama?" he said.

"Oh, you!" She tickled him in the side.

Hearing the rhyme in his sleep, Prince Pineapple did a powerful backflip, knocking over the lean-to and clicking his heels when he was airborne. He landed in an angry heap in the rubble of the lean-to. "What the hell?" he said, still not fully awake. Moments later: "Who said a rhyme!"

"Uh … sorry," Javik said. "You heard that in your sleep?"

"That's the most dangerous time, when my muscles are relaxed!" Angrily, he pushed the twisted lean-to away and curled up on the ground.

Javik straightened the lean-to and set up resting places under it again for himself and Namaba.

"You can call me Nama, too," Namaba said, suppressing a giggle.

Javik stretched out on a pad next to her. "Are you sure?" he asked.

"I wish you would."

O O O

Wizzy lost all sense of time. His memories faded like the decaying thoughts of an old man. His attention span grew baby short. He was a rock now, condemned to sleep in a bed of slime.

Bursts of anger from the life remaining in him were drowned out in a muddy death that permeated every cell of his magical body. Like a dying fleshcarrier looking for a warm place to curl up and die, he burrowed deeper in the mud. Soon he reached firm, moist soil.

Then, in a quick, angry thrust of his remaining energy, he darted a short distance between two rocks, pushing soil behind him as he went. This blocked the short tunnel he had dug, preventing Bottomless Bog's slime from advancing through it.

Only barely conscious, Wizzy found himself in a tiny, dry underground chamber. He glowed a sickly shade of yellow, then flickered out. It was the quietest, darkest place in the universe.

# CHAPTER FOURTEEN

*Often it is a matter of degree. It is wrong, but not that wrong; right, but not that right. It seems that black and white are ideals, obtainable only by paint pigments, and even there …*

A Timeless Truth

It was nearly time for Lord Abercrombie's final soil immersion. He moved from metal man to metal woman, inspecting his meckies for the last time. Using a chamois cloth, he burnished a brass "REBUILT" plaque here, flicked dust off a shoulder there. It was a solemn occasion, with all the meckies standing in three neat rows near Lord Abercrombie's throne.

Wearing a cardinal red caftan with gold scrollwork on the sleeve and half collar, Lord Abercrombie glided to his throne. He felt a final urge to sit upon it and look out at his underground mechanical staff. The black satin cushions felt soft beneath his half bottom. "I'm leaving soon," he said.

A blue female meckie rolled forward from the ranks, asking, "You've made a decision, Lord?" This was the artistically programmed linguistics expert, the one with the gargling voice.

"I have."

"Flesh or Magic?" the meckie asked.

"Magic. It may not be the correct decision, but at least it's a decision. That's something, anyway."

"Good luck, Lord Abercrombie. What should I put on the history wall?"

"I'll take care of that myself. If I turn into any sort of a decent magical planet, that should be a minor matter." Lord Abercrombie felt a tear welling up in his human eye. The thought of never seeing his recycling facility again was a burden. Then he remembered the visual sensors he would have when he became the planet. Still, it would not be the same.

The blue meckie rolled back into the ranks.

"You've all done your best," Lord Abercrombie said. "I want each of you to know that." He rubbed his eye.

"Goodbye, Lord," the meckies said in unison. They waved stiffly and noisily, clanking their metal arms.

Lord Abercrombie glided to the corridor. He heard mechanical voices behind him in the main chamber, and poked his head back in. The linguistics meckie was touching the arm of his throne, acting as though she wanted to sit upon it.

"Go ahead," Lord Abercrombie said, smiling softly in his half-faced way.

She started. Turning to face him, she said, "You mean sit on it?"

"Sure. Why not? It's of no use to me anymore." He turned and left.

As he negotiated the intricate maze of passageways leading to the Soil Immersion Chamber, Lord Abercrombie did not feel happy or sad. It was a numb, neutral feeling, possibly in preparation for the killing of his remaining fleshy self.

Minutes later, he dropped into the immersion hole with more than a little trepidation. Sitting down, he covered his fleshy leg with dirt. The soil was warm. He closed his human eye and visual sensors and lay back in the hole. Warmth greeted his fleshy half-backside.

In a flurry, Abercrombie used his hand to pull dirt over the rest of his exposed skin. His hand was last in. It remained outside for several seconds. Then it made a waving motion and pulled itself into the hole.

*Goodbye,* Abercrombie thought. *And hello.*

O O O

After a short nap, Javik recharged. He felt fresh. Returning to the lean-to, he nudged Namaba to awaken her. "We'd better get going," he said. "Should try to cover more ground before dark."

She sat up and yawned.

O O O

Namaba was just completing her recharge when she noticed Rebo loping toward them from uptrail.

"You've got to see this," Rebo shouted. "It's just up the trail."

"What's up the trail?" Namaba asked, handing the folding shovel and barbed cord to Javik.

"You've got to see it," Rebo said.

"You're not making any sense," Javik said.

Prince Pineapple stirred from his nap and sat up. "What's all the commotion?" he asked.

"Come with me," Rebo said, almost too excited to speak. He pulled at Javik's arm.

"All right, all right," Javik said. He secured the nutrient kit to his belt.

"Wait," Prince Pineapple said, rising to his feet. "I need a recharge."

"Hurry," Rebo said. "No one will believe this."

Javik tossed the nutrient kit to Prince Pineapple. "Make it quick, Prince."

While Prince Pineapple recharged, Javik mentoed the lean-to and pads. With a crisp snap, they popped back into the tiny yellow cube. Javik replaced the cube in a side pocket of his survival pack. Seeing an empty bio bar wrapper in the pack, he tossed it out on the meadow.

After Prince Pineapple was allowed an abbreviated recharge, they all went with Rebo. The meadow sweltered in the afternoon heat of three Corkian suns. Soon Javik was perspiring again. Waves of hot air danced ahead of them, blurring features on the white cliff.

At the rear, Prince Pineapple complained about the shortness of his recharge. His bag of junk clattered as he walked.

Rebo ran ahead, then waved and called for the others to hurry.

"Rebo's gone mad," Javik said. "His brain is sun-baked."

"I've never seen him like this," Namaba said.

"We'd better catch him," Javik said. "And make him lie down in the . . ." Javik stopped in mid-sentence. Rebo had disappeared!

"Where'd he go?" Namaba asked.

"Magic!" Prince Pineapple said.

They heard Rebo's voice now, but could not see him. It seemed to come from the trail just ahead. But the meadow was perfectly flat here, with no places that might conceal Rebo's large body.

"Rebo!" Namaba shouted. "Where are you?"

"A little way up the trail. Keep going."

They walked cautiously, following Javik. He took each step with care, testing the ground before committing the weight of his body.

"There is magic in this meadow," Prince Pineapple said.

"Hey!" Namaba said, running into Javik's back.

He had stopped suddenly in front of her. "My foot!" Javik said. "Look at it!"

Namaba saw the back half of his foot. But the front was gone. When Javik pulled his foot back, she saw it in its entirety.

"An invisible barrier," Javik said. He reached back and took Prince Pineapple's bag of junk. While the prince protested, Javik threw the bag forward. It disappeared, landing somewhere with a loud clatter.

"Quit throwing things at me," Rebo said, still unseen. "That darn near hit me!"

Javik took a deep breath and stuck his face through. There was no physical sensation at all. He saw Rebo standing on a piece of white shale at the base of a towering cliff. Above, the sheer face of the escarpment was profiled against a deep blue sky. The scene was so awesome and so surprising that Javik felt a shortness of breath.

"Don't hold back," Rebo said.

Javik stepped through, followed by the others. A series of "oohs," "aahs," and "wows" followed,

"I told you it was magic," Prince Pineapple said. He found his sack of trash and swung it noisily over one shoulder.

"We were getting close to this cliff all day," Rebo said, "but didn't know it." He touched a triangular dot pattern on the cliff at his side, then pointed to Javik's left, where a trail ran between the cliff and the edge of the meadow. "More dots that way," Rebo said.

"We might have given up and turned back," Javik said, scratching his head. "And it was here all the time."

"What do you think, Prince?" Rebo asked. "Did the magicians create that illusion, or was it Lord Abercrombie?"

"I don't know," Prince Pineapple said. His black button eyes squinted as he stared up the face of the cliff.

"How far up the trail did you go, Rebo?" Namaba asked. The yellow and black polka-dotted ribbon fell from her mane and fluttered away in the wind, unnoticed by her or the others.

"Not far," Rebo said, "Moha should be ahead, whatever that is."

"Moha," Prince Pineapple said, feeling a chill run down his back. "Something is coming back to me. A Moha is spoken of in one of our epics. It is a fearsome thing—a terrible monster."

"It would have been nice to know this earlier," Javik said, staring at the prince with his hands on his hips. "Don't suppose we have much choice now, though. No way to cross that bog again."

"What sort of monster is it?" Namaba asked.

"I don't know," Prince Pineapple said. "Didn't pay much attention to epics in school. It destroyed a Fruit army, I think."

"It is best not to hesitate," Rebo said, recalling his gang warfare days. "Sometimes the thought of a thing can be more terrifying than the reality."

They set out along the trail at the base of the cliff, looking for three-dot markings.

O O O

With the decision to commit himself, Lord Abercrombie changed rapidly. His fleshy half disappeared entirely. His mind became more expansive, capable of deeper, more significant thought. He was the planet Cork now, more than ever before. His face became the face of the planet that was exposed to the heavens.

With his visual sensors, he looked out upon the grays and blacks of night on one side of Cork. On the other side, he observed varying shades of color, from sky blues to the oranges, reds, and yellows of dawn and sunset. He told himself he was thinking about important things. Cosmic things.

*I have a comparatively large planet,* he thought. *Some are bigger than mine, but most are smaller. Earth is smaller!*

The comparison with Earth made him happy, for it seemed to him that he was more important now than Uncle Rosy or any other Earthian. It was a territorial thing: The guy with the most turf was superior.

*Maybe this can be a stepping stone to something greater,* he thought. *A method of conquering other worlds could occur to me.*

He rubbed the plates of two continents together to relieve an itch. It was an automatic movement, and it surprised him.

*Hmm,* he thought. *Think I'll try that again.* He rubbed the continents together again in just the same way.

*I'll bet I can wipe out Brother Carrot now,* he thought. *And Prince Pineapple, too! I might have done it earlier, if I hadn't been afraid to commit myself.*

But this prospect did not appeal to him very much. It seemed beneath him, a trapping of his former self. Besides, with Abercrombie soil-immersed, the chamber entrance leading down from the surface of the planet was sealed.

*A major planet does not concern itself with fleas,* he thought.

So Lord Abercrombie concentrated on more important matters. On the night side of his planet, he saw deep space, with more stars and bright planets than all the grains of sand in his deserts. He wondered who out there might be plotting at that very moment to invade his territory via the Dimensional Tunnel.

*I can't seal the damned thing,* he thought. *Anyone entering the Dimensional Tunnel from another planet could land on my doorstep. Uninvited. Well, go ahead and try. I'll give you one hell of a fight.*

His paranoia raged anew, but on a much larger scale than before. He recalled having laughed at the foolishness of his own fears when he thought he had seen the Big Picture. His laughter roared across the surface of the planet then. But nothing seemed at all funny to him anymore.

A cloud of silver meteorites passed near Cork on the dark side, and Lord Abercrombie could see that they were going to miss him by a good fifty thousand kilometers.

*This way!* he thought, wanting more bulk for his surface.

But the meteorites went on their inconsiderate way, leaving a space trail of sparkling silver embers.

When the embers had died out, a flash of orange lit up the blackness of space. Something was approaching at high speed, growing larger and more brilliant with each passing second. Lord Abercrombie's joy overflowed, like the anticipation of a spider about to ensnare a tasty fly. It was a large orange ball, bearing down on him.

*Nice meteor,* he thought. *Come a little closer.*

Seconds later, Lord Abercrombie blinked his visual sensors. *Wait,* he thought. *It's getting too big. My God! It's huge!*

He began to wonder who was ensnaring whom.

The orange fireball became so bright that Lord Abercrombie could not keep his visual sensors open. At the last moment the fireball turned and went the other way. When Abercrombie next looked, through slit-wide sensors, he saw a great orange comet, with a long, translucent tail that stretched across the sky in a graceful, orange thread of light.

The comet swung around to Abercrombie's daylight side and headed toward him again. Again he was forced to close his visual sensors in the brightness. Abercrombie felt the comet sear through his atmosphere. He smelled sulfur and waited for the impact. Strangely, he felt no heat on his surface.

O O O

Sidney the comet swooped over Bottomless Bog, then returned and hovered there. The cadmium yellow outline of a face appeared across his flaming orange nucleus. Sidney smiled gently.

*Be patient, Wizzy,* he thought, looking down on the bog tenderly. *A million years is but a moment. You' II be free someday, my son. Then you'll do wondrous things.*

O O O

Lord Abercrombie tried to open all his visual sensors, but repeatedly was blinded by the brightness of the Great Comet. The comet irritated him. It hovered in his face like a giant, fat mosquito, and he had no arms with which to swat it.

Lord Abercrombie searched his surface until he found a bank of visual sensors he could keep open. As chance would have it, these sensors were on decaying plants floating just beneath the surface of Bottomless Bog. He peered through the murky water of the bog, using the water as a fleshcarrier uses sunglasses.

He saw the smile on the face of the comet now, and it seemed to be smiling directly at the sensors he had open. *It knows I can't do anything,* Abercrombie thought. *It's laughing at me.*

Lord Abercrombie created a hurricane. It was quite a powerful hurricane, and it broadsided the comet, bringing with it a gathering of cumulonimbus clouds. This did not bother the intruder at all. The comet continued to smile.

*It thinks it's superior to me,* Abercrombie thought, fuming. *It's prettier, more mobile.*

Now Abercrombie built formations of towering, anvil-topped clouds around the sides of the comet. Bolts of lightning lanced into the comet. Thunder roared across the sky. Abercrombie attacked until he felt fatigue. Again, this did not faze the comet.

*It must have a weakness,* the frustrated planet thought. *But what could it be?*

Lord Abercrombie considered letting loose a torrential downpour on the comet. But he felt rock weary, and the thought of such an attack seemed ludicrous to him. The fireball was so immense that only part of it was in the planet's atmosphere; much of it extended into deep space.

O O O

Just before the appearance of the comet, Prince Pineapple insisted on another recharge. The charge he had received earlier that afternoon had been short because of all the excitement generated by Rebo. It needed augmentation, and he selected a spot along the trail at the base of the white cliff.

Prince Pineapple closed his eyes and went into a trance during his recharge, as he was wont to do. It was at the height of this ecstasy that the Great Comet appeared in the sky over this side of the planet.

When the sky flashed orange, Javik and the Moravians covered their eyes and dove for the ground. Namaba cried out that the sky was on fire.

"I don't think so," Javik said, unable to look. "My guess is that it's a comet or a big meteor. And it's awfully close."

They heard the pounding of thunder in the distance and wondered if this was the end for them.

O O O

Lord Abercrombie wanted the minerals, gases, and other materials in the comet. With them he would be infinitely larger, infinitely more powerful. A force to be respected in the universe.

*I must move out of orbit,* he thought, *if I'm going to make any sort of a showing in battle. Why isn't the comet attacking? Is it teasing me?*

Lord Abercrombie tried to move his planet out of orbit. "Uuumph!" he grunted.

Cork did not budge.

*Now that would really be something,* he thought. *To move around wherever I want, whenever I want.*

The thought of this so appealed to him that he tried again. Over and over he tried. But Lord Abercrombie did not budge one centimeter out of orbit.

*Maybe I just need to try a little harder,* he thought.

So he concentrated every bit of energy he had. The nutrients on Cork's surface began flowing to his core as Lord Abercrombie called upon them for support.

*These nutrients are mine,* he thought. *No more sharing them with fleas on my surface!*

O O O

Sidney the comet focused his attention on the meadow of scarlet flowers. He saw Javik covering his eyes and prone on the ground at the other end of the meadow, at the base of the white cliff.

*My lifelong friend,* Sidney thought. *May good fortune grace your steps.*

It troubled Sidney that Javik would have to die comparatively soon, limited as he was by the frailties of flesh. Sidney wished he could offer Javik the longer life of a comet or perhaps a small star so that they might spend more time together.

But it was only a passing thought, one of those space dreams that magical comets are known to have. Sidney looked back down at Bottomless Bog.

O O O

Lord Abercrombie felt the nutrients of living forms surge into his core. He was absorbing entire flowers, small trees, and shrubs, along with many Fruits and Vegetables who were recharging at that moment. Many of the hardier flowers on the planet held out against his gluttony, as did most of the large plants.

O O O

With one foot in the ground, Prince Pineapple was at the height of his recharge. It was that euphoric point where all the juices from the soil flowed at full force through his pineapple veins. With his eyes closed, he leaned back on both elbows and savored the moment.

Then he screamed. "Eeeeah! Eeeeah!" The skin on his exposed foot stretched nearly to the breaking point. Something powerful was pulling at it! He tried to open his eyes, but a blinding fire across the sky prevented it.

"Help!" Prince Pineapple shouted. "For God's sake, hurry!"

Javik followed the sound and crawled to Prince Pineapple's side. "What's wrong?" Javik asked. Shielding his eyes, he squinted to look at the prince. A cluster of flowers within Javik's narrow range of vision disappeared into the ground with a loud *fwwwp-pop* suction noise. He heard the pops of suction all around and saw the ground color lighten.

Prince Pineapple did not respond. He was unconscious. But his bare foot was moving sporadically, jerking like a bodily limb consumed with the throes of death.

*I've got to get him out of there,* Javik thought.

Flowers were disappearing beneath the surface at a furious pace now, leaving all the ground that Javik could see denuded.

Javik pulled on Prince Pineapple's arms. Then he realized that his hands were stuck to the prince. He could not pull them free and could not get Prince Pineapple out of the hole.

"It's got me, too!" Javik yelled. "Knock me away, somebody! Use that survival pack I left on the rock!"

Since Namaba was closest, she felt with her eyes closed until she found the pack. Then she felt Rebo's firm grip on her arm.

"This is *my* duty," Rebo said. He took the pack and crawled rapidly over to Javik. Keeping his eyes closed, he swung the pack until it struck Javik.

"Harder!" Javik screamed.

Rebo gave the survival pack a mighty swing, knocking Javik free. Prince Pineapple remained stuck to Javik, so he, too, was knocked away from the hole.

"It's … the end of the world," Prince Pineapple said, rolling on the ground and moaning. He was short of breath.

"I think we're okay," Javik said, catching his breath. "If that's the comet, it's probably over the bog where Wizzy was lost."

They spoke without opening their eyes, like people in a dark room.

"You mean it's Wizzy's dad?" Namaba asked. She squeezed Javik's hand.

"That's what I'm thinkin'," Javik said.

"I was almost recharged," Prince Pineapple said after a while, beginning to breathe regularly. "Something started pulling on my foot … sucking on it. I might have been pulled underground."

"We're even now, Rebo," Javik said. "You're no longer indebted to me."

"My obligation did not end when I saved you," Rebo said. "That is not our way. It is a lifelong thing."

A furious rhythm came from the meadow now, drowning out all conversation.

*Fwwwp-pop!*

*Fwwwp-fwwwp-pop!*

*Fwwwpop-da-dee-pop!*

*Fwwwp-pop-ditty-pop-ditty-pop-pop-pop!*

In the next instant, the ground rumbled. Then everything fell silent. The sucking sounds stopped, and there seemed to be no life in the vicinity other than their own.

O O O

Lord Abercrombie exploded out of his immersion hole, bouncing off the rock ceiling of the cavern. Dirt flew everywhere.

His scream echoed through the passageway. "Eeeeah!"

Abercrombie floated back down in slow motion, supported by a parachute of magical air. His naked body was different now. It still was partly magical and partly fleshy. But now it was a mixture, with splotches of skin next to empty spaces … a knuckle here … a knee there … both thighs … two hands but only one arm … the top of his skull …

Gradually, all the fleshy places filled in. When Abercrombie landed, his body was entirely flesh again. In an awakening haze, he tried to crawl back in the hole. But unseen hands pushed him away, gently but firmly.

*I'm rejected,* Abercrombie thought. *The Realm of Magic does not want me!*

Wearing nothing but his wardrobe ring, he stumbled out of the Soil Immersion Chamber into the labyrinth of passageways. The maze had once been second nature to him. But now he walked aimlessly in wrong directions, tripping and falling often. He scraped his knees, shins, and arms on the hard, rocky ground. The pain made his sensation of rejection even more acute. Only fleshcarriers felt such pain.

O O O

Sidney the comet arched heavenward, leaving Cork and all its problems behind. As Sidney left the atmosphere and accelerated in the vacuum of space, he thought about how glad he was to have found his present life. It was a prize far greater than anything offered by Earth's Bureau of Freeness, an existence never before contemplated by an Earthian.

Sidney remembered wishing for a Bu-Free prize, and now it struck him as funny. Tragically funny. He wanted to tell millions of Earthians how foolish they were to waste, their lives hoping for such things. He thought of the problems on Cork too, and considered interjecting to set things straight.

Then he changed his mind. *I can't worry about that stuff,* he thought. *One comet can only do so much.*

Gracefully, he streaked across the starcloth of space at many times the speed of light.

O O O

"It's gone," Javik said, opening his eyes. He rose with the others and squinted to look around. The sky was pastel blue, with three Corkian suns just above the horizon. But there was no warmth from the suns. A chill wind blew dust over the desolate expanse that once had been a pristine meadow.

"My God!" Namaba exclaimed. "Every flower is gone!"

Javik shivered, despite having on the vari-temp coat. "Let's get out of here," he said. "There's death in the air."

The trail at the base of the cliff ran alongside the denuded meadow for a short distance. Occasional broken flower petals, leaves, and stems on the ground were reminders of what once had been. The three-dot markings were clear along the shale cliff here, and appeared more frequently than before—as if to reassure them that they were going in the right direction.

Walking ahead of the others, Javik harbored deep doubts. Even with the certainty of the markings, he was not at all convinced that this was where they should be. And as he glanced back at Namaba, Rebo, and the prince, he saw it on their faces too: wide-eyed expressions mirroring his own fear.

They skirted a sizable pile of loose rocks which had fallen across the path. Nervously, Javik looked up at the white cliff before returning to its base. The broken pieces of shale showed evidence of having fallen recently, with flat, unweathered surfaces.

After they had gone a little farther, Javik thought he heard low, chanting voices. He stopped and raised his hand. "Listen!" he said.

The others stood still. The only sound was a rattle from Prince Pineapple's bag of garbage.

"Shhh!" Javik said.

Somewhere a rock tumbled down the face of the cliff. Javik's gaze darted in all directions. "I don't hear it now," he said.

"Maybe it's the wind," Namaba suggested, "whistling over the rocks."

"Yeah," Javik said.

The trail rose up an embankment now, leading them to a high area which was not all that wide. Down a steep incline to their left a deep blue lake began to emerge beneath a curved section of trail. The lake sparkled in the late afternoon suns as if fine jewels had been encrusted just below its surface.

"I christen thee Jewel Lake," Javik announced. He made the sign of the cross, touching his forehead, shoulders, and chest.

"It gets narrower," Prince Pineapple said, pointing ahead.

The incline falling off to Jewel Lake became a sheer dropoff less than a kilometer uptrail, leaving them only a narrow trail. Above and to the right a stark white cliff looked out uncaringly.

*That's a long way down,* Javik thought.

When they reached the beginning of the narrow trail, Prince Pineapple found three black dots on the side of the cliff. There could be no doubt. Ahead the trail wound around a jutting portion of cliff. Javik heard low, chanting voices again, louder this time and unmistakable—voices that seemed to come from somewhere uptrail, or perhaps overhead. He craned his neck to look up, but saw only clouds moving against the sky along the top of the cliff.

"I hear it now," Namaba said. "Deep voices."

"Magicians," Prince Pineapple said. "Or their spirits."

"The wind, more likely," Javik said. He sighed and faced the precipitous trail. "Good sense tells me to camp here for the night. We're losing daylight and there's a flat spot back a ways … just wide enough for the tent. But I want to get away from this place."

The others agreed. As they started out with Javik in front, Javik heard Prince Pineapple reminding everyone to avoid rhymes. *I ought to wait for the worst dropoff and really lay one on him,* Javik thought. *Wonder if he'd hit the lake on the fly.*

"I know some good rhymes," Javik said. "Do you prefer Mother Goose or dirty limericks?"

"Neither!" Prince Pineapple squealed, plugging his ears with his stubby fingers. In his excitement, he dropped the bag containing his possessions. It clattered over the edge, gone forever. "Now see what you made me do!" he wailed.

"I'm sorry" Javik said. "I didn't mean to do that. Maybe we'll find another canister ahead. Millions of them were catapulted."

"That was a particularly nice selection," the prince gruffed.

"Better the bag than you," Javik said.

Javik turned his attention to the trail. Footing was becoming more treacherous, with many loose pieces of shale. The wind-chant grew louder as they rounded a bend. Then, inexplicably, the noise died out. The lake had narrowed to no more than the width of a river below them, with portions of it in shade as the suns dropped.

"It's too quiet," Namaba said.

"I see the pass," Javik said. His voice was an excited whisper.

A split in the white cliff was clearly visible only a few kilometers uptrail. With blackened areas on each side of the divide, it appeared to have been cut out of the white shale by a bolt of lightning.

"We'd better pick up our pace," Javik said. "I don't want to be on this trail after dark," He began to quick-step.

"And the Moha?" Prince Pineapple said. "The monster of legend? You would rather share an evening with that?"

"My service automatic packs a hell of a wallop," Javik said. "It's a baby cannon."

"Maybe we should turn back," Namaba said. "It seems more sensible to face this Moha in the daylight."

"What does your yenta say?" Javik asked, slowing to a walk.

"It's been giving me trouble since we left the meadow. I get no indication now at all."

"Back a ways, all I could think about was getting the hell out," Javik said. "Now I'm not so sure I did the right thing." He paused and looked back.

Just then a cacophony of angry voices rose from the rear. Javik saw something bright red on the cliff just above Prince Pineapple. A group of tubby little creatures stood on a ledge up there. They shouted in froglike voices and waved their arms angrily.

*Strawberry people?* Javik thought

Prince Pineapple looked up. "Outcasts!" he yelled. He ran uptrail to get away from them. A thrown rock glanced off his back.

Javik and the others ran until they were out of range of the hurled missiles.

"They live in caves up there," Prince Pineapple said, looking back. "I think we interrupted a sacred ceremony. That's why the chanting stopped. They're mutants that grow on the ground. His voice became a hiss as he added, "Like Vegetables."

"I remember your argument with Wizzy," Javik said. "But don't melons grow on the ground, too? I saw several in the royal court."

"I'm not going to tell you a melon person is as good as any other Fruit," Prince Pineapple said. "We've all heard of melonheads. But a melon is much better than a strawberry."

"How so?" Javik asked.

"It just is, that's all."

"I guess we're not turning back," Javik said, seeing strawberry people swing down to the trail on ropes. They gathered there, chattering excitedly in throaty, croaky voices that made them sound like a pond full of bullfrogs.

Prince Pineapple's mouth curled downward in revulsion as he looked at them. "Mutants," he snarled.

The strawberry horde moved closer. They took a few steps, chattered nervously, then took more steps. They appeared to be building up courage.

"Maybe we could block them off with a rockslide," Rebo suggested, pointing up the wall. "Aim your thunder piece about there, Captain."

"We may have to come back this way," Javik said. He began to run uptrail. "Let's go!" he said.

The quartet took short, quick steps, looking down constantly to keep from taking a misstep on the loose trail. Just centimeters to their left the sheer dropoff waited like a predator toying with its prey.

They didn't have to look back to know the strawberry people were in pursuit. Angry grunts and the scuffling of many feet told them this. A small rock glanced off the back of Javik's head. He heard Prince Pineapple and the others curse as they were pelted. Javik's implanted mento unit throbbed.

Javik broke into a full run. His feet skipped over loose slabs of shale. Some pieces fell from the trail toward the ribbon of blue lake far below. The trail began to drop down steeply now, and it was all Javik could do to keep from tumbling forward head over heels.

They ran down, ever down, in daylight that was fast becoming dusk. Javik's knees ached. Quick glances back told him the pursuers were slow, and he was relieved at this. The lake was far behind them now, and the trail widened. The sheer dropoff became more of a gradual incline across white granite.

With the strawberry people out of sight, Javik and his group were nearing the bottom. In shadows ahead, Javik saw the pass between the cliffs. Charred streaks along each side of the pass told a story only the planet knew. Layers of orange covered the sky.

They slowed to a walk, passing near a cluster of AmFed garbage canisters. Prince Pineapple gave them a longing look, but did not ask to stop. One was split wide open, with government forms and pamphlets spread around. The other canisters were basically intact, with only a few bright objects showing.

As they neared the pass, it became apparent that something on the ground was wedged between the cliffs. It was round and large, but somewhat difficult to see in the waning light.

"A big boulder?" Javik said, in a low voice.

"We'd better be careful," Prince Pineapple said.

The excited voices of strawberry people behind them caused them to quicken their steps. Javik was just about to bolt when he glanced back and saw that the pursuers were stopped on the trail.

"Mo-ha!" they chanted. "Mo-ha!"

"I told you," Prince Pineapple said, looking around nervously.

"Mo-ha … Mo-ha … Mo-ha … Mo-ha … Mo-ha … Mo-ha … Moha-Moha-Moha!" Faster and faster they chanted, sounding to Javik like the tape of an old-style train that Sidney Malloy had played for him once. It was one of the illegal things in Sidney's safe.

"The Moha is here somewhere," Prince Pineapple said. "The scroll said where the cliffs meet."

Javik started when dozens of long tentacles popped out of the boulderlike mound. "That's no rock," he said.

The quartet approached carefully, with their small complement of weapons drawn. This amounted to no more than Javik's automatic pistol and Rebo's switchblade knife. Namaba and Prince Pineapple found heavy stones. The mound was less than fifty meters in front of them now, and in the dim light they saw eyes on the tip of each tentacle. The eyes had black pupils with white corneas. Each tentacle was poised, cobralike, and the eyes stared sullenly at Javik's group.

"Why," Namaba said, leaning forward to get a better look, "it's a … a potato! A giant potato!"

"Yeccch!" Prince Pineapple exclaimed, feeling disgust. "A Vegetable mutant!"

"Is there any chance it might be friendly?" Rebo asked.

"Not this monster!" Prince Pineapple said. "If I remember my epic right, it destroyed an entire Fruit army."

Rebo's dark eyebrows furrowed. "But should we assume…?"

"*You* get close enough to find out," Prince Pineapple said to Rebo. "Then we'll know for sure."

"I'm gonna do that," Rebo said. He dropped his knife. Looking at one of the potato monster's eyes, Rebo decided it was sad. Rebo felt honor-bound to protect Javik from the monster, and he still felt love for Namaba. But he also felt something else: an inexplicable desire to understand the creature.

"Wait," Javik said, catching Rebo's arm. "One of those tentacles could strangle you. The eyes don't look friendly at all."

"Maybe he's just afraid," Rebo said. "A protective posture. I've seen it many times in gang combat." He looked at Namaba.

"My yenta is not working," she said. "It's been out since we passed through the magic barrier in the meadow." She thought for a moment, then dropped her rock. "I'm going with you."

"Don't," Javik said.

"I'm going," she said simply. It was the female tone of determination Javik had heard from Earth women, the mindset that could not be resisted by mortal man.

Rebo and Namaba approached the Moha. They walked slowly. "Don't show fear," Rebo whispered. From the hill far behind them, Namaba heard the strawberry people's chant: "Mo-ha! Mo-ha! Mo-ha!" With each step, Namaba's steam engine heart raced faster, pumping air and water through her system. She felt pressure building. Then it released as steam shot out of her cuplike ears. *Show no fear,* she thought.

Rebo extended his arms to the Moha in a friendly gesture. "Friends," he said in a soothing tone. "We are your friends."

The tentacles coiled back and looked to Namaba as if they were about to lash out. The Moha seemed to be waiting for them to get closer.

Namaba closed her eyes with each step, occasionally opening them narrowly to peer at the potato monster. Its lumpy skin was the rich brown color of the soil.

"Friends," Rebo repeated. "We are your friends."

Namaba squinted, afraid to see fully what was going to happen next. They were only a few steps from the Moha now, well within reach of its tentacles.

To Namaba's surprise, the tentacles relaxed and started swaying gracefully. She opened her eyes all the way.

Rebo laughed. "That's a good fellow," he said. "No one's going to hurt you." He stroked the Moha's side.

"Thank God," Namaba said. "I didn't think you could do it."

Rebo looked at her with eyes that burned from hurt. "You didn't? You came with me out of *duty*?"

"Well, you did save my—"

"You owe *me* nothing," Rebo said, still stroking the Moha. "That obligation is to the other Rebo, the one I left on Morovia."

Namaba was sorry she had not met Rebo later in her life. They had done too many bad things together. It all seemed so long ago. She had to have someone new, someone untainted by the terrible old memories of Moro City. She looked back at Javik.

Javik slid his service pistol back into his holster, then retrieved Rebo's knife. Seeing Prince Pineapple was still holding a large rock, Javik told him to drop it.

Prince Pineapple knew he had no choice—not if he wanted to reach the Magician's Chamber. Grudgingly, he complied. As he joined Javik, however, a thought struck him. "I am a Fruit," Prince Pineapple said. "And that is a potentially ferocious Vegetable. There are natural hatreds between us."

"Just don't call it any names," Javik said. "And no quick movements."

"If the Moha tries to strangle me," Prince Pineapple said, "will you use your gun against it?"

"Maybe," Javik said. He was not teasing the prince this time. Javik honestly was not sure what he would do if such a thing occurred. "Let's hope it doesn't happen," he said.

Prince Pineapple said a little prayer as he walked with Javik to the Moha. Rebo was being lifted high by one of the tentacles.

"Gently," Rebo said, stroking the suction-cup-covered tentacle. "Up and over." The tentacle lifted him to the other side, out of view of the others. "That's it," Rebo was heard to say.

Prince Pineapple and Javik were beneath the Moha's swaying tentacles now. The prince shook with fear. A Moha eye was just centimeters away, looking at him intently.

"Go with him, Namaba," Rebo yelled from the other side. "I'm safe on the ground now."

Soon all the adventurers, even a perspiration-covered pineapple prince, had been lifted over the top and deposited safely on the other side.

"He just needed a little love," Rebo said. "Most folks probably throw rocks at him."

They camped nearby for the night.

# Chapter Fifteen

*Five magician trainees were discussing the comparative storage capacities of a rock, a grain of sand, and an atom. All knew from their lessons that no correlation existed between size and storage capacity. But then a black-robed magician appeared, asserting that a rock afforded far more storage capacity and ease of data retrieval than its smaller brothers. Through a series of elaborate demonstrations, the magician proceeded to prove his assertion. At the height of his audience's confusion, he admitted it was all a practical joke, that he was not a magician after all. "Actually," he said, "I am a droplet of Markesian slime brought in on one of your shoes."*

One of the Rejected Stories

As they broke camp the following morning, the suns seemed cheerier to Rebo. He was not certain whether they reflected what lay in store for the group, but felt some part of their brilliance had to emanate from what he had done the previous evening.

While Javik loaded his survival pack, Rebo looked back at the Moha. The Moha was not moving now, having withdrawn its tentacles.

*Poor ugly, lonely fellow,* Rebo thought. On the cliff trail beyond the Moha, there was no sign of the strawberry people. Rebo wondered if they had seen the Moha lift them over its back.

*That will be the stuff of legends,* Rebo thought. *They'll say we were magicians, of course.*

Although it amused Rebo to think of himself as the subject of a legend, he knew it was not an important thing. Namaba was the thing of most consequence to him now, but she no longer wanted anything to do with him. Hearing Javik and Namaba laughing together behind him, Rebo thought sadly, *Perhaps the suns sparkle for them.*

O O O

Beyond the white cliffs and across the denuded meadow-land, Wizzy remained in the underground compartment he had dug with his last spurts of strength. As Wizzy awoke now, he had no idea how long he had been asleep. It might have been a million years. Or only a million deci-seconds. It occurred to him that time was virtually meaningless so far beneath the surface. No suns marked the passing of days, and there was no variation in the temperature. Without visible cycles of life and death, happiness and sadness were muted.

Wizzy felt only one reality: He was buried and forgotten.

So it was in this cold and lonely place that Wizzy stirred and opened his cat's eye. In the white glow light of his rested body, he surveyed the specks of dirt along the ceiling of the tiny chamber. The specks looked very large to him, since they were exceedingly close. He studied them in minute detail, noting a most unusual crystalline shape.

*Insoluble silicon,* he thought. *With aluminum, oxygen, hydrogen, iron, calcium, magnesium, potassium … so much in such a small space!*

Wizzy may have stared at this speck of soil for only a few moments. Or perhaps it occupied him for the better part of a thousand years. Eventually he did look away, for one can only stare at something like that for so long before losing interest.

He stretched and yawned, then stretched again. "Oh my!" he exclaimed. "I wonder what has happened above?"

Wizzy envisioned Javik and the others long dead now, among many skeletons bleached white on the surface and visited often by the suns, the wind, and the rain.

He cried out at this thought. The sob of a millennium nearly overwhelmed him. But Wizzy held his tears, fearing even mercuric moisture might harm him. Soon his sadness passed.

Then it occurred to him that he could call upon his data banks to see how long he had been buried. So Wizzy glowed bright red, filling his little space with a warm glow. *Let me see,* he thought. *How many millions of years was it?* His microminiature magical circuits brought forth the startling answer.

"Thirty-eight hours!" Wizzy said, bellowing so loudly that it made his tympanic sensors ring. "Can it be?"

He verified the data. It was correct.

Wizzy moved around a little bit in the cramped quarters, trying to find the most comfortable position. For a while, he lay upside down, then on each side, then again on his bottom. No position seemed particularly satisfactory.

He spent some time wondering what to do next. Then he realized that he had been burrowing into the soil overhead. Pieces of dry dirt were being displaced in this unconscious maneuver, moving down along the sides of his lumpy body and piling up beneath him.

He stopped moving, afraid to twitch for fear of breaking through into Bottomless Bog. *How long have I been doing this?* he wondered. *How far am I from the bog?*

Then he remembered how close he had been to the shore when he fell in, and recalled the straight dropoff he had bounced into just before hitting bottom. Maybe he was no longer directly beneath the bog. Possibly it was a natural survival instinct that had moved him, causing him to burrow laterally just enough to get under dry land. If that had happened, he only needed to rise straight up to freedom. Wizzy knew up from down, being able to sense the pull of gravity.

*But what if I'm beneath a curved portion of the bog bottom?* he wondered. There was only one way to find out. If he became wet again, he could burrow back down and go to sleep for another thirty-eight hours.

Now Wizzy made a conscious effort at burrowing upward. He moved slowly at first, afraid that he would break through the bog at any moment. After traveling a good two meters, Wizzy became confident and increased his speed. This led to another increase seconds later. Soon Wizzy was a molten orange fireball, rising upward at a high rate of speed. Encountering rocks in his path, he dodged the larger ones. The smaller stones embedded themselves in his malleable skin.

Wizzy exploded out of the soil into the clear, cerulean blue sky above Cork. Three suns undimmed by clouds warmed his body. He rose a thousand meters above the planet, then did a series of joyous loops, trailing white smoke behind him.

*It's wonderful here!* he thought. *A great time to be alive!*

Recalling the map on the Sacred Scroll of Cork, Wizzy flew over the barren land that once had been a meadow. *The planet has changed in a short time,* he thought. *There are no flowers on this portion.*

Fresh doubts struck him concerning how long he had been entombed. He felt strong now, perhaps too strong for having been asleep only thirty-eight hours. *Maybe my data banks have been damaged,* he thought. *And I've been asleep for a long time.*

In the distance, Wizzy saw a high white cliff. He flew toward it. After a while, he noticed that the cliff did not seem to be drawing nearer. He increased his speed.

A short time later he burst through the magical barrier and hit the face of the cliff. His momentum and bulk broke away large pieces of shale, and he tumbled to the ground among them.

Wizzy felt embarrassed as he emerged from the rubble, although certainly no one had witnessed his faux pas. He alighted on a flat piece of shale to think.

Something colorful on the ground caught his eye. It was black with yellow polka dots—a strip of cloth. A thought struck him, but he dismissed it immediately. It couldn't be that!

He moved closer to it.

*The ribbon from Namaba's mane!* he realized. It looked fresh and nearly new. It hadn't been there long.

On the cliff just overhead, Wizzy saw a three-dot trail marking. *They've been this way,* he thought. *Recently.*

O O O

Reaching the cavernous Dimensional Tunnel room, a nude, dirty, and thoroughly disheartened Lord Abercrombie tried to compose himself. Shivering in front of a wall mirror, he saw that his body was completely flesh, without a single magical void. *I may as well make the best of it,* he thought, seeing the reflection of his packed train of trunks in the mirror. *I can't stay on this planet.* The galactic wind howled behind him.

Wanting to freshen up for his Dimensional Tunnel trip, Lord Abercrombie mentoed his wardrobe ring and took a dry shower. The ring played its cheerful tune. It was a novelty for him to see electrolyzed dirt falling off the side of his fleshy body which had not been there only a short time before.

"It's fresh-up time!" Lord Abercrombie sang, following the tune played by the ring. "It's fresh-up time!"

He began to feel better.

At his next mento command, a bright yellow caftan with black braiding on the arms and neck stitched itself around his body, followed by white satin slippers and a full thistle crown. His powers were diminished now, but at least he looked more regal than before. He turned before the mirror, admiring each angle.

Petulantly, he decided to change the outfit.

At his mento command, the old outfit disappeared in a *poof* and everything except the standard-issue thistle crown changed. His caftan became bright purple with slender gold stripes. Gold slippers adorned his feet.

He turned in front of the mirror and decided that this looked very nice. But improvements could be made. So he changed the outfit. Then he changed again. A dazzling array of colorful caftans and slippers flashed in front of the mirror as Lord Abercrombie put on a one-man fashion show.

But none of them suited him to perfection. An inexplicable element was missing each time. So Lord Abercrombie made a ferocious, pouting face in the mirror and leaned towards the glass with his hands on his hips.

"None of these outfits will do for my trip!" he shouted. "None will do at all!"

The glassplex mirror became hazy. Then it rippled. Seeing his reflection distorting in the mirror, Lord Abercrombie stepped back, alarmed. Distant, cackling laughter echoed inside his skull. It grew louder. He threw his hands over his ears, but this did no good.

"Stop it!" he screamed.

His caftan, slippers, and thistle crown disintegrated in a small explosion that startled him. He had not mentoed this. Then the wardrobe ring slipped from his finger and flew across the cavern, disappearing into the blackness of the Dimensional Tunnel.

His brain reverberated with laughter. Red and white striped crew socks appeared on his feet, then disappeared. Next, a royal purple ascot wrapped itself around his neck, pulling itself tighter and tighter as the laughter continued.

"Guggg!" he said, gagging.

Now the ascot disappeared, leaving behind a red burn mark on Lord Abercrombie's neck. He rubbed it.

The laughing voices receded. All became quiet, with the exception of a slight, whistling wind from the Dimensional Tunnel.

"I didn't want to keep that ring anyway!" he exclaimed, laughing nervously. This became two short laughs. Then two longer laughs and a confident chuckle. Soon he was howling, with his nude body bent over in mirth.

"A-ha. A-ha-ha. Aha-ha-ha-ha-ha-ha-ha-ha-ha!" His glee bounced off the cavern walls and entered the Dimensional Tunnel, ending up who knows where.

Lord Abercrombie thought of his laughter reverberating across the universe. This struck him as so funny that he laughed even harder.

"Well!" he finally said. "This has been a good joke on me!"

He scampered into the outer passageway, intending to find something recycled to wear and a meckie to accompany him on the trip.

O O O

Before setting out that morning, Javik and the others found that they could again recharge. No one understood what had happened the day before, when Prince Pineapple and Javik had almost been sucked into the ground. They theorized that it had been a peculiarity of the meadow.

Everyone, even Prince Pineapple, said goodbye to the Moha and thanked him for being so helpful. Shortly after they set out for their final assault on the Magician's Chamber and the Dimensional Tunnel, Rebo ran back to pat the Moha again. There was no response from the potato creature other than a graceful waving of its tentacles, so no one was certain how much intelligence it had.

"I really liked that guy," Rebo said as he rejoined the group.

They turned uptrail, moving into agate country, with sparse and gnarled noble fir trees dotting the way. In all directions they saw massive slabs and hills of translucent, ochre-colored stone. Morning sunlight permeated the agate rocks, making them appear liquid.

Soon they reached a one-story oriental gazebo that had a wooden wall on the side facing the trail. The other side of the structure opened in a half circle. Eight neat stacks of dark brown fabric were spaced evenly around this half circle, under the shelter of the roof.

Javik found a sign on the inside of the wall, written in three languages, each of which he recognized with the aid of his language mixer pendant. "Interesting," he said. "It's in English, Morovian, and Corker."

The others gathered around and verified this.

Reading one of the versions, this is what Javik saw:

**THESE ARE THE EIGHT FOLDING PATHS
SELECT A PATH.
PUSH IT OPEN.
IT WILL UNFOLD BEFORE YOU
WALK ON IT.**

No one knew which trail to select, so each unfolded two paths. They flip-flopped open into the distance like the binding displays of an encyclopedia salesman. When all were open, they found that one had three-dot markings every few hundred meters. The others were unmarked.

They set out along this path, with Prince Pineapple forging into the lead. "The Magician's Chamber is close," he said. "I know it."

Soon the path became a dirt trail. As they reached dirt, the cloth path folded up behind them, returning to the gazebo. On both sides they watched the other paths flop back as well.

After only a few more steps, Prince Pineapple was forced to stop suddenly, for a large wooden sign painted with white letters had sprung up in his path. This was printed in the three languages of the group.

"'Go back!'" Prince Pineapple said, reading the Corkian version. "'Wrong way!'" He scratched his head.

After a moment of thoughtful silence, Javik said, "I don't believe it, Prince. Go around."

Prince Pineapple agreed. "An Abercrombie trick," he said. He started around the sign.

But the sign moved to block his path.

Javik tried to go around the other way, but the sign split into two neat halves, with a wooden portion blocking both him and the prince.

Namaba and Rebo made attempts, too. But now the sign split into four pieces, with one in front of each of them.

"Do not be alarmed," an omnipresent voice said. "I am attempting to help you."

"Who said that?" Javik asked, startled.

The quartet backed away from the sign pieces, gathering together a short distance back.

The sign pieces drew themselves together again.

"Many months ago," the voice said, "Lord Abercrombie sent his meckies to the gazebo. They switched the paths around. You need to move over two paths to your left."

"You are not Lord Abercrombie?" Prince Pineapple asked, one eyebrow lifted inquisitively.

"Certainly not. I am a magician's helper, left here aeons ago to watch over the area. This is a galactic park, you know. I'm sort of a park ranger, you might say."

"You are invisible?" Namaba asked.

"No more than you, dear. I am the beautiful rock to your left."

Namaba looked down and saw two medium-sized agates on the ground. She touched one. "Is this you?" she asked. The rock was smooth and sun-warmed.

"Certainly not! That is a common agate. I, on the other hand, am a history stone—a repository of all the legends and data concerning this quadrant of the starfield. Now Abercrombie is washed up, rejected by the Realm of Magic."

They gathered around the stone and looked down at it. This rock looked no different from any other in the vicinity. It was about the size of Javik's hand, yellow ochre in color.

Prince Pineapple felt a rush of excitement at the thought of Lord Abercrombie being rejected by the Realm of Magic. For the first time the prince consciously considered the possibility of stepping into Abercrombie's place. Before this he had felt only generalized anger, a desire to throw Abercrombie out. Now he felt something entirely different. He wanted to be lord.

*They were right about me,* Prince Pineapple thought, looking at each of the others. *They saw it in my eyes.*

Javik looked at him.

Prince Pineapple looked at the talking agate and asked, "How do we know we can trust you?"

The agate laughed, its voice seeming to come from all around. "You don't. But then, what choices do you have?"

Javik lifted the stone and stood up with it. "I could toss you in a ravine," Javik said. "There's one just over there." He nodded to indicate direction.

"I could place barriers in your way to prevent it," the agate said. "I'll tell you what, though. If you want to take this trail, go right ahead."

"You won't stop us?" Prince Pineapple asked.

"No. But do you really think that would be wise, Prince Pineapple? Do you, Namaba?"

"It knows our names!" Namaba said, surprised. She looked around.

"Someone around here knows our languages, too," Rebo said.

"This could all be Lord Abercrombie's doing," Prince Pineapple said. "We've all recharged. He knows everything about us now from the connection."

Namaba wrinkled her hair-framed face into a frown. "I think my yenta is working again," she said. "It tells me we should trust the agate."

"You're certain?" Javik asked. He leaned over and put the stone back where he had found it. "We don't have much to go on," he said, rubbing his tongue across his lower lip. The lip was chapped.

"I think I agree," Rebo said. "This agate might have threatened us, or tried to bluff us with its magic. It didn't do either of those things."

"Do you mind if we continue on this trail a little way?" Namaba asked, leaning over the agate, "and then make our own decision?"

The sign disappeared. There was no response other than this.

Namaba loped ahead to where the sign had been, then passed beyond. "Let's take the other trail," she said.

All agreed, and they set off across a field of rock. Here they encountered occasional long-stemmed yellow flowers that had six round petals apiece. Javik picked a flower and used a piece of twine to secure it to Namaba's mane. "This will replace the ribbon you lost," he said.

O O O

Glowing bright pink with a yellow tail, Wizzy skirted the base of the white cliff, following the three-dot trail markings. He flew above the blue lake, which narrowed to a ribbon of water, then paused at the beginning of the precipice trail. From there he passed the cliff dwellings of the strawberry people. Three of them ran out to watch him as he flew by.

Wizzy was a good deal larger now than he had been, and his translucent tail extended a good five meters behind his nucleus. This must have been quite a sight for the outcast strawberry people, especially following so closely on the heels of the episode with Javik's party.

Wizzy left the strawberry people in the wink of a cat's eye. He swooped low over the Moha now, passing through the opening in the cliffs. This agitated the Moha, and it waved its tentacles wildly. One tentacle passed harmlessly through Wizzy's gaseous tail.

Reaching the eight folding paths, Wizzy nudged them open. In doing this, he clumsily destroyed the gazebo with the fire from his nucleus. Fortunately, a foresighted magician had treated the cloth paths with flame retardant.

While the gazebo burned, Wizzy checked each path. Quickly he located the one with three-dot markings. Streaking along this path, he reached the dirt area so rapidly that the magical agate did not have time to warn him.

"Wait!" the agate called out. "Not that way!"

But Wizzy was so far uptrail that he did not hear the agate.

O O O

With Prince Pineapple trudging ahead and Rebo bringing up the rear, Javik and Namaba walked beside one another holding hands. At first the lovers found this difficult to do, owing to the markedly different cadence of their steps. Namaba's gait was more of a lope, with her head bobbing up and down, while Javik walked erectly and smoothly in the Earthian manner. After a kilometer or so, they found a middle ground, with Namaba moving more smoothly and Javik herky-jerking it.

"We'll be married in Moro City," Namaba said. "My minister can do it." The light brown fur on her mane was gold-tinged from the sunlight.

"Where would I work?" Javik asked, squinting. "Is there a Moravian Space Patrol?

"We have an Air Guard," she said. "But Moravian ships are more primitive than yours. And we have nothing to compare with the technology in your wardrobe ring."

"That's not technology," Javik said with a wink. "It's magic."

She smiled.

"I don't mind if the place is a little backward," Javik said. "Just as long as we're together." He thought about how sappy his words might have sounded to him once. But it struck him that the really important things in life were sappy.

Catching up, Rebo said, "It won't be easy for you on Morovia. I'm not saying that out of jealousy. Most folks will be afraid of Tom."

Namaba's eyes flared. "They can all go to Morovian Hell."

"It's easy to say that," Rebo said. "But you'd better think it over carefully. They'll think Tom is a freak."

"Then I'll make my living touring the planet," Javik said flippantly. "We'll make enough money off freak shows to build a rocket and get the hell out of there."

"We're not doing any sideshows," Namaba said. "You're no freak. A Moravian on Earth would face the same situation. You're different, that's all. We'll prove to people that different is not bad." She squeezed his hand tightly. "We'll make them understand," she said. Her lips were a thin, determined line.

"Good luck to both of you," Rebo said. "Maybe I can help, when we all get back—if the Dimensional Tunnel works out the way we hope."

Namaba glanced back at Rebo and saw sincerity in his eyes. They glowed a soft shade of red.

"Say," Rebo said, looking at Namaba. "Do you remember Jamaro? Remember how he came back all deformed after the Hoka Wars?" His expression became troubled as he realized he had placed himself into a hole.

"Jamaro returned with only two legs," Namaba explained, glancing at Javik.

"Pretty horrible, eh?" Javik said.

"I used a bad example," Rebo said, biting nervously at his lower lip. "I was just thinking I could work with those kinda guys—you know, in therapy."

Javik thought of Sidney.

"Sounds fine, Rebo," Namaba said. "You'll do fine. All of us will!"

"We have wars on Earth, too," Javik said. "I was good at that game. Seems like a long time ago, though." He reflected upon the Atheist Wars, when he and Brent Stafford swaggered across half the star system. "Hell, I'd be a young general now if I'd been able to keep my nose clean."

Seeing Namaba looking at him curiously, Javik forced a laugh. "Guess I'm pretty funny, eh?" he said. "Someday, Namaba, we'll be gray-haired, sitting in rockers on our front porch. A little Moravian kid'll be sitting on the steps, and I'll be starting to tell a war story. You'll say, 'Not that one again!' Or maybe you'll smile softly and leave, knowing I've changed the story with each telling, making more of myself than there really was."

"Anything worth saying is worth exaggerating," Namaba said, nodding her head. "That's what Grandma used to say."

"Sounds like your grandpa told his share of tall tales."

Namaba laughed. "Maybe that little Moravian kid will be our grandchild."

"That'd be somethin'," Javik said. "Yessir. That'd be some-thin'!"

Engrossed in the conversation, Javik suddenly realized they had fallen far behind Prince Pineapple. He could just see the top of the prince's helicopter beanie beyond a rise in the path. Then Prince Pineapple turned and ran back toward them. When the prince's face came into view, Javik saw that he was shouting something. The words were lost in the wind.

"Looks like he's found something," Rebo said.

They picked up their pace and moments later found Prince Pineapple standing over a pile of sun-bleached bones.

"A Yanni tribal burial ground," Prince Pineapple said, brimming with excitement. "With long goat bones in a triangular pattern."

"There's a significance to that?" Javik asked.

Prince Pineapple looked full in his face with the expression of a scolding Freeness Studies instructor. "Triangle … three dots."

"Oh, sure," Javik said. "A magical sign. What do you think it means?"

"It's a sign that we're close," Prince Pineapple said.

"Speaking of signs," Namaba said, pointing uptrail. "I see another one."

As she spoke, a wooden sign was rising slowly from the ground beside the trail just a few meters ahead. When it was all the way up, she saw it rested on two legs and was red with white lettering,

Javik walked up to it and read. It was printed in English:

**DIMENSIONAL TUNNEL**
**2 KILOMETERS**

Javik stepped aside so Rebo and Namaba could read it. Now it changed to Moravian. When Prince Pineapple read it, the printing became Corkian.

"Three languages again," Javik said.

They set off, and soon were out of sight of the sign. Minutes later they heard rapid footsteps approaching from downtrail. Turning their heads, they were surprised to see the sign running after them. Two arms had sprung from the edges of the signboard, and its legs had big, clumpy feet. Jumbled letters were shaped in the form of a cherubic, smiling face.

As Javik's jaw grazed his boot tops, he watched the sign run by and plant itself in the ground a few paces uptrail. The sign's arms folded in and melded with the board. The facial letters formed English words. the feet disappeared, leaving two rigid board legs planted in the ground. Here is the message Javik saw:

**DIMENSIONAL TUNNEL**
**1 KILOMETER**
**Approach at own risk.**
**Strong galactic currents.**

They continued on their way. A few minutes later the sign again rushed past. This time it planted itself in front of a large flat stone and began to glow like a New City neon sign. There was a new message:

**DIMENSIONAL TUNNEL**
**LAUGH TO ENTER**

They searched the base of the flat stone, looking for a tunnel or a doorway. Seeing nothing, they looked at one another and shrugged.

"Guess we'd better laugh," Prince Pineapple said.

So they laughed.

And laughed.

And laughed some more.

Their laughter echoed off the rocks, trees, and shrubs around them. They laughed so hard that the sign broke into uncontrollable giggles. Its lettering became a muddled, unreadable mess.

With tears in his eyes, Javik saw two humanlike puffy white clouds drop feet first from the sky. They were not very large as clouds go, being perhaps twice as tall as Javik. But they were quite muscular. Ceremoniously, with stern expressions on their puffy faces, they took positions on each side of the giant slab of stone.

"It's under the rock!" Prince Pineapple said.

Javik wiped tears from his eyes and cheeks.

Using its little finger, one of the clouds lifted a corner of the slab and peeked under it. "Oooh!" the cloud squealed, dropping the slab. "A big worm touched me!"

"Oooh!" the other cloud said.

"Oooh!" the sign said. And the sign jumped completely out of the ground, landing in a clump of bushes.

Now the clouds leaped high in the air and were carried off by the wind. Soon they had floated out of sight.

The sign crawled out of the bushes and ran downtrail. Soon it was gone too, leaving the travelers in a most bewildered state.

Just then Javik heard a faint little chuckle. He didn't know where it came from. Looking at the solemn and confused expressions of his companions, he knew they hadn't done it.

You must realize that this was perhaps the tiniest chuckle in the Aluminum Starfield. It might have been trapped beneath a pebble and then kicked free by someone's foot. Or maybe it was simply a slow echo, having just completed its bouncing journey from surface to surface.

Whatever the source, it was just enough of a chuckle to complete the required amount of laughter. As Javik looked at his companions, he became aware of a creaking noise. It came from the large slab of rock.

"It's moving!" Namaba exclaimed.

Sure enough, the stone was lifting like a megalithic hatch, creaking higher and higher until it fell over the other way on its top. It might not have creaked so much if only someone had been there to oil its magical hinges. Unfortunately, there was a decided shortage of magician's helpers in this part of the universe.

Moving to the edge, Javik saw steps leading down from all sides of a square hole. It resembled an inverted, hollow pyramid. In a wild flight of fantasy, he envisioned a pyramid rocket landing here and plowing into the ground. It was a preposterous thought, causing Javik to wonder if a magician was playing tricks with his mind.

Prince Pineapple started down the steps.

"Hold it, Prince," Javik. said, grasping Prince Pineapple's arm firmly. "I want you to wait here." Javik released the prince.

"What do you mean?" Prince Pineapple asked. "We were going to get rid of Abercrombie together."

"I'm going to see what Abercrombie's been up to," Javik said. "If he's no threat to Earth, I'll leave him and enter the Dimensional Tunnel with Rebo and Namaba."

Prince Pineapple's black button eyes opened wide in shock. "*Leave him?* You can't do that!"

"I'm not going to get rid of him for you," Javik said. "I've never trusted you." Javik removed his Tasnard rope from the pack and mentoed it. The black and white striped rope looped around Prince Pineapple's arms and torso, pulling his arms tight against his body. Javik pulled the struggling prince to the surface.

"Now see here!" Prince Pineapple said. "You can't—"

"Shut up," Javik snapped. He mentoed the rope again, instructing it to tie the prince to a nearby willow sapling.

The Tasnard rope curled out of Javik's grasp and dragged Prince Pineapple to the tree. It tied him there in a standing position.

"Earthian bastard!" Prince Pineapple said. He pulled at the rope and kicked, but it held him fast.

"That'll keep you on ice," Javik said. He turned to Namaba. "Stay here," he said. "It might be dangerous."

"I agree," Rebo said.

Namaba leaned down and gave Javik a kiss on the mouth. "I'll watch the prince," she said.

"And this is one tough lady," Rebo said.

Namaba half smiled. Her eyes were full of concern for Javik and Rebo. "I should go with you, Rebo," she said. "My Moravian obligation

"You can help by staying here," Rebo said. "Keep an eye on Prince Pineapple. We can't have him getting in the way."

"All right," she said softly.

Javik and Rebo stepped carefully into the hole. The upside-down pyramid was larger than it appeared to be, and soon Namaba saw their forms diminishing in size as they proceeded. She lost her sense of perspective. For a moment she thought they were climbing up the steps.

With her back to Prince Pineapple, Namaba did not see that the Tasnard rope was beginning to slip. Something in the bog had damaged the rope's delicate mechanism. Quietly, Prince Pineapple removed the rope from his arms and torso, pulling it over his head. He pulled a long goat bone out from under his coat. It was sharp on one end, having been broken in the indeterminate past.

*They plan to leave me on the surface!* the prince thought desperately.

Javik and Rebo reached the base of the hole now. Namaba watched as Javik leaned down and looked inside a square, black hole. He jumped into it, followed by Rebo.

Prince Pineapple swung the bone mightily, hitting Namaba on the side of her skull and slashing her skin sack with the sharp portion of bone. It was a mortal blow.

A loud sound of releasing steam came from Namaba. Her body took off like a discharging balloon, looping in the air and wetting Prince Pineapple's face and clothing with steam. Soon Namaba's body was no more than an empty, hairy bag of flesh. It dropped to one side of the entrance.

The Sacred Scroll of Cork fell from Prince Pineapple's coat, unnoticed by him. He leaped down the steps with the zeal of a fanatic, carrying the long goat bone. "It's mine!" he said. "The Magician's Chamber is mine!"

O O O

Wizzy's path brought him to a Vegetable village by the sea. Here tiny white stucco houses clung to hillsides and to cliffs overlooking the blue water. Over the center of town, Wizzy looked down on a cobblestone square thronging with thousands of Vegetable people.

Glowing kelly green from his flaming nucleus to the tip of his wispy tail, Wizzy dipped low over the square. He heard the excited conversation of the people.

"Did you hear the news?" a voice said. "Brother Carrot is victorious."

"Wonderful!"

"Death to the Fruits!"

"Things will be different now!"

While Wizzy had grown to many times his original size, he still was not such a large comet. At first only a few Vegetables noticed him over their heads. Gradually, however, the word was passed and fingers began to point. Soon, Wizzy had become the center of attention.

"I must have taken a wrong turn somewhere," Wizzy mumbled. He felt embarrassed. His nucleus changed to a bright shade of crimson, and his tail matched that.

In the next hour and a half he retraced his flight carefully, finally arriving back at the burned-out gazebo. Flying slowly along each of the eight folding paths now, Wizzy encountered a wooden sign which had sprung up in his path.

Wizzy burst right through it.

"You foolish fellow!" the magical agate yelled after him. "Come back here!"

Sheepishly, Wizzy returned and spoke with the agate. Wizzy had his faults, but he knew the truth when he heard it. Shortly he was on the correct path.

*How stupid of me,* Wizzy thought as he sped along the path in a bright green blur. *All that wasted time.*

"Curious fellow," the magical agate said, watching Wizzy flash in the distance. The agate felt warm in the rays of three suns. Now, as it grew quiet once again, he drifted off to sleep, his history storehouse just a little bit richer.

O O O

With weapons brandished, Javik and Rebo dropped to a rocky passageway surface. The passageway walls were gray stone, dimly lit from unseen sources. Rebo's eyes glowed bright red, casting an eerie light. Seeing darkness in one direction and light in the other, they walked toward the light.

It was cold here, so Javik paused to mento on a pair of vari-temp pants, matching his orange coat. "You want anything?" he asked, looking at Rebo.

"Naw. I'm fine." Rebo was cold, but decided he didn't need more than his club jacket.

The passageway opened into a wide, well-lit cavern. One wall of the cavern faced a series of clear glassplex tubes.

"This place looks familiar," Rebo said.

Moving around a stocky pillar, they came upon a gray rock throne with black satin cushions. Junk sculptures made of scrap pieces of metal, plastic, and glassplex flanked the throne.

"Of course," Rebo said, touching a throne cushion. It was smooth and cool. "The half-faced creature sat here."

"Half-faced?"

"Namaba and I were in those tubes out there, going around and around. Then we landed next to your ship." Rebo's red eyes darted around nervously. "He's here somewhere."

"Abercrombie? You think it was Abercrombie?"

"I don't know. But he was very angry with us."

O O O

On the other side of the chamber they found another passageway. They moved from light to dark in this passageway, not speaking. It was very quiet. It was colder here, and Javik saw Rebo shiver.

"You sure you don't want something to wear?" Javik asked.

Rebo did not answer. He moved ahead of Javik, extending his knife in front of him in the low light of the passageway. Rebo glanced back often as they proceeded, revealing fear in his face. Presently they came upon a side cavern full of silent machinery. Meckies were piled near the doorway. Nothing moved in the room.

"I thought I heard something," Javik said, pointing up the passageway.

Rebo listened intently for a moment. Then he shrugged his big shoulders. "I don't hear anything."

"I don't hear it now," Javik said. "Let's go on."

They passed dozens of other caverns similar to the first. Inside each it was the same: meckies piled motionless near the doorway and not a gear moving anywhere.

Soon the passageway widened like a funnel opening and grew lighter. They rounded a turn and were in another cavern. This cavern had three mirrored walls. The fourth side was black, with no wall visible. Javik heard wind noises in the room and felt cold through his vari-temp clothing.

Judging from the shadows, Javik decided this cavern was illuminated from above. There was a considerable amount of light where he and Rebo were, contrasting with the darkened fourth side of the room. Oddly, however, when Javik looked up he saw only dark gray rock with no source of illumination. A long train of trunks was in the center of the cavern. Javik saw something move behind one of the trunks.

"You there!" Javik barked, dropping to his belly and holding the gun out with both hands. "Step out where I can see you!" Unnoticed by Javik, the folding shovel and barbed cord slipped out of their sheath and fell to the ground.

A human figure wearing dark coveralls emerged from the shadows. This was a bearded man, much shorter than Javik, stepping forward with his arms folded across his chest. Javik heard Rebo's heavy breathing at his side.

"I've been expecting you," the man shouted. He walked toward Javik. His beard was dark, of indeterminate color.

"Stay back," Javik said. "Keep your distance."

But the man came closer. He was not armed, and appeared harmless enough to Javik. "I was just about to go on a trip," the man said, nodding toward the trunks. "Everything is packed."

"You're Winston Abercrombie, aren't you?" Javik asked, looking closely at the man's eyes. They were widely set and large. Javik stood up, still aiming the gun.

"That is correct," Abercrombie said. His voice was distant and unconcerned. It almost seemed to come from the wind that howled around them. A phosphorescent, pink label on his shoulder flashed this message:

**100%**
**recycled**
**material**

"It's the same man," Rebo said. "But his face … It's complete!"

Abercrombie unfolded his arms and gestured toward the blackness behind, him. "That, gentleman, is the famous Dimensional Tunnel." A smile touched the corners of his mouth, then dropped to steely hardness.

"I am from Earth," Javik said, gripping the gun handle too tightly. He felt perspiration on his palms. "Sent to investigate the garbage situation … and your disappearance."

"But I have not disappeared," Abercrombie exclaimed. "Do I look invisible to you?"

"No."

"I'm quite visible, quite fleshy now." He laughed. It was a piercing, cackling laugh. The laugh of a crazy man.

"I think you'd better come with me," Javik said, motioning with his gun barrel.

"Come and get me," Abercrombie squealed. He stepped back into shadows.

"Hold it!" Javik snapped.

Rebo followed Abercrombie.

Javik moved forward now too and saw Abercrombie stepping backward, approaching the blackness of the Dimensional Tunnel. Abercrombie cackled with laughter.

Rebo was close to him now, but stopped short when he saw the edge of the tunnel just a few steps behind Abercrombie. "Be careful!" Rebo warned.

"I know where I am," Abercrombie said. "I don't like to travel without luggage, but we do as we must."

Rebo switched his knife to his other hand and reached out until his fingertips nearly touched Abercrombie.

"Let him go," Javik said.

"I'm five times the size of this little feller," Rebo said. "You want to question him, don't you?"

"Yes, but …"

Javik stopped when he saw Rebo grab one of Abercrombie's arms. Rebo towered over Abercrombie and was many times his bulk. Rebo pulled.

But Abercrombie did not budge. He smiled diabolically.

Rebo dropped his knife and grabbed hold with both hands. He dug his paws into the ground and pulled again.

Abercrombie still did not budge. "Heh-heh-heh!" he cackled.

"Let go of him!" Javik shouted.

But it was too late. In one ferocious flip, Abercrombie pulled Rebo over his shoulder and hurled him into the Dimensional Tunnel.

"Aaaiy!" Rebo screamed. Then he was gone.

"I have the strength of fifty," Abercrombie said, approaching Javik. "You are in my domain."

Javik pulled the trigger. The gun jammed. He turned and ran, with Abercrombie in pursuit. Javik knew why Abercrombie was so strong. He was insane.

"This is *my* chamber!" Abercrombie squealed. "*Mine*, Earthian."

Suddenly, Javik dropped to his knees, turned, and fired. This time a flash of orange flame shot out of the gun barrel. A thunderclap reverberated off the walls.

The laser shell hit Abercrombie square in the shoulder. He fell to the ground, unconscious.

Javik tied Abercrombie's hands and feet with mento-produced strips of heavy cloth from his wardrobe ring. Then he brought the first-aid kit out of his pistol handle and caulked Abercrombie's shoulder wound.

Since Abercrombie was a small man, Javik lifted him easily over one shoulder. When he reached the passageway, Javik saw Prince Pineapple running toward him at full tilt, waving a long, sharp bone. The big pineapple man had the same crazed expression as Abercrombie, and was approaching fast.

"What are you doing down here?" Javik shouted. "I told you ..." He ducked. The bone whistled by his ear. Javik dropped Abercrombie to the ground and reached for his gun. Then a thought struck Javik and he screamed, "There was a young lady of Rhodes!... Who sinned in unusual modes!"

Prince Pineapple did a high backflip, landing neatly on his feet. "Damn you!" he said.

Javik continued: "At the height of her fame!... She abruptly became!... The mother of four dozen toads!"

The angry prince did a double backflip.

Then Javik attacked with more dirty Irish limericks, sending the hapless prince backflipping into the distance of the corridor. Javik heard his rhymes echo, and surmised this would keep Prince Pineapple occupied for a while.

As Javik reached down to lift Abercrombie, he thought of Namaba. He walked rapidly. Then he broke into a full run. Reaching the base of the inverted pyramid, he lifted Abercrombie up to the lowest step. Then he crawled up and again lifted Abercrombie's limp form over his shoulder.

Javik sprinted up the steps. Reaching daylight, he called Namaba's name. There was no answer.

"Namaba!" he repeated. "Namaba!"

Then he saw it on the top step at the opposite side of the pyramid: a tiny bag of fleshy fur with a yellow flower attached to it. He dropped Abercrombie on the ground and ran to her. "Namaba!" he moaned. "My God!"

Something creaked, but Javik paid it no mind.

"My love!" he wailed, overcome with grief. Javik knelt over her deflated, lifeless body and took the flower from her mane. He pressed it against his nostrils. It still smelled sweet. She had been alive only minutes ago.

A loud creak caused him to look up. The stone was dropping! A shadow had moved halfway across the opening.

Javik's mind raced. *In or out?* he wondered. *Shall I take her and jump in the Dimensional Tunnel?*

The stone lid continued to drop. It was three-quarters shut. Javik was completely in shadow.

*But she's dead,* Javik thought. *I couldn't live on Morovia without her.*

At the last possible moment, Javik grabbed Namaba's body and rolled into the sunlight above.

With a loud *plop* the stone dropped over the opening. Dust rose from the area.

Javik did not want to move. He lay on his back with Namaba against his chest. The warmth of three suns caressed the backs of his hands. Namaba's body was light, without substance. He wondered how someone so alive and so vibrant could be reduced to this.

A tear ran down his cheek.

In the settling dust, a parchment rose silently skyward, unseen by Javik. It was beginning its journey back to Sacred Pond. But Wizzy saw it when he flew up. And he saw Javik lying on the ground holding Namaba's body.

"Captain Tom!" Wizzy squealed, streaking down in a bright green flash. "Captain Tom!"

O O O

Far beneath the surface of Cork, Prince Pineapple was lying on the ground, recovering from a nearly fatal attack of backflips. In a daze, he staggered to his feet. He ran one way, then the other, searching every passageway, every cavern. No one else was there. Locating the base of the pyramid steps, he stared up into darkness.

His head throbbed. He needed time to think.

O O O

Rebo wished he had accepted the vari-temp clothing when Javik offered it to him. He was cold. Damned cold. Freezing air rushed at him through the vacuum of an immense, universe-wide tunnel. Storms of gray and blue raged across his brain. Pinpricks of cold stabbed him. It was so cold that he felt hot. He remembered feeling this before, after falling into the maw of the Parduvian flytrap.

His body rolled into the shape of a three-legged fetus, just as it had before. Then it straightened, and he saw twinkling stars in the shadowy blue distance. The blues, greens, and browns of planets appeared and receded. Great suns came and went, blinding him with their intensity.

But the suns were cold. He wanted to get warm more than anything else. His brain became foggy.

Short visions of Namaba's face flashed in front of him like props in an amusement park tunnel, then splintered as Rebo hurtled through them.

Now he was a fetus again, spinning, spinning, spinning. He was a baby, newborn and ready to start his life.

*I can still be useful,* he thought. *It's not too late.*

He tried to shout this thought. It was pure truth and needed to be heard. But his voice made no sound.

In his muddled mind's eye, he envisioned a ward full of disabled war veterans. Inexplicably, all the veterans were children, as if they had gone to war before growing up. Rebo was on a platform, delivering a motivational talk. Everyone respected and loved him.

The tunnel became a great ocean wave, contracting and swelling. It pulled him forward. Inexorably, painfully forward. His brain became the ocean wave, pulling him back to Moro City. He wanted to go back. There were important things to be accomplished.

He broke free of the water and ran through the tunnel in immense, loping strides—strides that carried him millions of kilometers at a time. Eternity pressed in on him. He had to hurry.

He sensed warm yellow and orange colors in place of the grays and blues. His body tingled as the cold dissipated through his pores. His frantic strides became slow-motion easy, with his muscles pulling him forward in tremendous, smooth bursts. He felt sleepy, and a calmness came over him.

Rebo remembered the magical meadow, wishing he had been the one to frolic with Namaba. It might have been that way … might have been that way … might have been …

A red flash tore across his eyelids, and he was hot. Intensely hot. So hot that it seemed cold. He shivered, then felt his body temperature normalize.

Rebo opened his eyes. A scowling Morovian police officer stared down at him.

"I got one!" the police officer yelled. "It's one of those Southside Hawks." He pushed Rebo over roughly and cuffed his hands.

Rebo saw a brass plaque just centimeters from his face. It read: "PARDUVIAN FLYTRAP."

*I'm back,* he thought. *Back!*

The police officer stood him up.

"Listen to me," Rebo said. "I must tell you something."

"Plenty of time for that in court," the officer said. "They'll pop you certain for what you did to that poor old guy."

Rebo felt the officer's grip tighten on his arm. Uncontrolled rage twisted the officer's face.

*No one will believe me,* Rebo thought. *I've changed, and no one will know.*

# Epilogue

*Maybe Hoover was right.*

Graffiti on New City park bench

Wizzy buzzed low over the prone, face-up form of Javik. "Captain Tom!" he said. "You okay, Captain Tom?"

Javik sat up dejectedly and placed Namaba's body on the ground next to him. He mentoed for a soft terry-cloth bathrobe, and a white one wound its way around his arms and torso. Then he removed the robe and wrapped Namaba's body in it. His movements were gentle, reverent.

"She's gone," Javik said. He stared at the survival pack, which lay nearby on the ground. *Sleep,* he thought, thinking of the tent and beds inside.

"God, I'm sorry," Wizzy said.

"I loved her," Javik said. "Prince Pineapple's gone, too. He went crazy." Javik brightened for a moment as he focused on Wizzy. "You're larger," he said. "And your tail …"

Wizzy flew in a little circle.

Javik ducked to avoid the gas of Wizzy's tail. "That's a nice shade of green, too," Javik said.

Abercrombie started to regain consciousness. His eyes blinked. Still tied at his wrists and ankles, he rolled over from his back to his side.

"I have a much better color selection than before," Wizzy said. "Many more nuances of the spectrum, with still others waiting to be discovered."

Javik's face darkened. "Where the hell have you been, anyway?"

"I know what you're thinking," Wizzy said, glowing light red to study Javik's thoughts. "If I'd been here earlier, Namaba might still be alive."

"It crossed my mind," Javik said. He lifted Namaba's wrapped and lifeless form and carried it to a shady place beneath a pine tree, overlooking the big rock slab. He reached for the folding shovel on his hip, planning to dig a grave for her. But the shovel wasn't there.

"Something wrong?" Wizzy asked.

"The shovel and barbed cord," Javik said, looking around. "Must have dropped them someplace."

With Wizzy's help, they searched the entire area. Nothing was found.

"Where was the last time you saw them?" Wizzy asked.

"I'm sure I had them before entering the Magician's Chamber." He looked at the rock slab. "Damn, I hope we don't have to open that again. I've gotta find that stuff or I don't eat."

"I can dig a hole," Wizzy said. He flew to the spot Javik had selected and burrowed approximately a meter and a half into the soil, throwing dirt out in a pile beside the hole.

Javik did not say anything. He lifted Namaba's body and placed it gently in the hole. Not knowing any religious words, he stood there for a minute, looking down at her and crying. Then he knelt and pushed dirt over her, packing it down with his boots afterward.

"I think you expected too much of me," Wizzy said, hovering nearby. "After all, I'm only a little over seven days old. And I've tried to help you."

"Big deal," Javik said. He looked around for a marker, settling on a sizable agate.

"I think you could have shown more appreciation," Wizzy said. He watched Javik grunt as he pushed the agate to the grave site.

Javik horsed the rock until he had it in place. "Maybe it's a magical agate," Javik said. "Someone for her to talk with."

"Uh huh," Wizzy said.

*I've lived more in these few days than in my whole life before that,* Javik thought, staring down at the gravestone. *And now I've died, too. Prince Pineapple killed both of us at once.*

"I still don't understand all the emotions," Wizzy said. "I've made progress, though. You're experiencing sadness now."

Javik searched the area until he found a yellow flower like the one he had given Namaba. Digging up the entire root system with his bare hands, he took it back and planted it over her body.

*It's done,* he thought.

Looking around, Javik did not see Wizzy. Then something bright green flashed in the sky, catching his eye. It was Wizzy, sparkling in the sun and streaking away. Approaching Wizzy from deep space and growing larger by the moment, Javik recognized the Great Comet, burning white-hot, with a wispy, smoke-white tail.

Hearing the roar of rocket engines behind him, Javik looked back. An AmFed space cruiser with full para-flaps extended was setting down by the rock slab. A cloud of dust rose overhead.

"How'd they find me?" Javik mumbled. He tasted dust.

Then he looked skyward and knew the answer to his question.

"Goodbye!" the Great Comet wrote, making a trail of smoky letters across the blue sky.

"Goodbye!" Wizzy wrote, in smaller, more uneven letters.

Javik smiled as he squinted to watch the comets swoop high overhead, like a pair of fighter plane pilots. It was a joyous maneuver, shared by a proud parent and a proud child.

"Hey, fella," Abercrombie shouted, getting up on one elbow. "You're gonna be a goddamn hero, bringing me back and all. You know that?"

Two crewmen appeared in the open main hatch of the space cruiser.

"Yeah," Javik said, showing no enthusiasm. Wearily, he went to Abercrombie and removed the heavy cloth from his ankles.

They trudged together through the dust toward the waiting cruiser. The crewmen waved and yelled something.

*Maybe I was a little hard on Wizzy, Javik thought.*

# About the Author

Brian Herbert, the son of Frank Herbert, is the author of multiple New York Times bestsellers. He has won numerous literary honors and has been nominated for the highest awards in science fiction. In 2003, he published *Dreamer of Dune*, a moving biography of his father that was nominated for the Hugo Award. After writing ten Dune-universe novels with coauthor Kevin J. Anderson, Brian began his own galaxy-spanning science fiction series in 2006, Timeweb. His other acclaimed solo novels include *Sudanna, Sudanna* and *The Race for God*. He co-wrote *Man of Two Worlds* with Frank Herbert.

# If You Liked . . .

If you liked *The Comet Chronicles,* you might also enjoy:

*Dangerous Worlds*
*Sudanna Sudanna*
*Timeweb Chronicles Omnibus*

# Other WordFire Press Titles by Brian Herbert

*The Race for God*

*The Stolen Gospels 1: The Stolen Gospels*

*The Stolen Gospels 2: The Lost Apostles*

*Timeweb Chronicles Omnibus*

**Marie Landis & Brian Herbert**

*Memorymakers*

**Bruce Taylor & Brian Herbert**

*Storm World*

**Brian Herbert & Kevin J. Anderson**

*Tales of Dune*

www.ingramcontent.com/pod-product-compliance
Lightning Source LLC
Chambersburg PA
CBHW050058120726
47904CB00004B/1138